THE PATH OF THE FORGOTTEN

Creation of Legends

EMMA BINSFIELD

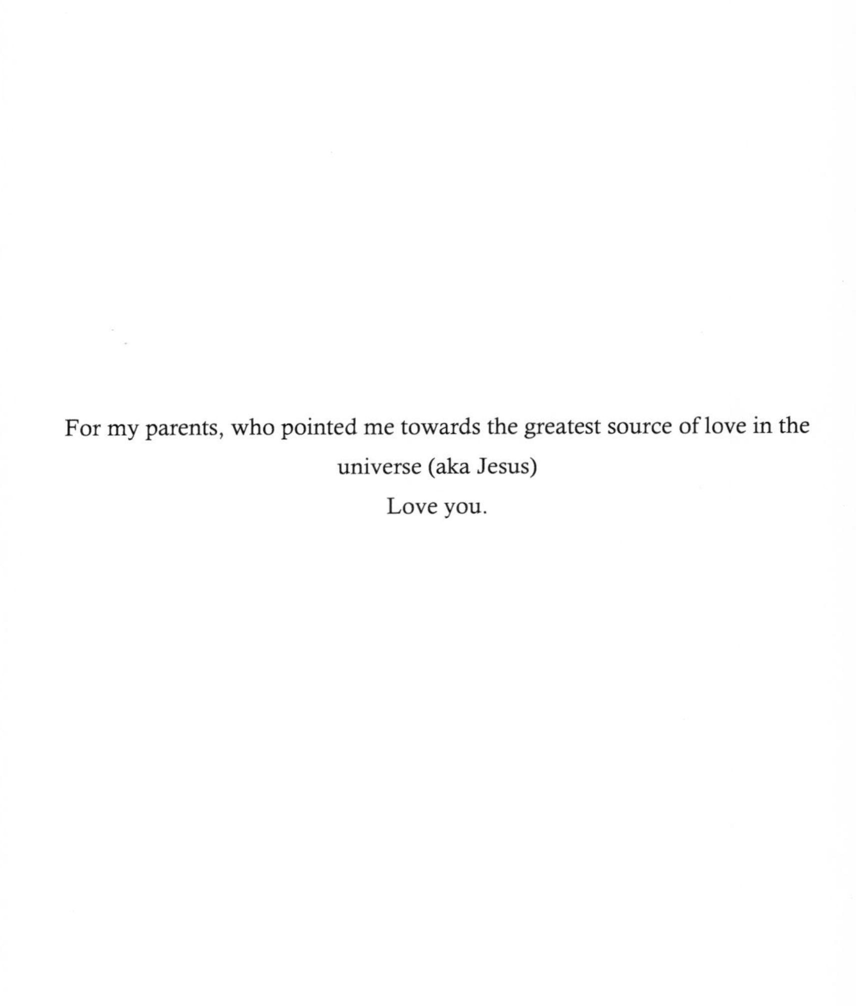

For my parents, who pointed me towards the greatest source of love in the universe (aka Jesus)

Love you.

Table of Contents

Prologue

I remember that day well, almost as if it were yesterday because of the pain attached. One might think that after seventeen years I would move on. I expect most people would accept the situation. That was not the case for me. This was something that I would never forgive nor forget.

It was the day that my parents were killed.

The pain churned inside me years afterward. It gnawed away at me as if draining my very life force. It took away any joy or happiness that I could find. No matter what I tried, I always felt empty; nothing could fill the void that had been created inside me.

It was very difficult to find anything that seemed to be worthwhile. The only thing that eased the pain was hunting. It no longer mattered to me whether it was as an employed mercenary or just to bring extra food to the table. The day that my parents died had permanently changed something in me.

I had been four at that time of their deaths—not that it made any difference. Being a human-fox hybrid in the Kingdom of Palee, I had the tendency to be one of the more intelligent children. I wasn't as smart as an owl or turtle hybrid, but I was nowhere near as dim as creatures such as squirrel hybrids. Hybrid children, by nature, mature faster than other races, so my mind at four could have been the equal of a twelve-year-old human.

Because of my species, I am incredibly clever—at least my grandmother told me I was. If I was really as clever as she believed, I likely could have prevented my parents' death or at least been there to aid them or die trying. Maybe so many gruesome things that had become part of my childhood wouldn't have happened if I had just been there.

That fateful day was perfect from an unsuspecting perspective.

Nothing seemed like it could possibly go wrong—the sun was shining and there wasn't a cloud in the sky.

I had been playing with a pack of wolf pups on that fine afternoon. I vaguely recall that they cheated at some game and refused to admit their offense. It was funny considering that I was the fox in the game and generally we are the untrustworthy ones. And yet there I was—innocent from the conspiracy in that ordeal. That fact both amused and irritated me. I hate being judged just because of my species.

I was explaining the rules of the game (again) when we heard shrill screams coming from the eastern town of Leshee. Everyone jerked around to look in the direction of the city. Panicked glances were exchanged before the wolves scampered off in various directions.

Wolf pups are such cowards, I thought. I had met rabbit hybrids that were braver than them.

I didn't run away like a scared cat. My family lived in Leshee and I had a growing fear for their safety. I didn't like the fact that the screams steadily continued as I ran across the grassy fields as fast as my short legs would carry me as the wind picked up. My long hair whipped around my face in the wind blowing against me.

The wind continued its brisk pace through the fields, but I could not hear any more screams traveling on the racing gust. I could hear nothing save for the wind flying past my furry ears. When I arrived, there was no sound to be heard for miles around. Even after wandering the whole town, I didn't discover anything. It was as if the city had become a ghost town. It reminded me of ruined towns that I would read about in old books that I occasionally found unguarded in the library.

I needed to investigate more, so the first place I went to was the town square. On any given day, it was the busiest place in town no matter what time it was. I figured that if anyone was anywhere, it would have to be there. Someone had to know what was going on, right?

Wrong. There was absolutely no one in the normally bustling courtyard. The only things that greeted me were tipped over and smashed carts, splattered produce sprayed on every nearby surface, and flying papers of would-be transactions.

Since the true meaning of what was going on was nebulous to me, I decided to move on to another part of town that was usually busy. It was one place that my family and I rarely visited because it was so crowded: the park. I had only been there a handful of times, so it took me a good deal of time to try to figure out where in the world I was going.

As I had expected deep down inside, but did not want to admit to myself, there was nothing at the park when I got there. However, instead of smashed produce and carts, all I found was multiple splintered benches. All of the trees and shrubs were battered as if a fight had taken place. Of course, as a four-year-old child—even one who knew a lot for their age—I was too stupid to realize that my suspicions were correct.

Naturally, like any child would, I just continued on my merry way, completely oblivious to what was really occurring. I mean, seriously! After seeing two different places that were *completely* abandoned, you would think that I would realize what the heck was going on. Unfortunately not, because I just went to the library to see if there were really people there.

There were not. The library was just as abandoned as everywhere else in Leshee. However, this time, it wasn't so much that it was abandoned that bothered me. What bothered me more was the way the books were strewn everywhere. Almost every single book had been taken off the shelves, and they all seemed to be covering the floor in large mounds.

Curiosity overcame me, so I stepped closer to one of the largest mounds. It was also one closest to the door, so I didn't have to walk far. I picked up one of the books only to see another beneath it. Unsatisfied with my discovery, I started throwing aside more books in hopes of reaching the bottom of the pile. After throwing about fifteen more books behind me I noticed something pale stick out from underneath. I continued to frantically pull books off until I saw something absolutely harrowing.

It was the body of an owl hybrid. I recognized the hybrid as one of the librarians that I had spent countless hours with during the days I could just waste away. The lenses of his circular spectacles were cracked and turned into powder that was sprinkled all over the floor near his head. I frantically moved the remainder of the books off of him. I was perplexed when I saw some sort of sticky red liquid covering many of the books that had lain directly atop the librarian.

I eventually found the name tag of this familiar hybrid. His name was Howise, whom I remembered as one who had helped me find books about important foreign kingdoms, such as Salia or even ones as distant as Estal. As far as we knew, few hybrids had ever ventured there in the times of old. I had asked why, but even Howise had refused to tell me. He said that it wasn't proper for a child to know the answers to some of the world's great mysteries. Though, it was probably just some plain fact to the adults who refused to tell me anything when I was a child.

I don't know what came over me, but I found the nerve to speak.

Honestly, that was probably a stupid thing to do in the eerily silent library. Who knows what kind of fell creatures I could have drawn to myself?

"Howise? Can you hear me?" I asked quietly.

No response. I put my hand on his chest, which was covered in the same red substance as the books, but felt no movement. Howise was completely and utterly still.

Over the next few minutes, I tried everything that I could think of that might possibly make the librarian answer me. Despite my best efforts, he still said nothing and showed no signs that he would be moving anytime soon.

By that time, I had begun to grow very frightened. I made up my mind that I was done looking for signs of people in this forsaken city and decided I wanted to go home. I exited the library in a mess of emotions that was only as complex as my four-year-old mind could allow.

What had happened in the short period of time that it took me to run here from that field? What was that red stuff that was all over Howise and some of the books that had been near him? Why was the city so silent? What happened to all of the residents who lived there? Was everyone hiding? Were my parents and grandmother okay? Had they been kidnapped or worse?

I had too many questions swirling around in my head for me to think straight. I started getting a headache both from my racing mind as well as the red substance on my hands. It then began to smell of iron, like the swords at the blacksmith's forges. The smell of the substance confused me. What sort of liquid could be bright red and still smell of metal?

Uncomfortable with all of the questions boggling my mind, I picked up the pace to make sure I could get across town before anything terrible could happen to me. I didn't like the look of Howise in the library and I didn't want that to happen to me or the ones that I loved. I hoped with all my heart that nothing unfortunate had befallen them.

However, as I trudged through town and saw that it was all demolished and abandoned, my hopes began to sink. The terribly pessimistic part of me could not help but believe that there was nobody alive in the town. Even if there was somebody still alive, something dreadful must befallen them. I forced myself to believe that my family was okay and that nothing had happened to them that would put them in danger.

There were only more signs of an attack of some sort as I got closer to home. Being naïve, I couldn't tell to what extent the attack had been, but I knew that there definitely had been a struggle. There were broken carts and even furniture; there was even broken glass from some of the windows that now lay in shattered pieces on the street. The sticky red substance speckled numerous objects I passed on my trek through the ruined town. I was careful to avoid it as I turned the corner to go down my road.

It was hardly a road, to be honest. It was probably about four feet wide at the opening and narrowed into a doorframe. The majority of my home was underground where there were no windows save for a couple of skylights that enabled us to know what time of day it was.

My family had lived in this same home for generations. My mother said that she had no intention of moving and my father had agreed with her. My grandmother just went along with it because she never saw the point in arguing. I, however, always wanted to see what the other parts of the world were like, even if it was only different parts of Palee. Any adult I ever told that to would only shake their head and tell me I could hope for the day I would have the opportunity to discover it. It wasn't until years later that I would actually realize what they meant by that.

I turned the corner and stopped dead in my tracks. There at the end of the alley were two forms that were lying as still as the stones that made up the surrounding walls. Around them were pieces of broken pottery, shattered glass, and splintered wood. I couldn't force my legs to move. All I had been able to do was stare at the appalling sight.

When I finally regained control of my shaking limbs, I rushed toward the two forms that lay on the ground. One was a young woman with fiery red hair and pale skin. Freckles covered her face and her arms. She wore a long, orangey dress on her lithe figure. She was also slathered in the same red substance that covered my hands.

Beside the woman lay a man with a thin, but strong looking frame. His hair was strawberry blond with strands of gold throughout it. He was just as pale as the woman and wore an outfit in a similar orange color. A dagger was close to his hand covered in the same red substance.

Once again, curiosity overtook me and I decided to find out more about the figures and the red, iron-smelling substance that covered them. That had been the second time that day that I had seen this sticky red liquid. Now that I think about it, I had never seen this liquid before that day. Was it a liquid that you poured on something to preserve its life? All I could do was wonder where it came from.

My breath was taken from me when I rolled over the man. He was a heavy weight for me to move, but the strain was not what stole my breath. The man was my father. I clumsily moved to the woman and rolled her over onto her back. Like I feared, it was my mother. I didn't know what else to do with them so I just hugged them and begged them to wake up.

I don't know how long I sat there trying to rouse my beloved parents. For all I know, it could have been hours. Perhaps it was only minutes. I didn't care. I only wanted my parents to wake and speak to me. I longed to hear my mother's lilting voice and my father's jubilant laugh, but I had no idea how I was going to achieve my goal.

Soon, circumstances grew hopeless. The clear sky dimmed and a chill settled over the air. I shivered as tears trickled down my cheeks. I sniffled as I heard shuffling footsteps make their way down the alley. With tear-filled eyes, I saw my grandmother shuffling toward me.

"Come here, my child," she gently said as she gingerly sat upon the ground. After I reluctantly climbed into her lap, she gently wrapped her arms around me in a comforting embrace. Against my will, I began to cry again. "Hush, child. They might still be here. They might hear you."

"Who will hear me?" I sobbed softly as I made a small effort to dry my tears.

My grandmother looked at me with sorrowful eyes. It seemed to me, in that moment, that any hope of normality had vanished.

"Scarlet, my dear granddaughter, you are still too young for all the knowledge you seek," she had begun in a soft, soothing voice that calmed me immediately. "I promise you, when the time comes, I will tell you everything."

"Will you tell me one thing?" I asked softly as I looked into her amber eyes. My grandmother nodded. Only once, but it was enough to urge me on. "What is that red stuff on Mama and Daddy?"

My grandmother sighed a long and deeply. It was a sigh that could have emptied all the lakes and lagoons of the earth of all their water. It was a sigh filled with sorrow, even regret. Only now I recognize that it was a sigh of knowledge that she almost lamented having.

"Though it pains me to answer and will likely pain you even more so, I suppose I have to answer," she sighed.

For the first time in my life, I watched as a single, glistening tear rolled down her sallow cheek.

With a choking voice she continued. "That red substance is called blood. It is the life source of all living creatures. Lose too much of it, and you shall surely perish."

I gazed at her like a deer hybrid stares into the bright, dancing flame of candles. "Are they…?"

My voice drifted off, unable to finish the unbearable question. I couldn't lose two people that I held close to my heart. Surely the world wasn't cruel enough to do such a thing. As I later found out, it was. The world I lived in was not as perfect as other kingdoms would like to believe.

To my dismay, my grandmother nodded. A new wave of tears gushed as I buried my face into her silvery hair. She gently stroked my furry ears as an attempt to comfort me. However, in that moment, nothing helped. "Hush, child. It will be alright. You're safe with me."

I might have been safe with my grandmother for that time and the years to come, but my life wasn't the same. Something inside me snapped beyond repair. I was determined to grow up and avenge my parents, whether I lived or died trying.

Hate At First Fight

I walked through Palee's capital city of Vareh mostly minding my own business. I had been busy that morning collecting any fallen change on the street. By "fallen" I meant picking the pockets of hybrids that were considered wealthy in our culture.

It wasn't like we had very much of a culture, though. Palee had no superior leader save for chieftains that met every so often. Even then, the clans were not on the best terms; several were basically at war with each other. They didn't physically fight (most of the time), but they refused to be associated with each other.

I couldn't really blame them, though, since I myself was part in one of these cold wars that had erupted. The foxes and the wolves constantly argued and fought even though we were distant kinsmen. However, that did not stop the wolves from thinking that the foxes were the ones to blame for the attacks. They loved thinking that all fox hybrids were in league with elves. I vehemently argued that we hated the elves as much as everyone else.

I actually found it hard to believe that many of the wolves opposing me had been so-called "friends" of mine when I was a child. Now they were some of my biggest targets for spying or merely picking a fight. Many wolves could be sure that I had discreetly picked their pockets when I passed them on the road.

I strode down the main street of Vareh being careful to avoid getting dusty. It hadn't rained in this area for many days so all of the roads were basically just red dirt. Avoiding it was certainly a task, though. There were hybrids bustling around in every direction, each stirring up their own personal cloud. I'd finally had enough of it when I decided to just go through the back alleys in the city and find my way home from there.

My grandmother had been busy in our hometown of Leshee, so a few days prior, I decided that I would head north and go exploring. Ever since my parents' death all those years ago, I had been exceptionally curious about the outer reaches of Palee and the outside world because I felt like there was more that people hadn't told me. Sadly, many of the places I wanted to visit were in off-limit areas that were forbidden by the elders of the kingdom.

Officials always said that I would cause too many international incidents if I were seen. Not unlike when I was a child, they refused to tell me what was really going on because I was "too young." I had tried asking again recently and they used the same excuse. It was demoralizing to hear that stupid excuse yet again when I've been considered an adult for years.

I was making my way down the alley when I heard a nearly silent wingbeat and the thump of feet touching the ground. The whooshing sound alerted me that it was one of the hybrids capable of flight (and be able to fly far, at that), but that didn't stop me from being suspicious. One of the watchmen could have seen me pick somebody's pockets and were coming to press charges for petty crimes while mt big ones went unnoticed.

Not that I really cared about being fined or anything. Half the reason that I broke Palee's few laws was because I was intentionally trying to get myself exiled. If I wasn't allowed to leave the southern borders legally, I would just have to find a creative way to get out of this prison.

Of course, that might not make sense as to why I was hiding now. To make myself clear, I hide so I wouldn't get fined and placed under watch. Why? Well, so I could make sure whatever I pulled would be punishable by exile, of course.

I drew a dagger from my belt and waited a few seconds before I made a move. When I did, I spun and threw my weapon. I did not care if it was a friend (I had few, so that was unlikely) or foe. To be honest, I hoped that it was one of those wretched wolves that always seemed to be following me. No matter the case, I was eager to teach my adversary that it was not the wisest idea to sneak up on a fox.

Metal clanged against metal as my dagger met its target. I quickly inspected the figure that stood behind me with their arm held up, presenting a metal band on their arm. It was a raven hybrid. Her jet-black hair was pulled into a severe braid at the top of her head. The purple-dyed tips extended down to her hips and brushed against the glossy ebony feathers of her wings.

"Well, fancy meeting the infamous Scarlet Sutton here today," the woman said as she sauntered closer to me, lips curled into a mischievous smile. As she moved, the sunlight illuminated her flawless, porcelain skin.

I let down my guard a little bit by relaxing my shoulders and slightly releasing my grip on the dagger I held. I knew the girl and could easily deal with her.

"I could say the same to you, Razil," I stated with a pointed glance in her direction.

The woman smiled as she tilted her head. We both began to laugh as we embraced each other. This raven hybrid had been one of the few friends that I had grown up with that didn't absolutely despise me. If anything, everyone else hated her right along with me.

Razil hadn't had a difficult childhood. Rather, she was just one of those people who were exceptionally skilled at threatening those who opposed her. She was skilled on making good of those threats as well. That might have been part of the reason I liked her so much. Still, I was thankful I had at least one friend that I could completely let my guard down with.

"Indeed, you could," Razil laughed as she slung her arm over my shoulder. "So, what brings you north on this fine winter day?"

"My grandmother gave me leave to explore the kingdom for a while," I answered. Out of habit, I did not give her too many details. "I was actually heading back south again. I've been up here for three days already and should really be heading back. After all, it is at least ten-day journey when you're walking."

"True enough," she agreed. "Hey, let's have some fun before you head back. I can't imagine that you really want to return so soon, right?"

"Well, no…I don't…but my grandmother would start to get worried about me. She's too frail for something like that. The anxiety could kill her," I objected as I nervously bit my lip.

I didn't want to bring that kind of stress on my already-delicate grandmother since she was constantly worried about my safety and wouldn't be able to bear it if something happened to me.

After all, my grandmother was the woman who had taught me to read, write, and hunt. She had been the closest thing I had to a mother since I was a child. I had no stronger bond with any living creature than I did with her. I wasn't about to forsake that bond just because a friend wanted me to hang out with her for a few hours more. A personal rule of mine was that family came first, and I wasn't about to desert that rule for Razil.

"But you could just send a letter telling her that you'll be home a little bit later than you had previously expected," my friend suggested with a hopeful look on her face.

Her extraordinarily green eyes were practically begging me to send a letter to my grandmother and stay in Vareh. I wanted to stay and enjoy the company of my friend, but I knew that I had a duty to my grandmother to be back on time.

"I guess you're right," I sighed as I started pulling out a piece of paper and a quill from the satchel that I had been carrying.

I was in no mood to argue with Razil, and I also knew that I would be able to make up lost time, so I might as well start writing the letter and give it to the post master so it could be delivered in the next few days. I just hoped that it would actually reach Leshee before I got there so my poor grandmother wouldn't get too worried.

Mid-sentence, I sent Razil a pointed look. "I'm only staying for a couple more hours. I need to be leaving at sunset so I can still make it back punctually."

"Deal," she agreed as I signed and sealed my short letter.

I handed it to her and she launched into the air to deliver it to the post master. It was far safer to have her deliver it since I was a fugitive. As it was, I wore my cloak with the hood up nearly all the time so nobody would recognize me. I would need every day I had to figure out how to get out of this blasted kingdom, so I wasn't going to let my fiery red hair give me away.

Razil returned a few minutes later bursting with exuberance. If I didn't know any better, I would also say that there was a glimpse of mischief in her eyes as well. I knew the look better than anyone else since I had known her from when we were kids. I would be a fool to not recognize the look in someone's eye when they smelled trouble. In Razil's case, that was really all she could ever smell.

"What did you see?" I asked with a raised eyebrow.

Razil smiled somewhat evilly. I couldn't decide if that was good or not. However, with Razil, you never really could tell.

"There's a fight in the main courtyard," she explained as she pulled her hood up as well.

I admit it's rather amusing to see someone with giant wings wearing a cloak. Sometime, I would really have to ask her what it was like to do such a thing. I had been meaning to ask her for years, but I had always forgotten about it until moments where there was no chance of asking about it.

"Who's in the ring this time?" I questioned curiously, sheathing the dagger I'd thrown at Razil when she arrived.

Then we briskly crossed the city to reach the central courtyard. I'm sure that Razil would have rather flown, but that would have given away my position. And honestly, I had no intention of being found out.

"I think it's some wolves who seem to be going through some sort of civil war in their own clan," Razil answered with a nonchalant shrug.

On the outside, she seemed pretty calm about the fight and everything going on around us, but on the inside, I knew that she was one who longed to fight with a burning passion.

"Sounds interesting. Maybe I can get in on it," I commented with a cold laugh.

I rubbed my hands together in anticipation. Any fight that involved some of the wolves from various packs was interesting, but seeing a fight between wolves of the same pack would be even better. Oh, and were they fighting with weapons or merely fist-to-fist combat? I hoped it was the latter because then I would be able to teach them a lesson.

When we got there, I saw two grey wolf hybrids exchanging blows. The smaller one received a punch right as I reached the edge of the crowd. I almost felt sorry for him when I heard bone crunch. He reeled backward in pain and the other wolf towered over him, spitting insults. The larger hybrid started circling around the smaller one in a threatening manner.

I cocked my head, oh so desperately wanting to join the fight and smack the larger wolf. I had no especially warm feelings towards any members of the wolf clans, but I hated when anyone was spoken down to. That largely stemmed from the fact that I had been insulted all my life just because I was a fox hybrid.

It was actually quite interesting to see a grey wolf again. Despite their name, their hair was all sorts of colors. The only distinguishing mark that separated them from any of the other pack members was their streak of grey hair. Since I never really saw many grey wolves anymore, I knew that their numbers were either dwindling or they were becoming more reclusive. That was better for me in a way—less insults, but less fights to start as well.

This particular wolf hybrid (the larger one anyway) had blond hair with the typical grey streak. His hair itself was not something to get overly excited about, though. It was just boring old blond hair; it was his eyes that were more striking. He really only had one good eye—the left had a long scar that ran through it making it that pale blinded grey. The wolf's good eye was a brilliant blue color. It was the same blue as an August sky.

He might have been good-looking if a snarl wasn't showing his distinctive fangs as he stared toward the ground at the now-crouching wolf.

He had received another strong blow, but this time it had been aimed at his ribs. The smaller wolf coughed and spat out blood and—as I noticed—a tooth. Lovely.

The smaller wolf was certainly more striking in looks than his opponent, who just looked downright cruel. He had jet black hair with the grey streak, of course. Though, the streak of grey was far thinner than most hybrids of his species. He also had pale blue eyes that seemed to sparkle with hope as well as fury when he looked at his foe. I only noticed because I was trained to pay close attention to details. As a fighter, it was a helpful thing to understand how many fights an enemy had survived, since it altered how you had to take them down.

The smaller wolf sprang against his opponent again and successfully knocked him backwards. The larger wolf soon regained his balance and threw himself against the injured wolf, who pulled out a small dagger which was used to stab the snarling wolf in the thigh. He howled in agony as the blade gored deeper into his flesh.

Watching his face, I could almost feel the pain. But as sympathy pinged, I always remembered the anguish of seeing my parents lying dead the ground covered in blood. Fury always overcame sympathy.

The wolves swung their fists a few more times, hitting nothing. In my opinion, they had very poor form in fighting. The larger kept stumbling while the smaller appeared to be lightheaded from blood loss. Soon they had rested again and were back at it with hard punches and insults.

"Do you know who either of these two are?" I whispered in Razil's ear.

I had half a mind to join the fight, but I needed to know if she was friends with either one so I didn't injure the wrong one or anything. Personally, I wanted to see them both dead. The wolves had brought so much harm upon me and my family name that I only wanted something wicked to happen to them.

"I have no idea who the heck they are, but I feel like I should know them," she responded quietly. Razil didn't take her eyes off the battle the entire time that she spoke. Her curious eyes mostly followed the larger wolf. "Why do you ask?"

"I'm tempted to join their little skirmish to end it. Though, I don't really feel like killing anybody you know," I answered nonchalantly.

Razil laughed softly. "Thank you for that, Scarlet. I—"

She was cut off by another scream of agony. I whipped my head around to see what had happened. In the few seconds I was distracted, the battle had reached a crucial point. The smaller wolf hybrid now lay flat on the ground, most likely from an attack that had some extra force packed into it. The side of his blue tunic was slowly beginning to turn red. The smell of iron filled the air.

My instincts took over. I felt only the urge to kill. I had never tasted blood before, but I had killed many things in my lifetime. All I had to do was smell blood and my primal instincts kicked in—it happened every time.

I was an efficient hunter when I needed to be, but I was an even better mercenary. My grandmother did not know, nor would she ever, about my main occupation. If she knew I was killing for money, she would never let me out of her sight. It was just better for me to keep my business a secret so nobody else I loved would get hurt.

I pulled my dagger out again as I leapt into the fight zone. I collided with the larger wolf almost instantly. He flew backwards when he was struck with the full force of my weight. My knee was on his chest as soon as he hit the ground. He struggled to move, so I held my dagger to his neck. The razor-sharp blade was close to penetrating his skin several times. I let it. He still struggled, but to no avail. Blood started slowly dripping.

"Who are you?!" He shouted gruffly as he threw me off of him.

I rolled three times in the dust and jumped back up on my feet. This wasn't my first rodeo.

"Your worst nightmare, wolf," I hissed. I bared my own fangs, and even if they weren't as large, they were still incredibly sharp.

The wolf's eyes narrowed in anger and frustration. He pulled throwing stars from his belt and hurled three of them at me in swift succession. I was quick to dodge them, and that only made him angrier.

I continued to dodge his attacks while making my way closer to him so I could land a few blows. First, I targeted nerve centers in his arm (he screamed like a child when I hit my mark). Then I used the butt of my blade to hit him in the jaw.

Before I could land another punch, however, my adversary knocked me to the ground and held his fist to my neck, effectively blocking the air flow.

"Doesn't feel so great, does it?" he said scornfully as he pushed his hand onto my throat.

Black clouds rimmed my vision and I started having trouble breathing. I could hear the crowd cheering and shouting as we fought. I couldn't tell who they were cheering for, I just heard and hated it. Any moment I could become unconscious, if not worse. In one final attempt to regain dominance, I cut the arm holding me down with the back of my blade. The wolf wailed in pain as he jumped backward. I took my chance and rolled away from him.

I was about to begin another attack when the crowd started to part. Town officials came running toward us shouting, "Stop in the name of the law!"

Of course, Palee and its cities had few laws, and this fact was pointed out by many of the members of our ever-growing audience. I could have sworn that I saw Razil mutter something, too. This exasperated the officials greatly. It merely amused me.

The lead official was a wolf hybrid, and he was quite noticeably one of the grey wolves. His bone structure also matched the younger wolves very closely, so they had to be either related or of the same species. Besides that, his eyes narrowed when he saw my enemy. It seemed as if they knew each other and most likely had a…interesting relationship.

He glanced toward me. His hand roved closer to his belt where his weapon hung. "Is this man giving you trouble, miss?"

Thankful that he hadn't recognized me, I answered in as steady a voice as possible. "Not until the end there when he was cutting off air from my lungs. No, I merely stepped in because he couldn't defend himself anymore."

I nodded to the other wolf-man that now lay near Razil. He was still struggling for breath while Razil tried to stop the blood. I glanced at Razil and gave her a subtle nod. I wanted her to tend to the other man so the officials would think we were friends. Really though, I only wanted to question him when given an opportunity. After looking at him more carefully, I felt like I recognized the unfortunate wolf.

"Ah, I see," he stated.

He inspected the condition of me, the man Razil was tending to, and the hybrid that I had faced off against. He grunted when he was inspecting me. He looked me in the eye, almost daring me to defy him to which I subtly tilted my head and smiled politely.

He turned away. "I'd be happy to take this low-life off your hands if you would like to get your friend there some medical help. I can see that he needs it."

"Yes, of course. Thank you," I answered.

I restrained myself from saying anything to the wolf that I had beaten. If I did, I was sure that I would give myself away, and that was *not* preferable. Instead, I watched as the officials bound him and led him down a different street to the more developed part of the city.

As he was being hauled off, the wolf hybrid shouted at me, "We know who you are and our retribution *will* be swift."

Deciding it was a comment intended only to scare me, I turned back to Razil and the other hybrid. He was fading fast. As a pool of blood welled beneath him, I remembered what my grandmother had told me about blood all those years ago: lose too much of it and you'll die. I had a sinking feeling that it might happen to this man if we didn't do something in the next few minutes. He wouldn't be able to hold on for much longer.

"Come on, Razil. We need to get him somewhere where we can help him and I won't be discovered," I whispered as we started lifting the man off the ground.

The man groaned softly as we raised him into the air. I almost hated moving him, but it really couldn't be helped. As much as I didn't like people, least of all wolves, I couldn't let this man die because of an injustice that had been done to him.

In addition, there was no way that I was going to stay in the open for longer than I needed to. I had already drawn enough attention to myself for one day. I didn't need any more. What I needed was to focus my attention on making sure that this hybrid lived to see the sun rise again.

Razil and I managed to drag the man to one of the shadier parts of town. Strangely enough, Razil took us directly to her house.

That surprised me greatly, because bringing a potential enemy to my living quarters was the last thing I would ever do. It was dangerous. Then again, Razil didn't seem to think anything was wrong with this guy. Besides, it was her risk in bringing him here. She could be the one to deal with the consequences.

We laid him down on a tough mat on the floor. He didn't seem to notice that it was hard and uneven, but then again, he was in pain. He looked like he was approaching Death's doorstep. His wounds were still steadily bleeding and I didn't think he would have much blood left in him for too much longer.

"Come on. We have to do something," Razil stated urgently as she tossed a container of herbs to me.

"What am I supposed to do with these?" I demanded in confusion as she started making a cold compress with a cloth.

"It's a leaf called *serekin*. It has the power to stop bleeding when it is rubbed on the wound," the raven-woman replied as she set the cold compress on his head. "Okay, now apply it."

Then she started getting wet cloths to clean the man's wounds. He grunted softly when the cold cloth made contact with his skin. I could only imagine how it stung. I remember times when my grandmother had done the same thing to me as a child when I was sick.

"I don't see how a stupid leaf is supposed to stop bleeding like this, but fine," I said through gritted teeth.

My eyes widened in surprise when the leaves actually did what Razil said they would. Within seconds, the flowing blood had clotted completely. I was stunned to learn that some plants had such potent healing power.

"Wow. That actually worked," I muttered.

Razil grinned smugly. "You'd be surprised at all the crazy plants that exist."

I nodded in acknowledgement.

The man jerked into a sitting position and looked at us with wild eyes. He jumped up and made a desperate dash to the door, but I blocked him and slammed the door shut. I glared at him and he recoiled. He then started looking around the small house as if in hopes of finding any alternate escape routes. Judging by the look on Razil's face, I knew that it was a vain search. The door was the only way out of her home.

"Where am I? Who are you people?" the man asked as his eyes darted from me to Razil and back to me.

It was obvious that he didn't trust us, and I didn't blame him. Who would trust somebody who dragged you to their house after you were knocked out in a fight and only minutes away from death?

"Relax, you're safe. Just—"

The man cut her off by drawing a dagger from a sheath that I had just realized was inside his boot. He glared at both of us threateningly.

"Tell me your names, *now*," he demanded. He would have seemed pretty intimidating if I hadn't noticed that his ear twitched anxiously, giving away his emotions. He had an edgy posture, so I knew I had nothing to worry about with this jumpy hybrid. He did not seem brave enough to make good on his implied threats.

"My name is Razil. That's Scarlet," Razil answered. "We brought you back here because you were badly injured."

I glared at her when she introduced me. She pretended to take no notice, but I *know* she saw me glaring at her. I hated it when she did things like that.

"I don't care if I was injured. I had everything under control," the man said as he adjusted his grip on his blade. His knuckles were turning white from the pressure that he was applying. He was really bad about hiding what he was feeling. Then again, I doubt the normal eye would notice half the stuff that I do. I was a trained professional who knew how to spot all the little details other people would easily miss.

"Hmph! I seem to recall saving your life back there," I commented with a defiant stare toward the man.

He raised his eyebrows in surprise and then started fidgeting. He sheathed his dagger again before he started wringing his hands restlessly.

"Oh, uh, I guess you did," he said quietly, not making eye contact with either one of us. His attitude changed in the blink of an eye. "My name is Rennan, by the way. Thank you for what you did to help me, but I really should be heading home now."

I raised my eyebrow in surprise. Now would be my only chance to question this jumpy wolf hybrid, even if I would not be able to ask many questions. I didn't want him telling the authorities about me. "Oh? Where do you live?"

Rennan chuckled nervously as he scratched the back of his neck. "That is a very stalkerish question, but I suppose that I must answer since I am indebted to you for saving my life. I live in Leshee."

"How perfect! That's where Scarlet lives, too!" Razil said as she clapped her hands in delight, perhaps a little bit too cheerfully.

Once again, I glared at her.

However, this time she only met my eye for a second and grinned evilly. "The two of you should just head back down there together."

"I don't need a babysitter," I muttered under my breath.

"Of course not judging from the way you held your ground in that fight," Razil said with a nonchalant shrug, "but wouldn't it be safer if you traveled with someone instead of just by yourself? There are all sorts of unsavory characters between here and Leshee. Believe me, I would know."

I instantly felt the need to point out that I had met far more unsavory characters in my travels than she had. Of course, I met them once and never saw them again. *Nobody* ever saw them again.

"As much as I hate to agree with somebody who I literally just met for the first time in my life," Rennan began, "she's right. The countryside has grown wild and incredibly dangerous in the last few months."

"Then I guess Rennan is coming with me," I sighed as I stalked out of the room.

Little did I know that I then began the journey that would change my life forever.

Ambush

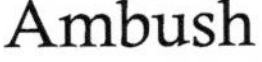

Razil lent Rennan one of her cloaks so that neither one of us would be recognized if we ran into trouble. Well, I doubted the wolf was the type to cause mischief as an attempt to get himself exiled. Still, I wanted to make sure that every precaution was taken care of.

We waved good-bye to Razil at a quarter until dusk. Rennan had wanted to leave sooner, but I dismissed any argument that he tried to start. I knew that we would be safer traveling under the cover of darkness. Naturally, Rennan argued that it was not nearly as safe as traveling during the day. In response, I simply overruled him by telling him I was in charge.

In his frustration, I believe he specifically said, "You could trip on a root or get caught in a pit or fall into a stream or step on a mysterious slime."

I—not being in the mood to argue with a wolf hybrid, of all people—told him that there was no possible way in any of the kingdoms that we would step on a mysterious slime. I hadn't wanted him to travel with me to begin with, so he should have considered himself lucky that I hadn't already found a way to get rid of him. I was in charge, and that was final.

The moon was out and the sky was perfectly clear that night. The winter had been cold but without snow. For that I was thankful. It's difficult to hide my bright red hair amidst any landscape save for fire. Snow only made it harder. Since I didn't dare light a fire, I just pulled my fur-lined cloak closer to myself.

"So…how long have you lived in Leshee?" Rennan asked, breaking the beautiful silence.

"Always. I don't remember seeing you there at any point in time," I answered somewhat shortly.

The wolves had fled Leshee not long after the callous massacre. I had no knowledge of any of them moving back in recent years. Then again, I was usually traveling under my pretense of trader to pay attention to other clans.

"It's actually quite interesting you say that—I vaguely remember a young fox-hybrid by your same name. The last time I saw her, we had been playing a game in the fields. Then we heard screams coming from the city and the rest of my pack bolted and never went back," Rennan laughed softly. His voice was quiet, yet it still carried through the expansive plains—reminding me of empty memories.

But what Rennan said stuck with me. Had he been one of the wolf pups that I had last seen when I was four? Unable to find a suitable reply, I remained quiet.

Rennan continued while trying not to pick at his scabs from the afternoon's fight. "Heh, this is kind of awkward, considering your kind is basically the mortal enemy of the wolves, but thanks for saving me back there."

"Uh, sure. It's no problem, I guess," I muttered.

I hadn't jumped into that fight to save him. Actually, I didn't know why I joined that fight. I had no special love for the wolves. Though, I couldn't let Rennan suffer like that. It wouldn't be fair to him or anything that I valued.

I asked, "Who was that other man, anyway?"

"Oh, him. Just the most notorious grey wolf hybrid in Palee. We've been trying to get him into custody for months, yet somehow, he evades all capture. It's like he has a super skilled group of warriors to bail him out or something," Rennan laughed coldly. "His name is Wayne. He's not the nicest person you're ever going to meet."

"Why do you want him in custody?" I asked curiously.

I tried to restrain my pleasure of how much information I was dragging out of the wolf since I had a feeling that sooner or later he would reveal something of use to me. I knew it wasn't any of my business, but the professional killer part of me argued that the information could be useful.

"He was involved in some pretty shady stuff throughout the kingdom," Rennan replied. "I honestly didn't think he'd show up in Vareh today. Last I knew of, he was on the west side of the Swamp of Solitude."

"One never expects to meet their enemy until they are forced to face them. And even then, they wish that they weren't there," I commented, my voice as dark as my mood.

My mind turned to the small part that didn't want to face my parent's murderer. I still wasn't exactly sure that I wanted to know who did it, terrified that it would be somebody that I knew. But then there was the part of me that wanted vengeance for all the wrong that had been done to my family.

I shook my head to snap out of my thoughts. "Why was this Wayne character fighting you?"

Rennan clicked his tongue. "So many questions from you, Scarlet, but I'll answer nonetheless. I was in Vareh to pick up a few supplies that I could only get there but couldn't find, and then Wayne came along and was like, '*Rennan, you coward, fight me.*' I told him no, but he started throwing punches at me anyway, not caring what I said. The only reason I went down was because I thought I recognized you, Unfortunately, the few seconds I froze for were exactly what Wayne needed to deliver the finishing blow."

I looked at the wolf in shock. "So…this is all my fault?"

Rennan shook his head violently. Then he clutched his side where we had wrapped bindings mere hours ago. He winced before he spoke, quite fast might I add. "No! You had no fault in this matter. It was entirely my own for letting my curiosity get the better of me…as usual. I'm just glad that you stepped in when you did—I don't think I would be here right now if you hadn't. That's why I wanted to thank you."

"Oh, then in that case, I guess you're welcome," I said quietly as my cheeks flushed pink. I didn't really like the thought that somebody's curiosity about me had almost killed them. I forced my mind to return to the task at hand. "It's at least ten days of a trek to Leshee. We had better stop and make a camp for the night unless we want to freeze to death before the night is even over."

"That is probably a good idea," Rennan agreed with a nod.

We put down the small packs that we had been carrying with us and were quick to make a shelter before our fingers became like icicles. I didn't know about Rennan, but I liked having feeling in my fingers.

After a few minutes, Rennan turned back to me. "Which one of us should get firewood? And did we eat anything before we left?"

I looked at him like prey. "No, we did not. We were leaving before we ran into any other kinds of trouble. You can go get the firewood while I'll go find something that we can cook over the fire."

"I suppose that works," he agreed as he meandered off into the small grove of trees where we were camping for the night. He wandered back about twenty seconds later.

"What is it? Where's the firewood?" I asked with a raised eyebrow.

Rennan smiled strangely before he scratched his neck nervously. "Do you, by any chance, have a dagger that I can borrow?"

I rolled my eyes. "Why? I thought you had one."

"I did, but Wayne stole it in our fight. Vareh's officials probably have it now. And the one in my boot is far too small to chop any branches or twigs with."

"I thought you were a wolf, though. Couldn't you just break branches with your bare hands and call it good?"

"Heh, I'm sure you've noticed, but I am not the strongest wolf out there by a long shot," Rennan chuckled quietly.

I sighed, unsheathed one of my daggers, and handed it to him.

He smiled awkwardly. "Thanks. I'll have a fire going by the time you come back."

"Good. Don't lose that dagger. I'm going to need it later," I stated as I started walking off.

"You're not going to skin me, are you?" he called in a joking tone.

I smirked slightly, deciding then that I enjoyed Rennan's company. "No, I was going to skin whatever I catch with the knife you get to borrow because it has a longer blade."

"Okay," he said as we parted ways so we could accomplish our respective tasks.

Even if I knew it would only be for a short amount of time, it was nice only having to pay attention to my own activities. I wasn't used to having to look after or keep track of other people, and concluded that I wasn't fond of it. Not to say I didn't like the people themselves (most of the time. I am not a people person)—I just preferred to be on my own. I didn't want to cause other people to suffer if I made a life-threatening mistake.

I took a deep breath of the night air, fully enjoying the chill that it possessed. I cleared my mind and began listening for any movement across the plain. The only sound I heard was a soft breeze blowing through the tree boughs and sweeping across the tall grass, making a melodic swishing noise.

As the wind blew strands of my hair into my face, I opened my eyes and saw a flock of game birds land in the wide plain. I figured that if I were able to catch two of them, we would have enough to eat tonight and perhaps something for breakfast in the morning. I was sure Rennan would appreciate breakfast since he was so eager for dinner. Meanwhile, I probably could have gone all night without eating anything and just stopped in a small village in the morning to pick something up. However, I preferred to be prepared for that sort of thing rather than hear Rennan's complaints all night.

I crept closer to the animals. They couldn't see me through the tall grass, but I could see them. I was so close that when they jerked their heads in my direction, they spread their wings. I panicked as they flew off so I lunged in hopes of catching one.

The birds flew away as I crept out of the little shelter that I had been hiding in. I tried jumping in order to catch one, but I was unable to propel myself high enough to snag one of the winged creatures. When I saw that they were too far away for me to catch, I sighed and threw a rock in frustration.

"Child, what are you doing?" a melodic voice asked from behind me.

I turned around to see my parents standing there. Their expressions were gentle and slightly amused.

"I was trying to catch the birds," I replied as I pointed to the sky.

By now, the birds were so far away that they were only black specks on the horizon.

My father smiled as he sat down on a rock. I immediately climbed up into his lap. My mother knelt beside us.

"What harm did the birds ever do to you, Scarlet?" my father asked gently.

I looked up into his amber-toned eyes before I answered. "None. I just wanted to see if I could catch it."

"What would you have done with the bird if you had caught it?"

"I would have played with it or brought it to you."

My mother and father looked at each other for a mere second before turning their focus back to me.

My mother spoke this time. "Scarlet, do you think the bird likes its freedom?"

"What's freedom?" I asked in confusion. I had never heard the word before.

Father sighed softly. "Freedom is being able to do things without being controlled or restrained from outside forces. So, do you think that bird would have wanted to stay here when it has friends of its own to play with?"

I shook my head sadly. "No, I don't think it would have wanted to stay here. Will you stay here and play with me instead?"

"Of course, my child," Mother smiled as she kissed the top of my head. "We'll stay here for as long as we can."

I came to my senses when I felt my eyes welling with tears at the memory of the heartfelt moment that I had shared with my parents all those years ago. I was three when they told me that. What's more, that was one of my final memories with them before my fourth birthday—their death day.

I watched the birds fly off into the night sky and shook my head sadly.

I would just find some winter berries or something to eat instead. After remembering the last time I tried to catch fleeing birds, I no longer felt like hunting them. I would rather suffer a less filling meal than take away the bird's freedom for the present moment. I was sure that I would have to catch one eventually, but I had no motivation to do it then.

Later, I returned to the camp holding a small pouch full of roots and berries that we could cook to make a little bit sweeter (I had already tasted the berries and discovered they were immensely tart). Rennan had succeeded in lighting the fire, so I was pleased that I wouldn't have to do that as well. Since I didn't think he would have the guts to hunt, it was a good thing to know he could light a fire.

Rennan looked away from the fire to the direction I was approaching from. He smiled proudly when he saw me. "I got the firewood and started the fire! And I didn't burn anything other than what I needed to!"

"I can see that," I said as I sat down on a log across from him. I could also smell no traces of anything burnt, so that was nice. Burnt smells made me sick.

"So, what's in the bag?" Rennan asked curiously.

I sent him a skeptical look before I opened the sack. I quickly scanned the contents to remind myself of what it contained.

"It's just a bunch of roots and berries that we can cook. I gathered as many as I could find," I responded as I tossed him the closed bag.

He caught it after fumbling to keep a grip on it. I restrained my laughter concerning his "grace."

"Were you unable to find meat?" he asked as he pulled out a couple of sharp sticks. He probably whittled them while I had been hunting.

I didn't have the heart to tell him that I hadn't felt like hunting animals after that memory had resurfaced. It was too personal to tell someone I barely knew.

"Well, I was on the trail of some, but they saw me and bolted too quickly for me to catch. I couldn't find anything else within a reasonable distance so I found those," I replied with a nonchalant shrug.

Rennan nodded thoughtfully as his attention returned to the blazing fire. He didn't question me further, which I found relieving.

"So…what's the plan?" Rennan asked as he handed me one of the sticks with berries on it.

I took it and pulled one off. It wasn't nearly as hot as I thought it'd be, so I popped it into my mouth. As I had hoped, it was much sweeter than the raw berries. I took my time in answering his latest question.

"We go to sleep, get up early, and keep trekking," I answered when I had stalled long enough. Though he was somewhat oblivious, I knew that Rennan was not stupid and he would know when I was stalling. Wolves were smart enough for that.

Rennan groaned. "I assume that's the plan for the next nine days as well?"

I nodded, much to his disappointment. "You're welcome to stay here and make your own way back home if you don't want to wake so early."

"No, I'll come, but we will be stopping for meals, correct?"

"Just breakfast and supper. We'll take several breaks for water, but beyond that, we continue moving. If a storm comes, I don't want to be caught out in the open," I stated, looking up at the sky. The wind had picked up again and it was bringing clouds along with it.

"Okay. Well, I guess I'm going to call it a night. Good night, Scarlet," Rennan said with a small smile. I nodded in acknowledgment, but I didn't return the smile. I was just going to blame it on the cold weather and didn't want to show my chattering teeth.

"Night. Make sure to wrap your hands. The last thing that we need out here is hypothermia," I stated.

He nodded and grabbed a couple of loose cloths from his pack. Then he went on his side of the shelter and laid down to try and sleep in the glacial cold.

Though I was physically exhausted from hiking and the fight, I couldn't seem to make myself sleep. I had a lot on my mind from what had happened that day. I couldn't help thinking about Razil not acting like her typical self, the fight seeming off, and Rennan suddenly joining me. Still, what bothered me the most was Razil. She had seemed jumpy, not as jumpy as Rennan seemed to be, but jumpy. It was like she was hiding something, but did not—or could not—tell me what it was.

Eventually I got tired of thinking of the possibilities, so I decided to turn in for the night. I knew that I had sat there for hours and it would only be a few more until we had to get up again, but a little bit of sleep was better than none at all. I would regret it later if I did not sleep, so I entered the shelter and curled up as far away from Rennan as I could. Then I fell asleep and awaited the next few days of endless hiking.

We reached Leshee eight days later—a day sooner than I had

anticipated.

I would explain all the details, but there isn't much to say. We traveled through the endless plains until we reached some of the scattered woodland that was north of the city. From there we journeyed through the "dark, scary forest," as Rennan called it, for a whole day. I had better luck hunting there so Rennan's spirits were high for the duration of our woodland hike. We also ran into some of the forest hybrids, but we passed by peacefully and continued on our way.

The city was loud and busy when we arrived. Rennan and I both pulled our hoods up so we wouldn't be recognized. I wanted to make a quiet entrance so I wouldn't cause a huge uproar in the town. People didn't always take well to my presence. Since Rennan and I both lived on the south side of Leshee, we decided to take a short cut right through the heart of town instead of lengthening our trip by going around everything.

It appeared to be a market day. There were carts set up all around the square with buyers and sellers bargaining away. I noticed Rennan watching almost longingly so I elbowed his arm and gave him a questioning look. He looked down at me and briefly smiled.

"Sorry. My parents are merchants and come here every so often," Rennan replied as he looked at the ground.

"So, your pack doesn't live here?" I questioned in surprise.

Most members of wolf packs lived in the same city, if not the same den. Rennan nodded to confirm my suspicions.

"I'm the lone wolf of my pack, so to speak," he said quietly. "I left a few years ago because that den wasn't enough for me. I've always been one who likes to travel. I was also one of the youngest pups, so I didn't really have all that great of a time growing up either."

"Yeah, I kind of know how that is," I replied with a sigh. I wish I didn't, but I did. And sadly, there was no possible way to change that appalling fact.

We were almost out of the town square and the marketplace when trouble started to arise. Screams started on the east side of town and steadily travelled to the west. Rennan and I looked at each other before sprinting to find a decent hiding place. I had no intention of fleeing and would fight if I needed to, but I had to see what was going on first. All of it reminded me too much of the day my parents died. This could tell me what had happened.

Before we could determine the cause of the chaos, cloaked figures in all shapes and sizes came rampaging through the square. They all wore hoods that covered their faces so I couldn't identify any of them.

All I knew is that none were elves. If legends were correct, we would never know what hit us if they were elves. These rogues weren't nearly as graceful as the stories claimed that elves were. All the individuals had drawn swords which they promptly used to smash all the carts, produce, and wares into little pieces.

I sat there, completely stunned when the cloaked people turned to the citizens. In mere seconds, there were bloody corpses strewn across the stone blocks and wooden planks. The whole scene echoed the memories that scarred my mind. My chest heaved and my stomach churned while I watched the whole thing. I couldn't bear to see so much injustice done to these innocent people. I wasn't particularly fond of any of them, but they did not deserve to die.

Then fury and adrenaline took over. I unsheathed my longest dagger and gritted my teeth. I started to move, but Rennan grabbed hold of my arm. He gave a look that implored me to remain hidden, but I ignored him. I was the only one with the skills to drive the attackers off. I knew what needed to be done, and he had no choice but to follow me.

I slipped out of our hiding place and threw myself into the swarm of cloaked figures. I raised my dagger and swung, slicing the cloth to shreds as well as the muscle beneath. Some dropped dead on the spot; others tried to fight back, but died in the process. The majority cried out in agony and fled in terror.

When they were all gone, I turned to Rennan, who stared at me in shock.

"I cannot believe that you just did that," he said in awe as he looked at everything around us. "I don't know how you can do that."

"Practice, I guess," I muttered as I cleaned my blade on one of the cloaks I had torn.

I might as well use that instead of soiling my own cloak. The blood would dry darker on mine anyway, what with it being a fairly light shade of orange. My grandmother always called it a pumpkin orange.

My eyes widened with fear for my grandmother. "We need to find her."

"Find who?" Rennan asked as I started running to the south side of town.

I needed to make it home before it was too late. I didn't answer the wolf, but I knew that he was following close behind me. Soon we reached the alleyway that lead to my front door. It was utterly empty.

"Scarlet, where are we?" Rennan demanded, scanning all shadows for the mysterious mercenaries.

"A place that she should have come to a long time ago," a cold voice stated boldly from behind us.

My spine tingled when I recognized the voice. I tightened my grip on my dagger as I turned to face my newest adversary.

She, like the others, wore a long, dark cloak, though it looked quite strange on her because of a large set of feathered wings that were as black as night. She threw her hood back and laughed. "Yes, it's me. Don't look so surprised!"

"What are you doing here, Razil?" I hissed through gritted teeth.

My ears were flat against my skull. I was just waiting for her to make one wrong move so I could pounce on my enemy—if she proved to be one.

"I'm finishing the job that should have been done years ago," she said, revealing her true colors. "Now step aside and nobody gets hurt."

"Never," I seethed as I unsheathed the second dagger. I had a feeling that I would have need of it yet.

Razil narrowed her eyes as she pulled a long, sharp object out of one of her pockets.

I immediately recognized it as a tranquilizer dart. "What is that?"

She grinned evilly. "I told you about the amazing powers of herbs, did I not? Yes, I know I did. Well, this is just another example of one of their great abilities. The plant that I used to make this is called *relek*. It has the phenomenal power to paralyze anything it comes in contact with in only a few seconds. Kills in minutes. Remarkable, isn't it?"

"I would say that it is, but that's giving you something you want," I sneered, giving her an icy glare. She frowned when I said, "Get out of here. I won't let you finish whatever it is that you came for."

Razil laughed a long, empty, hollow laugh. "Don't you see? It's already happening" —she whistled— "Bring her up!"

The door behind us slammed open as a man (an actual human, not any sort of hybrid) carried out a limp form. The man himself had dark skin and hair, clearly from another kingdom. He wasn't particularly young either; perhaps he was still younger than most people, but certainly not as young as Rennan or I. Razil shoved past us to stand beside the man.

"If you so much as touch me, she dies," the raven announced callously. She raised a dagger above the limp form that the man held in his arms.

I took a good look at it and gasped when I realized who it was: my grandmother!

"Scarlet, child, come here," my grandmother pleaded in a frail voice.

It sounded like she was just barely holding onto life. What had they done to her in the time it had taken me to get here?

"May I have a word with my grandmother?" I asked with mock-politeness.

Razil looked at her associate and nodded. They stepped back a few feet and pretended not to notice us.

I rushed to my grandmother and knelt down beside where the man laid her. "Grandmother. Please speak to me."

"Child, I told you once that I would tell you all that you wanted to know," she began with a frail voice, "I now see that I should have told you years ago…."

"No, please, don't leave me," I begged as tears filled my eyes.

I couldn't bear losing my grandmother. This couldn't be the end. I wouldn't let it be the end. I didn't know what I would do if I lost her. She had been with me every stage in my life and I wouldn't know what to do or where to go without her loving guidance. I had a feeling in the pit of my stomach that I would be lost without her.

"Ugh, enough already!" Rennan shouted as he pulled out his own small throwing stars.

He hurled one at Razil and it hit her in the arm. She cried out in horror when she saw bright red blood trickle down her arm in small streams. Her eyes became wild as she started shouting curses. Then, to my dismay, she threw her tranquilizer dart at my grandmother and hit her neck. Razil grabbed her partner in crime and flew up above the tops of the buildings and flew out of sight.

"Grandmother!" I shrieked. I probably shouldn't have since it betrayed my feelings when my enemies were still far too close for comfort, but I couldn't help it. I was shocked and angry. Beyond that, I could practically see the life leaving Grandmother's eyes. "No, please don't leave me now. You have to survive this."

"Child, there comes a time where everyone must pass into the halls of their ancestors," my grandmother said quietly. She reached up and gingerly put a hand on my face. "This is my time to join them. I've lived my life; it's time for you to live yours now."

"This can't be the end!" I protested desperately.

"But it is," she countered. She drew in a long breath before saying, "I wanted to tell you so much, but now there is little time."

She hesitated long enough for me to think that she was drifting away.

I panicked. "Grandmother, what did you want to tell me?"

"Don't hold on to the past for too long, my child. Don't let it drag you down. Remember it, but let it shape you for the life you still have to live. Thrive!"

With that, my grandmother breathed her last.

I just sat on the ground with my grandmother, mourning the loss that I once again had suffered. This was the woman who had taught me to read, write, and so many other things as I grew up. I couldn't just lose her and not feel the pain! First my parents had been taken from me when I was a child. Then my longest known "friend" had betrayed me and murdered my grandmother right before my eyes. I couldn't help but wonder what horrible thing would happen next.

My grandmother's death tore at me inside. Fires seemed to rage, wanting to destroy everything in its path. My head started spinning in the realization that I was alone in this dark, terrible world with nobody to stand by me from my own family. I was the sole survivor and nothing could ever change that.

In that moment, I swore I wouldn't go down nearly as easily as my parents or grandmother. If anyone came after me and sought to end my life, I was determined to give them gruesome memories that they would never forget. That is, if they lived to remember me.

"Scarlet, I'm *so* sorry. I shouldn't have forced her hand," Rennan profusely apologized.

I could barely pay attention to him due to my grief. I let my tears freely flow down my cheeks as I held my grandmother close to me.

"There's nothing you could have done," I sniffled a few minutes later. "There's nothing you can do. She's always going to get away with it no matter what we try."

"Mm, I wouldn't say that," a new voice said. It was a deep, accented, and almost enchanting voice that obviously belonged to someone young and educated.

I rose to my feet and Rennan and I turned to face the stranger.

He emerged from the shadows at the head of the alley and walked over to where the two of us stood. He was a head and a half taller than me and at least half a head taller than Rennan. The man threw his hood back and I gasped in shock and anger. Before me stood a member of the race that I hated the most.

An elf.

Desperate Path

"Who are you? What are you doing here? Did you cause all of this?" I demanded, frantically gesturing toward the entire scene around us.

The elf looked at me with mild amusement. He ran his hand through his dark hair and cracked a small smile. He was a very tall man, taller than any who lived in Palee. He had piercing grey eyes and slightly unkempt brown hair that reflected gold and a little bit of red tones in the sunlight. It hung just past his shoulders and directly contrasted his outfit. He was dressed all in black, which made him seem even more suspicious.

Armor covered his shoulders and he carried a pack filled with weapons on his back. Surprisingly, he did not carry a single broad sword with him. Instead, it looked like his main weapon was the massive scythe slung over his back. One side was a long, perilous silver blade and on the other was a griffin claw that was just as sharp. His face looked kind when he smiled, but otherwise it was as still as stone and showed no emotion whatsoever. Despite the fact that he looked approachable, I didn't trust him as far as I could see him.

"Typical for a hybrid to think an elf would do this," he said in a relatively firm voice. He looked me dead in the eye. "I assure you; I did *not* orchestrate this. I would never lead a massacre."

I narrowed my eyes. "Then why are you here? You of all people wouldn't be in Palee unless you were following through with an attack on innocent people!"

"I didn't do it!" the elf shouted, his voice becoming fierce while shadows crept into his face.

Out of the corner of my eye, I noticed that Rennan shrank back a little bit.

The elf shook his head as if snapping out of a trance and the shadows retreated. His voice became low-toned again. "I am here because I've been following these assassins since Scottsdale, Tralia. I don't know who came here to lead this massacre, but I do know who sent them in the first place."

"Then by all means tell us! And while you're at it, tell us who you are," I commanded impatiently.

The elf sighed and looked everywhere but at Rennan or I. Resentment filled his eyes, but somehow, I got the feeling that it was not directed toward us.

"Fine, I'll tell you what you need to know," the elf said, eyes as gloomy as a thunderstorm. "Just a warning, you won't like it any more than I do."

"Well, then, you had better get started," Rennan stated bitterly.

From what I had learned about Rennan in the last few days of traveling with him, he didn't like the elves any more than me. They were stuck-up, snotty, and conceited beings that cared only for themselves. They didn't have any second thoughts for people like the hybrids who were basically locked in a prison every day of their lives.

"My name is Cameron Woods. As you've already noticed, I'm an elf, but it's not like you think," he added quickly when Rennan and I both glared at him. "I'm an elf, yes, but not one with active status in Heviah" — he laughed bitterly before it turned into a snarl— "I used to, but no longer. I was exiled for constantly pointing out the flaws in our society without hesitation. But, as expected, nobody listened to me because they were all too arrogant to consider anything other than their own status and 'tradition.' Not even my own family stood by me when I was given my sentence."

I snickered in understanding. Rennan nodded and sighed. We both knew what it felt like to be abandoned by the ones we loved. My experiences were something a little different than theirs, but the same core feelings remained.

I muttered, "Yeah, tell us about it."

"That's part of the reason I'm here. Like I said before, I've been following these killers since they reached the capital of Tralia. They stopped there for supplies or something before coming north over the mountains. I-I forget what you call them," Cameron said as he ran his hand through his hair again. A shining metal band on his index finger glittered in the sunlight.

"The Forgotten Mountains?" Rennan suggested with a questioning look.

Cameron snapped his fingers. "Yes, that's the name. Sorry, I'm usually better at remembering details like that. Anyway, I know who sent those assassins and I wanted to follow them to see just how corrupt things in Heviah have become in the last five years or so."

"Okay, that's great and all, but why are you here for us? We're nothing special among our people. Heh, we're probably a couple of the least respected people in this blasted kingdom," Rennan said.

He sent a quick glance at me as if saying *no offense*. I didn't take any since he spoke the truth. Nobody really liked either of us.

"Yes, I was coming to that. From careful work I uncovered from my research around here is that you two are from lesser known families who have...*difficult* backgrounds. I came here because I need your help," Cameron said as he stood up a little bit straighter.

I don't know why he did, unless he was trying to be more assertive. But still, what would an elf want to do with hybrids like us? It didn't make sense that he would want the help of two outcasts.

"But that doesn't explain how you know who the heck we are. You said you uncovered information, but *how*?" I demanded.

I didn't like how he just casually talked about knowing who we were. I had worked undercover jobs long enough to know how much information to get out of the target before killing them. I don't know how dangerous of a guy this elf was, but this was one of those times that I wasn't going to take any chances.

I glared at him. "You don't just say that you know people without further explaining *how* you know them."

Cameron shifted his weight and looked me dead in the eye. "A guy has a lot of time on his hands when he's exiled for eternity. Do you really think I would spend five years doing nothing when there was so much work to be done?"

"No. Get to the point," Rennan growled.

"Fine. I spent a year or so just wandering the wilderness exploring. From there I made it to Sala and spent a year there doing more diplomatic research and establishing an alliance with one of the eastern kingdoms of Galerah. Since then, I've journeyed all over Palee looking for anyone that might be willing to help me in my quest."

"Why do you need our help? You're an elf. Can't you do everything on your own?" I asked, not caring if I came across rude or not.

Cameron hung his head in humiliation.

"No elf can do everything on their own. I've tried to do all that I could to make other people see the light and how corrupt our world has become. I wouldn't be here right now if there was no other way. And I don't say that because you two are my last option. I say it because this world needs change," he said quietly. "Please, Scarlet and Rennan. I need your help."

Rennan and I turned to each other and stepped out of earshot from the elf. I didn't like that he was here so soon after the latest attack, so I was incredibly wary to trust him. It was one thing for me to learn to trust Rennan like I had, but it was another thing entirely to learn to trust an elf, the sworn enemy of my kind.

I had discovered (mostly by sneaking into the restricted areas of the library late at night) that the elves were one of the leading reasons that the hybrids in Palee were basically prisoners.

Several centuries ago, there had been a war started by the hybrids that was launched against the elves because of the laws of their dictator-led culture. The elves, of course, tricked everyone else into thinking that we hybrids were the ones to blame for all the evil in the world. The hybrids lost the war and were locked up in the Kingdom of Palee where we would never again be let out. Things had only deteriorated more in the last hundred years or so.

Rennan shook my shoulders. "Earth to Scarlet! You in there?"

"Yeah," I said quietly.

I didn't want to say anything concerning what I had been thinking of and Rennan seemed to notice. He didn't push for any information either.

"What do you think we should do?" the wolf asked quietly.

He subtly nodded in Cameron's direction. The elf stood there staring off into the sky with a childlike fascination with the fluffy white clouds that were scattered throughout the great vastness of blue.

I sighed. "I don't know, and I don't trust him—at all."

"I know. I don't trust him either. But think of it this way: he's offering us a way to get out of this wretched kingdom. This may never happen again, Scarlet," Rennan pointed out.

It was a decent argument—even I had to admit that.

"I guess there is some logic to that," I reluctantly admitted as I shifted my weight to my other leg. "I say we get some more information out of this elf before we agree to anything. I don't know about you, but I don't feel like following him to my death."

"Agreed. I'm not ready to die either," Rennan stated.

We turned back to the elf, who looked both nervous and hopeful.

"I really hope you haven't decided to kill me here and now," Cameron said in a half-joking tone.

I narrowed my eyes at him and his smile faded. He quickly became serious again.

"We'd like to know what we're going to be getting ourselves into if we agree," Rennan diplomatically expressed.

I didn't know the jumpy wolf hybrid had it in him to sound so professional!

At any rate, it worked because Cameron nodded his head.

"I understand that. Knowledge of another person's motives is key to trusting them, and I know that neither one of you trust me because I'm an elf. I wish that I wasn't one in times like this. Still, I saw no point in pretending I was anything else. If we trust each other, nothing can be hidden," he sighed sadly as he looked away.

He remained silent for a couple minutes before saying, "A small portion of information is currently clear to me. All I know right now is that this world is falling apart and it will destroy itself if we don't do something soon. All of Galerah is in a state of unrest that will crumble into chaos if something isn't done. I was hoping that I would be able to find you and see if you would help me since I believe that we can repair the bridge between our two species."

"How did you even know where to find us and who we are? I doubt Heviah has records on every single hybrid here given how much they hate us," I asked suspiciously.

The fact that Cameron had specifically chosen Rennan and I to ask for help seemed odd, considering how many more reliable hybrids there were in this kingdom.

Cameron smiled wryly. "They don't. I learned about you two on my own. I've been in Palee several times before, actually. I was trying to figure out why everyone distrusts the hybrids so much, and I honestly don't see what everyone's so afraid of. I've seen more virtue here than in most kingdoms. But that isn't what you asked me. You asked how I know who you are. Well, Rennan, I've talked to people who have mentioned you to me as a guy who is quite amiable and looking for a way to make things better for Palee as a whole."

Rennan's eyes widened in surprise. "Well, that's not wrong. But how were you here before without being recognized? Any hybrid would to recognize an elf any day of the week. Not to mention smell one."

Cameron smirked. "So…we smell now, too?"

"That's not what I meant!" Rennan cried quickly with an expression that clearly communicated that the elf had caught him off guard.

Cameron laughed with a smile at the hilarity of Rennan's rushed cry.

"I know it wasn't, and don't worry, I know what you mean," the elf assured the wolf with a wink. Rennan blushed.

"What about me?" I questioned. I glared at the elf. "How did you know about me?"

"I'll be perfectly honest with you, Scarlet," he began. "It was a lot harder to put a precise pin on who you are. The more I travelled throughout Palee, the more I heard of a killer who struck in the dead of night and was never or seldom seen. Curiosity overcame me, so I looked into different accounts of the people each target knew.

"The only city relatively safe from these assassinations was Leshee. From there, different people told me about a young woman who kept to herself and rarely talked to anyone. I've been around elves and other such people long enough to know that when they're withdrawn, something foul is never far behind. So that's how I learned about you. Is there anything else you would like me to explain now?"

I was shocked that he was so quick to nail me as an mercenary. While there were still many things about this elf I would love to know about, I decided not to ask any more questions now. In addition, I was not ready to give any of my background when he had given me so little of his. So, I just said, "No. Now answer Rennan's question."

"Fair enough. I was here and unrecognized because I have a rare gift among the elves. I'm the only one in recorded history to ever have received it."

"What is it?" I asked.

My curiosity was beginning to get the better of me. I had read in several books that elves of noble blood received special gifts, and often times they were unique either to a family or an individual. The fact that this elf had one that had never been recorded in history intrigued me greatly. I mean, I knew more about the other kingdoms than most hybrids my age, but ancient books can only teach me so much.

Then I realized something. "Wait, since you have a power, does that mean you are royalty?"

Cameron flushed red. Apparently, I caught him off guard with a question that he didn't think I would ask. "N-no! Of course not! I was a knight in the king's court. Some members of my family were royalty at one point, so I guess that's how I got one. And to answer your first question, I have the ability to shape-shift. It's something that proves very useful when you don't want to be found by scouts in cities you're not technically supposed to be in."

"Okay, that's good to know, but now we've gotten off track. What do you need our help with?" Rennan asked when we had passed through a period of awkward silence.

Cameron continued to make strange faces (like the ones a person makes when they're internally talking to themselves) until he seemed to come up with an answer.

"I need your help to find evidence that the Elven monarchy is truly corrupt and help me overthrow them," Cameron stated with a little more assertiveness in his deep voice. "Nobody believes me, but based on the fact that you two are pretty biased against the elves, you might be able to help me find evidence and see through their lies."

I looked to Rennan again and he nodded his head ever so slightly.

"Okay, we'll help you, under a few conditions," I stated.

"Anything."

"If we succeed, you will find a way to declare the hybrids free to live and travel wherever they desire. I also don't want to be controlled or silenced on this quest either."

"Done. Anything else?"

"Yes. You have to get us out of this kingdom as soon as possible."

Cameron laughed. "Then I guess we set out in the next hour."

"Don't make us regret this decision," Rennan stated in a threatening manner. He would have looked quite intimidating if he had actually been taller than the elf. Instead, it was quite a comical sight. The shorter guy was threatening the tall one.

"I promise you won't regret a thing," Cameron said solemnly.

For his sake, I hoped he spoke truly.

We had to gather supplies before we left so we split up to gather anything we needed. Rennan went to his own apartment to get anything for this journey and Cameron went somewhere else in town to gather food supplies and weapons. I personally did not see why he would need more weapons when he already had a scythe, a bow, arrows, throwing stars, and countless daggers. He didn't give me a reason why either.

I, meanwhile, had the most difficult task among the three of us: deal with my den and grandmother. I ended up finding a cart that was still in decent condition and I gingerly put my grandmother in it with a cloth over her. I didn't want anybody to ask questions if I passed by. All I wanted to do was give my grandmother a proper burial and then get out of town. I didn't want to linger in this town that reeked of death any longer than I had to.

I wheeled the cart out into one of the fields surrounding Leshee. I specifically took it to the same place we had buried my parents all those years ago. It was in a grassy area scattered with colorful flowers, which made the graves relatively cheerful. The graves themselves, at this point in time anyway, were just large mounds in the otherwise flat plain.

I laid the cart down and started digging a pit large enough to put my grandmother's body in. It was slow, grueling work, but I eventually was able to make a large enough hole next to my parents. I gently laid the body in and covered it with the loose earth I had already moved. Then I transplanted one of the flowering plants and planted it atop my grandmother's mound.

I stepped back and looked over their graves, barely believing I had just buried the last living member of my blood family. Now I was completely on my own and could do what I needed to. Heh, it was a bittersweet feeling. I had the freedom I had always wanted, but I had lost the only thing I had stayed here for.

"I know how it feels," a deep voice said from behind me.

I turned around to see Cameron standing behind me in the form of a musk deer hybrid. For a second, I seriously thought he was a real one because he didn't show any signs that he was an elf. He was several inches shorter to match the size of the actual species. Now he was more of

Rennan's height instead of the normal, towering one of the elves. Even the fangs were spot on. His ears weren't even pointy! The only thing giving him away as the elf I had met earlier was his thunderous grey eyes that were too curious for his own good.

He offered a sympathetic smile. "I too know what it is like to lose people I love."

I remained quiet until I could think of something to say. It was strange to find myself relating about something like this with an elf. "I wouldn't expect elves to lose those they love to assassins or death of old age."

"Not old age since we're immortal. That fact also makes my exile incredibly long if the current king isn't overthrown. But assassinations do occur in Heviah every once in a while. I lost an aunt to a bounty hunter a few years ago. She was the only one who sided with me when it came to pointing out the corruption in our kingdom. The king had her killed secretly one night and I never heard of her again," Cameron said quietly. "But yeah, I know the pain you're feeling."

I looked at him and I saw genuine sadness, and also bitterness, in his grey eyes.

"Yeah," I said almost silently.

I noiselessly prayed for the souls of my family before I turned away to head back to my den to grab anything else I wanted to take with me before we left. I had no intention of coming back to Palee for a long time. Honestly, I didn't ever want to come back. It was a feeling of utter hiraeth.

"Did you get everything that you needed?" I asked him.

"Yeah, I have it all. I assume we're going back to your den to grab anything you need before heading out?" Cameron replied while he followed a few feet behind me.

"Yes, I need to take care of a few things," I replied.

We were nearing my den now. I started walking down the alley to the door, but the elf hung back at the opening to the narrow street.

I turned back to face him. "Since you're not coming, why don't you go find Rennan?"

"That's a good idea," he agreed as he walked off to a different part of the fairly large town.

Once he was gone, I sighed and turned back to the door. It was a heavy wooden door with a few carvings of trees and leaves as well as our family crest: a simple paw print made up of complex designs. There was an amber-colored stone set dead in the middle of the print. I remember the day my mother carved it. I fondly remember her embrace as she told me I would never get lost so long as I knew our crest.

I never forgot the symbol on the door that I had come to know so well. Seeing the print of the Sutton family always gave me a sense of peace and belonging. It saddened me to think I would never see this beautiful door again, but perhaps it would be for the better. Perhaps I would finally move on from everything that has happened.

I pushed past the door and stepped into the small, cluttered den. Much of the furniture was in pieces and many scraps of cloth were torn and tattered. I sighed heavily when I saw the damage done to the home I loved dearly. Despite the urge I felt to clean it up before I left (I had been in charge of much of the cleaning because my grandmother was quite frail and I could not stand it when things were not in their designated places), I just wandered through the building to the back. That was where my bedroom was located.

I had a small room filled with books and little things I had brought home from my travels. It only consisted of small objects like strange rocks or gemstones that could be found in the specific areas in the wilderness of Palee, but I always liked them. Beyond that, there wasn't really anything that screamed, *This is Scarlet's room!* It was just a simple room that had served its purpose while I lived here.

I was quick to grab necessary belongings. Really, it wasn't much. It was just a few extra clothes and additional weapons I was able to tuck into my boots or the pack I would be carrying. I was almost ready to leave the den when my eyes passed over something on my nightstand. I slowly walked over to it and picked up the small, smooth object. It was a charcoal sketch of me and my family when I was a baby. They all looked so happy, like nothing could ever go wrong.

"*Scarlet?*" Cameron's voice called through the den.

I didn't say anything because I was too taken in by the peace I felt by looking at that picture. My parents were alive and well, my grandmother looked strong as if nothing would stop her, and I was safe in my father's arms. And here I was now, the last one left who belonged to the Sutton name. I heard Cameron and Rennan's footsteps approach.

"Scarlet, we're ready to go whenever you are," the elf's voice informed me.

"Okay, I'll be out there in just a minute," I stated as I shoved the picture into the pocket of my fur-lined cloak.

There was no way in Galerah I was going to leave this picture behind. It might have been part of my past, but I was going to remember it as long as I lived. I might as well have something to remind me of the love I recalled feeling when I was little, even if I doubted I would ever feel such love again.

I quickly strode out of the den and into the cool, evening air. I closed the door to my past and sighed. This would be the last time I would stand in this spot for a long time. I closed my eyes and pulled out the amber stone in the middle of the paw print. I felt somehow that it would connect me in a small way to my parents, so I felt the desire to take it with me. I put it in the same pocket as the picture before I turned to face Rennan and Cameron.

"Ready to go?" Rennan asked as he shouldered the pack that had been sitting near his feet.

I nodded my head as I followed them both out of the alleyway. I looked back one last time at the home I had grown up in. It looked small and sad, and I couldn't bear to see it that way.

Cameron put his hand on my shoulder. I looked up into his steel grey eyes, which were kind and compassionate and understanding.

Then we looked to make sure nobody was watching us before we sprinted out of town.

We trekked on through Palee for weeks after that. Our journey south was a calm one, as we found out. Cameron chose a quiet route for us to travel. He said few people knew about it and even fewer took it. I wasn't entirely sure if I thought that was good or bad. I was afraid wild animals, or crazy hybrids for that matter, would attack us at some point in the night.

Thankfully, the elf assured us that would not happen. And if it did, however unlikely it was, he would be ready with his bow.

Rennan relaxed significantly when he saw all of the weapons Cameron had been carrying with him. Honestly, the wolf hybrid was shaping up to be quite an amusing person. He was so clueless at times that he made me want to laugh without a care in the world. Other times, his cluelessness was going to be the end of me. However, I certainly respected him much more than I had when I had first met him when he woke up in that traitor's house.

We made camp early one night. Once we had gotten tents set up and a fire started, Rennan decided that he was going to go exploring a little bit. While he did that, Cameron and I remained in our camp, sharpening some of our weapons. For a while, it seemed like neither one of us had any intention to strike up conversation.

That is, until Cameron asked, "So. How long have you lived in Leshee?"

I put down my whetstone and stared at the elf. I tried to determine the intent of his question, but I couldn't place it. Finally, I reluctantly responded, "Almost my whole life. After my parents died, my grandmother and I moved around a lot, but we always ended up back in Leshee."

"Were you close to her?" he asked quietly.

I didn't want to respond, but I couldn't help whispering, "Yes."

The elf nodded. "Love is an interesting concept, don't you think?"

"Why are you asking me this?" I demanded.

I didn't like how closely he was hedging around my motives. He already knew I was a mercenary. I hadn't told him I was driven by desire to avenge my dear parents either, but he seemed to have keyed in on it. He didn't need to know more.

"To start a conversation. I don't like small talk," Cameron shrugged as he inspected his blade. "I just find it interesting that love can create such a strong bond between two people who dearly care for each other one minute, and rip them apart the next. It seems fickle, doesn't it?"

"I can think of many words to describe love, but fickle is not one of the first that comes to mind," I answered coldly.

"Fair enough. I find that while it can be fickle, it is still a driving factor in life—even if it isn't always used in the best sense of the word. People can love each other dearly, but I fear more people in this world are loving wealth and power more than the simple things," Cameron sighed.

I looked up from my blade to see him staring into the fire. "That's why you found us and asked us to join your quest, isn't it?"

"Yes. Forgive me for making assumptions, but I think you may have become a mercenary because you're still hurting from a loss. That's why I wanted to find you—because you can empathize people in similar situations," Cam explained. "As for Rennan, he is just pure passion for what he holds dear. I haven't known either of you long, but I just have a feeling that those things are true about you. Those qualities make you ideal people to change the world—but you can't do that if you're trapped in a forgotten kingdom, can you?"

"No, we can't," I agreed with a twitch of a smile. "Tell me, Cameron, why do you think you're an ideal person to lead this quest?"

"You already know I was exiled, but thirst for power isn't my motivation. I know this sounds crazy, but I feel like there's darkness and poison spreading outwards from Heviah. I've seen it everywhere in my travels. It bothers me, and I've never been the type to just sit by while the world falls apart," the elf replied. "But as for morals and how those relate to motives, I'm not all that different from you. I've been deeply hurt in my own past, which fuels a conflict that goes back millennium in my line. I desire to make things right in Heviah and Palee. I just can't do it alone."

I sat back a little bit, thinking about what the elf had told me. Remarkably, I didn't take issue with anything he had said. He was very fair in how he viewed things. He wasn't wrong in how he had perceived Rennan and I either. From that alone, I figured that he was far more perceptive and intelligent than he let on. I'd rather be on his side in these strange times than against him.

"We seem to agree on something, elf," I stated a few minutes later.

He raised an eyebrow. "Oh?"

"This world needs to change, and we three are the ones to bring it."

The next morning, we set out at the break of dawn.

Since Rennan and Cameron were in no mood for conversation that early in the day, I had time to think about the origin of this quest. My mind was primarily focused on the betrayal I had experienced from Razil. Oh, how angry that made me. How long had she been working for the enemy? Was she ever my friend? Was she really raised in some sort of evil organization who sought to wipe out anybody who didn't conform to their corrupt standards?

Rennan and Cameron said that I had rambled on such questions to myself for the majority of the hike. I know my face had flushed red in embarrassment when they told me that. Rennan had said that he thought that she had been my friend for a certain amount of time, but had only recently joined the enemy under force.

Strangely enough, the elf thought she was raised in a secret organization that wanted to wipe out those who didn't conform. When I asked him why, he didn't answer and instead remained silent after shrugging his broad shoulders. I'm just going to say right now that it is impossible to drag anything out of the elf that he did not want you to know.

Soon we decided to make a camp for the night. After all, this was the third week straight that Rennan and I had been traveling through Palee on foot without much of a rest. Cameron was reluctant to stop for the night, but in the end (after a very a long debate where Rennan and I had to thoroughly convince him otherwise) we managed to win the case. Cameron is *not* an easy person to win over.

We set up a tent and once again, I sent Rennan to retrieve firewood from some of the nearby trees. Just like last time, he came back mere seconds later asking if he could borrow my dagger. I gave it to him again and he went back to the woods.

"Why does he not have a dagger with him? He should have grabbed one from the blacksmith before we left Leshee," Cameron asked as he slipped out of the shadows.

I jumped because I had not realized that he had returned. He had gone off somewhere to see if there was fresh water we could drink.

"I have no idea. I honestly should just give him one of mine to keep.

Just not that one," I stated as I pulled out one of my many daggers from my left boot. I'd probably end up giving him that one.

Cameron raised an eyebrow at my curious choice of weapon storage as he set a pan of water down.

I raised an eyebrow in surprise. "What? Don't tell me I'm the only one who does that."

Cameron laughed as he began to take one of the leather guards off his wrist. Beneath it was an incredibly thin dagger; it was almost thin enough to resemble some sort of rapier-like weapon. "No, of course not. Any good hunter—or huntress—knows how to effectively store weapons."

"Indeed. Now we should see if we can actually teach Rennan how to use a dagger to fight instead of just cut wood," I remarked as I watched Rennan try (and fail) to climb a tree to get a fairly thick, dead bough even though there was one of the same size not far away from his pile. I heard Cameron snicker.

"Quite an interesting person, isn't he?" Cameron commented with a hint of amusement in his voice.

"Indeed, but I'm sure you have enough of your own stories you could tell," I stated slyly.

Or, not so slyly since Cameron's head immediately whipped around to stare at me. It was like laser vision because the glare from his steel grey eyes was so intense.

"I have said all that I need to say for the present time!" he snapped quickly.

Then he stalked off back into the shadows before I could call him back. I stared after him as he walked into the trees in the opposite direction of Rennan.

"What's his problem?" Rennan asked out of nowhere.

I turned around to see him kneeling and trying to set up the fire. I watched him try to make a tepee sort of structure before actually igniting the dry wood.

I shrugged as I sat down opposite from the other hybrid. I didn't want to tell Rennan all of the details, but I knew I had to tell him something. "I don't really know. We were just having a conversation and then he just got irritated and stalked away."

"Huh, weird," Rennan said as he started beating rocks together in an attempt to make a spark.

I watched as he continued failing at his fairly simple job. I was just about to help him when a spark fell on the dry twigs. All the dead wood around it ignited with a large *whoosh*.

"Wahoo!" He cheered.

His excitement was almost infectious, but I couldn't bring myself to smile.

After that, we just stayed near the fire and cooked whatever small pieces of food that we had left in our packs from this morning's meal.

I realized that I should have put more food in the packs before we left Leshee, but Rennan said that we would probably be passing by some small town before we left Palee. He figured that we could just pick up some more food supplies somewhere like that. I couldn't argue with his valid point.

From there, Rennan and I set out a couple of blankets to sleep on and we turned in for the night, even if it was still early. Rennan fell asleep almost instantly, but it took me a long while to get comfortable.

No matter what I tried, nothing worked. In the end I just decided to lay there and just think about life. As it turned out, that just depressed me further so I just watched the sky.

Cameron returned much later. The sky had long since gone from a pale blue, to bright pinks and oranges, to a deep blue in his absence. Stars dotted the sky and the moon beamed down upon us. However, he did not come to the shelter immediately. Instead, he went and sat down near the dying embers and stared into them for what seemed to be an eternity.

The entire time he sat there, he said nothing. All he did was stare at the embers as if he were trying to turn them into ice.

I wondered what he was thinking about that made him remain still for so long with such a stern expression. I ended up falling asleep long before I could figure out what it was that made him so different from anyone I had ever met. Whatever it was, I was determined to figure out.

Wolf Hunt

I was shaken awake, much to my surprise and irritation. It was only hours after I had fallen into a restless asleep. The sky was dark, alluding to it being early, yet none of the stars had disappeared from the sky. I groggily sat up and looked to my side to see Rennan fast asleep next to me. Looking further, I saw Cameron standing a few paces away and staring in wonder off into the trees.

"Scarlet, come here," he whispered urgently.

I got up very wobbly and tried to walk over to where he stood. I am reluctant to admit that I failed in doing so, since getting up so fast made my head dizzy. Cameron saw me and quickly walked over to me and led me where he wanted me to stand. My vision cleared a few seconds later.

"Look up into the sky," Cameron directed me.

"All I see is blue and stars," I said in confusion.

Was the elf going mad or was I missing something?

"No! Well, yes. Look over there in the direction of Leshee. What can you see?" he asked me as I followed the direction in which he pointed his finger.

I squinted, but I still could not see anything due to darkness. Honestly, I was a little surprised that we could still see Leshee after close to two weeks of hiking. Then again, Palee had a higher altitude the further south one goes.

"Still nothing. Are elf eyes prone to imagining nonsense?"

Cameron sighed and started leading me closer to whatever it was that he was waiting for. Soon he began to quicken his pace. I could not for the life of me understand what was so important that he had to wake me up in the middle of the night. If it was just some stupid star he wanted me to see, I swear I was going to lose it.

"Okay, we're closer so you should be able to see it," he stated as he worked to regain his breath. The cold air made it hard to breathe and run at the same time. "Again, look in the sky. There should be a bright star any second now."

"And how do you know—oh…," my voice drifted off.

Just as Cameron predicted, a bright star started to fall in the direction of Leshee. I watched in wonder, awe, and shock as it disappeared from sight beyond the dark horizon. Seconds later, a fiery inferno consumed the city full of wood buildings and thatched roofs.

"The city is burning," I breathed numbly.

"It wasn't supposed to break," Cameron said in a small voice. His hand moved to cover his mouth in shock. "It was supposed to just fly by, not land on Leshee. Those poor people…."

A faraway look entered the elf's eyes as he watched the city burn. I was silent from the shock of it all. If we had not left Leshee when we did, that could have been *us* burning in the heat of a fallen star. I silently thanked the elf for approaching us when he had. Otherwise, Rennan and I would be dead.

"How did you know that would happen?" I asked with a choking voice.

I was having a hard time believing everything was real—that I was alive and outside Leshee. Then again, I was probably just reacting from the shock of what I had just witnessed.

"I knew from various studies that there would be shooting star tonight, but I didn't know it was going to break through the atmosphere. All reports said it would stay suspended in space," Cameron said as he stared at the ground.

I could feel my lips quivering in the cold and I had forgotten my cloak back in our camp. The elf realized I was cold and offered me his cloak, which I accepted gratefully.

He continued. "Since shooting stars don't come around that often, I wanted you to see it. It was supposed to be a sign of friendship if you're willing to give it. You two are important, I have a feeling."

"Cameron—"

"Please, call me Cam."

"Okay, but what made you so sure that it was us that you needed to find? We're just two hybrids that nobody ever pays attention to since once is a misfit and the other is an outcast. What would make us so special?"

"I needed to find you and Rennan because I knew you had to be important. All rumors about you and stories from locals about Rennan just gave me a strong, positive feeling. In all honesty, I don't know the exact reason why I was led to you two, but we will find out," he stated as he continued to watch the flames consume the town.

He fell silent for several minutes, which left what seemed like eternity to stare at the blazing flames.

Then he turned to face me again. "I've seen many things, Scarlet, and I know I'll see a whole lot more by the time this journey ends. You will, too. I hope we can stick together as a team."

"We can. I don't plan on going anywhere now. After all, there is nowhere I can go."

"Thank you, Scarlet."

I briefly smiled at him and nodded.

He returned the smile and then we walked back to the camp where we tried to grab a few hours of sleep.

I gave the cloak back to the elf and quickly wrapped up in my own cloak before I could freeze any more. I had no intention of becoming a foxsicle. It had almost happened to me before when I didn't pack necessary supplies when I camped in the Forgotten Mountains, but I wasn't going to let that happen again. Besides, I had a feeling I would need my energy for a long day of journeying south to prove how fallen our world had become.

"Good morning! Time for another long day of hiking through the southern plains of Palee where we'll meet our deaths if we don't find civilization soon!" an overly cheerful voice announced.

I slowly opened my tired eyes to see the sky turning pink in the east. Based on the position of the stars, I hadn't been asleep for very long. Regardless, I just wanted to close my eyes and stay there for a few hours, even if it was bitterly cold.

I sat up to see Rennan standing in the middle of our camp. He had gotten a fire going and he seemed proud that he had done it without any help or instructions from me or the elf. He looked like he had gotten sleep, but then again, he hadn't been woken up in the middle of the night to watch a star fall on and burn his hometown.

Speaking of the elf, he was sitting on one of the logs staring off into space. From the look on his face, I could tell that he barely slept at all. His hair was more unkempt and he had massive dark circles beneath his grey eyes. He appeared to be lost in some sort of world that only existed in his mind and was ignoring everything else.

I got up and walked over to the dancing flames and sat opposite of Cam. He didn't notice my presence at all. On the other hand, Rennan acknowledged me and sat down to my left. His face was amazingly cheerful given the circumstances. I secretly envied how he could maintain such a positive attitude when it was more than likely that we were traveling to our doom. I wondered if the elf was going to tell him what had happened mere hours ago....

"How did you sleep, Scarlet?" the wolf asked as he pulled small berries we had collected a few days ago out of his pack.

I had completely forgotten we had left berries in there. However, because the berries appeared black and shriveled, Rennan grimaced and threw them into the fire.

"Fine, I guess," I sighed as I ran my hand through my thick hair.

I released the braid it was in so I could redo it. I didn't feel like dealing with my crazy hair when we would be hiking until sunset. I silently groaned at the thought of traveling through the cold, wet plains at the heat of the day with few or no rests.

"That's good," Rennan said. Then he turned to Cameron. "What about you?"

Cam looked up in a daze. It was like he didn't entirely know that he had been spoken to. Though, the surprised look on his face was priceless. I never thought the elves, who were supposed to act regal and poised, had the ability to make such expressions. Cam was just a different story altogether.

His expression still blank, he asked, "Wait, what did you say?"

"How did you sleep?" the wolf repeated.

"I didn't," Cam said as he turned away because he didn't want to elaborate any further.

He didn't say anything else after that, but neither did we. None of us seemed to be able to find a conversation that wouldn't end awkwardly.

Eventually, Cam broke the silence. "We should probably see if we can track something down to cook. That way, we'll have something for lunch later."

"I'm all for that idea, but...uh...this is really bad timing: I don't know how to hunt," Rennan said sheepishly.

Cam smirked slightly, and I laughed to myself. I should have guessed Rennan would have no idea how to hunt. It was unlikely he had ever been in a situation where it was kill or be killed.

"Well, come on then. It's time for you to learn the most basic skill when you live in exile," Cam said as he got up and walked over to his pack of weapons.

He unfastened the cloth that had been holding it all together and displayed everything he had been carrying with him. I couldn't believe how many he had. It was like an entire arsenal of military-grade weaponry. How he managed to carry all that metal around with him, I didn't know. The only logical reason my brain could comprehend was that he was forced to get used to carrying everything with him at all times since he lived in exile. He had to be really strong if he had been doing that for a while.

"How have you been carrying all those weapons?" Rennan asked in shock as he stared at Cam's extensive collection of pointy objects.

Heh, he had read my mind. In response to Rennan's question, all Cam did was smirk.

"These are only the big ones. I have small ones all over camp," the elf stated as he made a large sweeping gesture to the rest of our small camp. To my surprise, he pulled a couple of throwing stars out from underneath the log he had been sitting on a couple minutes earlier. Rennan's mouth hung open, much to Cam's delight. "Yes, I'm sure that would stun an average person…no offense. I've been doing this for years; I know how to hide weapons by now."

"Wow, that is incredible," Rennan breathed as he ran his hand through his hair.

I really wondered how many weapons Rennan had seen in one place at once. This was likely the first time he had seen anything more than a couple of daggers and some throwing stars together. The last time I had seen so many weapons in one place, I was in the blacksmith's shop in Leshee picking up my custom-made dagger with serrated edges. Oh, how I loved that blade!

"Yes, but that's enough about that. I want to get hunting before the sun rises too much," Cam stated as he started sealing up his case again. He had left his bow and quiver out, so I assumed that was what he was going to take hunting.

He also left out a dagger which he gave to Rennan a couple minutes later. It was actually quite amusing watching Rennan try to strap on the belt for it. It was Elvin made, so it was a little bit different (and in my opinion, slightly disgraceful) to see such equipment on a hybrid.

Soon, we set out a short way from camp. Cam had transformed back into his musk deer form so the animals wouldn't smell him as much. Somehow, he had managed to do that when neither Rennan nor I were looking.

I wondered how often he did that, honestly. Was he one of the types who talked to himself more than other living people? Wait, that was a stupid question. Of course he was! He had lived in exile for five years and had likely talked to few people since leaving Heviah. As far as I knew, not that many people in any of the kingdoms are very friendly to strangers outside their species.

How old was Cam anyway? He seemed young, but elves were immortal, so there was no telling how old he really was. Normally by now I would know, but Cam was very good at not revealing anything about himself without a good reason. I had to give him that. He had skills when it came to keeping secrets. Unfortunately for him, I was good at unearthing secrets. I was determined to learn more regarding the mysterious elf.

"I can't believe you've never been hunting before," I commented when the silence got too awkward for even me to handle.

Rennan looked at me with a nervous grin, and Cam dropped back to join the conversation. At that point, all three of us were walking side by side in a perfect line.

"Heh, yeah. I guess it is kind of crazy considering what I've wanted to do for years," Rennan chuckled. Cam raised an eyebrow at the wolf hybrid in a questioning manner. "I've always wanted to be an assassin to help protect my people from enemies."

"Ha!" I barked a loud laugh.

Rennan? An assassin? I don't know why that amused me so much, but it did. There was no possible way that Rennan was cut out to be cold-blooded killer. I just knew it. He was too caring to be able to kill without mercy.

"And what do you think is so funny?" Cam asked with an amused expression.

He probably guessed what I thought was amusing, but I figured it was best if I just explained it. After all, Rennan was looking at me with such an innocent, questioning face. I couldn't believe that a wolf hybrid could be so clueless! I began to respect these men more and more....

"I could give you pointers on being an assassin, Rennan," I offered with a fleeting smile. I didn't want my amusement to show through too much.

Maybe that was why Cameron remained so quiet—perhaps he didn't want to show us what he was feeling deep down.

"How would you know anything about being an assassin?" Rennan asked with a puzzled expression.

He really could not guess? Oh, I would have to teach him a thing or two about picking up on the obvious in the near future. Otherwise, I doubt he would last long out here.

"I *am* a mercenary," I stated in a relatively mysterious voice.

Cam's eyebrows flew up and Rennan stopped dead in his tracks. Rennan's face was so priceless that another grin spread across my face.

"You're a *mercenary*?!" Rennan cried out.

In the distance, birds squawked and flew out of the trees.

Cam turned and glared at the wolf.

The wolf's ears fell flat against his head. Then, in a quieter voice, he said, "*You're a mercenary*?!"

"Yes, and that is not how you remain incognito," I stated with a pointed stare at my jumpy companion.

"Sorry, Scarlet, I just think that's kind of interesting," Rennan said with a sheepish grin. He ran his hand through his hair as if he were trying to process information. Then he turned to Cameron, who was on his left, and grinned. "Any secrets you want to share, so I don't have to keep being shocked?"

Cam smirked. "Nice try, but no secrets are being revealed from me anytime soon."

"But you have secrets?"

"Everybody has secrets."

"What kind of secrets do you have then?"

"The kind I cannot tell you."

"Are they deep, dark secrets?"

"I'm not telling you, Rennan."

"Darn it."

"Yeah, good luck trying that again," Cam laughed quietly as he clapped Rennan on the shoulder.

He became silent again, and a faraway look returned to his grey eyes. The elf's face darkened as he gazed on the fields ahead of us. Then they seemed to come back to reality.

"Come on, I see something," he announced softly.

"What is it? How big is it?" I whispered as we crept through the tall grass.

Standing up straight, it came up to the guys' waists and a little bit higher for me. It gave us sufficient hunting cover. We moved stealthily, ever closer to whatever we were following.

"Looks like a deer or something," Cam murmured as he peeked above the tips of the giant stalks of grass. Cam looked out across the plain, and one of his currently-furry ears twitched. I didn't know if he was hunting by sight or sound, but I could tell he was good at it. He gazed over to his left. "I need to make it over to that bluff so I can get a clear shot."

"Okay, let's go," Rennan nodded.

He and Cam went on ahead while I stayed back. I drew my daggers just in case something jumped out of the grass towards me, knowing it would be very, very bad news if I wasn't ready for anything out here. Much of southern Palee was unpopulated since it was so close to the borders. There was no telling what might happen.

One second, everything was calm around me, and the guys had everything under control. The next I heard a bow twang and Cam's voice shout, "Watch out!"

Then I heard loud thumps and felt vibrations that were steadily growing closer to where I stood. Following the vibrations, a large mass flew out of the grass and barreled straight toward me. I screamed as I narrowly dodged the flying animal.

The animal was not a deer like Cam had thought, but was actually a wild wolf. Not a hybrid, but an actual gray wolf. And boy, was it mad. It had a broken arrow shaft sticking out of its hind leg and foam coming from its mouth. The wolf's eyes were wild with rage as it fixed me in its glare. It snarled as I raised my daggers into a defensive position.

The next thing I knew, the wolf vaulted towards me. Its yellowed teeth were borne, and its eyes turned black as it flew through the air. I barely had enough time to leap out of the way and slit its throat with one of my blades. Even still, I felt its claws cut through my cloak and skin. I hissed and tried to ignore the stinging cuts.

The beast slowed for a few seconds before it started circling me, undoubtedly for another attack. The wolf leapt toward me again and caught the corner of my cloak. I had no choice but to unclasp it so I wouldn't be choked from the pull of the heavy fabric.

The rabid wolf managed to get itself wrapped up in the fabric, and was subdued for a few precious seconds. I called out to Cam and Rennan, who were still searching for their prey, so they would come to where I was fighting the rabid animal as soon as possible. I had no intention of fighting this thing alone. One bite and I would be infected. I couldn't afford for that to happen since none of us had medical supplies except whatever we found near our campsites every night.

The wolf tore the fabric and released itself from its hold with greater speed than I thought possible. It fixed me with a beady glare once again. I raised my daggers and taunted it to come near me. I would have to be able to hold my ground until my friends could get over there, so I had no choice but to fight.

But I never had to strike the mad animal again. The elf flew through the air with a remarkably sharp blade and swung it at the beast. It yelped upon impact and slunk backward. It growled again as Cam threw his blade on the ground and nocked an arrow to his string. He raised the bow, took aim, and fired immediately. The wolf staggered backward and snarled as the arrow pierced its thick hide. Cam loosed three more arrows in quick succession, giving the creature little time to react. The wolf fell dead after the third hit, falling on the ground in a heap.

The elf cautiously lowered his bow. He never took his eyes off the dead animal that lay only a few yards away from us. Cameron's hand shook as he picked up his dagger and returned it to its sheath. Seconds later, Rennan ran back toward us and sharply inhaled when he saw the lifeless wolf in front of him. His face paled to almost the same tone as his ice-blue eyes.

"It was a wolf," the other hybrid said in an astonished tone. He was quite taken aback by all of this. He turned to Cam and frowned gravely. He looked betrayed. "I thought you said it was a deer."

"To be fair, I *did* see a deer," Cameron said as he, in turn, faced Rennan. Irritation shone through his steel eyes and a shadow spread over his face. "That's what I was trying to shoot before Scarlet yelled at us to come over here."

"Then why are there four arrows in that wolf? All of them are yours!" Rennan practically shouted.

All of his features were rigid, and his face was beginning to become pink from more than just the cold. Rennan's eyes shone with a colder light than any I had seen before in the short time I had known him.

Cameron didn't look too much happier. There were almost more shadows than elf at this point. His jaw was clenched, and his head held low in fury and wrath. He was deadly enough to strike at any point in time, almost not caring whether he hit friend or foe.

"I shot the wolf because it was mad and it was about to kill the lot of us!" Cam shouted. Then he composed himself. "Tell me, would you like to be dead right now if I hadn't shot it? It's still as lethal dead as it is alive. I'd be happy to introduce you to him."

"You cold-hearted, merciless elf! How dare you?!" Rennan shrieked as hot tears started dripping down his face. He clumsily drew his dagger and pointed it at the elf's neck.

Cam raised his chin so that the dagger would not pierce his unnaturally pale skin.

Rennan hissed. "You speak just as any other elf would. You care nothing for those you deem lesser than yourself!"

"Hold your tongue," Cameron seethed as he slowly lowered the blade Rennan held in his hand by the leather guard on his wrist. Cam's face was dark and twisted as he looked down his nose to stare Rennan in the eye. "I've told you where my allegiance lies. Nothing I have told you has been a falsehood. I would never kill an animal without a good reason."

"But you did!"

"I killed it because if I didn't, it would have killed Scarlet!" the elf shouted. He stole a brief glance at me before his gaze returned to the wolf hybrid.

I could do nothing but stand there in shock as they sent insults and accusations back and forth for the next several minutes. I wasn't about to step in and make things worse.

"Yeah, well maybe we would be better off if you had never come in the first place!" Rennan shouted as he started swinging his dagger perilously close to Cameron's face.

Eventually, he hit the elf and blood started gushing down his perfectly white skin. Cameron gingerly reached up to touch his temple and lowered a shaking hand when he saw that it was covered in bright red blood. He became bleak—almost evil looking.

"If I had never come and found you, where would you be now?" the elf asked in a very low voice. He didn't make eye contact with anybody as he spoke. Shadows crept over his whole face and only continued to get darker. He became more and more threatening by the minute.

Rennan looked at him in confusion and was speechless for a few seconds. All he could do was make faces as he tried to formulate some sort of answer for the elf. "I don't know! Back in Leshee where I don't have any problems! Where I would be free of *you*!"

Cameron laughed darkly before he snapped his head up and looked Rennan in the eye. "I hate to break it to you, but Leshee is no more. It burned to the ground last night after a star fell and hit it. Your home is destroyed. *You have nowhere to run.*"

Rennan stared at the elf in shock and horror. His jaw dropped when he realized what Cameron meant. The wolf's expressions shifted from anger, to sorrow, to fury in mere seconds. He clearly had no idea what to say. Cameron himself didn't look sorry for what he had said. The shadows shrouding his face did not disappear.

"I can't believe you," Rennan muttered as he lowered his arm.

Before I knew what was happening, he lunged at Cameron and swung his arm.

Blood of Elves

I would be lying if I said that it was all sunshine and rainbows. The air was thick with disbelief and betrayal and anger. It seemed like storm clouds wheeled overhead even though there wasn't a single cloud in the sky. Blood was scattered on the ground from the dead wolf and my arm while plastered on the side of Cam's face where Rennan had cut him.

"How dare you?!" Rennan shrieked as he swung his dagger at Cameron again.

The elf had only a few seconds to draw his own knife and raise it in defense. He had to be quick, for Rennan kept throwing fast, wild attacks at him. If Cameron had not been such an agile warrior, he wouldn't have remained unscathed.

"How *dare* you kill that wolf?! Why didn't you tell us Leshee is destroyed?!" Rennan yelled again.

"I already told you, I wouldn't have killed it without reason! Besides, would you have even believed an elf like me?" Cam spat as he knocked Rennan backwards with a well-aimed kick to the ankles.

He fell with a yelp, but quickly rolled over and jumped back up to his feet, his eyes wild with rage. I could only imagine what was going on inside his mind as he prepared another attack.

"What would you have done in my place? Kill it or become infected?" Cam demanded, stalking forward.

"I'd rather let it go! It could die on its own!" Rennan cried.

Once again, Cameron knocked him backward. Rennan panted heavily as he tried to regain his breath, but Cameron was so inhumanly motionless that it was scary. Rennan still looked exceptionally angry, and Cam was unreadable. However, shadows crawled across his face as he raised his dagger again. That was when I finally stepped in.

"Rennan! Cam! Enough! This is ridiculous to be fighting over a wild wolf!" I shouted as I forced myself between their blades.

I knew that neither one of them would strike me no matter how angry they were at each other. I hadn't known either of them for very long, but I knew they wouldn't harm somebody that they considered a friend or ally. Well, except for the fact that they were allies and they were attacking each other in a fight to the death.

Rennan growled in a low tone. "It's ridiculous for him to kill an animal of *my* species when he said he was going after a *deer*. He should have just stuck with the deer instead of killing that wolf."

"Yeah? Well, I didn't have a choice, Rennan. It was a kill or be killed moment, and we all kind of need to stay alive," Cameron said quietly.

Once again, he made eye contact with no one, and the shadows remained as a cover on his face. They seemed to be retreating, though, so that seemed to be a good sign.

"Will you try to talk it out without killing each other? Fighting will get you nowhere," I pointed out.

Rennan scoffed. "So says the trained mercenary who kills to make a living."

I glared at him and restrained my own rage. He had a point—I did make a living by fighting, but I couldn't let that instinct control me now when I needed to try to end *their* fight! Getting dragged into this because of Rennan's aggressive remarks was not going to help anything.

"Would you just knock it off?" Cameron muttered as he started picking his weapons up. He pulled the arrows out of the wolf and wrapped them in a cloth. Then he started walking away from us.

Rennan mumbled something under his breath as he watched the elf stalk away from us.

"And where are you going?" Rennan shouted.

He asked it in a tone implying that he didn't really care if he received an answer or not. It seemed he asked the question only to fill the empty air surrounding us on all sides and perhaps to satisfy his own frustration. His voice filled the void for a second, but the wind carried it away ere it could linger for too long.

"I'm going to find solitude of the only one here who has any sense!" Cam shouted over the wind. It had picked up and the air was becoming chilly again even with the sun coming up.

"And who is that?"

"Myself!"

Rennan muttered something I didn't catch before he turned away.

I sighed and rolled my eyes. I had no choice but to follow one of them and see where he went.

I followed Rennan first just because he was the one that seemed to be the angriest out of all of us (I started to get irritated by how foolish both men were being). It would be better to get him calm before I even tried to reason with the unpredictable elf.

"I know you're following me," Rennan sighed.

I didn't say anything in hopes that he would turn around. I wanted him to see how foolishly he had just acted, but I couldn't do that unless he spoke first. I mean, come on! The wild wolf was clearly mad!

"Scarlet."

"Okay, yes, I'm behind you," I admitted as I fell in stride next to the wolf. He grunted but didn't say anything. Great, I guess that meant that I would be the one who would have to say something first. "So. What just happened?"

"Cameron killed a grey wolf, didn't you see?" Rennan asked bitterly. His voice was mixed with sorrow, but I also sensed some form of betrayal.

I inwardly sighed. It was going to be much more difficult to reason with the hybrid than I had previously thought.

"Uh, yeah, I felt it, too," I said, gesturing to my arm, which was still bleeding from where the wolf had clawed me.

Rennan's eyes widened in dismay before he scowled at the sight, but he did nothing nor did he offer me anything to stop the bleeding with. Still, that was not my priority.

"Why were you so angry back there?" I asked him.

"Well, it's not so much that he killed the wolf, more that he didn't tell me my hometown burned down last night," Rennan said quietly. He looked down at the still half-frozen ground as he spoke. "Do you know what became of it?"

"Unfortunately, yes. I do. I watched as a star fell on the city, fire leap from roof to roof, and everything burning to cinders," I replied in a grave voice. "Rennan, we have nowhere to go now if we decide to abandon this quest."

"If *you* abandon this quest, you mean. I have somewhere I can go at least…even if it is not my first option," he whispered.

I guess he was right. The last of my home and my family were gone; I was completely on my own now. I owed allegiance to nobody and was tied down to nothing. Meanwhile, Rennan had living relatives in some other places in Palee.

"You aren't leaving, are you?"

"Not yet. I just want time to sit and think—alone."

"I guess I'll go then."

I was turning to go back to where the dead wolf lay when Rennan stopped me. He looked like he was about to say something, but then stopped himself.

He did eventually speak but still seemed hesitao t in doing so. "Do you, uh, want my cloak or anything? Yours got kinda shredded."

"I'm fine. Thanks though," I said with a fleeting smile.

Rennan shrugged, and we parted ways. He was right about needing to think. So much had happened in the last few minutes that I also needed time to sit and analyze everything and try to plan my path ahead.

I slowly walked back to where the wolf was killed and found Cameron leaning over it.

He held my shredded cloak in one hand. In his other hand were the family picture and the amber stone I had shoved in my pocket before leaving Leshee. He shoved both into his own pocket. The cloak itself was stained with blood and grass. There was absolutely no way that I was going to wear that thing again. It didn't matter how long it had been in my possession—it was disgusting, and I wasn't going to touch it.

As for Cameron himself, he was standing as still as a stone statue while he held my cloak in his hands. He seemed solemn, like nothing in the world mattered anymore. I couldn't see his face, but I could imagine what it looked like. His posture was slumped over and stiff, like he had been there for several minutes already. He was also shaking—I guessed it was from the frigidity of the air, but I couldn't be sure without seeing his expression.

I silently stepped up next to him, not saying a word as I did so. He turned his head to look at me, but quickly looked away. He gently set my cloak on the ground before backing away from the wolf. He grabbed his bow and slung it over his head and began to walk away from me.

"Where are you going?" I asked him.

The wind blew my hair in my face, and I struggled to pull it back into its rightful place. Cam sighed and walked behind me. Then he gently took hold of my hair and started doing something with it.

I became confused. "What are you doing?"

"I'm rebraiding it for you so it won't be in your face," he replied almost silently.

I have to admit, I was touched he would take the time to do that for me, especially given the circumstances. Right then I decided this elf wasn't so bad after all.

"As to where I'm going, I'm just going somewhere else where I won't bother you," he answered quietly. "I understand if you don't want to help me anymore. I am not worthy of your aid."

My jaw dropped in amazement. "Why are you not worthy of our aid? Cam, I've only known you for a couple of weeks, but you seem like a person who I would willingly help to the end of the line."

"But you saw what happened back there. Rennan clearly does not want to be anywhere near me. I doubt he wants to speak to me either after what I just did," Cam answered. He let go of my hair and walked in front of me again, shouldering his additional weapons. He bit his lower lip and shook his head. “I should have known he would react negatively to those shots, but I didn’t have a choice. Besides, I’m an elf whether I’m in exile or not. Hybrids generally don’t like us anyway.”

“It’s not the dead wolf that bothered him the most—though, that did play a part in this whole ordeal,” I stated as I fingered the intricate braid the elf had just completed.

Cam looked up at me and slightly tilted his head. He winced, and his hand went up to where his forehead was still oozing blood. I could feel his pain. I’d had targets deal me similar kinds of blows to what the elf had just received.

“Why then.”

“He’s upset that you didn’t tell him about Leshee burning down last night.”

The elf sighed. “How would I have told him, Scarlet? I was trying not to bring you into it so you wouldn’t have to face Rennan’s wrath. I had no chance to mention it to him either and ruin his mood. This is the way it had to be.”

“But that doesn’t mean that you have to leave! Reconciliation isn’t impossible. Please don’t go, Cam. You were right in saying one thing: we have nowhere to go.”

Cameron looked at me in surprise. His steel eyes were clouded over with remorse as well as something that seemed to be curiosity. They looked at me, as if searching for a deeper answer to some question he had asked me in his mind. “You...want me to stay?”

“Yes, because you’re the best chance we’ve got at changing this world and making everyone see how dark it has all become. I’m sick of being treated like dirt, as is my whole race. It's high time this world had a perspective change," Rennan's voice said over the now-gentle wind.

Cam and I both looked in the direction of the voice and saw the wolf hybrid standing a short distance away. He looked like he was unsure of what to say to us. He didn't exactly look mad, but I could still see some traces of his earlier irritation. Rennan mostly just looked worried. Worried about what, I could not say. I could just see it in his face.

"You came back. Why?" Cam asked in disbelief as Rennan walked towards us.

He remained a few feet away from the elf. Both men looked somewhat nervous to be so near each other again so soon after their fight. They probably thought the other would start another struggle to make everything even worse, and I honestly didn't blame them. I had the same thought in the back of my own mind and was on guard in case it came to pass.

"Thanks to Scarlet, I now realize that it was stupid of me to react so foolishly. Sure, it was a wolf that shouldn't have been shot, but I guess it's better the wolf is dead than Scarlet and for us to be alive rather than burned to death," Rennan shrugged with an apologetic expression.

Cam's shoulders relaxed from the tenseness I hadn't realized he had been holding. Rennan, however, still seemed to be pretty uneasy, but he gradually became more relaxed.

"As I told you, I wouldn't have killed it if I hadn't had a very good reason," Cam said with a very uneasy laugh.

The tips of Rennan's mouth twitched upward before they became a straight line again.

Cam grew serious. "But answer me this: why are you still here? I understand if you want to continue your lives in Palee and not get caught up in my quest for justice."

Rennan and I sent a look to each other. We both knew exactly what we wanted to do, regardless of what had happened in the last half hour.

I was the one who spoke next. "That's the thing, though. Cam, you and I both saw a star fall on Leshee last night. We have nowhere to go."

"Yeah, and we have absolutely no intention of staying in this blasted kingdom either," Rennan stated. "We spent our childhoods, like most adventurous hybrid children, planning ways to get out of here. This is our chance to leave now. You're just lucky Scarlet didn't succeed in one of her plans to escape, otherwise, you would have lost Palee's most cunning warrior."

"For the record, I never told you any of that—"

"But was I right?"

"Yes, Rennan."

"Thought so. You may continue."

"Anyway, I did have plans, but this is the only one that is going to work for the good of all of us and hopefully the other kingdoms—if we succeed, that is," I said with a chuckle.

Rennan smiled for real this time and Cam smirked. The tension was slowly vanishing.

"Well, if you guys stay, I appreciate it very much," Cam said with a grateful smile.

Rennan and I managed to smile a little bit, too.

"Okay, totally random change of subject, but am I the only one who hates the sight of blood?" Rennan asked out of the blue, completely startling us out of our somber moment.

I was glad, though. I didn't know how much more of that sweetness I would be able to take.

"It's just you," I commented.

"Yeah, and don't take this the wrong way, but I think 'assassin' might be the wrong career for you if you don't like the sight of blood," Cam smirked.

Rennan just smiled one of his typical, goofy grins.

"So…where are we supposed to be going?" Rennan asked once again as we journeyed through southern Palee.

At this point in the day, the sun was beating down like it was trying to murder us. It had risen high in the sky only hours after we had broken camp.

I'll rehash our morning quickly: neither elf nor wolf seemed to be holding anything against each other now; they continued as if nothing had happened. Although, I suspected that Cam still held a grudge to some degree, even though he didn't show it. Anyway, we had packed up our camp quickly after hunting (we didn't catch anything) and set out again.

The sun was high overhead in the clear blue sky. If it hadn't been in the middle of winter, the direct sunlight in the open plains would have been unbearable. Thanks to the naturally cold season as well as a strong breeze coming down from the north, we remained fairly cool during our cross-country hike. Yet despite the ideal conditions, Rennan somehow managed to find something to complain about. I couldn't have cared less because I wasn't listening to him, but I could tell from the look on his face that Cam was beginning to lose his mind.

"For the last time, Rennan, we're heading toward the base of the mountains!" the elf cried in exasperation. He threw his hands up in the air, which ended up jingling the arrows in his quiver so much that I thought a few might fall out.

"Okay, but after the mountains, where are we going?" the wolf asked as he started rummaging in his pack.

I had no idea what the heck he was looking for, and I had no desire to know, especially if it was food. None of us had eaten breakfast and we were paying the price for it now. I wished we had eaten something, even if it was minimal. We had seen no wildlife that would have been possible for us to hunt, so we were solely relying on what we had in our packs or whatever edible vegetation we were able to find.

"Well, from here there are two places that we could go. We're basically at a fork in the road," Cam said as he stopped in the shade of a few lone trees.

We followed his example and set our packs down for the few precious minutes that we could. My shoulders were beginning to become very sore from constantly carrying mine for weeks on end.

"Okay, what are the two options?" I inquired as I pulled out my nearly empty canteen of water.

I really needed to fill it up next time we came across a stream with clean water; otherwise, we wouldn't last very long out there in the sun.

Even with the wind from the north, the direct sunlight was a bit much.

"We're either going to head southeast and travel into Sala, Kevay or we're going to continue on the path we're on and reach Scottsdale, Tralia in a few weeks," Cam replied.

I didn't really want to head down into Tralia (especially since it was giant country) unless we absolutely had to. Rumors from mountain scouts said King Umber wasn't exactly the greatest with foreigners or rebels. The giants and the hybrids weren't enemies, but it certainly would not end well if some international incident occurred.

"What kinds of creatures live in Kevay again?" Rennan asked with a very thoughtful expression on his face.

Cam raised an intrigued eyebrow. It was like he couldn't manage to understand how Rennan didn't know something that seemed to be very commonplace information.

"I can't believe you don't know or have forgotten, but Kevay is the kingdom of the water dwellers—mermaids and such creatures. I believe some water nymphs live there, too. Well, ones that moved from Salia," Cam responded.

I snickered in amusement that I had totally called it. Cam *did* think it was common knowledge! The elf sent me a strange look but didn't say anything.

"All right, I don't feel like seeing giants yet, so I guess we just head toward Kevay," Rennan shrugged. He looked to me. "What do you think, Scarlet?"

"I have to agree with Rennan, I'm not quite ready to face giants either," I concurred.

Cam nodded his head as he shouldered his weapons again. He changed the direction of our course, and we were off again. "Okay, then on to Sala we go."

"Are we there yet…?" Rennan whined.

He had been saying that same phrase repeatedly all afternoon, even though we yelled "no" at him every single time. At that point, we were all exhausted. Rennan complained he was hungry and sore, I was irritated from the repetitive whining, and Cam was beyond frustrated by all of Rennan's questions and the snappish answers I had given him.

"No! We're not! That is the last time I'm going to answer any question like that!" Cam cried as he ran his hands through his hair.

He looked even more disheveled than he had this morning. I'm sure he didn't feel too great, either, what with his lack of sleep and food. If he did, he was very good at disguising his discomfort.

"How much longer are we going to hike then? I'm—"

"Don't you *dare* make one more complaint, Rennan!" I stated firmly as I turned around to glare at the wolf, who was dragging himself along behind us. He looked exhausted, but weren't we all? "We'll get there when we get there. No sooner."

"Ugh, fine, but how soon is 'soon?'" Rennan asked in a dismal voice.

I couldn't help but wonder the same question. We had been walking all day with hardly a moment's rest, and there was no sign of stopping. Maybe that was the elf's plan all along—to make us reach our deaths by hiking with no rest. No, that idea is actually rather absurd. Though he was an elf (who by nature can be cruel), Cam wasn't nearly as nasty as many of the Paleean stories say that elves are.

"I think it might come sooner than we think," Cam said, narrowing his eyes. He seemed to be looking a long way ahead of us, as if searching for what path we needed to take. He pointed straight ahead. "Is that a village, or has he sun finally addled my mind after all these years of exile?"

I gazed in the direction that Cam's finger was pointing.

On the horizon, I could see dark shapes against the bright pink sky. Unless I was also losing it, I was pretty sure that Cam was right; it *was* a village. It was probably just one of the small towns that weren't large or populated enough to appear on many of the maps of the entire kingdom of Palee. Then again, I wasn't exactly sure Palee had a map of itself anywhere except in the Old Books (our unofficial history books), and those were ancient and perhaps not entirely up to date.

I fought a relieved grin. "You know, I think you may be right, Cam."

Cam smiled broadly at me. "Then that is where we're heading!"

"So…we finally have an end in sight?" Rennan asked hopefully.

Cam sent me a helpless look before he turned back to our friend and nodded his head.

Rennan pumped his fists in the air in some sort of celebration. "Then what are we waiting for? Let's go!!"

Cameron and I had no choice but to follow Rennan as he picked up the pace. The village on the horizon was still a few miles away, but Rennan was determined to reach it before we needed to set up camp for the night. To my dismay, that meant running for nearly two more hours. The village turned out to be farther away than we had previously anticipated.

As darkness fell, we had to make a light so we could cross the uneven terrain. Though, we didn't need it for that long since we reached the outermost gates of the town not long afterwards. I assumed the only reason the town had walls and gates and such was to protect it against robbers from around the kingdom. It was one of the few smart villages that had them, especially since it was further south than most Paleeans dared to go in their entire lifetimes.

The walls themselves were about eight feet tall and made of dark wood. Cam seemed to be nearly as tall as them in his normal elvish form and easily could have scaled the walls, but he needed to be in a hybrid form in order to keep his cover. If an elf were discovered to be in Palee, they would literally lose their head. The only Paleean laws that were kept were trespassing laws and that was because their penalty was death. Hybrids have enough murders in our kingdom; we didn't want to risk losing any lives that could have been saved by just keeping a law.

Anyway, before I started talking about the death penalties in Palee, I was talking about the gates and wall! Yes, that. Because of the risks of scaling the wall in the dark, we were forced to walk around the whole town before we came upon the gates, which were on the southern edges of the small village.

Since Rennan was so eager to reach the village, we let him be the one who got to knock on the gate. He did so and latches clicked open a couple of minutes later. A very, very beady little eye gazed at us from the other side of the panel that opened after the latches clicked. Seconds later, a small side door was open a few inches, and a small, wrinkled woman stepped out. She seemed to be some sort of wingless bird hybrid.

"Name your clan!" She squawked. Yup, definitely an old bird hybrid.

Then a thought struck me. I didn't know any clans of musk deer. In other words, Cam's flawless disguise now had a flaw.

I subtly leaned over to him and whispered, "Transform into a fox hybrid. Now."

"Why?" he hissed as he stepped into the shadows. He seemed like he was doing what I asked him, but was still a tad bit reluctant.

Instead of replying, I glared at him as if to say, *Transform now or else.*

He nodded in acknowledgement and completely disappeared into the shadows where he couldn't be seen. I doubted the old woman even noticed that he disappeared. Cam returned seconds later sporting an even lither frame and a pair of furry ears like mine. His bone structure seemed to be more fox-like, too. He was good—very good.

"Your clans!" she shouted again in an even more shrill voice.

Rennan glanced at me and then answered. "Penbrooke and Sutton."

The woman looked at us the three of us in a questioning manner. I nearly burst out laughing while she inspected us with one very wide eye and the other a very squinty eye. The guys seemed to be having the same problem and it was nearly too much to handle. Thankfully, though, the woman's eyes returned to normal and she stepped back a few inches.

"That's two names. There are three of you," she observed with a suspicious gleam in her pale green eyes.

Rennan and Cam both sucked in a breath and looked to me. They knew I would be able to create a cover story in mere seconds due to the training when I first became a mercenary.

"He's from the Penbrooke clan of grey wolves," I repeated, gesturing towards Rennan. He was the easy part of this whole cover story. Then I pointed to Cam. "He and I are from the Sutton clan of common foxes. He's my cousin on my mother's side."

"I see," the woman said in an even more scratchy voice, if that was even possible. At least it wasn't as terrible as a cat's nails on a chalkboard in one of the schoolhouses that used to be in Leshee. "Why do you three want to enter this here town? No outside folk ever dares knock on my gate so long after dark."

"We are travelers in the kingdom, and we saw your village on the horizon not two hours past. Instead of pitching a camp in the cold, we thought we could seek shelter inside your gates," I replied coolly.

Rennan tried to hide his impressed face but didn't succeed until Cam elbowed him in the arm. The disguised elf only smirked.

"Well, in that case, you youngsters had better come on in. Can't have you catching your deaths in this cold. Bitter wind tonight," the woman relented as she ushered us inside the gates. "There's an inn in town. There's sure to be a couple of rooms open for you."

"Thank you, enjoy your night," I said as we walked further into the town.

Rennan and Cam walked on either side of me. When we were out of sight and out of earshot from the gatehouse, both men cheered and threw their arms around my shoulders. I was shocked they didn't wake up the townsfolk.

"That was amazing, Scarlet!" Rennan cried in delight. "How did you think to say that Cam is your cousin? That was brilliant!"

I smiled at his enthusiasm. At least I knew I could do something useful on this quest.

"I just thought it would be easier to explain a member of my clan nobody knows exists rather than make up a clan of musk deer that could be seen through if given enough thought," I answered with a quiet giggle.

Cam grinned and laughed as well.

"Rennan's right, that *was* brilliant. Though, I am glad we aren't cousins," Cam stated with a hint of a smile.

I raised an inquisitive eyebrow.

He hastily continued his thought. "No offense, of course. I just don't know how you can deal with these ears!"

He reached up and touched the tips of his furry ears that matched mine. I couldn't help but laugh at his face. It was so amusingly childlike that anybody with a decent sense of humor would have to laugh at him.

"Well, I don't know. I have never known any other type of ears!"

"Okay, I hate to change the subject from Scarlet's brilliance and Cam's weird opinion of fox ears, but can we get to that inn the lady mentioned?" Rennan pleaded as he rubbed his hands together to warm them. "I am cold, starving, and exhausted."

"Yeah, let's get there as quick as possible and see if they have a room or two to spare," Cam agreed.

Rennan naturally ran up ahead to look at everything, forcing Cam and me to match his pace once again.

Ode to Fly Soup

We reached the Blackshell Inn about five minutes later thanks to the quick pace Rennan set for us. The wolf hybrid seemed to be more than eager to get somewhere with fire and food he did not have to hunt. Cam and I could only chuckle at him. However, it definitely reminded us that we needed to give Rennan proper instructions on how to survive in the wild when there were no cities or villages to stop in. He'd have to get used to a wanderer's lifestyle.

Cam pushed open the door to the large inn and was kind enough to allow Rennan and I to enter the building first. He quietly closed the door behind the three of us and followed Rennan down the short, dimly lit hallway. There were hooks for cloaks and such things on the walls, but none of us felt comfortable enough to leave any of our things where anybody could touch them. Cam chose to carry his weapons in with him rather than leaving them stowed away in the entry.

We eventually reached a sort of check-in counter with a glowing green flame in a bowl. I looked around the establishment to take in every detail I could. There were plenty of other people there, so it would be easy to blend in once we figured out what we were doing for the night. Most stood near the fire laughing heartily about some joke that probably wasn't even that funny.

To our left, there was a long hallway that led to two flights of stairs. One led upwards to a second floor and the other to a basement. I figured the basement was more for hybrids that preferred utter darkness at night and no sunlight upon waking up in the morning.

"I guess this would be an okay place to stay for the night," Cam whispered to me after Rennan rung the bell. The elf seemed to be on his guard for anything unexpected.

"I suppose," I agreed in a tone as low as his. "Though, if we have a choice, I want to be at the end of the building on the top floor in case we need to make a quick getaway."

I didn't want to be overheard in this place. I had stayed at my fair share of inns (including this one), and as an mercenary, I couldn't afford to be caught and fined. It would be incredibly bad if anyone in this place recognized me.

"Agreed," Cam stated, seemingly understanding the reasons why I needed to have a backup plan for this stay. "I'll see what I can do."

"Actually, I think it might be better for Rennan or me to do the talking here," I objected.

Cam cocked his head in confusion. He narrowed his eyes and made a face that urged me to continue.

"You're still pretty new to the kingdom. It would be better for a hybrid to deal with any business here. Besides, we would be the ones to understand the social cues," I explained.

"As much as I hate to admit it, you're right," Cam sighed.

Though, he seemed to be thinking of something else. The expression he wore gave me the feeling that he still thought he should do it himself.

Cam and I both looked to Rennan, who in turn just stared at us with his wide, ice-blue eyes.

A smile graced Cam's face. "I think I know who would be the perfect man to do the talking here."

"Why me?" Rennan cried out in a low tone. "Why do I have to do the talking? Why can't Scarlet do it?"

He looked around at other guests to make sure no one had overheard him. Nobody noticed since they were too caught up in their own noisy conversations to pay attention to those of anybody else.

"I told you guys what I do for a living. If I'm recognized, we're dead. We can't risk our mission because of me. It's far safer to have you do it since you're new here. Besides, I have stayed here before, and the innkeeper might recognize my voice," I stated.

Rennan reluctantly nodded.

"Hey, since that wild wolf tore your cloak and you haven't been wearing one, won't you be recognized?" Cam asked.

"I don't think so, since I'm usually in disguise when I come," I said with a slightly uneasy shrug. I bit my lip as I tried to remember what I had been wearing the last few times that I had stayed in this particular inn.

Cam didn't look convinced. He remained silent for a few seconds before he suddenly took off his pack of weapons.

"Will you take my cloak? I don't want to take any unnecessary risks," he requested as he started unhooking his cloak's pin.

He held his black cloak out to me. I was loath to accept it as I didn't think it was necessary at that point in time. Though, I could understand his concern and figured I didn't have a choice in the matter.

"Fine, but—"

A fat man come out from behind the reception desk. He wore all brown colors and had the beadiest yellow eyes that I had ever seen in my life. His wardrobe certainly conveyed that he was working class, but they were in a nice enough condition to show that he didn't have to work too horribly hard. Due to his eyes and the strange indentations on his skin, I could tell the short man was some sort of reptilian hybrid. It was hard to tell what kind since there were so many different variations within the kingdom, though.

"Ah! Guests! Welcome to the Blackshell Inn. I am the innkeeper. What can I do for you three young travelers tonight?" the man asked with a pleasant smile.

Though, his smile faded and his eyes widened dramatically when they settled on the elf. I looked at Cam out of the corner of my eye and he appeared relatively amused by our host.

"Do you, uh, have any rooms available for rent tonight?" Rennan asked in a very shaky voice. He looked to me and Cam for support and we nodded him on. "Preferably on the second floor?"

"Well! Aren't you lucky? A guest just so happened to leave the inn from one of the top rooms. I'd be happy to clean it out for you. When do you need it by?" the innkeeper asked with an eager smile.

Perhaps it was too eager, but that could just be me. Plus, there was something in me that sensed a double meaning to another guest "leaving." He couldn't be genuinely pleasant all the time, especially since he kept glancing at Cam apprehensively.

"Any time tonight is fine by us," Rennan answered.

The innkeeper nodded as he pulled out a couple of pieces of paper, wrote down a couple of notes, and turned back to us. He smiled a relatively creepy smile. "I'll have that room ready for you in an hour or so. Until then, you can go rest in the tavern. You must be weary from your travels."

"Thank you, sir," Rennan stated he paid for the room.

The innkeeper then walked down the hall and up the stairs.

Meanwhile, the guys and I walked into the tavern. The green fire from the hearth provided an eerie green glow that shone around the entire room. Many people were illuminated by the green light, such as a petite woman with dark skin and bleached blonde hair standing next to a man who looked just like her. They had seemed to have just walked in. Beginning to ignore everyone else, my friends and I took a table in the corner where it was the darkest and furthest away from the fire.

"Well, that was an interesting man," Cam stated as he gazed around the room. He was looking at everyone—except for us—as he spoke. His slight smirk revealed that he knew more about this place than he was telling us.

I nodded my head in agreement. "I'm telling you, it was a lizard hybrid if I ever did see one—and a very creepy one at that."

"Oh, most definitely! My hands were shaking the entire time I was talking. It was really hard to look him in the eye," Rennan said with a timid laugh. He pulled a small rock out of his pocket and started messing with it as he continued. "This whole place is creepy. It's dark."

"Yeah, it isn't so much the fact that it's so dark in here that bothers me," Cam commented, his eyes and ears were fully alert to anything that could possibly happen. He fingered the arm guard concealing a dagger underneath. (Side note: he was still carrying his weapons and now the satchel was lying underneath the table. I was using it as a footrest.) The elf looked uneasy.

"What is it then?" I asked.

To be honest, this was not the best inn that I had ever stayed at. It was one that was generally filled with low lives who stayed up all night drinking with their friends. However, it did provide the perfect cover while we stayed here. Because of that, I was curious to hear Cam's reason for why he was uneasy.

"I can't explain it, but I can't help but think something bad is going to happen tonight that is absolutely impossible for us to avoid," he explained as he sat back in his unforgiving chair.

Now he looked uneasy and uncomfortable! These were the worst chairs I had sat on in a long while.

Rennan put his rock back in his pocket and looked across the room, narrowing his eyes a few seconds later. "Yeah, I know what you mean. Nothing here seems safe."

"Just be on your guard," the elf muttered, running his hand over his face to keep himself awake.

He opened his mouth to speak again, but he never got the chance to. Another lizard-like man shuffled out of a side room and hobbled in our direction. He was bone thin and short, unlike the innkeeper who had been stout and of average height. His right leg seemed to be lame or paralyzed, so he clumsily dragged it along with the rest of him. He came to the table that we were sitting around.

"What you want to eat?" he asked in a gruff voice. He produced a scraggly looking notepad out of his apron pocket as well as a small, broken pencil. I guessed he was the cook, but I had a hard time believing it. He looked more like an old, dying man than a cook.

"What do you have?" Rennan politely inquired.

I noticed that his hands were under the table again. They must have still been shaking. Actually, all of Rennan's body was shaking. It could have been nervousness, or it could have been fear—I couldn't tell which. Cam, on the other hand, was deadly silent as he studied the spooky cook with his piercing grey eyes. I was as relaxed as I possibly could be. I had been in situations like this before, so I didn't have problems keeping my cool.

The cook grunted as he pulled another worn piece of paper out of his pocket. He squinted at the small paper like he couldn't read the writing. It had to have been the menu for this place. "Soup, salad, bird meat."

Well, that was relatively helpful, so I decided that I'd answer. There couldn't be a huge risk in saying just a few words, right? Besides, Rennan looked so panicked that he was about to lose his mind.

"We'll just have the soup," I said with a pleasant smile.

The cook grunted and then scuffled back in the direction he came from and disappeared through the mysterious door. All three of us exhaled as soon as he was out of sight. The tension had thickened the air around us. It was so suffocating that I was all too eager to suck in a breath of air—even if it wasn't too fresh.

"I take that back. The innkeeper is not nearly as creepy as that dude," Rennan whispered after a couple minutes.

Cam and I immediately agreed. Now I could see what the elf had meant by this place being weird. The people running it were incredibly strange and were enough to make even the most unemotional people feel uncomfortable. I hadn't noticed it when I had been here before, but the longer I was in this place now, the more weirdness I picked up on.

"Yeah, if we weren't on edge before, we certainly are now," I murmured.

Cam nodded his head before going back to watching the people around us. They all chatted pleasantly and tried to keep their focus away from the newcomers (us) in the corner. We remained silent as we watched them.

After a few minutes of silence, things began to get interesting. A thin woman meandered through the crowd and glanced at us. She had thick black hair that cascaded over her shoulders and dark purple clothes that offset her greenish-yellow eyes quite well. Her eyelashes, as I noticed, were well-defined and a bold black. Her long nails looked like they had been painted purple. To my dismay, she continued strolling along in our direction and soon sat down right next to Rennan.

"Well, well, well! What do we have here? Two foxes and a wolf—how cute," she purred in a silky voice. "Where are you three from?"

She batted her eyelashes in a manner I found annoying. To my left, Cam shifted uncomfortably in his seat—and it wasn't just from the stiff wood. His eyes were fixed on the serpent-shaped necklace around the woman's neck. The woman looked at him sweetly, but he refused to make eye contact with her.

"We're travelers from the north," I answered shortly.

I had a bad feeling about this cat-like woman, and I had no intention of telling her anything else. She had something about her that made her seem untrustworthy. There was no way I would risk our quest for something like that. It would be stupid if any of us told her anything of importance.

"The north, you say? You wouldn't happen to be from Leshee, would you?" she purred in an apathetic tone. She looked at her nails as if she were uninterested to hear whatever answer we gave. "I heard that it was hit by a falling star last night. Isn't that something? There hasn't been a fallen star anywhere in Galerah for millennia."

"We're not," I lied. I hated how she spoke of the former city as if it meant absolutely nothing.

I could feel my cheeks burning red even in the dim light. Cam nudged my knee with his in a subtle effort to calm me. I took a deep breath and then moved his leg.

"Good to know. Enjoy your stay," the woman said as she got up from our table.

She smiled slyly and walked away to join some conversation on the other side of the room. Good riddance. I still watched her to make sure she had no ill motive that might possibly force me to break my cover.

After a few minutes of seeing nothing out of the ordinary, I relaxed slightly and turned back to my friends. They seemed to be just as pleased as I was to see that cat hybrid gone—Cam especially. He had frozen when he had seen the woman's necklace and her flirty smile. Thankfully, he had no interest in her whatsoever. Well, at least I assumed so since he was even more silent than usual and had refused to say a word when she was sitting at our table.

Moments later, yet another lizard hybrid brought out a tray carrying three steaming bowls. His appearance resembled both the cook and the innkeeper, but he had a kinder expression than both of them combined on his reptilian face. He smiled amiably as he set the bowls down on our table. His toothy grin was friendly, but to a person who had never seen lizard hybrids before, it could have been very unsettling.

"Three bowls of fly soup, as ordered!" the lizard stated cheerfully.

I looked at my bowl and saw transparent objects floating in the frothy liquid. There were also spots of green that reminded me far too much of mold. I could only guess what else was drifting around as one of the contents of this meal. My friends and I looked at each other as if we were having some sort of telepathic conversation. Finally, Cam was the one who spoke.

"*Fly soup*? I hate to be rude, but nobody told us it was fly soup," he stated.

I was shocked to hear his deep voice with no accent at all. Instead, it was more like my clan's dialect. There was no way anybody would think he was something other than a fox hybrid.

"I assume it was the cook who told you the menu?" the server sighed.

Cam nodded his head.

"In that case, don't mind old Gob. He takes too much pleasure in disgusting the guests with all of the weird concoctions he creates in his free time," the lizard sighed.

"I'm sorry, but what kind of name is 'Gob?'" Rennan asked curiously.

The tips of his mouth curved upwards and hinted at a smile. There was a similar expression appearing on Cameron's face as well.

"Ah, well, he prefers that to 'Gobbledygook.' Likewise, I go by Hob, and the innkeeper goes by Bob—short for 'Hobnob' and 'Thingamabob,'" the server chuckled. "See, the three of us are brothers, and we had very creative parents. Anywho, enjoy the soup!"

The server left us after that and we stared at each other in horror again. I didn't know about the other two, but there was absolutely no way I was ever going to eat *fly soup*. Just from the nauseated look on his face, I could tell Cam and I shared the same mindset. Rennan, on the other hand, didn't look bothered in the least. In fact, he seemed to be pleased.

"Please do not tell me that you have actually eaten fly soup," Cam pleaded with an appalled expression.

His accent had returned to his voice now that we were alone again. To Cam's dismay, Rennan nodded his head. The elf looked so green (both from the lighting and disgust) that I patted his shoulder sympathetically. He made a weak attempt to smile at me.

"My pack used to have friends who were lizard hybrids. Every time we went over to their place, they served fly soup or something with insects," Rennan shrugged. "I guess I'm just used to it."

Cam's face was still sickened and I admit I did make a face when Rennan took a bite of his soup and smiled.

"And now I'm not hungry anymore," Cam sighed as he pushed his bowl away and slumped down in his chair. He looked completely and utterly miserable.

"You should probably eat something. Neither one of you has eaten anything today," Rennan commented, his spoon pointed at both of us.

Cam and I glanced at each other and wordlessly came to an agreement.

"I would far rather eat something that has been in our packs for a few days than eat fly soup," I stated as I pushed my bowl away.

Before Rennan could argue anything else, we were interrupted by the innkeeper named "Thingamabob."

"Ah! Enjoying Gob's special, are we? Well, eat up quickly. I've prepared your room," the lizard hybrid said as he fixed us in his yellow-eyed gaze.

Rennan smiled pleasantly (he was in a much better position to deal with people after he had eaten).

"Thank you. Just leave the keys here and we'll go up in a few minutes," Rennan stated with a friendly smile.

I couldn't help but be amazed that this was the same wolf who had been freaking out a little while earlier. Thingamabob raised a curious eyebrow (if it could really be called an eyebrow since they were only raised scales), but shrugged in agreement as he tossed a set of keys to Cam. I wondered if he threw the keys to Cam as a peace offering.

"Your room is number fifteen. Enjoy your stay at the Blackshell Inn!" the innkeeper cheerily informed us as he walked out of the room again.

Cam was quick to put the keys in the pocket of his satchel so they would not be stolen by any of the other questionable hybrids in the room.

And that was when a cry rang up through the entire inn. Not like a cry of terror—more like a cheer. However, to us, that was almost worse. Cheering meant things would get heated and leaving the tavern would become difficult. I don't know about the guys, but I would rather keep the cover we had worked so hard to build rather than lose it needlessly.

Cam seemed to share my thoughts since he gestured towards the exit of the large room. Rennan took one last bite of his soup and got up as well. Cam grabbed his weapons (taking his massive scythe out in the process) and swung them onto his back again. I could tell that the elf was eager to leave and get to the relative safety of our room.

We were halfway across the room when the only exit was blocked by two figures in dark hoods. One was tall and the other was about my height.

The taller one was a man. His one blue eye and another blinded eye was enough for us to recognize him. Rennan and I immediately sucked in a breath when we saw Wayne, the wolf hybrid that Rennan had been fighting when I first met him. The other figure was female. She too threw her hood back to reveal long, shiny black hair with purple streaks. She also had wings that made her cloak look incredibly awkward. I instantly knew it was Razil.

"You're both tense. What is it?" Cam asked in a hushed voice.

We had retreated back to the corner where we wouldn't be seen as easily. We needed a plan before we did anything else. Wondering how much we should tell the elf, Rennan and I exchanged worried glances.

"Those two people that just entered are enemies who we've fought in the past under...problematic circumstances. The girl's name is Razil and she can't be trusted," Rennan stated as he watched both of the shady figures mingle with the rest of the crowd. He shook his head in irritation. "The other is a grey wolf named Wayne. He's a member of my pack—my cousin, unfortunately. I can't believe he's already managed to get himself out of custody."

"You never told me that," I commented as I looked at Rennan with a questioning gaze.

He just shrugged it off. He must not have thought that piece of information was really important in the grand scheme of things. I suppose it really wasn't—I just liked knowing all different relations in whatever circumstance I'm in.

"Okay, so they're two bad people and you want to avoid them. Got it," Cam stated with a nod of his head. He seemed to be remarkably understanding about all of this. I mean, he didn't even require an explanation! Well, I guess he probably would later on. "What's the plan of action? I can't imagine either one of you would want to stay here until they retire to their rooms."

I bit my lip. "Not really—they're too close for comfort. I'd rather get out of here without either one of them noticing us and starting a brawl or something. Thankfully, they won't recognize you, Cam, no matter what form you're in. However, Rennan and I need to keep our hoods up so we can get out of this inn without butting heads with Wayne and Razil."

"Yeah. What she said," Rennan agreed.

Both of us just wanted to get out of that tavern and get to our room where we would not be bothered by anybody. Cam was of the same mind.

"Okay, why don't we just try to casually walk out of the room?" Cam suggested calmly. The tone of his voice made me relax enough to trick my stubborn brain into thinking everything would be okay. "I doubt they would even think to suspect three passers-by as their enemies. Besides, since there are three of us, wouldn't they just let us go because last they saw you it was only the two of you?"

"The elf has a point," I whispered to Rennan, who nodded in agreement. "I think that plan is worth a shot, Cam. Let's give it a go."

Cam shouldered his weapons again, and Rennan and I grabbed our packs from the floor. We two hybrids made sure that our hoods were up so that shadows fell on our faces. The lighting (if it could barely even be called that) was on our side because it cast more shadows than regular torches would. In that sense, we were well protected. However, Razil and Wayne were still near the doorway, which wasn't all that wide. We would have to make it through in a single file line without touching them.

Rennan and I had both made it through the narrow space when everything started spiraling downward. Wayne took a step back and knocked into Cam, who was still holding his scythe. The sharp point hit Wayne's arm and created a deep, bloody slash in his flesh. Then I noticed Wayne had a bracelet in the likeness of a serpent. Was serpent jewelry suddenly in style or something?

The wolf cried out in agony before he turned around to glare at Cam. The elf just looked at Wayne with an emotionless face. It was impossible to tell what he was thinking or what he felt like at that moment.

"Put that weapon away, fool! You'll regret it if you don't," Wayne snarled furiously.

Cam held up his hands as if to say he was innocent. I caught a brief glint of mischief in his eye before he turned back to the other wolf hybrid, and I got the feeling that he wasn't as innocent as he wanted himself to appear.

"I'm sorry, sir, but you were the one who stepped backward into me," Cam said politely. Once again, he spoke in a Paleean dialect instead of his own, crisp accent.

Wayne glared at the disguised elf. The glare would have sent chills down even my spine if it had been directed at me.

"Listen, just watch where you wave that thing. You could have killed me!" the wolf snapped with an icy glare.

Cam just shrugged nonchalantly much to Wayne's chagrin. I could see that the other wolf intensely hated the elf now, and I really hoped nothing else would happen. Cam needed to get out without compromising our cover.

"How about I watch my weapon if you watch where you're walking?" Cam shot back.

Now both men were glaring at each other without moving a single muscle. To my dismay, Razil started chanting *fight, fight, fight* and all of the other guests chanted it along with her.

Before I could do anything to help, Wayne threw a swift punch toward Cam's jaw. Cam jerked his head to the side and rubbed his jaw, which was sure to bruise.

Cam glowered at Wayne. "You are going to be sorry you did that."

"Try me," Wayne taunted.

Cam's left eye twitched before he swung his leg toward Wayne's ankles. The fall knocked the wolf off balance and gave Cam a moment to plan out his next move. Soon Wayne was up again and trying to throw more punches towards the elf, which Cam dodged every single time. Eventually, Wayne just threw himself at Cam in a tackle position and successfully knocked the elf over.

At this point, all of the other guests were shouting and cheering and making bets on who would win the fight. They had even pushed tables and chairs out of the way to make more room for Wayne and Cam to fight.

Speaking of them, Cam was now underneath the wolf and was struggling to throw him off. Wayne was taking his opportunity to throw more punches at my friend. Cam was doing an excellent job of dodging and blocking them, but he wouldn't be able to keep it up indefinitely.

Cameron had shifted back into his normal form, so he would be recognized as an elf. The only thing that saved him from being noticed was the sorry excuse for lighting. Otherwise, everyone in the inn would have seen an elf and ganged up against him.

Wayne jumped at Cam, and the elf dodged him again. This sent Wayne flying into the hearth. The wolf howled in agony as he rubbed his surely-sprained wrist. He turned to glare at Cam who watched him with taunting eyes. Cam was agile in sidestepping the next attempted punch from Wayne and gave him a blow in return for the ones he had already received. Cam tackled the wolf to the floor but was soon on the bottom again.

Out of the corner of my eye, I saw Razil draw a dagger out of a sheath inside her cloak. She silently stepped nearer to the aggressive fighters. She lowered the dagger so she would be able to stab Cam in the side. I don't know what came over me, but I lunged at Razil to prevent her from stabbing the elf.

She grunted as she pushed me off of her. I slid and rolled to my feet and sent a glance to Rennan in the doorway to signal not to enter the fight unless everything else went downhill. All the while, I tried not to knock into a small group of people, including a really tall man with curly black hair who seemed to be protecting a fair-skinned woman with a shocked expression.

In the process of rolling, my hood was thrown off, thus exposing my identity. The raven narrowed her eyes when she realized who I was. She snarled at me, and I was pleased to return the gesture. I drew one of my own daggers and lunged at her. I would keep her away from Cam if it was the last thing I did.

"Just like when we were younger, isn't it?" Razil asked with an evil grin. She took great joy in bringing back cheerful memories gone sour from my childhood.

I glared at her before I started laughing bitterly.

"Yes, and I recall beating you in the knife fights every single time," I muttered as I dodged one of her novice slashes.

I grabbed her wrist and pulled it up between her shoulder blades. I probably should have done things differently after that, but at that moment my eyes were too clouded by fury to see things any other way. I pulled out my serrated blade and made one quick cut to Razil's wings. It was enough to permanently damage them, but not enough to slice them clean off. Razil cried out in anguish as I released her from my grasp. Stripping Razil of her ability to fly was the only thing I could think of to stop her.

She reached back to the base of her wings and her eyes went wide. She pulled her hand back only to see that it was covered in bright ruby blood. Her eyes went wild as she turned back to me. Razil shrieked as she threw herself at me with one final wing beat. It was the chance I needed to knock her out cold. So, I did. I dodged her jump and gave her an extra push into the wall.

"Scarlet, if you're done with her, I could use a little help!" Cam grunted.

He was still beneath Wayne, and I could tell that his strength was failing fast. Another few minutes without aid, and he would not make it out with only minor injuries. As it was, Cam was bleeding from the same spot where Rennan had hit him that morning, and it was gushing again. Needless to say, it was going to scar.

"Right," I murmured as I ran toward him.

I pushed Wayne off of the elf and knocked him out with one well-aimed punch. Cam had already done a good job of beating up the wolf, so I just had to finish him off. I nodded to Rennan, and he picked up the rest of Cam's weapons. At the same time, I offered Cam a hand in getting up. We needed to get out of there quickly as Razil and Wayne were already beginning to stir. Many of the other guests started whispering as well. I scowled to myself; I was not pleased with how the night had progressed.

We ran through the inn with shouts following us from behind. I almost ran into two women as I rushed up the stairs. One made eye contact with me. She was the same one with dark skin and ombre hair from earlier—and she stared at me with a wide-eyed expression.

But she wasn't what I needed to focus on. We needed to make it to our room and lock ourselves in. From there, we would be able to figure out our next plan of action.

We were scarcely up the stairs and down the hall when we heard pounding following us. Cam whipped out the keys, unlocked the door, and shoved it open with his shoulder. Once all three of us were in, he slammed the door shut and locked it.

"Okay, we have about two minutes to make a plan before we absolutely have to get the heck out of dodge," Cam stated breathlessly. He held his arm up to his forehead in an effort to stop the bleeding with the fabric. "What are we going to do?"

"Well, maybe we could—wait. Do you guys smell smoke?" Rennan asked.

Cam and I both sniffed the air.

The building was on fire.

"Okay, we escape out the window," I decided as I worked to unlock it. When it wouldn't open, I turned around to see if we had anything that would help. "Cam, your scythe."

Cam handed me his scythe and I used the tip to jam the lock into a breaking point. We had the window open mere seconds after that. We had even less time to get Rennan and me out the window and onto the roof.

Once we were out, Cam climbed out the window and put his scythe back in his stash of weapons. He carefully closed the window before nodding to me. He and I jumped off the roof and landed on the ground perfectly. Rennan was more hesitant than we were, but we eventually got him down with the right amount of coaxing and encouragement.

"Sorry, guys, we need to make it to the other side of the mountains before we can rest in safety again," Cam said as soon as we were all safely on the ground. I looked at him questioningly. "We're going to have all sorts of trouble chasing us if we don't."

"How in the world are we supposed to reach the other side of the mountains on foot by morning? We'll be caught as sure as death," I stated as Cam started walking off away from the inn. Smoke rose from the roof and shouts could be heard coming from inside.

"Um, guys?" Rennan interrupted.

"Not now," Cam hissed. He looked at me. "We'll just have to move faster than we did getting here."

"But that's still going to take hours! They'll catch us!"

"Not if—"

"Guys!" Rennan shouted with a slight scowl on his face.

Cam and I turned to glare at him.

"What?" we both shouted in unison.

Rennan pointed to a large building behind him. "There are stables right behind us. Couldn't we just steal a couple of horses and use them to get over the mountains by sunrise?"

"Rennan, you're a genius!" Cam cried with a smile as we all ran toward the long, one-story building.

Inside, there were several horses that were in excellent condition for running several miles at once. However, one in particular caught my eye.

Cam must have seen it too because he sharply inhaled and said, "Am I seeing what I think I'm seeing?"

"If you're seeing an alicorn, then yes, you are seeing what you think you're seeing," I replied as Cam rushed toward its stall and picked the lock. The silver alicorn was out seconds later.

Cam looked around the rest of the large stable.

"Rennan, get the pegasus in the corner stall. Those wings will help you get over the mountains faster," he instructed.

Rennan nodded and did exactly as the elf instructed him. The black-coated pegasus looked pleased to be out as it was led to the front of the stable.

Both the pegasus and the alicorn spread their wings as we mounted them. Since I had never ridden a horse before, I climbed up on the alicorn behind Cam. Cam himself was obviously an expert when it came to riding equestrian animals, and Rennan was pretty good, too. Well, Rennan was better at riding the pegasus (which is really quite different than riding a regular horse because you have to watch out for its wings) than he was at fighting with blades.

As soon as we were ready to go, we galloped through the small town and headed towards the southern gate. That was the fastest way to get out of the town and the shortest route to the mountains.

We certainly caused a major ruckus in our haste to leave. Many of the townsfolk had lit lanterns to see what was going on, and the town officials ran out of their homes trying to catch us. I'm pretty sure we had awakened the whole town.

Or at least Wayne and Razil had since they had been the ones to start the fire. They were evidently unconcerned about the fire so they tried to chase us on foot. Thankfully, the alicorn and pegasus were far faster than even Wayne so we were out of town before they could get their hands on us.

I could only relax when we were a long way away from that village and over the mountains. We crossed them far sooner than I thought we would and ended up pitching camp on the south side of the highest ridge. It was the side farthest away from a fort of any kind.

In my heart, I knew that if Rennan or I ever tried to enter Palee again, we would not have an easy time. We would most likely become fugitives within the kingdom and wouldn't receive a moment's rest until we had been executed for crimes we had not committed.

We had no choice but to travel to Kevay.

Memory

When we landed on the other side of the mountains, we were quick to establish a camp. The entire time we set it up, Cam would not look anyone in the eye or say a single word. He was beyond silent, which seemed to worried me for reasons that I did not comprehend. Furthermore, he was sullen. Something weighed on him that he didn't like and refused to talk about.

Unfortunately, I was unable to ask him anything because he noiselessly insisted upon being far away from me. Eventually, I started wondering if I had angered him, but there was nothing that I could think of that could have possibly offended the elf.

Rennan was in good spirits, though. His wide smile was ever-present. He appeared to be fond of the company of the winged creatures that we had escaped with. The three of them were entirely carefree now that we were on the opposite side of the mountains that formed the borders of Palee.

Through all of that, I wasn't quite sure what to think now that we were out of the kingdom. I mean, I was thrilled I was no longer stuck in the kingdom that kept me behind bars, but at the same time, I felt…empty. I had all I had ever wanted, but not in the way I wanted it. It was completely bittersweet. The only thing that had been holding me back was gone forever.

Cam sat down next to me without saying a word and I relaxed ever so slightly. Just his presence was calming. He seemed to be just as relaxed as I was as he gazed into the fire in front of us. I found it funny that we both felt that way even though neither of us said a word to the other. Perhaps we just silently realized that the other had genuine intentions.

"Hi," he said quietly after a while, keeping his eyes glued on the blazing fire.

The flames danced and yellow light was cast across the entire camp. It was an eerie light, but nowhere near as eerie the green fire in the Blackshell Inn. I much preferred to see the orange flames I was accustomed to. But back to my previous train of thought, Cam remained still as he sat beside me on the decaying log.

"Hello," I answered just as softly.

I couldn't think of anything else to say, so we fell silent again.

It's not that I didn't want to talk to the elf—I just couldn't think of anything to say that didn't concern who he was or what the plan for our quest was. I wasn't exactly great with friendly conversation. I was far more at ease receiving orders and getting the job done. Besides, it wasn't a time for details. We needed to regroup.

Cam ran his hands over his face and sighed. "I am so sorry for screwing things up back there. If I hadn't started that fight, we might be sleeping on real beds instead of on frozen ground. I shouldn't have been so cocky and...and I don't know. I shouldn't have done that."

I looked over at the elf and watched him in the firelight. He seemed to be paler than I had ever seen him. I guessed that it was due to the blood he had lost in the fight with Wayne—the blows he received had not been kind. Many of them had drawn blood, which was now plastered on his face and hands, but he didn't seem to notice it. Well, that or he was ignoring it.

"I don't think there was anything you could have done differently, Cam," I whispered.

Cam turned his head and looked at me with an expression that made his self-reproach evident. I think pain is what I picked up on the most, though. It was emotional as well as physical because of fresh wounds and his growing regret.

I sighed. "Knowing Razil and Wayne, they would have found someone to start a fight with anyway. Unfortunately, you were the one who grazed Wayne's arm as you walked by him. It was just an accident that led to conflict."

Cam laughed bitterly. Familiar shadows darkened his face as he turned away from me and back to the fire.

He continued in a hushed voice. "Was it an accident though? I did exactly what I meant to do. There was no accident on my part when I ran into Wayne. Slicing his arm with my scythe was intentional."

I gaped at the elf in shock; I would never have thought that Cam would be cold enough to harm someone who had never hurt him for no apparent reason. Well, something that dangerous anyway. Cam didn't tell anyone his reasons.

"Why did you do that then?" I asked.

"Scarlet, I did it for reasons far too complicated to explain at this point in time."

"But *why*, Cam?"

He shook his head and bit his lip. Once again, he looked away. "I don't want to talk about it."

I sighed, knowing I couldn't drag another word out of the stubborn elf. If he was done talking, he was done for however long he decided. There was no telling when that would be.

"I will say only this: the biggest reason was that those two hurt you and Rennan. I haven't known you two for long, but I consider both of you to be my friends—and I won't tolerate anybody who hurts my friends,"

Cam said quietly, finally looking me in the eye. His grey eyes were dark and filled with pain. He shifted in his seat. "So…I guess that's why I did it."

"Thank you," I said.

Cam looked at me in befuddlement. "What have I done to deserve your gratitude?"

"You got us out of Palee and were willing to sacrifice your life for a couple of low-lives like us. Not everyone does willingly," I stated with as much of a smile as I could muster. Though it was very minimal, the sentiment I tried to express was genuine—the first one I had the courage to offer for a long time. "I consider you as a friend, too."

The right side of Cam's mouth tipped upward slightly as he looked at his feet.

"Thanks, Scarlet," Cam said nearly inaudibly. He quickly squeezed my arm and then let go before a smile graced his face. "We'd better get some rest. It's getting late, and we have a busy day tomorrow. I want to reach Sala before the end of the week."

"Will we be safe there?"

"Safe enough."

I was awoken early the next morning by somebody shaking my shoulder. I opened my bleary eyes to see Cam standing above me. Like all other mornings we had traveled together, he had fierce dark circles beneath his eyes and his hair was relatively wild. However, this time, he had a smile on his face. It was more amusement than joy, but it was still a smile. That was better than the somber and remorseful look he had worn last night.

"Mm, what time is it?" I asked with a yawn as I wrapped a fluffy cloak around me.

Then I realized that it was Cam's cloak I was still wearing. Cam had to have been freezing last night since he only had his normal winter clothes and not the added warmth and protection of his heavy, fur-lined cloak. Though, the more I thought about it, the more I was sure that he shapeshifted to keep warm.

"First of all, I know what you're thinking. Go ahead and keep my cloak until we get to Sala. I can get you a new one there because—I see you blushing—you keeping it for now is really a non-issue," Cam stated with a slight smirk. "Second, Rennan and the horses—well, magical horses—are ready to go."

Remember when I said the elf was perceptive? Well, he most certainly was if he could guess what I was thinking without even needing to ask.

"I assume he wants to go now?" I asked as I sat up and began to gather my sleeping pad and items that needed to return to my pack.

One thing I had learned about Rennan was that when he wanted something, he was going to go after it with everything he had. Out of the corner of my eye, I noticed Cam nodding his head to confirm my assumption.

"Here, let me help you," Cam suddenly offered as he held open my pack.

I raised an eyebrow at him but didn't stop him from helping while I folded my blankets so I could just stuff them all in. For the life of me, I was unable to figure out what Cam was doing by jumping into something that I had under control. A couple minutes later, we had my entire space cleaned up and neatly packed away.

"You know, you didn't have to assist me with that," I commented with a small smile.

Cam just shrugged and grinned. It was the first real grin I had seen since I met him a few weeks ago. Granted, that wasn't very long, but that smile was a sign he trusted us. It was a sign that he trusted *me.*

"I suppose I didn't, but can't a friend help a friend?" he asked as he shouldered his own weapons.

He started walking away from our small camp. The fire was already out, and everything else we had brought in our hasty escape was dealt with efficiently.

He waved his hand for me to come. "Come on, Rennan has the rest of the things we brought with us if you were wondering. He is seriously eager to get to Kevay."

"Technically, aren't we in Kevay now?" I curiously questioned.

I had always been under the impression that the Forgotten Mountains formed the border between Palee, Mahe, Kevay, and Tralia. I had never been told anything else to alter that impression. Then again, I knew very little of the outside world except for the fact that Heviah, Salia, and Estal wanted to keep us hybrids in our own lands where we couldn't cause any "trouble."

"Well, sort of. There are still a few empty, unpopulated plains we need to cross before we're completely out of Palee. The border with Kevay is literally where the waters meet the land. But don't worry, it won't be a far ride," Cam explained.

As he continued explaining borders, I wondered how he knew of all of these things about Galerah if he had only been a knight in the king's court in Heviah. Cam seemed to know more about the Eight Kingdom's than most scholars. But how could a mere knight know so much?

"How long do you think it will take?"

"Eh, a few hours at the most. As I said, it isn't a far ride if we're flying. On foot, the journey could take a little over a week. The plains are pretty empty from here to the bridge."

"Bridge?"

Cam looked at me. I just made a confused face and hoped he would explain what he meant by "bridge." I didn't know why in the world we needed to make it to one.

"You don't know about it?" He was shocked.

"I don't know much about anything except what goes on within Palee and ancient history," I admitted with a shrug.

Cam sighed but nodded. "Okay, then I'll explain it when we eventually find Rennan."

"You don't want to explain it, do you?"

"Nope! I want you to see it!" Cam grinned.

I chuckled softly as I looked at his amused face. If only all elves were this friendly. Then there would be no reason for all the strife and war in Galerah's history. Half the conflict everyone faced wouldn't even exist. "Then I guess we need to find Rennan so we can get moving, don't we?"

"Novel idea!" Cam agreed enthusiastically.

"Well, look no further! I'm right here!" Rennan's voice shouted from somewhere above us.

I looked up to see him seated on the pegasus and riding around as if they didn't have a care in the world. Rennan looked beyond excited. His mood seemed like he had certainly gotten a decent amount of sleep.

"Rennan! What in the world are you doing up there?!" I shouted as I watched as him circle overhead on the pegasus.

Instead of answering me, Rennan leaned forward and whispered something into the winged creature's ear, and they began to descend with such skill that it made Rennan look like an expert rider. When they had landed, Rennan jumped off the pegasus' back and bowed so extravagantly that Cam started cracking up. I didn't know what to think of either one of them.

I stared blankly. "I don't even know how to respond."

"Well, he only knows how to respond to all of this with laughter. I don't believe he's said much else to me, actually," Rennan stated with an ear to ear grin.

Cam knew it was directed towards him and eventually composed himself to a wide smile.

Rennan continued. "I just thought it would be a wise idea to get some practice riding a winged horse before I would be on one by myself for most of the day. Or however long it takes us to get to Sala."

"Should I have learned to ride…?" my voice drifted off as Cam shook his head.

Now I felt bad for sleeping while the guys had been riding. Would that be a problem later on if I ever needed to take the reins?

"No, as long as two of us know how, we'll be fine," Cam explained as he figuratively waved my worries away. "Besides, you'll be sitting behind me on the alicorn."

He flashed me a smile assuring me that I had no reason to worry about anything in the coming days. I really hoped he was right. I didn't think I could handle something terrible happening, forcing us to deal with it with little food or rest in our systems.

I was about to speak in surprise, but Rennan interrupted my thoughts with one of his questions I had come to know well.

"You know they have names, right?" Rennan asked.

"You mean the alicorn and the pegasus?" Cam asked with a confused look on his face.

"Yes, them."

"What are they, then?"

"Take a guess."

"How am I supposed to guess what their names are? I'm not telepathic!"

"So? Just guess!"

"Ugh, fine. Betty and Joe?"

"Not even close. Guess again."

"Rennan, tell me."

"Cam, guess."

"Why are you being so difficult about this?!" Cam cried in exasperation. He ran his hands through his hair as he stared at Rennan. "Will you just tell me their names?"

Rennan himself just shrugged with a half innocent, half amused smile. I could only imagine what was going on in their heads.

"Well, I'll tell you that neither one of them is Frank or Suzie. Or Bob and Sara for that matter," Rennan began.

I know I gave him a strange look on that one. Never in my life would I expect two magnificent creatures to have such commonplace names. And that was coming from a person who had read plenty of documents about people with names like "Bufferbell" or "Zippernete!"

"Okaaaaay…then what are they?"

"The pegasus' name is Thornebrook, but he likes Thorne better," Rennan explained. "The alicorn's name is Angelica."

"Okay, I need to ask this: how do you know that?" I questioned Rennan.

I honestly wondered how the heck the wolf knew what these names were and what the animals preferred. He grinned as both the pegasus and alicorn trotted up beside him on either side. None of this was really making much sense to me.

"He knows because we told him," the pegasus stated in a voice as clear as birdsong on a spring night.

I gaped at them, not knowing what to think or how to respond. I had never heard of an animal talking before. At least, not in a speech that any of the intelligent species could understand.

"You…can talk?" I managed.

I couldn't believe my eyes when both of the winged creatures nodded their heads. I looked to Rennan, and he merely stood there grinning like a fool. Cam, on the other hand, was just as shocked as I was that these flying horses were talking to us like we might to each other.

"I'd heard of the stories where great winged horses could speak in the tongues of men, but in all of my travels I have never had the pleasure to meet one," Cam said in wonder. "To meet two at once is a rare pleasure."

Cam bowed to them in the typical elvish fashion that I had read about in books. In Palee, if anyone were to bow, it was a full bow at the waist. In Hevian culture, they held one arm firm in front of their chest and did a sort of a half-bow.

Still, that sort of thing was something only high-ranking nobles or royalty did. The elf continued to amaze me with little things he did with no explanation. Not only that, but Thorne and Angelica both bowed to Cam. He had to be more than a knight.

"The pleasure is ours, my liege," Angelica said with a voice as sweet honeysuckle nectar in the springtime. Her silver coat and wings shimmered in the rising sunlight, while her eyes twinkled with joy and hope.

Thorne also bowed. He was no less majestic than Angelica with his shiny black coat and wings. His blue eyes were as clear as the August sky.

Both of the winged horses seemed to know something I didn't. Cam confirmed my suspicion when he nodded to the horses with a look in his eyes begging them not to say anything. What he didn't want them to reveal, however, was a mystery to me. I doubted the elf would be willing to crack it for me. Even if he was, I suspected it would not be for a long time.

Cam cleared his throat and changed the subject. The horses stood up straight again and flapped their wings eagerly. They and Rennan were all itching to set out. Cam seemed to be eager to start moving as well, but I was still unsure of everything.

I didn't know what the plan was and Cam had already refused to tell me anything. I probably should have questioned him a little bit more, but I had no choice but to go with it. I just had to wait and see what happened when we got to the Palee-Kevay border.

Rennan and Cam mounted, but I hung back. I was incredibly hesitant to get up on Angelica. Cam must have noticed because he jumped down and strode near me. He smiled slightly and offered me his left hand, the one with the small band of silver on his index finger. I still wondered what it represented.

"Come on, Scarlet. You'll be safe with Angelica and me. I promise," the elf stated gently.

I slowly took his hand, and he led me over to where the silver alicorn stood.

He gestured to the alicorn. "Do you want me to help you up? Or are you able to do it yourself?"

I wanted to say that I could to do it myself, but I had never ridden a horse in my life before yesterday, and I hadn't even been the one steering! I had zero experience on how to mount one. I mean, I had mounted last night in a hurry, but that was instinct. There was no way I was going to be able to do it again without making a fool of myself.

When I didn't say anything, Cam cocked his head and gestured toward the alicorn. I just stood there and didn't move. I could only look at the ground. Eventually, I made up my mind to let Cam help. I'd far rather accept his help than failing to mount Angelica and embarrassing myself.

"You don't know how to mount, do you?" Cam asked as his smile faltered a little bit.

I shook my head.

To my surprise, he nodded in gentle understanding. "Okay. Let me help you."

He mounted Angelica again and then offered me his hand. I took it, and he pulled me up with a firm, but tender, grip. I was surprised to see that such a ascetic man like Cam could have such a gentle grasp. Most people with a build like his that I had come across did not have a grip nearly as kind as his.

The more interaction that I had with Cameron, the more I liked and respected him. I was glad to have met him, and not just because he had helped Rennan and I escape Palee without being caught. He was someone who genuinely wanted to see the world change for the better, and I was growing more determined to help him achieve it.

"There you go. That wasn't so bad, was it?" Cam asked with a smile when I had safely mounted.

I shook my head.

Cam smiled, then focused his attention on Rennan and Thorne. "Alright, everyone. Our path to Sala lies to the southeast. We need to get moving if we're going to get there before tomorrow's dusk. We spent more time here than I anticipated."

"You mean before lunch?" Rennan asked as Thorne and Angelica spread their wings and took to the skies. Rennan's smile was almost playful when Cam turned to glare at him.

"Lunch is not our priority!" Cam shouted over the wind.

"Not 'our' priority! *My* priority!"

Cam muttered something under his breath and returned his gaze to the path ahead.

Looking down at the ground, I could see everything we would have come across if we had been traveling on foot. There were small forests, large rivers, giant rocks, and countless other things that would take all day to describe. I was absolutely stunned to see how beautiful the world outside of Palee was. Its beauty was something I never would have expected to exist outside of the desolate wastelands of my home kingdom. To put it simply, the world outside seemed to be breathtaking and full of opportunities for our success.

From that point on, we rode in silence to the bridge that Cam had spoken of only half an hour earlier.

Somehow Rennan managed to get his way after all. By some mysterious means, he persuaded Cam to let us stop.

Actually, it wasn't a mystery.

Rennan brought up the topic of lunch every fifteen minutes, so the only logical way to end all his pestering was to land near Kevay and eat lunch. Cam only agreed because he was sick of Rennan's complaining and we were apparently moving much faster than he had anticipated.

We landed in a hidden valley that was located in one of the small forests in the area. The thick pine trees made it impossible for anybody to find us on the ground. Cam was sure nobody would be able to make it far enough into the forest to find our little circle. There were also waterfalls and small rivers in the clearing, each gushing forth hundreds of gallons of water. The gurgling sound they made was relaxing and put me in a much calmer mood instantly.

Rennan—oh, Rennan—had kicked off his boots and jumped into the river where he proceeded to swim around and splash us. I didn't mind since the water felt relatively warm despite the winter weather. Now that we were further south, it was warmer everywhere. Angelica and Thorne enjoyed the water and jumped under the waterfall as well.

And then there was Cam. The instant the water splashed him, he withdrew into himself. He climbed up one of the sturdier trees near us and watched from a few branches above. From then on, I knew that Cam and water did not mix.

"Come on, Cam! Climb down from your tree and join in!" Rennan called in delight.

Cam smirked and shook his head. Instead of coming down, he ascended a few more branches without saying a word.

Not wanting the elf to feel abandoned, I got out of the shallow water and wrapped up in my borrowed cloak. Then I climbed up the tree to join him.

Eventually, I got high enough to where Cam was only sitting a few branches above me. He looked down at me, smiled slightly, and then looked up again at the clear blue sky. The wind tousled his hair as it blew through the top of the tree. Cam was far happier up here than he had been on the ground near the water.

"Hello," I said, climbing up a few more branches.

Cam grunted, but said nothing and did not make eye contact.

I continued climbing until I was at eye level with the elf. "Is everything okay? You've seemed a little distant all day."

"Yeah, I'm fine. I just have a lot going through my mind right now," Cam sighed as he glanced at me, offering a weak smile.

I didn't believe him for a second. From being around him so long, I was beginning to figure out when something was bothering him. He just wasn't saying a word about it. Stubborn elf.

"Are you sure?" I pushed. I wanted to see if I could help in any way, and I found myself somewhat surprised at that. After all, I had never really been a person who wanted to help others. If anything, I harmed more than I helped, especially given the fact that I was a successful mercenary. I guess Cam was just a person who I thought was worth helping. He seemed to appreciate it even if he didn't outright say it. "Can I help in any way?"

"I'm okay. Memories are just flooding back. It's so much to take in again," Cam admitted as he rubbed the bridge of his nose. "It was a lot to take in the first time, but now...now it's even harder."

"What is it, Cam? What resurfaced?"

"It's from when I was a child. I was playing in the garden one morning when I saw two winged horses flying overhead. I was in awe and tried to tell the others what I had seen, but nobody believed me. I've never been able to tell if it was a dream or reality, but I'm starting to think it was the latter," Cam said quietly. He stared at the sky the entire time that he spoke and his eyes were filled with a youthful light. "I was maybe five at the time."

"You were young," I said almost silently. I wondered if my parents were alive and well, at that time. I wondered what life as a child must have been like for Cam. Had it been enjoyable or like my childhood, which was full of sadness and heartbreak? "Cam, can I ask you a question?"

Cam snickered softly, still not making eye contact. "Technically, you just asked me a question. And before you start talking about how that's not what you meant, I know it's not. You want to ask me something else, no?"

"I did," I answered, not really knowing how to respond. I recovered my wits a moment later. "How old are you now and when were you exiled?"

"Ah, ah! That's two questions at once!" Cam laughed, finally looking me in the eye. He smiled and wagged his finger in a joking manner, then sighed and went back to the stone-like expression that I had come to know so well. "Nevertheless, I will answer your questions. I've been exiled since I was nineteen, which was five years ago. I suppose that makes me twenty-four. At least I think that's accurate—it's hard to track years when you're in exile."

I looked at him blankly. A knight at nineteen or younger was unheard of. My brain refused to accept that fact as I asked, "When did you become a knight, then? You must have been very young if you were exiled at nineteen."

Cam smiled sadly. His grey eyes shone with the light of happy years that had long since gone by.

Then he quietly explained, "I *was* young when I was knighted. Like I said before when you asked about my rare gift to shape-shift, I come from a family with several members in the nobility and even some who were royalty in past generations. My father wanted me knighted early on in life so I could live up to the family name. As a result, I was knighted at thirteen."

"Wow. That is insane to think about. You have great strength to have survived so long," I said quietly. "Thank you for being willing to share."

Now my mind had countless other questions racing through it. I wanted to ask more questions, but I didn't think Cam would take it very well. He had already told me more than he ever had at any one time.

"We should probably be going again. We've lingered here long enough," I whispered a few minutes later.

"I'll be down in a few minutes," Cam stated. "And Scarlet?"

I looked up at the elf again. His eyes were full of longing and something else I couldn't quite place. "Yes, Cam?"

"Please don't tell any of what I just told you to Rennan or anyone else. I don't like talking about my past, and when I say something about it, I don't tell just anybody. I trust you not to say a word," Cam said as his voice became suddenly quiet.

I nodded my head in understanding and silently swore that I would not tell anybody about anything Cam had just disclosed.

"I won't," I promised as I continued my descent from the tree.

Rennan was waiting for me at the bottom. He looked relaxed and even happy in these dark times. I don't know how long he had been waiting, but his hair and some of his clothes looked slightly drier than when I had last seen him.

"Is Cam ready to go yet?" Rennan asked as he jumped up to his feet. "The horses and I are ready to continue on our way."

"He said he'll be down in a few minutes, so I assume we'll leave just after that," I answered.

I walked past him so I could gather up everything we had gotten out during our time in the clearing. There was no way I was going to leave any trace of our presence for hunters or anyone else to find. I knew how to cover my tracks.

"Okay. What's he doing in the tree anyway? You know, other than avoiding the water," Rennan questioned as he followed me aimlessly.

I'll grant that that sounds weird. He followed me, yes, but he had a look in his eyes that made it seem like his mind was very far away.

"I can answer that question myself," Cam called from across the clearing.

I turned around in time to see him jump down from one of the lower branches that was about five feet from the ground. He showed no sign of the sorrow that he had exhibited only minutes ago; he was very good at hiding his emotions.

Cam walked closer to us and began to speak again. "I hate water and I've always been more comfortable in high trees. So, I figured I would climb a tree to prevent getting wet."

"Told you," I smugly whispered to Rennan.

"…And that was how I managed to find my knife again!" Rennan shouted over the wind.

For the entire ride, all we had been hearing about was the time when Rennan was a child and had lost his favorite dagger. However, since he was only six, it was not actually a dagger but a stick. Cam had muttered to me that the fact that it was only a stick was a lot safer than giving the wolf a real blade. I agreed since Rennan was not the most skilled when it came to weapons.

"Okay, please no more stories from when you were young. I don't think I can take hearing any more stories about losing something," Cam yelled, his voice conveying equal levels of irritation and amusement.

I was with him, though. I had come very close to yelling the same thing several times in the last hour.

"But I thought you guys liked my stories!" Rennan cried as he feigned a look of offense.

Cam made a strange noise that I could only assume was the restraint of laughter. Still…that sound coming from the elf seemed slightly suspicious to me. I wanted to know what amused him so much about Rennan! It seemed like every time Rennan did something remotely amusing, Cam was right there to laugh at it. Well, smirk at it. Rarely did Cam actually emit any sort of noise outside of conversation other than the occasional grunt or weird sound. I think that was one of the consequences of being in exile for five years—lack of knowledge of interaction with other people.

"I never said we didn't! I just want silence for the last few minutes of this flight!" Cam shouted in response.

Rennan's eyes went wide in realization of what Cam had just said.

"Only a few minutes left? What are we waiting for?! Come on, Thorne!" Rennan hollered in excitement.

The pegasus did not move any faster. In fact, I think he was moving slower. Whether it was out of spite or exhaustion, I did not know.

"My lords—and ladies," the pegasus said, glancing at me and Angelica. "If we winged horses could have a word?"

"By all means speak, friend pegasus," Cam urged with a thick accent in his deep voice.

Once again, I felt like I was close to figuring out the answers from the elf I wanted, but at the same time, I felt farther away from the truth. It was baffling.

"If it pleases you, Angelica and I would like to land and continue on foot since we are so near to our destination. I am unsure how much longer my wings can last," Thorne explained in his typical tone of grandeur and nobility. He certainly had polite manners.

"Of course. You've carried us this far. I don't see why we can't do something to would relieve you," Cam stated with a nod of his head.

Both fliers nodded to the elf as they began their downward spiral. It was only a brisk walk from where we landed to the bridge Cam had spoken of earlier. Cam seemed pleased that we had reached the bridge much faster by air rather than the week he had anticipated on foot.

The bridge seemed to be miles long and made out of some sort of shining substance. It stood high above the water, but I didn't see anything in the water that could support such a structure. The wind had picked up, but it didn't rock the bridge whatsoever. This surprised me since I had always read in books that bridges of this size had a tendency to sway in strong gales.

Cam turned to us and smiled. "The bridge to Sala is made out of the finest pearl and is supported by columns of corals beneath the surface of the water. The Mer-people built it centuries ago before Palee became a forbidden kingdom. An identical bridge lies to the west and leads north into Mahe."

"So that's our road to Sala?" I asked, looking skeptically at the grey-eyed elf.

He nodded, and I sighed in an attempt to steady my nerves. I was not an anxious person, but I was nervous now. It was like something was telling me to go into the city, but I couldn't explain what it was or exactly what it was saying to me. I just knew that I had to follow it.

"I guess we had better get going then," I commented.

And so, we picked up our packs from our short rest and headed toward the city once again. Cam led in front followed directly by Rennan and myself. Thorne and Angelica followed behind us and were able to walk side by side due to the tremendous size of the bridge. We walked in silence for what seemed like an eternity until we finally reached a massive gate. The gate to Sala, the capital city of Kevay, was our first destination outside of Palee in our quest to return light and justice to Galerah.

Royalty

Cam stepped forward to knock on the gate. It barely made a noise in the clear air, but it sent vibrations that could have knocked me off my feet. Through it all, Cam stood there as if he didn't notice the shaking.

Even the water beneath the bridge was moving, but I later realized it wasn't from the bridge. For a long while, I couldn't see what was making the water rise and ripple. It seemed as though some unseen, underwater force was controlling it. Never in my wildest dreams would I have thought that was the actual cause of the amazing movement of water.

Eight living creatures jumped out of the water in a blinding flash of blue and green light. I covered my eyes so I wouldn't be blinded by whatever was happening around us. I was thankful I closed them since the light got increasingly brighter and more splashing noises could be heard.

When the lights finally disappeared, there was a troop of soldiers pointing jagged spearheads at us. Rennan sharply inhaled as one approached his throat. The same thing happened to me, but I wasn't scared like he was. Instead, I held my ground with a cold look on my face. It wouldn't be wise to show fear to these apparently fearless warriors.

I scanned the troop of water-dwelling soldiers to take note of any detail I possibly could. Their armor was made out of a shining material skillfully woven together to create durable chest plates that could no doubt survive many battles. Any fabric they wore was lightweight and could dry very quickly once it was out of the water. Their captain wore a helmet with a plume of something resembling purple seaweed or kelp.

The captain of these transforming sea folk leveled his spear right at Cam.

The elf did not move a muscle nor change expression when asked,

"Who are you, and why do you knock on the doors of the Kevayan capital of Sala?"

Cam, being the diplomat he is, was the one who answered the aggressive question from the seemingly irritable sea captain. The spear point touched his throat when he opened his mouth to speak—likely to ensure that Cam wouldn't cast a spell. Cam held up his hand as a sign of peace. I suppose he also wanted it to mean that we wouldn't harm anyone, but I wasn't in favor of that side of the gesture. I didn't like being held back physically or verbally, as my first instinct was to fight.

"We are travelers who seek to stay the night in the safety of your splendid walls. We mean no harm and we will not cause you any trouble," Cam stated politely.

The captain narrowed his eyes and looked the elf over from head to toe. Eventually, his eyes widened again and he dipped into a low bow.

"Of course, my liege. I will alert the queen of your arrival," the captain reverently replied. "Please wait here until we can escort you inside the gates."

I cocked my head slightly because of the strange reaction from the captain and the even stranger reaction of Cam. Cam just nodded, his eyes begging the water dweller not to say anything more about something I could not clue into. This strange behavior from the elf—first with the horses and now with the guards—puzzled me greatly.

"Of course. Thank you, captain," Cam said gratefully, as he nodded his head.

The guards and their captain jumped over the railing and into the water. As they did so, they morphed into their water forms beneath the surface, so there was no blinding flash that could possibly damage our eyesight.

"Okay, who was that, and what was it all about?" I asked when I could restrain my curiosity no longer.

Rennan nodded his head in agreement to my question. He was just as eager for an answer. Cam, however, was less than enthusiastic. His face turned pink.

"Oh, that? That's the captain of Queen Coral's guard. The majority of her court and the city are underwater, so they dove back down to report land-dwelling visitors," Cam explained as he scratched the back of his neck.

I had a feeling he was either far more nervous about this visit than he let on, or he was hiding something from us.

"But he seemed to *know* you," I pointed out with the beginnings of a scowl on my face. "Why is that?"

Now Cam's face seemed to pale, but some of the color returned before he had the chance to speak again.

"This isn't exactly the first time I've been to Sala, so he recognizes me from those visits. Normally I enter the city on the other side," Cam answered with a forced laugh.

I knew there was more that he wasn't telling us. I just *knew* it.

"Knowing and recognizing are two different things, Cameron. That captain seemed to know you. Perhaps not personally, but he acted like he's had friendly conversations with you before," I pushed with growing annoyance. "What aren't you telling us?"

I tried not to let annoyance show for fear that the elf would not reveal the answers I desired. I hated trying to pry things out of him, but he left me no other choice. He certainly wasn't making it easy, either.

Cam opened his mouth to speak, but he never got the chance.

The massive gates started to open, demanding our silence. I watched in wonder as the gates, which must have weighed several tons, effortlessly swung open across the bridge. They were wider than the bridge allowed, but that didn't stop them. The bridge changed shape to allow for the movement of the heavy golden gates.

On the other side, the sea captain and a few of his men waited for us. The men were at attention, and the captain himself held a small, leather pouch. He beckoned for us to come closer. In his gesture, he included Thorne and Angelica, who had remained silent up until that point. I assumed they didn't want anybody to know they could speak.

"These crystals will make it known that you five are allowed to be here. That includes you, pegasus and alicorn. I know you can speak—you have an intelligent look in your eyes," the captain stated with a small grin. "These crystals will allow the hybrids and the elf to transform in case they decide to visit the underwater part of the city."

The captain handed out little multicolored crystals. They were on chains so we had to wear them as necklaces. The horses didn't seem to mind their new accessories. For the most part, I didn't either. From pure curiosity, I noticed that the horses' crystals were both bright shades of blue that stood out against their coats. Rennan got a pink crystal, the one I received was green, and Cam's was a platinum color. I had no idea if the colors had any significance or not, but I was curious.

I wanted to know a lot of things, but I highly doubted most of my questions would be answered in my lifetime. It was more likely that I would receive few answers, merely leading to more questions in my already crowded mind. I was only a hybrid in a world revolving around people who thought they were better than me.

I shook my head to rid myself of depressing thoughts. There was too much going on at that moment to be focusing on little things that didn't matter in the greater scheme of the quest.

"The palace of the queen should be easy to find. As your elvish friend knows, it's on the top of the hill," the captain informed us as he pointed to the steep hill that rose up from the center of the large island. "Just go through the market, and you'll be at its gates. The queen is expecting you. Farewell."

The captain and his men bowed to Cam and then closed the gate behind us. Then they marched in the opposite direction. I was confused as to why they were bowing to the elf, but I decided to let the matter slide for now. I hated that Palee was a forsaken kingdom that knew nothing of current affairs between kingdoms. I feel like if I knew all the relations, things would be much easier to understand. Like perhaps the merfolk were just bowing to Cam because he was an elf. I would have asked Cam, but I filed that sort of query under the category of *Answers Cam Was Not Yet Ready To Give.*

"I guess I get to play tour guide," Cam muttered as he started fidgeting with the edge of his black sleeve. "Well, come on."

He didn't look entirely pleased that he was the one leading us through the city. Or perhaps there was another reason he was less than happy—I couldn't tell.

We followed him through the streets of the island-city. Along the way, he explained that he hadn't been there in ages and things were far different than he remembered. The king had died and his wife, Queen Coral, was now the head monarch of the kingdom. Cam also mentioned that the queen and her late husband had a daughter who was a little bit younger than me, but I didn't catch her name. I just kept nodding my head, only half-listening to the conversation. Rennan was genuinely interested by all of it, but I wasn't nearly as enthusiastic.

The more we walked through the city, the more I realized I didn't belong. Many of the townspeople were either human, had some sort of fey blood, or were one of the merfolk that had morphed to be on land. Cam belonged to some degree since he looked like some species of the fey.

But Rennan and I? We were drastically different than everyone else, largely because of our furry ears and our small fangs when we opened our mouths to smile or speak.

"Scarlet, you coming?" Cam asked me, walking back.

I came back to reality to see him and everyone else far ahead. He must have given the directions to Rennan so he could come back to me. I nodded my head and jogged to catch up to him.

He pivoted on his heel to walk in the same direction as me, then watched me intensely for a moment. "What's wrong?"

I sighed, not bothering to make eye contact. "Rennan and I don't belong here."

Cam narrowed his eyes, not in confusion, but trying to process what I had said. "You know, I don't either. Technically, since I'm in exile, I shouldn't be allowed into any city in any kingdom. I'm supposed to be restricted to the extreme wilderness. But why do you say that?"

"Look around. We look drastically different from all the other people here. Besides, won't we be recognized as hybrids, the species that is confined to their own borders? Won't we be sent back?"

"Nah, the Kevayans don't care who enters their lands—or seas—as long as they don't cause any trouble. The late king didn't sign the treaty saying that all hybrids were prohibited from entering his kingdom and Coral refuses to ignore that fact," Cam said with a shake of his head. "I wouldn't worry about anything here. We're just here to search the libraries in the palace for anything that can help prove that Heviah is corrupt."

I was about to speak, but then I heard Rennan's voice shout, "WHAT?!" through the city. The market was too loud for anyone else to hear and take notice, but Cam and I were so accustomed to Rennan's shouts that we heard it loud and clear.

We looked at each other with concern in our eyes and ran ahead to see what was the matter. When we got there, my eyebrows flew up, and Cam muttered something under his breath.

Only a few feet in front of Rennan stood a man—or rather an elf—who bore a striking resemblance to Cam. He had dark brown hair that reflected gold and chocolate tones in the sunlight. His slate-grey eyes were almost as dazzling as the smile stretched across his face. This new elf wore teal and bluish-grey colors with little to no armor. Actually, when I looked at him more closely, he had no armor and no scars anywhere on his flawless tan skin.

Cam growled and stalked over to the other elf. They both drew themselves up to their full height, and I saw that Cam was an inch or so taller than the newcomer. I also noticed how alike they were in appearance.

The only differences were that Cam was much paler (despite his years of exile), his hair was longer and a bit messier, had several scars and cuts, and was far more muscular than his double. The other elf's grey eyes were also filled with a colder, more assertive light and his features weren't as sharp as Cam's. Besides those minor differences, they couldn't have been more alike.

"Why are there two of you? There isn't a mirror here, is there?" Rennan asked with a thoroughly confused face.

Thank goodness the wolf had spoken when he did, because Cam was in the process of subtly pulling out one of his well-hidden daggers. The look in Cam's eyes was almost murderous while he wordlessly watched his double.

Cam-but-not-Cam smirked slightly. The real Cam took a step back and took a deep breath. Neither one of them was particularly happy for reasons I did not yet know—the key word being "yet."

"He's my twin brother," the newcomer stated with a grin, though it was not a happy one.

He seemed to be more amused at Rennan than anything else. But really, the more important point was that *Cam has an identical twin brother?!* Why hadn't he told us that sooner?

Yeah…I must have made a face since Cam looked at me with a fleeting expression of regret. Then he turned back to his brother and opened his mouth. Still, he did not speak due to Rennan interrupting him.

"No, that can't be right. What's the real reason? This has to be some type of magic, right?" Rennan demanded as he made a face.

He looked so sure there was some kind of mistake. Unfortunately, there was not. I hoped this was all just a bad dream that we would wake up from soon, but the awakening never came. Time continued, and nobody woke up from reality.

Cam sighed a long, sad, disappointed sigh. "It's not magic. I wish he was lying, Rennan, but sadly he is not. He *is* my twin brother; his name is Carter. Or rather, *was* my brother since you all disowned me five years ago and sent me to exile, never again to return to a kingdom that is rightfully mine!"

"Wait, what?" I said in confusion.

A kingdom rightfully belonging to Cam?

Just when I thought I had something figured out, it was tipped upside down, leaving me to rethink everything again.

"He didn't tell you?" Carter asked with an astonished, yet amused expression. Cam muttered something under his breath before his brother continued. "Cameron was the heir to our father's throne before he was exiled. Sadly, he was too foolish to realize that all of his stupid rallies—or, as he called them, 'remonstrations'—were actually detrimental to his standing in Heviah. I'm sure he kept his signet ring, didn't you, brother?"

Carter grabbed Cam's left hand to look at the metal band on his index finger. Of course, it was a signet ring! He had probably kept it in case his banishment was ever lifted. If that ever happened, he would be the king of Heviah, I'm assuming.

Now that I was able to catch a better look at it, I could see clearly what it was. The metal band was fashioned to depict leaves curling around each other, holding a single sapphire stone in place. It was nearly as stunning as Cam's eyes. Somehow, despite his years of exile, the ring was still in flawless condition, like it was brand new.

How could I be so blind? First his lack of personal information and mysterious ring, then the horses and the captain calling him "liege," and now this…it all made sense. Too much sense. Blood drained from my face when I realized I had been in the presence of a would-be king and hadn't even known it.

"Knock it off, Carter. And they weren't stupid. They were necessary—I don't regret being exiled," Cam mumbled as he snatched his hand out of his brother's reach.

Carter shrugged and went on with his story. He didn't seem to notice whatsoever when Cam started reaching for his scythe. Hopefully, they wouldn't start fighting right in the middle of the street…Actually, I sort of hoped they did. Then I could whoop this sucker for making Cam's life miserable. Carter didn't seem like the fighting type.

"Fine. I shall continue now. Cameron is my brother, but you'd never tell by the way he acted in Heviah when he was living there. He always went strutting around as if he were a peacock," Carter explained.

When he demonstrated, Rennan looked at him in horror, and Cam rolled his eyes. Then he pulled his brother back by the collar of his shirt. I honestly could not imagine Cam doing anything like that. Ever. He was not nearly as arrogant as his brother painted him to be. If anything, Carter was the one who came across as self-absorbed and prideful.

"No, that was *you*. I was always too busy helping other people to ever have any time by myself," Cam corrected as he reluctantly let go of his brother, who just rolled his eyes. "Meanwhile, you were always nagging at everybody else to do what *you* wanted and never thinking of anyone other than yourself. Oh wait, that's just like everybody else in that blasted kingdom of selfish, self-absorbed jerks!

"That's why I was banished. I was different; I was strange. Nobody wanted to see past their own selfish desires to even hear what I had to say! Instead, what did you do? Listen for once when I lost my lid that one time? Seriously. One. Time. *Ever*!!

"No, you all just went on with your lives, acting as if nothing was wrong and you didn't have a care in the world. You pretended everything was perfect; you pretended *you* were perfect. Well, news flash! Nothing is perfect! Did you ever think about the other kingdoms and how the elves have ruined everything for places like Palee? Murders happen so often. Soon, their entire race will be wiped out and forgotten in history.

"It would be so much better if it was the *elves* who were wiped out. Then we could see what everything would be like and how the world would be different. We would see how much the elves have truly messed up everything in this world with their conceited ways of dealing with even the smallest things. It's all '*do this, not that!*' or '*I didn't want this, get me a different one*' without so much as a please or any sign of gratitude afterward. Who would want to associate with people like that, honestly? I know that if I were anybody else, I wouldn't want to deal with people from Heviah! I'm genuinely surprised more people haven't cut ties with Heviah already."

Cam shook his head with a sour expression. "Everyone back 'home' is so snotty that I honestly cannot believe I'm the only one who sees the corruption. I tried for *years* to help people see the downward spiral many of the kingdoms are falling into. But, as usual, I was never heard—much less given a second thought. It didn't even matter that I was the crown prince.

"All I was ever known as was 'the radical prince' or 'dear, sweet, delusional Cameron.' I even heard the council mock me once. I felt like an absolute nobody when they told me that my dreams of helping people would never be achieved or when they told me it was a child's dream. They said I should just work on my lessons and not to worry about things that aren't my concern."

Cam took only a second to breath before continuing. "But what nobody understands is that it *is* my concern. One day, whether through times of peace or by war, I *will* be king. Father cannot withhold that right from me. I could care less about the title, but what I *do* care about is helping people as best I can. How can I help when all I was told to do was study? I couldn't follow that order, so I continued my work through the shadows and was eventually discovered and exiled for *helping* the less fortunate. Judge me when you're perfect.

"If anything, exile has made me stronger than ever and I am ready to take back my position as heir, even if it costs me my life. I would rather die for a noble cause than be locked up in a palace and pretend that nothing is going on, biding my time for the rest of eternity.

"And what is it all for, really? Why are elves the ones who run everything? We're no smarter than the wizards or some of the fairy folk. No, the only way we're different from everybody else is the horrible way that we treat others. There are people who are starving, homeless, seeking aid anywhere they can find it. What have we done to help?" Cam scowled again before he snorted, "Heh, nothing. What do we hope to gain from it all? Bigger egos? Even more power and wealth? Imagine if we didn't have all that. Imagine if all our fancy clothes and mansions and castles and fortunes were all gone tomorrow. What would we be left with? Think about it."

Then he stalked away with his hands in his pockets, leaving us all speechless.

I personally was absolutely stunned by what had just transpired. That was the longest time I had heard Cam speak uninterrupted in the entire time I had known him. It wasn't just that he had said so much, but he had also been mad. Not irritated or reclusive like I had seen him at certain times in the past few days, but *livid.*

In that instant, I worried for Cam. Now I could see why he didn't mention anything from his past life in Heviah, including the fact that he kept most of his true identity as the heir to the throne a secret. He already had a very, very irritating and snobbish brother. All he had wanted was a friend who truly understood and listened to him without titles being involved.

"Well, that could have been handled better. I don't understand why he got so upset. But I suppose he was always like that," Carter said thoughtfully.

Rennan and I looked at him in horror. Did he use his brain at all? Did he even have one? Did he hear the words that he was speaking? Now I could really understand Cam's struggle. Carter was impossible to tolerate.

"*'Handled better?'* Handled better! Ha!" I laughed harshly. "You must be a fool if you don't realize what's happening. Rennan, stay here and don't let him out of your sight."

It was the first time I had spoken since Carter had appeared. He seemed to go into a daze, like it was the first time he had noticed me. His eyes became wide and filled with a softer light. I found I preferred the cold light that had been shining through his steel eyes earlier rather than what now appeared.

"Understood," Rennan acknowledged as he unsheathed the dagger that Cam had given him. Rennan backed Carter against a wall and Angelica held him there with her long horn.

Seeing that they had this new elf under control, I pivoted on my heel and headed out to find Cam.

He was probably in bad shape after his rant. Whenever I ranted with myself on missions working with other people, I always sought solitude afterward so I could collect my thoughts. It occurred to me that Cam might do the same thing, so I tried to find a park or garden with trees fit for climbing. Because he seemed to like the trees, I thought it might be a good place to start. I just hoped that I would have a little bit of luck to find him before the sun set.

After a long while of meandering around Sala, I found a large, spacious park area with primordial oaks and maples. There were trees as ancient as the mountains, yet sturdier than many stones. There were several sections of the park with shaped topiaries representing many aspects of underwater life. I guess it made sense since for the above-ground part of the city to reflect happenings of the culture beneath the water's surface.

Sure enough, I found Cam sitting by himself in the higher branches of a rather peculiar oak tree with indigo leaves. Ignoring the strange leaves, I started climbing up the branches. I was only two branches up when I realized I wasn't tall enough to climb any higher. Frustrated, I looked up into the loftier parts of the canopy to try to figure out where Cam had gone.

He was nowhere in sight now.

Then I heard shaking boughs behind my head. I swiftly whipped around to find myself staring into the most striking grey eyes I had ever seen. I realized that they belonged to Cam, who was now hanging upside down from one of the higher limbs. His eyes shone with a mixture of relief and amusement, but his face was as emotionless as a rock. I'll admit that I did cry out when he suddenly appeared.

"What are you doing?" he asked me in a smooth tone.

From the way he spoke, one would never know that he had just had a major rant not even twenty minutes ago. He seemed like he was just having a quiet afternoon to himself. I looked at him with curiosity. Here he was, asking what I was doing when he was hanging from his knees in a tree. He went so far as to cross his arms—he knew it amused me because a slight smirk appeared on his lips. The fact that his long hair was loosely hanging in the air didn't help a whole lot either.

"You know, I could ask the same of you," I pointed out, forcing a small smile.

Cam grinned before he swung himself up so he was sitting upright on the branch above me. He held out his hand and I took it. He pulled me up so I was sitting right next to him.

"I knew you would come looking for me, Scarlet, and I'm glad that it was you and not Rennan and especially not *him*," Cam said.

When he referred to Carter, his voice dripped with venom. Shadows crawled over his face like maggots crawling and worming their way through rotten flesh. I sharply inhaled with slight fear for what might come, but he shook himself out of his trance and looked me in the eyes. He looked apologetic, but in his grey eyes was pain and a hint to a power that could be unleashed at any moment. He smiled as if to say, *There's no reason to worry. You're safe.*

"If you don't mind my asking, what exactly happened back there?"

"I'm sorry you had to be there for all of that, really I am. I never meant for you to see any of it. My brother has had that coming for a long time," Cam explained with a saddened look on his face. It was clear he regretted blowing up in front of us. "I just didn't think he would get it today."

"You're absolutely right, though; you just showed me the opposition we will face in this journey and why we need to stick together through all of it. You've also shown me that this quest—if or when it succeeds—will be worthwhile. Everyone will benefit," I stated with a smile.

I was going to stick with my friends and fight for them no matter what. We all had to count on each other in order to live, survive, and thrive.

"Thanks, Scarlet. I know we'll be stronger together than we are apart," Cam said as he wrapped his arm around my shoulders and gave me a brief hug.

After being on my own for so long, it reminded me of when I was little and my grandmother would comfort me whenever I was hurt or upset. It was like a small piece of her was still with me when he showed that small bit of kindness.

Then Cam smiled out of nowhere. "Okay, grip the branch with your legs."

"Why?"

"Just do it."

"Okay," I agreed reluctantly. "What are we doing?"

I had absolutely no idea where this was going, but I went with it anyway. It couldn't hurt, right? As soon as I had a strong enough grip on the branch, Cam scooted himself a foot away and grabbed my hand. Then he swung us backward until we were hanging from the tree—just like how I had found him.

"Seeing everything from a new perspective."

"We're just looking at everything upside down."

"I know. It's still a new perspective."

"Cam, what is the point of this?"

"To have fun."

"This is a bizarre way to have fun."

"Aww, come on, Scarlet! Just admit that this is awesome," Cam said with a playful grin. "Admit it. You're enjoying this."

I couldn't help but smile back. His good mood was infectious.

"Oo!! Swinging from trees!! Fun!!" a new voice cheered.

Cam and I looked down to see an average-sized girl climbing up the tree. Her pink eyes sparkled like sun on a lake as she practically danced up the branches. She climbed up right next to us and hung upside down on the other side of Cam.

Her face was practically glowing with excitement. "Such a beautiful perspective, isn't it?"

Cam smirked smugly as he turned his head toward me. "Told you."

"Who are you?" I blurted out.

I wanted to know who she was, where she came from, and why she randomly appeared right beneath us. The girl looked at me from the other side of Cam's head. Her grin was both innocent and mischievous at the same time. I didn't like her. That smile reminded me too much of Razil.

The girl giggled as if she thought I or something I had said was utterly hilarious. I, on the other hand, did not find anything nearly so funny.

To my chagrin, Cam was smirking in amusement as he brushed some of his hair out of his face. I sent him a clear plea, but he pretended not to notice the desperation in my eyes. He just jumped (or rather, backflipped) down from the branch. The girl and I had no choice to follow him.

Well, I didn't. I didn't want to be left alone with this crazy girl. She could stay in the tree for all I cared.

"You must be new here if you don't know who I am," she relentlessly giggled. "Well, you are, miss. Cameron knows who I am!"

"All too well, princess. All too well," Cameron smiled as he dipped into a playful bow.

The princess exchanged the bow for an elegant curtsey. I hoped I wouldn't ever have to do that while we were here. Anything remotely like proper was not in my wheelhouse. Need a weapon? Sure, got that. Need a quick solution to a problem? Not an issue. But being fancy and polite? Count me out.

Cam straightened and cleared his throat. "Scarlet, this is Princess Valerie. Valerie, this is Scarlet."

"Oo!! Hi!! Nice to meet you! As Cameron said, I'm Valerie and I'm actually a mermaid in my land form," Valerie stated at a breakneck speed. The words seemed to tumble out of her mouth like rock towers when knocked off balance. "Where are you from?"

"Uh...," I looked to Cam for help.

I didn't want to tell Valerie that I was part of a forbidden species and have her tell everyone we met along the way, even though my ears would give me away anyway. That would expose far too much information I wanted to keep secret. Cam met my eyes and nodded.

"Valerie, that shouldn't be something you ask immediately when you first meet someone," Cam gently chastised.

Valerie laughed and waved him off.

"Oh, you're so uptight, Cam! Loosen up a little and have some fun!!" Valerie cried in a sing-song voice.

Then she started dancing in circles around Cam, who was beginning to look very uncomfortable.

She kept going, too. Like she pulled out flowers and started singing extremely ridiculous songs that made absolutely no sense to me. But Valerie didn't take any notice of us as she enjoyed herself.

Eventually, when Cam seemed to reach his breaking point, he walked behind me.

"Nah. I'll stay the way I am, thanks," he said quietly. He wrapped his arm around my shoulder, leaned down, and whispered, "Try not to mind her too much. I know she's crazy, but she means well. Besides, her mother might be able to help us."

"Okay, fine. I just hope you know what you're doing," I agreed begrudgingly. I didn't really like Valerie, but I would be kind and polite if Cam wanted me to be. I was no diplomat, but he definitely was. Whatever Cam said in a situation like this was an order to be followed.

"Thank you. Trust me, I've got this all under control," he whispered again.

He straightened once more and got Valerie's attention. I distinctly noticed that his arm was still wrapped around my shoulder. I tried not to act so awkward that Cam's ploy wouldn't work.

In a louder voice he said, "Well, Scarlet, had better get back to the rest of our companions."

"Oo! Can I come? I love meeting new people!" Valerie asked in an overly excited voice.

Cam nodded, and she started jumping up and down, clapping her hands like an overly caffeinated child. She then started dancing in circles around us, as Cam and I walked through the park towards the exit. We slowly made our way out of the park to find our friends. Well, friends plus Carter the Utter Annoyance.

"Okay, who the heck is she?" Rennan asked when we approached them.

I sighed and looked behind me to see Valerie skipping and throwing little orange flowers everywhere. She had been doing so since we left the park. Meanwhile, I tried to ignore her many, many comments to Cam. I think the elf was beginning to lose his mind, honestly. Half the time, he didn't even bother answering the mermaid.

"This is Princess Valerie. She's Queen Coral's daughter," Cam explained to the wolf. Cam's voice was relatively tight, so I knew his patience for the mermaid princess was beginning to wear thin.

Rennan nodded slowly as he watched the princess start dancing in circles. Cam and I just rolled our eyes. It was the fifth time she had done so already.

"Oh, I know who she is," Carter stated as he walked up to the princess. He took her hand and gently kissed the top. "How are you, princess?"

Valerie's cheeks blushed purple as Carter smiled at her with a bow. She curtseyed in return. Cam just grunted in response.

"Very well, sir," she chirped with a broad smile.

Her eyes were shining with joy as she spoke to the annoying elf. I could see why she could drive somebody crazy. Man, I hoped her mother wasn't the same type of person (and by that, I mean always dancing around). I appreciate a leader being relatively calm when dealing with professional matters. Plus, I don't think I would be able to handle another Valerie....

"Okay, well, we need to go to the palace and meet with your mother, Valerie," Cam stated to distract the incredibly excitable girl.

She jerked her head away from Carter and stared at Cam. Then she grinned and clapped her hands joyfully. Cam smiled, but I could tell he was in no mood to give a real smile. It looked far more forced than natural.

"Hooray! Mother will be thrilled to see you, Cameron!" She cheered with a beaming smile. The blue-haired girl then turned toward Carter. "Are you coming, too, Carter? You all appear to be in a group."

I was hoping Carter would be smart enough to realize that if he came with us, we would be stuck with each other for an indefinite amount of time. There was no way I was going to stay sane around him of all people. To be perfectly honest, I would love to tie him to one of the highest turrets of the palace and leave him there to rot for the rest of his long life. Just from knowing him for a little bit, I could tell that imprisonment would serve him well.

Unfortunately, he was smart enough to clue into what was going on and said, "Yes, of course. I'll come with you."

"Can you hit him with your knife?" Rennan whispered to Cam, who did actually have a long knife drawn, though I wasn't entirely sure I wanted to know why. Especially since Carter and Valerie had turned their backs to us.

"I believe the technical term is 'stab,'" Cam stated with a pointed look at the wolf. "Besides, I have more of a mind to punch him in the face."

"That would not be the wisest idea," I stated as I looked at the elf. "We're in the middle of a city, and we don't exactly blend in here."

"I hate that fact," Cam muttered as we followed the princess through the town's market.

It was slow because Valerie and Carter stopped at every other cart to say hello to the vendor. At that point, Cam had to hide his blade or else he would raise suspicion. Well, probably not much suspicion; it was likely that many of the people there already knew he was the heir to the throne of Heviah. Still, he couldn't go around a city with a drawn knife and a massive scythe on his back and not freak someone out.

Cam looked ahead wistfully. "Are you sure I can't punch him in the face?"

"Yes."

"What if I just break his nose a little?"

"Unless you want something really bad to happen to you, no. Sadly, he has the law on his side because you're exiled."

"Scarlet! Stop being so right!"

"If you want me to stop being so right, stop being so wrong!" I joked with a laugh.

Cam smirked in amusement as he sheathed the blade he was carrying. All you could see of his weapons were the tips of his arrows, bow, and the head of his massive scythe.

It was strange, really, how kingly he actually looked now that I knew the truth. He appeared far nobler than before, especially now that I saw him next to his cowardly brother. His face was fairer, both in complexion and kindness. Cam was the type who would stop at nothing to help somebody he cared about, even if it meant his own demise. He was a friend that would stick by you when everyone else seemed to disappear.

Valerie and Carter seemed to know the way to the palace like the back of their hands. Eventually, Valerie stopped greeting all of the vendors in the market and turned her attention to Carter as we trudged up the hill. Seeing how energized they were, I envied them. All Cam, Rennan, and I had been doing for the past weeks was hiking through the countryside, constantly in danger of being discovered. It was likely that Valerie and Carter had never known danger in their entire lives. Everything must have been absolutely perfect for them, thinking they never did anything wrong.

They were royalty. What were we? Rennan and I were fugitives, and Cam was an exiled heir. It was strange and frankly wrong being led through the city behind a prince and princess. In most cases, I easily would have taken them both hostage and questioned them until I had gotten the answers I wanted. However, since we were trying to keep our cover and had a quest to complete, I was forced to be polite. I wasn't doing it for them, but rather for Rennan and Cam who expected me to do the right thing.

"So how long will you be staying this time, Cameron?" Valerie asked as she began dancing around us again.

I was going to stick out my foot and trip her, but she stopped her strangeness and fell in step on the other side of Cam.

The elf slowly moved closer to me. He was wary of the mermaid.

"I don't know," he replied somewhat shortly. "I guess we'll be here however long we need to be here."

"You should stay here for the winter!! Mother says the storms are going to be bad this year and nobody should really be traveling around the northern kingdoms. Except, of course, those who live in Tralia or Estal. They're always too warm for the storms to affect them for long," Valerie stated. She continued talking for a long time after that, but I didn't care enough to listen to everything she said.

From the looks of it, Cam didn't either. We both withdrew into our own thoughts and ignored the outside world.

I looked over to Rennan at one point and noticed that he was watching Valerie's every move, like nothing else around intrigued him in the slightest. I would have thought nothing of it if we hadn't been passing some pretty impressive structures built out of precious stones and coral-like materials that would impress even the most clueless individual. Instead, his eyes remained on the mermaid princess.

I elbowed him in the ribs, and he turned and scowled at me. Even then, he glanced back to the blue-haired girl before his attention remained with me.

"What was that for?" Rennan hissed his demand.

"Why are you staring at the princess?"

"I don't know."

"I don't believe you."

"Too bad."

I was going to speak more, but Rennan refused to look back at me. His strange behavior made no sense to me. Well, it made about as much sense as the night when Cam had gotten angry and stalked away into the trees. Neither of those events made logical sense to me, so I ignored them for the present. I had more important things to worry about while we were in Sala.

We would soon be in the presence of the queen, and we'd have to figure out what to do from there. It appeared to be a long, dark path ahead of us, even though our goal was hopefully to restore light to Galerah.

I wasn't one to let myself hope for things, but I got a light, airy feeling in my chest as I wondered about how things might turn out for us all. If we failed in everything else, the one thing I hoped for was that we would all survive. I didn't think life would be very great if we set out on this journey for justice and one or more of us died. There might be no one else to carry on the arduous work we three had set out to do.

Cam startled me out of my thoughts by gently tugging on the edge of my borrowed cloak.

I looked up at him and noticed that his eyes were fixed in front of us, but he would send me sidelong glances. I raised my eyebrows to urge him into speaking his mind. Well, part of it anyway; there was no way he would ever speak his whole mind.

Quietly, he asked, "What's your opinion of staying here for the winter?"

I thought for a minute before I answered. I wasn't entirely opposed to it, but I did have hesitations. It was actually a very logical idea, but it also had its downsides. The main one I could think of was being forced to stay around Valerie for two or more months. I couldn't imagine how on earth I would be able to survive.

Finally, I shrugged. "I guess we could."

"Okay, I'm thinking that might be our best course of action. It gives us time to rest, recuperate, and research whatever we need for our quest," Cam stated quietly, glancing down at me a few times. "I also need to talk to the queen at length about several matters, and there's no way we'll be able to accomplish everything needing to be done in only a few days. I also—heh, look at Rennan."

As directed, I looked at Rennan. He was watching as Valerie started dancing around and throwing flowers again with a large smile. He looked so hilarious that I wanted to laugh and startle him out of his fantastical daydream. He had eyes for the princess—that was most certainly obvious. Soon he would be floating after her with little hearts trailing after him.

"Rennan needs help," I whispered with a grin on my face. Cam snorted but nodded in agreement.

"Leave him be for now," Cam stated in a tone that was both firm and gentle. "We can interrogate him about it later."

I didn't know how he did that. I knew one tone: firm. I couldn't be gentle at the same time. It wasn't in my nature. Or maybe it was, and I was just severely out of practice.

"I like that plan."

"I hope you're all done talking," Carter began as he turned around to face us all.

Valerie turned around as well.

The annoyance's eyes regarded all of us before he continued speaking. I hated the fact that his grey eyes lingered on me the longest. It made me want to punch him in the nose like Cam had wanted to do earlier. The fact that both of us restrained ourselves was amazing.

He smiled. "We're approaching the gates to the palace."

Unwanted Company

Once again, the sound of gigantic pearl-like gates creaking open filled the air. Though, this time they opened normally and nothing changed shape to accommodate the large doors. I was still stunned that palace gates were being opened to me. It wasn't something that happened to a fox hybrid. I would probably be the only one to experience this. Even then, it was largely due to the fact that I was part of a group including merfolk and elvish royalty.

"You nervous?" Cam whispered to me while the gates were opening.

I hesitantly looked up at him and nodded my head. I didn't want to admit it, but I really was nervous. Never in my life had I stood in front of formal royalty.

Cam, Carter, and Valerie were different. They were around my age and couldn't care less (well, in Cam and Valerie's cases) if they were treated like royalty or not. They wanted to be seen as equals (I'm guessing that for the mermaid. I still couldn't decide what to make of her). Carter, on the other hand, was just what I had expected from an elf.

"Yeah, this is one of the first times I've met somebody who technically has authority over me," I answered quietly.

Cam's lips twitched and hinted at a small smile, but they never curled into one.

"You know, since I was wrongly exiled, you are technically still under my authority," he commented as he started twisting the ring on his index finger.

I looked at the elf in a questioning manner. "What do you mean? I didn't think you held any power like that."

Cam's face grew darker and his subtle smile faded. I sighed as he turned away from me.

"I'm sorry, I misspoke; I didn't mean it like that."

"I know you didn't. I guess I deserve that since I've told you almost nothing of what this quest will accomplish if we succeed. Just let me talk to the queen about a few things," Cam sighed. "But don't worry about having to answer to me—I won't order you around like my brother might. Speaking of which, never do anything he tells you without running it by me. There is no telling what motives he may be covering up. He's a master of trickery, so don't let yourself fall prey to the poisonous words he speaks."

"Okay," I agreed.

Cam retreated further into his mind. He usually dwelled in the deeper, darker recesses, so I hated to see him go any further into it. I was afraid I had offended him and he was withdrawing because of the words I had so recklessly spoken. In the future, I would be far more aware of thinking before I spoke.

The gate continued to open and soon it was lined with aquatic soldiers in their land form. They held trumpet-like instruments with purple and blue flags hanging off them. They were embroidered with the image of a green colored shell bearing a glittering pearl. I could only guess that this was the crest of the royal family. Their armor sported the same colors and fashion of the guards we had met at the eastern entrance to the city. However, these guards seemed more welcoming to guests than the captain and his men had been. I suppose it might be because we were not seen as a threat to Kevay's security any longer.

The horns blasted a sort of fanfare unique to Kevay. I had never heard a tune quite like that before and I doubted I would ever again unless I returned here as a guest of the queen. There was one other way that I might stay as a guest in this kingdom, but I hated the thought of it.

I hated it almost as much as I hated the person who could make it happen. The only other way it could come about is if Valerie dragged me back to Sala as her friend. I mentally gagged at the thought and hoped with all my might that my face didn't express the same feeling.

Valerie, being Valerie, skipped right into the courtyard of the palace and started humming along to the fanfare. Her eyes mainly were set on Cam or Carter as she twirled around us. Rennan's pale blue eyes followed her every move.

Meanwhile, I chose to pay attention to the scenery around us. Out of the corner of my eye, I observed what the twins were doing. Cam was staring blankly at the palace, deep in his own thoughts. On the other hand, Carter was watching me with a wistful expression on his face. I scowled in his direction and he quickly looked away.

"Come on, everyone!! I'll give you a tour of the palace before my mother sends for us!" Valerie called out when she was done dancing and humming.

Rennan followed immediately with Carter close behind. Cam and I moved at a slower pace, but we kept the other three well within our sights.

Cam didn't say a word, but he didn't have an air about him causing me to think he was angry or irritated with me. No, actually, it seemed more like he was pondering what I had carelessly said. Strangely, he still wanted me near him. I couldn't imagine why, though. If someone had said something like that to me, I wouldn't want to see them at all, much less be around them.

“What in the world is going through your head to make you so quiet?” I asked, half to myself and half to Cam. I cursed myself when I realized I had done exactly what I was trying to avoid.

Cam jerked his head toward me and caught me in his probing gaze. He looked at me with a searching expression that showed no emotion.

“I can’t tell you that, Scarlet, as much as I’d like to,” Cam answered in a much softer tone than I expected. He sighed and seemed to shrink in the process. He ran his hand through his hair and then looked back at me. “There are still too many unknowns. It’s just not the right time.”

“Okay,” I sighed, deciding not to take the matter further. I didn’t want to create a second incident for today or push him any closer to the thin edge he was already balancing on. “I’m sorry for earlier, Cam. I really didn’t mean it like that. I really need work on keeping my mouth shut.”

Cam, to my surprise, laughed softly. “You’re forgiven, Scarlet. It isn’t a big deal. I can’t expect anything other than your comment when you barely know anything about my past and what my future holds. I’d love to tell you, but I’m still unsure of how everything will play out. I can guess, but I won’t know for sure until it all comes to pass. And really, speak your mind, especially to Carter if it involves how annoying he is. You made me promise that I wouldn’t silence you on this quest, after all. I want to be held fully accountable to that oath.”

“Thanks, Cam,” I said with a grateful smile. He nodded with his usual half-smile. “And believe me, the first chance I get, I’m going to let him have it. Your brother is seriously difficult. How did you live with him?”

“He certainly is. And like I said earlier, I was too busy helping other people to ever pay attention to the things my brother pulled. He loves making it out like I'm the problem child. As the older twin, I'm naturally assumed to be the responsible one," Cam explained with a shrug.

I raised my eyebrows in slight surprise. I had no idea that Cam was the older twin, but I should have figured that out since he was Heviah's heir. Still, it was another piece of information in this sea of madness that I was drowning in.

"Hmm, interesting."

"You know what I think will be even more interesting?"

"What?"

"Finding out what my jerk of a brother is doing here at the same time we are," Cam answered. Some of the shadows came back to his face and it darkened once more. "Doesn't it seem suspicious to you? It was like he was looking for us."

"It is suspicious. I didn't trust him the moment I laid eyes on him…."

"But he looks like me!! Are you saying you don't trust me?!" Cam interrupted, faking offense as he threw his hand up to his chest, clutching his heart.

"I trust you. Now let me finish!" I laughed half-heartedly as I lightly punched his arm.

He only grinned with a mischievous light in his steel eyes. He appeared to be back to his relatively cheerful and light-hearted self. Well, for the moment, at least.

My thoughts wandered a little bit. "It is suspicious he's here at the same time as us. Was it me or did your brother seem almost pleased to see us?"

"It wasn't just you; I noticed the same thing," Cam replied as the gloom returned to his face. It twisted into a thoughtful expression leading to a place that only he knew how to access. "Considering how we got along when we were younger, it is highly doubtful he's genuinely happy to see us. Be on your guard and do not trust anything he says."

I was about to reply, but Valerie ran back towards us from the other side of the courtyard. She had more flowers in hand, so I was wary of what she was going to do with them. Was she going to start singing or dancing? Or both?! Oh, heavens, I hoped it wasn't both. I'm pretty sure I'd die if I heard one more Valerie song today.

"Come on, guys!!! You're going to get lost in the palace if you don't hurry up and come!!!" she practically shouted as she grabbed Cam's wrists and dragged him away at full speed.

He sent me a pleading look for help, but all I could do was jog to catch up.

Soon we had rejoined the rest of our curious group in the main hall of the palace. It was mainly constructed of precious stones like pearl and aquamarine. Many of the supporting columns were created out of strong corals that were some of the brightest colors I had ever seen—I couldn't recall ever seeing brighter greens, pinks, and oranges.

Being in Kevay had truly opened my eyes to sights I'd never thought possible…even if they were pointed out by an extremely hyperactive mermaid who was constantly singing, dancing, throwing colorful flowers everywhere, and greeting everyone she met in the hallways. I never thought I would meet somebody like that. Now look at where I was.

"So. Where do you guys want to start?" Valerie asked cheerfully as she planted her hands on her hips. Her grin was way too pleasant for me to be at ease like the guys were. I would forever be on my guard around her. There was something about her I didn't like and I wouldn't rest easy until I figured out what the heck it was.

"I believe your royal mother would like you to start in her throne room," a rich voice said from behind us.

We turned around to see a green skinned man wearing grand, flowing clothes. He wasn't royalty, but he certainly was a noble. This may sound weird, but I could practically smell the pompousness emanating from him. Seriously, he was wearing some extremely pungent cologne. I wanted to gag.

"Oh, Fredster, don't be dull! Live a little!" Valerie cried out as she started dancing yet again.

I wanted to die right then. Seriously, I wanted a lightning bolt to strike me through the ceiling and to fall dead on the spot. Unfortunately, that didn't happen and Valerie continued her latest dance around the snotty, uptight dude. Cam sensed my irritation and he put his hand on my shoulder for a brief instant. It was enough to remind me that I wasn't the only sane person here.

"Your highness, your mother is waiting for you and your friends," the man stated in an uninterested tone. He must have had a lot of patience if he was close enough to the princess to be called "Fredster." Though, even I had to admit that it was a pretty brilliant nickname for someone who obviously hated it. "She requests your presence immediately."

"Then off we go!! Let's go, friends!" Valerie said in her sing-songy voice as she skipped down one of the halls with Carter and a love-sick Rennan chasing after her.

Cam and I began to follow, but the man grabbed the elf's wrist. Cam gave him a questioning look.

"Unhand me," Cam demanded as he narrowed his eyes. He slowly reached for one of the daggers that hung at his belt. Cam fully unsheathed and held it to the green man's throat. "Who are you and what do you want with me?"

"Forgive me, my liege," the man said with an extravagant bow. "My name is Frederico. I wanted to inform you that your equestrian friends are in stables with our top groomers looking after them. You should not have to worry about them while you stay in the palace."

Cam and I relaxed slightly, but we kept our blades drawn as a precaution. "Thank you for the information. If you'll excuse us."

We stepped past him and briskly walked down the hall to catch up with the others. We didn't slow our quick pace until the green-skinned man was out of sight. Despite the bright colors he was dressed in, he seemed incredibly shady to me. He would not receive the slightest shred of my trust.

"Well, that was weird," I commented.

"Indeed," Cam agreed. He ran a hand through his hair. "Then again, maybe I'm overly cautious. I've been in exile too long."

Soon we reached the others who waited near a large, jewel-encrusted door. I assumed that it was the door leading to Queen Coral's throne room.

Valerie confirmed my assumption when she said, "Here we are: the door to my mother's throne room. I hope you're ready, 'cause I'm opening it in three…two…one!!"

On cue, she pushed the door open and sprinted into the large room. It was far more majestic and breathtaking than anything I had ever seen. Half the room was dry land but the other half was filled with water. The half-submerged throne had several gigantic, glowing green gemstones laid within it. The throne itself was made from a substance like gold, but yet shone with an even brighter light.

A woman with pale blue skin like the princess sat on the throne. A jeweled silver crown sat atop her indigo-purple hair. She had striking pink eyes and long, deep blue eyelashes. She wore flowing robes just like Federico had. However, the most stunning thing about the woman was her long, fishlike purple tail.

"Welcome princes from afar and neighbors to the north," the woman stated in a voice as soft as the finest silk. Her trilling voice was easy to listen to and almost pleasurable. "I see a fox and a wolf hybrid among you. Welcome! You are safe here. Tell me, what are your names?"

"My name is Rennan. I come from the Penbrooke clan of grey wolves," Rennan answered with a respectful bow. He stepped back a second or two later and looked to me.

I inhaled a shaky breath and stepped toward the throne. I clumsily bowed as I said, "Scarlet Sutton, a common fox. I am the last surviving member of my clan."

Rennan sharply inhaled behind me and even the queen raised her eyebrows in surprise. I realized that nobody knew of the constant death that had wiped out my suffering clan. We had been small to begin with, but the attacks against foxes had increased in recent years and more died every month. I didn't even know how many fox hybrids were still breathing relatively free air.

"Welcome, then, Scarlet and Rennan. It is an honor to have such a worthy species as guests in my halls. I hope you enjoy your time in Kevay," the queen stated. Then her pink eyes settled on the twins. A small smile spread across her lips. "I see the Woods brothers are here as well. It is a pleasure to see you here again, my friends."

"The pleasure is all mine, Queen Coral," Cameron insisted with a polite smile as he raised his head from its bowed position. "Thank you so much for your hospitality."

The queen smiled happily at the elf. "Of course. How long will you be staying this time, my princes?"

Cam looked to me and I nodded. He turned back to the mermaid queen. "With your permission, we'd like to remain in Sala for the rest of the winter. I fear the winter storms rapidly approaching from the north will derail us significantly if we were to keep traveling. By my calculations, it will soon cover the northern plains and likely will not thaw for weeks."

"You speak truly," the queen agreed. "My sky readers have seen the signs and they share your mindset. The northern storms approach swiftly this year. I would hate to see such excellent warriors and travelers such as yourselves become trapped in unforgiving weather. You four are more than welcome to stay here until spring arrives."

"Thank you, Queen Coral," Cam said as he bowed again.

The queen smiled and nodded her head. She turned her gaze towards Valerie, who looked all too pleased that we would be staying. As much as I hated it, I had given my consent to Cam and I had to live with my choice. The weather was against us in this instance and there was no way I had the power to deny it.

"Valerie, why don't you find our guests a block of rooms? They look weary after traveling," the queen suggested.

Valerie smiled and nodded excitedly.

"Or from a long afternoon of listening to Valerie sing and dance around us while throwing flowers everywhere," I muttered.

Cam snickered in agreement. Thankfully, the queen didn't hear us. Or, if she did, she paid us no attention.

"Of course, Mother," Valerie agreed as we left the room.

And so began the next part of that very, very long day. All I hoped was it would end soon. I didn't know how much more Valerie I could take.

As it turned out, Valerie found us a block of rooms in the same corridor as her bedroom. I wasn't originally very happy when she told us, but I was a little bit less irritated when I found out that I was on the opposite end from her room. Rennan's room was to the left of mine and Cam's was directly across the hall.

"You four can request anything you need while you stay here, and I'm happy to get it for you myself if I can," Valerie explained with friendly smile.

Perhaps it was a little bit too friendly. She stared at Cam and Carter the entire time she spoke without so much as a second glance at me and Rennan (who, naturally, was watching her every move).

"Thank you, princess," Rennan stated in an effort to draw her attention away from the elves.

Valerie blinked owlishly and smiled at the wolf, who looked all too pleased to have received a smile from the princess. She nodded and then we five each went into our separate rooms.

I pushed open the door to my room and was astounded to see how much of it resembled my family's den in Palee. The outside walls matched everything around us. There was no doubt in my mind about magic affecting this room. How else could it look like a place in Palee? There was a hearth that looked just like mine and even the furniture looked and felt like something that would have been found in Leshee.

One difference was that the furniture was so much nicer than anything I'd experienced in my life. Another thing I noticed later on was the giant, four poster bed in the corner of the room. It was far softer than what we had back home. Feeling exhausted, I decided to lie down for a few minutes.

"There you go, child. All safe and warm," my grandmother whispered as she tucked me into my small bed. I looked up into her amber eyes and saw so much love. I couldn't help but smile.

"And you're sure they won't come for us again?" I asked with a shaky voice.

There had been several attacks that week and I was afraid of the people behind it would coming again to specifically look for us. All I could think of was their dark cloaks, hidden faces, and bare knives. I shuddered at the thought.

"Yes, my child. No danger will come to you tonight," Grandmother assured me as she kissed my forehead. She pulled my blankets up further so I would be in a perfect cocoon of warmth. "There will be no one breaking in here to harm us."

"Do you promise?"

"Yes, I promise. I'll always be with you when you need me."

Tears filled my eyes when the memory faded. I remember being six or so at the time. I was so small and vulnerable; I didn't know how to fight or fend for myself. My grandmother was always there with me making sure nothing went wrong while she was around.

Now that she was gone, my heart felt empty. It was filled with the same cold feeling I had gotten when my parents died. It was all my fault. I hadn't been there when I lost my parents and I had been too late when I lost my grandmother. It could have been avoided if I had been there. I could have let their killer take me so they could live instead.

Though a knock echoed through the large room, I didn't feel like getting up to answer it.

"Who is it?" I yelled, only caring enough to sit up and wipe my eyes. Nobody needed to see those shameful tears. I didn't want to be pitied by anyone.

"It's Cam and Rennan," Cam's accented voice shouted through the door.

I had half of a mind to get up and open it. That is, until I heard the next voices.

"It's also Carter," I heard him say.

"And Valerie!!" The mermaid shouted in a sing-song voice. "We're heading to the dining hall for dinner and we came to get you so you don't miss out!"

Now I had no intention of answering the door. I liked moping in my room more than talking to other people at the moment.

"I'll come later!" I shouted back.

Really, I had no intention of getting anything to eat. My stomach was in too many knots to attempt keeping any food down.

"Okay, just come when you're ready, Scarlet," Rennan's voice instructed.

Then I heard footsteps walking down the hall and away from my room. I thought the coast was clear when I heard another soft knock on my door. Knowing I wouldn't be left alone until I answered it this time, I reluctantly got up to see who was on the other side of the door. I opened it to see a worried Cam.

"You don't have any intention of going down there, do you?" he asked immediately.

I shook my head but said nothing.

Cam sighed. "Fair enough."

"Why are you still here? Didn't you go with the others?" I asked suspiciously.

Cam just cocked his head with a relatively calm expression on his face. He sighed again and stuck his hand into the pocket of his tunic. He hadn't changed into anything nicer since we got here, so he was still dressed in his rugged traveling clothes. I'm willing to bet he was also still armed.

"I, uh, wanted to give you this," the elf answered as he handed me a folded piece of paper and a small rock.

I looked at him quizzically before I opened it. My jaw dropped in surprise when I saw that it was the family picture and amber stone I had brought from Palee. I vaguely recalled him grabbing them from my ruined cloak, but I hadn't realized that he still had them.

He fidgeted with his ring. "Sorry it got a little wrinkled. I tried to keep it in good condition for you."

"Wow. I can't believe you still have these," I said quietly. I looked up at him, tears pricking my eyes. "I don't know how to thank you."

I couldn't believe that he had carried the picture with him for all of the miles we had travelled. It was heartwarming to think that he cared enough to do something like that for a lowly fox hybrid like me. The small gesture meant a lot to me.

"You don't have to," he answered with a brief smile. He turned to leave, but then turned to face me again. "If you don't come and join us, just stay in your room until you hear us come back. I'm kinda wary of some of the nobles right now—I don't recognize a lot of them—so just be on your guard."

"Okay, I will. Thank you again, Cam," I agreed with a nod of my head.

He smiled and nodded before walking away with his hands in his pockets. I closed the door again and sank down to the floor. This was going to be a long night of waiting.

Yeah, I just sat in my room looking through books on Kevayan history all evening. I had nothing better to do and I didn't feel like getting anything to eat or sleeping. Though I was exhausted and sleep sounded nice, I couldn't force my eyes to remain closed. All I could do was sit around doing nothing and waiting for something to happen.

Eventually, my patience was rewarded when I heard footsteps and cheerful conversation floating down the hallways. It sounded like disembodied voices looking for people to stalk. Okay, that was a bit weird, even for me and the strange thoughts constantly floating through my head.

I heard another knock on my door and got up to answer it. On the other side of the door stood Rennan. Unlike Cam, Rennan had taken the time to change into the fresh clothes provided for him in his room. He looked at ease in them, but I could never see myself wearing anything so nice. Now I understood why Cam hadn't changed either.

"Hey, you didn't come down with us," Rennan commented with a worried tone to his voice. His face expressed the same concern, but I couldn't make myself sorry for causing him anxiety; I wasn't bothered by staying in my room all night. "Are you feeling okay?"

"I'm fine, just tired from our journey and what not," I answered with a small smile. I couldn't muster anything more.

Rennan didn't seem to believe me, but he dropped the subject. I was glad because I really didn't want to explain that a large part of the reason I didn't go was because I didn't want to be stuck with Valerie longer than I had to. It was all too obvious that Rennan liked the princess and as much as I didn't like her, I didn't want to ruin it for him…much.

"Okay, well, I guess I'll see you tomorrow. Night, Scarlet," Rennan sighed as he walked back down the hall and into his room.

I was about to close my door when I saw Cam and Carter coming down the hall. I quickly closed the door just enough so I could still see them but they couldn't see me. I wanted to see how they interacted without me around. Honestly, it was sort of how I expected it, but also not. Carter didn't really seem to care about anything, that is, until he muttered something that made his brother mad. As for Cam, he ignored Carter until aggravated.

"I don't recall you ever saying you would help me get out of exile.

You never said a word to defend me while I lived in Trehi," Cam hissed in a low voice. His eyes were narrowed and the shadows were creeping back into his features, making him look much deadlier than normal.

Carter just rolled his eyes and stopped walking.

Cam stopped right in front of him and glared daggers at his younger brother. "What are you doing here, Carter? Be honest."

"It's hard to be honest with you, Cameron, since you already know everything," Carter muttered as he glared at his brother. Both of them looked ready to strike at any moment. "And since you know everything, wouldn't you know why I'm here?"

"I *don't* know everything, Carter. That's why I asked you a question. What are you doing here?"

"Since you're obviously too dumb to figure it out, I'm simply not going to tell you," Carter remarked aggressively as he started walking past Cam again.

The elder grabbed the younger's wrist and they found themselves in a stare off. Then Carter yanked his wrist out of Cam's grasp, stalked off to his room, and slammed his door shut. After watching their exchange, I didn't think it was wise to have put the twins in rooms right next to each other.

Cam muttered something inaudibly before vanishing into his own quarters for the night.

I heard a *click* noise signaling the door being locked from the inside. Cam had probably locked it to keep his pest of a brother out of his space for as long as possible. I could understand the feeling since it was what I had wanted to do to Valerie several times. The only difference was that I wanted to lock it from the outside and trap her so she could never escape without help.

I really don't like Valerie.

As soon as the coast was clear on both sides of the hall, I swiftly opened my own door and dashed across. For a second, I considered turning back since I was acting solely upon sudden whim. I didn't really know what I was doing and I had no idea what it would accomplish if Cam opened the door. In a rush of adrenaline, I knocked. He opened it seconds later.

"What are you doing here?" Cam whispered quickly.

He looked down the hall in both directions before he pulled me into his room. It was dimmer than the hall had been so it took me a minute to adjust to the lighting. When I did, however, I was shocked at the design and décor of the elf's room.

It was large and not at all what I had expected. I would have thought that it would be grand like bedrooms in palaces, but it was really quite the opposite. It was homey, sort of like thatch-roofed cottages in small towns. There was a fair-sized hearth on the far side of the room with a couple of high-backed arm chairs near it. Candles lit different walls and glowed red. There was also a large four poster bed with side tables bearing lit candles.

Cam must have noticed my surprise and awe because he shuffled uncomfortably out of the light of the doorway. He quickly closed the heavy door and locked it again so no one would be able to get in without his consent. He tucked the key into his right pocket before walking up beside me.

"Not what you were expecting is it?" he said with a small laugh.

I shook my head and he smiled slightly.

Cam stuck his hands in his pockets and strode across the room to plop down in one of the arm chairs. He nodded towards the other one and I sat down. He looked sort of awkward, probably since we were sitting only a few feet away from each other with no one else in the room.

"Not that I'm trying to get rid of you or anything…but why are you here?" he asked a few minutes later.

"Well…don't hate me, but I overheard your short conversation with Carter a few minutes ago," I began hesitantly.

Cam sighed as he stared into the fire while the flames danced in an ever-changing waltz. They captivated the elf for several seconds before he shook his head and looked me dead in the eye.

"I don't hate you, Scarlet. I never truly could. I may get irritated, but it's never hate," Cam answered solemnly with a firm tone to his deep voice. He meant what he said. "But yeah, *that.* I already guessed you overheard it."

I looked at him in confusion. He hadn't seen me in the hall and there was no other possible way that he would have known about it. Carter hadn't seen me and even if he had, I doubted that he cared enough to tell his brother. "How did you know?"

Cam shrugged. "You're aware of most out of the ordinary happenings. Besides, I saw that your door was slightly open. But doesn't it seem to support our suspicion that it's strange he randomly showed up here at the same time as us?"

"Yes, and it doesn't make any sort of logical sense," I replied as I rubbed the bridge of my nose.

I could usually figure out why something was happening just by seeing signs around me. However, this time, it was so much more difficult. I felt like the answer was right in front of me, but my mind couldn't grasp what the answer was.

"It doesn't necessarily have to be logical. Very rarely are things ever completely 'logical,'" Cam pointed out as he sent a quick glace to me before turning his attention back to the fire that continued to burn in the hearth. In the brief second he looked at me, I could have sworn he was grinning with amusement.

"That...hurts my brain," I chuckled quietly.

Cam set his eyes on me again and smiled slightly. It was a kind of half-smile, really. Only the right side of his mouth curved upwards. But I still knew it was a smile because of the playful glimmer in his eyes. I didn't know whether to take his comment about being logical seriously or not.

Cam opened his mouth to say something else, but just then we heard strange thumping noises on the other side of the wall. Now, it wouldn't have been strange if it were on the right side of the room; I would have just assumed it was some other person who lived in the palace. But it wasn't. It was the wall that divided the twins' rooms from each other.

Cam's head whipped around to the wall in question.

The only thing there was several large bookshelves stuffed to the brim with books. For a brief second, my mind flashed back to when I had explored the library the day my parents died. I was quick to suppress the memory again. The last thing I wanted was to be thinking about childhood horrors. We had more pressing matters to attend to.

"Did you hear that?" Cam whispered as he slowly rose from his armchair.

He was looking in the direction of the wall where the noise had originated. He glanced at me and I nodded my head. I didn't like the sound of it, either. The elf crept towards his bed and started throwing the pillows under the blankets and sheets. He also set his weapons out in a strange arrangement on the floor before he returned to my side.

"What are you doing? Why did you randomly place your weapons everywhere and put pillows under your blankets?" I asked in a hushed tone. I couldn't seem to wrap my brain around the situation. I mean really, did putting pillows underneath the blankets make any sense?

Cam cocked his head and narrowed his eyes at me, but said nothing for the moment. Instead, he grabbed my wrist and dragged me over to an area where I could barely be seen from anywhere in the room. There was a table and chairs that blocked me from sight.

"Just stay here and don't move or say anything until I direct you otherwise," Cam instructed with a firm tone and a raised eyebrow. He said it in a way that made it seem like he knew I didn't like listening to direct orders and would do just about anything to defy them.

However, I was surprised to find myself complying with his instructions. I just nodded and watched as Cam hid in one of the darker shadows of the room, his black outfit helping him blend in.

Soon, we heard more thumping coming from the wall. It was followed a few minutes later by a long creaking noise that echoed throughout the large room. I wanted to cover my ears at that point, but I remembered that I wasn't supposed to move so I just tried to ignore the horrible, agonizing sound. In the end, I ended up grinding my teeth together because I couldn't take it anymore. I'm pretty sure I wore down the points of my fangs.

I was shocked to see the walls beside the bookshelves slide open to reveal a secret door. It led straight to Carter's room and vice versa. I couldn't help but look over to the corner where Cam was hiding, but I didn't see him anywhere. It was like he had totally disappeared from the room and left no trace of where he had gone. If he had left the room through the main door, I hadn't heard it open and close—much less be unlocked!

All I could do was keep watching the strange door to see what would happen. Admittedly, I was relatively disturbed to be in the same room as someone who could quite possibly be looking to kill others. It was weird, considering that's what I did for a living.

A cloaked figure stumbled into the room with something long and shiny as the hidden door closed behind his. I couldn't make out his features, but I knew it was a male just from how wide the shoulders were. However, they weren't overly wide so the figure was either young or just didn't have that strong of a frame. I figured the latter would be more likely if it was any citizen or noble in Kevay who had just found their way into my friend's room.

The figure clumsily stumbled over something as he walked into the room. He bent over and picked up a small, flat, metal object and held it up to the light. I immediately recognized it as one of the throwing stars Cam kept tucked into his belt's pouch for emergencies. The figure must have thought nothing of it since he just dropped it and it clattered on the ground. That was a bad idea since I had a feeling Cam had left the weapon there as a warning.

I watched curiously as the figure slowly made his way over to the four-poster bed. He approached and raised whatever object he held in his hand. That's when I recognized it as a dagger. He raised it above his head and let it slice through the air until it plunged into the bed.

Then I understood what Cam had done. He had taken a precaution so that anyone who came into the room would think he was fast asleep in bed. It certainly looked like a body now….

The figure must have realized it too since he suddenly became very edgy and started looking for a way to open up the secret passageway again. When he could find no other way to open it, he started to slowly back up towards the wall. That's when Cam's tall form manifested itself behind the figure, which jumped and shouted something in a different language.

"Going somewhere?" Cam asked with a dark looking expression as he drew one of his many hidden daggers. This one came from underneath one of the armguards he wore on his wrists.

The figure said nothing, but started slinking towards the main door. Cam made no movement save for tilting his head to one side as he watched his uninvited guest try to find a way out. The elf started stroking the tip of his especially sharp dagger.

Cam laughed bitterly. "Aw, don't go. Our fun is just starting!"

Cam stalked towards the figure, who backed himself into the door. There was no way to move away from the point of Cam's dagger. Cam's eyes looked downright wicked as he crouched down in an attempt to look the strange figure in the eye. The elf shook his head, but I didn't think it was in amusement this time. It looked to be one of disappointment or even concern. To my surprise, Cam started talking to the figure he had pinned to the door.

"You know, I had hopes for you. Hopes that one day you would see the light and not be so self-absorbed as to do something like this," Cam sighed. Then his face turned as cold as the glaciers that constantly surrounded the Mount of Death in northern Palee. "Instead, you turned out to be exactly what I always knew you'd become. You care nothing for others—only for yourself and moving up the ranks in Heviah. You aren't here to be peaceful, are you? You came here to murder me and take my throne, didn't you? Carter?"

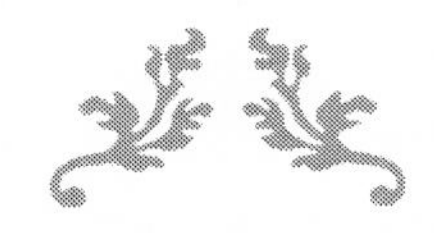

The Spiral of Doom

With that final question, Cam pulled down the figure's hood to reveal none other than Carter Woods.

I fought the urge to gasp when I saw the twisted face of that terrible elf. There was no possible way I would have thought he had the guts to kill his own brother. I had always known the elves were a corrupt race, but I never thought one of their highest-ranking members would stoop so low. Honesty, I should have expected it. Yet there we were, me hiding in the shadows while the two brothers were in a stare down that seemed to send years of memory and anguish swirling around them.

"Of course, I'm not here to be peaceful," Carter spat as he attempted to bat away Cam's dagger (which only accomplished a slit in his palm). His face twisted into a scowl when he glared at the dagger hovering mere inches from his face.

I had a feeling he intended to appear frightening, but that didn't come across very well. He only looked pitiful. Besides, I could think of nothing more terrifying than the murderous look in Cam's steel eyes.

Carter glared at Cam. "Surely you aren't stupid enough to think that the next in line would just sit back and let the crown slip away from him."

Cam laughed darkly as the shadows flowed across his face like a raging river flooding an open valley. "And surely *you* wouldn't be stupid enough to come in here thinking I don't have a plan to deal with intruders."

Carter looked confused. "I don't see any precautions. All your weapons are scattered across the floor waiting for anybody to pick them up. I wouldn't call that a plan."

The elder twin smiled evilly. "In this room, my only limit is my imagination. Unfortunately for you, it is incredibly wide. Father did me a favor by exiling me—all those years alone gave me the chance to expand it into ranges people could never conceive. I've seen things that people think are myths, you know. I assure you, everything is quite real, just like anything that I put my mind to in here."

"That still doesn't explain your precautions."

"Doesn't it?" Cam inquired.

He raised his hand as if to strike—Carter even braced for it—but the stroke never came. Instead, Cam merely snapped his fingers.

Carter, who had his eyes closed, opened them slowly to see…nothing. Nothing had happened in that brief instant. I couldn't see Cam's face either because the shadows had grown too thick around him.

"Nothing happened. You're bluffing," Carter stated in a tone obviously intended to be offensive. He stood up and pushed his brother back a few steps before proceeding to brush off his cloak, suspiciously eyeing Cam a few times.

Cam, however, just stood there watching his brother skeptically. His head was cocked and his fierce eyes were burning with intense revulsion. Still, he did not retaliate. To my surprise, he started laughing a cold, hollow laugh that echoed about the large space. It was the most alarming sound I had heard in a long while.

"Nothing? Of course not. I was giving you a final chance to explain yourself before I decide to do things the hard way."

"You hold *no* power."

"Ah, and that is where you are wrong. I hold a vast wealth of power—I just choose not to use it. That's not how I work and you know that, Carter. You have to give me a really good reason to use my power and sadly, you just gave it to me," Cam replied as he shook his head.

Fear entered Carter's eyes as the shadows around them thickened. Soon I could only see their vague outlines. Then I heard a clang and a cry. I assumed it came from the coward. The shadows cleared to reveal a caged Carter and an emotionless Cam, who turned to face my direction. All ill-will had vanished from his eyes and was replaced with a gentler light.

Cam looked me straight in the eye. "You can come out now, Scarlet."

"She was in here, too?!" cried a very confused Carter.

Cam rolled his eyes and urged me to come closer. I nodded in agreement, but I didn't take another step until I had drawn one of my own daggers. I knew Cam had his, but I didn't trust the deceitful elf as far as I could see him. It didn't matter if he was in a cage or not—there was no harm in being cautious.

"Yes, I was in here, too," I stated through gritted teeth. "And I saw what you were trying to do. It was pathetic."

This pusillanimous man frustrated me beyond what I could comprehend. He cared nothing for others, and while I was guilty of the same fault from time to time, I still found compassion for those close to me. Carter received no compassion. He had no honor. I had seen him attempt to murder his own brother.

If I were anyone else, I might have considered giving the lily-livered elf lessons on how to hide oneself in the shadows and then strike their target or proper fundamentals of the art of killing. However, I was far too disgusted to ever consider the possibility. There was no way I would ever teach this snotty prince how to do anything. I would far rather let him fail.

"Just tell us why you're really here and why you tried to kill me,

Carter, and I'll consider releasing you with little injury," Cam stated nonchalantly as he inspected the sharpness of his still-drawn dagger.

The elder twin seemed calm, but something about the way he spoke betrayed his outward appearance. Cam always reminded me of a fierce river being held back by the smallest possible dam—one wrong move and it would blow.

"Why would I ever tell you? It's not like you care," Carter pouted within his steel cage.

I sent him an icy glare and he recoiled into his wretched self even more. To my pleasure, Carter scooted back away from us. He dared not move nor make eye contact with anyone. His eyes were firmly fixed upon the stone flooring and it was obvious that he was thinking of something, but I didn't even want to guess what it pertained to. Apparently, Cam's imagination hadn't thought to have designed smoother floors for his quarters.

"I wish you wouldn't be so difficult," Cam muttered as he fully faced his pitiful brother again.

Almost as suddenly as it had materialized, the cage disappeared. It left behind a cloud I found suspiciously similar to shadows. Carter looked shocked that it was gone as he stood up. Cam crossed his arms in front of his chest and glared at his younger brother relentlessly.

"You're letting me go?" Carter asked, not quite daring to hope.

"No, of course I'm not letting you go. I haven't received the answers I want and you obviously don't want to do things the easy way," Cam stated with a sickeningly light tone of voice. The dark gleam in his eyes told me that whatever was going through his mind directly contradicted his tone.

"You? Do things the hard way? Please, you're too—oof!" Carter cried out as Cam unexpectedly slammed his twin against the wall, which had unexpectedly become raw, rough rock.

Had it been the same material before and I just hadn't noticed it? Or had Cam just changed it to something that could seriously inflict damage on someone?

"'Too soft?' Is that what you were going to say?" Cam suggested with a grim smile as he released his brother. He took a step back and watched as Carter slid down to the floor to try to regain his breath. "Get up."

In the darkness, I noticed Cam fighting to control the wild light in his eyes.

"Why?" Carter rasped.

"*Get up.*"

Carter got up, but he had help. Well, I think the more accurate statement is to say that he was dragged to his feet by Cam. Cam grabbed the collar of Carter's teal jerkin and yanked him up off the floor. As he did so, I noticed the room starting to change again.

Wind swirled around us, enveloping us in a gust so powerful that it nearly cost me my balance. I had to inch my way towards a solid wall to prevent myself from falling. I watched this new scene unfold while a hole started appearing in the floor. It glowed red, like there was some sort of inferno blazing far within the deepening pit. I was too stunned to do anything when I saw Cam grab Carter. He dragged him toward the edge of the red-lighted crater.

"Cam, what are you doing?" I cried out over the howling wind.

Any sort of loose object was caught up in the squall circling around the large room. Books even flew off their shelves and became dangerous projectiles that could potentially gouge somebody's eye out. I steered clear of the shelves for fear I would become the victim of one of those heavy books.

Cam didn't answer me. Instead, he continued to pull his brother toward the edge of the glowing abyss. He held his grip, but Carter constantly struggled against it. As much as I hated Carter, I didn't think it was right to send him to a fiery death.

"Cameron, don't do this!" Carter pleaded as he continued to resist his brother's iron grip. "Please, Cam. Why are you doing this?"

For the first time since I had met him, Carter looked genuine. Genuinely frightened, that is.

Cam's face was dour as he looked down at his identical twin. Only a light of pure hatred could be seen blazing in his eyes. It wasn't the same Cam I knew—not in the slightest. This was a far darker, more twisted version of him. He was utterly unforgiving.

"You thought I was too soft. If I were, would I be doing this?" Cameron asked. His voice was quite hollow, like all of the true Cam had been sucked right out of him. All that was left was a shell containing only malice and hatred. "You doubted my power, so I will show it to you. Gaze upon the Spiral of Doom! One false move in any direction and I'll drop you."

"Please, Cam! Don't do this!" I shouted again.

This time, the elf seemed to hear me. He jerked around in an inhuman fashion and caught me with his callous gaze. I recoiled slightly when I locked eyes with him. Cam said nothing, but his glare spoke volumes—he didn't want me involved.

He was warning me to stay away from him.

Despite that, I slowly crept closer as the two brothers went back to bickering and yelling at each other. I had to be able to do something, even if it was minimal.

The defenseless Carter begged the merciless Cameron to let him go, but the elder brother would do no such thing. He seemed to be set on one thing and one thing only: make Carter suffer revenge for the injustice inflected upon him. Their shouting rose above the wind again.

"You still didn't tell me why you're doing this!" Carter yelled.

I had obviously missed some parts of the conversation if I just heard that. That also meant I didn't know if Cam had said anything that might prove to be important in the future.

"I'm doing this because you deserve it! You are a spoiled, selfish pig that should never have come in here. Just give me answers!" Cam shrieked as he dropped his brother to the ground. Cam stumbled back a step.

Carter panicked and cowered in the shadows that began to swell around us. For a moment, he looked like he wasn't going to answer. However, his mindset quickly changed when Cam's knife-hand twitched.

"Fine! Father sent me to kill you if you were still alive. Under no circumstance was I to return to Trehi without a token proving your death!" Carter admitted quickly as Cam raised one of his daggers.

Cam's eyes blazed with hate, but they changed in the slightest way—one I couldn't identify—when his brother spoke.

"What token specifically and what would happen if you returned without it?" Cameron demanded savagely. I doubted Carter was able to tell, but in that inquiry, some of Cam's defenses were lowered and his eyes became less…fiery. They were still anything but soft, however.

"Your head, preferably. He also wanted your signet ring that you stole when you were exiled," Carter answered quietly. He rubbed the back of his hand nervously as he thought about his second answer.

For his sake, I hoped that it was a good one. I doubted Cam would be merciful to his idiot brother. If I were in his place, I doubted I would show mercy to somebody like Carter. I would get it done and over with as quickly as possible.

"But if you returned without it, what would happen?"

Carter swallowed his courage. He continued in a quiet, raspy voice. "I would be dead on the spot. They fear you, Cam. They don't want to see you alive in Heviah ever again."

"Why didn't you tell me this earlier?" Cam questioned as he slowly lowered both his daggers. His features softened.

Unfortunately, they softened a little bit too soon. As soon as he saw his chance, Carter landed a punch to Cam's nose. Blood streaked down the elf's pale face and the wild look returned to his eyes.

"Coward!" Cam bellowed as he tackled his brother again.

Carter was forced close to the edge of the Spiral of Doom, as Cam had called it. Smoke hissed out from the top of the crater and the flames within it crackled. They seemed to promise a slow, excruciatingly painful death to anyone who fell into it.

That was when I recovered my wits. After cautiously scrambling around the pit, I forcefully pulled Cam off of Carter and shoved him backwards. I had to make sure that he was far enough away so that he wouldn't retaliate against me as well as get closer to his younger brother. I didn't feel like dealing with this new side of Cam. It was pure madness.

Cam was stunned when I knocked him backwards—so much so that he stayed there. I turned my attention to Carter, whose fear flickered across his features. I grinned an all-too-pleased smile as I punched him in the face, knocking him out cold.

Once I was sure it was lights out for Carter, I turned back to Cam. I glared at him in a way communicating that I wanted the room restored to how it was when I came in. He did so willingly. Soon, the room looked normal. The wooden floors shone with polish and the pale grey walls gave them contrast even in the dim candlelight. Everything the wind had knocked down was put back in the shelves and no cloth looked windblown.

All the while, Cam didn't bother to look at me. He did, however, grab his brother and drag him back to his own room. When he returned, he locked the main door and stalked over to the secret entrance. The doorway that led to Carter's room was promptly blocked with a bookshelf. When he was done, Cam sat back down in his armchair and gazed into the fire as if nothing life changing had occurred in the last half hour.

"What just happened?" I asked bluntly. I would not sit idly while my mind demanded answers.

Cam glanced at me nervously, obviously thinking that I wouldn't be watching him. I was, and as soon as he noticed, he looked back towards the fire.

"I…I don't know anymore," Cam sighed as he buried his face in his hands.

I felt sympathy for him; he had to be an absolute wreck. After all, he just learned that his father had sent his brother to murder him. That wouldn't be an easy thing for anyone to grasp, no matter how much they had endured over time.

"That's not really an answer," I stated shortly, much colder than I had meant to come across. I wanted to try to be somewhat comforting, but it wasn't in my nature.

Cam looked up at me with a blank expression. However, I could tell that his mind was anything but blank. In his eyes I could see thoughts racing around, almost sending him off course into a spiral of despair. He looked like his expression, and his sanity, would crack at any moment.

"I know it's not an answer. I just don't know what to say except I'm so sorry you saw that," Cam answered quietly. His accented voice hitched several times—he suffered emotionally far more than he let on. "I never meant for you to see any of it."

"Evidently, you don't mean for me to see a lot of things," I commented.

He looked at me in slight confusion. He wanted me to continue my thought and explain.

"You told me the same thing after your rant earlier," I clarified. "So, tell me, is there anything else about your past that you want to say now?"

Cam paled tremendously, but nodded his head. I knew he would explain some things, but he wouldn't tell me all of it. There was always something more when it came to this elf. Still, I knew it would only be a matter of time before he gave in and told me more. I gave him a chance to collect his thoughts.

"Like you already know, I was banished five years ago by my own father…very kind of him. It couldn't have been more unfortunate timing. Since elves are immortal, a problem arises when it comes to the monarchy. If we don't die, how will the crown change bearers? It wouldn't without a special law demanding kings to reign for a total of five hundred years if they aren't killed or step down first," Cam stated, barely making eye contact.

I cocked my head, not understanding why it was a problem. It sounded like a solid system. "But how could that be unfortunate timing if elves reign for a really, really long time?"

Cam laughed bitterly, as if the world was coming to an end and he knew how it would happen. "That's the thing. Five years ago was my father's four hundred and ninety-fifth year of reign. And before you ask, Carter and I are young because most elves don't generally marry until they're around three hundred; my father waited much longer than that because he wanted to be the sole monarch for all of his long reign. Part of me doubts that even Carter has married at this point. Our father wouldn't want to risk his sons or possible grandsons taking his throne.

"Yeah, that so didn't happen with my parents, though. He met my mother at a meeting with the different rulers of large elven cities. She's the daughter of Ladefindel, one of my father's top generals. They saw each other and immediately fell in love," Cam explained. "She stayed in Trehi after that, leaving her high-ranking family in Lyka. You can guess what happened from there. Anyway, I'm supposed to ascend to the throne this year on my birthday in November, which means we have about eleven months to get to Heviah and complete our task."

"I'm still confused. Why is all this a problem?"

Cam looked at me and sighed, seemingly expecting me to know

exactly what was going on, but forgetting that I knew nothing of current laws and politics. "My father has grown so corrupt since Carter and I were born. He wants his reign to go on forever. Everyone in Heviah, like Carter said, fears me. They've always known that I was different. They kept me at arm's length because they were afraid I might turn on them."

"Would you?"

"Would I what?"

"Would you have turned on them?" I asked curiously.

I decided I wasn't angry anymore. That feeling had been replaced with a sense of curiosity and intrigue.

Cam smiled wryly as he considered his answer to my question. He chuckled and met my eyes, then shook his head saying that he wouldn't.

"*I* wouldn't have turned on them. Nay, *they* turned on me. I've told you how it got to be that way, but I didn't tell you how I left," Cam stated as his face turned back towards the blazing fire. He smiled at some memory that I doubted he would tell me. "I left the capital after darkness had fallen on the night I was sentenced. I couldn't risk anybody seeing me. When an elf is exiled, it's the same as a death sentence. If I had been seen, I'd be dead right now.

"I literally only had an hour to gather sufficient belongings for my long journey. I grabbed only the weapons I carry with me now and a few other things—one of which was my signet ring. Without it, I wouldn't be able to reclaim the throne if I ever have the chance," Cam finished. He sat back in his chair and stared at me, long and hard.

"That explains a lot of Carter's motives," I said after a few minutes of awkward silence.

Cam scowled, but nodded in agreement. He had no sympathy for his brother.

"Yeah, and he deserved everything I threw at him just now," Cam remarked with a sour expression on his face. His eyes grew dark again and shadows slithered onto his face like a snake pulling itself over a rock in order to catch its prey. "I regret nothing."

"Do you realize that every time you do that, shadows crawl over your face?" I blurted before I could stop myself.

I clapped my hand over my mouth before my traitorous tongue could utter anything else that I might regret.

Cam, who was noticeably taken aback, swerved his head toward me and once again. I didn't dare open my mouth.

"I know," Cam sighed as the warmth reappeared in his features. A sad light filled his eyes as he seemed to reassess everything. "I'm so sorry, Scarlet. I can't control those shadows all the time."

"What are they?" I asked quietly.

A somber feeling had settled over both of us. Neither one of us wanted to converse for unspoken reasons. Cam stood up and walked to the floor-to-ceiling window. He looked out upon the city. Only a few lanterns were lit at this time of night. His face looked both reflective of the recent events and worried for what the future might hold.

Cam's voice was unsteady when he answered me next. "Sometimes I can't hide the demons that I face. I can try to control them, but they always seem to find a way to make themselves known, much to the fear of others. I didn't realize they started physically manifesting themselves."

He sat back in his chair, an empty look in his eyes. "I am the architect of my own destruction."

I was about to offer him reassurance, but I never got the chance. A knock made Cam reluctantly trudge over to answer the door. Any confidence in his step was gone and replaced with pain and misery. Cam pulled the key out of one of his pockets, placed it in the lock, and turned it. He opened the door and who did we see? None other than Carter himself.

"Can I, uh, come in?" Carter asked uneasily. He glanced at me (I had my daggers out again and was on the defensive) and then back to Cam.

Cam, to my surprise, let his brother in. They kept a far distance from each other, however, so I knew Carter remembered some of what happened minutes earlier. Even if he didn't have the entire memory, he would have figured out some since his cheekbone was starting to bruise.

"So…about what happened…," Carter began awkwardly.

"It seems we're all in the same boat," Cam said grimly from the shadows of the room.

I don't think he trusted himself anywhere but there. Though, the shadows didn't come from him, so I guess that was good. He wasn't slipping into his darker power. In fact, I think he was actually exhausted from all of the craziness.

"What do you mean?" Carter and I asked in unison.

I glared daggers at him and he immediately turned his pining eyes away from me. I hated that he was paying so much attention to me when I made it quite obvious that I was not interested in him whatsoever.

"Think about it. Scarlet and Rennan can't go back to Palee because of the confinement laws that the elves were too eager to sign. You can't go back, Carter, without a token, and there is *no* way you're going to kill me,"

Cam explained slowly, his exhaustion obviously catching up to him. His words were becoming more slurred than they had been. "And I can't go back because I'd be dead as soon as they see me."

"So, what do we do then?" Carter asked.

All malice he had displayed earlier was gone and replaced with remorse. I guess he had some sort of heart—no matter how strange or twisted it might be—after all. Well, that or he was so self-absorbed that he was doing this to save his own skin.

"First of all, Carter has to swear that he won't try to kill me again," Cam stated firmly. He slunk a short way out of the shadows he had been lurking in. "*I* will swear that if you inflict any injury on me or my friends, I will repay it two-fold."

"Deal," Carter agreed instantly.

"Good. You will join us in overthrowing our father so I can retake the throne. You will be loyal to us and not leak any information about our true intent," continued Cam as he began to pace the length of the room.

Since I didn't have to take any oaths, I assumed Cam considered me loyal.

"Agreed," Carter nodded. He looked at the floor and bit his lip. "Cameron, can I talk to you in private for a few minutes?"

"Yes," Cam agreed. He looked toward me. "You're free to leave, Scarlet. I see the look of worry in your eyes. I'll be fine. Get some rest and come to breakfast with us tomorrow morning."

"I'll be there," I promised as I slowly departed from the room.

I didn't want to leave, but I had to trust that Cam would be able to handle his brother on his own. There was a part of me that feared they would start arguing again and come to blows that would be more dangerous than the first time, but I couldn't help that.

There was nothing else I could do to help him tonight, so I opted to get ready for bed and attempt to get some decent sleep for the first time in a while.

I awoke early the next morning. Pink light streamed in through the cracks in the barely open curtains. Though it was early, I did not feel weary despite the Spiral of Doom incident.

I reluctantly got up from my soft bed and stretched. I had gotten better sleep in a foreign bed than I ever had in my life. Was it affected by some sort of magic, too, or had I just been overly exhausted last night? I was just grateful I had been able to get some sort of rest. The stay in the palace would be one of the precious few times I would be able to sleep in a real bed.

In walking over to the window to look outside, I realized I was still in the clothes I had been wearing for the last few days. I knew there was clothing provided for me, but I didn't feel like putting them on. Still, there was a part of my mind that knew it would be rude to my hostess if I didn't use what was supplied.

I found garments dyed in my clan's colors in the drawer. There was nothing to represent Kevay such as the pinks, purples, dark blues, and greens that appeared to be their national colors. Instead, they were the colors unique to the Sutton family.

I admit it was touching to see that the merfolk had thought to use those colors for me. I unfolded it and was able to find a long, red tunic with grey leggings that fit perfectly underneath the tall boots I always wore.

Right after I was finished dressing, I heard somebody rapidly knock on my door. I turned on my heel and quickly walked towards the door. Since it wasn't locked like Cam's door, I just had to open it to see who wanted to bother me this time.

"Good morning!" Rennan said cheerfully.

Right after he spoke, Valerie did some sort of dance that seemed to involve running right behind Rennan. She threw flowers at him as she, too called, "Good morning, wonderful people!"

Once I had gotten past the initial surprise of seeing both Rennan and Valerie outside my door at such an early hour, I mustered up the strength to smile. Rennan looked especially nice this morning. Apparently, the colors of his clan were not the grey I had expected. Instead, they were pale blues that went quite well with his skin and blue eyes. Or maybe he just liked those colors. My point is that he looked nice.

Rennan was grinning widely when he saw that I was in a relatively good mood. I wasn't typically a morning person after long hikes.

"Uh, good morning?" I responded with slight hesitation.

It wasn't a habit to use that specific expression. It seemed foreign as it rolled off my tongue. Valerie stopped dancing and came up beside Rennan and he started grinning like a fool all over again. The thoughts going through his mind were way too obvious.

"Do you know if the twins are up yet? I was thinking we could do an early breakfast before I give you newcomers a tour of the city!" Valerie asked excitedly.

I struggled to keep the smile on my face. It was going to be a long day if she was going to be this chipper the entire time.

A door shut on the other side of the hallway. Thankfully, it took all the attention away from me, much to my relief. I didn't like being in the spotlight if I could help it. I glanced toward the door that had closed to see Carter. He looked about as worn out as my mind felt. The circles beneath his eyes weren't nearly as dark as I'd seen Cam's, but I could tell that he hadn't slept much. In addition, the bruises I gave him were barely visible, so no one could learn anything about our crazy night.

"I'm up, and I'm sure my brother is, too. He probably would want us to go on without him," Carter answered. His voice sounded confident while speaking, but I could see his fingers shaking as he strode over to us.

Valerie shrugged. "Okay! Then I guess we're going to head to the dining hall! Come on, Carter!"

With that, she pulled on Carter's wrist and ran down the hallway with him in tow. I shook my head. Thank goodness she hadn't decided to grab me. She still hadn't earned my trust and after what happened last night, I was reluctant to give it to anyone new. Though, there was a part of me glad to see that Carter's suffering, no matter how minimal, would continue for a while longer.

"So, what was going on with you last night? You seemed cold and sorta distant," Rennan asked.

I looked up at him in surprise, but he didn't look at me. He kept his head facing forward the entire time.

"I just didn't feel very sociable last night," I answered vaguely.

I didn't feel like giving him the details of what had happened. Cam hadn't explicitly stated that he didn't want it shared, but I had a feeling that it was better to err on the side of caution. I kept my mouth firmly clamped shut so I wouldn't make a mistake and blurt out what I was thinking again. If I did that, I would have to explain everything to Rennan, and who knew how he would take it?

"Mhmm. I see. And Cam? What was he doing? Don't pretend like you don't know what was going on. I'm not that dumb. I know you were in there. Same with Carter."

"How did you know?"

"You want me to list everything?"

"Why not?"

"Okay, here goes: first, I saw you go into Cam's room after we got back from dinner. Second, I heard yelling and banging. Third, I heard and watched Cam drag a seemingly unconscious Carter back to his room. Fourth, I heard Carter go back into Cam's room a while later. Fifth, I heard Cam banging around in his room early this morning. Accurate?"

"Very," I sighed. Rennan was too smart for his own good. I figured there was no way to hide anything that had happened last night, so I mentally agreed to answer any questions that were asked. "Your wolf ears serve you well."

"I guess. Why didn't you come get me? I could have helped," Rennan asked as he scratched the back of his ear quite suddenly. Wolf hybrids had strange habits, just saying. In all seriousness, however, Rennan's face was grim and I could tell that he had been hurt. His expression caused a wave of guilt to spread through me.

"I thought you had gone to bed already and I didn't want to wake you up," I answered quietly. I could feel his icy stare on the side of my neck. I wanted to shudder, but didn't want to show what I was feeling. "I'm sorry, Rennan. I won't do it again."

"Good. Remember that for future events like this. I want to be one of the first to know about things when they're happening so I can help," Rennan stated sternly.

I nodded my head in agreement and tried to swallow the lump that had grown in my throat.

His voice became soft. "Now that the hard, awkward part is over, is Cam okay?"

"I think so. Why?"

"Well, he sounded ticked off this morning when I first heard him. How was he last night?"

"To be perfectly honest, terrifying."

"How so?"

I hesitated before answering. I wasn't quite sure what to say. "Sooo…you know how shadows seem to surround him when he's mad or upset?"

Rennan gazed down at me with a puzzled look. "Yes, I remember those specific shadows quite well. But what do they have to do with Cam's current condition? Other than that perfectly horrid scar I gave him during my own slip into madness."

"Well, it appears that we are looking directly at his raw power when those shadows creep into his features," I began. "The rooms we're staying in are magic and Cam knows how to manipulate it. Basically, what happened was that Carter tried to murder Cam last night—"

"He did?!"

"Yes! Now let me finish! Carter failed, obviously, but that was after Cam went sort of wild. Cam created what he called the 'Spiral of Doom' and he was going to throw Carter down it if he didn't get answers. He seriously went insane. It was absolutely terrifying to see someone who's generally so level-headed do something so...*vicious* to a blood relative. I didn't think he would ever do something like that," I shuddered.

Rennan seemed to share the discomfort I felt. Neither one of us spoke for the next few minutes, though we did keep the princess and younger prince in sight.

"Wow. I never would have suspected that," Rennan commented a few minutes later.

He was still in shock. I nodded my head in agreement right before we heard footsteps running through the majestic halls. We whipped around to see Cam sprinting towards us, dressed all in black as usual. He looked pale (more so than usual) and breathless.

"Where are the other two?" Cam asked, panting for breath.

He had evidently run a far distant at a fast pace in order to be this winded. I wondered if he was just running late or running from danger. His immediate question didn't appear to indicate either.

"They're down the hall. Why? Is everything okay?" I asked just as quickly.

The elf didn't seem to be nervous, but there was definitely something on his mind. He started turning in circles, inspecting everything before he uttered another word. Just as well. He still needed to catch his breath.

Cam looked at Rennan, eyeing him somewhat suspiciously. "I assume you know? About what happened last night and this morning?"

"I know about last night, but not details of this morning," Rennan answered quietly. "I'm so sorry to hear about it."

His ear twitched twice in sympathy. He looked uneasy around the elf now. I couldn't exactly blame him. I'm sure I would have acted the same way if someone had told me that a close friend of mine had gone mad mere hours earlier.

Cam waved him off. However, he still seemed to be touchy about the subject. I was afraid that he was planning something rash, but then I remembered that Cam would always weigh out the risks beforehand. Still, it seemed too soon to be so nonchalant about those events.

He shrugged. "Don't be. He had it coming. However, I should have controlled myself better and for that I apologize to you, Scarlet, and to you, Rennan, for not coming to get you."

"To be honest, I'd quite rather you don't come for me during any incident with magic or knife fights. I'm no fighter, we all know that," Rennan said quietly and with a slight smile. "We three know about that scar I haphazardly gave you."

Cam seemed to instinctively reach up and touch the place on his left temple where the long, jagged scar was. It was still very red. Unfortunately, it was a deep cut that would scar his face for decades. Meanwhile, Rennan flinched and revealed his guilt for causing the elf's injury.

I think they both learned something from each other that day, though. Cam learned not to shoot wolves and Rennan learned not to tick off this particular elf.

"I know, but you *will* know about things in the future," Cam stated firmly. He cleared his throat to change the subject. "So, the reason I'm here is because I'm eating breakfast with you and then I'm going to be in meetings with the queen all day. Wish me luck to stay sane in there. Merfolk love to argue."

"You mean more than you and Carter?" I said jokingly.

Cam sent me a sidelong glare.

I recoiled. "Too soon?"

"No, perfect timing actually," Cam answered, smiling from ear to ear. I did not expect him to do that. "Nice attempt at humor, Scarlet. But yes, they argue more than my brother and I."

"So, what are we supposed to do while you're in meetings?" Rennan queried.

I was glad somebody was asking questions. My stupid brain couldn't seem to come up with any good ones that would be useful.

Cam shrugged. "I don't know, really. Follow Valerie on her tour of the city. You'll need some patience if you choose to go that route."

"We don't have a choice. But I thought you and the princess were close?"

"*Close*? Is that what you thought yesterday?"

"Yes? Was I wrong?"

"Yes, quite wrong, Rennan. I merely tolerate the princess."

"Why?"

"She's crazy! That's why."

"Nah, I think you are, Cam. Valerie is an angel."

"An angel who delivers craziness into the world."

Their friendly argument went on for a long while after that and all throughout breakfast. After that, Cam went off to his meetings with the merfolk and Rennan and I were forced to go with Valerie and Carter on a tour of the city. Valerie, as was to be expected, was overly cheerful when we were in the park and Carter was also ridiculous, just not in the same way.

In short, I was surrounded by craziness.

Aqua Excursion

I heard a knock on my door early in the morning.

At that point, it wasn't uncommon for that to happen in the early hours of the day. We had only been in Sala for a week, and I have already been awoken way too early for too many days in a row. Usually it was by Cam because he was giving me an update on his plans for the day. But his weren't the only wakeup calls I got every day. I also received a second call two hours later when Valerie and Rennan practically came banging down my door.

That was true of this morning. I groaned to myself and reluctantly rolled out of bed to answer the door. Well, after I finger-combed my hair to make it look relatively presentable. I unlocked the heavy door and pulled it open to see none other than the pale elf. He was already starting to get the dark circles under his eyes again, but somehow, he had a smile on his face.

"Hey, sorry to wake you," he whispered sheepishly. "I came to tell you my plans."

I shrugged as I let him in. I closed the door again and he went to sit in one of my armchairs.

"Okay, let me guess this time," I said before he got started. I continued when I saw the corners of his mouth twitch. "You have meetings, meetings, and more meetings? Oh, wait, and maybe some more meetings after that."

Cam snorted and smirked slightly. "I wish I could say that you're wrong, but as usual, you're dead on. No wonder you're a good mercenary."

"Ha," I said.

That was debatable because I've had my fair share of failed missions, but I guess he was right. I was usually accurate with my guesses and plans. I changed my train of thought because I wanted to go back to sleep for a while before Rennan and Valerie came to bombard me with excitement.

"So, do you have any other plans for today?" I asked, changing the subject slightly.

"Eh...I don't really know yet," Cam sighed. "I know I have at least three two-hour meetings today, but I don't have any plans otherwise. Coral says she wants me to try to enjoy myself for a little while, but I told her enjoying myself is hard to do when I'm breaking the laws of my exile. I always expect some of my father's soldiers to come find me here and kill me on the spot."

He had a valid point. I always had the worry in the back of my mind that someone would recognize me and turn me in for being a hybrid and a mercenary. I couldn't blame him for such thoughts when he had a really good reason to be afraid of the outcome. He was lucky Coral had shown him compassion; otherwise, none of us would have a good source of information or a decent shelter for the winter.

"Anyway, I'll probably be able to have meals with you all today. Like even breakfast," the elf continued with an absent-minded wave of his hand.

I raised my eyebrows in surprise. Cam hadn't come to eat breakfast with us since the first morning we were in Sala. Even then, I don't think he had eaten much—if he had eaten anything at all.

Still, it would be nice to see Cam for more than just a few minutes a day. All of Cam's time and patience was consumed by serving the merfolk as their mediator, so I agreed with Coral—he needed some time to unwind.

"Are you actually going to eat something this time or are you going to sit there awkwardly watching everyone else eat?" I questioned with a jovial smile.

“I’ll eat, but probably not a whole lot,” Cam smiled back. He looked out the window and sighed. He stood up and said, “Well, I should be off. I have a meeting to go to underwater.”

“Wait, you’re actually going underwater?” I asked quickly, now interested. I got up so I could follow him.

“Yes, and I’m not happy about it. I was really hoping that it would be on land, but Coral said that there was no way that she was going to be able to change it. So! I get to shapeshift to have gills,” Cam responded with mock-excitement. He ran a hand through his hair. “Gills are really itchy. My hair always aggravates it, too.”

“So why don’t you cut your hair?”

“Because I tried once and didn’t like it. Plus, it acts as a barrier when I don’t want people to recognize me on the street.”

“But you can shapeshift.”

“Yeah, but that doesn’t mean I want to shapeshift all the time. It’s too noticeable in public. And it means I have to constantly focus on what I’m doing.”

“If you say so,” I shrugged.

“I do say so,” he stated defiantly.

I rolled my eyes.

I liked Cam because he had sound logic and didn’t usually mess around like everyone else around me. However, it was times like this where I just wanted to smack him upside the head because he was so difficult. Still, I let his antics go this time because he was probably restraining himself from any level of sarcasm in all of the meetings he was forced to sit through. I didn't envy him—I would not want to trade places even if it meant that I was still stuck with Valerie.

"Okay, well, I'll see you in a couple of hours," I stated as Cam opened my door.

He nodded and then left without a word.

Deciding not to think too much about Cam's strange habits, I locked my door and climbed back into my bed to try to catch another couple hours of sleep. As I pulled the blankets over my head to block out the rays of the rising sun, I wondered what craziness there was in store for me ....

Who would have guessed that my door was beat upon not an hour later?

Oh wait, just about anyone who knew Rennan and Valerie would guess that. Seriously, did they have to be so determined to wake me up at unearthly hours when I was totally willing to waste time in this city? Why couldn't they channel that determination towards Carter? Sadly, it was almost always directed towards me.

"Scarlet! Are you awake yet?" Rennan called through the door.

"I am now," I muttered to myself.

I dragged myself out of bed so I could get dressed really fast. I highly doubted I would have the chance to get ready for the day after I opened the door. I pulled on my boots and stalked over to the door, unbolted it, and swung it open.

On the other side, Rennan stood by himself. I was shocked Valerie wasn't with him.

"Where's the mermaid?" I asked.

"She's downstairs already, and I think Carter is with her," Rennan explained with a shrug. Strange wolf. He was so happy whenever Valerie was in his company, but the second that she decided to focus on the twins, Rennan got super moody. He really *did* have it bad for the mermaid princess. "She sent me up here to get you so we can go get breakfast."

"Ah," I nodded my head.

Since I didn't say anything else (I didn't feel like starting a conversation), Rennan continued. "Have you seen Cam today? He didn't wake me up this morning to tell me his daily plan. I doubt he would have gone to his meetings without telling at least one of us what his schedule is like."

"Yeah, he came by and told me," I responded with a slight sigh. I was glad he told me, but not at the cost of my sleep! "He says he has a few meetings today, but otherwise Queen Coral told him he needs to relax."

"It's about time he actually did that. Relax, I mean," Rennan clarified his statement with a grin. "He is involved with way too many matters within the merfolk's business than he really needs to be."

"To be fair, though, he is also the rightful king of Heviah. That sort of thing would be required of him," I countered.

We began to walk downstairs to meet the others for breakfast.

Rennan's ear twitched. "It's still kind of weird to think of Cam as the king of the elves. I don't think I'm ever going to get my head wrapped around that one."

"I kind of wish he would have told us that when he first approached us in Leshee, but at least we found out before we got to Heviah," I said with a shrug. "I agree with you though, it is a little bit strange to think that we've been in the company of a king and didn't realize it."

There were many things I wish Cam would have explained sooner, but there wasn't any way I was going to be able to change that now. I would just have to deal with what he did tell me and go from there.

"Ha, and we should have," Rennan chuckled.

I raised an eyebrow, so he took that as consent to continue speaking.

He smiled to himself. "Well, you should have since, you know, you're the type of person to figure things like that out. Thinking back on everything now, he said quite a few things that should have tipped us off."

"You mean besides the fact that he refuses to talk about his family? Yes."

"Yeah, but after meeting Carter and finding out what a jerk he is, I can see why Cam never mentioned anything about him," Rennan stated as we started descending a flight of spiraling stairs. "Regardless, it will be good for him to try to relax for a little while."

Before I could say anything else, heavy footfalls echoed through the hallway we had just exited. My hand immediately went to one of the knives I kept tucked inside my boot and Rennan shifted his weight to the balls of his feet so he could run if he had to.

I looked to Rennan and tilted my head toward the wall. He got the hint and backed up to it, waiting for whoever was running down the hall. I was about to walk up the stairs, but I was prevented by a man barreling into me. Thank goodness Rennan was right there to catch me. If he hadn't, I definitely would have fallen backwards down the stairs.

"Oh my word, I'm so sorry, Scarlet!" Cam said quickly as he helped pull me up into the hallway to be on level ground. "I didn't know you were right there. I didn't mean to almost send you flying down the stairs. Are you okay?"

"Yeah, I'm fine," I answered with a slight grin. "I just didn't expect you to come running down the hallway and then rocket down the stairs. I thought you were in a meeting?"

The elf made me laugh when he got so flustered. It was hard to be mad at him when he was apologizing this profusely.

Cam's face went from a flushed red to a deathly white. He fidgeted with his signet ring before saying, "Yeah, well, that's the thing. Coral forbade me from coming to any of the meetings today."

I looked at him in astonishment. "What?! Why would she do that?"

"Believe me, she wouldn't have done it unless she had a very good reason," Cam explained rather calmly.

For a moment, I was shocked that he could keep such a level head after being forbidden from doing something by a queen. Then I realized who it was that I was talking to. Cam, by nature, wasn't fazed by a whole lot. I decided to trust him and not freak out.

He continued. "The reason she forbade me from today's and probably tomorrow's meetings are because a small squad of elves and a couple of officials rode in unexpectedly about half an hour ago. They're demanding to meet with the queen on various matters."

"Okay, so that's that explanation," Rennan said somewhat thoughtfully, "But what was Queen Coral's reasoning behind it?"

"She thought it would be best for me not to be anywhere near the elves in case they recognize me—even in the slightest. I wasn't willing to risk my whole mission on a small chance like that, so I agreed with the queen. So, long story short, I get a complete day off," Cam answered with a shrug.

We wordlessly decided to head to the dining hall to meet up with Carter and Valerie.

Cam sighed a minute later. "As much as I'd like to do some research today, I don't think I really should."

"I'm in agreement," Rennan nodded. "It will be good for you to get a day to rest, Cam. You never take enough time for yourself to recharge."

Out of the corner of my eye, I noticed the wolf sending Cam a pointed look—I'm sure Cam caught that glare.

"To be perfectly honest, I've never been allowed the chance to go off somewhere by myself and recharge at all. I'm relatively unfamiliar with the concept, but I'm willing to give it a shot for today since I physically don't feel like doing a whole lot," Cam shot back.

Rennan rolled his eyes, but did not argue.

I snorted to myself before saying, "I know you'd like to do nothing, but we're spending the day with Valerie. She's bound to have some sort of folly planned. There won't be any escaping it, but maybe you can convince her to let you sit some of it out."

"Eh, it's Valerie. She'll let me have my way because she's so obsessed with me and my brother," Cam snickered as we reached the bottom of the stairs.

I nodded, and my heart rose in my chest—only a few hundred more yards and I would be subject to the whim of a mermaid princess for the next several hours. Cam looked about as apprehensive as I felt.

Valerie's hug came sooner than I would have liked. As soon as we had rounded the corner to get to the dining hall, she practically suffocated me. I know she was merely happy to see me, but I still wanted to punch her in the throat. I was not fond of people touching me, much less smothering me in a hug.

Cam looked like he shared the sentiment (especially since Valerie always hugged him around the stomach). Rennan, on the other hand, thoroughly enjoyed every second of the mermaid's embrace. Have I mentioned before that he had it bad for Valerie? I probably have. But now I've said it again so it's even truer.

"Hi!! You made it!" Valerie cheered jubilantly. She yelled into the dining hall, "Carter! All three of them came!"

Carter's voice shouted back, "*Cam is actually going to eat breakfast?!*"

Cam rolled his eyes and stalked into the dining hall without saying a word to Valerie.

She tried to act like she didn't notice, but I saw her deflate a little when Cam didn't even say 'hi.' She turned to me and Rennan looking somewhat rational.

"Not that I'm displeased to see Cam or anything, but why is he here right now? I thought he was in meetings with my mother all morning and wouldn't catch a break until mid-afternoon?" she asked with a slightly confused expression on her face.

"See, and that's what Scarlet said, too," Rennan began. "He said a squad of elves rode in this morning, demanding to meet with your mother. She forbade him from attending those meetings in any form, and he agreed with her call. So! Cam gets to spend the day with us!"

Valerie's face lit up quite noticeably. She clapped her hands before saying, "Yay! I have such amazing plans for today, too! I was going to take you all to the underwater part of the city so you can experience the best of both worlds while you stay in Sala. Now Cam can join the fun!!"

Rennan engaged Valerie in conversation further, but I soon tired of all the enthusiastic exclamations, so I decided to go find Cam to see what he was doing. Well, more to see how he was faring with Carter. I suspected Cam would be talking with his twin just to make sure there was no trouble rising up between them again. The last thing we needed was another incident like the Spiral of Doom on our hands.

I walked in to see Cam and Carter in what appeared to be a civil conversation. Neither elf looked agitated, so I took that as a good sign. Maybe Carter really was going to turn over a new leaf and help his brother. I smiled to myself, hoping Carter was really going to live up to the expectations Cam had placed on him. As I got closer to where the twins were sitting, I heard the two of them talking.

"Have you seen avocado toast anywhere here?" Carter mused, half to himself.

Cam looked at Carter like he was crazy (I still think he was). "No, Carter, I have not seen avocado toast."

"Will you help me find some?"

"No," Cam snorted. "Why do you even want avocado toast?"

"Because it's good!"

"How?! It tastes like flavorless paste on bread!"

"You obviously have been in exile long enough to lose your refined palate," Carter declared rather dramatically.

Cam merely rolled his eyes. "You know what, I'm not going to argue this. I'm just not going to help you find your stupid avocado toast."

I pulled up a chair and sat down right as I sensed another major twin argument about to blow up.

Somehow, they were both relieved that the argument didn't have a chance to escalate further. They dropped the avocado toast discussion (I was glad they hadn't asked my opinion, because I don't mind avocado toast and actually would have taken Carter's rather than Cam's side).

At one point, Cam discretely knocked a paper off their small table when Carter wasn't paying attention.

"I'll get it," Carter said as he bent over to grab it.

"What's on the back of your head?" Cam asked when Carter looked down.

Carter abruptly turned to look at Cam. Somehow, his face was both suspicious and panicked. "Uh, the rest of my head?"

"Ha, okay," Cam snorted with a smile.

Carter's hand practically flew up to the back of his head. Cam laughed hysterically.

Carter glared at his brother when he realized nothing was there. "You jerk. There's nothing on the back of my head!"

"That was the point, Carter," Cam continued laughing. "I just wanted to see if you would actually fall for the trick. Turns out you are gullible enough to still listen to me."

"Cameron, I never know when you're messing with me or not, so it is always safe to listen to you," Carter said in nearly a mumbling tone.

Cam just smirked.

"I don't know. Cam said to trust him, so we did. Then he got us lost in the woods more than once when we were traveling to get here," I told Carter.

This time, Carter laughed and Cam rolled his eyes.

Cam shot back, "I recall that happening *once*. At night. When I was tired. You expect me to navigate dark woods perfectly when I was physically and mentally exhausted? You and Rennan weren't much help either."

I shrugged. "It still happened. Besides, Rennan is no use when it comes to navigating and I didn't recognize that part of the woods."

"Ha, she's giving you some grief, Cam. She must do it pretty often for you to take it this well," Carter commented with a smile to his brother.

Cam just stared at Carter, but didn't say a word.

"What's he talking about, Cam?" I asked curiously.

Cam ran a hand through his hair and smiled faintly. "He's referring to when I was younger and barely knew how to handle teasing in Trehi's academy for nobility. Though, if you must know, I've grown out of it, Carter."

"Well, I'd hope you would at this point. We're twenty-four now, so yeah," Carter shrugged. "Anyway, good morning, Scarlet."

"How is that the first time you've said 'good morning' to me?" I asked with a snicker.

"In my defense, I don't usually see you in the morning."

"Morning?! Good morning, everyone!!" Valerie sang as she danced into the room. "I have a wonderful time planned for you all today!"

Cam and Carter sighed audibly when they saw the bouncy mermaid enter. No doubt they had to be thinking of what attention they were going to get from the princess today.

"Of course, she does," Carter muttered. Cam nodded his head in acknowledgement.

"So! I'm thinking we're going to start off with getting your crystals activated and then we're going to go underwater. I want you guys to see the larger part of the city today. It is absolutely stunning down there and really isn't something I would recommend skipping," Valerie explained with her ever-present smile. She became thoughtful. "Oo, but skipping there sounds like a lot of fun."

"She wouldn't recommend passing on anything," Cam whispered to his twin.

Carter stifled laughter. I decided to ignore them.

"Does anyone have anything they want to add to today's plan of fun?" Valerie inquired of us.

I wanted to ask if I could sit the whole underwater thing out, but I decided not to say anything because Rennan would drag me under against my will. He's stubborn like that.

"Uh, just one comment," Cam spoke up. Valerie grinned and ecstatically nodded for him to continue. "I will not be using a crystal. I will be shape-shifting."

Carter's head whipped towards Cam. He had wide eyes and his mouth gaped. "Whoa, did you actually come up with a way to deal with your hydro-anxiety thing?"

Cam was about to say something, and then thought better of it.

"*Hydro-anxiety*?"

"Yeah. You don't like being in the water. Did you get over it?"

"No, I still don't like it. I'll have to surface every once and awhile because I'll start subconsciously thinking I'm suffocating," Cam explained with a shrug. Well, that explained why he didn't like going underwater at all.

"Okay, fair enough," Carter relented.

"So, whenever you all are ready to leave, let me know and we'll head to the lower levels of the above-ground part of the palace," Valerie stated.

Then she skipped off towards the tables bearing food with Rennan right on her heels.

"See, she'll skip but she won't pass," Cam snickered.

I rolled my eyes, and then we enjoyed a relatively uneventful breakfast.

"Okay!! Are we all ready to go under water?" Valerie asked us with a wide grin. She was so excited to take us underwater that it was making me nervous.

Now, I'm not a nervous person, but when someone was so excited, I became overly concerned I would mess something up. But now that we were in the moment, I could understand why Cam didn't want to go underwater. I felt like my own fear of suffocating under the water was starting to develop.

"Yes! So, how do these crystal thingies work?" Rennan questioned as he started fidgeting with his pink crystal. He was trying to make it work by pressing the bottom in case there was a button.

"So, what you have to do is put the crystal on your wrist like a bracelet and jump straight into the water," Valerie responded with a smile.

"Yeah, that can work for you people. I'm shape-shifting, so see 'ya!" Cam shouted as he dove into the pool.

Valerie laughed joyfully and jumped in after him. Rennan, Carter, and I all looked at each other in bewilderment. None of us knew exactly how to respond to what we had just seen.

"Okay, so I guess we just give it a shot," Rennan said as he looked at the crystal one more time. He looked up and stared at Carter. "Have you ever done this before?"

The elf shook his head. "No, I've done things a lot of people wouldn't normally do, but this isn't one of them. Temporarily becoming a merman is going to be a first for me."

"Or you could be a mer-elf," Rennan suggested with an impish grin.

"You have got to have the most childish sense of humor of anyone I have ever met in my life," Carter stated matter-of-factly.

"You have no idea," I muttered.

Rennan pretended he hadn't heard me and said, "I know you all love me, so I'm going to take that as a compliment."

Valerie poked her head out of the water and a pink fin followed a second later. She grinned expectantly. "Are you guys coming? You're missing quite the show down here."

"What's happening?" Carter inquired curiously.

"The fish seem to love Cam."

"Ha, he can be the king of fish."

"Oo!! Let's call him 'King Fishyfan!'" Valerie cheered with a wide grin.

"That doesn't even make any sense!" I argued.

Carter stared at me, completely deadpan. "It doesn't have to make sense. Cam himself doesn't make any. Therefore, we are calling him King Fishyfan."

"Ugh," I groaned in defeat as I put my crystal on my wrist.

Then I stepped towards the water and dove in. Almost immediately, bubbles and light swirled around me. I don't really remember the whole process of the transformation, but I remember my legs felt really weird and my neck was super itchy. When the light cleared, I looked down to see a long, delicate fish's tail the color of amber.

I breathed, "Whoa."

"I know, it's kind of crazy to get used to," Cam's deep voice said to me.

I heard the voice as clearly as if we were on land, which didn't make much sense to me. Then I panicked. Did I not have my furry ears?!

He laughed. "The fins are hard to adjust to as well, just in case you were wondering."

Lo and behold, I had fins for ears instead of my furry, fox ones. The fact unsettled me, but I ended up deciding the change might be for the best while I was underwater since I didn't want bothersome water to get into my ears. When I looked down at my new tail, I also noticed that instead of the red leather coat I had been wearing earlier, it was replaced with a simple red top with slightly billowy sleeves. I couldn't believe how thorough the merfolk's magic was to make changes to my wardrobe and anatomy.

I looked up to see Valerie's pink tail swishing around. She was obviously still talking to Rennan and Carter, who hadn't yet transformed. Deciding not to worry about them, I looked in the direction of the voice.

Naturally, Cam was just floating in the water. His chestnut hair hung around his face in soft looking locks. I was surprised to see him with fins for ears as well. He didn't seem horribly bothered by it. Then again, this probably wasn't the first time he had been underwater like this. In addition to the fins, Cam had changed his wardrobe to a simple tunic that really only covered his torso. It was pinned at the top and exposed the top of his chest and arms. His sparkling silver tail was eye-catching as it reflected all of the light shining through the water.

"That was a very weird sensation," I commented. I didn't blame him for wanting to shape-shift; I would have done the same thing if I had the ability. "Also, Valerie and Carter have decided to call you King Fishyfan. Just thought I would let you know."

Cam looked at me, momentarily confused. Then he rolled his eyes as he swatted a bright yellow fish away from his face. "It's because all the fish swarm around me, isn't it? They always do. Queen Coral always has to have guards keep the fish out of the room when we have underwater meetings."

"Why do they like you so much?" I asked with a stifled laugh.

Another fish—this time a bright pink one—tried coming very close to Cameron's head. He was less than happy to see it.

"Heck if I know," he growled as he swam away from the fish. "All I know is that I hate their constant pursuit of me. Why can't they follow

Valerie?!"

"Why can't who follow me?" the mermaid princess asked as she swam down to join us.

"The stupid fish! Who else?" Cam shouted in agitation.

Valerie giggled. "But you're King Fishyfan! Of course, they're going to follow you!"

I smiled smugly at the elf. "I told you."

He rolled his eyes and exhaled deeply. "That you did."

Carter and Rennan appeared seconds later. Rennan kept going on and on about how amazing it was to be underwater without suffocating, thus boring Carter out of his mind. Though, I'd be shocked if anybody else present wasn't bored. I knew I was, and looking at Cameron, he was of the same mindset. Valerie, on the other hand, was just as enthusiastic as Rennan.

"Okay!" Valerie exclaimed in a bubbly voice.

When I looked at her, she had her hands planted on her hips, waiting for the boys' attention. Cam was still busy batting away colorful fish to pay much heed to her.

Valerie started on her explanation of hectic plans. "So, what I'm thinking is that we all will go in one group and just swim around the city looking and all the awesome, glittery things. And then—"

Cam held up a hand once the fish abandoned him. "I'm going to stop you right there, Val. While Rennan and Scarlet haven't been here before, I'm sure they have very different ideas about what they want to see in the city."

"So, what would you suggest, Cameron?" the mermaid princess asked with a raised eyebrow. She seemed slightly irritated that Cam had thrown a wrench in her plans.

"Why don't you take Rennan to see nearly everything down here? Since Carter and I have been here before, we'll take Scarlet to go to whatever she wants to see," Cam suggested calmly. If he knew he had irritated the mermaid, he was wise to not engage her frustration.

Valerie considered that for a minute. Then she nodded. "Fine. We'll meet back here around dinnertime. Does that sound good for everyone?"

"Yes! 'Cause then we can get dinner afterwards and it will be a wonderful end to a great day!" Rennan readily agreed with a huge grin on his face.

I rolled my eyes. "You say that because you'll just want food after swimming around for hours."

"Of course!" he cheered. "Come on, Valerie! Let's go!!"

Carter shook his head as they swam off at top speed. He muttered something to himself before saying to Cam and I, "They are such strange people."

"You have no idea," Cam snickered. Once Rennan and Valerie were completely out of sight, Cam turned to face me. "So, where do you want to go, Scarlet?"

"I don't know, mostly because I have no clue what all is here. You guys are better off taking me to whatever you think is interesting," I shrugged.

The twins immediately looked at each other and smiled. I wasn't quite sure I wanted to know what they were agreeing about. In the short time I had known Carter and knowing what I did about Cam, it had to be something spectacular if both of them agreed in an instant.

I tried not to sound unenthused as I asked, "What did you just think of?"

"Bubble fountain?" Cam asked his brother.

"Bubble fountain," Carter agreed.

I couldn't argue with them since both men had agreed with each other (I didn't want to tip their balance and cause a city-wide disturbance), so I had no choice but to follow. They led me through the palace and out into the city. As soon as we had gotten into the courtyard, I could see why Valerie had wanted to bring us down here.

The underwater part of the city was absolutely huge and utterly breathtaking. I had never seen anything like it before in my life.

All throughout the city, fish and merfolk alike worked together in harmony. There was no chaos anywhere to be seen in the shining city. There were jubilant voices floating along with the currents, and when they reached my ears, I couldn't help but smile. The entirety of the coral-covered, pearl-encrusted city was simply spectacular. It was a joyful place, which I found to be very refreshing after my life in dreary Palee.

"Not quite what you expected, is it?" Cam chuckled when he saw my awestruck expression.

Carter couldn't help but grin at me as well.

"No, it isn't," I admitted as we swam out over the palace gates. "It is much more beautiful than I ever anticipated. Though, it is even more sparkly than I thought it would be."

Carter snickered. "I can't say I blame you. But if you think this is sparkly, you should see Trehi."

I looked over to him and was slightly surprised to realize his tail was a teal color and he wore no tunic. I couldn't help but laugh to myself when I noticed that Cam had a much more toned figure than his brother. The first weird thought that came to my mind was Carter having stick arms while Cam had some serious biceps.

But back to what is actually relevant....

"So where are we going?" I asked the twins.

"Bubble fountain!" Cam replied with a grin.

After that, neither twin gave me any explanation for what we were doing. They took me through the markets, the underwater parks, and to see various parts of the extensive palace grounds. Still, they were fixated about the bubble fountain they kept referencing. If I asked questions, they would only respond by saying, "bubble fountain." Though, when we got to the center of the city where this fountain supposedly was, I could see why they didn't want to tell me anything about it. Any description they would have given me wouldn't have made any sense.

The bubble fountain in question was huge. It was easily five yards on all sides in an octagonal shape. The sheer size of it made me wonder how long the merfolk had spent to engineer such a feat. Bubbles continually flowed out of the gemstone-studded tip of the fountain in copious amounts. Some sort of magic had to be involved for it to pump out that many bubbles in a minute, not to mention the spectacular arrangement of precious stones found exclusively under the water's surface.

"This is amazing," I breathed.

My mind couldn't focus on just one thing. The whole fountain was absolutely breathtaking.

"See? I knew you'd like it," Cam smiled. He and Carter bumped fists, and I just laughed. "Queen Coral showed me this when I first came underwater. She knew I would appreciate the beauty of it since it reminded me a little bit of the fountains in Nesha and Heviah I've always been so fond of. Since then, it's kind of been a place I come back to whenever I'm underwater."

"That's actually kind of nice," I mused to myself.

"And relatively normal," Carter added. Carter just laughed when Cam sent him a sidelong glare. "What? I'm just saying normal people do stuff like that!"

Cam stared at his brother. Then he smiled. "And how would you know what normal is? You never knew how to act normal when we were at the academy."

Carter flushed slightly when he became flustered. "To be fair, I was under the age of seventeen and extremely awkward as a kid."

I stage-whispered, "If you were to ask me, I'd say he's awkward anyway."

Both twins heard me, as was intended. Cam just busted out laughing while Carter floated there taking his brother's laughter bravely. If we had been on solid ground, I'm sure Cam would have fallen on the ground with laughter. Honestly, I had expected Cam to find some amusement with my comment, but I didn't think he was going to be laughing so hard.

"Okay, that is a good one," Cam managed when he had relatively composed himself. "And accurate, considering last night I heard Carter talking in his sleep."

Carter scowled. "I did not!"

"Yeah, you did," Cam responded with a huge grin. "You were going on about something misty. I don't know. I was too busy reading when I heard you."

Carter's face totally went red, even in the strange underwater lights. "Okay, we are dropping this topic right now. Cam, let's take Scarlet to the gardens."

Cam didn't say anything, but shrugged and followed his brother as he swam away. Then Cam's face lit up and he rushed forward to catch his brother. They conversed quickly, and then Cam swam back towards me.

"What were you doing?" I asked him when he rejoined me.

"I'm taking you to the gardens while Carter goes to the city center," he replied.

I was confused. "I thought he was going to be with us all day?"

Cam snickered. "Are you kidding? He and I are siblings. We will take any opportunity to get rid of each other. So, we just mutually agreed to ditch each other."

"I will never understand you two," I sighed with an eyeroll.

"Of course not. You've never had siblings."

"All I had was Rennan's pack until the Leshee massacre," I stated. The thought was both depressing and normal. Depressingly normal. I hated it. "But I think if I actually had siblings or close family around my age, I would never understand them."

"It would be fun though, you have to admit, to have someone to hang out and get along with," Cam shrugged. "In better times when Carter and I were younger, we did have fun with each other. We'd always play games and compete in the gardens."

"That does sound nice," I decided with a small smile.

"Yeah. There was one time when we accidentally hit my father's statue with a ball. Took him two months to realize there was a ball stuck within that stone crown," Cam remembered with a smile. "So yeah, it's kind of fun."

We fell silent for a few minutes, but then Cam asked me, "Have you seen the aboveground gardens yet?"

"Sort of, but it was late in the day and I was tired of hearing Valerie shout about doing each other's hair," I responded with as little of a groan as I could manage. I was so not going to have my hair be done by the princess. She'd make it so bouncy that I would be driven insane by it.

"I can understand the emotion," Cam nodded. "She once tried to put my hair in a bun. I told her never to do it again. So far, she hasn't."

"Uh huh…," I said with slight hesitation.

I won't deny it, I was trying to imagine Cam's long hair in a bun. Yeah. That thought did not compute.

"Don't even think about telling her to do it again. I will kill something if anyone tries touching my hair," Cam warned.

I held my hands up in surrender—there was no way I was going to send Valerie against Cam when he obviously had a firm stance on this topic.

Cam's mood changed quickly. "Anyway! We're going to the gardens. Since you're one who likes being outdoors, you might enjoy it."

"Okay then. Let's get to the gardens, so then I can behold the beauty you think it is," I said with a smile.

So, we just swam on until we reached the gardens.

It was an interesting place, really. There were so many types of interesting plant life that would never survive above ground. There were trees kind of reminiscent of willows, but these had leaves all sorts of colors and they seemed to be made of some translucent material that gave them a pretty shimmer. Not only that, but there were more types of glittering seaweed than I could count.

"Wow, you were right, Cam," I breathed in wonder.

I just kept gaping at (and touching) everything because it was so cool. This place was absolutely stunning. You know, for a mermaid city full of overly chipper fish people.

"Of course, I'm right," Cam snorted behind me. "But what were you referring to?"

I snorted a laugh. "You were right about me liking these gardens. They're so pretty."

"Oh, I know right?" Cam said. He appeared beside me and moved his hair out of his face. "As energetic as the people here can be, they really know how to design gardens."

"They really do," I nodded in agreement.

I swam towards one of the benches I had spotted from a short distance away. Cam followed and sat beside me.

"How many times have you been here?" I asked him. "Underwater, I mean."

"Not many times," he said with a shrug. "I try to avoid coming underwater as much as possible just because I can never shake the thought of drowning or losing my focus to shapeshift. However, when I am underwater, I like coming here. It's nice to have someone with me this time, though."

I smiled. "It's nice of you to bring me here with you. I feel like this is one of the only calm places I've been in for the last week. Or maybe that's because I'm just with you."

Cam just smiled for a minute, not saying anything. "It's my pleasure. And you're right, it's calm because it's just you and me."

"Yeah, it's not just you two anymore," Carter said with a smirk as he appeared on Cam's other side. The elder twin's face flushed red, but Carter ignored him. "You said to meet in the garden, brother, but you never said when."

Cam mumbled something under his breath, but neither Carter nor I understood what he was saying.

Finally, at a volume we could all hear, Cam asked, "How was your swim around the city center?"

"Boring. And loud. Since it was boring and loud, I came back here to find you two," Carter replied with a shrug.

I couldn't blame him for coming back when he was faced with those circumstances, but at the same time, I wasn't totally thrilled that Carter had rejoined us either. Like Cam and I had agreed on, things were so much calmer when it was just the two of us.

Cam still seemed irritated that his brother was already back, but he didn't say anything else about it. "So, where to now?"

Before Carter or I could respond, we heard loud voices coming from the gates to the castle. We looked in that direction to see a bunch of merpeople swimming through the town towards us. The eyes of the twins went wide.

"Hide," Cam hissed as he dragged us into a building adjacent to the area the garden was in. I don't know what they had seen, but I doubt it was good. Cam only had this type of reaction if there was some kind of danger.

"What's going on?" I demanded quietly.

"The elvish soldiers I told you about earlier. They're here now," Cam whispered, keeping his eyes glued to the armored mermen swimming through city.

"We can't afford to let them see you," Carter stated, also watching the transformed elves. He turned to his brother. "If they do, you'll be killed on the spot and I'll be put on trial for fraternizing with you."

"Yeah, let's avoid that," Cam muttered in agreement. He watched the elves pass by and then said, "Let's go. I'm going back up to the surface where it's easier to hide."

"Agreed," I nodded.

However, as soon as we were out in the open again, a voice shouted, "Cameron Woods!!"

Our heads whipped around in the direction of the voices. Valerie and Rennan were swimming towards us at top speed, excitement plainly written on their faces. Cam narrowed his eyes and bolted off towards him.

Carter and I remained behind to make sure the elvish soldiers didn't hear our impulsive friends. They turned around, thinking they were hearing things, and then they returned to whatever business they were trying to accomplish. I nodded to Carter when I decided the coast was clear.

We rejoined the others, and Cam was in the middle of a lecture about yelling his name across public spaces.

"It's dangerous," he was saying when we swam up. "If I'm recognized, I will be killed. Then they'll the lot of you because you've all helped me break the rules of exile."

Rennan groaned. "Sorry, Cam, we were just really excited."

"You're always excited," I pointed out with a touch of irritation.

We were so close to being discovered and all because Rennan was *excited*? I should have known better, but I couldn't help but shake my head in dismay.

Rennan considered my comment and then grinned sheepishly. "You have a point, but this time it's something worth being excited about."

"What was it this time?" Carter asked apathetically.

For once, I couldn't blame him for expressing that emotion. We had witnessed Rennan being excited so many times in the last week that we didn't know what else in Sala was going to wind him up.

"We found a duckling."

Cam scowled. "Why was there a duckling underwater?"

"Oh, it wasn't underwater," Valerie cut in with a grin. "We swam up to the surface because Rennan wanted to see how far away from the main island we were, and there was this duckling just floating on the top of the water. It looked lonely, so we decided to say hi to it and then it followed us back here!"

"The little guy is as tame as a pet, and he is so sweet!" Rennan added with his ever-present smile.

The twins and I exchanged a look.

I sighed. "Well, we'd better go see this duckling of yours."

Valerie and Rennan cheered and then swam off. The rest of us followed, rolling our eyes and muttering under our breath about how ridiculous of a pair Valerie and Rennan made. They took us back up to the room where we first entered the underwater part of Sala.

After transforming to obtain legs again (I silently rejoiced in the change), I looked around the room. It's pretty safe to say I prefer dry land to water.

Anyway, there was a duckling sitting in the middle of the room.

"So…this is the duckling?" Carter asked, clearly unimpressed by the small creature.

It was a duckling, which by nature are small. I don't know why Carter was expecting anything else.

"Yep!" Rennan smiled. He walked over to the little guy and picked him up. Rennan hugged the little bird and it seemed to be happy to see him.

"Have you named him?" Cam snickered.

I couldn't help but smirk.

"No, but I do know that he only eats grapes."

I just stared at him. "How is that relevant when we are talking about the duck's name?"

"It's still about the duck," Rennan answered matter-of-factly. "Just for that Scarlet, I will name him Firecracker because of you."

I rolled my eyes and let the wolf continue with his ridiculousness.

"I don't know whether that is a compliment or an insult," I muttered.

"I'd suggest taking it as the former," Carter whispered to me.

For once, I agreed with him.

"No, here's an even better name: Firequacker. 'Cause he's a duck," Cam grinned mischievously.

"Do not encourage them," I warned Cam.

"They are not obliged to listen to me," he said, his eyes twinkling.

Valerie laughed and clapped excitedly. "Yes! That shall be his name!"

I glared at Cam for giving the two crazies the idea. He just smiled and waved.

If we were going to be in Sala for the winter, it was going to be a long two months....

The Queen's Decision

Let me just tell you, beautiful though it was, Sala was full of way too many dances, royal events, meetings, and colorful flowers to ever make me feel totally comfortable. Don't get me wrong, all the people in Sala were nice, but they were *way* too perky for me.

Plus, being forced to spend half my time with Valerie tested my patience. She had a good heart, but it was buried beneath all of her quirks and oddities. Besides, when I saw her too-wide grin, all I could think of was the last smile Razil had given me before I left Vareh. It was also completely obvious that she was hitting on Carter. He didn't suspect the princess at all, but I could see it every blasted time Valerie looked at him.

As for Carter himself, he hadn't tried anything like the first night we had entered the city. He had kept to himself mostly. However, during meals, he often made a point to start arguing with his brother. I wasn't quite sure if it was because he really wanted to argue or because he wanted to make it seem like things were normal between him and his brother. Honestly, it could have been a little bit of both.

On occasion, I had been left alone with Valerie and Carter when Cam had taken Rennan somewhere in the city. Originally, I had been very irritated because Cam knew I didn't like either of those crazy people. But it wasn't entirely useless. I had discovered that Carter had not manifested an ability like Cam's. That information was great and all, but what was really interesting was that Cam and Carter's father had the ability to become whatever substance he could think of. That was useful information because one day, we would have to face him.

Cam's presence remained elusive. Most of the time, he was in meetings with Queen Coral and her officials, somewhere in the extensive libraries in the palace, around the city on some royal task, or somewhere off by himself. Occasionally, he would set time aside to try to be normal with me and Rennan. Even still, he was always on edge about something. The only times we really saw him were at meals, and he was absolutely exhausted during every single one of them even if he didn't always show it.

Though, in our rare times to relax, we were able to learn more about each other. Even if Cam still said very little about himself, he did disclose small facts like his enjoyment of shooting his bow in the woods or that he despised the sun. Through small things like those, I felt like I got to know him better.

Only Rennan was genuinely happy to be here. Except for Valerie, but she was an exception since she lived here. She was always happy to be in the city. Anyway, Rennan enjoyed himself greatly. He also enjoyed the company of Firequacker. That is, until he had to release the duckling so it could go on with its life.

I heard that he went to the underwater half of the city using the power of his identification crystal a few more times since the first and only time I had gone with him. Each time, he came back more and more excited about the world that he had yet to discover. Though he loved the city of the merfolk, I knew the wolf was eager to set out again and see more of the wide world we had yet to discover.

One night, only a couple of days before we were to leave, we received anonymous notes. And by "we," I meant Rennan, Cam, and I. I thought I was the only one who had gotten one, but as I later discovered when Rennan came crashing into my suite, we had both received a mysterious message.

"Hey, sorry to interrupt your afternoon again, but did you get a random note that only had one phrase on it?" Rennan asked curiously when he entered my room.

I had been trying to do some reading to relax for the first time in years, and I kept getting interrupted. Finally, I gave up so I could talk to Rennan.

"I did. Why? Did you get one?"

"Yeah. All it says is 'watch the silver bird,'" Rennan answered with a confused expression on his face.

"I feel like that has nothing to do with what I received," I stated with furrowed eyebrows.

A knock distracted us from our conversation. I gave whoever was outside my door consent to enter, and Cam quietly slipped in.

"Okay, please tell me I'm not the only one who got a weird note today," he demanded as he crossed the room in four long strides.

"Nope, we both did," Rennan responded. "Actually, we were just talking about them. Mine just says, 'watch the silver bird.' What does yours say?"

Cam made a face. "It just says, 'fly into war.' If you ask me, I'd tell you that it is a precursor to whatever is going to happen in the near future. Scarlet, tell us yours."

"It reads, 'and into freedom's unknowns.' Wait, I think they're all part of one message. Think about it, we all got a fragment of a sentence on the same afternoon. That has to mean something, right?" I questioned.

"You could be correct," Cam acknowledged, a thoughtful expression on his face.

"Sooo...," Rennan began, "the full message would read, 'watch the silver bird fly into war and into freedom's unknowns?' I feel like there should be more to that statement!"

As soon as Rennan finished speaking, he yelped as a bright light flashed in front of the three of us. When it dissipated, all that remained was a folded piece of parchment paper on the floor. Cam kneeled to pick it up and break the seal. He read the message and then dropped it on the floor.

"What?" I asked. "What does it say?"

Cam answered with a colorless face. "'Watch the silver bird fly into war and into freedom's unknowns. Watch the fox discover more than bones. Watch as the wolf's skills hone. Nothing can be stopped; it is all in motion. Persevere, or question the notion.' That's all it says. Read it for yourselves if you don't believe me."

"I believe you, Cam," I said quietly. "I don't think it was a mistake for this to come to us. This is obviously something meant either to urge us on or to warn us. But Cam, tell me, have you ever been a silver bird?"

He shrugged. "Once or twice. One of the first things I ever shapeshifted into was a silver hawk. I'm going to assume it means me anyway because it also specified fox and wolf. So. This is something to be taken seriously, no?"

Rennan made a face. "I'd say we should keep this tucked away in the back of our minds, but not worry too much about it. I'm sure everything will sort itself out."

"Yeah, you're probably right," I agreed.

Cam nodded his head, and then we dropped the subject.

Still, I couldn't help but wonder to myself the significance of the silver bird, the fox, and the wolf. It meant us, but in what way? I stayed up a good portion of the night thinking about it, but when I got nowhere in my train of thought, I put it out of my mind.

The next morning was when we had decided to leave.

Cam had one last meeting with the merfolk and he said he would send for us afterward. He had all those meetings, but never told us anything about them. He only mentioned that there were a lot of disagreements. At any rate, Rennan and I would be summoned to the main library afterward.

A servant boy came and told us that Lord Cameron had sent for us. I still found it strange to think of Cam as a prince and the first heir to the elvish throne—or with any royal title, really. It was also unnerving to go to a huge library even after seventeen years. I still had nightmares about that day, but the regrets followed me even more.

"Well, I hope we're finally going to know what the plan is," Rennan commented to break the silence we had fallen into.

I nodded my head, but I didn't say anything. My nerves were too out of control to really say anything coherent and relevant.

Rennan sent me a sidelong glance out of the corner of his eye. "Is something bothering you, Scarlet? You seem really quiet. Well, quieter than usual."

I was hesitant to answer. I didn't want Rennan to think that I was a coward. "Well, uh, libraries kind of make me anxious. It makes me really uneasy and...and I don't really know how to say any of this."

Rennan looked at me skeptically and I didn't dare to make eye contact with him. I was afraid of him laughing at my stupid fear of libraries. Eventually, I managed to look up and see a compassionate light in his pale blue eyes. Even though his eyes reminded me of ice on a frozen river, they shone with the same kindness a child would show people they loved.

"I'm not going to press you for details—you and Cam both hate it when I do that—but I will say that you are one of the bravest people I've ever met. I know that you can survive another little while in a library," Rennan said quietly. He didn't seem amused at all, nor did he think I sounded ridiculous. He sounded sincere in everything that he said to me. "Will you tell me a little bit, though? Not everything, mind you, but just enough that I can know how to help."

"When I was almost four, there was a major attack on Leshee. You probably remember it," I began. "How old were you when that happened? Nine?"

"Around there, yeah," he interrupted.

I sighed and continued with a shudder. "After all you wolves fled, I wandered back through the main areas of the city: the town square, the park, and the library. When I got to the library, I saw mounds of books strewn across the floor and they were covered with blood. All of the librarians were killed and buried in tombs of books. It was an absolute massacre that took my parents from me. It's kind of my motivation for a lot of things I do."

Rennan remained silent for a while. Eventually, he spoke right as we reached the door to the library. "I see. Listen, if you make it through our time in the library, you can do anything you want to me."

"You'd willingly submit yourself to my kind of amusement? And what if I don't make it?"

"Meh. I'd do just about anything to help. Besides, you'll make it. I'm sure of it," Rennan answered with a confident grin.

I mustered a smile as the locked doors clicked open.

We turned to see Cam standing between them. He looked pleased to see us, but appeared nervous at the same time.

He smiled weakly, like it was taking all of his energy just to stay awake. Then I noticed that he was even more worn-out than he looked. His face was paler than usual and he had brutal dark circles under his eyes, giving him the appearance of one who hadn't slept in weeks—and his messy hair confirmed that fact. The dagger and most of his other small weapons that hung at his side were noticeably missing from his side as well.

Cam opened the door wider so we could slip inside. Rennan snuck in and I ducked under Cam's arm. The elf looked both ways out into the hallway and briskly closed the doors behind us. Cam produced a massive set of jingling keys from his pocket, which he used to lock the doors from the inside.

Then Cam led us to a table strewn with all sorts of books, quills, and papers. Before I could get a good look at any, Cam swiftly gathered them all to put them somewhere else in the library.

"I see you got my message," the elf said in a voice so low I thought he was talking to himself.

Rennan, on the other hand, didn't take it that way and instead responded with, "Yup!"

Cam shook his head ever so slightly, muttering as he did so. He gestured to three seats around a small, circular table near a corner of the library, and the three of us sat down without saying a word. Nobody spoke for a few minutes afterward.

"You look like you've had quite the night," I commented.

Cameron snickered. "That's one way to put it."

"Soo…what's the plan?" Rennan asked, breaking the silence. "Have we found any evidence pointing toward the fact that the kingdoms grow more and more corrupt as time passes?"

He looked at both of us. I didn't meet his gaze and Cam suddenly became very interested in the floor.

Cam bit his lip and remained silent for a few seconds before shifting in his chair. "Yeah, about that. I learned some, but there was less here to draw from than I thought there'd be. Kevay has either become very good at guarding their information from me, or the other kingdoms don't do much with the merfolk that would possibly hint at them being corrupt. It's probably the lattr because what good is the word of one kingdom against six others?"

"Okay. Then why don't you tell us what you were doing in all of those meetings you've been in for the last few months? Surely you heard something there that would be beneficial. Rennan and I haven't heard anything in the city that is of any use to our quest," I urged.

Rennan nodded his head sadly to back me up. Cam looked like he was about to argue and object, but he closed his mouth and nodded in agreement.

"Well, I was mostly in those meetings to settle arguments among the nobles. Believe me, there were a lot of arguments needing to be solved.

Kevay and its people aren't quite as perfect as Queen Coral would like to believe," the elf muttered. "Anyway, the only impression I got from them was that formalities could certainly be much fairer and smoother when it comes to international trade.

"Besides that, all I really got was there's unrest with an unknown cause in Heviah. Apparently, elvish trade and interaction has been inconsistent for the past year and a half. Beyond that, I know nothing about my father and his personal doings."

"So basically, in the two months we've been here, we've accomplished nothing?" I clarified. I knew I was scowling. After all, who wouldn't when they realized they had been stuck somewhere they hated for two months for no helpful reason?

Cam made a face. "Well…I wouldn't exactly say *nothing*. Sure, we could have been met with more progress, but we obviously weren't meant to find it at this time. However, in some private discussions with the queen, I did discover a few things."

"Like?" Rennan prompted with a hopeful expression on his face.

"Queen Coral and I were talking a couple days ago—I see the look you're giving me, Scarlet—anyway, we were talking about different things we've heard in the kingdoms over the last few years," Cam said with a slight tone of hope in his voice. "Come to find out, we've both heard rumors about some sort of rebellion spreading. Nobody knows the 'why' or 'how' behind it, but we do know that this rebellion is comprised of citizens from all over Galerah. We also know that their intentions are anything but good."

I processed what he had said. "So, there's a rebellion in the kingdoms and nobody knows what it's rebelling against?"

"I'd say that pretty much sums it up. There used to be a rebellion in Heviah when I lived there, but I don't know if this is the same one. So never mind that, I guess. We should just keep our eyes peeled for anything particularly suspicious," Cam answered as he ran his hand through his already messy hair before trying to fix it.

Now it was sticking out in all directions like he had been struck by lightning. I can't see Cam ever getting struck by lightning, though.

"But what are we going to do? It's not like we can go to Heviah or something and research any of this. You know what will happen, Cam. If you're spotted, you're dead," Rennan pointed out as he glanced between me and the elf.

I just watched them and Cam's eyebrows drew closer together as he formulated a plan.

Rennan continued. "Is there any other place we can go to look into this? After all, I doubt Heviah will just flat out say 'we're corrupt! Come defeat us!' From everything Cam has told us, they're going to hold on to their power until the last second. There's still too much that we can accomplish with a little more research and effort. I know we can succeed if we keep trying."

"I know we can, too. It'll just be far more dangerous than it might have been here. I can bend the laws a little bit since I'm a trusted ally of the merfolk and a personal friend of the queen. I don't have the same liberties in the other kingdoms," Cam began to explain. Then he stopped to think about his unspoken idea some more. "Still, there *are* a few places we can go where we might be able to uncover some information."

"Where?" I asked.

"You already know that Heviah and Palee are out. I don't think Estal would be the greatest place to go because mankind is very similar to the elves in several respects—unpredictability being one. I probably wouldn't be allowed within the borders of Salia either, for reasons that we don't need to get into right now," Cam continued, "but there may be some helpful people in Tralia, Nesha, and Mahe."

"Then I guess we head to one of those," I stated with a slight sigh. Part of me didn't want to continue traveling because of the chance of something happening to send us off course.

"I vote we head to Mahe first. Going to Nesha or Tralia will involve a several week journey by boat, and that isn't appealing to me. Plus, we don't have that kind of time to waste right now," Cam decided as he stood up again. He started pacing the length of the room.

"Then on we go to Mahe," Rennan agreed as he too stood.

Just then, a loud knock echoed throughout the library.

Cam covered the distance with a few long strides and pulled the massive key set out of his pocket again. He unlocked the heavy, wooden doors to reveal a servant boy on the other side. He bowed to Cam, who inclined his head in return.

"Lord Cameron, Queen Coral requests the presence of you and your companions in the throne room," the child informed him.

Cam smiled and instructed the boy to tell the queen we would be there momentarily. Then the servant boy left us alone—not that we lingered there for very long. We set out soon after to reach the throne room in time for this visit with the queen of the merfolk.

We arrived outside the throne room a few minutes later. I had only seen the doors a handful of times during our visit, but they enchanted me every time I saw them.

In front of the doors, Valerie and Carter were standing there waiting for us. Carter held himself up a little bit taller when he saw us. I didn't know if it was more for me or for Cam, but I didn't like how arrogant it made him seem. Valerie, on the other hand, lit up when she saw that Cam was with us for once. She flew to his side and immediately seized his arm.

"Oh, Cam! Mother called you, too! Come inside! Carter and I were waiting for Rennan and Starlet to get here because we thought it would be just them! We're so happy to see you!!" Valerie cried happily.

I tried not to scowl when she called me "Starlet" instead of "Scarlet." Surely it wasn't on purpose, right? Was she just that ignorant?

"Yeah… 'happy,'" Carter muttered.

We all ignored him.

"Er, yes, Valerie. I'm here as well," Cam stated with a weary look on his face.

I highly doubted he was in any sort of mood to deal with the hyperactive princess. If I were in his place, I would've probably been harsh and told her to keep quiet. Unfortunately, Cam was just as polite as he was lethal in swordplay (Rennan had learned that the hard way on one of our free afternoons).

"Now can you please let go of my arm?" he pleaded. "I feel like the circulation to my hand is being cut off."

"Oh, sorry! Now come on! We mustn't keep Mother dearest waiting!" Valerie said in her sing-song voice.

Before I move on, let me just say that she did *not* release Cam's wrist. All she did was loosen her grip before dragging him into the throne room. Carter, Rennan, and I had no choice but to follow them.

Queen Coral was sitting in her elegant jewel-encrusted throne when we entered the room for the second time. This time, she looked very official with her hair intricately braided and crown resting on her head (made of her namesake, I assumed). She wore jewelry that made her look more regal than the few other times I had seen her. She also had attendants and officials surrounding her, who were just as adorned as she.

"Ah, I see you have received the summons," Coral stated as the five of us bowed at the edge of the water half of the room.

We waited patiently (except Valerie) for Queen Coral to speak again. I admit I was quite curious to see what the queen would say about our quest, though. I hoped we would be allowed to leave the city instead of being forced to stay and rot until we died. Or, as it would be in Cam's case, a slow punishment of captivity for the rest of his eternal years.

Okay, that's an exaggeration. I hoped we would be given aid as we left instead of being sent into the wild to die and rot.

"Indeed, we have, Mother," Valerie agreed, stepping forward and curtseying again.

A gleeful grin spread across her face as she turned to face us as well as her mother. To be perfectly honest, in the back of my mind, I wondered if she was an automation running on underwater squirrels—sea squirrels? Did they eat sea acorns?

A hopeful light danced in Valerie's eyes. "Have you and the Marine Council come to a decision yet?"

"Wait, what decision? Coral, with all due respect, you never mentioned anything about a decision," Cam interrupted with a very confused look on his face. He was obviously trying to comprehend what was going on and figure out a solution. That was a reoccurring thing with him—he always tried to be ahead of the curve.

Queen Coral's eyebrows knitted together. "Yes, my daughter speaks the truth. The council and I have been thinking about your quest for the last two months and have finally come to a decision on whether we will support it or not."

Cam's face became pale with dread. He swallowed before speaking again. "What did you decide?"

One of the queen's officials stepped forward. He had deep green hair, almost black, that seemed extreme against his pale, human-like skin. I thought that he must be some sort of half breed who obviously came from a noble family. His eyes shone with wisdom and compassion, but his face was grave when he whispered something in the queen's ear.

"We have been discussing what the outcomes of your quest may be. Some members of the Marine Council believe such a mission is folly and should not be attempted. However, there are others, including myself, who believe that you five are the catalysts this world needs to change," the man began. "We voted on what Kevay would do if this turned into a full-scale war."

"What was the result?" Cam questioned, anxious.

His voice made me suspicious that he didn't think this mission of ours would ever be approved, but there was something in me that doubted that. It was like he had some speculation about the matter beforehand and simply wanted it confirmed.

"The votes were nearly equal. Yet, in the end, we came to the agreement that Kevay will support you in battle against Heviah, should it come to that. The elves, save for your grace" —he bowed to Cam (taking no notice of Carter)— "are no friends of ours. They treat us similarly to how they treat hybrids like Master Penbrooke and Mistress Sutton. To a degree, we are hybrids as we walk on both land and water. My queen will not stand for such treatment to her people and will fight for the amendment of such actions."

"Indeed," the queen agreed. She looked at each of us with her bright pink eyes. They twinkled with hope and sorrow like she was sorry to see us go. "You have my blessing on your quest. My people will help in any way we can."

We all sighed in relief. I was able to release a breath I hadn't realized I had been holding.

Cam turned to me and Rennan with a look in his eyes that said, *We'll be out of here by nightfall and hopefully not in a creepy base with mutant creatures.* Obviously, a reference to the Blackshell Inn being the last time we'd have shelter by nightfall. Rennan was noticeably assured. I knew he was also excited to leave and explore new parts of the world.

Queen Coral turned to her daughter and looked skeptical. "Daughter, have you made your final decision?"

We all looked to Valerie, who was at a loss for words for the first time in her life. She looked more nervous than I had ever seen her, too. Still, she put on a bold face and stepped forward to address the council and her mother. I noticed her fingers shaking as she held her arms behind her back to steady herself.

"I have made my decision, Mother. I will join my friends on their quest and aid them as a symbol of peace from Kevay," Valerie stated solemnly. Then the mischievous gleam returned to her eyes. "I promise not to be a party foul or lead them to their deaths like the sirens in the old stories."

"That would be helpful," Rennan muttered to himself.

Cam subtly nodded in agreement.

Cam then stepped forward to the queen. For the briefest second, Valerie grinned widely, before she controlled herself. Her expression quickly became neutral again. Cam took no notice of her (though, I suspected he did indeed see the expressions princess was making) and shifted his attention back to Queen Coral.

"Forgive me, Your Highnesses, but is it truly necessary for the princess to come with us? The path we're taking is dangerous and no place for those who cannot fight—no offense to Valerie, of course. My point is: I do not desire taking any risks if they are unnecessary," Cam pointed out. His voice was steady, but his eyes remained uncertain. He was withholding something from us to keep us safe.

"I understand your concern, Lord Cameron, but Princess Valerie's presence is a necessary risk. You will have to teach her to fight along with the two others who require the same training. However, you will need her if you ever stray into a town. A noble with current standing will be of use in your ranks," Coral stated firmly. "My lord, you of all people know the risks and challenges you will face. Only you can make the right decision when the time comes."

Cam's expression looked like he wanted to argue and he even opened his mouth to begin the protest against the queen (I told him later on that it would have been a risky move since she was already doing so much to help us), but no words came.

He slowly closed his mouth and bowed deeply. "As you wish."

"Friends, it is now time for you all to depart. I wish I could be of more help to you, but know that you can return here any time you need to," Coral stated. "Be safe. Take anything you may need to succeed for your quest."

The five of us bowed to the queen and her officials and then exited the throne room. The massive doors closed behind us as soon as we were out of the doorway. Before we could say anything to each other, Rennan and Valerie ran in separate directions. I could only guess that they were going to grab their things so we could set out. That, of course, left me with the Woods twins.

Once Valerie and Rennan were out of earshot, Cam reeled on his brother. Neither one of them looked happy in the least. Carter looked nervous for what was about to happen. Cam must have seriously terrified his brother that first night in order for Carter to be this frightened. Cam himself looked more ticked off than anything.

"WHY are you coming with us? You know you aren't welcome!" Cam spat angrily.

Ouch. He was harsher than I thought he'd be.

Carter flinched, but that was the natural reaction of anybody who had just been told by their sibling that they weren't welcome.

Carter's shoulders sagged slightly. "I know I'm not, but I don't have anything else to do. You know I can't go home empty-handed, Cam.

Besides, I might have a few things I can offer your little team. Well, in addition to my stunning good looks."

I mentally gagged and Cam's right eye twitched. Sometimes, I couldn't believe how annoying this younger elf could be. Cam had to be thinking the same thing. It must have been hard growing up in the same palace as Carter for more reasons than one. He was not an easy person to get along with, and he was so spoiled that listening to all of his little complaints about daily occurrences were hard.

"Fine, you can stay with us, but *I'm* in charge. Not you. You are not allowed to question my leadership or try to do things your way. *Am I understood*?" Cam demanded with an icy glare in his eyes.

Carter nodded his head and then took off down the hallway.

Cam muttered something under his breath and shook his head as we watched his cowardly brother run away. Then he turned to look at me. His gaze was far gentler now.

"You'd better go gather your things so we can leave soon. I want to get to land by sundown," he stated.

"I have everything I need," I answered as I fell into step next to him. All I needed was my cloak and my daggers, which I was already wearing. The picture of me and my family was in my pocket as well. I was ready to leave Sala at a moment's notice. "Do you want my help with any of your things?"

Cam was about to decline my help, but then thought better of it. With a loathe expression, he said, "Fine. I guess you can help. Follow me."

I followed him all the way back to his room. He unlocked his door (at this point, I was wondering exactly how many keys this elf actually had in his pockets) and pushed it open. All the while, he was busy muttering to himself.

I couldn't figure out why until I looked up. Books covered every available service. They were stacked in piles on the floor and opened ones were everywhere. The best thing, however, was the fortress of books in the corner of the room. I smirked when I saw it and Cam blushed.

"I can explain that," he offered quietly.

He began to move slowly as if he were both hoping and dreading that I would want to hear it. Cam was the kind of person who wanted to say so much but couldn't find the words to express it.

"Do tell," I urged as I sat down in one of the plush arm chairs near the fiery hearth.

Cam muttered to himself as he started picking up books he had left scattered all over his floor. He seemed to regret his offer already. I laughed, much to his irritation. He sent me a look that clearly showed how annoyed and amused he was.

"Well, as you can see, I've been doing a lot of reading at night."

"Which explains the dark circles under your eyes."

"Yeah, those."

"Have you gotten enough sleep recently?"

"Yeah."

"Liar."

"Maybe so, but I needed to read all these. It's not like I can carry hundreds of books with me when I'm in exile. I don't have a bottomless satchel," he shrugged casually, but there was a pointed look in my direction. I let the matter slide and gestured for him to continue. "I'm actually really bad about taking all the books back to the library, so I ended up with piles growing everywhere so I decided to make a fort out of them like when…."

His voice drifted off as his shoulders sagged under the weight of memories. Cam seemed to age about ten years, if that was even possible for an elf. Storms of sorrow gathered in his eyes. I also noticed the tips of his pointed ears turning pink. But he wasn't angry—he was sad.

"Like when?" I prodded him.

He didn't answer immediately. Instead, he sunk to his knees and started fingering some of the books he still held in his hands.

"It's nothing," he managed after a while. "I just decided to make a fort so I could go read in there. There's a chair with candles inside, too. I spent hours in there. Anyway, we're here to get my weapons."

My elvish friend changed the subject so quickly that I almost didn't realize what was happening when Rennan burst into the room. That was when the commotion began.

Rennan, who didn't realize how fast he was running, slammed right into Cam and knocked him to the floor. Cam was quick to throw Rennan off, but sent the wolf flying into the fortress of books in the corner. Rennan knocked out the supports and the whole structure came tumbling down on top of him.

"I'm okay!" he announced as he popped his head out of the pile of books.

The elf looked over at him and started laughing. I would have laughed if it hadn't reminded me of the library in Leshee all those years ago…I shuddered at the memory. If either of the guys noticed my expression, they didn't say anything. I wanted to keep it that way.

"That's good," Cam managed to say through his laughter. He stood up to give Rennan a hand in getting out of the pile of books. "What brings you here, my flying friend?"

Rennan grinned broadly, likely quite amused with himself. His smile could have made anyone perk up a bit. "I got all of my stuff ready to go! Val and Carter have, too. I'm sure you can hear the princess singing another one of her beautiful songs from here. But anyway, I was coming to see if you were ready to go yet. I'm so excited to see more of Galerah!!"

"We know you are, Rennan. You've made it quite clear," Cam chuckled as he slipped a couple of daggers into his boots. Then he picked up his scythe and strapped it across his back, along with his bow and quiver of arrows. Lastly, he hung a new weapon at his side: a long, silver dagger with a beautiful scabbard. "I'm nearly ready and Scarlet is prepared to leave any time."

"Okay! I'll let the others know and we'll prepare to set out!" Rennan beamed.

He was about to run out of the room, but Cam caught the collar of the wolf's pale blue jerkin.

Rennan yelped softly and rubbed his throat. "What was that for?"

"Don't leave; I'm not done with you," Cam stated calmly.

Rennan raised an eyebrow, but stayed.

Cam looked between us and sighed. "Look, if I lose it around the other two, just remain calm and please try not to push me any further. I'll try to keep my cool, but even I have a breaking point."

I cocked my head. "Of course, you have a breaking point. We all do. Yours is just much harder to reach than others. We'll try not to do the same thing, won't we? Rennan?"

I sent him a look that said, *efy me if you dare.* He caught the message and quickly nodded. Cam smiled and looked up at us again as Rennan slung his arm over the elf's shoulder.

"Always trust the hybrids to be true to their word," Cam said quietly. Then he pulled away from Rennan and paced towards the window. He gazed out silently. "You know, Angelica and Thorne are still in the stables. What are we going to tell them?"

"Well, I don't think it would be the best thing if we had two massive, winged horses with us when there are already two elves, two hybrids, and a mermaid. We'll be spotted for sure," I answered. I personally thought it would be much better if the horses remained in Sala during our quest.

Cam nodded in agreement, but said nothing. Instead, he looked to Rennan.

"As much as I'd love to have them come with us, Scarlet has a point. We'd be spotted with them. So yeah, it's probably best for them to stay here."

"Then we're in agreement?" Cam asked, eyebrows in a perfect arch. Perfect, just like the rest of his pale face.

Rennan and I nodded our heads.

Cam nodded his as well as he grabbed his satchel. "Okay then. I'm ready to go when you guys are."

"Then let's goooooooo!" Rennan shouted as he began running out of the room again.

"Walk, Rennan!" the elf shouted in warning. Cam rolled his eyes like he knew what was going to happen.

"I'll be...," Rennan's voice drifted off and sure enough, we heard a huge *thud* a few seconds later. "*I'm okay!*"

Cam and I grinned at our excitable friend and raced off to see what trouble he had found himself in this time.

It was nothing more than a few bruises, as we discovered. Rennan had crashed into Carter in the hallway as he had been exiting Cam's room. I nearly died of laughter when I saw the wolf and the younger elf in a heap on the floor. Valerie had raced out to see what all the commotion was and nearly passed out when she saw "poor, sweet Carter" splayed out on the floor. Cam just watched with a very amused smirk. That smirk seemed to be his trademark expression.

However, I noticed that Cam wasn't surprised at what Rennan had done this time. It was like he knew it would happen regardless of the warning he gave. I knew elves with noble blood had amazing powers, so I was honestly starting to wonder if foresight was one of Cam's. Too many things like that had happened since the time I had met him for me to believe otherwise.

I was deep in thought about that subject when I noticed Cam staring at me with his head cocked to one side. He seemed to be studying me like a specimen with secrets that he couldn't wait to discover. Our eyes met and he gave me a knowing look. Though, it wasn't a calm one. A fire burned behind the grey depths that plainly told me to stop questioning his powers.

Fascinating.

We left the palace soon thereafter.

Cam, Rennan, and I had stopped by the stables to say farewell to the horses and explain what we were doing. They were upset that they couldn't serve their king (meaning Cam), but they agreed to stay unless they were needed. After that, we set out from Sala and crossed the bridge with greater speed than I thought we would. Then again, the bridge leading into Mahe was shorter than the one that led to the shores of Palee.

Part of me wondered if I would ever see my homeland again. I wanted to go back and help everyone—to protect everyone. But I knew that I had a place in the ranks of my friends and I had a duty to them. Our quest came first. We needed to restore light and justice to the world. After that, Rennan and I, if he was willing, would travel back to Palee and help rebuild our kingdom. That is, if we survived.

I shook those depressing thoughts out of my mind and focused on the path ahead. I knew my place and I had to keep it. I raised my head to the sky and took a deep breath. I was back in free air, heading toward freedom.

I hoped.

Selfless Sacrifice

As could be expected, we hiked until Rennan hit his threshold and started complaining. He whined that he was hungry (about an hour after we had stopped for lunch), his feet hurt (after hiking for two hours), and the sun was too bright.

However, this time, it was so, *so* much worse.

Valerie was one of those types who liked to point out everything that she passed and what it reminded her of. Carter would engage in conversation with Rennan and Valerie, but it would be filled with comments on Cam's so-called "leadership" and such remarks.

Being the leader of the mission, all these complaints, observations, and remarks were directed toward Cam. He endured it without saying hardly anything. He just kept walking in front of everyone else, not bothering to turn around. If he did, it was rare and brief. He mostly forced the other three work out their differences by themselves.

I myself tried to behave and not start any more fights than were necessary. I already knew Cam was worn thin and it hadn't even been a week since we had left. I didn't want to push him beyond his limits.

Though, that's not to say that I didn't throw in my own sarcastic remarks from time to time. Those were mostly directed toward Carter and Valerie. I spared Rennan from my comments. Valerie and Carter, however, were too dumb to realize the meaning of what had been said to them. I certainly had a *lot* to say to them, too.

The day wore on and it began to grow late. "Late" being about dinner time, according to Rennan's inner clock. I suspected that it was his stomach giving him an excuse for making us stop again (he had already made us stop several times, which caused us to lose time and energy that could have been used for pressing forward).

"Cam. Cam. Cam. Cam. Cam. Cam. *Cam.* CAM!!" Valerie sang as she danced around the elf.

By that point, I was walking beside him and I could clearly see his face. Our fearless leader was *not* amused. Valerie, on the other hand, was grinning ear to ear, if what she had could even be called ears. Hearing fins? I don't know. Something weird. Anyway, she was poking his arms while singing another one of her ridiculous songs.

Finally, Cam couldn't take it anymore. He swatted Valerie away and sidestepped her, nearly knocking me over in the process. He sent an apologetic glance my way.

Then his gaze zeroed in on Valerie. "Gah! What *is* it?!"

The mermaid pouted at the harsh tone Cam had used, but then shook it off in a matter of seconds. Her ever-present smile returned and her curly blue hair bounced as she started dancing again.

She was almost bashful as she said, "I was asking you when we can set up camp or something. I'm so dreadfully exhausted and I was hoping you could help in some, er, small way?"

She batted her eyelashes as if she thought that would win Cameron over.

I don't care how long either one of us had known Cam; she might have known him longer than I, but I knew Cam would not be swayed by some flirty mermaid who was too naïve to grasp the gravity of anything outside of her own, rainbow-filled world.

Cam wasn't soft enough to do anything for just anybody. He weighed out the risks and pondered everything thoroughly before making a decision.

I doubted he would find Valerie's requests worthwhile. I know I wouldn't.

Carter and Rennan stopped walking so they could watch the exchange between Valerie and Cam. With curious eyes, they wondered if the elf would actually be persuaded by this vivacious princess.

Cam's lips curled upwards in a tight smile. To the undiscerning eye, he looked like he was going to grant Valerie's request and do anything she asked. However, as a person who knew how to read emotions, I could see a mischievous, even spiteful, light in his steel eyes. The shadows starting to creep into his features. Thankfully, they retreated seconds later when Cam mustered a half-hearted, bitter laugh.

I half-expected him to say, "Foolish girl! You know not to whom you speak!" and then go all crazy powerful like he had the night Carter had seriously ticked him off. Although, the shadows had been controlling Cam at the time and I still didn't know how much he remembered from that night. I still would have liked to see him scare the living daylights out of this childish princess.

Despite his friendly smile, Cam's voice was lower than usual when he turned to all of us and said, "You know what? We might as well camp here for the night since *some* people" —he glared at his brother and Rennan— "can't seem to find the energy to go on. We're in Mahe. We can continue in the morning."

Rennan cheered and got to work setting up camp. The twins and I pitched in and got everything set up within minutes. Valerie was the only one who didn't help. Stupid girl. She was too spoiled for her own good.

After the tents and everything were set up, Cam sent the crazy people into the nearby woods to search for some firewood. That left only me and

Cam in our small encampment. I didn't know why he hadn't sent me to keep an eye on them. I didn't trust something bad not to happen. However, I had to obey orders when Cam told me to find some fresh water for our camp.

I had gone down to the creek to fetch some of the cool water, which meant I would be gone for a few minutes. When I got back, I found Cam high up in the tree we were camped around. I chuckled to myself, thinking about how much Cam liked trees. Every time he was moody, I would find him in a tree with a stone-like face. This time he was up there fingering something small that he held in his hands.

I sighed and set my buckets at the foot of the gnarled oak the elf had decided to climb. Once again, he was so lost in thought that he still didn't notice me. However, I noticed his intricate dagger still hung at his side, so I knew my chances of being impaled were high if I wasn't careful. The last thing I wanted to do was startle and force him to draw his weapon thinking I was one of the others or worse yet, an enemy.

I climbed up to the higher branches behind Cam so I could try to talk to him. I knew he probably wasn't in a mood for conversation, but hey! It was worth a shot, right? At the very least, it might cheer him up. I swung myself down so I was looking Cam dead in the eyes. He didn't notice me for a minute because his eyes were glued to whatever he was holding.

"Fancy seeing you up here," Cam muttered in an uninterested tone. He didn't look up at me.

I dropped down onto a branch level with the elf's. There was no point in hanging upside down indefinitely. "Why do you say that? I'm the only other person here and you expect me not to follow you when you're up in a tree?"

Cam smiled wryly but didn't look at me. "You set yourself up for disaster. They'll figure it out soon enough."

I looked at him in confusion, not sure what he was talking about. "What disaster? Who will figure it out?"

He waved away my questions. "Bah, don't listen to me. I'm speaking nonsense again. Come on, we should get down from this tree and wait for the others without looking suspicious."

"And how would we not look suspicious?"

"As much as I hate it, small talk."

"About what?"

"I don't know. I just told you I hate it. I'm bad at it 'cause, you know, I've been exiled for years?"

"Okay then."

We jumped down from the tree and landed on the ground. Almost immediately, noises drifted in from around us, but wasn't the voices of our friends. They were deeper echoes and sounded much, much more dangerous. I watched the borders for anything that could possibly be a threat, but saw nothing.

I glanced at Cam and saw that his back was entirely rigid. Whatever I had heard, he had as well. His hand rested on the hilt of his dagger, ready to draw it immediately. There was no need, however, because we were unable to hear the echoing sound a few minutes later. We relaxed and let our hands leave the sides of our daggers.

Soon our friends returned to the camp with firewood. Since Carter and Valerie (being so inexperienced) didn't know how to light a fire or anything like that, Rennan decided that he would be the one to teach them.

It was funny, really, watching Rennan, the complete klutz, trying to teach palace children an essential tool to survive in the wild. They watched the wolf in fascination and Rennan seemed to enjoy the attention. That made one of us. Cam and I just sat back and watched the three of them look absolutely ridiculous as they tried to get sparks to kindle by grating the bluntest of rocks together. Amateurs.

We ate a dinner of wild deer a little while later since Cam had managed to catch one within an hour. This time, there was no major crisis of a dead, rabid wolf. Rennan referenced that to the amusement of Cam, and I enjoyed seeing Carter so confused. I admit, seeing Carter being clueless and not so arrogant was the high point of my day.

"So. We've got a few hours before we should get some sleep," Rennan stated.

All eyes turned to him. Surprisingly, it included the pink eyes of the princess, who rarely gave Rennan a second look. I'm sorry to say Rennan noticed.

"Is anyone actually tired enough to sleep?" he asked.

None of us were.

"What's your point, Rennan?" I questioned. "Surely you don't want to continue west, do you?"

"Of course not! Don't be absurd, Scarlet!" Rennan replied, quite loudly might I add, with a shocked expression on his face. He acted like he couldn't believe I would suggest such a thing to him. "I was thinking we could find some way to entertain ourselves."

"What were you thinking?" Carter asked, a hungry look gleaming in his eyes.

The difference in emotion shown in the eyes of the two brothers never ceased to amaze me. Cam's grey eyes sparkled with compassion, knowledge, and fury for those he deemed worthy to fight; Carter's steel eyes were generally full of bitterness, lust, and arrogance. It seemed so hard to imagine that they were twins, much less that there could have been a time where they didn't want to kill each other.

Rennan smiled as he suggested, "Maybe…something for us men to prove our worth?"

To the ones we fancy, I mentally added.

Rennan needed to work on being subtle. He was really, really bad at it. Luckily for him, Valerie was too distractible to pick up on the double meaning of many of the wolf's comments.

Cam smirked at the idea. "I hope you weren't thinking a test of arms. I'd overpower both of you without even trying."

I thought he sounded somewhat prideful like his brother with that bold statement, but I knew what he meant.

Rennan thought for a couple of minutes before he snapped his fingers. He had evidently come up with some sort of great idea that would supposedly solve the problem.

For once, Valerie and I shared a look agreeing that this idea of his was one that we would certainly laugh at without shame. The mermaid and I never agree on anything, so that was saying something.

"Speak, wolf," I urged.

The wolf pretended not to hear me.

"You said 'test of arms,'" Rennan began, grin starting to spread.

"Yeah, so?" Cam questioned, a hesitant expression on his face.

"What if it wasn't a test of arms, like weapons, but a test of *arms*?" he asked with a foolish looking grin.

I rolled my eyes but smiled. Rennan certainly had an interesting interpretation of things. It was refreshing at times to have his ridiculousness break our tense mood. Rennan never failed to amuse us…or at least Cam.

"I'm game if you are," Carter agreed.

Rennan smiled and he and Carter looked toward Cam, who was sitting under the tree, far away from the fire. Natural shadows covered him like blankets so I couldn't see if any of his inner shadows were at work. I found myself strangely wanting to prevent those shadows from ever terrorizing my friend again.

"Why not? We have nothing better to do," Cam sighed as he got up.

He tried to sound uninterested in Rennan's whole proposition to pass the time, but even in the dim firelight I could see a glimmer of amusement and even faint expectation of something in his eyes. He moved closer to the fire and sat down opposite of me. His eyes were glued to the flames. They grew wide before he shook his head to snap himself out of whatever trance he had fallen into.

He raised his head to meet eyes with Carter and Rennan. "So, who goes first?"

"If he's willing, Carter and I will," Rennan offered.

I stifled a laugh when I saw how desperately hopeful the offer was. Rennan wanted to prove to Valerie that he was worthy of her affection. I doubt she would even pay attention to him. If Rennan won, she would only be concerned about seeing if "poor, sweet Carter" was alright. Still, it was a brave move for Rennan to be willing to risk his ego.

"Might as well. I'm pretty sure I'll win anyway," Carter agreed with an overly confident smile that exposed many of his shining white teeth.

Cam made his gag quite obvious. Carter simply ignored his brother.

Rennan smiled as they settled themselves into good positions. Conveniently, there was a large rock in the middle of our campsite that was fairly even on the top.

Cam watched from the shadows while Valerie and I stood closer so we could see everything a little bit better. I was supposed to be their referee just to make sure neither one of them cheated. Well, to make sure Carter wouldn't cheat. Rennan was too desperate for mermaid attention to even try. He'd want to win fairly.

"Ready?" I asked when they were in position.

"Yep," they answered in unison.

"Begin!"

Rennan and Carter's faces contorted with strain almost immediately. I was good at guessing how different things would go down, but I couldn't see any hint as to who might win this match of arm wrestling. Rennan had a thin, sort of lanky frame, but Carter was a palace boy who didn't really know how to do anything. They were pretty evenly matched for two people who weren't the fighting or wrestling types.

Valerie was cheering for Carter during the whole thing. Needless to say, she did a lot of dancing as well. I don't know where she found the flowers, but somehow, she had gotten her hands on beautiful lilies that didn't deserve to be plucked and tossed in the air. I ignored her as usual.

Cam, on the other hand, watched in anticipation. Under normal circumstances, or with people who weren't occasionally controlled by shadows, this would have been a common sight. However, the description of "normal" was not accurate for Cam. As he watched the match, his eyes were glowing. Not only from excitement, but literally *glowing*. There were no shadows in his features to be seen, but those glowing grey eyes alarmed me greatly.

I took it upon myself to unsuspiciously go over there and see what the heck was going through the elf's head to make his eyes glow. The only way that I figured I could get close enough without distracting Rennan and Carter (well, Rennan. I didn't care if I distracted Carter) or getting hit in the face by Valerie's swinging arms was to slowly circle around them. And I did exactly that until I was standing right beside Cam.

"Your eyes are glowing," I stated plainly.

I found no point in trying to be subtle. Those eyes of his were seriously freaking me out, and that's saying a lot. They looked like some sort of sea creature or swamp monster with stormy grey eyes that shone out like lamps in the darkness.

"I don't know what you're talking about," Cam replied, not looking at me. His voice sounded strange, almost distant as he spoke. It didn't have the same thick accent it usually had, either.

I pursed my lips. "Yes, Cameron, you do. Snap out of it."

"I told you, I don't know what you're talking about," Cam snarled. He clasped his hands to the sides of his hands.

His shoulders shuddered with some sort of foreign power. I took a small step back, scared to find out what would happen next. This wasn't the Cam I knew and I didn't like it. It was more like something, or some*one*, else fought for control of my friend.

"YES!!" Rennan shouted as he threw his hands up in the air.

I jerked my head to look in his direction, which momentarily distracted me from the glowy-eyed Cam. Carter was sulking, Valerie stood stone-still, and Rennan was the one dancing for once. I almost couldn't believe my eyes: Rennan had won against Carter.

"I can't believe you won," Carter said incredulously. His eyes were wide with shock and a hint of disgust.

Part of me was glad to see him like that because he deserved it. Same with seeing Valerie so heartbroken that her precious Carter had lost. And then there was the other part of me that was sorry to see them so down. My softer side disgusted me.

"That was a good match! Nice job!" Rennan said cheerfully as he held out his hand for Carter to shake.

The elf looked at him as if thinking, *Is this guy serious?* Then he reluctantly shook the wolf's hand and moved so he could switch places with Cam. All the while, Carter's face was sullen and gloomy. He was obviously disappointed with how his match had finished.

Rennan turned to Cam. "Are you ready?"

"I might as well be," Cam replied as he got up from the log.

His eyes now ceased to glow, and I was starting to think I was the only one who had seen it. If anyone else did, they didn't mention it. He got into position with Rennan and began the match before I told them counted them off.

The strain on Rennan's face was obvious. Cam posed far more of a challenge than Carter had. Rennan was struggling to keep his arm upright. I couldn't see any chance for him to be able to keep his arm up, much less push Cam's down.

It was like there was some other kind of strength that was controlling the elf's arm in this match. However, there were no shadows to be seen, nor were his eyes glowing anymore. Cam was doing all of this using his own brute strength. I was terrified by the implications, but also impressed.

All of a sudden, the sky grew dark with furious clouds blocking out the setting sun. Thunder pealed through the valley. Lightning crackled through the sky and zapped various spots on the ground that were a long way off, but were still too close for comfort.

Rennan yelped when Cam forcefully slammed down their arms, thereby winning the match. But that didn't matter anymore.

Cam and I had already drawn our weapons and were ready to face any threat that came our way. Carter nervously drew the sword he had brought from Sala. Valerie just stood frozen in fear. She screamed when a massive gust of wind blew out our fire as easily as a candle.

The hair on everyone's necks stood on end when some feral beast roared from the woods to our left. It wasn't a wolf, but something much, much bigger.

"What was that?!" Rennan shouted above the roaring wind.

"I don't know, but I don't want it to find us first!" Cam yelled back as he sheathed his dagger and pulled out his bow instead. He carefully nocked an arrow before creeping forward. "Rennan, come with me. Scarlet, stay back with Carter and Valerie and guard the camp."

Rennan and I nodded. The elf and wolf crept out into the woods (I hoped they wouldn't be struck with one of those highly charged blasts) and I turned back to the heart of camp.

"Where are they going?" Carter demanded.

He tried to sound tough (I don't know if it was to impress me or to get Valerie off of him), but any noise made him jump skyward. Plus, it didn't help that Valerie was freaking out and refusing to give him a moment's rest. I doubted she would let go any time soon.

"They're trying to find out what made that sound," I responded bluntly. "Valerie."

She looked out from behind Carter's shoulder. Her eyes were slightly purple (I guess that's what mermaids looked like when they cried?) and tears were running down her cheeks. Her perfect face was contorted with panic.

She sniffled. "Hmm?"

I pulled out a smaller dagger and handed it to her. I didn't like the mermaid, but she needed to have something to defend herself with if she ever faced the need. She didn't deserve to die just because she was attacked and unprepared.

"Take this. If something attacks us, you may need it," I stated as I handed her the small blade.

Her pink eyes widened with greater fear (she must not have ever held a weapon), but she nodded anyway as she gripped the dagger like her life depended on it. I nodded to attempt to reassure her. Even with all my skills, I didn't know if I had the ability to defend three people.

"What's the plan?" Carter asked. His knuckles were white from gripping the handle of his sword so hard.

I was about to answer, but a large *crack* split the air around us. Some sort of large animal bounded out of the brush.

"Hit the dirt!" I yelled as I forced both of them onto their knees.

I rolled on the ground twice before I was able to rise to my feet and face the beast. What I saw took my breath away: in front of me stood a dragon. The magnificent beasts were thought to have been wiped out hundreds of years ago, and yet here one was, ready to kill all three of us with one swift stroke of its jagged claws.

It was beautiful, in a terrifying sense. It primarily had pitch black scales with green scales scattered all over its head and massive wings that were folded against its back. Eerie yellow eyes glared down at us and promised death if we made any move. I held my breath as I watched the majestic beast heat up its throat that would surely produce flame to roast us.

The dragon began to open its mouth. Small flames rushed out and flew into the air. Valerie shrieked, which caused the dragon to focus its beady eyes on her. It regarded her carefully, no doubt sizing up a perfect snack. It reminded me of a dwarf's eyes lighting up when they saw roasted mutton on a feast night. The gigantic, fire breathing form pushed itself to where it could almost snap up the mermaid in one huge bite. Once again, Valerie shrieked and started running around our clearing. The black dragon chased after her, destroying over half the camp in the process.

"We have to get that thing away from her!" Carter hissed to me.

I glanced at the dragon, hoping it didn't hear us. Fortunately, it was too busy trying to catch Valerie as a pre-dinner snack, so that wasn't an issue. I turned back to Carter, whose eyes were filled with terror.

"Yeah, but I have no idea how we're going to kill it," I muttered, keeping an eye on the dragon. "The only thing I can think of doing that would make any difference would be to distract it."

It kept itself guarded, which made it really hard to plan an attack that would do serious damage. Not to mention the thick, fire proof scales that all dragons had.

"You want us to *distract* a beast that can *breathe fire*?! We don't even stand a chance against that thing! Are you crazy, hybrid?!" Carter practically shrieked as he ran a shaky hand over his face.

"It's your choice, elfling: die a cowardly death or die trying to save a friend," I hissed threateningly, jerking him down to where I could speak directly into his ear.

He cowered at my firm grasp on his shoulder. He reluctantly agreed. "Fine. We distract that thing."

I let go of his shoulder and drew the second dagger I kept in my tall boot. I would need all the weapons I could get if I was going to distract this beast. I slunk close enough to where I could jump on top of the brute.

Valerie kept shrieking and running, so the dragon kept bounding after her. Its expression vaguely reminded me of domesticated dogs that would run around chasing their owner and begging for treats. However, this dragon was much wilder than that. Its primary instinct was to kill anything it considered good eating. In other words, Valerie.

Would you just stop moving for one second so I could get a grip on you? I thought to myself.

It would be so much easier if I wasn't riding this thing like a bucking horse I. Slowly, I managed to climb close enough to slice the base of both wings. Even if my blade hadn't penetrated very deeply, the dragon roared in agony and threw me off its back.

Valerie fled into the trees and I hit the ground with a hard thud. The fall knocked the breath out of me, but I didn't have the luxury of staying there for long. Furthermore, I had no idea to where Carter had disappeared.

I had no time to wonder. Seconds later, battle cries grew louder. I immediately recognized the higher pitch of Rennan's shouts and the elvish (though, I didn't understand it) that Cam always muttered when he was angry. Rennan flew out of the trees and immediately stabbed the dragon somewhere in the webbing between its toes. It roared in agony. Cam hurried to my side and helped me up before rushing into the battle with the dragon.

He effortlessly swung himself up to its back and began his assault. Out of nowhere, a shining rope appeared and Cam swung it around the mouth of the dragon. When Cam tightened the rope, the dragon shook like a muzzled animal and spread its wings. Cam held his ground as the dragon prepared to launch into the air. Three wing beats and they were twenty feet off the ground.

"Cam!" I shouted up at him.

Either he didn't hear me or he chose to ignore me. Whatever the case, he had just gotten himself into serious danger. The dragon was thrashing through the sky and refused to let up trying to free itself from the magical bonds. Cam almost fell off several times, but he managed to keep his grip on to the rope restraining the dragon's mouth.

To my horror, the dragon set itself completely on fire. Valerie (who had run out into the clearing when the dragon became airborne) and I yelled at him to jump off and try to land safely or something, but Cam would do no such thing.

He held on to the dragon and was able to draw his scythe. Another wall of flames surrounding the worm prevented me from seeing Cam's movements. One last eardrum-shattering roar blasted through the air. Then, the fireball went out and they fell straight out of the sky.

The trees beyond the clearing were splintered into smoldering toothpicks seconds later. The four of us sent each other looks of panic before we sprinted into the forest to try to find the bodies. As we ran, my heart leapt into my throat. I tried to suppress the hated fear that Cam would be dead when we found him. He had saved us all from the beast. There was no way he could just die.

We found the smoking body of the dragon. It had snapped several sturdy trees in half and had brought down even more branches from neighboring foliage. Even with all the soft vegetation, it wouldn't have been a soft enough landing pad for Cam to live. He would have been skewered by one of those things if he landed even slightly wrong.

"Does anybody see any sign of Cam?" Valerie asked in a shaky voice.

I didn't know if she was more traumatized from that blasted dragon chasing her or being faced with the idea that Cam may or may not be dead. I was kind of struggling with the same thing, to be honest. I was more shaken because Cam had selflessly sacrificed himself in that fight with the dragon.

"Nothing," Rennan answered from the other side of the wreckage.

His face was ashen as he sifted through the thick branches. I noticed that he was shaking just as much as Carter was. Carter was searching through the wreckage as well, but I figured it was more for his selfish reasons rather than trying to see if his brother was still alive. He was probably looking for the signet ring so he could return to his old life in Heviah where everything was all happy and perfect.

The massive corpse moved slightly. I caught Rennan's eye and we rushed toward the corpse. Silver blood soaked the branches, so I knew without a shadow of a doubt that the dragon was definitely dead. It appeared that Cam was even more deadly with his scythe on senseless beasts than he was with his bow.

The wolf and I struggled to move the carcass, but after several strenuous minutes we finally managed to move it off the immense pile of firewood.

Where the dragon had lain only a few minutes earlier lay the limp form of Cameron Woods. His eyes were closed and he looked as white as a sheet. I couldn't see any burns or anywhere his bones could have been broken. The only injury I could see was his broken nose, which had to have been inflicted when he was crushed by the body. Beyond that, Cam looked almost normal when Rennan and I picked him up to get him off the branches.

"Is he breathing?" Rennan asked as he felt for the elf's pulse.

"I don't know," I answered. I put my head down to his chest so I could try to feel any sort of movement. I heard his faint heart beat and, after an eternity of waiting, a shallow breath. "He's barely hanging on."

"Sit him up," Rennan ordered firmly.

We hastily propped Cam up into a sitting position and gingerly moved him to where he was sitting up against one of the colossal oak trees just like the one we had been sitting in only an hour earlier. So much had happened since that short conversation....

"How long do you think he has?" I whispered to the wolf. I didn't want Carter and Valerie to hear me. Even knowing that he was holding on to his life, I wasn't really optimistic. I didn't know how much longer he was going to keep breathing.

Rennan sent me a sidelong glance. Worry flickered in his pale blue eyes as he inspected Cam. Rennan put his hand on Cam's forehead, and quickly pulled it away. "He's burning up."

"Fever?"

"Yeah. A really, really bad one."

"Is everything okay?" Valerie asked softly.

Rennan sent me a worried glance. I could tell that he didn't want to break the news to them, even though we knew Carter probably wouldn't care very much if his brother was dead.

"Uh…about that…," Rennan began. He chewed his lip before opening his mouth again.

"Well, I must sincerely thank you for killing that dragon for me," an educated, slightly sarcastic sounding voice said from behind us.

We whipped around to see a tall man standing against one of the giant oaks. He had copper colored hair and purplish-blue eyes. He wore a long, dark blue cloak that hung down to the tops of his heavy black boots. At one point, his clothes might have been brighter colors, but now they were muted from several coatings of dirt that hinted at extended use.

"Who are you?" I demanded as I pointed one of my daggers at the newcomer.

Rennan grabbed my wrist as a warning, but I didn't listen to him. I was too angry about losing Cam to bother showing any mercy to any potential threat.

The strange man smirked. "I'm not a threat, if that's what you're thinking. I've been following that dragon for days because I needed to collect some of its blood."

"Why would you need some of the dragon's blood?" Carter asked with a confused expression.

The man looked at the elf as if he thought the answer was the most obvious thing in the entire world. The look he gave Carter was pretty epic, so he gained a little of my respect.

"Dragon's blood serves as a base for many spells and is an excellent poison," the man answered. His eyes locked on Cam's nearly lifeless form and cocked his head. "Hmm. It doesn't usually act so fast on an immortal being."

"What do you mean? What is your name? Speak!" I demanded again.

The man took no notice of me and instead strode toward Cam and kneeled down next to him. The stranger curiously inspected Cam's limp form as if he were a perfect specimen.

"Excuse me, where are my manners? My name is Andrew Ca-er. Cardell. Yeah. Drew Cardell. I'm a sorcerer and currently the only person who knows how to save your friend from dragon blood poisoning," the man named Drew stated. His name and introduction were sort of sketchy, but I decided to let it pass because I was far more concerned with keeping Cam alive than to pick meaningless fights.

"Cam is *poisoned*?" Valerie squeaked and promptly fainted into Carter's arms.

Carter just rolled his eyes and set her gently on the ground. No matter. He would still be the one to carry the mermaid back to camp when the time came.

"I'm afraid so. It's a rare thing to be poisoned by dragon blood, mostly because dragons themselves are so rare no matter what realm—er, kingdom you're in," Drew stated as he pulled something out of the small pouch that hung from his belt. "Since I know you'll ask, my lady, this is a balm that should help slow the poison. I believe the name is *akele.*"

"Will that stop the poison completely?" Rennan asked curiously.

I would have said something as well, but I was far too stunned to be called "my lady." I mean, he was a complete stranger! I think that was mostly because, being a hybrid and all, we aren't usually spoken to with titles of respect.

"Sadly, it will not, but I know someone who can help," Drew stated with a gloomy voice. He caught himself when he realized what he had said. "That is, if you're willing to accept the help of someone you just met and probably don't trust. Oh, don't look so surprised. I see it written quite plainly on all of your faces. None of you trust me."

"Forgive us, but no. We don't," I replied rather bluntly.

Rennan sighed and pulled me aside. I glared up at him. His pale blue eyes were downright icy as he gave me a look that clearly meant, *Shut up.*

"What is it?" I demanded with a slight scowl.

"I know you don't trust him, but Drew might be the best chance we have of saving Cam," Rennan stated quietly.

The hope in his eyes was evident and it almost made me want to do whatever the wolf said just so I didn't have to face any wrath that could unexpectedly come from this surprising hybrid.

He continued. "Like it or not, we need his help. What's more important to you: not trusting someone and letting your friend die or trusting someone who might be able to save our friend? Remember: Cameron is my friend, too. I want to see him alive as much as you."

"I guess you're right, but—"

"There are no 'buts,' I am right."

"Fine. You're right and I'm wrong. We'll trust Drew to help Cam and hopefully continue this quest soon."

"Believe me, if Cam holds on, he'll be back to making us hike pretty dang soon. Sometimes I think he makes us keep pushing on just to hear me complain."

"Oh, he doesn't do it to make you complain. You do that enough anyway and it drives him crazy," I replied with a smirk genuine enough to make a smile crawl across Rennan's lips.

"Do we have a deal then?"

"Yeah, I guess."

Rennan and I turned back to Drew, who was still kneeling beside Cam. The elf had managed to get much paler than even a few minutes before. We were losing him at an alarming rate.

"I hope you've come to a decision, 'cause this guy isn't going to hold on forever," Drew informed us with a gesture in Cam's direction.

I bit my lip. I hated seeing Cam this helpless. He was one of the strongest people I had ever had the pleasure to meet. It was too early for me to say good-bye to him for good.

"Take us to your friend. We need this guy alive," I responded.

Drew nodded his head and began to return all of his little objects to his pouch while Rennan, Carter, and I hustled to pick up our camp. The setting sun was beginning to lengthen the shadows as we packed up. We only took what we needed most because we had to carry Cam.

We met back in the new clearing a few minutes later.

Valerie had woken up and was now nervously watching Drew bandage some of Cam's small wounds that Rennan and I had missed. We handed the mermaid a pack and for once, she took it and didn't try giving it to Carter or complain. She kept it for herself, and I appreciated the fact that she was willing to pitch in and help the rest of the team in dire moments like this.

I looked down at Cam's nearly lifeless face—barely any color remained. I feared we would lose him before reaching help. I put my hand on his forehead and realized what Rennan had meant. Cam *was* burning up, and all because of that blasted dragon that Drew had wanted blood from. I just prayed that Cam would keep fighting the poison and hold out long enough for us to help him.

Just hang in there, Cam, I thought, *just hang in there.*

Arguments and Arrests

"So. You're sure you're not leading us straight into a death trap?" Rennan asked for the fourth time.

Sometimes, I don't understand him. Personally, I didn't think it made much sense to ask if something was a death trap after following a person we didn't trust for several miles. Wouldn't that be something to ask beforehand? Just a thought....

"Yes, you are perfectly safe with me. I assure you I am not leading any of you to your deaths. I am more eager to help your friend come *away* from the doorstep of Death," the strange man ("Drew" he called himself) said in a firm tone. He seemed to be relatively good at speaking with people, but he wasn't relaxed around them.

I couldn't help but steal a glance at Cameron. He was sprawled over the back of the horse Drew had with him. His face was ashen and his forehead was beaded with sweat. Without thinking, I pulled a small cloth from my satchel and wiped his brow with it.

The elf seemed to sense my touch because he made the slightest movement as if protesting against me. I almost laughed because I could totally imagine him doing that if he was conscious, but I didn't have the heart. I was more worried he wouldn't wake from his poison-induced slumber.

Carter caught my eye and raised an eyebrow. I ignored him and went back to dealing with Cam. His breaths were becoming shallower as we trudged on and it greatly concerned me. In the back of my mind, I was sure he'd die before we reached our final destination—wherever that was. It might have been pessimistic, but it's how I operated. I had no intention of getting my hopes up just to have them crushed. No thank you.

“Where are we going, anyway?” I questioned, eager to know the time frame we were working with.

Drew turned his head slightly so he could look at me through the corner of his eye. It was kind of creepy, but then again, I knew I had a similar effect on people when I did the same thing.

“We’re going to try to reach a small village with a medic who can help us,” he replied as he turned his attention forward again.

Very helpful. That told me only what we had already gone over several times, thanks to Rennan’s constant questions. It might have been the wolf's attempt to get Drew to converse, but it was kind of…lacking.

“Okay then,” I sighed. “While we’re walking, why don’t you tell us about yourself so we might be able to trust you? You seem smart. Surely you know none of us hold you in high regard.”

Drew sighed. “True, but none of you are very open to talking either.”

Blood rushed to my face in irritation. “Well, I’m sorry that we’re concerned for our friend and want to make sure he lives!”

“Some of you are worried,” I heard Carter mutter under his breath. I turned on him and glared at him threateningly.

“What was that?” I hissed, daring him to speak again.

He recoiled. “Nothing.”

“I thought so.”

“Okay, I get it. I’m being insensitive,” Drew said quietly.

He looked away, but I could have sworn that a tear was trickling down his face. I hated myself for feeling sympathetic, but I couldn’t help it. I did feel kind of bad for the guy, but I couldn’t get over my resentment for his insensitivity to the rest of us.

He dismally asked, "What would you like to know?"

"I don't know. Exactly where we're going, who you are, your back story, why the heck we should trust you in the first place. You know, just normal stuff people would ask when they meet a strange man wanting the poisonous blood of a dragon for his collection or whatever!" I answered somewhat angrily.

I was too infuriated to care about being polite or minding my manners in that moment. Rennan sent me another warning look, but I ignored him.

"Fine. I'd love to try to make it to Hila, but I highly doubt that's going to happen, seeing the condition of the elf," Drew said, casting a glance in the direction of Cam. He had a point and I hated it. "Instead, we're going to have to stop at the first small village we come across. Hopefully somebody will be able to help us there."

"Just anybody? What if there are no doctors?" Rennan inquired with a shocked expression on his face.

His mind didn't seem to like the thought of staying in an uncivilized town that might be the death site of our friend any more than mine.

Drew laughed humorlessly. "That brings us to another one of the lady's many questions: we're in Mahe. Several of the townsfolk are wizards with excellent skills in medicine. I am a sorcerer, but a young one. I don't know the full capabilities of healing magic, but I'm learning. I do not want to risk my skills on your friend because you seem to be very defensive of him. I'd rather not be the recipient of your blame if he perishes."

It's understandable if you don't trust me now—or ever, really," Drew shrugged. "If I were in your place, I would probably be of the same mind. Only…for other reasons. There. You have your answers. Now, can I ask for your names? None of you told me."

"Since no one else is volunteering the information, I suppose I'll start," Rennan offered. "My name is Rennan Penbrooke of the grey wolves. I lived in the northern Kingdom of Palee until recently."

He didn't go into details of what had happened, which I thanked him for. I felt like talking about it would be ripping some sort of plaster off my bare skin. In other words, it was too painful (I speak from experience with the plaster thing. Sometimes my dear grandmother let me do too many things by myself). Drew didn't ask for any further explanation, either.

Instead, he turned to Carter and Valerie. "Sir elf, what is your name and story?"

Carter cleared his throat and mustered a smile. I knew he wanted his brother dead for his own selfish reasons. He must not have thought his job would be so easy (coward). "Prince Carter Woods of Heviah, son of King Tristan Woods. I was staying in Sala as a guest of Queen Coral when these four decided to go on a quest and drag me along with them."

Valerie tried to protest. "Hey! That's not—"

Carter elbowed her in the side and gave her a look that clearly communicated, *Shut up*.

I wondered if Cam would allow me to punch his brother in the face again even if he was currently dying from poison. Gosh. I should not have let my mind go there.

"And your name, maiden?" Drew asked quickly to distract Valerie and Carter. He seemed to pick up on the tension that was spreading through the air, but he didn't point anything out. It was a wise move on his part as it also prevented Carter from getting punched in the face again.

"I'm Princess Valerie of Sala, daughter of the great Queen Coral herself. I come in peace!" she smiled despite the nasty look Carter had given her mere seconds ago.

I had to hand it to her; Valerie could shake off negativity quickly. That was probably a skill I would never have the patience to learn.

"It's lovely to meet you all; truly it is. I've never met such an interesting bunch of people," Drew stated politely. He had nice manners for someone who wanted dragon's blood as poison. Eventually, he turned back to me. "Now, I still do not know the names of you and your, er, dying comrade."

Rennan snorted and I immediately sent him an exasperated look. He laughed. "I'm sorry; this probably isn't the time, but *comrade*. I just thought, 'what if it was *Camrade* instead?' Wouldn't that be hilarious? Sorry."

"You're right about the timing, but that's a really good one, Rennan. When he wakes up—if he ever wakes up—you'll have to tell him that," I commented with a breaking voice.

I tried to keep it together for the sake of myself and Rennan, but I found it difficult when I was making contact with his truly genuine eyes. Then I took a deep breath, determined to make Cam proud for his introduction (of sorts).

As boldly as I could manage, I said, "My name is Scarlet Sutton of the common foxes of central Palee. Like Rennan, I lived there until only recently when this elf found us." —I gestured to Cam's limp form— "He is Prince Cameron Woods, the heir to the elvish throne of Heviah."

Drew raised his eyebrows, but didn't argue the fact that Cam was the heir to the Hevian throne. He didn't even seem surprised by two hybrids traveling in the company of elves. Usually, such a thing was unheard of and, depending whose view it was, impossible.

I thought it was strange, really, since all Maheans knew of the difficult relationship (if there was enough interaction between the two species to call it that) between elves and hybrids. After all, they served as the original historians of Galerah. Either Drew was oblivious, he chose not to bring it up, or he opposed the conflict just as much as the hybrids did.

"It's an honor that so noble a people would trust me to provide aid to them," Drew stated with a slight bow.

Carter smiled rather smugly. "The honor is—"

Drew scowled at him and it quickly shut the elf up. He closed his mouth and stepped back a little bit to get out of the sorcerer's range.

"With all due respect, your majesty, I wasn't talking to you," Drew informed him rather solemnly. He turned away from Carter and instead looked between Rennan and I with admiration in his eyes. "I've always had a great respect for the hybrids—a species able to master both worlds of man and animal. A perfect mix, if you ask me. It's an honor to be in your company. You both serve a noble cause."

I searched the depths of the sorcerer's purplish-blue eyes for truth. They sparkled neither completely purple nor blue, or even a periwinkle color. They were a color all their own with power and magic shining through them. In them, I discovered Drew's intent entirely matched what he said. There was no malice behind his polite words.

"I'm gonna be honest, I don't know what to say to that but 'thanks!'" Rennan admitted with a laugh.

That's one thing I liked about Rennan: he was good at keeping the mood light. I had a feeling he was trying to do that for my sake. I appreciated it, really, I did, but I couldn't keep my mind from wandering back to Cam.

His condition continued to deteriorate. His temperature constantly fluctuated between being ice cold like a corpse and the fiery fever he had been fighting. There was no color left in his face and for some reason, his hair was slowly turning grey. I didn't see how dragon blood could cause such a thing, but I didn't like it and had no interest in trying to understand the science behind it.

Drew caught my eye. He smiled sympathetically. "Don't worry, Miss Scarlet. We'll get him back on his feet in no time. There's no reason to worry."

He was trying to be comforting and reassuring, but I still found myself worrying. I had no idea if he would die before we reached Hila, or even a small town like Drew had talked about. I just didn't know. I didn't really feel like finding out, but just going at a snail's pace like we weren't even trying to save him. If I didn't try and he died, I would never forgive myself.

"How much longer until we reach a town?" I asked in a dismal tone.

The smile on Rennan's face fell and Valerie looked towards the ground; Carter looked unfazed and Drew looked at me somewhat curiously. If Cam were conscious, I had a feeling that he would be giving me a look saying, *What in the world were you thinking to get everyone's eyes on you?*

"Not too much longer if we're lucky," Drew answered as he began searching the horizon for any sort of civilization we could seek help from for the night.

"I know you haven't known us for that long," Rennan said, "but you should know that luck does not generally run in our favor."

"Good to know," the magic-wielder commented.

Seriously! The guy was decent enough, sure, but there was something strange about Drew that made him different than other people in Galerah. For some reason, though, I found myself less curious about Drew's past and back story than Cam's...and that thought made my heart ache for my friend all over again.

After another hour of hiking (and in my case, constantly checking to see if Cam was breathing), we finally saw buildings on the horizon. They were still a long way off, but they gave me some hope that we would be able to make it and find help. If I had been on my own, I would have run to the gates and begged to be let in. I cared more about my friend than my own sore feet.

Unfortunately, the moment we saw those rooftops was also the moment we saw trouble. And not normal trouble like when you can't find your shoe or something, but rather life-threatening trouble. I didn't think that boded well since our most valuable fighter was incredibly sick, two of us didn't know how to fight, Drew's fighting skills were unknown, and Rennan barely knew the basics. I would be the sole protector until we were (hopefully) able to get Cam back on his feet.

Anyway, tonight's trouble was in the form of hunting birds soaring through the night sky bearing riders who held some pretty fierce looking torches. Even from a distance, I could tell they also carried some sort of weapon that could fire projectiles. But, get this, those hunting birds and their riders weren't the only things out in the valley! There were also ground patrols on wolves that looked ready to tear anything they caught apart limb from limb!

Rennan whimpered when he saw the ground patrols and their wolves. The last incident with a giant wolf had to have come to mind. It came to mine. I just hoped that we would be able to go in for the kill without Rennan getting mad at us for slaying his brethren this time.

I digress. We managed to make it into the cover of a thick grove of trees that was able to hide five people, a horse, and an unconscious elf. Thankfully, the darkness helped out. Enemies would have to be right on us to see through our cover. No one spoke a word until we were sure we were completely hidden from unwanted eyes.

"So...what are we supposed to do now?" Carter asked.

"Well, we have the village we needed to find. We just have to cross the valley to get to it," I replied, "Only, you know, without getting killed in the process. I happen to like living."

"Yeah, ditto," Rennan agreed.

"That short exchange has gotten us nowhere," Drew commented bluntly. "Scarlet's right: we have the village. Now the issue becomes getting there. I doubt those lovely night patrols would be kind enough to let us into their gates without proper identification."

"Wait, *identification*?" Valerie interrupted. "Why would we need identifications to get into the village?"

"Magic-wielders are paranoid that outsiders will steal their work, so each village council sets up patrols and what not to guard their research. It's a safety precaution I find to be quite ridiculous at times. I have ways to protect my research without needing any additional security measures," Drew explained. "Anyway, we need to get in there somehow."

"But how? You said so yourself: it's unlikely they're going to let us in out of the goodness of their hearts," I pointed out. "There is no way all five of us plus the horse and Cam are going make it into that city unseen."

Drew was thoughtful for a moment. "True. I know you'll probably hate this idea, but I think the best thing to do will be to split up. You know, divide and conquer."

"Yup. I hate the plan already," I agreed.

Drew rolled his eyes and began to open his mouth to argue, but Rennan never gave him the chance.

"Okay, we get that Scarlet doesn't like Drew's idea. Hypothetically speaking, if we were to go through with that plan, how would we split up and who would be doing what?" Rennan questioned.

Can I just stop for a second and say how much I wanted to slap Rennan in the face for interrupting what was going to be an excellent argument? I would have liked to hear all of Drew's thoughts on this plan and present my own. Sadly, we didn't have time for it.

"I would take Cameron and the horse into the village and get him help. After all, I'm the only one with identification papers and would actually be able to get in. They shouldn't question Cameron if I tell them he is seriously ill and needs help. He's also an elf, so few would be bold enough to basically say 'get lost' to the most terrifying of the eight kingdoms. Sorcerers are paranoid, but most of us aren't heartless," Drew answered. "However, they won't let you in regardless of if I'm with you. You four would be distracting the patrols so I can get to the city safely."

Rennan looked to be in agreement already, but I wasn't quite sold. The sorcerer made a good point, but I would need more to convince me that this plan was going to work.

"But how do we know you're not going to betray us and kill Cam yourself?" I demanded.

Drew straightened and held me in a gaze for several seconds before he narrowed his eyes and turned to everyone else.

"I assure you I am no traitor and I wouldn't kill anyone in cold blood. You can trust that I want to help you succeed. I have no intention of letting your friend die, by my hand or otherwise," Drew stated firmly, as if daring any of us to argue. "Any other questions?"

"If we do this, who would go with who between the four of us?" Carter piped up. For once he asked a helpful question.

"First of all, is everyone in agreement with this idea?" Drew asked, his gaze passing over us all.

Rennan, Carter, and Valerie all nodded their heads in agreement. All eyes turned to me.

"I still don't like it, but fine," I muttered, fingering the hilt of one of my daggers. At least this stupid plan would give me the chance to actually fight something that I could kill. And even if I couldn't kill it, I would at least be able to make it scream in terror or agony. Whichever happened first, I guess.

"Okay then. I was thinking perhaps Rennan and Carter could go together and Valerie and Scarlet would pair up as well," Drew offered.

Rennan's eyes went wide with horror before he miserably agreed. I smirked. I knew he wanted to be with Valerie for his own personal reasons, but I didn't think it would be a good idea if they were a team on the battle field. Valerie didn't know how to fight and Rennan would get distracted.

A hint of a smile crossed Drew's lips. "Since nobody is objecting, I'll take that as a yes. Is everyone ready?"

We all nodded our heads. Drew gave everything on the horse one last check before he mounted behind the still unconscious Cam. I couldn't bear to look at him as they rode off. I just hoped that Drew would be able to get Cam help in time and that he wouldn't die on us. If he did…I knew without a shadow of a doubt that I wouldn't be able to say goodbye. Cam meant something to me, and I wasn't going to let him go.

We wouldn't have much time before Drew alerted the patrols, so we needed to be ready when we heard the alarms. The idea was that Rennan and Carter would take off in a westward direction while Valerie and I headed east. We split up as soon as Drew and the horse took off from the clearing. I think he used a cloaking spell or something because he didn't alert the patrols at all. I kind of took that as a sign that we needed to get into the city on our own.

"Come on, Valerie," I whispered when the coast was temporarily clear. It probably wouldn't stay like that for long once Rennan and Carter got out into the open.

Let's just say I should not have opened up conversation with the mermaid.

"There once was a guy named Cam, who liked to eat eggs and ham. But he buried a bone, and he felt all alone, and that was the end of Cam," she randomly recited as we crept through the underbrush.

I felt my cheeks flare red. "How could you be making jokes when he's almost dead?"

"Trying to keep us upbeat, you know?" she shrugged. Then she continued with her poem or whatever she was making up this time. "There once was a girl named Scarlet, who became a world-famous starlet. But she wore bad cosmetics and looked so pathetic, and that was the heartbreak of Scarlet."

"Okay, Valerie, seriously. Why do you—"

"Wait! I'm not done!" She said as she clamped her hand over my mouth. Her voice became sickeningly sweet when she continued. "There was a great man named Carter, who, compared to his brother, was smarter. His heart was well-made for a certain mermaid, and that is the greatness of Carter!"

"That is literally the most ridiculous thing I have ever heard come out of your mouth," I grunted, pulling a branch back so it would hit Valerie in the face as she walked behind me. I'm pleased to say that it did.

"You just don't understand the amazingness of art. You're just jealous because you never have tiger nights," the mermaid stated rather haughtily.

"That cannot be a real thing."

"Wanna bet?"

I turned to snarl at her when we heard horns blasting. I looked out into the field to see Rennan and Carter randomly swinging their swords towards the patrols. They weren't going to last very long if they kept that up. I rolled my eyes and sighed. We needed to help them even if we were going to get caught in the process.

Blast their insolence, I thought to myself as I pulled out one of my many daggers.

It would meet a target before it went back to its sheath. That was a fact.

"Where are you going?" Valerie demanded. Her perfect face was twisted into a scowl as she watched me with hard, pink eyes. Her hands were planted on her hips.

"I'm trying to save them before they get themselves killed," I replied shortly. "You have a choice: come and help me or stay here out of the way."

"I'll stay here if you don't mind, hybrid."

I glared at her before I ran out of the grove of trees. I saw Rennan and Carter fighting for their lives. Rennan had a slight limp, so he either was injured in their little battle or he had been his regular klutzy self and tripped on a rock.

The sentries saw me and immediately sent a small squad to attack. I smiled. That was exactly what I wanted them to do. I drew another dagger and swung it right as one of the wolf riders thrust their spear at me. The shaft snapped in half from my tremendously sharp blade.

Instead of letting them pass me just to circle around again, I grabbed the rider, pulled him off, and took his place in the saddle. I'm not sorry to say that I trampled him with his own wolf. I couldn't get myself to care much. My concerns and priorities were to keep myself, Rennan, and Cam from dying. The other two could be casualties for all I cared.

More riders began to swarm together. I drove the first wolf into them and killed a few that way. They eventually shot my wolf dead. I fell to the ground and rolled a few times. Thankfully, I didn't land on my blade and kill myself. Nay, I was a master at avoiding blades while the birds screeched above me. I just kept going as soon as I was back up on my feet again. There was no time to lose.

I was surrounded. Where most people would be panicking because they thought they were near death, I was thriving. I knew my abilities. I knew I could take down every one of the patrols. I doubted a lot of them were fighters. Most scholars can't fight, and that leaves them with weaknesses. However, the fighter who is intelligent can take down even the deadliest of foes.

Moonlight glinted off their silver helmets and spears. Clouds hid most of the light, but enough shone through for me to see the details etched into their armor and the grim expressions on their faces.

Many looked young, but that could mean just about anything for this immortal race. Any of these warriors could be twenty or two hundred and not look a day older than sixteen. I didn't know how many battles they had seen, but I could see the terror in their eyes as I crossed their paths. I was a force to be reckoned with.

Another soldier attacked me from the back of a giant hawk. I couldn't tell exactly what type of hawk it was, but the priority was to distract them from Rennan and Carter. I grabbed his spear and flipped him off the back of his winged steed. He screamed as he fell and crashed into the ground. I didn't give him a second look after I stabbed him.

The rest fell like dominoes. They all made the same mistake as their companions: attack me one by one instead of fighting like a well-oiled machine. Rennan told me later on that I didn't look mortal on that battlefield. He said that I looked like some sort of spirit dancing with blades as I took out all the wizard warriors. All I remember was spinning and slicing with perfect accuracy in the cool night air.

Soon they were all dead. Rennan and Carter slunk out from where they had been hiding and met up with me in the middle of the field. Carter and Valerie were both shaken and stunned after seeing what I could accomplish with just daggers. Their reactions amused me. Rennan, on the other hand, looked proud of me. It was strange, as no one has ever been *proud* of my battle skills….

"Scarlet, that was incredible!" Rennan grinned widely when we were sure no one else would attack.

Even if nothing else was coming at me, I didn't want to let my guard down. I kept scanning the horizon and the woods and everywhere in between to make sure nothing caught us by surprise. I had no intention of getting myself captured after killing more than twenty patrols.

"Yeah. Felt nice," I muttered as I wiped the blood off them. "Shouldn't we be moving on now?"

"Yes, you should, intruders," a voice said from behind us.

We whirled around to see two wizards standing in front of us—one male and one female. The man had soft green eyes that I thought were too kindly for a patrol. He looked nice enough, but sadly, the same could not be said of his companion.

She had creamy brown skin and perfectly straight black hair. Her eyes were a striking sea foam color, but they were just about as cold as a glacier in northern Palee. I had seen ice in Rennan's eyes, but nothing like the glaciers from this girl. She seemed to be like me, in a sense—ready to kill at a moment's notice.

"You four are under arrest for disturbing the peace and attempting to steal research from the residents of Caso," the woman announced, voice as hard as stone. It was just as unforgiving, too.

I gripped the hilt of my dagger, but Rennan held out his hand to stay me. I didn't want to listen, but I knew I probably should this time.

"Look, there's been a misunderstanding. We haven't come to steal your research," Rennan began, taking a bold step closer to the wizards.

They tightened their grip on their spears, which they pointed at the wolf. Rennan raised his arms as a sign of surrender.

"You must be joking. Twenty patrols lie dead in that field. Why else would you kill them unless you were coming to steal our research?" the woman demanded, eyes wild with a burning passion.

"We didn't come to steal it," I repeated firmly.

The woman locked eyes with me and scowled. She instantly seemed to size me up as a threat—which I was—and readied herself for any move that I might make. That meant I would have to come up with something quickly if I was going to try to outwit these fierce scholars.

"Really? Then why did you kill them? Did they harm you?"

"They were hostile forces coming to attack us!" I argued.

"They thought you were going to steal our work!"

"Well, we're not!" I barked.

Everyone around me shrank back. They say a bark can be worse than a bite, but my bite was far worse and would come out in a moment. I wanted to settle things with a battle to the death.

"Silence, hybrid!" the woman shouted, pointing her spear at me.

I growled savagely as my fingers moved to one of my hidden darts.

"What my friend is trying to say," Rennan cut in to try to take control of the situation again, "was that we were trying to make it into the city but were attacked halfway by your patrols. She thought they were the enemy so she did what she had to and launched her own counterattack."

"Why were you trying to get into the city in the first place?" the man asked with a confused look on his face. "Even if you made it to the outskirts of the city, you need the proper clearance to get you inside. Do you have identification papers to prove that you are worthy to enter Caso?"

"Um, no, we don't…."

"Then I'm sorry, but you are under arrest until you can get proper identification," the woman stated bluntly as she tied my hands behind my back.

Soon, all four of us were bound with shackles and were being led back to the city. Rennan was right when he told Drew that luck was not on our side. We were now on our way to a jail cell for who knew how long.

Carter sighed. "Well, that could have gone far better."

A Turn of Events

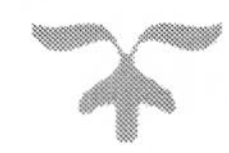

"Really, there has to be some sort of misunderstanding!"

That was our plea, but was it heard? No, of course not. I had thought the feline hybrids I'd met in Palee were pretty stiff necked, but I had never encountered any species as stubborn as these wizards. They were great scholars, sure, but they knew nothing about emotions or how to react to them.

They threw all four of us into one cell in the darkest, deepest, dampest corner of their abominable prison. There was one torch at our end of the hall to alert the guards that they had prisoners, but beyond that, there wasn't much for scenery.

Honestly, I was offended they put me with the other idiots (meaning Carter and Valerie, not Rennan). I would have thought they would put me in a solitary, heavily guarded cell because of the damage I had caused them. Obviously, they thought I was on the same danger level as the others since I was stuck here with two people I despised most.

One day, everyone would know the consequences of underestimating me.

Valerie didn't seem to be too happy about being in the same space as me either. She claimed several times that my pessimism made her hair lose its curl and bounce. I told her plainly that her claim was a lot of rubbish. She made a sour face and refused to acknowledge me afterwards.

"Well, this is a fine change of scenery," Carter commented when we were sure the guards were no longer paying attention to us.

"We are literally stuck in a room made of brick blocks and are being held captive in a prison. You call that a change of scenery?" I questioned bitterly.

It wasn't too great being stuck in a cell doing nothing when we could be helping save our friend! But no...we were here wasting time as usual.

"I was being sarcastic," Carter replied nonchalantly.

My left eye twitched.

"Your own brother is *dying* and you're sitting here being...*sarcastic*?!" I shouted angrily. "You are absolutely heartless!"

Carter's face turned to stone and Rennan was frantically warning me not to do anything else that could attract attention. But, of course, I didn't listen.

Valerie lost it. "So says the one who doesn't even care enough to thank those who try to keep moods and atmospheres light! Since I met you, I've seen nothing but constant negativity coming from you, hybrid!"

I growled. "I'm sorry, not everybody likes people who always sing and dance and throw rainbow flowers everywhere! Not everything in this world is sunshine and rainbows! That's fine if you're in Sala or a softer kingdom, but in the wild, you're at its mercy. If you had seen the things I have—"

"I don't want to if it means becoming the monster you are!" Valerie shrieked.

Both of us rose to our feet and kept shouting insults—the heat growing ever hotter. For a while, Carter and Rennan stayed out of it, hoping we could solve this argument ourselves. However, when it kept going, they were forced to step in.

"Look, maybe there's a way you guys can see eye to eye on this," Rennan stated in a gentle tone.

He distracted Valerie for half a second, but then she went back to glaring at me. I, on the other hand, silently cursed everything that had happened thus far to get me there.

"There is no way I will ever see eye to eye with this…this…she-devil!" Valerie seethed.

The mermaid promptly turned her back to me and refused to turn around, even when Carter was whispering sweet nothings in her hearing fins. I couldn't have cared less if she did.

"Now, Valerie…," Carter began.

The apathetic tone of his voice indicated that he cared nothing for what happened to anyone involved with this ordeal, whether it was me or Valerie or Cam. He was selfish and stuck up.

"You care nothing for us, do you? You only care about getting yourself out of this cell," Valerie muttered, as if she was just coming to her senses and realizing that the world was not as perfect as she once thought. It was as if this realization had just dawned on her and shocked every nerve in her body.

Carter was in a tight spot. He looked to me and Rennan for help, but I refused to give him any. This was his to solve. I wasn't going to get in the middle of it, especially if it involved the mermaid's feelings. At least, not her positive feelings. I would have been content to keep inflicting negative ones on her, but I had a feeling nobody would appreciate hearing things like that coming. I was pretty sure I just made enemies of everyone I knew.

"No, of course I care for all of you!" Carter protested.

He wasn't genuine. Anybody with eyes could see that. But Valerie didn't hear his lie and chose to believe him. Bad move. It would come back to bite her later and she would regret it.

Then Carter turned and reeled on me. "Apologize to her."

"No."

"What did you say to me?" Carter demanded, grey eyes becoming slits.

"I said, 'no,'" I repeated defiantly. My chin stuck up in the air stubbornly. Rennan put his hand on my shoulder and turned me to where I was looking up at him. I cocked my head, demanding he speak.

"Scarlet, too far. You need to back down," the wolf whispered.

"No, not too far," I began in a voice loud enough for everyone to hear. "She needs to learn that not everything is perfect and that no one can always be a positive light."

With that, the mermaid was reduced to tears. Rennan sighed and moved to Valerie's side to try to comfort her.

If I were any less stubborn, I would have been offended that my fellow hybrid chose to support of the mermaid instead of me. But I didn't care in the moment. I didn't want to be quieted. My chaos would continue.

"Scarlet, why don't you sit and think for a few minutes?" Rennan suggested quietly. He wouldn't make eye contact with me, and for some reason, that infuriated me even more.

"What? Am I a child now, too?" I asked through gritted teeth. I couldn't think properly through my rage. "Just some plaything to be thrown about until you have use of me?"

Rennan's jaw tightened and his gaze became cold. "I never said that."

"You clearly meant it!"

"You're speaking nonsense! Do you even hear yourself right now?" Rennan shouted at me.

I scowled. I could hear well enough to know when I wasn't wanted. I couldn't make myself care—I was used to the feeling of rejection. I was abandoned for so much of my life that it didn't make much difference now.

"Maybe I would if...."

The rest of my insult was cut off by my own sharp shriek, since the stone floor beneath me suddenly gave out. I fell for several seconds with the voices of my so-called friends calling after me.

Then my head hit the ground and I blacked out.

I woke up in a dark underground tunnel.

Though it was dark, I was able to make out some sort of light at the far end of it. It looked to be a pretty short distance away, but then again, my vision was still fuzzy from my fall. My head didn't throb much, so I didn't think I had a concussion. Still, I didn't know how long I was out, but I still didn't care. I was away from the people who I had previously called my friends. Maybe they still were—I didn't know.

But that was something I could worry about later. For now, my priority was to find a way out of this subterranean tunnel. I stood up, but immediately decided to sit back onto the damp ground. My ankle hurt like I had landed on it the wrong way. As far as I could tell, it wasn't broken, but it was at least sprained. I just wasn't sure how badly. I supposed I could still walk, but it didn't exactly do me much good. Limping was just making it worse.

"Well, well, well. What do we have here?" a familiar voice echoed through the tunnels.

I pulled out one of my daggers just in case I needed it. Sometimes, familiar voices were the most dangerous, a fact I learned all too recently from that scheming raven woman. Nevermore would anybody fool me that easily. At the end of the hall, there was a dark form of a man.

"Now, now, Sutton. There'll be none of that."

I recognized the smooth voice, but I couldn't place it. I felt like I knew it well, and yet I didn't. I stood up, purposefully keeping my weight on my good foot. If it was sprained, I didn't want to make it any worse. There was enough on my mind for me to worry about. Bats screeched and flew in circles around my head when I stood. I cursed under my breath as I crept forward towards the man.

"Who are you?" I demanded, keeping my dagger in my hand with a firm grip.

I studied the man more closely as I approached him. His olive toned skin reflected a sickly glow when he smiled, a webbed net of scars warping across his face.

The man faked offense. "Sutton! I'm shocked you don't remember me! But, then again, we've really only seen each other directly a couple of times in past years. And even then, it was brief."

My eyes widened in realization. The scars of this man belonged to someone I fought once when I was around twelve years old.

I ran from the man—he had been following me for miles around the city now. His scarred face scared me, but I knew I couldn't let it show. People like him wanted to be feared. That was how they conducted business.

Knowing I couldn't lead him straight back to my home, I tried leading this blond-haired stranger out of town. I reached the outskirts of the woods that made up the northern border. I had been forbidden to go there alone, but in that moment, I had no choice. The woods were the only way I could escape and circle back to the city.

I looked over my shoulder to see my stalker weaving his way through the thick crowd. If he was a hybrid, I didn't think he was a full blooded one. He had no distinctly animalistic qualities like most Paleeans. However, his eyes were pale and full of more knowledge than the average mortal. To my horror, his eyes locked with mine and he began to quicken his pace.

Deeper in the forest, the shadows taunted me. They wanted me to enter. It was like they were alive and calling out to me.

"Come," they seemed to beckon me.

They weaved back and forth like they were swaying in the wind, but there was no gust strong enough to come from the other side of the forest. There was no wind to my back, either. I figured it was a trick of the mind—something wanting to get me to fall prey to it.

I wouldn't. I needed to make it home.

I gulped and kept my hand on the small knife that my grandmother had given me for self-defense. She said it had belonged to my father, which I found mildly encouraging. I plunged into the forest and quickly hid in some of the underbrush. I would wait out the stalker and then run home after he left.

He reached the clearing a few minutes later.

"Young one, come out!" he called, scanning the forest landscape with his sparkling golden eyes. Just when I didn't think that man couldn't get any creepier, the shadows taunting me seemed to seep into his features, twisting him into a monster. His voice became harsh as he cried out, "Show yourself!"

Terrified, I stayed where I was. Sadly, the stalker found me a couple minutes later despite my best efforts to remain hidden in the bushes. I yelped as he forcefully snatched me out of the hiding place. The sharp branches cut my arms and drew blood. I almost dropped my dagger, but I kept my hold on it, fearing failure.

"Let me go!" I cried as I struggled to free myself.

He laughed evilly. "Never. You're brave—for a child. My master will appreciate that. He is always looking for more recruits."

Suddenly, this man didn't seem like the one who had been following me. He had a sense of elegance and etiquette to him. This new being seemed to malicious and wanted only to hurt me. I struggled to get loose from his iron clutches so I could go home.

"I don't want to go with you," I muttered as I kicked him in the face.

He cried out in agony and dropped me to the ground. Before he could recover, I sliced his ankle with the knife that had once been wielded by my father. I hoped I could do him proud with it. I tried to remember what my grandmother had taught me about fighting: stay balanced, always be ready for anything, and never give up.

The man slowly rose again before he threw himself at me. I raised my knife and sliced at his face, leaving two identical gashes in his olive toned skin. He howled in anger as he drew his own sword to swing it at me. I ducked below it and turned so I could swing and hit him in the back of the head.

Apparently, I must have more strength than I realized because he crumpled to the ground. He didn't look conscious. I made sure of it by kicking him in the legs and carefully turning him over. He was definitely out cold, but something else was very much awake in him. The shadows poured out of this strange man and onto the ground where they disappeared without a trace.

The man's eyelids fluttered open mere seconds later. "W-where am I?"

I didn't know if I should answer or not, so I remained silent, carefully keeping my distance from the dual-personalitied man. There was no way what he was doing was normal—not even in the slightest. I didn't want to take my chances with something so obviously volatile.

The man looked up and smiled warmly at me. I didn't trust him, but I also didn't run away. I was frozen with confusion, and couldn't do anything particularly useful.

"Ah, there you are," he said gently, "I've been looking for you for quite a while, my dear."

"Why would you be looking for me?" I questioned with uncertainty. Panic choked my throat.

"I heard about your potential, and I wanted to see if it was true. I know about your little incident."

I paled. "You mean the town square? I'm sorry, I didn't mean to. I can explain...."

"Hush, child," he said.

I hated my immediate calmness in recognizing one of my grandmother's favorite things to say to me.

He smiled. "What you did is why I'm here. We're always looking for new talent."

"You said your master would be pleased."

His face contorted with confusion. "I don't have a master. I work for myself—as do my operatives. At least they better not, those sorry little—"

"Okay, I get it. You work for yourself. But how does that involve me?" I asked, putting on my best business face like I had seen Grandmother do when she was bartering with various merchants in town.

"Ah, yes. You show great potential."

"For what?"

"Have you ever wanted to be an assassin?"

I looked at him in shock. I had indeed considered it with the hopes of getting revenge on those who had killed my parents. I hadn't let that go, and I wouldn't ever. *Not until the person who had killed my parents had paid dearly. My grip on my little knife tightened.*

"Yes. I have considered the possibility."

The man smiled. "Good. We could always use new fighters like you, if you would like to join. Do we have a deal?"

I nodded my head.

"Good," he said with a smile. "Call me Mongwau. I'll be your mentor in fighting techniques."

The memory faded away and I found myself in the damp tunnel, ankle still throbbing. In front of me, I saw someone who had taken me under their wing and taught me everything I know. I don't think I had been more pleased to see anyone in my whole life.

"Well, fancy meeting you here!" I said with a smile to my superior. "Long time, no see."

Though he was the head of a guild of assassins, Mongwau was the type who did a lot of the work himself, so he didn't just delegate tasks. He was the kind of boss who was fair, even though it meant taking lives. It couldn't be helped when it was your business.

"Indeed," he agreed. He grabbed the torch off the wall and held out his hand. "Come, walk with me."

I winced as I moved my ankle again. Mongwau noticed and frowned.

"May I help?" he asked.

I nodded, fearing he might try to realign it like he had done to my shoulder a few years back. That's a story for a different time. Instead, Mongwau laid his hand on my ankle and a warm tingle spread through my foot and leg. Soon, my ankle felt as good as new.

He looked up at me. "Better?"

"Much. Thank you," I said gratefully. I regarded him curiously. "How did you do that? I thought you were a hybrid?"

Mongwau smiled wryly. "I suppose I must explain since you've asked. I'm only half-owl hybrid. I'm also half-wizard and I normally live here instead of Palee."

"That's interesting, but I…don't know how to respond to that."

"Then don't. We have more important matters to discuss."

"Like?"

"The group you travel with--Penbrooke, the Kevayan princess, Cardell, and the Woods princes—are a curious company. However did you become involved with them?" Mongwau asked with a sidelong glance as we walked through the tunnels.

Each turn looked exactly like the one before it, so there would be no possible way for me to find my way back to where we had started.

"It's a long story," I answered.

I didn't say anything more about our mission. I trusted Mongwau, but he was still a bounty driven mercenary. Despite our code, he could easily place a bounty on my head if I said anything he didn't like. Besides, I didn't intend to endanger Cam or Rennan.

"I see. Anyway, I've got a job for you," Mongwau stated in a glum tone.

"I know that voice. This is from an outside employer, isn't it?" I asked.

"Sadly, yes. But he offered the job at a price I couldn't possibly refuse."

"How much?"

"Triple both our weights in gold and precious stones," he responded with a hungry look in his eyes. "Scarlet, if you succeed, we could be rich. Neither one of us would ever have to work again."

"Yeah? What's the catch? There's always one when it comes to a reward that big," I pushed. If it was within reasonable limits, I would have no problem carrying out this task for Mongwau while I was on the quest.

"There is none. It's a simple objective, really."

"What is it?"

"Collect the heads of the Woods twins and bring them back to me in Hila in three weeks' time."

I stopped dead in my tracks. So much for a simple task. "Mongwau, I can't do that. They're my friends. I can't just kill them—even if it means collecting a massive reward ensuring well-being for the rest of my life."

Mongwau scowled. "Sutton, I trained you better than that. If I've told you once, I've told you a thousand times: assassins don't have friends. It's not in our nature. We can't have anyone close to our hearts because tomorrow, they could be gone."

"They deserve their freedom."

"Freedom is life's great lie. Once you accept that in your heart, you will know peace."

"Peace is another one of life's great lies. There is always a war brewing. Someone is always planning attacks, betrayals, assassinations, whatever. There's no stopping war," I argued. "I can't take that job. They're still my friends. They mean more to me than any reward ever could. There is no convincing me otherwise."

Mongwau clicked his tongue. "Fine. Assume they *are* your friends. What have they ever done for you? They've done nothing except give you a hard time. They don't see your true capabilities like I do. I always have. Listen to me, Scarlet."

"I...won't listen...," my voice sounded distant to my own ears.

It was like there was something messing with my ability to focus on the words coming from someone who wasn't even three feet away. My head felt like I had been spun around in circles for hours and was just now released.

"You have a choice: bring me the heads of the elves or face the consequences of the Master in due time," Mongwau stated grimly. He took my hand and held it for a second. "Think about it."

I felt a foreign energy rush from him into me. Soon it dissipated and I could think clearly again. I took a deep breath and just kept breathing.

"Fine," I said through gritted teeth. "I will."

I didn't like the thought of betraying Cam just to get a really nice reward, but I didn't have a problem getting rid of Carter. He had done nothing for us except make our lives miserable since he first met us in Sala. His presence wouldn't be missed if I were able to land a perfect, clean stroke on his neck to separate his head from his shoulders. What could go wrong with that plan? All I would have to do was wait for the cover of darkness and then....

Wait.

What was I thinking? Those weren't thoughts I should be having while Cam was still dying from the poison. Besides, Carter *was* Cam's brother. Cam never really showed it, but I knew he *did* care for his twin in an uninvolved way. I couldn't just take that from him with a single stroke of one of my daggers. Not when so much else had already been taken from him.

"I should get back," I murmured, staring down the tunnel into endless nothing.

"Remember what I said, Scarlet, and you would be wise to listen to another piece of information," Mongwau warned. I raised an eyebrow, and he gravely continued. "I know what it is Cameron Woods suffers from. Do not let him play it off just as a harmless force he can perfectly control. He holds greater power than anyone knows. Don't be foolish and assume that you are safe with him. Nay, know that he is the most dangerous person you will ever meet."

I looked at Mongwau, and for a single second, I could swear I saw shadows crawling across his face. They were the same shadows that had possessed Cam the night of the Spiral of Doom.

I blinked, hoping that my eyes were playing a trick on me, but when I opened them, I wasn't in the tunnel and Mongwau wasn't standing beside me. Instead, I was in the middle of a street outside a small, blue building. It had two stories made of stone and few windows, but one was lit from within on the second floor. On the door hung a sign that read, *Drew Cardell, Amateur Magician.*

Panic and hope coursed through me as I ran to the door to knock. I received no answer at first. I was about to knock again when the door opened. Drew stood in the doorway with a genuinely shocked expression.

"Scarlet? What are you doing here? Where are the others?"

"They're locked up in a cell. I fell through the floor and wandered through underground tunnels. Then I found myself here," I explained. I saw no need to explain about a price being offered for Cam and Carter or my conversation with Mongwau.

Drew muttered something under his breath. "Okay, fine. I'm going to go get them out of custody. I have a feeling your mermaid friend doesn't like confined spaces. Just go upstairs and watch Cameron."

"Is he any better?" I asked hopefully.

To my disappointment, Drew bit his lip and shook his head sadly.

"No. If anything, he's in worse condition than when I got him here," the sorcerer admitted. "Since the medic hasn't been able to come yet, I gave him everything I could think of, but nothing has worked so far. All you can do is sit with him and see if anything changes."

"Okay. Good luck getting them all out of custody. I'll be here," I stated quietly.

Drew nodded and then ran off into the streets. He pulled up the hood to his cloak and then disappeared into the shadows cast by the buildings in the bright moonlight.

I sighed and went inside. I nearly had a heart attack when I entered the main room of Drew's small house. It was a complete and utter mess. Papers and writing utensils were strewn everywhere along with every color of jewel and crystal you could think of.

I forced myself to ignore it and trudged up the stairs to the second floor. It was far cleaner than the ground level, but it still had stacks of books everywhere. Some were closed and others lay open with several markers scattered throughout the yellowed pages. If Cam could see it all, he and Drew would be discussing theories on random subjects for hours on end.

Speaking of Cam, he was sprawled out on the bed, paler than ever. Drew obviously hadn't thought to disarm him, so all of his knives and daggers were still strapped to him. The only things missing were his bow, quiver, and scythe, which were on the ground next to the bed.

His eyebrows were knitted together in pain, but other than that, his face showed no expression. The way that his skin and hair were losing color rapidly worried me. Very little of his deep, chestnut brown hair remained. It was mostly white or gray. He looked so close to death....

If I truly believed what Mongwau had said about Cam being the most dangerous person I would ever meet, it would be in my best interest to kill him now and be done with it. It would be easy to play it off like he had died from the poison. I would just have to find another time that would make killing Carter very easy.

Blast! Why am I thinking that?!

I sighed and choked back a remorseful sob. Cam meant more to me than most other people had in my life. He had believed that I was a good person, despite my strange tendencies and not being the greatest at trusting people.

Our friendship was something else, too. It was proof that even the greatest of enemies could get along without trying to kill each other. If Cam died, I would lose an understanding, genuine friend. I would be stuck with only Drew to keep me sane. I would say Rennan also, but he had his moments of being crazy.

Oh…Rennan. How could I be so nasty to him? Cam wasn't the only one who believed in me—Rennan had, too. Rennan had been trying to keep me level-headed, and apparently the way I repaid him was to destroy everything that we had worked to build. I had probably done that with everybody in the last couple of hours.

A sickened feeling filled me when I realized I had ruined everything that had been months in the making.

I knelt down next to Cam's side and gingerly stroked his left hand. His signet ring shone in the dim light, the dark blue stone looking almost like the Paleean sky at midnight during the winter months. I don't know if I imagined it or not, but I could almost see the stars twinkling back at me through the stone. I held Cam's corpselike hand in mine. I tightly closed my eyes and tried not to let my mind wander down paths I didn't have the heart to tread. That wouldn't get me anywhere good.

Then there was a surge of energy flowing through us. The room exploded into pitch darkness before it became a blazing fire. However, the fire was no threat to me. It just swirled around Cam, enveloping him in its many tongues.

I screamed and stumbled backwards when Cam's eyes began to glow. They were fully open and pure white light shone out, radiating light through the small room. The light from his eyes tried to cut through the darkness, but to no avail. The shadows were far too strong for a light that seemed weak in comparison.

Winds picked up in the room, even though that should be impossible. We were indoors, after all. Plus, the wind seemed to be coming from inside the building rather than through the windows, which were firmly latched shut. I screamed again as books flew through the air, ducking under the desk so I wouldn't get hit.

What came next was more horrifying than anything I had seen yet. Still, all I could do was watch with wide eyes as Cam started floating above his bed and yelling what I assumed to be the elvish phrase '*utinu en lokirim*' over and over again. I tried to yell his name, but I couldn't even hear myself over the wind. I think the shadows were muffling any sound trying to travel through the room.

Finally, one of my screams fully echoed through the small room when the intensity of the shadows wavered. The light in Cam's eyes faded back to the normal grey when the sound of my voice registered in his mind. His previously stone expression melted into something of concern when our eyes met.

"Scarlet…?" he tried to say, but then fell back into the bed in the same condition he had been in moments earlier. In other words, almost dead.

It was only a matter of time before he was gone for good. The poison had been in his system for far too long for him to recover. I knew in that moment it would impossible for Cam to make it back from Death's doorstep this time. I felt completely helpless knowing he had fought that dragon to keep us safe and now there was absolutely nothing I could do for him.

The tears flowed loose as I wrapped my arms around the elf. Between sobs I managed to say, "Please, Cam, don't leave us. Don't leave me."

I almost screamed again when I felt Cam's barely warm fingers curl around my wrist. With wide eyes, I flung myself backwards and onto my feet to watch this new scene unfold. Cam sat up and coughed. This would have been totally normal if he hadn't been coughing out smoke as well.

I quickly scanned the room for water and miraculously found an unspilled jar on the desk. I handed it to him and he took it gratefully.

"What happened?" he questioned in a hoarse voice after he had downed the whole jar. "I mean, after I took on the dragon?"

"No, you can't be real right now. Am I dreaming? You were almost dead!" I rasped out.

My mind was pretty much everywhere at once. Nothing formulating in my mind made any logical sense. Cam had been *seconds* away from death, then he starts coughing out smoke and demands to know what had happened since he had been unconscious! Surely, I had to be dreaming!

"I'm very much alive, Scarlet," Cam stated with a very confused look on his face. "How long was I out?"

I turned to look at him. Almost all the color had returned to his hair, but his face was still amazingly pale. His eyes weren't glowing with the white light and there were no shadows to be seen. However, there was a troubled cloud in his grey eyes. I decided not to worry about it now and instead be happy that the elf was alive and breathing.

"You were out for way too long. I had…I had given you up. I thought you were dead," I choked out. Fresh tears welled in my eyes. "Why did you take on the dragon by yourself?"

Cam's lips twitched and he patted the side of his bed. He lay back down as I sat at the edge of the mattress. He had to be exhausted after his last episode with the shadows on top of the effects of the poison.

"I knew you would ask that. I had to do it, Scarlet. I'm the only one who has taken on one of those foul beasts before and lived to tell the tale,"

Cam scowled at some old memory he obviously didn't want to talk about. "I wanted to protect you."

"And you did, but you almost died in the process."

"Can we skip the little details?"

"Cameron! You almost *died*!"

"I know. It's nothing new for me. Please tell me what has happened since I was knocked out by that accursed poison," Cam pleaded as he wrapped his hand around mine again. His grey eyes were so wide that I almost didn't need convincing.

I sighed, but agreed. I told him everything except my memory, the price on his head, and my conversation with Mongwau about him being the most dangerous man I would ever meet. I still had a choice to make about the bounty, but I figured that it could wait until the morning. I had enough conflicting emotions concerning Cam to deal with in the present.

Cam sighed when I was done. "Wow. I'm so sorry. If I had known...."

"If you had known, you still would have done it."

"Yeah, I guess you're right. But sorry doesn't begin to cover how much turmoil I put you through. I should have told you what I was doing before I ran in there like a fool," Cam muttered as he looked out the window into the dark sky.

"If you're a fool, you're a brave fool," I commented with a small smile.

Cam lips twitched slightly. He had sat up while I was explaining everything that had happened, but he laid back down when he heard footsteps thumping up the stairs.

He sighed. "Please don't tell anyone about our conversation. I want to talk to you more later about what happened a few minutes ago."

I looked at him in shock. "You mean about what literally almost drained the last of your life force?"

"Yes, that."

"Okay."

The door burst open and I quickly pulled my hand out of Cam's. To create a cover as to why I was sitting on the bed, I put my hand on his forehead. Cam's lip twitched like he thought it was funny. I thought it was a good cover up, though.

Carter was the first one through the door. His face fell slightly when he saw his brother awake. "Oh. You're still alive."

Cam snorted, even though it sounded terrible. He must have still had dragon smoke in his lungs. "Don't sound so disappointed. I might think you don't like me."

Carter was about to open his mouth to protest, but Valerie raced in through the door. She ran toward Cam and threw her arms around his neck. Cam made a gagging noise and coughed again. When Valerie eventually realized she had caused Cam pain (or she had enough of her exceptionally long hug), she pulled away and smiled. I was painfully aware of her refusal to acknowledge my presence.

"Thank the stars you're alive!" she cried happily.

Still grinning, she stepped back slightly to allow Rennan and Drew to squeeze into the room. It quickly became very cramped in there. I was just glad I was right next to Cam.

"How on earth did you survive the poison?" Rennan questioned. His dark eyebrows furrowed. "You should be dead right now."

Rennan didn't look at me either, from what I observed. I didn't blame him or even Valerie for not wanting to interact with me. I had been nasty to them.

As Cam explained everything he was feeling to Drew (the sorcerer wanted to make a supply run but he needed to know what to get), I managed to slip outside. I didn't want to be in a place where I wasn't really welcomed by the others. They could have their time with Cam—I could wait.

I was outside for what seemed like forever when the front door closed softly behind me. I didn't bother to look behind me to see who had come out. If it was Drew, I doubted he would say hello to me as he walked off to get his supplies. He wasn't the conversational type, just like me. I couldn't help but appreciate that quality in him.

"Mind if I join you?" a deep, accented voice asked.

Surprised, I looked up to see Cam standing behind me. He was smirking in the moonlight as he watched me sitting on the steps. He was wrapped in a thick blanket.

"How long have you been standing there?"

"Longer than you'd like. Can I sit here or not?"

"I'm not going to stop you."

"Yay," he said, and promptly sat down beside me. He wrapped the blanket over his head like a child might, and I almost laughed because he looked so comical. He must have realized he did and enjoyed it because he did nothing to change the position of the blanket. Well, that or he was just cold. "So. Can we talk now?"

"You're already talking, aren't you?" I answered rather dejectedly. Cam tilted his head and stared at me.

"You're thinking about earlier this evening, aren't you?"

"That's one thing, yes. But how would you know about that? You were unconscious."

"Rennan told me about what happened and Valerie is sitting still for once."

"Oh."

"I'm calling him out here."

I looked at him in a panic. "No, please don't. He hates me right now."

"Is that what you think?" Cam questioned, some sort of unidentifiable emotion in his eyes.

I nodded sadly.

He shook his head. "He doesn't hate you, Scarlet. He's just worried for you. You've been off all evening."

"How can you tell?" I asked quietly.

I thought I had done a good job of sealing off anything I'd experienced after I had fallen into the tunnel with Mongwau. His words still echoed through my mind, unwilling to let me feel any sort of peace. But like I said, there was no such thing as true peace. There was always something lurking in the darker places of the world.

Don't be foolish and assume that you are safe with him. Nay, know that he is the most dangerous person you will ever meet.

It was hard to believe that statement now after sitting with Cameron for a few minutes. When I looked into his eyes, I could see his care and concern for others. He was like a gentle soul, who didn't care if he got hurt in the process. I had already seen several times that he was willing to sacrifice himself for his friends. Then again, I had seen the darkness inside of Cam come out before, and it was the most terrifying thing I had ever seen in my entire life.

"You just seem distant, that's all," he replied with a shrug. He picked up a small rock and held it in one hand. He grinned mischievously. "Watch this."

Then he lightly threw the rock at the door and waited to see what would happen with an eager smirk. Crazy thoughts and ideas must have been bouncing around in his head to make him do such a thing. He was normally very, *very* reserved. He never threw anything, much less a rock, unless he was forced to.

"Why did you do that?" I inquired.

Cam turned to me and smiled in a manner I had seen painted on Rennan's face many a time. It pained me to make the comparison.

"You see, Rennan and I discovered that your friend Drew—great guy, by the way. Studies the Ancient Magic like I do—is a tad bit particular."

I raised an eyebrow in confusion.

"He likes certain things a certain way, but totally lets the rest of the mess take over," Cam explained. He threw another pebble at the door. "Rennan and I have been messing with him ever since we found out about it. Now. Just listen and perhaps we'll hear the sorcerer himself yelling at me to stop throwing pebbles and get back inside where it's warm."

As if on cue, Drew's voice yelled through the door, *"Cameron Woods! I swear if I hear another thud coming from you, I'm going to tie you to a chair and not untie you until Wraeo gets here tomorrow morning!"*

"Not a chance! And send the wolf out here! I want to talk to him!" Cam yelled back.

"No! You should be inside resting! If you want to speak with him, come inside!"

Cam was about to get up and go inside, but the doorknob turned and opened to reveal the one and only Rennan. He held his finger to his lips and closed the door behind him—likely so Drew couldn't hear our conversation.

"He's putting everything on lockdown mode so he can sleep. We have a few minutes out here, tops," Rennan explained in a hushed tone. He spoke directly to Cam, not offering me a second glance.

Cam nodded and then turned his steely gaze on me. It would have been fearsome if he hadn't been wrapped up in a blanket looking like a five-year-old.

I sighed. "I'm sorry, Rennan."

It was barely audible, but Rennan looked at me out of the corner of his eyes. His head was lowered, so I couldn't tell what emotion he was displaying: anger or sorrow. He didn't make any noise for a few minutes. For that matter, neither did Cam or I. I had a feeling that Cam wanted us to smooth out our problem on our own. I just didn't have any words fitting to say to him.

"I know you're sorry. I am, too. I should have made sure you were okay during all of that instead of immediately taking sides and trying to get you to calm down. You were right, though. Not everything in this world is perfect. I've come to realize that now," Rennan stated softly. "Ever since that skirmish with the wild wolf, I've been thinking."

"About?" Cam urged, now obviously choosing to get involved.

"I've been thinking about how I reacted and now how Scarlet responded to all of Valerie's nonsense. Yes, I mean it. I might have a soft spot for the mermaid, I'll admit that, but I do realize that she's a bit energetic," Rennan said with a pointed look at both of us, as if daring us to tease him. "We reacted because we thought things were being done to us unfairly, or at least in Val's case. Scarlet and I reacted because we were pushed beyond our limits. I don't think we can finish this thing without causing some sort of chaos to push people beyond their limits."

"I think you're on to something there," Cam muttered, half to himself and half to us. "When people are pushed beyond their limits, they have a tendency to admit their mistakes and someone might actually slip and tell us what we need to know to take down my father and his inner circle! It's like using their fear to our advantage! Rennan, you're a genius!"

Rennan smirked. "I get that a lot."

I rolled my eyes. "So, that's the new plan? We cause enough chaos to make people uncomfortable so they'll slip and tell us valuable information? I hate to be pessimistic, but that doesn't sound like the strongest plan."

Cam nodded in acknowledgement. "I know the feeling, but that is the best we can cobble up for now. We can work out more ideas tomorrow when I actually have full thinking capabilities."

"Yeah, we should all probably get some rest," I agreed. It had been a long day for us, but I was still reluctant to let Cam out of my sight. I didn't want him to leave unexpectedly during the night and not come back, whether it was by his will or not. "You should go first, Cam."

"But—"

"No buts. She's right," Rennan said with a twinkle in his eye. My cheeks warmed, glad that Rennan was siding with me on this matter.

Cam made a face but consented. He seemed to float back inside with the blanket trailing after him. It had to be a long blanket if it could cover Cam's head and still trail behind him. He was seriously tall. I jokingly wondered if the blanket had magical capabilities.

"Look, Rennan…," I began. He held up his hand to silence me.

"Say no more. You're forgiven, Scarlet. Just tell me next time you're hitting a wall, please."

"I will."

"Good," he said, giving me a quick side hug. "Now, come on. We need to get inside before Drew loses his head about us being out here for so long."

"Wise idea."

We both went inside and found small beds made for us. Valerie and Carter were already fast asleep on the ground floor and I assumed Drew was upstairs in his own bed. Cam was in the middle of the floor with one of his daggers by his side. I decided to think nothing of it and laid down in a pile of blankets a few feet from him.

I was almost asleep when I heard an accented voice whisper my name. I rolled over to see Cam staring at me through the darkness. Once again, the elf looked comical with his crazy hair and blanket wrapped around him.

"Yes?" I whispered back.

"Thanks for believing I could hold on. I don't think I would have been able to come back if it weren't for you."

"But I told you I had given you up…."

"The conscious part of you might have, but in your heart, you still believed I was alive. My subconscious somehow managed to connect to yours and I was able to wake up from that slumber. I'm glad you came when you did. I don't know how much more I would have been able to take of those dreams."

"Dreams?"

"Bah, don't listen to me. I'll tell you about the dreams some other time…maybe. Point is: thank you. I'm indebted to you."

"Think nothing of it, please. I'm just glad I could help."

"You'll help me far more than you'll ever know," Cam said distantly. He rolled onto his back. "Good night, Scarlet."

"Night, Cam."

No Weapon, Perfect Distraction

Sun shone through the windows early the next morning. I opened my eyes and saw the ceiling far above me. For a second, I almost forgot where I was. A complete mess surrounded me and I had the inexplicable urge to try to clean it up. There were papers covering every available surface and books stacked beside chairs and tables...and *on* tables.

Then I remembered where the heck I was: the home of the sorcerer Drew.

Everyone I had shared a room with was still fast asleep. Rennan was sprawled out on the only sofa in the room, face buried in blankets and pillows (which was good because he snores really loudly...but you didn't hear that from me. You heard it from Valerie). Carter and Valerie, however, had makeshift mattresses that they were conked out on.

The only people who weren't present were Drew and Cam. Drew, I assumed, was still sleeping upstairs in his own bed, but Cam? I had no idea where he would be on a sunny morning like this one. I doubted he was outside in the sun because he hated it. If he had his way, he would only travel by the shadows of night. But there were no shadows and definitely no Cam.

That is, until I heard a yell from upstairs. Somehow, nobody else was woken up by the commotion above us. Even Rennan, who wasn't exactly a deep sleeper, didn't wake up.

I wasn't going to do anything to help (which sounds terrible), until I heard a huge *thud* on the floor and then the sound of thrashing limbs and snippets of elvish phrases. That's when I ran upstairs and saw something absolutely strange.

Now, I'd guess that Cam was roughly six and a half feet tall. And yet,

I saw him thrashing around on the floor, Drew trying to subdue him, and a little humanoid creature the size of a toddler sitting on Cam's chest. From what I could tell, Cam looked like he was trying to reach one of his daggers that had been flung across the floor during his struggle.

"Oh, good, you're here. You can help us restrain him," Drew grunted as Cam purposefully kicked at him.

Cam wrapped his feet around Drew's neck and pulled him down. The magic-wielder almost hit his head on the windowsill, but narrowly missed it.

"Why is he like this?" I asked curiously.

I looked at Cam and tried to figure something out. There was a wild look in his eyes and pale shadows crawled over his face. I sucked in a breath, and somehow brought myself back under control. I wanted to slap those shadows right out of him just because of the fear that welled up inside me.

"The eelfleng suffahs from terrable nightmahres," the little creature answered as he forced a thick pink sludge down Cam's throat.

The elf coughed and tried to spit it back out, but the small being forced his mouth closed until Cam absolutely had to swallow the stuff if he wanted to breathe.

When he was pleased with his work, the creature announced, "There ya go. Ralease 'im, Cahdell."

Drew released the elf.

In a swift motion, Cam dragged Drew down again to punch him in the jaw before retreating to the darkest corner of the room. He looked like a scared animal while he cowered in the darkness. I could barely see his expression, but I saw enough to tell it was his regular stone one. He didn't move for several minutes.

"Ugh, fine. Can I punch him now? I owe him revenge for the one he just landed on my jaw," Drew grumbled as he rubbed the left side of his face.

When he removed his hand, I noticed that the area was swollen and turning a subtle shade of purple. When the little creature shook his head, Drew muttered something under his breath and started cleaning up the trashed space.

"Sooo...what exactly were you doing to Cam?" I asked when I mustered up the courage.

That question came only after several minutes of sitting on a stool doing absolutely nothing except sitting and watching them clean. I had no desire to be given the same treatment Cam was experiencing.

The little dude turned to me.

"Naw, come down ahn' seet so ah cahn teel ya," the creature instructed.

After seeing him force the sludge down Cam's throat, I decided to obey. I didn't really feel like being this guy's next victim. Drew was cleaning in the background and constantly sending glances in Cam's direction as if making sure that no attack was coming. After seeing the wild look in Cam's eyes, I had a feeling he was trying to sort something out instead of planning any kind of attack.

The small one said with flourish, "Ya see, ahm tha sohrt of creetcha tha' ya humahns cahll 'gneffels.'"

"First of all, I'm not a human; I'm a hybrid. Second, what's a gneffel?"

The gneffel thing grunted. "Tha' mahkes na daffance ta me! Ya lahk humahn ena' fer me ta teel! Naw, whaht was ah sahing?"

"You were telling her about what you were doing to Cam," Drew answered helpfully from the other side of the room.

He had finished cleaning up the mess and he was now sitting in an armchair across from the corner where Cam was huddled up, rocking back and forth, and muttering under his breath.

"Yas! Ah remembah naw!" the gneffel stated with a wicked grin. His teeth shone white against his tanned skin. His long (for a foot and a half tall creature, that is) hair was neatly combed back and put into place using some sort of gel. I didn't want to know what was in it after seeing the sludge's appearance. "Yas, yohr freend wahs mahshing—"

"Thrashing," Drew corrected.

"Mahshing, thrahshing, na daffance! Ahnywah, yohr freend was thrahshing on tha fler. Muttahed semtheng abat, what wahs it, Cahdell?"

"He kept muttering the phrase '*utinu en lokirim*' over and over again. I think it's elvish, but I can't be sure," Drew answered. "Wraeo, I'll take over from here. You're welcome to leave now."

"Buht ah cald be af heelp!" the gneffel protested.

"You've helped enough," Drew shot back with a pointed glare.

"Fahn. Teel meh ef thah eelfleng nads ahnatha smahck apsade tha heed," Wraeo muttered as he stomped off down the stairs and then out the front door.

As soon as I knew he was gone, I let out a breath I hadn't realized I had been holding.

"Sorry about Wraeo. He's crazy, but he means well. He's the best medic this village has. Plus, he's treated patients suffering from dragon blood poisoning several times. Unfortunately, they all died. Cameron is the first person to ever survive. He's stronger than anyone I've ever seen," Drew explained.

Drew watched the elf curl and uncurl his fingers around his own wrist. Cam didn't look all that great to me. It was sort of like he had been brainwashed and all of his intelligence was taken from him, basically turning him a toddler stuck in a grown man's body. Drew just shook his head.

"But what were you doing to him? Wraeo's accent was thicker than Cam's, so I barely understood a word he said," I questioned as I rubbed the bridge of my nose.

The gneffel was certainly an interesting character. Although Drew said the creature had meant well, I wasn't sure if I would want such an excitable thing treating me.

"Well, he kept walking around last night. But he was sleepwalking and I didn't trust him not to hurt himself or somehow escape my house. So, I brought him up here and disarmed him. Did you know that he always has two daggers under his armguards?" Drew asked in shock.

I nodded my head.

Drew continued. "Interesting. I didn't find that out until a few minutes ago when he pulled one out to try to defend himself.

"Anyway, as soon as I dragged Cam up here last night, I sent a message to Wraeo to bring the treatments for dragon poisoning. When Wraeo got here this morning, Cam started thrashing around in his sleep and was muttering the phrase '*utinu en lokirim.*' Sadly, it's a different form of elvish than what I'm accustomed to, so I couldn't understand any of it. Do you know what it means?"

"I don't know, but when I was here with Cam yesterday, he kinda burst into flames and was repeating the same phrase," I admitted.

Drew stared out the window and fingered the necklace I just now noticed he wore. It was a simple locket with small pictures carved into it. There were two small runes I couldn't understand. I would have asked what it was, but I didn't feel like it was the right time.

"That's very concerning. So much so that I'm going to have to snap him out of his trance," Drew decided suddenly.

"Wait, you mean he's been in a trance since I came up here?" I asked in disbelief.

"How else were we going to get that disgusting pink sludge down his throat? Again, he's a very strong fighter. More powerful than any I've seen in even my re—time. In my time," Drew shrugged with a self-loathing glare at his feet. He was going to say something else, but he quickly caught himself.

I was too preoccupied with my own thoughts to care.

Don't be foolish and assume that you are safe with him. Nay, know that he is the most dangerous person you will ever meet.

Maybe there was some truth to those words after all.

Drew crossed the room to Cam's corner and stood over him. Cam took no notice of the sorcerer. Instead, he kept swaying from side to side and muttering in elvish under his breath. Before I could protest anything, Drew slapped Cam's face.

"There. It's done," Drew said with a self-satisfied smirk.

Cam, meanwhile, was out cold on the floor.

"Was that really necessary?"

"Tell me, Scarlet, if someone had been irritating you, had just punched you in the jaw, and they were under a trance, would you break the spell like that?"

"Well, yes, I would. Who wouldn't?"

"Then there's your answer," Drew stated as he sat back down in his armchair, patiently waiting for Cam to come to. His purplish-blue eyes soon rested on me. "I know what's on your mind. The bounty on the Woods twins troubles you."

"How? You can't read minds, can you?" I demanded, eyes narrowing immediately. I prepared to be on my guard for any dirty tricks the sorcerer might play.

His eyes twinkled mysteriously, but not necessarily in a good way. There was a level of darkness to them that I didn't want to delve into. I had enough of it in my own mind. Surely that same darkness could be multiplied in a sorcerer's mind. "There are some things I cannot talk about here, Scarlet. In due time you will find out the meaning of my statement. But for the present, I would encourage you to think very carefully about the bounty. Choose wisely."

I stubbornly did not respond.

A few minutes later, Cam started moaning on the floor. I wanted to rush forward and help him sit up, but I didn't think he would appreciate it much if I did. He was too independent to admit needing help to do something as simple as sitting up. He tried to push himself up off the ground, but soon found that he was still too weak. I had to help, so I stepped towards him.

He recoiled as if expecting another attack, but then realized it was me and partially relaxed. I gently helped him sit up. I noticed that his cheeks were flushed slightly pink, but I decided not to read into it much. They could have been pink for any reason, but it probably wasn't my business to know why right now. He could have just been warm or still recovering from the poison.

"Okay, I'm just going to say that that stuff was absolutely disgusting. I hate medicine," Cam managed to rasp out a few seconds later. Then he looked to Drew and they made eye contact. "Also, you have a good swing, sorcerer."

"I find it amazing that you can come so close to dying and yet you always maintain a sense of humor," Drew stated with a slight smirk.

Cam returned the expression for a brief second.

"Yeah, I guess. But I wouldn't get used to it. There won't be much to laugh about in the coming weeks," Cam warned mysteriously.

By this point, he was sitting up and was rearming himself. Drew didn't make any comments, but I could tell that he was wary of the elf carrying weapons so soon after he almost died again.

"What are you talking about, Cam?" I questioned softly. I already knew Cam didn't like questions, but I needed to know what was going on.

"I...can't explain. I wish I could, Scarlet, I do. But just be prepared for the, er, *misfortune* to come," Cam answered, looking anywhere but at me.

I couldn't figure out what in the world he was talking about to save my life, but thankfully I didn't have to wonder about it for very long.

Drew shifted in his seat and cleared his throat. "Since we're in a solemn mood, I need to talk to you, elf."

Cam narrowed his eyes. "Don't call me that."

"You just called me 'sorcerer.' Therefore, I have the right to call you 'elf.'"

"Then I will come up with another name for you. Just don't call me that to my face. I'd rather not be labeled with a word connected to evil even if I am of that race."

"Fine, fine. Let's not get sidetracked."

"What did you want to know?" Cam asked glumly, sitting back against the wall. He was playing with one of his many small knives, so it was hard to tell how much he was really paying attention to the conversation. His mind could have been a million miles away like I knew it tended to be.

"You keep muttering the elvish phrase '*utinu en lokirim*' whenever you're knocked unconscious. I want to know what it translates to," Drew explained.

Cam paled tremendously. His fear was obvious. It was the strongest emotion he had exhibited besides anger that I had ever seen. Not only that, but it extremely rare for Cam to experience such a vulnerable emotion, so when he did, it was wise to be on guard.

"Under what circumstances did I say that?" Cam demanded in a shaky voice. His fingers no longer skimmed over his knife; they were completely still. His face became almost ghost-like when Drew asked his question. I hated how much life had been drained out of Cam when he heard the phrase.

"The first time was when you burst into flames in the shadow storm and your eyes were glowing," I began.

"And the second time you were in here yelling and thrashing in your sleep," Drew finished.

"We need to get out of here," Cam whispered almost to himself.

Cam's eyes had gone wide as something clicked in his head. If there had been any blood left in his face, it completely drained out of it now. He immediately jumped up, grabbed his weapons, and ran downstairs. Drew and I had no choice but to follow. As soon as we were downstairs, Drew bolted out the front door without looking back.

"What do you mean 'we need to leave now'?" I demanded to know.

"No time to explain. Get the others awake," Cam instructed as he began shaking everyone awake.

Rennan was wide awake in a few seconds, but it took far longer to wake up Carter and Valerie. I had a feeling neither one of them were used to getting up so early in the morning. Heh, they should have been warned that Cam likes to get up and hike at unearthly hours.

I managed to pull Cam aside a few minutes later. "Cam."

"What?" he asked. I had expected him to be panicked or even irritated, but I was surprised to find his tone calm and almost soothing.

"You know you're scaring me right now. Why do we need to leave right this second?"

Cam ran his hands through his hair and then over his face. A small part of me wanted to laugh at the face he made as he did so, but I didn't think this was an appropriate time for such a reaction.

"I know I'm scaring you, and I'm really not trying to. Knowing what I said when the shadows were in control…it alarms me. That phrase, '*utinu en lokirim*,' means 'son of snakes.' There's a certain rebellion in the Hevian kingdom who chose snakes as their military representative, and they just so happen to hate me—they've even tried hunting me during my exile," Cam explained, spinning his signet ring on his finger several times. "Remember when you were rambling about Razil being raised in a rebellion? I'm pretty sure she's a part of it, and was probably sent to hunt me down. I must have been dreaming about them—"

"Cam."

"Yes, Scarlet?"

"We'll get out into the wilderness and go somewhere else. I promise you'll be safe."

"It's not me I worry about," the elf admitted, biting his lower lip. He glanced toward Carter, who was still trying to wake up from his dead sleep. His hair looked like some cat had attacked his head and then used it as a bed.

"I thought he swore that he wouldn't try to murder you or anything?" I questioned in confusion.

As far as I knew, Carter had kept his oath. If he hadn't, he would be in some serious trouble with me. Even if he didn't intend to keep his promise to Cam, I would. And if that meant dealing with Carter, so be it. Maybe I could still bring his head to Mongwau and receive part of the bounty….

"Well, he's been rather finicky about it," Cam admitted with a slight scowl. He evidently felt useless just standing there whispering to me, so he started to help gather up our supplies and flawlessly organize the packs so we could carry as much as possible. "He hasn't tried another attempt like that one night when I created the, uh, Spiral of Doom. Blast, that was a bad night for me. Anyway, he continues to make threats."

"Does that count as breaking his oath?"

"Sort of. I guess it would mean that he was breaking his oath a little bit."

"Am I allowed to make threats in return?"

"You know your kind of threats usually involve some sort of injury, right?"

"Yeah, so?"

Cam laughed. "Scarlet, as much as I know you want to see Carter come to some tragic demise, he's still my brother. I won't deny that there is still a part of me that believes he can change his ways. After all, you are the single most stubborn person I have ever met in my life. You were so resilient and independent when I met you, but now you've warmed up to other people. Mostly. And you know who I'm referring to."

I flinched at the memory. "You heard about that, too?"

Cam sighed slightly and turned away from his work. He took my hand and looked me dead in the eye. I couldn't help but blush when I was obliged to look at him. He looked dead serious, and I wasn't quite sure what to say. Or think. Or feel.

"Scarlet, I know you don't like Valerie, but I really need you to try to get along with her. If not for your own friendship, will you at least do it for me?" Cam asked with an earnest light in his eyes. "Please?"

"Fine, but only because you're asking me," I relented with a sigh.

Cam smiled and released his hold on my hand.

"Right, because if Rennan had asked you to play nice with the mermaid, you would not have listened to the request as willingly," the elf commented with a smirk, ruining what was almost a sweet moment.

He looked very pleased with himself as he watched Rennan following Valerie around again. The poor wolf. He had to deal with so much rejection from the princess. I doubted I would ever fall for any guy, but I knew if did, I would certainly say so.

"Yeah, you may have a slight point there," I agreed with a small grin.

Cam returned the smile and went back to his work. His fingers moved deftly as he sharpened one of the small daggers that he kept in his boots on a whetstone. By the time he was done, they were nearly as sharp as a needle or a thorn on a rose bush.

"That's the Scarlet I know and love," Cam stated half to himself. "I know you'll do what's right."

I would have said something in reply, but his words hit me too deeply to be able to say anything other than "um." He trusted me to do the right thing, and yet here I was, wondering if I should follow through with the orders my boss had given me. I can't deny that I wondered what would happen if I brought in half of the requirements—if I killed Carter and let Cam live—and try to claim part of the bounty. But then Mongwau could easily send somebody else out to kill Cam and collect it for himself. Mongwau might include my head in those orders as well.

But how could I do the right thing with that weighing on me? I didn't like Valerie; I didn't like Carter. But I did respect Cam and his wishes. If he truly wanted me to try to be friends with the mermaid (I internally gagged at the thought), then I guess I would until I got the perfect chance to try something else.

"Hellooooooo…earth to Scarlet!" a voice called, startling me out of my thoughts.

When I realized that I had been staring at the floor for the last few minutes (or however long I had been staring at the floor), I snapped my head up to see Rennan's face in mine. A small cry escaped my lips as I pushed him backward.

"Gah! What is it, Rennan?" I demanded, planting my hands on my hips.

Rennan's lip twitched, hinting at a smile. "We're ready to go whenever you are."

"Define 'we.'"

"The whole group: me, Cam, Val, and Carter."

"Blast. Okay."

"Why such a dismal reaction?"

"I was hoping Carter would get some sense and decide to stay here. Or go back to Sala. I don't really care where."

Rennan snorted. "I'm in total agreement. The dude's spoiled. He's even more inexperienced than me when it comes to adventuring! Gosh, is this how you and Cam felt when I was learning to start fires with damp twigs?"

I laughed relatively light-heartedly. "Not exactly. You weren't quite as annoying and you were far more amusing to watch than Carter ever will be."

"Well then, I'm glad to know that I'm good for something other than being an awesome sidekick," Rennan grinned. "I'm just along for the comic relief."

I cocked my head and stared at him. "You're not a sidekick, Rennan. You're your own person on this team. You bring your own skills and talents."

"Sure, the talents of a sidekick."

"You're not a sidekick!"

"Hey, are you guys coming?" Carter asked, sticking his head into the house again. He still looked sleepy, and his hair was barely tamed. He couldn't pull off the same unbrushed adventurer look that Cam could. He just looked like a wannabe Cam. "Everyone is waiting for you outside. Drew will be back in a couple minutes to see us off."

"See us off or take joy in getting rid of us?" I snickered as I walked past Carter with my pack in hand.

Rennan nodded his head in agreement. Despite the drivel we were giving the sorcerer, I respected the guy. If we survived this crazy plan of ours, he was somebody I would be inclined to come back to visit.

We stepped out into the sunshine just in time to see Drew running down the road back towards his blue house. He was too far away for us to see his expression, but I got the feeling that something wasn't quite right. 'Cause you know, it was just our luck to have something go wrong right as we were about to leave to head towards the capital. I chose to blame the fact that Carter was with us and he was a magnet for bad luck.

Cam's guarded expression seemed to confirm my thoughts. His hand moved to his side where his beautiful dagger hung. He was ready to draw it and fight at a moment's notice. "Is it me, or does he look worried?"

"I was thinking the same thing," I grimly concurred as my hands curled around a dagger.

Carter and Rennan gripped the hilts of their swords after seeing me and Cam do the same. Valerie, being the only one who didn't have a weapon, pretended to do the same motion before dissolving into giggles.

Drew quickly approached, breathless. "So, uh, got some change of plans. I'm coming with you."

"Why? You weren't supposed to. You were going to stay here and only come if there was an absolute emergency," Cam questioned immediately. He didn't even pause to let the sorcerer catch his breath!

"Well…I may or may not be in trouble with the guards again…."

"What did you do?" Cam demanded, fury rising.

"All I did was get your friends out of their cell!"

"*What did you do?!*"

"Okay, all I did was impersonate one of their superiors and sneak them out using secret passageways under the city…and then proceed to wipe everyone's memory," Drew explained quickly. He glanced nervously at Carter, Valerie, and Rennan as if to say, *Sorry.*

Now I was really glad I had fallen down into those passageways before everyone else. It sounds like I had escaped some of the chaos.

Cam wrung his hands in frustration. "I can't believe you did that. You're supposed to be a sorcerer! You're supposed to do things with tact! Now there are angry guards with magical powers on our tails who probably want to see us dead!"

"Hey, that doesn't necessarily mean I'm a good one," Drew scowled. I couldn't help but feel like there was something he wasn't telling us. "Now wouldn't it be better to get out of town before they find us?"

"Too late," a voice said from behind us.

We spun around to see the same guards who had brought us into the city. The girl's eyes sparkled with hate and ruthlessness while the guy just looked apologetic.

The woman spoke. "We've already found you."

Drew managed to draw himself up a little bit taller before he tried to reason with his fellow magic-wielders. "Look, Dione, I'm just talking to my friends here…."

"The *friends* you busted out of prison last night? Andrew, you know that's against the rules and the Code of the Ancients," the one named Dione stated bitterly. "I thought you valued your research instead of pulling stupid stunts like you attempted last time."

"Wait, just out of curiosity, what did he do last time?" Rennan questioned with a curious look on his face. His eyes sparkled with interest. However, he shrunk back slightly when Dione glared seemingly straight into his soul. Drew's eyes showed a fraction of the same emotion towards Rennan.

The blond guy, however, was happy to answer Rennan's inquiry. "Well, the last time he pulled something 'stupid,' he was busy working for weeks on a project. At one point, Dione had brought him a platter of cheese to snack on, but Drew didn't touch it. It stayed there in the sun until it became some sort of super fancy, weird cheese. The officials liked it so it's some sort of huge success. Congratulations for that, by the way, Drew buddy."

"Thanks, Krolor," Drew muttered to himself. He turned back to Dione. "Look, if you just let us get out of town, we won't bother you ever again."

Something flashed in Dione's eyes, but I couldn't place the emotion. Cam apparently could because I heard him snicker from behind me. I couldn't imagine how it could be something funny enough to make so serious an elf snicker at one of the craziest possible times.

"Andrew, you know we cannot do such a thing for you again. You've already used up all your excuses for absence from meetings and all of the other events we hold. You already have a reputation for being late to everything we know you don't want to be at. The council says—"

"The *council* can say what they wish, I'm not going to listen to them," Drew snarled. It seemed like some old memory of his was resurfacing and affecting the way he interacted with the rest of us. He cleared his throat and continued. "But I'm not speaking to the council. Dione, I'm speaking to you as my friend—"

"I'm not your friend!" Dione shouted, her cheeks flushing pink. "I never will be, not after what you did! Do what you want, Cardell! I don't care! But mark my words: I *will* be reporting this incident."

With that sudden outburst, she stalked off into the heart of the city. Krolor remained with us in front of Drew's residence. Drew muttered something in a different language and the blond man nodded his head in agreement. They exchanged a few words and then Drew turned back to us.

"Krolor is going to buy us some time while they inform the blasted Council I'm helping a bunch of escapees get out of town," Drew explained as he shouldered the satchel he had been holding. "But we don't have forever. We need to get the heck out of here."

Cam followed the example and lifted his pack onto his back. The rest of us did likewise.

"Andrew, I may have something that will be of use to you. You may find that heading to Hila will be helpful. Find the emissary from Estal and start there. I have reason to believe that mankind is in league with the blasted Hevians—no offense, my good elves—and that you should pursue something there," Krolor explained in a rather disjointed manner.

I had trouble keeping up with the flow of conversation there.

"Thank you for that very helpful piece of information," Cam stated with a forced smile.

He looked about ready to bolt, and thankfully, Drew noticed. He said a few more things to the guard in their language before sending him off and turning back to us. He specifically turned to the elf.

Cam scowled. "Well, don't look at me! It's your wretched city! It's your duty to get us out of here."

"Fair enough, but you will be taking the lead as soon as we're out of Caso like we agreed," Drew stated decisively.

Cam made some sort of weird noise, but he didn't verbally protest the "order" the sorcerer gave him.

Drew half-smiled to himself. "Since you're not complaining, I'll take that as a form of compliance."

"I will never *comply* with anything," Cam announced irritably.

He kept his hands in his pockets as we walked. He was very careful not to say anything else, either. I suspected he had a lot more words he would have loved to get out, but he just didn't think it was the right time to do so.

After a while of sneaking through the city, which consisted mostly of ducking in and out of shopping squares in the most congested part of town, somebody finally decided to break the awkward silence. Only, of course, after we had been in a clear zone for a few minutes. Surprisingly, it was Valerie who had the brains to say something sensible.

That was a first.

"Dione seemed very hostile toward you, Drew. Why is that?"

Drew sighed. "That woman… has not made it easy for me in this realm—*town*. It's a town, Andrew. Anyway, she has not made it easy for me here. When I first moved to this place, she showed me around and immediately felt something for me that I knew I couldn't keep alive. Her feelings weren't exactly my priority."

"But you live in a house by yourself! Wouldn't you want to share life with someone as magical as her?" Valerie questioned with a shocked expression on her face.

And now she was back to her regular, dim self. The sensibility was nice while it lasted.

Drew's face flushed red and he wouldn't look at anyone. His hand rose up to the locket that hung around his neck. "No. I don't want to share it with anyone here."

"That must be very lonely for you."

"Nobody has any idea of what it's like."

"That's not true," Cam piped up from the back of the party. "The exile too know constant loneliness."

I turned around so I could see him. He was nervous speaking so boldly in front of several people, a feeling made obvious by his pink cheeks and fidgeting hands.

At that, Valerie's expression softened and she ran back to Cam and enveloped him in a massive hug. He looked even more uncomfortable with her arms wrapped around his sides, but the hug kept going on until Cam looked incredibly close to pushing her away. Meanwhile, Carter and Rennan looked jealous of the hug that had been bestowed upon Cameron.

Cam cleared his throat. "Yeah. Anyway, I know the feeling, Drew."

"Glad I'm not the only one," Drew grunted as we ducked into a back alley.

We were able to catch our breath for about four seconds before alarms started blaring through the city. Cam cursed under his breath and unsheathed his main dagger. Though it was a pretty thing, it was a weapon of war.

"Get ready to run," Cam directed. He quickly started preparing for any sort of confrontation.

Everyone followed his orders, but I hung back. Cam didn't even move from his position to go with us, giving me the sneaking suspicion that he was about to do something foolish.

"What are you going to do?" I asked him quickly. Without meaning to, my tone came across far harsher than I had intended.

Cam withered slightly, but he didn't get defensive like usual. "I'm going to create a distraction for you."

Valerie squealed behind us. We whipped around and stared at her in confusion. She danced over to us and started circling Cam. I thought she looked disgustingly flirty, so I pushed the thought out of my mind. The poor elf must have felt so awkward around the mermaid before he had met us....

"No! I'll create the most perfectest, brightest, most flower-filled distraction for you!!" she volunteered eagerly.

"Creating a distraction is very dangerous and you're one of the fugitives!" Rennan argued adamantly.

He had said that he "might have" a thing for the princess, but that was an understatement. He seemed to consider himself her protector. Funny thing, she didn't even register the concern in the wolf's voice.

"Well, if somebody gets caught, it might as well be me. I have no weapons and I'm not a fighter," Valerie began, more dignified than usual, "but I am a princess and that comes with certain privileges. When they find out they've been keeping royalty captive, they'll regret it."

"That's still dangerous."

"I'm willing to do it," Valerie stated firmly.

Rennan was about to argue more, but Drew never gave him the chance.

"Rennan, let her go. It's her choice to run into something so risky," Drew instructed quickly. "Besides, we don't exactly have all day to stay here and argue about it."

He was constantly scanning the surrounding area to make sure there were no guards rushing toward us. The alarms kept blaring.

Rennan sent Valerie one last glance as if making sure she was really alright to be the distraction. If Valerie was anybody else, I would have thought it was sweet for Rennan to be so concerned. I still didn't like the mermaid, but I remembered the earlier promise I had made to Cam. I would have to try to be friends with her if this quest was going to succeed.

But I also remembered the promise I had made to Mongwau all those years ago. It was impossible for me to ignore orders without punishment. At the preferable end of the scale, I would be brought in and whipped. At the more dangerous end of said scale, I would have a bounty on my head and be brought in to be tortured or worse. No matter what I chose, I would be a fugitive in some way. So, the question was: do I turn in the heads of the princes or do I ignore the orders and let them live?

"Alright. Be safe, Val," Rennan sighed.

Valerie nodded and ran off into the streets again. Minutes later, we heard shouting and figured it was a pretty good time to get out of there. Most of Valerie's distraction was on the east side of town, so we went west. Hopefully she knew we would be heading towards Hila and would meet us on the road there. Or at least she had the sense to head in that direction once she escaped.

We were out of town and a good way away minutes later, thanks to the "expert" directions from Drew. The sorcerer somehow managed to get us lost in the smallest part of town and Cam thought it had taken far too long to get out of there.

Due to his own frustration with being lost during a time crunch, Cam had shapeshifted into a falcon so he could guide us out of Caso. Until then, I hadn't realized that he could transform into a complete animal, not just a hybrid or any other humanoid creature. His ability was truly spectacular.

"Okay, is everyone here?" Cam said when we had met up with him again.

He had apparently been elf again for a few minutes and was still readjusting to his own fingers. Personally, I thought that was kind of amusing to watch. It almost made me think of last night when he had come outside wrapped up in a thick blanket. It was so childish and yet so sweet.

"We're all accounted for, minus the princess," Carter replied as he set his pack down in the shade of a tall pine tree. He seemed to be already exhausted from doing practically nothing. We would have a very long trek to Hila if he started complaining along with Rennan. I didn't think I would be able to handle that.

"Present!" called a bubbly voice.

Startled, we all looked around us, but we couldn't figure out where the voice was coming from. There was nobody in sight.

The voice called again, "Down here in the stream. The water is fairly cool if you want to put your feet in! All you have to do is avoid stepping on all the little fishies!"

The five of us slowly crept closer to the bank of the river to our right. We looked town to see Valerie treading water. Her long, pink tail flicked in different directions to keep her upright. Momentarily forgetting my resentment of the mermaid, I stared in awe at her tail. It sparkled like several thousand diamonds had been expertly attached.

"How did you get past the guards so quickly?" Cam questioned.

"Yeah, and why aren't the alarms still blaring?" Drew added.

Valerie smiled proudly. "To those of you who started this thing in Sala, remember when I promised that I wouldn't be like the sirens in the Old Stories?"

"Yes," Cam agreed shortly, "Continue."

"Well, that promise was directed to you guys, not people who held us captive," the mermaid stated with a mischievous grin. Cam's eyebrows flew up in surprise.

"Are you saying you actually managed to do it?" he demanded, taking a cautious step backwards. I also noticed that it was almost directly behind me. Valerie's eyes sparkled, seemingly confirming whatever Cam was afraid of. "What did you tell them to do?"

"First of all, I want to know what the elf is so scared of," Rennan interrupted as his impish grin spread across his face. "Second of all, what were you able to accomplish, Valerie?"

"Well, Rennan, I'm glad you asked! It's something my mom has been trying to teach me for years: the song of the ancient sirens. It enchants whoever hears it, and if they have a weak enough soul, they obey. It's manipulative, and we merfolk don't like to use it very much now," Valerie explained cheerfully. "And Cameron, I just told them all to turn the alarms off, forget about the escaped prisoners, and to all go take a nap."

If it was able to manipulate almost anyone into doing anything, I could see why Cam was somewhat wary. It was weird, though, because his powers were about a thousand times scarier and he seemed to be frightened by a simple enchantment.

"Okay, that's good. I was worried for a second that you had started a blood bath," Cam sighed with relief.

He tried for a teasing expression, but he didn't fool me. There was something on his mind, and it wasn't how he could make this conversation more humorous. No matter what it was, it was wise that he didn't bother voicing it to the rest of the group.

"So, you didn't convince them otherwise about my situation?" Drew asked quietly. He couldn't make eye contact with anybody. His shoulders sagged and his coppery hair hung into his face, almost blocking us from seeing his expression.

Valerie's aura of glee dimmed noticeably. Her jolly face fell and she looked down. She slowly pushed herself up out of the water and her tail gradually transformed into her legs. When they were completely solid and separate again, Valerie stood up and walked over to Drew.

She wrapped her arms around him in an apologetic hug. "I wasn't able to do anything that would make them forget you completely. You've been here longer than us, so it would take who knows how long to block all their memories of you."

"Were you able to do anything?" Drew asked again, not moving from Valerie's tight embrace. I didn't know if he didn't mind it or if he was too upset to do anything to get away from it.

"Well, I was able to make them think that you're just leaving town for a while and to just repurpose your house. Sorry. You didn't seem very happy there anyway," Valerie hesitantly admitted. She looked like she felt really bad.

To our surprise, Drew threw his head back and laughed. Carter and Rennan looked at him like he was crazy, Valerie was confused, Cam's face was as still as stone, and I just didn't know what to think.

Drew grinned. "Good! You're right; I did hate it there. I've always liked traveling abroad better. Now that they're repurposing everything, I can start journeying again."

"Where will you go?" Carter questioned. He was uneasy speaking for one of the first times today.

"I don't know yet. Wherever the path takes me, I guess. If you don't mind, I'll probably just follow you guys for a while," Drew answered, looking to Cam for his consent to join the quest.

"You helped save me from the poison, so I'm temporarily indebted to you," Cam began slowly, as if trying to articulate a perfect answer. "It would also be senseless if I declined the help of a sorcerer. So, if you choose to come with us, you're welcome to. Having another magic-wielder in our ranks probably wouldn't be a bad idea."

"Well, in that case, consider me the next person you're stuck with," Drew half-smiled.

Ending the Caso incident on a high note, we shouldered our packs and headed out again. We were proceeding to Hila to see if we could find out anything about this alliance between Heviah and Estal.

Last Second Rescue

"Are we there yet?" Rennan asked for the sixty-fifth time that afternoon.

I kid you not, I had kept track of every blasted time he uttered the question. Sixty-five might seem like a lot, but that was nothing to his total number of complaints. That number was off the charts. I hadn't bothered to keep track of it since I was already exhausted and my patience was worn thin. It also didn't help that Carter had been adding his own grumbling and aggressive comments into the mix.

"Rennan, I don't know how in all the kingdoms you manage to ask that same, stupid question so many times in the same afternoon," Cam mumbled in disbelief.

We had been walking since we had fled from Caso early in the morning. There had been a brief stop for lunch, but Cam had gotten us going again so we wouldn't be out in the open for too long. Since then, there had been never-ending complaints from Rennan and the "palace children," as I had come to call them.

"Maybe it's because I still haven't received a suitable answer," Rennan hinted, sending a sidelong glance at Cam.

The elf glared right back at him. "That is *so* not the reason and you know it."

"Man, I'm just trying to keep the mood light," Rennan chuckled, draping an arm around Cam's shoulders.

I would have expected Cam to react, but I think he was too exhausted to do anything other than keep walking.

"But seriously, are we there yet?" Rennan asked, deadpan.

"Okay, that's it!" Cam shouted as he ducked out from under Rennan's arm.

The wolf looked shocked at the quick action. Cam, however, was very irritated as he sprinted ahead of the rest of us. He didn't even look back once. Soon, he was just a small shadow on the horizon.

"What's his problem?" Carter asked apathetically.

I don't know what bothered me more: the fact that he didn't care for his brother at all or that he was just an all-around snobbish imbecile. I could teach him a thing or two about how to be helpful…hybrid style.

Ignoring Carter, I asked, "He does know how to get to Hila, right?"

Drew nodded as he stepped up to continue guiding us toward one of Mahe's larger cities. He almost seemed uncomfortable leading us. "Yeah, he knows where he's going. We were talking about it earlier, so he should be fine."

"Okay then."

I dropped back to the tail end of the group and cherished the quiet. I had some time, even if it was probably just a few seconds in the great scheme of things, to gather my thoughts and try to make sense of them. I tried to look at it logically, but the longer I tried, the more I realized Cam was right when he said that not everything was logical. I missed Cam already.

At one point, Rennan appeared at my side. I glanced at him in the corner of my eye, but I didn't think that he noticed.

He was worried and fidgety. Honestly? Part of me didn't want to know why. This guy could be so irritating, but he could also smell trouble with that extra powerful wolf nose of his.

"Do you think I offended him?"

"Who?" I asked, startled out of my thoughts.

"Cam."

"Oh, I don't know. I can never get a perfect read on that guy."

"I know. I can't either. He's very guarded. Or at least he has been recently," Rennan sighed, his head hung low. "We were friends, but now I think ruined everything."

"He has been more guarded recently, especially since he fought that dragon. That fight changed something in him," I agreed softly, "but Rennan, you didn't ruin everything. You *are* still friends. I thought I had ruined everything when I lost my temper, but we're still friends. True friends are the ones who go through dust ups and come out stronger."

"True, I guess, but friends don't always annoy the tar out of each other just for the fun of it. At least, not in the way I did. I pushed him too far after he asked me not to," Rennan managed quietly.

He couldn't bear to look up at me.

Awkwardly, I wrapped an arm around him. He did the same to me, and it didn't feel as awkward.

"Just wait until he comes back, then you can talk to him."

"Assuming he wants to talk to me again."

"Quit being pessimistic. That's my job. Just be kind to him."

"Okay. I'll make sure of it."

Cam returned about an hour or so later, but he didn't have much to say to anyone. Drew led us to Hila while Cam brought up the end of the group.

Rennan made no effort to go talk to Cam immediately, and the elf was the same way. Instead, they remained silent, walking on either side of me. I was literally in the middle of this thing between them and I had no intention of staying there. Deciding to make them sort out their differences, I walked ahead and fell in step with Drew.

"Hmm?" Drew asked out of the blue.

"I didn't say anything," I answered quickly.

He must have thought I said something when I appeared beside him. He must be used to being interrupted a lot if that was his automatic response.

"Oh, sorry," he said, running a hand through his coppery hair. It hung loosely around his face, shielding the sides of his expression from anyone who stood directly beside him. I could tell, however, that his purplish-blue eyes were trained on the terrain dead ahead. "Did Cameron come back?"

"Yes, did you not notice?"

"No, I was too busy thinking about what's happened in the last few weeks for me. It's been a nightmare," Drew hesitantly admitted. His shoulders sagged again, like a heavy load being placed on a table that didn't stand a chance of supporting it.

"I can understand that. My last few months have mostly been one disaster after another."

"Do you understand, though? Do you know what it's like to lose somebody you dearly love? It's hard for most people to know what such a thing feels like. Or at least it is in my culture."

"I've experienced more than some people will ever know. I lost my parents when I was four and my grandmother who raised me mere months ago. Not to mention I was betrayed by someone who was once a close friend. Believe me, I know what it's like to lose somebody you love and hold close to your heart. It takes a while for the hole to close again."

And yet, yours still *hasn't healed*, I thought to myself.

Yeah, like that was an encouraging thought at that moment. I didn't want to think about the family I had lost. That would distract me from the task at hand: get to Hila and figure out how to bust the elves and their allies.

"Scarlet, you have my respect for sharing something personal instead of saying 'I'm sorry for your loss' like most other people. You have a good heart," Drew commented, finally looking me in the eyes. "I'm sorry to cut the conversation short, but I can't force myself to talk about it anymore."

I don't know why, but it bothered me when people didn't make perfect eye contact when I was directly speaking to them. I just had a better feeling about the fact that they acknowledge me when they look at me.

"That's fine," I answered, relieved that he didn't want to keep talking about losses. I had handled nearly more than I could handle. It wasn't an easy thing to talk about.

I was lost in thought when a tall shadow crossed my path. I looked to my side to see Cam walking right next to me. "Did you talk to Rennan?"

"Yeah, things between us are good now. I just needed to get away from people for a while," Cam answered.

A wave of concern flooded through me. His eyes were anywhere but me, constantly scanning everything around us. I didn't know what he was so worried about.

Cam continued. "Rennan is fine now. He's going to talk to Valerie about…stuff. I don't know. I didn't pay attention when he was talking to me about her."

"Sounds like every other day to me," I snorted.

I admit I too ignored Rennan's conversations with Valerie when I could avoid it. This, thankfully, was pretty often. I didn't know what it was about that girl, other than the fact that her smile reminded me of Razil's way too much, that drove me absolutely insane.

But I soon grew serious. "But are you okay? You seem distant."

"Me? Distant? I don't know what you're—oh, who am I kidding? I'm not *trying* to be distant," Cam moped.

His head hung low and his hands were back in his pockets. He sighed. Drew somehow took a hint and started walking forward again to give us a little bit of space. Cam slowed his pace so everyone else would pass us as well. I didn't know what he was thinking, but it felt a little fishy for Drew to just leave me with Cam.

He whispered. "Are we friends?"

His question caught me by surprise. It took me a minute to figure out what he meant and then to form an answer. "Yes, Cam, of course we're friends. What makes you think otherwise?"

"You've seen the damage I can cause firsthand. I try to control it, but it happens anyway. I don't see how anyone can still be friends with somebody like me after so many disasters. I mean, the day I killed that wolf and lost it, when Carter ran into us in Sala and I lost it, the Spiral of Doom when I lost it, the dragon when I went crazy trying to take it on singlehandedly…you get the point," Cam noted dismally. A very heavy feeling settled over me before he continued. "I'm a monster who doesn't mix well with others."

"You're not a monster," I offered feebly.

Cam just laughed without humor.

I didn't know what else to say; I didn't want to say anything to make him think he was a villain or anything. However, He did have a point—he was different than other people I had met before. He had immense power that occasionally slipped from his control, sure, but I didn't see how anybody could be as powerful as him and completely restrain it. Still, I shuddered, thinking about the possibility of Cam letting all his power loose.

"Cam, you aren't a freak," I eventually managed. Why it was so hard for me to get the words out, I didn't know. Normally, I didn't have nearly as much trouble speaking quickly. "Please don't ever think that."

"Do you really believe that? Or are you just trying to console me?"

I hesitated, not knowing what to say, and Cam noticed. He hung his head, the tips of his ears slightly pink.

"Cam...," I reached towards him, but he panicked and jumped away from me.

"No! Don't make this worse. I already know I don't belong in your honorable company. I can't believe I thought we could actually do this. I...I'm not worth it," Cam said quickly, his voice breaking. He reacted like a cornered animal. "I beg of you, just let me go."

"Cam, no! We need you! This wasn't a mistake!" I protested desperately. "You are not a mistake!"

We wouldn't get anywhere in this quest without Cam. He was our peace, our justice, and our order. There would be no team if he didn't keep us from arguing from sunrise to sunset. Drew did what he could when Cam was absent, but there was something about Cam that couldn't be replaced.

Cam pulled away and shook his head forlornly. "No, Scarlet, I know where my place is, and it's not with you. I was exiled for a reason: I don't belong anywhere."

"Cam," I began gently, "you were exiled because you chose to follow your own path and not conform to a broken, empty, oblivious way of living. You chose to see things how they truly are and to do something about it! I don't know of anyone else who would do such a thing for somebody other than themselves. You genuinely care for others and we care for you…in our own special ways. Please don't abandon us. I doubt we'd get very far without your leadership. We need you, Cam."

I knew it was probably a lost cause, but I figured I might as well beg him to stay. It didn't seem like things could get any worse.

There was no way I would be able to figure out what Cam's mindset was, either. Rennan was absolutely right—it was hard to get a good read on Cam. His expression did not betray his thoughts or emotions.

At that point in time, he just stared at the ground directly in front of him with a stone face. I could have sworn that I saw a small tear run down his cheek.

"Blast. I'm sorry I'm such a failure to you guys. I don't know what I was thinking. There's no way I'm about to leave you—not when we've come so far," he apologized a few minutes later. His face was still somber, but he was sincere. "I'm staying and I won't leave. Please hold me to that. Also…thanks for listening, even if I shouldn't have said any of it. I appreciate it. You're a good friend, Scarlet."

"You're…welcome. You're always welcome around me, Cam. That

will never change," I answered.

I had done nothing to deserve his gratitude. Not after everything I had been planning to carry out the orders Mongwau had given me. I was just glad Cam was staying and wouldn't be abandoning us any time soon. I hoped he never would.

"Things will change in the coming weeks, Scarlet. I promise you that. But I would rather be facing them with you than on my own," Cam said quietly.

I looked up at him and he offered me a weak smile. The corners of my mouth twitched upwards, but they never reached a full grin.

Our quiet conversation was interrupted by an anxious Rennan approaching us. Cam's face became firm again, showing almost no sign of any of the emotions that had flown across his face seconds ago.

"What's wrong?" Cam demanded.

"So…uh…Hila is on the horizon…," Rennan began nervously.

His ears twitched like they always did when he was anxious. His pale blue eyes roved around, constantly scanning for something that wasn't there. I immediately tensed up and became on edge. I sensed that Cam did as well. His left hand moved towards his dagger.

"What is it?" the elf questioned again.

"Defenses—and a lot of them. These wizards seriously know how to protect their work."

"Well, that's just great," Cam stated sarcastically. He muttered some elvish under his breath. It was probably intentional that we did not understand it.

"What kind of defenses?" I asked.

Rennan looked at me for a brief second before his furry ears went back to twitching. How his hair didn't get messed up with all that twitching, I don't know. Rennan truly had skills for the most obscure things in the world.

"You wouldn't believe me if I told you. You need to see it for yourself."

"Then we'll come see it," Cam decided. Rennan nodded and ran up ahead to join the rest of the group. When it was just the two of us again, Cam pulled out the intricate dagger that hung at his side. He held it up to his face and it glimmered in the spring sunlight. "No matter what it is, I'm sure it will be an excellent chance to use Egladel."

"What in the world is Egladel?" I questioned in confusion. The name was foreign to my ears.

"My dagger! Its name is Egladel," he answered with raised eyebrows. "Did I not tell you?"

"No, you didn't! When did you do that and where did you get it? You didn't have it when I met you in Leshee."

"Queen Coral had it made for me when we stayed in Sala. She said, 'A true king needs a weapon just as great,'" Cam shrugged, perfectly mimicking Queen Coral's voice. I wondered if that was a skill that came with shape-shifting. Cam sheathed his dagger again. It truly was a magnificent weapon. "I really thought I told you."

"You didn't. You've been pretty distracted and all, what with almost dying again. How many times have you almost died, exactly?"

"Meh…I don't remember anymore. I used to keep a count, but I lost track of it about a year or two ago. Let's just say I know way more ways to die than the average person," Cam chuckled nervously. "Anyway. My dagger's name is Egladel."

"I don't recognize the name. What does it mean?" I asked, curiosity growing.

Cam smiled sheepishly. "It's elvish for 'forgotten horror.' I thought it would be a pretty fitting name considering my past."

"You are way too young to have a terrible past," I laughed quietly.

I half-expected Cam to get mad at me, but he actually laughed. It was a wonderful sound to hear him laugh in all the chaos shaping my reality.

"I know. It makes some things hard for me. I still think it's still a fitting name for the blade, though. Isn't it?"

"It is. It's a remarkable blade. Though, mine are still nicer," I said with a teasing smirk.

I knew that his dagger was a far higher quality than any of mine, but I had had my father's daggers since I was twelve. They were special to me, so I was relatively biased in my opinion. Cam just looked at me skeptically before he burst out laughing. I marveled at how quickly his mood could change in only a few minutes.

"Biased traitor!" he jokingly accused me. He kept laughing, but then controlled himself. However, once he controlled himself, he just started laughing again. I'll admit that I also started laughing. "Yeah, I think I need help."

"I think we're all going to need help if we're going to try to get into that blasted city," Carter stated sourly as we joined the rest of the group.

They were hiding in the brush looking out at the city. Cam immediately tensed up and returned to the normal state I was used to seeing him in: serious.

Carter asked, "Think you can get past this one, Mr. Wall Jumper?"

"Okay, I literally only heard the last statement. Why are you calling him 'Mr. Wall Jumper?'" Rennan interrupted with an evil grin on his face.

Cam glared at the wolf and his brother. I couldn't tell if he was daring them to say something else or just glaring at them to shut up.

Carter smiled mischievously. "Oh, he earned the name when we were twelve. We had been playing with one of our balls in the palace gardens and then he accidentally threw it over the wall—"

"You mean *you* accidentally threw it over the wall. Why must you always twist stories? I know I'm tall, but I wasn't tall enough to catch that horrible throw from you. What were you trying to do? Throw it to one of the wood nymphs on the other side? Everyone at the palace knew that you always flirted with them. Do you still do that?" Cam interrupted with a gleam in his eye that showed not only his own evil mischief, but his embarrassment of being talked about.

"N-no! I don't do that anymore!" the younger elf stammered, cheeks as red as a tomato. He cleared his throat and continued when he regained some of his dignity. "Anyway, we were trying to get the ball—"

"You may want to save story time for later, kids," Drew warned. "We have bigger problems at hand. How the heck are we going to get into the city? Those walls are way too high to get over stealthily, wall jumper or no."

He pointed to the tops of the walls where sentries were posted. They had some pretty ferocious looking beasts I did not want to face unarmed…or armed. They were nasty looking things.

"I could always cause a distraction again," Valerie volunteered, but she didn't exactly look too excited about it.

She must have thought that we could come up with something better or something. Or maybe there was something else going on in her head. Her pink eyes were darting around, looking at everything.

"Too dangerous," Cam stated, immediately dismissing the idea. "There are way too many sentries to distract. Even if she tried that, there's a ninety-nine to one chance all of us would make it through without injury or capture."

"Well, aren't you a little ray of pitch black?" Carter muttered.

Cam shot him a sidelong glare, but said nothing. Instead, the elder elf waited for anyone else to pipe up with a good idea.

Carter, surprisingly, was the next one to offer a plan. "We could always use magic to try to sneak through the gates."

We all looked to Drew, who flinched. "That would not be a wise idea. I already have a pretty bad track record and am notorious for pulling stuff like this. If I were to receive one more warning, well...."

He mimed getting his head cut off. We got the idea.

"Okay, so that got us nowhere," Cam declared sullenly.

No one had any other ideas to offer, so we were sort of at an impasse. We would have to wait in the bushes until we came up with something that might actually work.

"I have a solution," Rennan announced.

Cam sighed in relief. "Thank goodness."

"It involves fire."

"Absolutely not."

"Aw, why not?"

"Because we would cause unnecessary destruction when we're trying *not* to create any more enemies for ourselves. Wizards are bad enemies, right Drew?"

Drew nodded in agreement.

"So what? We already have a bunch of enemies. What's a few more?"

"How about…death! That's what a few more will equal."

"Then let's cheat death, shall we?"

"You're really going with this idea, aren't you?" Cam moaned as he ran his hands through his hair.

Rennan smiled and nodded his head ecstatically.

"The gates appear to be made of wood. We could easily throw a fireball or something over in the opposite direction and make for the gates while the sentries are all confused," Rennan explained quickly.

While he was speaking, Drew and Cam seemed to be weighing the risks and inspecting the visible areas of the gate for a possible weak spot. They seemed to converse telepathically before turning back to Rennan.

The wolf grinned. "So? Do you think it will work?"

"It will, but we're going to have to be fast to get in and get hidden," Cam started slowly. He hesitated and took one last look at everything before continuing. "We strike there and then sprint to the gate. Drew will have to put a cloaking device on us so we're not seen. Then we need to find somewhere to stay for the night."

"Got it. We're ready to go whenever you are," I stated with a nod of acknowledgement.

Cam sent me a small, encouraging smile before turning back to the others. He fidgeted with something in his satchel before pulling it out. It was a small, metal object with a red stone set into the middle of it. I guessed it was some object of mass destruction.

Cam nodded his head in approval for whatever he was holding. He looked around at us. "Is everyone ready?"

We all nodded.

"Alright," he said, "let's get this party started."

Drew put a cloaking device over us and we sprinted out of the bushes. Cam broke off from us at one point so he could throw his glowing metal device at the wall. He returned as soon as the wall erupted into tongues of fire.

Rennan and I stared at it in astonishment, no doubt imagining the destruction of our hometown. Cam wrapped his arms around us in a sympathetic manner. Putting grief aside, we rushed through the gates while all the sentries were distracted.

As it turned out, Drew's shield didn't last for very long. We were barely inside the city when we were spotted. We took off running down the side streets to try to escape all of the guards. I respected them for having so much security; I wished the Paleeans had a united force like that. I also despised them for making our job way more difficult than it needed to be.

We found ourselves at a fork in the road. There were several taller buildings surrounding us and we couldn't see where the path led unless Cam shapeshifted, which he plainly told us he would not do because it was too risky. He also seemed, at least to me, more drained of energy when he returned to his human form. Cam was adamant that we had to choose a direction, but before we could choose, we heard footsteps thumping down the alley.

Dirt got kicked up into my eyes, blinding me. I cried out for the others to wait up, but I don't think they did. A strong hand—I assumed it was Cam's—grabbed my arm and pulled me down the right-hand path. He led me through the streets until we huddled down in a shadowed corner. I only knew that because it was chillier there than in the dimming light of the rest of the city. Immediately, I started wiping the dirt out of my eyes so I would be able to see. I didn't want to be dragged around like a child.

"Did you get it all out?" an accented voice asked me.

But it wasn't Cam's. It wasn't nearly as deep and the accent wasn't as thick. I scowled when I realized who had actually helped me.

"I think so, but I'm going to need a few minutes to recover my sight," I muttered, rubbing the bridge of my nose. My eyes stung where the sandy dirt had hit them and tears gushed as they tried to completely purge the dirt out of my eyes. Minutes later, I had regained my sight. I looked up at the sky and around the alleyway. "Where are the others?"

"We got separated," Carter replied irritably.

I didn't know what disgusted me more—that Carter had tried to be kind to me or that he had actually touched my arm. I gagged thinking about it.

Carter continued. "I admit I got turned around when we were bolting and I thought they went this way."

"Well, you were wrong. It's too late and too dangerous to backtrack to them," I decided, getting to my feet and drawing one of my daggers. I wanted to be armed just in case.

I looked around the alley some more and discovered that this city was far more intricate than I had previously thought. It was far more advanced than the clay huts that I had grown up around. These were expertly carved stones that soared three or four levels into the sky.

I muttered, "They have to be overrun with guards and all kinds of sentries."

"You're probably right," Carter agreed, nervously fingering the handle to his sword. "Or maybe we were right and the others took the wrong way. If we can find them…maybe I still have a chance to redeem myself after all."

I scowled at him. "Are you still trying to get the signet ring so you can ascend to the throne? Are you still selfish enough to want to see your brother dead?"

"What? Scarlet, I know I haven't always had my brother's best interests at heart, but he's still blood family," Carter said quietly. His face showed signs of hurt and fear. The fear was rational since I kept twirling my knife in my hand, anticipating an attack. But the hurt in his eyes seemed forced. "I wouldn't want to see him dead. But wouldn't mind being redeemed from…."

"Stop. Talking," I growled. "You care nothing for others—only yourself!"

A new energy flowed through my veins, filling me with the urge to fight and kill this self-centered elf. Deep, deep in my soul, there was a burning feeling I couldn't describe. Carter refused to admit that he was still looking for the signet ring so he could be king. With that kind of power, who could stop him? Who could stop anyone who wielded it?

"Scarlet, that's not what I meant!" Carter protested. His grey eyes were wide with terror.

I followed his gaze to the long knife that I held in my right hand. It splashed pale light in various places in the alleyway. Moonlight wasn't the only thing it was capable of splashing.

I stared at my reflection in its sharp blade. If I carried out my orders right here and now and took the token to Mongwau, I could just blame it on the guards. I wouldn't have to worry about explaining how Carter died. I would just need to make sure that I had a perfect story constructed to cover up any missing details. My arm rose to strike.

"Scarlet, please don't," Carter pleaded.

I slowly raised my arm, establishing my aim. Carter realized what was going on and looked up at the point. His eyes fell to the ground when he understood what I was doing.

I snarled, "What's stopping me?"

"Me, that's what," another voice shouted coldly.

Whoever it belonged to blocked my strike. I glared at the newcomer. I looked up to see Cam's grey eyes glowering down at me. He held his blade where it stopped mine right before it reached Carter's chest. He completed a quick maneuver which lowered my blade back down to my side. I growled ferociously. I didn't want him to get in the way of me and orders that I needed to carry out.

He just stared at me. "Scarlet, this isn't you."

"For all you know, it is," I spat. "You elves are all the same. You only care for yourselves, not caring for lives you deem lesser than your own!"

Both elves looked at me in surprise, like they couldn't believe that I would be so openly blunt.

"Choose your next words very carefully," Cam uttered quietly.

"Otherwise, you'll force my hand."

He didn't make eye contact with me as he drew himself up to his full height. However, that didn't intimidate me in the least.

"Let her force your hand, brother. She isn't herself and this version of Scarlet scares me," Carter pleaded, grabbing hold of his brother's shoulder.

Cam shot a warning glance at his brother. Carter shrank back while Cam turned to me. "Scarlet, lower your daggers."

"I…I won't! I have orders that need to be carried out."

Cam cocked his head and his eyebrows drew closer together in his glare. "What orders? Speak!"

I grinned evilly, anticipating what was to come. I would attack when they least expected it. "Orders to kill you both. There's a reward being offered for your heads, you know. I'll be paid a pretty price if I turn in even one of you. Dead or alive—it doesn't matter."

"But I-I thought we were friends," Carter stammered in surprise.

"I was *never* your friend."

"You're right, brother," Cam stated. "The Scarlet I know would never turn in or harm her friends for a reward."

"Then you obviously don't know me!" I shouted. I could feel my face flushing red as blood rushed to my head.

When I couldn't take it anymore, I raised my dagger and rushed at Cam. He dodged the blade and kicked me back. I grunted and turned to face him again. His face was so serene that I couldn't tell what was going through his head. Whatever it was, it wouldn't be going through his head for much longer.

I snarled. "If you knew me, you would know what I truly felt!"

"I know what you feel, Scarlet. I know the pain from all those who betrayed you, hurt you, lied to you," Cam answered, landing a solid kick to my knee.

I yelped as my dagger flew out of my hand. I was too angry to retrieve it, so I just threw myself at Cam.

He caught my fist and looked at me apologetically. "Please, Scarlet, I really don't want to do this."

I gritted my teeth together. "Yeah? Well, I do. Do your worst, elf."

"You're both asking for trouble," Carter piped up from the corner.

That coward.

"I hate doing this so, *so* much," Cam sighed, releasing my fist and sheathing Egladel.

I looked at him in confusion when he took a step back and held his arms out wide. He looked like he was surrendering, but I knew he wasn't committing. The elf was too clever for that. This was some trick.

"What are you doing?" I demanded.

"I'm giving you a chance to fight."

"What? Do you think I'm not worthy enough of an adversary?"

"Well, you don't put up much of a challenge."

"Challenge?" I asked incredulously. I laughed darkly, and then went dead serious again. "*Challenge*. You want a challenge? I'll give you one!"

I swung my arm for another punch, right to his chest, but what should have been a direct hit sailed right through him. It was like he wasn't there. His form disappeared right in front of my eyes and appeared behind me. Not waiting for an explanation, I tried the same move again. The same thing happened.

"What are you doing? Those blows should have incapacitated you!" I shouted.

Cam smirked slightly. "All I did was use a skill that goes hand-in-hand with shape-shifting: rematerializing. You'll never hit me if I don't want you to."

"That's cheating!" I argued.

Cam sighed, long and pained.

While his eyes weren't on me, I unsheathed another dagger and held it to his throat. "Surrender. Now."

He slowly raised his hands in submission. Then he took me by surprise and laid his hand over my face. He began muttering phrases in elvish, which eventually grew louder and louder. I felt energy coursing through my veins again. The energy built until it felt like my head was going to explode.

Finally, I screamed as the energy completely left my body. I fell to the ground and started coughing because whatever Cam had done had ripped all the breath out of my lungs. When I mustered the strength, I looked up to see shadows swirling around Cam again. I couldn't comprehend what it meant.

He cried out as a funnel of shadows rose from the ground around him and took off into the sky. He was completely hidden from sight. I would have been obliterated if Carter hadn't rushed forward to drag me back into the safety of his corner.

Shadows flew everywhere and the winds picked up. They turned into a tornado of dark energy, but then a green lightning bolt split the sky and the shadows evaporated. The shadowy tornado left a drained Cam standing where it had once been.

Carter rushed forward to catch his brother before he fell over and hit his head.

"What did you just do?" Carter demanded from Cam when we had propped him against one of the walls.

Cam said nothing for the moment. Instead, he sat there, glaring at his brother and trying to regain the ability to speak.

"Other than attracting everyone in this place to us," I added quickly.

I pulled a canteen of water out of my satchel, which was lying nearby, and handed it to Cam. He took it gratefully. He ran his hands through his dark hair. It shone silver in the moonlight. The moon and stars had risen quickly, and we were now in the cover of darkness.

"Scarlet had a shadow demon," Cam eventually rasped out.

I stared at him numbly. I had had one of the same demons that Cam himself suffered from? Was that what had been affecting my judgment for the last day? I felt sick to my stomach.

He covered his face with his hand. "I took it from you. I didn't want to see you suffer...."

"No, you are not passing out on us now," Carter ordered, taking hold of his shoulders. "We need to get to the others, or at least find safety. Do you know where they are?"

Cam's eyes fluttered drowsily, but they flew open a second later.

"I don't," Cam admitted quietly. "When we realized you weren't with us, I ran back to try to find you guys."

Carter helped him up. It was almost touching to see Carter helping his twin, but then I remembered that Carter was still trying to redeem himself by getting the signet ring to Heviah. I would never let that happen.

"I'm glad you did," Carter said. "Otherwise, I don't think I would be breathing right now."

"Probably not," I agreed quietly. "You came in the nick of time."

I lowered my head in shame. I couldn't believe I had tried to accomplish Mongwau's orders. Carter was still a member of my team and he still had valuable information for us when we got to Heviah even if he wasn't my favorite person in the world.

"Glad I'm appreciated," Cam smiled weakly. "Now come on, let's get out of here. We've lingered too long."

"Agreed," Carter nodded.

We snuck out of the alleyway and tried to head towards the city library. Carter and I basically carried Cam through the streets for a while because he simply didn't have the ability to support himself. He had been drained of so much of his energy when the shadows took over. Still, I was glad he had purged mine from me. I had greater respect for what he faced day in and day out.

We were almost to the library when we heard scuffling boots behind us. Cam motioned for us to be silent as we slipped into another one of the back streets that was completely hidden in darkness. Cam was at the head of the side street, with me right next to him and Carter on my other side.

We patiently waited for whoever was running down the street to come into view. We didn't want to take any unnecessary chances and get ourselves killed long before our quest was complete.

Soon, the figures making the suspicious noise came into sight. We were overjoyed to see Drew, Rennan, and Valerie.

"Thank goodness you're alive!" Rennan cried out as loudly as he dared, capturing me in a hug. He lifted me off the ground in his excitement. When he eventually released me, he was grinning widely and his blue eyes sparkled with relief. "When we saw a shadowy tornado thing and the green lightning, we thought the sentries got you."

"Yeah, what happened with that, anyway?" Drew questioned as he slapped Cam on the back.

The elf flinched slightly, but tried not to show it. I think he was still more drained from the shadows than he let on. Drew sent me a knowing look and I lowered my eyes. He likely guessed what had happened. Before Cam got the chance to speak, however, Valerie crushed him with a hug. Then she moved right along to Carter.

"Uh, let's just say some chaos occurred. A guard or two attacked and I summoned some magic to help defeat them," Cam explained. He caught my eye and seemed to tell me, *I won't say a word if you don't mention anything.*

I nodded my head ever so slightly. Even Carter got the message.

Cam sent a questioning gaze to the others. "How did you get past those other guards?"

I had almost forgotten Cam had been with the others before he caught up with Carter and me to get us out of that mess. I'm glad he had shown up when he did, though. One more minute and Carter wouldn't be with us now and who knows what the shadow demons would have done to my sanity?

Drew cringed and made a face. "We had no choice but to slay them all."

Valerie looked apologetic and went over to give Drew a hug. He was so miserable that he didn't even notice. He couldn't make eye contact with anyone. When Valerie released him, however, he did smile at her appreciatively.

"We're sorry about your brethren, Drew," she began. Her usually bubbly voice was noticeably calm as she spoke. She was becoming far more level-headed than the flighty mermaid she had once been. "I hope you get a chance one day to visit again when our lives aren't in danger."

"Yeah, I would like to, but I don't think it will happen anytime soon," Drew sighed.

Cam nodded in agreement with the sorcerer's words.

"Drew is right. There are dark days ahead. We all need to be ready to face them, no matter what it takes. It will be physically and emotionally demanding as we pass through the desert into Estal to see what sort of corruption lies there. The endless desert will drive you mad in that kingdom," Cameron stated gravely.

All eyes turned to the elf dressed in black.

"You speak as if you've been there before," Rennan noted.

Cam's face became distant with a memory he had long since forgotten. It took a minute for the elf to come back, but when he did, he nodded. "I *have* been there—and not under peaceful circumstances. I don't want to dive into details, but what you need to know is that the Estalites are not the most welcoming people. They live in the burning desert, sure, but they're colder than the furthest reaches of the north."

"You're not talking about the Uncharted North, are you?" Carter asked with a shudder.

"That is exactly what I'm talking about."

"You've been there, too, haven't you?"

“I have. It’s not pleasant either.”

“We’ve gotten off track. We need to get into the library, find anything of use, and get out of here. We managed to buy ourselves some time with the walls and whatnot, but those aren’t going to last forever,” Drew warned us, moving closer to the library entrance. “Let’s get what we need and get a move on.”

“Drew is right,” Rennan affirmed. “Our greatest weapon here will be speed and efficiency.”

“Then let’s get to it. I have no intention of getting caught in another Mahean city,” Valerie agreed as she nervously wrung her hands.

Every single one of us agreed with her.

With that, we all crept up to the stairs of the library. The doors were locked, but Drew and Cam wouldn’t take no for an answer. They quickly found a way to break the lock (with a lot of bickering and muttering in other languages) and push the heavy mahogany doors open. The six of us gazed into the library.

We were in.

City On Fire

"Are we really here right now?" Cam breathed as he strode into the library. His head was lifted so he could see everything in the massive, book-filled structure.

While he was absorbing the glory of all that knowledge, I could only stand there numbly. My mind flashed back to the blood covered books in the library during the massacre that had taken my parents from me.

Rennan must have noticed my unease, because he laid a hand on my shoulder as if promising that everything was going to be alright.

"We are. I can't believe it," Drew answered with awe matching Cam's. "I've always wanted to come here."

I didn't know much about Drew—I doubted I ever would—but I got the feeling that libraries were some of his favorite places. Cam shared that opinion. I knew that after seeing the fortress of books that he had created back in Sala...and Rennan's crash into it.

"So have I," Cam whispered, half to himself. "It's a shame we can't stay here longer."

He and the sorcerer were in complete awe of the majesty of this place. They might have seen it as breathtaking, but all I saw was a potential tomb. Any of these shelves could be knocked over in an attack and we would be flattened like my grandmother's honey pancakes.

"I don't think that would be wise, brother. I know you love libraries—you always have—but this one reeks of something I can't put my finger on," Carter whispered, for once paying attention to something other than himself. Half the time, I expected him to pull some sort of portable mirror out of his pocket just to stare at his own reflection.

"It reeks of old secrets and danger," I stated.

My eyes were constantly alert for something that might not even be here. I kept thinking I heard footsteps on the further edges of the massive archive. I'll admit my hand kept moving to the hilt of one of my daggers. There was no way I would ever be caught unaware in a place like this. I wasn't about to let another library scar me for life.

Cam's shoulders sagged, as if all his joy had been stolen.

It wasn't like him to not notice something was off about his surroundings. He was always so good at identifying any problems or potential threats. Or maybe he had noticed it, but hadn't said anything because he didn't want to frighten us.

"I was really hoping you weren't going to mention it. I felt something wicked the moment we walked in, but I didn't want to alarm anyone. There's an ancient energy here and it is seriously bothering me," Cam admitted quietly. "We should just find the proof we're looking for and leave."

Called it. Was I good or what?

"I think that would be a wise decision," Rennan agreed, briefly glancing at me. He offered a sympathetic smile, and I appreciated his concern. It was nice to know that somebody was looking out for me even when I wasn't always looking out for others. "How are we going to go about it? Surely, we're not all going to stay together. It'll be faster if we split up."

"Like many times before now, the wolf is correct," Cam stated with a weak smile. It looked pained.

He turned to look at the rest of us, and we awaited his word. It was needless to say that we all looked to him as our leader. He was so kind and knowledgeable that I had no doubt he would make a wonderful king.

"We'll split up into three teams of two: Drew and Rennan; Valerie and Scarlet; and then Carter and I," Cam decided.

"Understood," I acknowledged, mildly annoyed that Cam had intentionally paired me with the mermaid. I knew what he was trying to do, but after nearly losing my mind to one of those filthy demons of mass destruction not even an hour ago, I didn't trust myself not to do anything stupid again. "What exactly do you want us to look for?"

"That's sort of where it becomes tricky. There's never been anything recorded or leaked in all the kingdoms of the elves doing anything illegal or oppressive because practically everyone sees them as being inspirational. Hopefully there are some records about my father and his deeds as a dictator that weren't destroyed centuries ago," Cam shrugged.

He tried to be nonchalant with his mentioning of his father, but he and Carter both tensed up. He was deeply disturbed about his father being our enemy. I couldn't blame him. I wouldn't want to have my parents be my mortal (or immortal, in Cam's case) enemy.

Cam turned to Drew. "The wizards record everything in Galerah, correct?"

"Affirmative," Drew nodded. "We document every major and minor event happening all over the known world. Since this is the capital of the kingdom that stands for knowledge and wisdom, surely we can find something that will guide us."

"Then there's our plan!" Cam stated, throwing his hands out, startling all of us out of our somber thoughts. For someone who was so good at blending into the shadows, he really knew how to grab someone's attention.

"Let's split up and start working. I have a feeling something will go wrong in the near future, and I'd rather not be here when it happens."

So, we split up into our separate pairs. Drew and Rennan took the loft area where there were a lot of the older books. Rennan later told me that Drew is a speed reader, so they covered a good portion of the room in only minutes. Cam and Carter claimed the right wing of the library while Valerie and I explored the left wing.

Neither one of us spoke to each other for a long while. We just scanned the shelves in silence, occasionally pulling an intriguing book off the shelf to skim through it only to find nothing useful. We silently agreed that she would work on one end of the aisle and I would work on the other. It was obvious neither one of us wanted to be closer than we had to.

After several minutes of searching, Valerie groaned and dropped the book she was holding on the floor. I didn't bother to turn around and look at her as I put the book I had been flipping through back on its dusty shelf.

"Too much reading for you?" I questioned unsympathetically as I began inspecting another book.

"No, it's not that...," her voice trailed off.

Valerie sighed behind me. Now I turned to look at her. Her pink eyes were distant and starting to fill with tears. She sniffled and wiped her eyes, concealing any sign that she had been about to cry.

I sighed and let my book fall to the floor to the floor. "Look, I'm sorry I was so nasty to you. I was scared and worried for Cam when we were captured, but I was wrong to take it out on you. So...gosh. This is really hard for me to say. I'm sorry, Valerie."

She looked up at me in surprise, a single tear rolling down her perfect face. I was shocked when she walked towards me and hugged me. "I'm sorry, too. I should have realized I was being a pest…I just wanted to make everyone happy. I was trying to be helpful, but my way of doing so is by keeping the mood light. I'm also sorry for calling you a monster. I never should have said that. You really aren't a monster, honest."

I looked at her for a few seconds, searching for honesty. There was no way the mermaid could have masked lies even if she tried. She was far too open. I smiled weakly. "You're forgiven. I'm so sorry I reacted that strongly to Cam almost dying."

"I forgive you, too. After all, what would we be without forgiveness?" Valerie said, offering a weak smile. "If you don't mind my asking, why did this near-death experience affect you so badly?"

"My parents died in an elf-led massacre when I was four and everyone I knew growing up always mysteriously disappeared. A couple months ago, my former best friend betrayed me and killed my grandmother, who was the last surviving relative who raised me. That was also the day Rennan and I met Cam. We've just been through so much together since then and I wasn't ready to lose another person I care about," I admitted when I had mustered enough courage.

Valerie blinked and hugged me again. This time, I didn't resist it.

"I personally know what it's like to lose someone you love. When my father died a few years ago, my mother and I were heartbroken. For the longest time, I couldn't believe one of the nobles had been trying to kill my whole family. So yeah, I know the feeling and it's not great. That's why I resort to cheerfulness—it makes everything less painful," Valerie explained softly.

I had totally forgotten that she had lost her father. Though, she was lucky enough to still have her mother.

She bit her lip. "As for Cameron…I also understand the worry for his life. I remember the first time he came to Sala after he was exiled. He was only nineteen, yet he seemed so strong and dignified."

"But why were you worried for him if he was so strong and dignified?" I inquired in confusion. I couldn't quite wrap my brain around the thought.

Valerie's lips hinted at a smile, but it never came. "That was after he had recovered. He came to us badly injured and near death. He wasn't nearly as stoic as he is now. He had lost a lot of blood during the weeks it had taken him to get to Sala. I'm still surprised he made it that long, really. Shows you Cameron is even stronger than he looks. Taking pity on him, my mother took the young heir in and helped treat his wounds, regardless of the laws concerning exile.

"He was timorous and angry when he came to us, barely knowing what to do with himself. He was also prone to being somewhat unnerving—he still has his moments, as I'm sure you know. Mother guided him and Sala has always been his safe haven. Still, he's come to us several times since then in increasingly dire conditions. My mother fears the day when there is no fight left in him. Though he's not our race, Cam is a beacon of hope to my people. It will be a sad day if that light is extinguished."

"He'd probably reprimand you for telling me so much about his past…especially a part he's never told me about," I mused. "Thanks for telling me about yours, though. I'm glad we made up. It's hard to keep an enemy when you're journeying with her."

Now Valerie truly smiled.

"Indeed, it is," she agreed. "And you're right, Cam would probably have some choice words for me if he found out, so let's not tell him. Our little secret?"

"Sure," I said with a smile.

A warm feeling washed over me, that is, until Carter came towards us with an urgent expression on his face. I looked up at him and scowled slightly. I still didn't hold him with the highest regard like I did with Cam or Rennan. He had to earn my respect.

My rough exterior returned as I asked, "What is it? None of you boys are dying, are you?"

Carter made a face, a rather surprised one, but shook his head. "Thankfully, nobody is dying. Including that brother of mine—unless you count his hatred of not taking books with him when we leave. However, Cameron did find something that may or may not be useful."

"I'm surprised he didn't start yelling in triumph," Valerie commented in an amused tone.

Carter snorted and nodded in agreement as we walked. I was confused, so I figured it was something only people who had known Cam for a long time would understand.

Valerie must have seen my face because she said, "He's loud when he declares victory, whether from creating something crazy or just because he's pleased."

"It doesn't happen often, though," Carter commented. "Or at least before he was exiled, really. Our parents were strict and never allowed open emotion from us."

I stopped and looked at him curiously. He seemed to take my hint.

"Val, go find Cam. I need to talk with Scarlet for a couple minutes," Carter instructed.

Valerie nodded and smiled at me reassuringly before she walked away through the maze of books. Hopefully she doesn't get lost in here.

Carter exhaled deeply. "Scarlet, I know you don't trust me."

"That's an understatement."

"And I know Cam doesn't trust me as far as he can see me—"

"Also an understatement."

"Let me talk!! *Anyway*...I know you guys don't trust me, and that's for good reason. The first night you met me, I tried to kill my only brother in cold blood from selfish orders given to me by my father. You have no idea how much I regret my actions. You have no idea how much I regret a lot of things."

"You? Feeling regret? Don't make me laugh."

"I'm serious."

"Hi, Serious."

"Okay, I get it. I deserve it, too. But really, Scarlet, I wanted to explain what I meant about redemption."

That caught my attention. I stopped being a nuisance and motioned for him to continue.

"I didn't mean redemption from my father by bringing the stupid signet ring to him. That is Cameron's burden, and I will have no part in it. I meant I wanted to redeem myself in my brother's eyes. I know he's always seen me as a disappointment. We're twins, for crying out loud. We're supposed to stick with each other through the thick and thin. Did I do that?

No. I stuck by *myself*, not the person who needed it most. It's especially horrible because he always had my back growing up," Carter shook his head. "I want to show him I'm sorry."

I couldn't believe that I was hearing something genuine coming from this elf's mouth. I still didn't trust him, but now I knew what he was trying to accomplish. He was putting forth the effort to make amends.

"If your actions match what you're feeling and you're really being honest about this, he might begin to trust you," I replied as we started walking again. "I appreciate you telling me that, but I won't be able to trust you completely until you prove yourself."

"Fair enough," he agreed reluctantly. There was a saddened and even wistful light remaining in his eyes. He sighed and straightened his shoulders. "Now come on, my brother is waiting for us."

We walked through several more aisles of books before we turned a corner to see Cam, Rennan, Drew, and Valerie all standing and waiting for us. It was almost like they were posing for something, though slightly less dramatically. Except for Cam, maybe. The guy just stood there grinning from ear to ear. His grin was unnerving, which made me thankful I usually only saw his smirk.

"Good, now we're all here," Cam stated in satisfaction. Though, I did notice that he sent his brother the slightest look of contempt.

"Why exactly did you call us down here, Camrade?" Rennan asked curiously.

Cam opened his mouth to speak, but then closed it. He looked at the wolf in confusion. Rennan only laughed uncontrollably. Meanwhile, the elf patiently waited for him to stop laughing so he could get an explanation.

"Do I even want to know what you just called me? What was it? *Camrade*?" Cam asked with an arched eyebrow.

He glanced at me, and I nodded my head. I wanted him to know just for the pure satisfaction of seeing Rennan try to explain his brilliance.

"So, the timing of this piece of genius was terrible, but I still think it's hilarious," Rennan chuckled with a jovial gleam in his eyes.

Nothing could dampen this guy's sprits...unless Valerie went to extremes to ignore him. Then he got moody and didn't talk to anyone. Regardless, he was currently lighthearted.

Cam blanched. "When was it?"

He didn't sound as terrified as he looked. It was almost like he knew what Rennan was going to say. My mind flashed back to the last time I had been wondering if Cam had the gift of foresight into dealings of the future. Then I remembered that venomous glare he had given me and shuddered. I looked at him again, and saw that he was indeed staring at me. Or maybe he was just telepathic....

"So, uh, it was when you were, uh, how do I say this? Nearly completely dead?" Rennan nervously explained.

Cam just stared at the wolf, staying dead silent and emotionless. It was another one of those moments when he was completely unsettling. No mortal could appear so much like a statue. Then I remembered: Cam isn't mortal! He's an immortal elf that will probably outlive us all. I don't know why, but that thought upset me, and I felt sort of disheartened by it.

Rennan shook off his nerves and grinned. "But anyway, Drew called you our comrade, so I thought, since you prefer to go by 'Cam,' you can be called 'Camrade' instead! Brilliant, isn't it?"

Cam chuckled softly. "Only you would come up with something like that, Rennan. Now, I will show you what I brought you down here for. That is, before Master Penbrooke decided to get me sidetracked."

"You decided to listen to me."

"It's because you are very distracting."

"You're very welcome."

Cam rolled his eyes. Then he turned to the rest of us. "Okay, in all seriousness, I found something."

"What did you find?" I asked, no longer able to keep my mouth shut. Cam smiled in a pleased manner.

"So, I was looking through one of the old books with Carter breathing down my neck," Cam began, stopping only to offer his brother a wicked grin.

Carter instinctively reached for his left arm. Cam must have done something, but whether out of malice or as a jest I did not know.

Cam continued. "And then I started reading about elvish crime in past centuries."

Drew gaped at Cam, who just smiled mysteriously. "Are you implying that elves had recorded secrets that weren't destroyed?"

"Indeed, I am, most noble sorcerer. In fact, there are a few people in the kingdom who have been around long enough to tell you that my entire bloodline has had corrupt kings since Kenelm the Great, the founder of my line," Cam replied. Then his face became grave and his whole body tensed up. It was like something else had entered his mind causing him to become extremely guarded again. "There's one thing, though: the book isn't complete. The really condemning part is locked away. I know where the entrance is, I just need ancient magic to open it."

"But you've studied the ancient magic and can use it like a weapon," Carter interrupted. His tone was adamant. "I've seen you do it before—you, uh, did it earlier—and you've been doing it for years. Surely you're as skilled as any master."

Cam's cheeks became slightly flushed from the praise. He clearly wasn't used to it. "Carter…please don't mention that. I am a master in the Ancient Arts, yes, but I prefer not to use that power. It's not wise for me to tap into powers so ancient. I would only use it in life or death situations."

"Life or death? I recall you returning to Sala several times in a near death condition," Valerie pointed out. "I'd say you've had plenty of chances to use it."

Cam flushed bright red, out of irritation this time.

"Believe me, you don't want me to use it right now—or ever. Only when all else fails would I be willing to use it. Am I clear?" Cameron demanded, eyes smoldering with a hidden fury.

We were quick to agree with him, lest the shadows return.

The fire in his eyes faded and his stone-like expression returned. "Now that that is clear, Drew: I need your help opening the gateway."

"You know crossing breaches into secured areas can result in death, right?" Drew asked, slowly stepping forward to stand next to Cam. Drew hurriedly waved his hands when the elf sent him a sidelong glare. "Okay, just asking. What do you want me to do?"

"Pull the book off the shelf and read it."

"Which book? There are literally hundreds on this wall alone!"

"*That one*!" Cam's voice boomed as he pointed to one of the leather-bound books.

Shadows erupted around him and swirled around his arms. For a split second, he blinked out of existence, only to come back a second later looking disoriented and terrified. He immediately snuffed out the shadows and stumbled back a few steps.

He quickly said in a smaller, much calmer, manner, "That one."

Drew reached out and pulled out the book Cam specified. He raised a skeptical eyebrow as he starting skimming pages. "So, there's a spell or something in here that will tell me how to open this gateway to condemning evidence or whatever?"

"In theory."

"In theory," Drew scoffed. "That's it? I just open it and read it?"

"Pretty much," Cam shrugged.

He didn't seem concerned about any other defenses that might be set. I wondered how the heck he was able to do it and keep his calm.

"Okay then. I guess I'll start."

"That won't be necessary," a sickeningly familiar voice called from behind us.

I closed my eyes and turned around. When I opened my eyes again, I saw a man whose face was obscured by a web of scars. He was the last person I wanted to see.

"Who are you?" Cameron demanded, pulling out his bow and nocking an arrow with amazing speed.

It was aimed straight at Mongwau's neck. Cam's features were rigid, as if expecting any type of attack to happen. Though, that was probably the case, since the elf was the master at planning for everything we might possibly need.

Mongwau looked directly at me, ignoring Cam's demand. "My, my, Scarlet. You never told them who I am? A pity, really. You could have saved me the trouble."

Cam turned his head to face me. He met my eyes with a piercing gaze that dared me to defy him. I hated that I was too weak to dare.

"Scarlet? Who is this man?" he demanded. "How do you know him?"

"This is Mongwau, my old mentor," I muttered. "He taught me everything I know about fighting. He also gave me orders to kill the twins for some 'amazing' reward."

I glared at Mongwau with all the venom I could muster. There was no way I was going to let him corrupt my friends with shadow demons like he had attempted to do with me.

Valerie gasped. Since she was standing next to me, she gently grabbed my wrist in sympathy.

My cheeks burned like fire. I was too ashamed to look at any of my friends. I could imagine the looks on their faces: terror from Valerie; shock from Carter; a stone-cold expression from Drew; and worst of all, anger and betrayal from Cam and Rennan. I couldn't face them.

"I don't care what you were to Scarlet, but you will leave. *Now*," Rennan stated firmly. There was no flexibility in his tone. I couldn't decipher anything beyond the determination ringing as loud as a bell tower. "We were here first, fair and square."

"My apologies, fellow hybrid, but I cannot allow that. My master has requested I bring you six to him," Mongwau said with mock-pity. "I would love to kill you now, but the boss wants you alive."

"Yeah? Who's your boss? I'd love to tell him 'hi,'" Cam snarled, keeping his bow drawn and ready to shoot. The flames in his eyes glowed intensely.

I was so glad his hatred and fury were not directed towards me. As skilled as I am, I wouldn't last long in a fight against Cam.

"You may yet have a chance, elfling," Mongwau said with a twisted smile.

My stomach churned. I couldn't believe that I had looked up to this man as a child. He was truly a monster.

Cam obviously didn't appreciate being called "elfling" any more than he enjoyed being called "elf," since he swiftly loosed the arrow he had nocked. It struck Mongwau in the shoulder and he cried out in agony. He cursed loudly as he pulled the arrow shaft out of his arm. Blood was dripping everywhere and the smell of iron filled the air. Horrors of my past were reborn.

"The master said only to bring you in alive. He never said anything about injured!" Mongwau roared as he charged at Cam. "Die, elvish scum!"

The elf immediately drew his scythe and blocked the blow that was coming from the sword. Cam knocked the him off his feet and sent him flying across the floor of the library. Mongwau scrambled to his feet, continuing to send fists flying.

"I happen to prefer living, thank you very much," Cam growled, masterfully avoiding everything the assassin threw at him.

It was like a dance, only with really sharp weapons that could take your head off at any point in time. I didn't feel like experiencing that today. Or ever.

Cam snorted, dodging an errant swing. "Surely you couldn't have been stupid enough to come on your own. One against six is hardly a fair fight. And even if the numbers were even, you would still be out-powered."

Mongwau laughed darkly. "Of course not, you imbecile! Any fighter knows to have loyal backup. And while these two warriors aren't from my circle of mercenaries, they are certainly skilled enough to be! Believe me, they are more than capable of slaughtering you."

He whistled, and for a second, nothing happened. Then, we heard the sound of two sets of feet running through the aisles of the library, searching for the fight. My heart sank when I saw who had rounded the corner: Wayne Penbrooke and Razil the traitorous bird.

Razil looked at me evilly. "Oh, Sutton. I've been waiting for this for a long time. It will feel so good to rip you to pieces like you did to my wings!"

Her wings were still fully attached to her back, which did not please me. The last time I had seen her in the Blackshell Inn, I had tried to cut off her wings to ground her for the rest of her life. To my dismay, she was still using them to her advantage.

To Razil's left stood Wayne. His blind eye looked whiter than usual in the dim light, and his good eye was ice cold as he looked around at all of us, lingering longest on me and Cam. He looked downright cruel as his gaze became fixed on his cousin. The larger wolf looked like he was ready to tear Rennan's head off.

"So. You're the one who slit my arm in that wretched inn. Figures you're an elf," Wayne snarled, looking Cam dead in the eye. Malice and hate glittered in his pale eye.

Cam was either incredibly brave or incredibly foolish to nod his head.

The elf kept his hands on his weapons, not daring to move a single muscle.

Wayne snickered. "I've looked forward to meeting you again, scum. I want to return what you did to me."

"You'd be stupid to try," Cam threatened.

He was frighteningly still, which meant he was planning something. Rennan put a hand on Cam's shoulder as a warning to stay calm, but Cam only gave him the briefest glance before turning back to the traitors.

Razil laughed wickedly. "Fools. You're fighting a losing battle. By the time the Master is done with you, you'll be wishing things had gone differently a long time ago."

"You've always fought a losing battle," I muttered.

Razil's green eyes zeroed in on me like an animal catching a glimpse of their prey. I knew her look of hate better than I would have liked. I readied myself for battle.

"You were all foolish to come in here and box yourselves into a corner," Mongwau commented.

Cam muttered something under his breath and Drew seemed to catch it. Drew was suddenly adamant that whatever it was Cam had muttered didn't happen.

The elf didn't listen, so he pulled something out of Drew's satchel against his will and threw it onto the ground. A purple force field appeared around us as smoke filled the air. Mongwau, Razil, and Wayne cried out in agony as the smoke surrounded them.

Meanwhile, the six of us seized our chance to make a break for it, so we picked up our gear and ran. We dashed through various aisles of books so we wouldn't get caught by the enemy. As soon as we were in the foyer again, Drew tossed something to Cam, who shoved it in his satchel. Once everyone and our things were accounted for, we bolted through the door.

Unfortunately, we ran straight into a barricade of Mongwau's assassins.

"Rennan, old buddy, you wanted a solution that involved fire," Cam stated hastily as the enemy started closing in on us.

Because of the pace, Rennan could barely afford a quick, questioning glance in our friend's direction.

"What are you thinking?" the wolf demanded, swiftly drawing his sword and blocking the blade of one of our attackers.

The rest of us with weapons unsheathed them and prepared to stand our ground. I just hoped we wouldn't have to deal with the other three jokers inside.

"We're using fire as our getaway," Carter realized with wide eyes.

Cam solemnly nodded, confirming Carter's suspicion.

"I hope you can control it, because too much heat is life threatening for me," Valerie informed us with a whimper. "The intense flames will dry out my scales."

Surprisingly, I didn't find myself irritated with her. Maybe it was because we both finally understood where the other was coming from.

"I'll make sure we don't harm you," Drew promised. Magic began glowing around his hands. The purple orbs already gave off some pretty extreme heat, so I knew they would do some serious damage. "Ready? *GO!*"

Drew blasted the building across the street with his inferno. The purple flames grew to massive sizes and then leapt to the next building. The fire spread from one building to another until the air had more smoke in it than we could breathe. We took that as a sign that we needed to get out of there.

As we ran out of town, I noticed that Cam kept looking behind us. Once when I turned around, I discovered that we were being followed by Mongwau's minions.

"We need to get them off our tails!" Cam yelled angrily.

He and Drew dropped back to the end of our group and stopped. I stopped along with them, motioning to Carter and Rennan to get Valerie out of the city before she died from the unnaturally hot temperature.

Cam noticed me and frowned. "No, Scarlet, go with the others."

"Not until I know what you're doing," I replied stubbornly.

Drew sent Cam a look.

The elf sighed. "Fine. I'm using magic to create some distance between us and Mongwau's cronies. I don't know about you, but I want to get out of this in one piece."

"You know full well that if you exert too much energy in your present state, you might as well die anyway," Drew pointedly remarked. "Cam, there's an easier way to do this."

"*No*! There may be easier ways, but they're not as effective," Cam argued. "Scarlet, go back with the others."

"No. I'm not leaving you. I will not lose you again, Cam."

We stared at each other unflinchingly for a few seconds.

An arrow zipped towards us before we could realize what was happening. Drew quickly used his magic to deflect it so none of us were impaled. Cam muttered something in thanks and I think Drew said something like "don't mention it."

"Fine. Scarlet stays. Drew, I'm ready when you are," Cam relented.

Drew nodded his head and ran in the opposite direction.

As fast as he could, Cam explained, "Before you ask, he's going to complete the other part to this plan. I can't be in two places at once without magic, so I needed his help. He knew this might happen since he discovered we were coming to Hila."

"Okay. What do you want me to do?" I asked. I wasn't going to stand there and do nothing. I wanted to help in whatever way I could.

"Just...don't hate me after this."

"I could never hate you, Cam."

"Thank you. Now prepare to brace yourself...and me when I'm done."

"Wait, what are you going—"

And then it happened. Cam's entire body burst into flames and shadows again. These flames were a thousand times hotter than the ones Drew had already mustered. I felt like my skin would have completely melted off if I hadn't jumped several feet away. The flames flew everywhere, carried by shadows stretching throughout the whole area. It was like the shadows became hands capable of placing the little balls of flame wherever Cam wanted them.

Buildings erupted into flames. Screams from people inside echoed throughout the streets. The assassins stopped dead in their tracks when they saw Cam on fire. A couple had the guts to come forward, but Cam turned his fiery gaze on them and threw fireballs at them. The entire group went up in an inferno of purple fire, and I watched in terror as the whole block of buildings was set ablaze in seconds.

Screaming continued until the flames and shadows surrounding and fueling my elvish friend faded away. I hadn't realized he had been floating again until his feet hit the ground with a thud. His knees buckled and I rushed forward to catch him. I was expecting him to be burning hot from the flames, but he was ice cold. I didn't know if that was good or bad.

"Cam…no, no, no. Don't you dare pass out," I commanded him, shaking his shoulders hard.

I didn't want to hurt him, but I also needed to keep him conscious. Looking around, I didn't know how much longer we would last in this burning town. We needed to get out of here before we became living candles.

"Did…it work?" Cam coughed a second later.

I almost cried in relief, but that wouldn't have done either of us any good. I nodded my head and helped him to his feet. Then we managed to make it out of town before the fire boxed us in.

When the others saw us emerge from the smoldering city, they jumped for joy and ran to hug us. We all had burns from the intense heat (Valerie had lost a few scales, but she said it was nothing to worry about and it wasn't as bad as it could have been), but none of us cared. I didn't even care that I had raw blisters that stung when I moved. We were all so shocked we had made it out with minimal injuries that we weren't even noticing the pain as we prepared to get away from Hila. Besides, that pain was easily healed by Drew when we found an opportunity to pause our trek.

Drew, who had gotten out of the city before us, congratulated Cam on a job well done, and the elf received it as best he could. After the brief time of celebration, we realized that we needed to get going sooner rather than later. We picked up our dwindling supplies and headed west towards Estal. We still hadn't found what we were looking for, but we needed get away from Hila and the enemy before we could figure anything out.

After about two hours of hiking through the darkness with nothing but one of Drew's purple fireballs to light our path, we pitched a camp in a grove of hardy maple trees. Nobody really chatted during supper. We were all too hungry to talk, I guess. But when we were finished, some conversation finally opened up.

"Guys, I hate saying this, but I felt like that entire trip was a bust," Rennan declared with a sigh.

Carter and I nodded our heads in agreement. Why did he always seem to agree with me...?

"Perhaps not a complete bust," Drew said with an expectant look at Cam. "Tell them what you found."

"But you never had time to tell Drew, did you, Cam?" I questioned.

Both men looked somewhat uncomfortable, and of course, neither one would say why. Cam only grunted in response. I decided I would have to question him later if I wanted to know more. There was no way he was going to answer me now in front of everyone else.

"I, uh, told him in that quick moment when I explained my plan," Cam hurriedly explained. "I found a book—and I brought with me. It's all about the alliances through the ages between Heviah and Estal. I barely skimmed through it, but it's really detailed. I might explain more about it tomorrow morning when I get the chance to read some of it."

I couldn't decide if anyone else bought it, but nobody pushed questions either.

"Okay, makes sense that you wouldn't read it tonight since you're probably physically and mentally exhausted," Carter began. "Though, will you at least tell us if you think any of it will be helpful?"

Cam muttered something else, but no one able to catch what it was.

"Oh, it might be. When the book was written, wizards were literally allowed to go anywhere. They were basically the historians for all of the kingdoms. So, because of that and their thoroughness of notetaking, there are some pretty detailed notes concerning alliances," Drew told us with a hopeful smile. That somehow answered Carter's question. Before anyone could start talking again, Drew said, "It's been a long day. We should all try to get some sleep."

"Yeah, you're right," Rennan agreed.

Drew started walking off, but Rennan stood up and stopped him.

A look of worry flickered across his face. "Though, I want to know one thing: what was that smoke Cam set off in the library?"

Drew hung his head. "It was a poison gas. I didn't want to take any chances so I gave some parcels of it to Cam. However, that didn't stop him from taking mine."

Rennan paled. His ears flattened next to his skull. "Are they…could they…."

"It depends on how strong they are," Drew answered, looking Rennan in the eye. "I'm sorry about your cousin."

"It's…it's fine. We should rest," Rennan mumbled.

He started shuffling away, but Valerie took it upon herself to follow him to his tent. She gave him a side-hug as they walked, and Rennan seemed eager to return the action. Poor guy. There was a chance he had lost his cousin, but he was still getting attention from the mermaid, at least.

"Well, I guess that's a sign this night is over," Carter stated as he too stood up and walked to his tent. "See you tomorrow, guys."

"Their spirits are low," Drew commented minutes later, glancing at Cam and I.

I looked at the sorcerer, but Cam didn't register he was being spoken to until I gently kicked his ankle. Then Cam looked up.

"You need a victory," Drew told him.

"Or even just something to go right without having to lose something else in the process," Cam sighed. He shook his head and went back to staring into the flames. "I just wish I could lead them like a king should, not reduce their hopes to almost nothing. Honestly, I feel horrible for bringing all of you into this."

"Don't you get it? You *are* leading like a king!" Drew exclaimed. "You're not arrogant like some kings or heirs I've met. You lead humbly, as a king should. Your doubt is showing that you're doing it right. Sure, you may be suffering some losses, but that always happens. All that matters is how you choose to come back from said losses and how you'll go forward."

Cam looked at him like he was joking.

"It's great you think that and all, but how am I supposed to know how to do that? I barely knew how to get through this one obstacle!" Cam cried as he buried his face in his hands.

Drew patted him on the back as he walked past.

"You'll know when the time comes, just as long as you embrace past experiences. No one gets far without them," the sorcerer stated, before walking off and disappearing into his own tent.

Cam and I remained at the fire. We sat there in silence for a few minutes.

Cam's hands dropped down into his lap after a while. His face was distraught. "Scarlet, I don't know what to do. All I do is destroy everything."

"Cam," I began gently. I got up and moved to sit next to him. "You don't destroy everything. Maybe some buildings, but not everything. If you did, you wouldn't have brought us all together."

"But I didn't. I ran into you and Rennan, really, and Carter and Valerie tagged along. Drew decided to come with us to escape his punishment," Cam said dismally. He gazed into the fire again.

We both watched the flames weave their intricate dance.

"But we all came to help *you*, Cam. We're going to stick by you no matter what. We all know that your cause is the right one—even that brother of yours is of the same mindset. We all believe you're the rightful king who deserves to rule."

"Even though I lose control of the shadows? Even though I lash out? Even though there's no possible way in the whole world I deserve you?"

"Yes. We'll always stick with you. Nothing changed back there. I saw you risk your life to defend us yet again. I'll never forget all the risks you've already taken to try to liberate Palee from your father's tyrant law."

Cam smiled weakly at me. His grey eyes shone with sadness, but also gratitude. "I'm glad I have you here with me, Scarlet. I don't think I'd be able to do half of this without you."

"Of course. I'm far happier doing something that helps everyone rather than sitting in Palee, grieving over my losses," I replied with a satisfied smile. I was happy to make some sort of difference. "I wanted to thank you for that, by the way. You helped me move on. You've helped me see the bigger picture."

Cam's smile faded slightly and his eyes filled with longing. "Scarlet. I don't deserve your gratitude. I'm around to help. It's just what I do. Please, when the time comes, remember that I did everything out of a desire to touch the lives of others. I would do so much more if I could. I just...."

I frowned. "You just what?"

"Never mind. Don't listen to me," he said, biting his lip and turning away. He resumed his position of facing me soon enough. "I guess I just wanted to let you know that I care."

For some weird reason, Valerie randomly walked by, humming some sort of strange tune. For some other weird reason, Cam reacted very strongly to the humming. His head snapped up and he stared at the mermaid with piercing eyes. It's amazing she didn't cower in his gaze. She just grinned mischievously.

"No. Don't you *dare* start singing that, Valerie Olivia Ciala," Cam firmly demanded.

Valerie smiled, pretending to be an angel.

"And if I do?" Valerie asked. She tapped her chin as if trying to remember something important. "What were the lines again? I think it was along the lines of expressing beautiful, sweet affection.'"

"Valerie...," Cam growled in a warning tone.

She ignored him. "Oo! I remember now! It was about a guy and a girl...."

"Okay, that is enough!" Cam decided, standing up suddenly.

"Wait, I am so confused. What the heck is she singing this time?" I asked in a perplexed tone. None of this made any sense, and frankly? I was too scared to ask about it. And yet there was still a part of me that wanted to know more so I could annoy Cam later....

"Oh, nothing, Scarlet," Valerie said with a slight smirk. "It's just something I learned as a little mermaid."

"Okay, then I am not going to question this," I decided.

If Valerie was intentionally acting stranger than usual, I'm not quite sure I wanted to know.

"That is a very wise decision, Scarlet," Cam agreed with an approving nod.

Valerie shrugged and started walking toward her completely blue tent. Before she went in, she mouthed something to Cam, but I was bad at lip reading (once I thought someone said "seagulls, stop it now"), so I didn't catch it. He just glared after her.

When Cam was calm again, he commented, "And by the way, that book is just on entrances into major cities in Heviah I already know about. It's not horribly important. So, on that note...I guess this is good night."

"Yeah, I guess so," I said. I offered him a smile, and he was able to muster one in return. "I'll see you in the morning."

"The same to you," he replied as we started walking in different directions.

(Our tents were on opposite sides of the camp, by the doing of Carter, whose tent was right next to mine. I still think Carter and Rennan set it up like that on purpose.)

"Oh, and Cam?" I said again, calling him back to where he would at least turn around to face me again.

He looked at me expectantly from the entry to his tent.

I smiled. "Don't worry. We'll figure everything out in the morning."

He half-smiled gratefully. "Thanks, Scarlet. That means a lot to me."

"Of course," I told him with a full smile.

With that, we both tried to get some sleep.

I was nearly out cold when I heard Cam yell in elvish (all I caught was Valerie's name), Valerie's bubbly laughter; and everyone else yelling at them to be quiet.

I just rolled my eyes at all of them and again attempted to rest.

They were all just some of the strangest people ever. I had somehow learned to accept that. Sure, Carter could be a brat, Rennan sure did know how to complain, Drew was painfully blunt, Valerie could drive you up a wall, Cam was beyond mysterious, and I didn't play well with others. We all had our quirks and flaws, but I think it helped us work better as a team.

I just hoped we would be able to survive the next few days, weeks, and months in one piece.

Prophecy Tree

The dreams came too soon after I closed my eyes.

I never really suffered from nightmares as a kid even though I had more than enough cause to. I always found a way to keep my mind and body calm as I slept—a great feat for me. However, this one dream—or more accurately called "nightmare"—was the worst I had ever experienced.

In my dreamscape, there were no lights anywhere. My dream self kept spinning around, trying figure out what was happening. Yeah. That didn't help anything. Everything remained pitch black.

I somehow knew I was in a small, confined space. Trying to figure out the layers of darkness surrounding me, I reached out to find nothing except the warm, suffocating gloom. The thought struck me to ascertain if I was even there. I wasn't. My mind could not grasp this new concept. It was almost too farfetched for me to comprehend. My brain hurt just thinking about it.

My focus shifted in a flash of blinding white light.

I saw myself standing on the edge of a massive cliff. Looking out, there were rusty colored canyons and a desert that stretched on for miles and miles. A turquoise river snaked below me, occasionally turning into white rapids. Gentle winds blew through the tops of the cliffs, but nothing drowned the sound of the rapids beneath me.

What am I doing here? I asked myself. *There is no way this can possibly be a dream.*

Nothing made sense to me. I wasn't one to dream often and nothing I ever dreamed up was this calm or serene.

"Oh, I can assure you, this *is* a dream," a gentle, but strong, voice announced from behind me. "Depending on what you see here, you may be glad of it."

I whirled around to see a woman with brown hair, tan skin, and brown eyes standing behind me. She wore a pale blue and purple dress with a sky-blue cloak over it. The hood was pulled up over her head, shadowing her face, but not enough to where I couldn't see it.

Who are you? How are you here and talking to me as if I were awake? I demanded.

My hands instinctively moved to where my daggers hung, but I was shocked to discover that I didn't have them. Actually, I didn't have *any* of my weapons. That was not good at all, especially considering I couldn't help but distrust this lady. She was too serene for anything truly living.

"Dreams are my domain, Scarlet Sutton," the woman replied, taking steps towards me. The earth rumbled beneath her feet as she moved. She was a powerful being. The only thing keeping the earth from fading to dust was the magic that the woman commanded.

She beckoned to me. "Come. I want to show you something."

How? You just appeared in my dream! How can you show me anything? I asked in confusion.

The woman cocked her head; her lips hinted at the slightest smile. "Just trust me. You will be glad to know about this when it comes to pass when you walk with open eyes."

That wasn't foreboding and gloomy at all....

She proceeded to lead me around the cliffs and into the forest beyond. Apparently, the massive pine trees were right behind us. I couldn't believe I hadn't noticed them before. I looked back toward the cliffs again, but they were nowhere to be seen. Instead, there were only trees. Again, I tried to wrap my brain around all the sudden changes. It was all so unreal....

Where are we? I inquired, scanning my surroundings for the second time. *How did we get here so fast?*

The cloaked lady turned around to look at me. She didn't look cruel, but she didn't exactly seem safe, either.

"That is only for me to know—even my brethren have yet to achieve mastery of this power. That is why dreams and such processes are mine to command," the woman replied calmly. She gestured for me to follow her into the woods. "As for where we are, we are in a dreamscape Mahe. We are in the woods you and your friends are currently camped on the eastern edge of."

How do you know where my friends and I are camped? Are you one of the enemy?

"I can assure you that I am *not* your enemy, Scarlet Sutton. I am only here to show you something. Then, it is up to you to decide where to go from there."

She led me further into the forest. We passed several small waterfalls, rivers, and caves in only a matter of seconds. I had looked into the real forest before the sun had set, and it had seemed very dark. However, in my dream, it was bright as daylight. It was like the canopy was made of glass that faded into open sky.

Eventually, we stopped at a massive cherry tree in full bloom. Giant pink flowers covered every possible surface of the tree's gigantic branches. I stared at it in awe, wondering how such a magnificent tree came to be in the depths of a forest. Why would you plant a tree like this in the middle of dark woods? Why not put it somewhere people could see it every day?

"I see that you take interest in Shakovi."

I turned around to see two more figures in hoods standing behind me. In addition to the figure in blue that had accompanied me thus far, there were also pink and grey cloaked women. The one in the pink cloak was a tall blonde hair and her eyes sparkled like peridots. Her face looked kind, but I sensed that she could be deadly if she chose to be.

Then there was the grey figure. There was a light in her blue eyes that revealed centuries, maybe even thousands of years of knowledge. Those depths seemed to reach wisdom so deep that there was no clear distinction between light and dark. Her silvery hair cascaded down her shoulders from underneath her hood like a waterfall in moonlight. The look on her face gave her away as the speaker.

Yes. Why is it here? It seems like a strange place for such a beautiful tree, I said in my nonexistent voice.

"Beautiful? Yes. Shakovi most certainly is that. It is also a good many other things," Pink One stated, gazing at the tree.

It was almost like she knew something nobody else did. Could she see the future?

Like? I prompted.

As soon as I spoke, Grey One shot me a warning look. I immediately got the feeling that I shouldn't try to pry anything from these ethereal beings.

"I will tell her," Pink One said in a tone clearly telling Grey One to relax. Blue One just kept an even expression as Pink One turned back to me. "While the tree is beautiful, its effects can be deadly if you are not prepared. Insanity, for example, can result from smelling the blossoms. When you come across it, make sure you are mentally prepared for what it will show you."

Show me? What do you mean?

"We cannot explain now. We have lingered here too long," Blue One said in an urgent tone. She and her fellow hooded figures started to fade into thin air. "Good luck, Scarlet Sutton, with the quest that will show you many more realities before it draws to a close."

Light from the sky started fading as the figures disappeared. I lost the ability to see all the details of everything around me. Even the tree called Shakovi, which was only a few feet from me disappeared from sight. Eventually, I was completely surrounded by darkness again. It was a stupid, warm, suffocating darkness.

"WHO ARE YOU TO THINK THAT YOU CAN DEFEAT ME?" a huge, rumbling voice boomed from every direction. "YOU AND YOUR PUNY FRIENDS WILL NEVER PREVAIL!"

I felt like my ears would go deaf at any moment from the trembling around me. I tried to find my voice, but no sound came out, nor could I even feel myself as the voice spoke. It wasn't like random voices that I had heard before.

This one was far colder, more powerful, and much crueler than anything I had ever heard in my life. Concern grew as I listened. For some reason, I feared not only for myself but for those I cared for. I had no desire for them to come face to face with this new monster.

"YOUR WORLD SHALL FALL. IT WILL BE CONSUMED BY MY FIRE!" the voice declared.

Flames exploded around me. The heat seared across my skin,

convincing me that I would wake up with more serious burns than I had gotten from the fires Drew and Cam started in Hila.

"YOU WILL BURN IN THE FIRESTORM."

I heard myself scream in the flames. Then, they disappeared as quickly as they came. I almost couldn't believe it had happened. Then, I could. In the places where I had felt severe burns, they were now turning to ice. Circulation stopped and my teeth chattered so violently I thought they'd chip.

Was this entity playing games with me?

"YOU CARE FOR YOUR FRIENDS MORE THAN YOU LET ON. WILL YOU REALLY KEEP THEM ALL ALIVE? OR WILL YOU FOLLOW THE PATH YOUR ANCESTORS SET FOR YOU?" the voice asked me. "THE ELF PRINCE WILL NEVER BE KING. HE IS A WEAPON ONLY. DON'T BELIEVE A WORD HE SAYS YOU TO, FOR EACH ONE WILL TURN YOU FARTHER AWAY FROM THE INEVITABLE REALITY."

No, I've heard enough, I wanted to say.

But no sound came. I was once again in a void of nothingness where I no longer existed and no sound was heard.

The cruel voice laughed. "FOOLISH GIRL. ONE DAY, YOU WILL SEE WHAT TRUE POWER LOOKS LIKE."

I woke up in a cold sweat.

My dagger, which had been lying on the ground next to me, was instantly in my hand and at the throat of whoever was shaking my shoulders. My eyes were too bleary to see who it was, but I could tell that it wasn't Valerie. Her hands were usually cold like they'd been in water. These hands were strong and warm.

"Whoa, Scarlet, it's just me. And since I'd like to live, can you please put the knife away?" the person chuckled softly.

I put my dagger down and rubbed my eyes so I could actually see who was sitting in front of me. When my vision cleared, I saw Rennan kneeling on the ground. He looked amused, but I didn't know if it was because of me or something else.

He cracked a smile. "Sorry, I didn't mean to scare you awake."

"No, it's fine," I said, putting the dagger back into its sheath where it would be safe. "I needed to get up anyway. What time is it?"

"No problem. And I dunno, but it's early since Carter and Val are still asleep. Drew and I, though ...we found something that we thought was pretty funny. I wanted to come wake you up so you could see before we disturb it."

"Should I be concerned for your mental sanity or whatever you found?" I asked in a teasing tone.

It probably wasn't very believable, but it was the best I could manage. The dream I had woken up from was unnerving. I shuddered at the memory of the dark voice rumbling through my head.

"You can decide for yourself," Rennan grinned mysteriously as he ducked out of my tent.

I sighed and wrapped my cloak (Valerie had gotten me a new one before we left Sala) around myself since it felt like a chilly spring morning.

Then I followed Rennan out of my tent and back into the common area.

Once out there, I saw Rennan and Drew standing over something. A small, purple light danced between Drew's hands.

"Okay, what in the world is going on?" I asked, taking a few steps closer.

Drew whirled around to look at me. They both sent amused looks to each other before turning back to me. Oh dear. Now I was scared to see what they were up to.

"Scarlet, come here, but be very light on your feet. I don't want to blow this," Drew whispered. He mouthed something to himself, and hurriedly said, "And also be quiet. Like deadly silent."

"You're asking a mercenary to be deadly silent," I mused with a smirk. "Done. Now what is it?"

I couldn't help but crack a smile. Their cluelessness guys could be pretty entertaining at times.

Rennan motioned for me to come nearer, so I did.

And then I looked down to see Cam lying up against one of the fallen logs. His black cloak was pulled over him like a blanket and a thick book was open right next to his head. Cam was still asleep, as far as I could tell, and he looked completely peaceful for once.

I found it amazing how peaceful and angelic he could look while asleep, yet be so stone faced and guarded in his waking hours. But I guess he was exhausted, too, given that he was still out. He was probably sleeping off his exhaustion from the shadow demon tornado.

"I thought he went to sleep in his tent?" I whispered.

I mean, I guess I hadn't seen him go into his tent and not come out last night. I had been too exhausted to pay attention to what he was doing after we had said good night.

"He did," Rennan agreed. "But apparently, he came out at some point to read by the dying embers of the fire. He must not have been able to sleep or something. We should have expected something like this to happen, though. After all, he's Cam."

"Yeah, I hate waking him up like this—wait. No, I don't. I'm going to enjoy this," Drew grinned evilly. The light in his hands glowed brighter, matching his mood.

Between his face and the fire, I could almost mistake Drew for the voice and fire I had witnessed in my dream. I took a step back just to be safe.

The sorcerer shrugged. "Anyway, I was going to wake him up and get some answers from our comrade."

"Camrade," Rennan corrected.

"Whatever," muttered Drew.

Drew dropped the light onto Cam. I don't know what it felt like, but whatever it was, Cam jolted awake. He shot to his feet and Egladel was fully drawn seconds later. Heh, fully drawn and being held to Drew's throat. Oh yeah, and there was another smaller dagger held to Rennan's throat as well. If the elf had any more arms, I expect that there would have been metal beneath my chin.

"Why did you do that?" Cam demanded with an icy glare.

He had only been awake for a few seconds and he was already firing on full cylinders. I marveled at that. I usually needed five minutes or so to wake up completely.

Rennan snickered and Cam's eyes darted over in his direction. "You fell asleep against the log with your book. We were waking you up like good friends would when they see you asleep on cold, hard ground."

"Good friends don't drop liquid fire on you," Cam muttered as he put his daggers back into their sheaths.

He didn't make eye contact with anything except the ground—probably for the best. His gaze was slightly murderous, and it was better for him to murder the ground than us!

"So that's what that was!" I exclaimed in surprise. Liquid fire was added to my list of things to ask Drew or Cam about later.

Cam blushed and his eyes widened when he saw me standing behind Rennan. His hands kind of fumbled with Egladel's handle, so I looked at him strangely.

He offered me an awkward half-smile. "Oh, Scarlet, I didn't see you there."

Drew smirked and whispered something in Cam's pointed ear. Cam blushed again, then scowled and punched the sorcerer in the arm. Yeah, I was definitely sure I didn't want to know what was happening. The guys confused me enough as it was; I didn't need more.

"Well...I guess I could go...," I started to say.

"*No*! No, you don't have to go," Cam said quickly. The tips of his ears were bright pink.

Rennan and Drew laughed at our friend for reasons that remained an enigma to me.

Cam scowled briefly. "You can stay."

"Real smooth, Camrade," Rennan laughed. Soon, he was clutching his sides because he had been laughing so hard.

"Yup. Very subtle indeed," Drew grinned.

"Will both of you just shut up? I don't know why you're even taking interest in this anyway!" Cam cried, throwing his hands up in the air.

Rennan and Drew just laughed harder. As for Cam, he sighed and gave up.

"Dude, we take interest because it is just hilarious," Rennan smiled.

Cam rolled his eyes. "You are no better than Valerie last night, you know that?"

"You're welcome!" Rennan stated cheerfully. Cam sighed again.

"Okay, I'm confused. What in Galerah is going on?" I demanded to know. I wanted answers this time.

"Nothing!" all three men exclaimed in unison.

Rennan said it in a way like it was an inside joke while Drew said it like he was too amused to explain; Cam just said it in a way that communicated, *Don't ask. They're being idiots.*

"Okay then."

"I feel like I'm missing something!" Valerie announced out of nowhere.

All of us, except for Cam, jumped in surprise from her sudden appearance. She was wearing a blue silk cloak as she stood on the fallen log right behind Cam (and even standing on the log, she failed to reach eye contact with the elf). Cam closed his eyes and tilted his head back up to the sky.

"What did I miss?" Valerie asked with a skeptical glance at the guys.

"You have missed nothing," Cam said, obviously trying to drop the subject.

"I missed something," Valerie insisted. She looked at Cam from head to toe, shook her head, and clicked her tongue as if disapproving of something. "You have it bad, I'm afraid. But never fear! Doctor Ciala is here! Come with me, good sir, and I will help treat your wounds."

Cam raised his eyebrow. "But they're not wounds...."

"COME WITH ME!"

"Okay, fine. I'm coming."

Valerie dragged poor Cam into her tent. Seconds later, Valerie's arm appeared in the doorway and thrust a sign into the ground that read, *"Doctor Ciala's Office. Do Not Enter Unless the Doctor Directs You To. Now Seeing: Cameron Woods."*

I honestly didn't know whether or not I should be confused about that or something else. (I wondered where she got the sign, at any rate.) Drew and Rennan, however, kept laughing their heads off. And they wouldn't even tell me why! They were frustratingly unhelpful in that regard.

"Morning, everyone!" Carter called cheerfully as he crawled out of his tent. "Ready for another fun day filled with murderous hiking and looking for things that most people think are nonexistent?"

We all looked behind us to see one very exhausted looking elf. Still, the expression of mock cheer on his face made me smirk.

"Remember when you said your brother was a little ray of pitch black?" I began.

Carter cocked his head in confusion, but nodded.

I continued. "Well, the same could be said of you right now."

"Meh, that still fits Cameron better, but whatever," Carter shrugged.

He sat down on the log near his tent and watched Rennan start a fire.

It was springtime, sure, but today was chilly. Still, I was hesitant to start a fire especially after my dream. Although, the warmth might be helpful in ensuring we wouldn't freeze to death.

"So. Does anyone know where my brother or Val is? Or what's for breakfast?"

Drew rolled his eyes. "I know the answer to both those questions. Cameron and Valerie are over there" —he pointed to Valerie's tent— "and I get to make breakfast. Yay."

"You don't make fly soup, do you?" Cam asked as he emerged from the tent with Valerie on his heels. "*Please* tell me you don't."

He looked on edge, and I didn't know from what. It could have been Valerie; it could have been something else. I didn't know.

"Or if you do, I want some!" Rennan stated with an eager grin.

Then he grinned wickedly at Cam, who looked positively green. I vividly remembered the last time we had an incident with fly soup. Yeah, that stuff is gross and I still can't believe that Rennan would willingly eat it.

Drew looked at Rennan and Cam in disgust. Then he looked at me in hopes of validating that they were seriously talking about fly soup. I nodded my head gravely. It was real and absolutely revolting.

Drew commented, "I have no idea what that is, and based on the look on Scarlet's face, I really don't want to find out. Nor will I be making it. Actually, we'll see if I can cook something that doesn't come out black."

"Black is still better than fly soup," Cam decided with a gagging noise. He walked across camp and sat next to me on the log. I found myself strangely pleased that he chose to sit there. "Though, never listen to

Rennan's opinion of it...."

"You just don't know what you're talking about," Rennan shrugged nonchalantly. "But what's really for breakfast, Drew?"

The sorcerer shrugged. "I really don't know. I've never been good at cooking. I always left the cooking to...never mind. I'll be back in a few minutes."

Drew walked off into the woods far enough away that we couldn't see where he went.

I suddenly grew concerned for him. He had a strong resolve, but the way that his voice cracked troubled me. It sounded like he was remembering something painful and was burying the secret.

"Where's he going?" Valerie asked as she emerged from her tent.

She was still wearing her silk cloak when she sat down next to Carter. Can I just say that she was sitting *very* close to him...? Even Carter looked slightly uncomfortable. Rennan wasn't too pleased about it either.

"We don't know. He just said that he would be back in a few minutes," I answered.

Valerie made a face, but said nothing.

"He had better be back in a few minutes, because he's been nominated to make breakfast," Cam muttered.

It was probably only loud enough for me to hear, and I was sitting right next to him. I gave him a strange look, not moving until he realized I was staring at him. "What?"

"When have you ever been so concerned about breakfast? You rarely eat it, and when you do, it's never much," I commented.

Cam shrugged, but the gleam in his eye was quite obviously

entertained by my comments.

"That's because I'm normally the one responsible for making it…and I'm indecisive so I never choose what to do. Don't judge me!" he exclaimed. His comment was obviously louder than he had intended because he buried his face in his hands.

Everyone looked at him funny and he shrunk into himself, pretending that he hadn't spoken. His cheeks were bright red and he began to drift away from me. I pulled him back, which only made his face redder.

When Rennan snickered from the other side of the fire, Cam, as could be expected, ferociously scowled at him.

"Calm down, I'm not judging you. And don't you dare move away," I ordered in a whisper.

Amazingly, Cam obeyed and did not try to move away again. He just stayed near me.

"Are you okay? What did Valerie want you for?" I whispered.

"Yeah, and nothing."

"Liar. What's wrong?"

He ran a hand through his hair, his exhaustion evident. And now that I was closer to him in daylight, I could see the dark circles beginning to form below his eyes again. I sighed mentally. Why couldn't the man just sleep?!

"I just keep thinking about yesterday," he admitted. "Those poor people…they didn't deserve to die."

"Cam, we're undoubtedly marching into war. War means casualties. Unfortunately, a lot of them are usually innocent townsfolk," I tried to say in a gentle tone. "There was nothing else you could have done to stop that."

"There has to be a way it could have gone differently. I, of all people, know that. It would be ridiculous if I didn't," Cam muttered. He shook his head. "And I did know other ways we could have acted. I was just too impulsive to do anything else. If I had...."

"Stop. Don't go there. Hindsight is a dangerous game," I stated firmly. Cam looked at me out of the corner of his eyes and hung his head. "You weren't being impulsive. Or at least, that's not the word I would use. You were trying to protect us and get us to safety."

"But...."

"No buts."

"Fine."

"So again. What did Valerie want?"

"Oh, she was just being Valerie," he replied, shooting a pointed look to the mermaid.

She caught it and just smiled and waved innocently. Cam shook his head and muttered something under his breath.

I raised an eyebrow. "What's that supposed to mean?"

"You can guess full well what that means."

"Um...okay?"

"Okay! I'm back now and I am giving breakfast duties to the lovely Princess Valerie. I'll do breakfast tomorrow," Drew announced as he dropped down onto the log Rennan was also sitting on.

"Assuming we even live that long," Cam added with a detached expression.

"See? I told you! Ray of pitch blackness, folks!" Carter shouted, jumping up to his feet and pointing at his brother. Cam glared at his twin and shadows started creeping into his features. He closed his eyes and bowed his head. Soon the shadows disappeared and only Cam remained.

"Thanks for that, Airhead," Cam said with a forced smile.

Carter made a face, but didn't say anything. Valerie chastised both of them for being annoying before getting up to start cooking. She told us she would make the delicacy of toast. Only, as she said, without the wonderful thing called a "toaster." Not a single one of us had any idea what she was talking about concerning this *toaster* thing. It seemed like a device that would only exist in a make-believe world.

Valerie was reaching into the bag that held all the food and cooking supplies. The burlap bag wasn't special. It just contained supplies that could be used for anything that we needed. Though, a small corner was singed from the first time that Rennan had tried to cook in the wild.

Yeah. *That* campsite was slightly black....

But yeah. It wasn't a special bag. However, I knew we were in for something crazy when Valerie's hand stopped moving inside of it. She grinned deviously—more deviously than I had previously thought possible for such a bubbly person. She looked up and around at the guys.

"Hey, people, guess what I found," she prodded with her usual beaming smile.

"What did you find?" Rennan asked in a slightly dreamy tone. He was still head over heels for that mermaid. Poor guy. He had strange taste in girls.

"Look!! A magical can of fly soup!" she exclaimed as she held up a silver can.

I doubted that's what it actually was, but I was quick to pick up on the fact that she saw this as a chance to mess around with Rennan and Cam. I understood why she did it, though—their reactions were priceless.

"Yes!! Make that!!" Rennan cried out with delight.

At the exact same time, Cam managed, "If I hear 'fly soup' one more time, I am going to be sick."

"Guys, you know she's messing with you, right?" Drew asked, obviously trying not to laugh.

I could completely relate to Drew. It was ridiculous, but I suffered because I still had a memory in the back of my mind about how disgusting fly soup actually is. How Rennan could stand smelling that stuff, much less eat it, I would never know. I would never ask for tips, either.

"Then it is a cruel joke," Rennan stated, quite over-dramatically.

"It is *so* not," Cam snickered.

It's safe to say that Rennan ignored him.

"Alright, enough both of you," Valerie interrupted with an amused smile.

Cam and Rennan stopped their bickering. Well, Rennan stopped. His attention was entirely focused on the mermaid princess. He watched attentively as Valerie pulled pieces of bread out from the bag and held them over the fire (from a distance so her scales wouldn't burn) until they were toasted. Then she put some butter on them (no idea where she got it) and handed them out.

When we had all taken a bite and decided it wasn't poisonous, she exclaimed, "See? Toast is good. Is this better than what you would have been able to accomplish, wizard?"

"Did I or did I not tell you that if I cooked, it would probably end up black?" Drew questioned. He had toast in his mouth as he spoke, so it really sounded more like, "Mid mi or mid mi not tell you thath if mi cooked, it mould promamly mend mup mlack?"

Cam snorted. "What was that?"

Drew scowled. "I said—oh, shut up, Cameron."

"You're welcome," Cam replied with an evil grin. Then he went back to nibbling on his toast.

He only ate about half of it (after peeling off the crust) before he put it down. Rennan made a face, as if sorry to see the other half of Cam's toast go to waste. The elf obviously knew what Rennan was thinking, because he made eye contact with the wolf right before he threw the remaining toast into the fire.

Cam wiped his hands together and then started messing with his signet ring—a nervous habit of his. He never told me, which can be expected because he never tells me anything about himself, but I had seen him play with it enough times to know when he was uneasy. The question was: what was he worried about this time?

"So…I hate to spoil the mood of the morning, but we should really pack up and move on," Cam announced after breakfast.

We all looked around at each other and nodded in agreement. We had already lingered (and made more noise than necessary) for long enough. I didn't want to risk being found by the guards in Hila.

"You're right. We had our rest. We need to keep going," Carter said, for once taking his brother's side.

Cam looked at him suspiciously, but did not question anything. The elder twin nodded and got up to go pack his tent.

Meanwhile, the rest of us immediately turned around to stare at Carter, none of us believing what we had just heard. We all knew Carter openly criticized Cam's plans. We couldn't believe that he had actually sided with the heir.

Carter didn't realize that all eyes were on him, so he sat there chewing his toast. That is, until he looked up to see four pairs of eyes staring at him. His eyes widened and he nearly choked on his breakfast. I'm not afraid to admit that I started laughing.

"What? Why are you all looking at me? Why is *she* laughing at me?" Carter demanded after he swallowed.

"Do I have something in my ears or did I actually hear you agree with your brother without argument?" Rennan questioned in amazement. His blue eyes were wide with wonder.

"You know, sometimes I can side with my brother on things. No one says I can't," Carter stated pointedly.

Rennan shrugged his shoulders.

Carter rolled his eyes. "I don't understand why you're all so shocked. Look, I'm trying to turn over a new leaf...figuratively. I don't want to touch an actual leaf."

Drew picked up on that. He began levitating a leaf from one of the surrounding trees. He levitated the leaf towards Carter. Cam must have heard the rustling noises, because he turned to see what was going on. Drew sent him a look and Cam said nothing. Seconds later, a wet leaf flew down Carter's neck, sending the elf screaming in panic.

"EWWW!!! WHAT THE HECK JUST FELL DOWN MY NECK?!?! IT'S SLIMY AND GROSS!! GET IT OFF! GET IT OFF!!"

Carter shrieked as he was jumping and running around the camp.

When he was nearly right behind Cam, the heir "accidentally" extended his leg and tripped Carter, who landed face first in the soft dirt.

"Ow," came Carter's muffled voice.

"Oops," Cam said with an evil smirk. He bent down next to Carter and pulled the leaf off his neck before flicking it away. Cam snickered. "You're welcome."

"Ugh, thanks," Carter muttered as his brother helped him up. Carter glared at Drew. "Expect revenge, sorcerer. It will find you."

"Oh, I'm sure it will," Drew said with mock-fear and a whole lot of sarcasm.

Carter fumed and stalked back to his tent.

Drew turned to me and grinned. "Well, I think that was well-handled."

I smiled from ear to ear. "Oh, yes. You made him scream, run around like a child, and then he got tripped. Very well done indeed."

"Even I have to admit that was pretty amazing. Nicely done, Sebastian!" Valerie cheered.

Rennan clapped excitedly to add to the effect.

Drew paled tremendously. "How did you know about that name?"

"Huh?"

"Sebastian. Why did you call me that?"

"Uh, so you would be obliged to sing in celebration with me?"

"Please don't ever call me that again."

"Erm, okay?"

Drew stalked off with the rest of us staring at him in befuddlement.

None of us had anything to say that would be helpful. Valerie and Rennan just brushed it off and went back to eating their toast. Carter tried to remain casual, but what Drew had done put him in a bad mood. Cam just sat there, staring into the burning flames as usual. And me? I didn't know what to make of it all.

Drew was a pretty laid-back guy who didn't like to talk about himself, but he was willing to help others as long as they didn't question him. And when questions were pushed or something was said wrong even in the slightest way, he would blow up and stalk off.

I nearly gasped when I realized that I was very similar in that sense. I was fine helping others as long as my motives were not in question. And when they were…it wasn't pretty. How was it realizing that gave me more respect for Drew?

"Earth to Scarlet," Rennan's voice called from somewhere far away.

I snapped out of my thoughts to find his hand right in front of my face. Since he kept snapping his fingers, I slapped his hand away. I scowled as I stood up and brushed off the back of my cloak.

Rennan smirked. "We're packing up to leave now. I was going to leave you and see how long you would sit there and stare into space, but Cam made me come and bring you back to reality. So, welcome back to the world of the living. May I take your order?"

"You're a strange person, Rennan," I muttered as I scanned the camp. Or rather, what was left of it since they had been efficient in dismantling it. There was no sign of Cameron anywhere. "Where is Cam anyway?"

"Oh, he went to go find Drew. Said he thought he might be able to find him," Rennan replied as I started pulling apart my tent.

Rennan might have been standing next to me, but his eyes were not following me. They were intent on Valerie. Big surprise, right? The poor guy was oblivious to the fact that she did not return his affection.

"I'm going to go help Valerie," Rennan announced.

"Are you going to help or are you going to keep making googly eyes at her?" I questioned nonchalantly while folding up fabrics and tent covers.

If Rennan was so dead set on Valerie, I might as well seize the chance to tease my close friend, right? I thought it was a pretty good opportunity to do so.

Rennan had been in mid-stride, but now he stopped and planted both of his feet on the ground. He raised a questioning eyebrow at me. "What do you mean? I'm being perfectly subtle. She doesn't know the difference."

"She might not, but the rest of us know your heart is chasing after that mermaid," I replied with a slight smile.

Rennan's face was pure shock. Subtlety was not his specialty.

I grinned and waved him off. "Oh, go on. Tell me if you actually manage to catch her."

"You're evil when you joke, but thanks, Scarlet," Rennan said with a side smile. He patted my shoulder and then ran off to supposedly help the mermaid.

I shook my head and smiled at the thought of what he might actually do to help…and if it really was help!

"That was nice of you," Carter commented from behind me. I silently sighed and decided not to give him the attention he wanted. I just went back to packing away my tent so we could get moving again.

"Yeah, I'm not some cold, heartless monster. I can do nice things for others occasionally," I stated rather shortly.

Carter snorted and sat down on the ground besides where I was working. And he happened to do it right as I was losing control of the poles, too. I grunted.

"Mind lending me a hand with this?" I grunted.

He was slow to register. "Oh! Sure. No problem, my lady."

"Don't call me that."

"Okay, okay, sorry. I won't call you that. What about—"

"No nicknames. Period, exclamation point. End of conversation."

"Okay then."

There was rustling in the bushes behind us. All four of us whipped around to see Cam, with an eager, yet wild, light in his eyes. His hair was full of leaves and twigs (which Valerie immediately brushed out, much to Cam's chagrin) and his dagger was in hand. He was slightly breathless, but I didn't know if it was from shock or excitement. I was never sure of anything with Cam.

"What is it? What's wrong?" I asked. I felt my hands moving to my knives just in case something ran out of the trees to attack us. With our luck, it was actually something that could happen.

"Drew found something I think you guys might want to see," Cam said breathlessly. "Leave all the equipment. With luck, we can come back for it. If not...we may find that we won't need it."

He might have been breathless and looking slightly crazy, but I got the feeling that this wasn't a friendly invitation to come. It was an order from our leader.

"What are you saying?" Carter demanded with narrowed eyes.

For a split second, I was stunned to see Cam panicking. But before anyone else could notice it, he was able to conceal what he was feeling and return to a relatively calm state. His eyes were calmer now, but a storm still raged in their gray depths.

Cam shook his head. "Don't worry about it. I'm sure everything will be fine. Just follow me so I can show you what Drew found."

We decided to follow Cam even if he was acting slightly weird. What were we going to do? He was our leader. He was the one who knew what we were doing out here in the middle of nowhere.

The maple trees that we had been camped under soon gave way to ancient pines. I marveled at the sheer size of them. It must have taken hundreds or even thousands of years for them to grow this huge. It would be a shame if a wild fire got loose in here. Everything would burn into cinders.

YOUR WORLD SHALL FALL… YOU WILL BURN IN THE FIRESTORM.

That horrible voice swirled around in my head, unable to escape. Or perhaps it didn't want to escape. Memory of my dream crashed through my mind, reminding me of what the Hooded Figures had told me. In this very forest, there was a "Great Tree"—Shakovi. I didn't know where it was located or why it would be important, but I had a sneaking suspicion everything was going to change. Whether for better or worse…that fate was still up in the air.

I realized how much this part of the woods resembled my dreamscape. The massive pines were one thing, since Palee had ones just like it. But these were different. There was almost a sense of…knowledge, I guess, about them that just couldn't be explained.

And then we turned around that blasted corner.

What did it lead to? You guessed it: a massive cherry tree standing proudly in the middle of the clearing. Pink blossoms covered every possible surface of the branches. Several hundred more petals were on the ground, creating a silky pink blanket. Drew himself was sitting under the tree, staring up into the branches. His eyes were narrowed, as if deep in thought about some philosophical matter.

"Welcome to Shakovi, the Great Tree of Prophecy," Drew greeted us with an excited smile when he realized we were there.

When he turned to us, his eyes were sparkling with hope. It seemed like there was a different Drew standing in front of us. He stood up and walked over to Cam, who I now realized shared the same expression. Seriously, there was something up with them.

"Why is there a cherry tree in the middle of a pine forest?" Rennan asked, gazing up at the petal filled boughs. He looked awestruck. "Doesn't it seem like a weird place for it to be? Does it hold any magical qualities?"

"Oh, that's the only reason why we brought you guys here. This tree does indeed have magical qualities," Cam answered. His eyes sparkled with something foreign. It wasn't the shadows, so I guess that was good. "With a single blossom, you're able to see something in your future. It's inevitable that it will happen, but you might have a little bit of time to prepare for it."

"So...do we each get a blossom or do we get one as a whole?" I asked.

"I'm assuming we would each get one," Drew shrugged. He stepped towards the tree. "There's only one way to find out. Everyone choose a blossom."

We all took one of the pale pink flowers. However, when we stood in a circle while holding the blossoms, nothing of interest actually happened. We just stood there, waiting for something, but nothing ever came.

I nearly smashed the flower because it didn't do anything. Before I could do that, though, Cam nudged my foot with his to get me to look at him. When I did, he gave me a warning look. So, I did not smash the flower.

"Why aren't they doing anything?" Valerie asked with a seriously baffled look on her face.

Okay, I'm going to be honest here, it was hilarious to see the mermaid holding a flower for so long and not actually throwing it or singing or dancing around the tree. I guess Valerie really had changed.

"I don't know," Drew answered. He muttered something under his breath, but then shrugged. "Maybe it doesn't work when we want them to or maybe we're not supposed to stand in a circle or we have to say a password."

"Ha, password!" Rennan laughed. Before he could say anything else, his eyes filled with white light and he seemed to go into a trance. He was under the spell of these blasted little flowers.

"Okay. So, there *are* passwords," Cam commented.

He shuddered, then whispered something and he fell into the same state that the wolf had. Carter and Valerie immediately followed suit. Their faces were eager when the light filled their eyes. Drew and I were the only ones left. He closed his eyes and whispered something. White light filled his eyes, too.

Then only I remained. I had no idea what in the world my flower's password would be. Rennan's had seemed to follow his sense of humor of "password" being the password, so was it something that had to do with one's self? Was it a part of us that we held on to like a lifeline? If it was that sort of thing, then I could only think of one word for me.

"Freedom," I murmured.

The flower glowed with warm light in my hands and the warmth surged up my arms and to my brain. Soon I was filled with warmth and my vision was pure white. That was when the flower started showing me things that were up there on the terrifying list with my latest dream.

The first thing that I saw was a huge valley. There was nothing but green grass for miles and miles as far as the eye could see. The only color other than green shades was blue. Not blue water or lakes or rivers, however. The only blue was skies with no clouds extending far above it. Birds of prey soared high above the valley.

In the middle of a grassy plain, I noticed ghostly white beings forming ranks. I couldn't tell who or what they were, but I guessed that it was going to be a major battle. In the front of the smaller army, was a man sitting on a pure white horse with wings and a horn. It reminded me of Angelica. The man had a bow on his back, daggers at his side, a scythe in hand, and a helmet and armor that would protect him in combat. He was very kingly.

The scene I was watching changed as the eerily beautiful forms charged into battle. I wanted to stay and watch, but the magic of the flower was not so kind to me. Well, that and I had the feeling that I wasn't supposed to know the outcome yet and that I would find out very soon.

The next thing I saw was a huge city. There was a massive, open palace in the middle of everything with another large open structure near it.

My vision got closer to the smaller structure. It was like a coliseum—

perfect for sending traitors to fight for their freedom.

As a child, I always wished that Vareh had one so I could prove my worth and show that there was still fight left in the fox clans. On the other hand, as an adult now, I could see how heartless the fights were. No crime should result in a fight for life or death.

There were more ghostly figures fighting in the coliseum—one male and one female. They had helmets on, so I couldn't see their faces. In the pit of my stomach, I felt like something was wrong. This fight shouldn't be happening, but there was nothing that the fighters could do to prevent it. They both fought fiercely, but the woman was the more experienced of the two, so she quickly gained the upper hand. Right when the fight reached a critical moment, the focus changed again.

This time, I found myself in a prison cell. Surrounding me were thick bars, a small window, and hard stone. There was no way any human would be able to break out of a place like this and make it out alive.

Though, for the life of me, I couldn't figure out why the magic of Shokavi would show me a prison cell.

Footsteps echoed through the corridor, coming in my direction.

Eventually, a tall man stopped in front of the door to the cell. A long, black cloak was draped over his shoulders. Pieces of silver armor occasionally glinted in the soft sunlight coming from somewhere I couldn't see. The billowing black hood was drawn up so I couldn't see any of his distinctive features.

I heard my own voice ask, "*Who are you?*"

I was the one who would be stuck in this cell?!

"*Death to some, life to others. Fear not. I am a friend and much more to you,*" the voice responded in a tone conveying nothing more than neutrality.

The voice was equal parts soothing and infuriating—neither of which seemed to do me any good. It was a voice that made so many emotions swirl inside me, but none of them meant what I hoped they did.

And then the vision ended.

Thank goodness we were still in the clearing when we "woke up" from our crazy visions. I had a momentary panic that some sort of flesh-eating beast was going to jump out of the bushes and devour us as an early morning snack when we were helpless.

I was so thankful when I saw that Rennan had already come back from his vision. There was a smile on his face, so I knew his had not been as strange as mine. Rennan was the only one "awake," though.

He ran over and hugged me, grinning widely. His furry ears were completely perked up in a cheerful manner. "Yay! You're back. How was your vision?"

"It was something all right. I wouldn't say that it was bad or anything, but it certainly wasn't good. It was more alarming than anything," I answered. I tried to explain it to him, but my tongue wouldn't form the words. It was like my voice wouldn't work. "That's odd. I can't explain the details."

"I think that's the magic of the tree. Our visions are completely ours and there's no sharing specific details," Rennan shrugged. He didn't seem bothered by it like I was. "I tried to tell Drew when he came back to consciousness, but it didn't work."

"He's awake, too? Where is he?" I questioned, looking around the clearing. There was no sign of the sorcerer anywhere. "But it would be weird if it works like that. It would be really bad if one of us saw something important, but couldn't warn the others about it so everyone else walks into it blindly."

"That is very true," Rennan agreed. Then he shifted his weight uncomfortably. "As for Drew…he came back to reality and seemed troubled about something. I'm guessing he saw something pretty crazy in his vision, 'cause he said he was going on a walk to clear his head and to wait for him to get back. He left a couple minutes ago."

"That's strange. I have a feeling that all of us are going to have something concerning in all our visions from those irritating little flowers," I commented, looking around at the camp.

As the twins and Valerie were still experiencing their visions, I saw how strange the six of us had looked. Our eyes had glowed pure white, brighter than the moon's rays on a clear night. Not only that, but we had stood as still as the trees surrounding us. Or we were just really good-looking zombies.

"Ahh!" Valerie squealed from behind us. We whipped around to see the mermaid on her knees. There was a fearful look in her pink eyes that made me wonder what she had seen in her vision. "There were…they…ugh! Why can't I talk about what I saw?!"

Rennan rushed to help her up. She blushed, but accepted the help gratefully. Rennan smiled happily. "It's the magic of Shokavi. We aren't allowed to tell others about what we saw. I don't know why and it doesn't make much sense to me, but those are the rules."

"I hate the rules," Carter coughed as he swayed back and forth like he had stood up too quickly. He put a hand to his head. "It would be really nice to tell you so we can take action."

"Action will come whether we want it or not," Cam stated firmly.

His sudden comment surprised me since I hadn't realized that he was awake. Had he been awake and remained silent this whole time, or he woke up when Carter started speaking? But the hollow tone of his voice surprised me most of all. The closer I looked at the elf, the more I could see the shadows fighting to appear and manifest. Cam was barely keeping them at bay.

"Where's Drew?" Cam demanded.

"I'm back. We need to get going," Drew instructed tightly as he rejoined us. "We're wasting travel time."

There was no nonsense with either elf or sorcerer. Rennan, as usual, was pretty cheerful. Meanwhile, Valerie and I didn't seem to know what to make of our visions. Drew looked frantic.

"You saw it, didn't you?" Cam demanded.

His eyes were staring straight at Drew, who had no choice but to meet the elf's steely gaze. Drew silently nodded his head, and Cam's face became more grave than usual.

Cam sighed sadly. "He's right. Take only what you need. We need to move far and fast."

"You'd better," a new voice rasped from behind us.

I had a sinking suspicion I knew exactly who it was. We turned our heads to see Mongwau, Razil, and the man who had been in Leshee the day my grandmother died.

Mongwau grinned evilly. "You don't have much more time to live."

Division

"*Run!*" Cam yelled urgently.

There wasn't time for us to go back and get our supplies, because that meant doubling back to try leading our enemy in circles. Personally, I wouldn't have made the effort to go back. I would have kept going on, but since some of the others had chosen to leave their weapons back at camp, we needed to get them. I just hoped our camp hadn't been ransacked.

"We need to split up to get them off our backs!" Drew yelled.

Perfect timing, since there was a fork in the path that would take us to our small camp. We just had to make it there.

"Wise idea, sorcerer!" Cam shouted, somehow managing to turn mid-stride and fling throwing stars at our adversaries. Their panic bought us some time.

Then he stopped and turned around to face our adversaries. Rennan and I stopped beside him while Carter and Valerie ran ahead with Drew to get back. Cam knelt down and started rummaging around in his satchel.

Without looking up, he commented, "You should have gone ahead with Drew."

"And leave you alone when you have a history of dangerous stunts? I think not," I snorted.

After seeing what Cam could really do with shadows and especially after his incident with the dragon, I was unwilling to leave him alone in such a risky situation. If he fell, I would rather go down with him.

"Yeah, what she said. Besides, we've been a team since Palee. You're one of our pack, Cam, and we don't intend to abandon you like we were abandoned," Rennan said in a firm tone.

Cam's hands stopped moving and he subtly smiled.

"Thanks guys," Cam whispered. "I wanted to tell you, in case we don't survive much longer, that I'm so glad I met you guys. You're the closest thing I've had to family in a really long time."

"You're welcome," Rennan grinned. He looked up to see Mongwau and Razil rounding a corner. Then his eyes narrowed and his grin faded. "But let's save the sentiment. We've got company. Should we hold them off?"

"Please do. Scarlet, take on Razil. Rennan, take Mongwau. Keep them away from me for as long as you can," Cam directed as he started working again.

Rennan and I sent a quick glance to each other before we looked down at the elf, who was fiercely concentrated on whatever he was doing.

"What are you going to do?" I demanded.

They were sixty yards away from us.

"I'm trying to create something that will distract them long enough for the others to get their weapons."

Forty yards.

"Are you sure that's going to work?" Rennan asked skeptically.

Twenty yards.

"Yes! Now go!"

We collided the instant weapons were drawn. Razil threw herself at me, but I had quick reflexes. In one smooth motion, I pushed the raven woman off of me and forced her away from Cam. That was my one task. I wasn't going to fail; otherwise there would be disastrous consequences for the rest of us.

"Why do you protect the elvish scum?" Razil spat as she thrust her spear in my direction.

Her blows were so predictable that they were pretty easy to dodge, especially since she took a few seconds to pull it back in a motion similar to repeated hyperextension.

She snarled, "Hybrids and elves are *not* supposed to get along, Sutton. You know that better than anyone. *Elves* were the ones who killed your parents. As children, we dreamed of getting our revenge. And now you're helping one? That's low, even for one of the lowest of hybrids."

"Yeah, it's nice to hear that coming from the person who betrayed me by killing my grandmother," I muttered. I kicked the back of Razil's knees and she fell backward. Immediately, I was on her and holding my knife to her throat. "Do you know what it feels like to have the last piece of comfort in your life ripped away from you by someone you thought had your back?"

"All young hybrids know some sort of pain like that. Everyone has family and friends until they get killed by the scheming elves. No one should trust them, least of all you. If you were ever the person I knew—the one who had so much potential—you would *never* side with an elf," Razil mumbled. She proceeded to nick my neck with one of her blades.

I was happy to return the favor, only much deeper. She screamed in agony.

Cam, who was still putting something together, caught my eye and sent me a questioning glance. I nodded my head, trying to tell him I had Razil under control. He shrugged and started working faster than ever.

Seriously. That man is skilled to be able to work that fast.

"If you ever knew me," I began, "you would know that I will always side with a just cause. Cameron has an impossible task that would bring the world peace and fairness if he succeeds. Think of it, no more pain and suffering in Palee. I don't know about you, *friend*, but that sounds like something worth fighting for."

"You are a traitor," the raven seethed.

"Says the traitor!" I screamed.

"I will not have dealings with your kind anymore. Oh! Silly me. How could I forget? You're the last of your clan. Once you're gone…nevermore."

I jabbed my dagger into her arm and Razil roared in anguish. There was not a single drop of sympathy in me as she clutched her arm and hobbled away from me. She gingerly wrapped her wings around herself, glaring at me. A small trail of blood followed her every movement. I moved in to finish the job.

"*Scarlet! Rennan! Get back!*" Cam shouted from behind us.

Rennan, who I hadn't realized had pinned my former boss to a tree (good on him), looked toward me and then we sprinted to get behind Cam. His little creation was complete, and it looked like a bunch of gemstones poked into a glowing bar of gold. Cam threw the clump into the area where Mongwau and Razil were stranded.

He commanded us, "Don't move!"

Before either one of us could ask what was happening, shadows swirled around the clearing like a cyclone. The gold bar exploded into a blazing light that seemed to cancel out some of the darkness.

I couldn't help but watch in awe as the shadows protected us from the blinding light. I had no doubt that anyone without any sort of eye protection would have lost their vision. But we still had our sight. The shadows were actually being used to *protect* us.

However, that safety did not extend to Razil and Mongwau. They received the full force of the blast.

Rennan and I were unharmed. The shadows and light vanished almost as suddenly as they had been summoned. The wolf and I looked at each other, awestruck and speechless. That is, until we realized that Cam had fallen onto his knees. We rushed to help him up.

"What in the world was that, elf?" Rennan demanded.

Cam didn't bother responding immediately. He looked more spent than any other time I could remember—there were have been many moments as of late where he looked absolutely drained.

"I...controlled the shadows," Cameron answered with wide eyes. He spoke as if he couldn't even believe himself.

Concern immediately grew in my mind. If controlling those shadows meant Cam getting weaker with each attempt, I didn't want him to keep doing it.

Cam looked up at us in panic. "Please tell me neither one of you are blind."

"We're not. We can still see, and I see that we need to get out of this blasted forest if we want to live," I commented.

Both men nodded in agreement. Cam struggled to his feet, then made sure that he had his satchel and then we were off again. Rennan, meanwhile, scanned the area for any potential attackers just to exercise caution.

Searching for the path back to camp, we ran through the brush. Three times we retraced our steps. Three times we couldn't find our way back. We were lost and the others were far ahead. Who knew if they had even gotten back to the camp? They could have been intercepted and had to fight hand-to-hand combat. I shuddered. They could be dead.

"Heh, this is like the time we were hiking south through Palee and we got lost in the woods," Rennan commented. He was trying to be cheerful, but I could sense some nervousness in his voice.

Cam could, too, because he hesitantly nodded his head.

"You're right, it is. Wasn't that the night Scarlet was trying to teach you how to actually use a dagger for more than just firewood?" Cam asked with a small smile.

"It was. He still can't fight properly, but he's better with a blade than when I first met him," I snorted with a joking eyeroll.

"I was so sore the next morning from falling over logs so many times," Rennan recollected with a content expression. "I was just the crazy guy with a sword."

"Yeah, well, you're our crazy guy with a sword," Cam said as he put his hand on Rennan's shoulder.

He laughed when Rennan clapped him on the shoulder. It wasn't the hollow laugh from the Spiral of Doom that I had heard before. Nay, it was a truly joyful and happy laugh—one that I seldom heard. Hearing it filled me with warmth I couldn't possibly explain.

"True, and I wouldn't have it any other way," Rennan decided, pulling me into a hug.

I don't know what it was about human contact, but it felt odd to me. I tried my best to hug Rennan back, but he just laughed at my failed attempt and playfully shoved me away.

"The three of us really are a team," I marveled.

It was amazing. A fox, a wolf, and an elf—all sworn enemies. Yet, we were brought together by a common goal. It made me think that maybe the world wasn't so bad. If we three could be friends, what else could be possible? Well, except for maybe the idea of there being several worlds that we interconnected and one person knew how to control the space between them.

"Yeah! We're the three musketeers!" Rennan cheered.

I laughed and even Cam's signature smirk made an appearance. That is, right before a blood curdling scream rang throughout the forest. Blood drained from our faces when we realized who the scream belonged to.

"Valerie," we said in unison.

Then we took off running in the direction that her scream had come from. Our path led through the bushes and over a couple of creeks. A few minutes and a lot of scratches later, we were on the edge of the forest again. I was about to run out and attack whatever had made the mermaid scream, but Cam pulled me back by my shoulders. He held his fingers to his lips—the universal sign for *quiet*.

In the middle of our camp, there were eight heavy-weight guards standing in a circle around the rest of our friends. One of them was holding Valerie in place by her wrist. Her expression was full of pain, so the guard had injured her enough to cause the scream. The guards watching Drew and Carter looked just as cruel. Then I realized they were rogue trolls from Nesha.

"Let us go, you big oafs!" Carter shouted as he struggled against the ropes tying him to Drew, who didn't look too happy about the situation either, but he didn't say a word.

I don't know how he managed that. I would have been yelling curses and trying to break out.

Cam got my attention. I made a face, and then he started whispering a plan. "I'm going to distract the guards while you two to sneak around and free the others."

"Killing is allowed, right?" I inquired with a raised eyebrow.

Cam stared at me with an emotionless expression. "No. You are not allowed to kill anyone."

"Dang it."

Cam chuckled and smiled at me. "Kill only if you need to and if there's no other way. Otherwise, leave them alive and their master can kill them for letting the prisoners get away."

"I can never tell when you're joking," I snickered, shoving Cam away.

He grinned, and then seemed to melt into the shadows. Seconds later, he emerged in a shapeshifted form: Carter's. I still don't know why wanted to look like his brother (especially since they were already identical twins), but he did. Though, in hindsight, it might have been because of the length difference of their hair and other distinct features.

"Good. I like to keep things interesting," Cam-as-Carter smirked.

Even his voice changed into the less-accented, higher-pitched voice of Carter! Cam's skill of mimicry knew no bounds.

He disappeared and then reappeared again on the other side of camp. He gave us the slightest nod before beginning to distract the trolls. Trolls are usually dimwitted, so I didn't think Cam had too difficult a task. However, there were some trolls that were far smarter than others and might not be so easily outwitted, which could easily be a possibility.

"You fools! You probably don't realize who you have in custody!" Cam-as-Carter shouted. All the trolls in the place whirled around to look in the direction of the voice.

"What the...," the real Carter tried to say.

He never got to finish the sentence because Drew elbowed him in the back. The younger elf muttered under his breath, but didn't say another word. Hopefully he realized that Cam was trying to distract their captors long enough for Rennan and me to release them.

"But...you're over there...," said one very confused troll.

Another one punched him in the ribs. If anyone but a troll received that hit, they would have knocked the wind out of them at the very least.

"You dolt! Of course, he's over there!" shouted the troll who held Valerie's wrist.

The princess looked like she was trying really hard to keep herself in check and not to start crying. For once, I felt sorry for her. Being held prisoner by a very large troll could not have been easy.

"Wait, Holg, why is he over there?" asked a third troll.

The second troll, Holg, shrugged and kept a firm grip on Valerie. His hand twisted slightly and the mermaid winced in pain.

Cam noticed, so he started talking again. Rennan and I took that as a hint to get moving.

"It's because I'm too fast for you to catch me, you idiot," Cam taunted.

The trolls growled and tried to catch him, but Cam *was* too fast. He deftly avoided any giant fists that tried to grab him with ease. He crossed the camp and back again without being touched once.

"I told you I was too fast. Why don't you just let them go and we'll have a real battle?" Cam grinned. He knew he was agitating the trolls.

The eight trolls looked at each other's warty faces in confusion. Some looked like they wanted to take the bait; others seemed to be trying to see through Cam's trick. Either way, none of them were sure what to do. Noting their hesitation, Cam continued his banter to keep the trolls confused and distracted.

"Rennan, do you think you can get Valerie out of that troll's grasp?" I whispered as we sneaked around the clearing, looking for the safest point to enter the camp.

Rennan bit his lip, but nodded.

"I think I'll be able to if Cam is able to get them away from the center of camp. I have a feeling that the troll holding Valerie is going to die in the next few minutes, and I don't want to put the rest of you at risk if I screw something up," Rennan replied, scanning the scene. "You need to free Carter and Drew first."

Cam was slowly luring the majority of the trolls away, but not enough were far away yet.

"Good idea. I'm going to go for it," I decided.

I pulled a dagger out so I wouldn't be caught unprepared if I was grabbed. For some reason, I was excited to see if I could take down a troll. I had never fought one before, so I fully intended to see how easily they fell in battle.

Rennan nodded. "Just be careful."

"I'll try."

Slowly, I crept away from where Rennan was hiding. All the trolls had moved a decent distance away from Drew and Carter thanks to Cam's derisions, so I thought I had a pretty good chance of freeing them.

Drew seemed pleased to see me. I figured he would be far more helpful than Carter, whose obstinance was starting to get annoying. He had become more helpful, but whatever he had seen in his vision had derailed his willingness. I mean, he had agreed with Cam just this morning, but now he was back to his old self!

"Took you long enough to get here," Drew whispered while I cut his bonds. Their hands were between their backs, so the trolls wouldn't notice that their bonds had been cut.

"Yeah, well, Cam got us lost," I replied with a slight smirk as I started working on Carter's ropes.

Carter snorted. "I'm assuming he didn't want to admit it so he just got you lost again?"

"Thrice. Now, don't move. If we launch an attack, I want you two to have the element of surprise," I instructed them. "I'm going to help Rennan with Valerie. I want you two to stay here like this until Cam actually starts a battle."

Carter muttered something about his brother, but I couldn't make out the words.

I lightly kicked his elbow. That made him stop muttering.

I quietly hissed, "What was that?"

"Nothing," he answered quickly.

Drew and I rolled our eyes. I nodded to Drew and then crept back into the bushes where Rennan was still hiding.

"Why haven't you gone yet?" I questioned the wolf.

"Because I haven't had a good opening," he answered.

"Then let's get Cam to make one," I suggested.

"Aw, but I think he's having fun mimicking his brother and insulting the trolls."

"That sounds like Cam, but he can play another time when Valerie's life isn't on the line."

"I can't believe you're willing to help her."

"People can change."

"You're right. Now get Cam's attention."

"Done," I agreed.

Cam was still bantering across the camp. I somehow managed to catch his gaze and I nodded my head. He smirked briefly and I saw the shadows flash into a physical form again.

For a second, I thought he was going to pull the shadow manipulation thing again, but he didn't. He just slashed at the nearest troll with Egladel. It drew some sort of blackened blood as the troll stumbled backwards, crying out in rage. Cam grinned smugly as he started swinging his blade.

"Let's do this," Cam taunted as he stabbed an oncoming troll with his dagger.

As fast as lightning, Egladel was sheathed and the troll was beheaded by the silver scythe the elf always carried. He looked fearsome as his form began to shimmer.

Shape-shifting in action, I realized.

Cam soon looked like himself again while he readied for another attack.

"Bring it on!" Cam roared.

Nearly all the other trolls rushed at Cam, figuring that he was the most dangerous enemy present. Drew and Carter wisely chose that moment to get up and fight. Drew produced a sword from nowhere and Carter reclaimed his own. They grouped up with Cameron, developed a quick plan, then took down several of the slower trolls.

Meanwhile, Rennan and I had the more difficult task of getting Valerie to safety. The troll was still holding her, which did not make our task any easier.

"Stab the troll's leg," I said quickly, "then we take out its arms so it'll be forced to release Valerie."

"That sounds risky…," Rennan began.

"Do you have a better plan?" I snapped.

Rennan's ears went flat against his skull. "Nope."

"So, then, let's go."

Instead of sneaking around like we had been doing, we charged straight at Holg. He was startled to see us, but kept Valerie's wrist firmly in his grasp. Valerie, on the other hand, burst into tears when she saw us. She might have been happy for rescue or it was the pain…or both.

As directed, Rennan sliced the back of Holg's legs. The troll howled and reached for a weapon with his free hand. That's when I came in and sliced his hand clean off. Blood spurted everywhere and dripped into tiny puddles at our feet.

While the troll was distracted by his lost hand, Valerie took her chance to escape. She pulled free with a scream and scrambled to find a weapon. Since there were none around us, the mermaid settled for a large rock, which she promptly threw at the troll's head. He fell over and lay still on the ground.

Rennan cautiously poked the troll with his foot. It didn't move.

That is, until it reached to its side with its good hand, pulled out a horn, and blew two quick blasts, surprising Rennan greatly.

Before a third could sound, an arrow appeared in Holg's throat. Our heads swung around to see Cam holding up his bow with another arrow ready to shoot. His face was ashen and his hands trembled.

The troll did not move again.

"We need to get out of here immediately," Cam warned us with a shaky voice. He slung his bow and scythe over his back and prepared to leave. "That was a call for reinforcements. I have no idea where they're going to come from, but I have no intention to remain here to find out."

"Agreed," I nodded my head.

Though we all agreed to leave, we stalled and waited a few more moments to catch our breath after the bit of excitement with the trolls. Luckily, no one had injuries that needed immediate attention (Valerie's wrist was fine—the troll had just held it at an unnatural angle).

Meanwhile, Cam kept pacing around the clearing without a second's rest. Frankly, it made me slightly twitchy because he was buzzing with nervous energy. He soon began to grow impatient.

"Okay, we really should go now," Cam urged. His face looked just as urgent as his voice sounded. He kept looking around as if anticipating something running out of the trees. "We've lingered too long."

Drew nodded solemnly. They knew something that we didn't.

Rennan and I seemed to be thinking the same thing since he was also watching both sorcerer and elf skeptically. He too sensed that something wasn't quite right. I doubted they would tell us what was going on, though.

With a final urge from Cam, we started walking. I knew in my bones that there would be more battles and hardships to come whether we wanted them to or not.

As we walked west, I felt like had been there before. That couldn't be right. I had never been anywhere near these woods before. Heck, I had never been out of Palee until I had met Cam.

"Why are you so edgy?" I demanded to know when I caught up to Cam.

He had been stalking far ahead, not bothering to say a word to any of us. I guess that would have been almost normal if we hadn't been hearing him mutter under his breath to himself. The rest of the group had nominated me to talk to him because they thought I would have the most influence on the sullen elf. Although, they refused to tell me why they believed that notion.

Cam responded with only a grunt.

"That doesn't tell me anything or answer my question," I pointed out. Again, my only response was a grunt. "Please tell me what's wrong. I don't like seeing you this way."

"I appreciate the concern, but there is nothing that you could do to help except…no. Never mind," he muttered, quickly looking away.

I gently touched his wrist. "Please, Cam. I want to help in any way that I can."

"Thanks, Scarlet. Just…keep being you, not anyone else," Cam whispered almost silently. "I wish I could tell you everything will work out, but I can't see beyond today."

"Nobody can—"

"I *can*, though. I have some foresight—only for a period of twenty-four hours—and I can't see anything beyond tonight!" he said, his voice dead serious. His eyes were as hard as titanium and as cold as the Uncharted North.

I *knew* he had foresight! I knew it! Somehow, I managed to keep myself calm.

Cam clearly regretted saying that. "I'm sorry. I shouldn't have told you. Forget this conversation ever happened."

"How could I forget it happened when it's you, Cam? You're hard to forget," I replied, offering a lighthearted smile.

In secret, I was concerned that the elf was in such a brooding mood and that he, as someone who could apparently see into the future, couldn't see past today. Did that mean that we were all going to die before the sun went down? I shuddered, my mind running wild with possibilities.

"So where are we going, exactly?" Rennan dared to ask from behind.

Cam turned around and started walking backwards so he could face everyone. The rest of us walked like normal people. Honestly, we were so used to this move from Cam that it wasn't unusual.

"Well, we were trying to go from Hila to Estal, so we keep going until we arrive," Cam answered.

Did I detect a tone of apprehension in his voice or did I imagine it?

"And how long is that?"

"However long it takes us to get there."

"That is *so* not helpful," Rennan complained.

Cam raised an eyebrow, but the conversation didn't go anywhere from there. Nobody really felt like talking since we were all so somber. After all, we had enemies on our tails and a few of us could very well be at Death's doorstep.

Cam and Carter suddenly stopped dead in their tracks for reasons they withheld for the time being. They sent each other panicked looks. Then Cam told his brother something in elvish and ran off somewhere into the trees. Carter quickly followed.

The rest of us looked at each other in confusion.

"Does anyone know what that was about?" Valerie asked with a puzzled look on her face.

I decided not to think about the small glimmer of hope and fascination in her eyes as she spoke about the twins. Then I marveled at myself, wondering why on earth I was having those thoughts and feelings. Being particularly emotional was never natural to me since I ignored my feelings growing up. They always led to memories of the pain I had suffered.

"How are we supposed to know? They're elves. Secrets are in their blood," Drew said with a shrug. He didn't seem thrilled either. "I'm not good with emotions; they're so messy."

"I think you're mistaking feelings for paint," Rennan pointed out with a slight smirk.

Even the corners of Valerie's mouth tipped upward.

Drew threw his hands up in the air. "Does it make any difference? I don't like either of them!"

"Okay, okay, we get it. You don't need to get so bent out of shape over it," Rennan muttered.

Drew shook his head with contempt.

Cam and Carter soon came running back to us.

"We need to pick up the pace. Now," Cam stated breathlessly.

"Why?" Rennan asked as we all began jogging away from the forest.

Rennan got his answer, but not from Cam. Horns and battle cries echoed in the distance. I knew immediately that it was Mongwau and his forces coming after us, so I could see why Cam and Carter were pushing us to get going. What I couldn't figure out was how they had known to check for pursuers.

"Okay! We're going!" Rennan shouted, breaking into a sprint to catch up with the elves.

I had to hand it to them; despite the last few days, they were exceptionally fast and light on their feet. Drew later informed me that all elves were like that and to not be surprised at their strange quirks.

We kept running for what felt like miles and miles. Time seemed to be at a stand-still, but the sun continued on its path. As it turned out, the sun was the point to our imaginary compass to Estal without getting ourselves lost along the way.

A few times, we took breaks to rest briefly and get water. None of us felt like eating because of exhaustion and how warm it was getting. It was a sure sign that we were nearing the desert every minute of the way. In my heart, I felt like that was an ominous fact. I could hear even the name "Estal" and a queasy, uneven feeling would fill my stomach. That alone was enough to ruin any appetite for the warm fruits I carried.

"We need to keep going," Carter said as he threw his few things back into his pack.

Cam sent a strange look to his brother, but I couldn't determine what it could possibly be. Discomfort? Fear? Anxiety?

"I really don't want to, but you're right," Cam sighed in agreement. He double-checked all his daggers before shouldering his pack again.

All of us reluctantly did the same as we started jogging again. I sympathized with Cam. I didn't want to go further tonight. My feet ached and I felt like I was going to topple over and die from exhaustion. A longer break would have been nice, at the very least.

Soon, much to our dismay, we heard battle cries behind us again. I turned around to see several trolls riding on monstrous beasts. They were grey and had shriveled, smashed faces with massive bugged-out eyes. The monsters opened their mouths to bark and howl, revealing rows of snaggle teeth that needed some serious dental care.

Mongwau and Razil led the charge, each riding a horse as black as night. The foam spilling around their mouths told me immediately that these horses would not easily be dealt with. They could have been influenced by the cruelty of their masters, magic, or even more horrible things I didn't dare imagine.

There was a murderous look in Razil's eyes. I knew she was looking for revenge for the blinding light Cam had unleashed along with the shadows. Who she wanted revenge on, Cam or me—or even both of us—was unclear. Her eyes were simply full of hate.

Carter saw them, too. He grabbed my wrist and pulled me. I snapped out of whatever trance my mind had gone into and started running again. The others weren't in sight, but I could hear their voices coming from somewhere. Were they fighting off an attack from the trolls and their foul beasts? If so, why was Carter leading me *away* from the battle?

"Where are we going?" I shouted over the wind.

I had no idea where it had come from. My best guess was that Drew or Cam had summoned it to throw off the arrows the enemy was firing at us.

"Safety" was all I got for a response.

We kept running, but we were constantly looking back so we didn't really see what was in front of us. We were too concerned with making sure nothing was on our heels. I looked forward at one point to see ruddy colored cliffs ahead of us. The grass was quickly transitioning into golden sand.

Then I realized where I was.

I was in the same place I had seen in the dream with the earth-shaking voice and those mysterious hooded figures. It was the same dream where that horrible voice had told me that it was going to consume the world in flames and that no one was going to survive. Thinking back on that nightmare filled me with terror that felt like it would never leave me.

My feet slipped on the loose sand. Naturally, I didn't think anything of it because I was mentally preparing myself to fight. My hands went to my daggers. Both Carter and I were ready—his sword was drawn and my twin daggers were unsheathed. I was determined to kill whatever came at me.

However, I wasn't prepared for what I would literally step into. I made the fatal mistake of setting a foot back so I could take off at a sprint.

The ground beneath gave out and I started falling. I threw my daggers into the ground and tried to catch the cliff, but I missed. Carter's reflexes were fast since he was able to grab hold of my wrists and hold me steady.

"Don't fall!" he shouted over the major wind gusts rushing through the canyon.

"I'm trying not to!" I shouted back.

Honestly, I was trying not to look down either. I didn't want to see the River of Division that was my potential deathbed. I normally loved water, but falling into it from this height? Not my idea of fun.

I started slipping from Carter's grasp.

He yelled, "Hold on!"

"Idiot!" I shouted. "That's what I'm trying to do! Pull me up!"

"I'm trying!" Carter exclaimed through gritted teeth. He was never going to make it, especially since his face was turning the same red as my hair.

"*Scarlet*!!" Cam's voice roared over the noise of the wind.

He came into sight a few seconds later. Blood was running down his face and hands, his cloak was torn in several places, and several arrows had been shot from his quiver.

His steel grey eyes were wild with fear and worry as he glared down at his brother. "What happened?!"

"Isn't it obvious?" Carter spat, still trying to pull me up. "She slipped and now I'm trying to pull her up again! Care to help?"

"I'll do more than help," Cam said, shadows creeping into his eyes again.

"No!" I begged earnestly. "Please don't use the shadows. The effort could kill you!"

Cam smiled sadly. "I'm dying one way or another. I can't escape the only thing that has ever been promised to me."

Then something happened that nobody anticipated.

The edge of the cliff right beneath Cam gave out and fell down into the valley below me. The heir barely caught himself on the edge of the cliff that hadn't deteriorated into dust. Cam grunted as he inched his way over to me. He grabbed my right wrist and helped my hand find the rock while at the same time trying not to plummet to his death.

I gripped it and tried to climb until my knuckles turned white.

All of a sudden, Cam's left hand slipped as the rocks gave way into dust. I screamed in fear for the elf. Meanwhile, he just grunted and attempted to climb back up—a task easier said than done. The wind was making it nearly impossible to keep our balance on this abominable cliff face.

"*Cam*!" I shouted with urgency.

I met his eyes and they were filled with something I had never seen before. I didn't know what it was, and I hated myself for my ignorance. Once I was sure that Carter still had a grip on me, I reached out.

"Take my hand!" I called to Cam.

"If I take your hand, the chances of us falling automatically increase! There's no way both of us are going to make it!" he yelled over the wind. His eyes were filled with a longing light.

"Don't *ever* tell me the odds!" I growled. "Please, Cam, take my hand before it's too late."

He closed his eyes and reached for my hand at just the right time. His right hand slipped and then we were both being held up by Carter alone. Carter cursed in elvish when we became hanging weights.

"I hope you have a plan," Carter said with a strained voice and expression, "because I don't know how long I can hold you up."

"I have one," Cam offered.

"Do tell—quickly!"

"Drop me."

"WHAT?!" I shouted.

I couldn't believe what I was hearing. There was no way in my sane mind that I was going to drop Cam even if all else seemed hopeless.

I was adamant. "We are NOT dropping you!"

"You have to! It's the only way you'll survive!" Cam pushed. He reached into one of his pockets and pulled something out. He slipped it into my boot. "Please, finish this for me."

I didn't think much of it then, but later I would find out just how important that small object was.

Tears filled my eyes. "There *has* to be another way. We can both make it up again. We can...."

Cam's voice was gentle but firm when he spoke again. He looked me directly in the eye. "There isn't. This is where my journey ends, Scarlet. This is what I saw in my vision. *I* can't escape this, but *you* can. Drop me."

"Why are you doing this?" I cried.

Tears were running down my face in miniature rivers. I tightened my grip around his wrist. I couldn't make myself let go. I was going to save him, too.

"*Because I love you*," he said.

My brain barely registered his voice.

He wrenched his wrist from my fist and began his plummet towards the water. His expression was apologetic, but I couldn't bring myself to feel anything other than shock. I legitimately thought I imagined those last words.

"*NO*!!" I screamed. I watched in horror as Cam's form became smaller and smaller.

He did nothing to save himself. He didn't even shape-shift into anything that could fly so he could save himself. He just kept falling until I heard a bone-shattering *CRASH* in the water far below.

"No. No, no, no, *no*, *NO*!!" I shrieked over the wind.

"Scarlet!" Rennan yelled in surprise. He somehow managed to catch my other wrist and started pulling.

Seconds later, I was back on solid ground while Rennan and Carter huffed beside me.

Rennan's brows knit together. "Where's Cam? I saw him run this way."

I looked at Carter, who shook his head but didn't look at me. I looked back at Rennan, whose eyes were full of genuine concern. "He...he fell."

Any light or hope in Rennan's bright eyes faded to a dull blue. Out of nowhere, Valerie appeared behind the wolf. She burst into tears when she realized what had happened and Rennan stood to comfort her. She cried into his chest with his arm wrapped around her. Drew stood a short distance away, just staring down into the river below.

"That's it then. It's over," Rennan whispered.

I couldn't move save to pull out whatever Cam had put in my boot. I curled my fist around it; unable to bring myself to look at whatever it was Cam had left me. Beyond that, I felt like I was paralyzed.

"He wanted us to continue on. He wants us to finish this quest for him," I said quietly.

"But if we succeed—and that's a huge 'if'—who would be king?" Rennan asked, his voice growing cold.

Carter cleared his throat and all reddened eyes turned to him.

"Since the first heir has...passed on," Carter began, "the next in line for the crown would be king."

"Ha! Don't make me laugh," Rennan growled. That was the harshest tone I had ever heard him use. Rennan was usually such a cheerful person; I was dismayed to see this side of him. "You've never had the guts to be a king."

Carter scowled. "Yeah? Well, you're just a hybrid! King or not, I still stand higher than you. You're the lowest of the lows, wolf!"

"Guys, please," Valerie sniffled. "This isn't going to help anything. Cam would want us to stop arguing and keep going."

Carter and Rennan immediately stopped arguing.

"She's right," Drew agreed, taking a few steps towards us. "We need to get to Estal and Heviah."

"Sadly, you'll only make it to one of those places," Mongwau's voice sneered.

I dejectedly turned around to see Mongwau and Razil staring at us triumphantly. I was starting to get tired of them interrupting all of our important conversations. Their weapons were drawn and ready for action, but my friends and I did nothing to fight back.

"And it's likely you'll never make it out."

I didn't have the heart to fight our capture, and evidently no one else did either because they came along quietly. Before we were entirely taken captive, I opened my fist to see what Cam had left me: the signet ring that secured his place as the elvish heir. I nearly choked when I realized the foreign emotion Cam had displayed only seconds before he sacrificed himself for me.

It was love.

Welcome to Estal

"So again, what are you doing in Estal, trespassers?" King Hezakah asked as he pinched the bridge of his nose.

We remained stubbornly silent. Hezakah had been trying to get us to talk for days now, but none of us would tell the king anything.

After Cam's sacrifice, Mongwau and his trolls had captured us and dragged us on a several week long trek to Bulshkan, Estal. From there, we were immediately taken to the king, questioned, and thrown into the muggy dungeon when we wouldn't talk. We'd been there for about a week already. We all wanted to get out, but we weren't going to be rash and create more trouble than was necessary. We were going to be methodical so we could slip out like cats in a tunnel.

Since we had arrived, Hezakah had questioned us every day, yet the only thing he managed to get was obstinate silence. For the most part, Hezakah had proved reasonable. He was slow to get angry and he had patience…to a certain degree. But I knew that patience would wear thin eventually.

A part of me feared that we wouldn't be so lucky to just keep being thrown in various cells. I doubted the king's mercy would extend so far. And since Mongwau and Razil seemed to be in his inner circle, our deaths could come at any point in time.

But at that point, I didn't really care. Being stuck in my cell had given me time to do a lot of thinking. It had also given me way too much time to grieve. Despite my best efforts, I had lost another person I cared deeply about. When I realized it was love that Cam had been showing me in the months since I'd met him, I was utterly heartbroken. I realized too late that what had grown in me for Cam was love, even if I hadn't realized I was capable of such affection.

The more I thought about it, I realized he was the only person who completely understood the loss and heartbreak that I felt. After all, he had lost his aunt in the same way I had lost my parents and grandmother. His presence had always filled me with warmth that I would ever find again.

Now that he was gone…I didn't know what to do. I had the signet ring, sure, but I had no idea what to do with it. All I had done was make a small pouch tied to my ankle inside my boot for fear of having it stolen. I had yet to come up with a decent plan to finish the quest and avenge Cam's death. The others were counting on me to be the leader and pull this whole thing off, but how could I lead them when I couldn't even manage my own thoughts and emotions?

In the present moment, my friends and I, bound and desperate, stood in front of King Hezakah. Though we knew the consequences of silence, we still refused to tell him a thing. Eventually, after a very long stare off, Hezakah groaned quite loudly. My heart rose to my throat. This was it. This was the moment that was going to decide our fates.

"After all of this pressure you still say nothing? How much longer will you try me?" he shouted angrily. "I don't even know your names so I can press charges to your kingdoms! How do you expect me to punish trespassers when they don't even give me adequate information to put on a warning poster?"

If he had this kind of temper all the time, no wonder his dark hair was beginning to grey. He didn't face us. Instead, he tore the crown off his head and flung it to the poor, clueless guard beside him.

Our nerves kept us utterly silent. I knew we were all worried about what would happen to us after this interrogation.

Well, most of us. Carter was the only one who didn't look like he feared for his life. Since he was usually a coward, I wondered what he was planning. Whatever it was, it couldn't be good. The last time I had seen this specific expression was when he had tried to take his own brother's life in Sala. Now he didn't have to worry about that task.

"That's it! You will receive death because that is so obviously what you want!" Hezakah raged. "I will grant it to you!"

"Wait!" Carter shouted. His voice echoed through the elevated hall.

All eyes turned to him. This was especially true of Rennan and Drew, who immediately knew something was amiss. The king raised a curious, but impatient, eyebrow. I didn't blame him. I would have sent Carter the same expression if not worse.

"The elfling speaks!" Hezakah announced in a loud voice and with demonstrative hand gestures. He quickly narrowed his eyes. "I had begun to think you were all mute and deaf. I'll humor you for the time being. Tell me why I shouldn't kill you in the morning."

Carter gulped nervously. Then his face became stern. "My lord Hezakah, I am Prince Carter Woods, son of King Tristan of Heviah. I bring these fiends to you to show my loyalty to my father's cause. They have openly plotted against the Hevian throne on several occasions and deserve death. I understand that you and my father are not currently on the best of terms, so take his enemies to him to regain the alliance my father once held with you."

I wanted to punch Carter for betraying us. Hezakah actually looked like he was considering Carter's request and proposition!

I never should have given him a shred of my trust. I should have thought to see this coming. After all, betrayal never comes from a stranger. I glared at Carter.

He only smiled at me wickedly.

After all this time of actually trying to be helpful, he ruined everything.

In that moment, I realized he had never wanted to help his brother and he only wanted the throne. He only wore the mask to trick us until he saw his opportunity. Carter was smarter than he let on, and he had done this intentionally. The dirty, underhanded, no good, dishonest elf! I needed more names to call him.

"Your request is granted and suggestion is eagerly supported," the king decided with a slight smile. He seemed glad to be rid of us.

And why wouldn't he be? Of course, we were bound to be prisoners after our friend had just died.

Carter grinned smugly. He sickened me.

Hezakah turned to the rest of us. "I'm going to start planning. I want to see if your father will come crawling back on his own or if I have to come on my hands and knees. Until then, Prince Woods will serve at my right hand and these prisoners will all meet their fates. The wizard shall have to work in the kitchens, the mermaid will be a maid, and the hybrids…they will face the traditional punishment for their kind. Dismissed!"

The guards immediately sprang into action. They made sure we were thoroughly bound and unable to escape before shoving us out of the doors. The four of us were led out of the throne room and back to the cells.

It made me more desperate to find a way to escape and to do

something terrible to Carter for betraying us.

No matter what, I would find a way to remedy this.

It was a couple days later when I finally heard the sound of another person walking towards my cell. It had been three days at least since I had eaten anything, so I had gone into a state of despair and forced sleep in hopes of warding off the sickening hunger. It had also helped me gain some sort of peace after the cliffside battle. I was mostly successful, too, until my concentration was broken by echoes in the hallway.

I sat up on my bed to try to relieve the pain of my growling stomach. I didn't know how much more I was going to be able to take. I could go without food, but I was starting to get dehydrated and there was no way I was going to survive in this desert city without water. That wasn't possible in this heat.

A cloaked figure stepped into view. From the blue cloak alone, I knew who it was immediately.

"Drew?" I whispered. "Is that you?"

"Shh," he said as he quietly started unlocking my cell door using magic.

He got it open a minute later, at which point he walked in and threw back his hood. His copper hair hung in his face, partially blocking his strange color shifting eyes.

He held a small package out to me. "I brought you some bread and water."

"How did you manage that?" I asked incredulously. Drew handed me the bread and I took it gratefully.

He shrugged. "I'm working in the kitchens now, but I don't know how often I'll be able to come down here. It probably won't be all that frequent what with a war looming on the horizon. Who knows? Hezakah might make me cook for his soldiers if I don't blow anything up here first."

We fell silent for a moment. Based on what Drew had told me about his cooking skills (or lack thereof), a disaster was not impossible."

"He and Tristan are not on good terms, and I doubt it will get better, even with Carter betraying and turning us in," Drew commented. "Wow, that was a depressing sentence, Andrew. She would never let me speak like…never mind. Point is face to face meetings will be rare."

"Okay," I said, slowly chewing on the soft bread. I looked up at the sorcerer. "Is there anything you can tell me now?"

"The Estalite ambassador is a bust. He was killed two weeks ago after siding with Coral on political issues concerning Palee. We're going to have to find our own way out of this mess," Drew sighed, taking a seat on the foot of my bed. He rubbed the bridge of his nose. "I don't know where to go from here. Normally I have some idea, but now…?"

"Now we're all at a loss," I finished quietly.

"Yeah," Drew whispered. "I can't believe he's gone."

"I can't either. But then again, I can," I replied, trying to keep my emotions in check. I didn't need to start crying again like I seemed to every time I thought of Cam. "I seem to lose everyone I care for at some point. Fate has a cruel sense of humor to take Cameron from me as well."

"I know what you mean. I lost someone I cared about once. My heart hasn't healed, and I doubt it ever really will. That's just the cost of love," Drew explained almost silently.

I looked over to him and watched him finger the silver locket that hung around his neck. It was a curious thing. He always wore it. It must have been given to him by whoever he held very close. He never spoke of the person, but I had a feeling that they had meant a lot to Drew to make him sympathetic to other people in the same situations.

He sighed. "I honestly didn't know what to do with myself when I lost her. Frankly, I still don't. I feel the same way now that Cam is gone, but slightly different. It's probably different for me than for you, since he meant something else to you, but you're not alone. You're not the only one his sacrifice has affected."

I just sighed and stared at the floor. "Drew, how are we supposed to lead the others? How are we going to defeat Tristan?"

The name was bitter as it rolled off my tongue. I hated it.

"I don't know, Scarlet. I really don't. We have to find a way to keep ourselves strong in this trial. We need to accept the fact that he's gone and move on. That is not to say we won't cherish the time that we had with him, but rather we use his memory to spur us on," Drew stated bluntly.

That stung more than I wanted to admit.

When I didn't say anything, the sorcerer continued. "Think about it. Would Cameron really want us to stay here and mope about everything that happened to him or would he want us to complete what he couldn't? I think he'd want us to press on and not grieve."

"His name needs to be remembered," I protested. My eyes were starting to tear up. "He can't be forgotten like my people."

"You hybrids know honor and glory well. Cam's name will see its own glory in later generations. I promise you that. But for now, his memory is what keeps us going. I intend to finish what he started," Drew stated firmly.

A new light sparked in his eyes—one that I knew well: revenge.

"Agreed. Tristan cannot prevail."

Drew smiled. "No, he cannot. Take heart, Scarlet. We're going to find a way to get out of here, no matter what."

I hate prisons, dungeons, and everything of the sort. I was in the dungeons of Bulshkan's palace for *eleven months*. It was torture.

Not only that, but Drew rarely came to talk after that one night. If he came, it was always brief because every single Estalite watched him like a hawk.

As a result, I had nothing to do except sit, think, sleep, and somehow keep my mouth shut. I would have *loved* to yell curses at the guards, but I needed the silence to think up a plan. I also had this stupid pendant that could electrocute me if I stepped out of line. I did it once and haven't done it again.

I just had to sit there and waste time when I'm sure we could have gotten so much further with our quest. I hate being used as nothing more than a toy, so I tried to keep myself from becoming desperate. There were several occasions where I was able to escape when the guards weren't paying attention. Sadly, I would always get caught and returned to my cell.

Not all the extra time was helpful since any plan I could come up with had a flaw. I liked the ones that involved killing the guards as they walked by so I could grab their keys, but even if I succeeded, I had no idea where my friend's cells were…or where to put the dead bodies.

Valerie and Drew were no help, either. They were able to walk by me as they were escorted up to the main levels, but we couldn't speak to each other. All they could do was offer calming looks that said, *we're going to get out of this.*

I wished I could believe them.

Footsteps echoed through the stone hallway leading to my cell. Soon, a figure in a long black cloak swept into view. His black cloak cast a shadow over his face that distorted any features beneath. I couldn't make out anything except the tip of a well-shaped, pale nose. He obviously wasn't an Estalite since his skin was so pale.

I stared at the man and he stared at me, neither one of us saying anything. I felt a strange feeling like I had been here in this moment before, but I tried to shake it off. For a moment, I really hoped that it was Cam in disguise and he was coming to free me from this blasted prison. I hated it more here than my entire life in Palee. At least in Palee I had been able to go everywhere!

"Who are you?" I demanded.

The man cocked his head, but I still couldn't see underneath. "Death to some, life to others. Fear not. I am a friend and much more to you."

"That doesn't tell me anything."

"It wasn't meant to," the figure stated. "My identity is for you to ascertain and not for me to tell."

His voice had a strangely familiar deepness, but the accent that I had been hoping for just wasn't there. Any hope that Cam had somehow survived the fall and had been hiding out somewhere was utterly crushed.

He left me alone again before I could ask any other question.

I guessed that it was about midday when two female guards came to get me. They didn't tell me what they were doing, but they insisted that I came with them. Naturally, I didn't trust them at all. If you had been through everything I had, would you?

The two women were nearly identical in every sense. They had strawberry blonde hair, amber colored eyes, and tanned skin dotted with dark freckles. They wore golden armor with crimson tunics and dark colored leggings. Their golden sandals sparkled in the low rays the sun cast through the dungeon. They looked amazingly familiar, but I couldn't put my finger on it.

"Who are you?" I demanded in a low tone when the two women sent each other a knowing look from beneath their helmets.

"Not here. Follow us," the one on the left directed quietly.

She started walking down the right hallway. The other lady beckoned for me to follow them. I followed, but only because anything was better than going back into the cell. I had had enough of seeing the same four walls day after day.

The two women led me into a small armory in what I guessed to be the east wing of the palace (it was warmer in there). Bronze armor and weapons hung on every available space. The only piece of furniture in the room, besides the racks of armor, was a small chair in the center.

"Again, who are you?" I asked, making sure I was a safe distance away from the two guards in case they tried to attack me or something.

As skilled a warrior as I was, I doubted that I would be able to take down two trained guards with weapons when all I had were my bare hands.

The women reached for their helmets. They pulled them off to reveal ears that looked exactly like mine.

My jaw dropped. These two women were from Palee. More importantly, *they were members of a fox clan.* That explained why I recognized them. They looked like my final memory of my father on the day that he died. They had his same hair color, but there's no way that they could have been my siblings. I was born an only child.

"We are Serena and Samantha Sutton of the common foxes of Palee. I'm Serena and that's Sam," the one named Serena explained. "When we discovered a fox hybrid being held captive, we worked very hard to find a way to get ourselves transferred here."

I was too shocked to say anything. After all, I thought that I was the last surviving member of my clan and then I found long lost cousins that I never knew existed!

"But why? This place is torture! I'm not worth all of that trouble," I argued.

"But you are, cousin," Samantha insisted.

My gaze shifted to her. They both had kind personalities so I found it hard to imagine them surviving in a place like this.

She pleaded, "Will you please tell us your name so we know what side of our family you're on? We know you are part of our bloodline, but there are some things we can't guess. We've spent years trying to find someone from our clan or anyone who might have news of it, and you're the first we've come across."

I didn't entirely trust them, whether they were blood family or not, but I found the means to tell them that I, too, was a Sutton. Eventually, we came to the conclusion that their father was my uncle and my father's brother. That would explain why we all looked alike and shared the same surname. I just couldn't believe I still had living blood relatives.

"Scarlet, we didn't bring you here just so we could tell you that you still have living family," Serena began with a penitent expression. "We wanted to warn you."

I scowled. "Warn me about what? I'm already facing certain death for plotting against the Hevian throne. How much more danger could I be in?"

My cousins looked at each other apprehensively. Sam was the one who continued explaining. "Heviah and Estal are on the verge of war. The alliance they once had is crumbling because that Woods scum found out that Hezakah has an army of hybrids. The elf king was furious, so hybrids have been in even greater danger recently. We heard rumors of even more raids and massacres being launched in Palee, just like the ones that killed our parents."

I thought for a minute or two, trying to process that information. "So…what exactly am I facing and why does this potential war involve me?"

Serena, gentle as ever, sighed. "Scarlet, the punishment you are facing is gladiator fights to the death. You've survived nearly a year in the dungeons to prove your hardiness, so now you'll be forced to fight until someone dies. There is no escape except for a bloody death on the battle field. As for the war…that applies to everyone who gets caught in the crossfire. You need to get your friends out of this city and continue on your quest."

"How do you even know about the quest?" I demanded.

My guard was completely up now. I wasn't taking any chances.

Sam smiled. "Your wolf friend mistook me for you and told me about his theories. I won't repeat them since they're full of all sorts of holes. Seriously, how can anyone think a wolf can be a better hunter than a fox?"

"Because they don't realize that a fox can use their own weapons against them. That sounds like Rennan, though," I snickered.

I would have to remember to punch Rennan next time I saw him for telling escape plans to strangers. Jeez, that wolf always managed to find himself in some sort of trouble. I was half amused that it was completely his own doing this time and Cam hadn't whispered anything in his furry ears. (That, by the way, has happened in the past. How else would the idea of "coconut bombs" get into the wolf's head?)

"Right. And you need to use that skill," Serena said with a worn smile.

She got up and started rummaging around in the countless stacks and piles of armor and weapons. She soon brought back a pile of armor that contained both metal and leather as well as several weapons that would be easy to carry.

I looked at her questioningly."Why do I need to use it now?"

"Because. We're going to get you ready for your first fight," she answered, inspecting different swords and heavy weaponry that seemed far too clunky to carry into close combat.

"It's easy once you figure out how your opponent fights," Sam shrugged as she began helping her sister.

Oh boy, I thought to myself, *this isn't going to end well….*

I waited in the hallway leading to the arena. Serena and Samantha had done an excellent job outfitting me for the fight that I would be forced to survive through. I had twin daggers hanging at my side and an axe slung across my back. They had suggested a bow to me, but I was no good with one. I'd tried it a few times, but I never hit the intended target. Besides, the thought of carrying both a bow and daggers was a reminder of a painful memory.

Eventually, they led me to the arena entrance.

Surprised, I realized this was the same arena that I had seen in the vision shown to me by the Great Tree.

If this was the same coliseum, then did that mean everything else I had seen in the vision was in Estal? If so, what was the timeline associated with it? Days? Months? Years? I shuddered. Part of me hoped that I wouldn't live long enough to find out. The other part wanted to keep living so I could make Cam proud even if he wasn't here to see it.

The sisters stopped right behind me.

I turned around and looked at them in confusion. "Aren't you coming?"

"This is as far as we're allowed to go. We'll be waiting here for you if you live through the fight," Serena replied.

"What she means is that *when* you survive," Samantha shot a pointed look at her sister, "we'll be waiting here to return you to your cell. We're now your permanent guards. Though, know this, we may not be able to show compassion all the time. Sometimes we may be forced to be rougher."

"Understood," I nodded. I was about to go into the waiting area, but I stopped again. "Do either of you know who I'm going to be facing?"

They both shook their heads.

"You could be facing another imprisoned hybrid or you may be facing one of the Estalite officers to see who's made of tougher steel," Sam explained with a sour expression. She regained her composure and brushed a strand of hair out of her face.

"I hate how they always think that Paleeans are just animals waiting to die," Serena spat. "I mean, we may have animal features, but we're still human. We still deserve a chance."

Sam and I agreed entirely.

"If my friends and I can get out of here and overthrow the kings, we'll make sure that Paleeans are treated more fairly, like we should be," I promised them.

It was the same promise Cam had made to me when I met him. Even if he hadn't survived this journey, I was intent upon keeping that promise for my generation and those that come after me.

"Thank you, cousin. You have a good heart," Serena said with a grateful smile. "Now get out there. You have a battle to win. Remember what we taught you."

"'Use their strengths against them,'" I recollected with a small smile. I was determined to win. "I'll make you proud and get my friends out of this prison."

Moreover, I was determined to make Cam proud. I owed him that.

With a last look of encouragement from my cousins, I stepped out into the bright sun and a cheering crowd. Doubtless they were cheering for my adversary. I didn't care who it was, as long as they actually presented me with a challenge. If it was an easy target...well, this battle wouldn't end well for them.

I was anticipating an actual test to my abilities rather than just a fight for entertainment. There was no honor in fighting for a prize. Things like that always brought out the worst in people and I liked to keep my honor. Surprising, considering I'm an mercenary and most of us will get the bounty no matter what.

I looked around the coliseum to try to determine any advantages I might have. It was just flat, sandy ground. The only advantage I had were my own skills. Even the sun wasn't helping. Normally I was fine with it, but today it seemed like it was just beating down mercilessly on everything.

I laughed halfheartedly to myself, imagining Cam hissing at the sun and Rennan teasing him about being a creature of the night. Then I sighed. I missed the good old days when it was just the three of us on our journey.

The cheering continued when I stepped out into the center of the coliseum. Hezakah's voice echoed through the open space seconds later, introducing me and my punishment. The cheering ceased and spectators started booing. The king motioned for silence and the crowd hushed.

"Yes, yes, I know you all disapprove of the existence of another hybrid. I do as well," Hezakah began.

The people in the stands murmured their agreement with the king as I muttered curses under my breath about the snobby, self-obsessed people who refused to see past flaws and appearances.

Hezakah ignored them. "Today we have a very…shall we say, *special* fighter in the lineup. May I present to you: Razil, a former commander of my army! May she keep her life and earn back her honor."

Razil was thrust out of a door on the opposite site of the arena. I had never seen her so ragged. Her hair was loose over her shoulders, her ebony wings were obviously missing several feathers, and even her typically tan skin looked pale. The hate that glowed in her eyes was intense as the guards pushed her into the ring. Despite me being her enemy, I had a feeling that this pent-up fury was directed entirely toward King Hezakah.

"*Fight!*" Hezakah shouted over the roar of the crowd.

Razil screeched and ran at me, pulling out twin katanas in seconds. Personally, I thought it was slightly unfair that her blades were longer than my daggers, but didn't I say I wanted a challenge? I responded to her attack with my battle axe. Its steel blade deflected her swords with a metal-on-metal screech.

"So, what did you do to get yourself in trouble this time?" I casually questioned as I deflected another one of her wild strokes.

"Me?! You're the reason I'm here in the first place!" she seethed.

"Really? I didn't betray my best friend by killing her grandmother! If you hadn't done that, I never would have left Palee!" I roared, shoving her to the ground and trying to stab her leg with the sharpened bottom of my axe.

The crowd bellowed in approval for me, but booed at Razil when she tried to get up again. I forced her back down until she answered my question.

"You were always so lucky," she muttered, escaping my grasp.

We circled each other, each with her weapons drawn.

"*Lucky*. That's a generous way to put it," I spat, jumping to dodge a throwing star the raven had thrown at me. I was not going to be caught off guard by the smallest weapon on the battle field. "How in the wide world could you think I was lucky?"

"My family never loved me, Scarlet. Even though you only had your grandmother, she cared for you. That elf cared deeply for you before he fell off the cliff. You were well cared for," she muttered. "I've always envied you for that."

We broke into a long exchange of quick blows. She landed one on my knee and I connected with her elbow.

"So, our whole friendship has been a lie, then?"

Razil blinked her eyes in shock for a few seconds. "I…no. It hasn't been a lie, but some things don't last forever. Like you!"

She flung herself at me with two wing beats to aid her. In a second, I had my axe out and I made a clean swing. I heard the sound of bone crunching and the raven woman fell to the ground with a hard thud and a scream of agony.

I stared in shock when I realized how close I had come to killing her. As much as I hated that woman, she didn't deserve to die by my hand. She had lost her wings to me. I refused to do more than that.

Razil brought a shaking hand to her shoulders. Her green eyes went wide when she pulled her blood-covered hand back. The air reeked of iron while blood gushed out of the fresh wound. The crowd went wild. The broken look in Razil's eyes obviously showed that she had no more fight left in her.

"Good-bye, Scarlet," she whispered as two guards rushed towards us. She didn't meet my eyes. "In case we never see each other again, I'm sorry. I never should have joined the Estalite army just to get revenge. I never should have joined the Serpent's Sons. It got Wayne killed, and I'm its next victim. Don't do what the king wants—he's mad."

The guards reached us and hauled Razil to her feet. It was horrifying to see all of the fight taken out of her. She offered me a genuinely apologetic smile before they dragged her somewhere dark and most likely dangerous.

I knew in my heart of hearts that this was the last time I would ever see Razil.

I couldn't believe I felt sorry for the person who had betrayed me just because of jealously. But I did.

"There you have it!" Hezakah's voice boomed over the cheering of the crowd.

I turned and scowled in the direction of the king's spectator box. Even from a distance I could tell that he was planning something and I wanted no part in it.

"We have today's winner," Hezakah grinned, his expression devious. "We'll see if she survives any more battles."

With that, he motioned for me to go back in the direction I came from. Sam and Serena were waiting for me in the corridor and congratulated me immediately.

I accepted their praise as well as I could, but it felt hollow. I had just taken down a friend and completely destroyed any chance she had at life. I felt horrible.

They took me back to my cell where I would wait for the next wicked order from Hezakah. Personally, I was glad for the solitude because it gave me a chance to think through all I knew for a second time.

I didn't know who to trust anymore.

Reckless Gambit

Drew nearly scared me out of my wits one night when he randomly appeared outside of my cell door.

I had been in a dead sleep after a strenuous fight, and the sudden clinking of iron keys startled me out of my slumber. At first, I didn't know what had happened or what time it was, but when my eyes adjusted to the dark light, I saw the tall sorcerer standing in the doorway. He was barely visible and there was a slight haze around him, so he must have been using a cloaking device.

"Drew?! What in Galerah are you doing here?!" I demanded when I had come to my senses.

Not that I was displeased to see him, but I didn't like people waking me up from my sleep. Last time that happened, Cam woke me up and we had watched my hometown burn to smoldering ashes. Oh, why did I have to think of Cam?

"Look, there's something happening tonight that needs to be investigated," Drew said quickly. He kept looking over his shoulder and out into the hall. I didn't know what was making him twitchy, but whatever it was, it had to be big.

"What's going on?" I asked, eyebrows furrowed.

"I heard rumors that officials from Heviah are going to be here for a night and they're meeting with Hezakah soon," Drew whispered in reply. "I don't have time to explain it here. Come with me and I'll tell you more."

"Shouldn't we get Rennan and Valerie?" I questioned as we swiftly fled the cell block.

"There isn't time."

"Then why did you get me?"

Drew stopped to look at me. "You have Cam's ring. I know you do. That thing is what is going to help us get the throne back. The one who has that ring is, by law, the next ruler of Heviah. Since Cam gave it to you, if we succeed in this venture, you're on the throne."

"But I'm a hybrid!" I protested. "Won't that be the same as conquering Heviah?"

"*It doesn't matter*!" Drew shouted, staring me dead in the eye. His face was inches away from mine. He blinked and withdrew. "Scarlet, that ring *cannot* fall into the wrong hands, especially those of any of the surviving Woods. You have to have the strength to persevere."

"Drew, I don't know if I can do that. I'm not a leader."

Drew leaned against the wall of the corridor and closed his eyes. "I'm not either. I'm not a hero, Scarlet. Anyone can attest to that. However, I do know when it's time to grow up and step into roles that force me to grow as a person. I've had to do that so many times that it's now second nature to become what I'm not. I'm not a leader, but I know what needs to be done. I hate to be blunt, but our leader is dead. He's never coming back. If he could, I'm sure he would have done so already. I can't change that, and neither can you. Cam entrusted you with that signet ring. He had faith that you could lead, and so do I."

My mood became grim at the mention of Cam. "You should not have put your faith in me, but fine. And I'm not doing this for you, Andrew. I'm doing this for Palee like I was to begin with and for Cam."

"Fair enough. Now let's go before we miss anything."

"What exactly are we doing, anyway?" I asked curiously.

Drew didn't say anything, but he pulled me into a side corridor when we heard fast-approaching footsteps.

Wrong move.

The footsteps were coming from that hallway, and there wasn't any time to escape or put a cloaking device around ourselves. We ended up running into them.

Whoever it was, they were tall. Like really tall—several inches over the six-foot mark. He seemed surprised to see us. His hood flapped back far enough for me to be able to see a shocked expression on the bottom half of his pale face. He obviously wasn't an Estalite native.

He muttered something of apology before briskly continuing on his way.

"That was weird," Drew muttered when the figure was gone.

"I just hope he doesn't tell anyone about a hybrid prisoner being loose in the palace," I breathed quietly. "That would mean the end of us all, most likely."

"That's true," Drew agreed with a nod of his head. His expression changed from surprise to one of austerity. "Is it me or did he seem really familiar?"

"Don't say it. That thought already crossed my mind, but there's no way it's possible," I argued. "I'm sure we're both just starting to hallucinate from being stuck in this palace for so long."

Cam was dead. Drew had already made that abundantly clear.

"Really? Both of us seeing the same thing at the same time? Those odds aren't exactly high, Scarlet," Drew pointed out with a raised eyebrow. "I highly doubt that was what just happened. And I'm not necessarily saying I take back everything I said about the elf."

I shrugged, deciding to ignore the Cam reference. "I don't care. All I care about is not getting caught. Can we just get on with this whole thing?"

"Yeah. You're right. We're both probably just tired," Drew relented.

Then he began leading me through the palace again. Soon, we reached expansive gardens in the heart of the entire palace. Everything was so lush and beautiful that I could have stayed there in peace for endless hours. Rennan would have enjoyed the fountain with its carvings of wild animals and all the water it poured out each second. I think Valerie would have gotten excited about the tropical flowers growing in all the beds. And then there was the great oak tree standing in the center of the garden. If he were here, Cam would have loved it.

And that was just the plant life. The architecture of the whole thing was equally, if not more, stunning than the fountain and the flower arrangements. The entire plot was surrounded by brilliantly carved stone pillars that stood a good twenty feet tall, which curved into sweeping, breathtaking arches.

I had never seen anything like them in all my travels. The wizards in Mahe took to simple wooden and stone buildings suited for their research, and the merfolk preferred ornate domes and high rising spires. The royal residence of Bulshkan favored ornate columns and buildings organized in a simple yet elegant fashion. It was truly unique.

"Where are we going, Drew?" I asked a few minutes later.

"I'm trying to get us to where Hezakah holds offices. I don't know when the Hevians are going to get here or when they'll start, but it's going to be soon. Elves function on fast paced, precision schedules, so they are going to be punctual," Drew replied shortly.

"No wonder Cam always kept us hiking at a pretty fast clip," I said half to myself. I had never known that about elves, but I guess it explained a lot of Cam's weird tendencies when it came to timing.

"So you can mention him but I can't?" Drew snorted bitterly.

I narrowed my eyes. "What?"

"Never mind," Drew mumbled. "But you're probably right. He grew up with it, and from all the time I spent with him, I noticed that his exile never broke his habits. Cam always functioned with a high awareness of the time."

"Too bad his depth perception wasn't that precise."

"Yeah."

We continued sneaking through the palace until we were walking through hallways that were each grander than the last. Soon we entered a more private wing, but I don't know if the lack of activity there was an advantage or foreboding. Drew didn't seem to be taken aback by any of it, but maybe that's because he had a tougher spirit than I.

The sorcerer led me down one final hallway. At the end was a large door. There were torches lit in the room beyond, which I determined by the illuminated cracks between the wooden slats of the door. Drew put his ear up against the door and smiled slightly.

"What is it?" I asked expectantly, careful to keep my voice low so nobody would hear me.

"We're going in," was his reply.

I stared at the sorcerer in shock. "Drew! Are you mad? We can't just walk in there like this! They'll recognize us immediately and they'll kill us on the spot!"

"If you would let me finish," Drew snapped with a sideways glare, "I'm going to use magic to disguise us so we won't be recognized. Please, I know I've made some mistakes since you met me, but this isn't one of them. I've known about this meeting for days and I've carefully made my plan."

I snarled. "If you knew for so long, why didn't you tell us sooner?"

Drew glowered back at me. "Because I was never originally going to bring you with me! The Hevian officials are going to be here to discuss searching for Cam's body in the bottom of the River of Division. They are convinced that since he's an elf, his body remained untouched by time after he died. They're trying to obtain the approval to access the river to retrieve their prince's body and that ring regardless of if he was exiled years ago or not."

"They're sickening," I grimaced.

"All the more reason for them to have a change in management," Drew stated shortly. "Now, are you going to continue being obstinate or are you going to actually help me get this information?"

"I'm seriously questioning your motivations, but I'm doing this. Trehi's forces cannot prevail at the cost of the hybrid kingdom's freedom," I answered brusquely.

Drew held his face inches away from mine again. Speaking slowly, he hissed, "If I didn't believe in justice, I wouldn't be here right now. Do you know how easy it would be to let you all rot here in this palace until you accept your own deaths? It's as easy as breathing for me.

"Do you know why I stayed? I gave my word to Cam to help and protect *you*, Scarlet. I made no promise for Carter, Valerie, or even Rennan. Cam asked me to stay for *you*. If you want, I could leave and force you to stand on your own two feet and get to Trehi yourself. It would be my pleasure."

More footsteps echoed through the halls. Drew muttered something under his breath and magic enveloped us. Seconds later, both of us looked exactly like Estalite guards. Somehow, the sorcerer even gave us spears. Though he was on my last nerve, I had to credit him for being clever.

Two leading elves turned down the hallway that we were standing in. One I recognized immediately, the other I had never seen before. The new elf had piercing grey eyes and light brown hair that cascaded down his shoulders. A small copper circlet held his hair out of his face. He and the other elf both wore elaborately embroidered clothes studded in jewels. Quite obviously was it Hevian fashion.

Oh, by now you probably want to know who the other elf was. Carter, naturally.

I was very thankful to be unrecognizable (it was weird having dark skin and hair), because I'm sure Carter would have known who I was immediately. Besides that, I'm sure I would have tried to attack him if Drew hadn't glared a warning at me with those color shifting eyes of his.

Instead, we allowed Carter, the other elf, and their squad of elvish soldiers past us. They entered the torch-lit room and closed the door behind them. Four of the Hevians remained outside in the hall with us. As soon as the door was closed, they all sighed in relief, which confused me greatly.

"I can't believe they made us travel north for two weeks just for us to stay a night," one elf said to his companion.

"And not only that, I hear they are bargaining for a long-dead corpse," another elf snickered.

“The king finally lost his marbles,” an elf beside me remarked.

The others nodded their heads.

“Forgive my intrusion, good elves,” Drew interrupted. Even his accent was now one of Estal. “But are you not loyal to Lord Tristan?”

“Do not speak that name to us,” the fourth elf warned. He took his helmet off to reveal cropped blond hair and blue eyes. His expression was kind enough for a Hevian warrior. “We four have always been loyal to the young prince. Not Carter, mind you, but Cameron, his elder brother.”

“Would it grieve you to learn that he is dead?” I asked tightly.

My own voice sounded strange coming out of my mouth. How Drew had managed that, I honestly didn’t know.

All four elves turned to me in shock, and even Drew sent me a cautioning glance.

“How do you know of this, lady?” the first elf asked. His voice was filled with astonishment.

“We were part of the ambush to capture him and his small group of allies. I myself saw him fall off the cliff and land in the River of Division. No doubt your sovereigns are bargaining for the right to acquire his corpse from the river,” I answered. It was growing increasingly difficult to keep my emotions in check.

“’Tis sorrowful news, no doubt,” the blond elf sighed. “I had been hoping our rightful king would end his father’s reign.”

“So were we all,” his companion agreed. “Who knows how much longer we’ll survive under Tristan’s tyranny before the world falls to his madness? Soon, he’ll force every kingdom to bow to his will. The king is mad. It is plain to all who aren’t blind with greed and complacency. He kills whoever he thinks opposes or may oppose him. His dictatorship is destroying everything. He cares nothing for those lesser than himself. Sadly, Lord Cameron's supporters are too few to make a difference in Heviah, so we must hope to the ones above that the tyrant's reign will end."

"That was well spoken, but I'm sure it was also treason," Drew commented with a slight smile from underneath his copper helmet.

"Indeed," one elf nodded. "As long as Ladefindel doesn't hear us, we're alright."

"Ladefindel?"

"Poor Queen Laralind's father. Mercy on her soul," the elf sighed. "He came here with Carter, as you saw."

"Ah," Drew nodded. "You can rest now. We'll take it from here."

"What?"

Without warning, Drew pulled a crystal out of his pocket and used it to create some sort of glittering mist that caused the Hevian soldiers to slump over and fall to the floor. They were out cold.

"Did you just kill them?" I demanded quietly.

"No. I merely put them to sleep since they're loyal to Cameron. If they weren't, well…you get the idea," Drew replied as he returned the crystal to his pocket. He stepped over the soldiers, motioning for me to follow quickly. "Come on, I'm going in."

I had no choice but to follow Drew. I noticed that he changed our appearances from guards to torch bearers. Nobody in the room suspected that we were anything other than what we appeared to be.

As we took our places on either side of the doors, I took note of the room. Half of it was open columns that looked over the city. In the center of the room was a large, round table. Hezakah, the one guy with an eye patch, Carter, and this Ladefindel character stood around it, debating with each other openly.

"The river is on *our* land, Ladefindel, and it is no easy task to get to the bottom," Hezakah was saying with a wary expression. He didn't seem to be in favor of whatever the elves were proposing.

"Hezakah, we know that. That's why we have only the most skilled spell casters in our country being prepared for such an endeavor," Ladefindel argued. "On behalf of my son-in-law and my fallen grandson, I demand to have clearance to the river."

"I doubt a dead man would want his body touched," the Estalite king stated pointedly. "You know the legends about dead elves—none of them end well."

"Sir, my people are well aware of the tales about King Kenelm and the people his ghost terrorized. No one would want that to happen to them. However, those are still just legend. I have no doubt that Kenelm was a real man—after all, he's one of my ancient ancestors—but the ghosts are the stuff of myth," Carter insisted sternly.

Then he pinched the bridge of his nose and sighed. "I'd take the chances here. This is my brother's body we're trying to retrieve. Exiled or not—traitor or not—he's the son of a king and his corpse shouldn't be rotting away at the bottom of a river."

"My prince, that is a very risky move," eye patch guy warned Carter. "That river is treacherous. Why do you think we never make raids or war in Mahe? It's almost impossible to cross the river without losing men. I lost several just trying to capture those traitors. Do you have any idea how difficult it would be to retrieve one man? There are probably hundreds of corpses down there!"

Carter just responded with a haughty glare.

"Enough, Bartholomew," Hezakah snapped.

The other Estalite closed his mouth and crossed his arms.

He didn't say anything more, so the king continued. "If Tristan wants the body of one of his sons so desperately, he should have come here to beg himself. I'm not about to allow safe passage through my lands to a man who will not speak to me in person. I know what it's like to lose family, but these are hard times that will lead to open war. I will not bring further death to my people or to yours."

"King Tristan would have come himself, but he had more pressing matters that he needed to attend to," Ladefindel stated with a scowl.

Hezakah scoffed. "You'd think that if he really wanted to honor the death of his son—no matter how strange your traditions concerning the exiled are—then it would be his first priority. Lord Cameron was his son by blood, so I have a very hard time believing Tristan would just leave him down there. Furthermore, it's been nearly a year since his death. Your king should have come to me months ago *before* he cut off all trade and alignments with Estal!"

"My father was too grieved for Cam to do anything short of secure his borders. He would have come, but his duty consumed his time," Carter tried to defend his father.

"Sure, and my father is going to let all the hybrids out tomorrow," Bartholomew snorted bitterly. He just rolled his eyes.

"Hey! You're not supposed to speak to me like that! You know full well who I am, and you would do well to respect me!" Carter scowled angrily.

"Really? Do you even hear yourself? You sound exactly like your father! You're just as stuck up and obnoxious as he is!" Bartholomew shouted back, making crazy gestures the entire time.

Carter's face turned bright red. "You don't know what you're talking about, you fool! I am Carter Woods, next in line for the throne of Heviah! I demand respect!"

"Ha! You'll never get to see the throne so long as your father keeps his corrupted rear end glued to it!"

"Of course, I will. I'm his son, and he knows the laws!"

"If he truly knew the laws, you would be king now. You're of age; his reign is legally over. So why does he continue to withhold from you the crown?"

For once, Carter was speechless. He had no other smart words in his arsenal, and Bartholomew knew it. He grinned smugly and announced his departure, briskly stepping past Drew and I to get through the door. He slammed it behind him.

While he did so, I glanced at Drew, and he sent me a look of surprise. I hadn't expected to have so much insight into Tristan's character at once. Or Carter's blindness, for that matter. I couldn't decide if it was a good or a bad thing.

"Now, where were we?" Hezakah sighed after a minute. His face retained the same stern expression it had worn thus far, but it was increasingly apparent that he was becoming weary of the elves' arguments.

"You were going to give us safe passage through the desert?"

Ladefindel pressed.

"Enough! You will not force my hand, you wicked elves!" the king bellowed. Neither elf moved. "I have had quite enough of your incessant pestering to get through my deserts. Try if you will to reach the river with your spell casters. I will send my men to slay every last one of them. No one will honor your dead."

"Now, Hezakah—"

"No. I will not listen to you anymore," Hezakah stated shortly, holding up his hand to the elves.

Ladefindel scowled and Carter remained neutral. Carter then whispered something to his grandfather, who seemed to agree.

"Fine. We will drop the subject. Should we now decide how we shall avoid war?" Ladefindel asked calmly. "We have our terms—"

"What did I just say? I am done with you wicked elves! I will let war break out if only to wipe the smug smiles off all of your faces. Estal is not some weak country you can take for granted! We are a people to be reckoned with!"

"Silence!" Carter shouted. "All we're asking for is the right to retrieve my brother's body."

"No, you're looking for a chance to conquer my country. I'm not having any of it."

"Blast you, Hezakah. You all deserve to die!" Carter cried as he gritted his teeth.

I wish I could have done something in the moment, but Drew and I were trying to keep our cover as torch bearers. Besides, I couldn't have done much else. If I had taken a step forward, there was a chance they might slay me instead.

An arrow zipped through the room between Carter and Hezakah. It flew into one of the massive tapestries and the force was enough to cleanly slice the fabric all the way through.

Hezakah glared at the elves. He pulled a dagger out from his robes and tried to throw it at Ladefindel, who caught it effortlessly and began to engage in a fight with the king. Carter managed to flee the room in all the chaos.

"We can't let him get away!" Drew cried.

He snuffed out our torches and we bolted outside and down the hallway in pursuit of Carter.

In the midst of everything, Drew managed to change us back to our true form. Even better, he gave us weapons that we were used to wielding. Though, in that moment, I would have taken a spear just so I could pin Carter to a wall.

"Left!" I called to Drew.

At that point, Carter and I had pulled ahead and Drew lagged behind. I had no idea what he was doing back there, but I was focused on Carter. That was when we reached the gardens.

The elf noticed he was being followed (I doubted he realized who we were) and was trying to shake us off his tail. He did so by trying to weave a complicated path through the flowers, but he couldn't fool a hybrid's nose. I tracked him down and caught up with him.

"What do you want from—oh...," Carter's voice trailed off when he turned and saw me standing behind him.

With his expression being both shocked and affectionate, he reminded me of how he was on the night of the Spiral of Doom. We were all so wrong to think that he could have abandoned his evil ways. Now here we were again, paying for his mistakes.

He managed to ask, "How did you get free?"

"There are some things you will never know, Carter Woods," I laughed bitterly, gripping my dagger tightly. I snarled at him. "Why did you betray us? You made a promise to your brother."

"Yeah, and that promise is exactly what cost me the last of my compassion towards others. My brother was always a fool who didn't see what true power looks like. It's a shame he realized it too late," Carter shrugged.

"Every single one of you Woods sickens me," I shook my head in disgust.

Carter frowned. "That doesn't seem to apply to Cameron. Or rather, didn't. He's gone now."

"Are you really sorry that he's gone?" I asked with lowered eyes.

I needed to know the truth, and now was likely the last time I was ever going to get the chance to hear it.

"I—"

"The truth, Carter."

"I'm torn. To be perfectly honest, I never liked my brother. Not because he was cruel to me, but because he was always so kind to me. And that's where it becomes hard. Our parents disapproved of open compassion from Cameron, and I never knew how to accept his continued compassion," Carter said quietly. "I've never agreed with Cameron about anything, but he showed me kindness and stood up for me even when our parents wouldn't.

Even after the Spiral of Doom, I saw the man he had become, and a small part of me was happy."

He ran a hand through his hair and sighed. "After everything that has happened, I've learned that we were meant for different things. Cam has always been one to make his own path, and it led to his downfall. Mine has been laid out before me, and I've chosen to take it to make a better future for myself and my line after me.

"That's kind of what happens when one son manifests with a gift, but the other doesn't. The one who doesn't has to do things the hard way. I was born to be a king, Scarlet. It's been a long time coming, but nothing can change that. But all good kings need a queen, and mine was taken from me. Give me the signet ring and I can make us the leaders of Heviah."

He held out his hand to me, but I refused to take it.

"I would never take you as my husband, you heartless worm," I spat in disgust.

Carter's face twisted into a scowl as he withdrew his hand. "Silence! I know what it is to lose the ones I love! I've suffered as much as that blasted brother of mine! Because of the audacity of my brother and the greed of my father, *my* line will never endure! We're all going to die, and it's their entire fault. I'm not going to let that happen. I will tear Trehi and Bulshkan to the ground brick by brick if it means seeing a future for the only one I have left!"

"You know, at one point I really thought that you could change. But you didn't, and now you're choosing to save yourself," I said with a choked voice. "Cam and I always hoped you would abandon your old ways and see the light that continues to fade. But now? Now I just see an elf so blinded by his own desire that he doesn't even value the life of his own kin—the life of his blood brother. For crying out loud, you are his twin and he is dead! He's dead because of you! Your selfishness is what drives you. I…I'm so done with you."

Carter flushed red. "No, he died because of *you*! I warned him of what would happen when his emotions would cloud his judgment, but did he listen to me? Of course not! Nobody ever does! That is why, when I am king, I intend to make an example of all of those who doubted me. They all feared my brother. They all fear my father and his father before him. They will learn to fear the name of Carter Woods! I will be the most powerful elf who has ever ruled Heviah. Just give me the signet ring and I can end your petty existence."

"No! You would take the ring to Tristan! Then all of us would be dead! Is that really what you want?!"

"Yes, that is what I want. If I can't kill you myself, I can just as easily have others kill you and Drew. That's right, I know he's around here somewhere. Why don't you show yourself, wizard?" Carter called through the gardens.

Silence. That is, until Drew rushed forth and tried to blast Carter with magic.

The elf scoffed when Drew missed. "Amateur. I'm a lot smarter than I seem, you know. Hevians are known for two things: prowess in battle and intelligence. While Cameron was gifted in the former, I received more of the latter, which was quite apparent in most of our decisions. His were always blind."

"You are poison!" I cried as I tried to stab the elf.

He caught my arm and elbowed me in the ribs. He forced me to my knees and wrenched my dagger out of my hands. The elf held it just beneath my throat. He glared at Drew, who had magic at the ready.

"Do it and she dies," Carter snarled.

From out of nowhere, a giant silver falcon flew down from the sky. It grabbed the collar of Carter's tunic in its talons, causing the elf to shriek as he was pulled backwards.

He tried to grab at the bird, but it was far stronger than him. The bird carried Carter above the ground and dropped him a few feet away from us. It alighted on the top of the fountain and gazed down at the elf with intensely focused grey eyes.

When Carter came to his senses, he glared at the bird. Then his eyes went wide with realization and he gripped the knife in his hand even tighter.

"You," Carter muttered. "You just want to ruin everything for me, don't you?"

I looked at Drew and he sent me a look that was as confused as I felt. I could only guess that Carter must have had some sort of run in with this bird before.

He rushed at the bird and it in turn swooped down, talons first. Carter realized this too late and the falcon's sharp talons cut three large gashes into the side of Carter's face. He screamed and fell to his knees as the bird flew off again.

"Blast you, you stupid bird!" Carter yelled into the air as he clutched the side of his face. Blood dripped through his fingers. Eventually, he tried to stand again.

The bird immediately returned and clawed the elf's neck. More yelling and curses. The process continued for a while longer before the giant silver falcon flew away into the night. I never saw it in Estal again.

Carter finally stopped paying attention to his gushing wounds and turned to us again. With the side of his face marred from the falcon's talons, it was like he was showing more of his true self. In other words, pure evil.

He stalked closer to us, dagger still in hand. Drew immediately made it disappear into thin air and smirked when Carter's eye twitched.

Carter muttered something about magic and wizards, but he stopped in his tracks. He pointed to us with one blood-covered finger. "This isn't over. Mark my words, Scarlet Sutton, I will be king whether you're alive to see it or not."

"No, you won't," I shot back.

"You're always so stubborn," Carter's face contorted into that wicked expression of his. "It won't be enough to save you this time. Know that I could have you killed, but my father may yet need you alive. Seize them!"

Strong hands grabbed me and Drew from behind. Estalite soldiers pulled hard to drag us away from each other. As we were forced in separate directions, Drew sent me an apologetic glance. I didn't return it.

As I was dragged back to my cell, I pondered everything that had happened that night. I came to one conclusion, and that is best stated in the form of a question: how much more could we take before the world burned?

Fight Night

A few more weeks passed and nothing really changed. I sort of lost track of time, but I think it was about a month, since I saw the moon change phases. The only time I got to see even that was when I was in the coliseum fighting for King Hezakah's amusement.

I swear I hate that man.

He just made me fight. He constantly stirred up bitterness by making me kill innocent hybrids who should never have been taken captive. It was unfair. Worst of all, I had risen to the top of the ranks—making me someone everyone else was trying to beat. That expectation caused all sorts of unnecessary stress. Above even that, Hezakah never mentioned war to anyone, nor did I hear rumors of it. All I know is that he was different than when we had first arrived in Bulshkan.

I never got to see Rennan. We hadn't faced each other in any fights. My cousins told me a Rennan Penbrooke was still in the lineups, but we weren't in the same bracket. I decided it was a good thing. The last thing I wanted was to face Rennan in a fight because it meant one or both of us would have to die.

I hadn't seen the others much either.

Especially Drew. After our escapade that one night, we had both been watched like the outbreak of a disease. We never had a moment of peace. Occasionally, Drew found the means to sneak down to the dungeons to tell us news. He also carried rare messages between Rennan and me. Still, I didn't know how much this place had affected the wolf and I was fearful that he would be crushed under the pressure.

Drew told us Valerie was doing better than the rest of us because she had her own quarters. Apparently, she had become far more responsible and even more logical since we were captured. The mermaid had taken a risk and told the king who she was and he was shocked that he had imprisoned royalty. She was no longer one of the maids, but she also didn't have free rein to go wherever she wanted nor was she allowed to leave the capital. She was, however, the one who found Drew and told him where we were being held.

I was amused to learn that Rennan kept telling Drew to send messages to Valerie and vice versa. I think in the romantic sense, things were looking up for Rennan and Valerie. Since the betrayal, Valerie evidently no longer had any positive feelings for Carter and had decided that Rennan was a good guy. I was happy for them, but it did make me wish Cam was here to tease Rennan relentlessly.

Personally, I was surprised Drew had agreed since he had become far more antisocial and secretive than when we had met him. It was strange that he had been willing to play the messenger between Rennan and Valerie of all people. Maybe he agreed because he was sort of a stalker and enjoyed hearing other people's business. I don't know. Drew was honestly just different than anyone I had ever met in my life. His volatility provided him both an annoyance and a will to survive.

Valerie did acknowledge me. She was often my colosseum fights. She also sent me a message once through Sam saying it was her way of showing that I wasn't forgotten. She supplied Sam and Serena with different pieces of information about daily life in the palace that she thought might prove useful. It was a small token of trust, but it was better than nothing from that girl. She had certainly changed for the better since I had first met her in Sala.

As for me, I know I had changed since Cam's death.

Death is a funny thing because it causes everyone to change in different ways. Carter turned bitter; Drew became secluded; I'm willing to bet Rennan became more pessimistic; Valerie took up responsibility; and me? My determination was now strong enough to move a mountain rock by rock if necessary—even with a hurting heart.

I was sitting pondering such things when a grey squirrel managed to find its way into my cell. It completely baffled me as to how it had found a way into the palace in the first place. This was not a rodent friendly place. The little creature just scuttled in and jumped up on my bed. It almost seemed like a flying squirrel considering how high it bounced.

"Shoo!" I shouted and pushed it off.

It retreated to the bars of the door and sat there. It stared up at me with intense grey eyes that seemed far too focused for a squirrel. It cocked its head at me and then ran out of the cell. The squirrel disappeared just as quickly as it had come.

I sighed and fell back onto my bed to stared at the ceiling.

Sam and Serena came by a while later with the midday meal of stale bread and an old canteen of what always tasted like dirty dishwasher. While I picked at the bread, they would tell me anything important about the day's fight. That was another thing I hated: there was never enough time to properly recover from wounds from previous fights before being flung into another one. I still had an open knife wound from a tiger hybrid I defeated yesterday.

"What news?" I asked with a bored tone.

I wasn't particularly excited. Drew had said things were ramping up in the palace and there were whisperings about open war between Estal and Heviah. He said he hoped it wouldn't come to that while we were imprisoned, but he wanted it to happen eventually because it left Trehi open to infiltrate.

"Hello to you, too, cousin," Samantha snickered. "You're cheerful today."

"Pardon, but I'm afraid I don't have much humor today," I answered as I sat up on my rock-hard bed. "Have you heard anything about tonight's fight?"

Serena sighed. "Sadly, no. There has been no leaked information that we've heard, and we haven't been together all day until now. Hezakah has remained stubbornly tight-lipped about tonight so I wonder what in Galerah he's planning."

"No good, I'll wager," Sam commented. She reached to grab the tray I handed her through the bars. "I wish we could stay longer, but there are new captives we're supposed to escort to their cells. With luck, we'll be back before your fight begins tonight."

"Okay, then I guess I'll see you later," I sighed.

My cousins nodded their heads and walked off, leaving me alone once more.

I looked at the bread and decided I would be better off starving or dying of exhaustion than to try eating the brick of flour. So, once again, I just flopped onto the bed, ignored the discomfort, and tried to relax and gain as much energy as possible.

At some point in the afternoon, a dove flitted into the window of my cell. I looked at it curiously. It was very different than the squirrel that had come earlier. I couldn't imagine why something as beautiful as a grey bird symbolizing peace would fly so near to a place so obviously poisoned with evil. The very air burned with hatred and reeked of the blood of gladiators who had lost their lives in the ring.

I still couldn't believe I had been forced to face Razil in the ring. That fight had constantly been brewing in my mind over the past year. I had little else to think of, so my mind always revisited her demise. I never would have thought that either of those things would have come to be.

The fight was something I had been waiting to happen for a long time. Now that it actually had…I didn't know what to think. The fact that Cam had also been right about Razil and Wayne joining the Serpent's Sons also bothered me because I didn't know how far the rebellion had spread.

Not to mention the whole ordeal with Ladefindel and Carter. That was a totally different level of unthinkable.

The bird flew down to my bedside, so I stroked the dove's smooth feathers. It was relatively amusing—and strangely calming—to see a symbol of peace in a place where it shouldn't exist. I could have imagined it, but it was like the bird was leaning into my hand—a very strange action for a bird. Usually it seemed like they always knew I was a hunter and they would flee at their first chance. Crafty creatures.

The bird's calmness reminded me strangely of Cam's. Though I knew Cam generally wasn't fond of people in the least, I knew he liked to be appreciated by them. For a split second, I marveled at myself for how much I had learned about the elf just by being around him. I wondered if he had intentionally let me learn so much….

My mind returned to its previous track. The bird's eyes were a steel gray and just about as intelligent as an owl's, sparkling with curiosity that couldn't be satisfied. I smiled sadly. They were so much like Cam's. The longer he was gone, the more I realized that what I had felt toward him was not only loyalty but love as well.

I hated myself for only realizing it once he was gone. No matter how hard I tried, I knew I would never be able to turn back the clock for a do-over. I was would never lose that yearning no matter how many times Drew told me to let my misery go. Cam meant too much to me to ever let his memory fade.

"I wish Cam were here," I whispered to the dove even if I knew it wouldn't respond.

It cocked its head at me in the same way the squirrel had. Were wild animals becoming smarter or was I just losing it? My eyes played a trick on me for a second because I thought the bird started shimmering in the dim light of the cell. It was another painful reminder of the shape-shifting elf I loved.

That's something you don't hear every day. Hybrids and elves never fell in love.

The dove flitted around the cell and my eyes followed it. It didn't do anything out of the ordinary—just things birds normally do. Eventually, it came back to me and perched on the windowsill. Again, to confuse me even further, it cocked its head and made a noise, as if beckoning me to continue.

Seeing as how I had nothing else to lose, I let everything spill out—tears included. "I can't hold this in anymore—even if I'm talking to a bird. Cam was the only person who I ever loved with all my heart. I mean, I love Rennan, too, but not in the same way. Rennan is like a brotherly love. Cam was just different than anything I had ever known. He cared for me in a way nobody else ever has. It wasn't care like my grandmother's preparation and training for life.

"No, it was care like genuinely supporting me and who I am, mercenary and all. He never questioned me about anything and he always there when I needed him. I never thought anyone would give themselves up for me like he did. It was so selfless. The look in his eyes was so genuine and heartfelt that I'm never going to forget it as long as I live. It was…unexpected and touching to know he cared so much. And the fact that he trusted me with the thing that could change the course of history? I'm undeserving of that honor."

I pulled out the signet ring and stared at it hopelessly. "I don't know what to do with this. I really don't. Obviously, he trusted me with it, but I'm not a leader; I never was. There's no way I could ever rule Heviah on my own—I've always been better at taking orders. We all looked to Cam and he led us like the true king he was born to be. It's not fair that he was taken from us so soon."

The bird appeared to nod.

I sighed and a tear rolled down my cheek. "I just wish he was here."

The bird cooed and flew to the other side of the room again. Seriously, I thought I was hallucinating for a second or two. The dove's form shimmered and began to change. Shadows wrapped around it, as if shielding the process from my unwanted eyes.

Seconds later, something, but definitely not a dove, stood in its place.

It was a man, standing a little over six and a half feet tall. He wore all black, with the exception of silver shoulder armor and stone-grey fingerless gloves underneath chestnut armguards. The hair that hung to his shoulders was deep chocolate shone with red and gold highlights in the evening sun. His steel eyes sparkled with curiosity that could never be quenched. A scar on his left temple ran down the side of his handsome, pale face. His expression was amused and almost joyful, given the fact that he was standing in the middle of a cell.

Though I was sure it was only a crazy illusion that my mind had conjured out of grief, I knew who it was immediately.

"How are you…how did you…but…you died!! And now you're here?!" I stammered, not quite able to form the words. Yes, I was very eloquent.

The man smiled wryly. He held out his arms in a sort of weak celebration or welcoming. "Surprise! I'm back from the dead!"

Just to make sure I wasn't dreaming, I walked across the small space and stared into his eyes. Then I slapped his face. He grinned like only he would and I yanked back my hand. Yep. He was definitely real. There was absolutely no denying the stinging feeling I felt in my fingers. I could only imagine what his face felt like! There was an outline on his cheek, almost looking like a burn in the shape of my hand.

"Can I just say *ow*?" Cam asked, still smirking.

Surely by now you would know that it was him. Only the elf would find a way to get in here and willingly be slapped in the face.

"You shouldn't be saying anything! I saw you die!" I cried.

Tears burned my eyes as they seemed to be clawing to get out. I restrained them for the time being. I didn't need to be crying when I needed an explanation more than anything.

"Yeah, well, it didn't stick. And let me tell you, hitting the freezing cold river was painful. Never let me do that again," he chuckled. His tone was light, but the look in his eyes was serious.

"I didn't want you to do it in the first place."

"I know. I didn't want to either."

"Then why did you?"

"To save you! And because it's what I saw in my vision from Shakovi. Whatever one sees in those visions always happens and there is no way to escape or change them," Cam said passionately. Then he shrugged. "And because I knew there was no way in Galerah Carter was going to be able to lift both of us back up."

"Carter I understand, but why were you so insistent? I'm not important enough for you to sacrifice yourself for. You're the rightful heir to a kingdom with a huge amount of influence and I'm just a hybrid from a country most people want to forget about," I stated adamantly.

He raised an eyebrow, so I decided not to push for more information on that topic.

I decided to address a different subject. "So, wait, please explain this to me: if you died and you're here now, did you really die? Or did you purposefully trick me?"

Cam shifted his weight uncomfortably. "I didn't trick you—I swear. It's kind of a long story."

I pursed my lips. "You made me think you were dead for over a year. I have time."

He sighed. "Fine. I'll do my best to explain what I can. I *did* actually die—a very painful death—and it wasn't a trick. I hit the water and every bone in my body was broken; I knew I was paralyzed. That's why I couldn't swim to the surface of that blasted river. That's why I drowned. You would not believe how agonizing those last few seconds were with the cold water burning my lungs, preventing me from breathing. In my final seconds, I felt Light and Shadow fighting for control and dominance over me. I've told you before that I'm forced to walk the fine line between darkness and life. My death there decided it."

"So, it *was* you that one day in the black cloak telling me you're death to some and life to others!" I exclaimed in realization. When he smirked and nodded, I slapped his arm. "No wonder you were so unhelpful! What have you been doing since then?"

"Just terrorizing palace workers and gathering information—the usual things a shape-shifter does. Anyway, the Light claimed dominance and power. I was taken to a heavenly stronghold where I was revived. I thought I was losing my mind for a minute there. After all, I was in Estal one minute and in a pristine white room built out of precious stone the next. I thought I was hallucinating."

"Like I am right now," I interrupted again, hardly believing my ears. It was all too surreal.

He sent me a pointed look. "You're not hallucinating. I *am* real. See?" He touched the side of my face with his warm fingers.

My rebellious heart fluttered, despite the tough exterior that I was trying to keep up. In all honesty, I felt like I was going to break sometime soon. There was no way I was going to be able to play this emotionless role forever—my emotions were slipping out more and more often.

Cam withdrew his fingers with a slight smile and continued. "I thought I was imagining things, especially when three women wearing cloaks came into the room. They explained to me that I was in their kingdom, forever chosen by the Light. They also told me that while I will never be rid of the shadows until the 'final hours of the world,' I am now able to control them without becoming so drained of energy.

"Regarding my ring, I gave it to you because I didn't know what would happen to me. I trusted you with it because I knew you would keep it safe. Even if you couldn't claim the throne with it, you would keep it as a memory…which I find to be very sweet."

"But how did you come back to life if you were dead?"

"They sent me back. It's as simple as that," he answered nonchalantly. "They let me return so I could help you guys change the world for the better. I still have a kingdom to reclaim. Speaking of which, can I have my ring back?"

"Oh, uh, yes. You can," I answered, fumbling as I pulled it out of my tunic pocket.

My hand was shaking so much that I dropped it on the floor. Cam and I both bent over to pick it up, awkwardly pausing with our hands touching.

I felt too humiliated to look him in the eye. "S-sorry."

"Don't be," he said. His face became soft, even hopeful. He slipped the signet ring back onto his left index finger where it belonged. Then he started fidgeting again. "What you were saying a few minutes ago…."

I probably blushed about as red as my hair. I felt some serious embarrassment for knowing he heard all the things I had said to him in dove form—even if it was all completely true. I hadn't expected to pour everything out just to have him come back seconds later. His shape-shifting ability was way too skillful for his own good. And mine, for that matter.

"Um…forget I ever said it," I mumbled.

"It's hard to forget when it's you, Scarlet. You're not that easy to forget," he whispered, repeating the words I had once used to describe him. "You were right, you know, about that last emotion you saw from me. It *was* love, and I'm not afraid to admit it, if only to you. I would never hear the end of it from the others."

"Is that what Valerie and Rennan teased you about?"

"Yes. And that doesn't change anything for me. I love you, Scarlet Sutton, even if the rules of this world say that it is forbidden for an elf to love a hybrid—even one as lovely as yourself."

I smiled, tears welling up again. He spoke with so much conviction that I found it difficult not to believe him.

"You've never been one to follow the rules," I chuckled.

He half-smiled. "No, I never have. I much prefer making my own."

I stepped closer to him, looking up into his silvery eyes. They were full of love, but he didn't show anything with his expression. His cheeks flushed slightly, but he didn't resist me like he was prone to do. I wrapped my arms around him and refused to let him go. He did the same, bending to where his chin rested on my head.

"I missed you, but words don't do any good to describe the feeling," I whispered into his pointed ear. "I never would have forgotten you."

"I know you wouldn't. I missed you, too," he replied, gently kissing the top of my head.

My body filled with the warmth of the happiness of being loved—a feeling I had been lacking for most of my childhood. Cam had a knack for making me feel complete.

He whispered, "I love you, Scarlet."

"I love you, too," I replied. I pulled back to where I could see his face again. "Please promise me that you won't die again. At least not for a very, very long time."

He smiled happily. "I'll try my very best to keep that promise. And I hate to ruin the mood, but that might be a difficult task. There's a war brewing and there's no telling what will happen."

"You mean there's no telling how many dangerous stunts you're going to pull," I corrected with a raised eyebrow.

He pondered the statement and then nodded. "True. I guess I pull a lot of those, huh?"

"Do you want me to make you a list of the ones I've seen just since I've met you?"

"Not particularly," he chuckled. Then he became serious again. "Do you know where the others are? I tried to find them all, but I only know where Rennan is. Drew and Valerie's whereabouts seem to evade me no matter what I try."

"I don't know where they are. Drew has been working in the kitchens or something like that and Valerie has been a guest of sorts since she told the king that she's royalty," I shrugged.

That was about as much as I knew. Drew wasn't able to talk long on the rare occasions I saw him. His information hadn't really been helpful, either.

"Have you talked to Rennan?" I asked.

"No," Cam bit his lower lip. "That's the thing, I haven't actually seen him."

"You *just* said you know where he is."

"Yeah, but I haven't seen him with my actual eyeballs!"

He paused to pull down the skin around his eyes. I held back a smile and tried to keep a straight face. For such a serious man, Cam could really surprise me with the random things he pulled. I felt so glad to have him back. Cam sensed my amusement and grinned.

Then he cleared his throat and continued. "Anyway, I haven't actually seen him. I've been by his cell, but he was never there. I know he's been in the coliseum a few times, but I haven't been at the fights because I never catch the time. I've been at yours, though. In disguise, of course. But I digress. Where's Carter? You never mentioned him."

I scowled and looked away. That rotten, miserable, no-good elf (I still need more adjectives). I hated him so much. If I had to fight anyone in the ring, it should be him! I found it difficult, however, to tell Cam just how far his younger brother had fallen. "Your brother betrayed us the second death was threatened. He told Hezakah that we openly plotted against the Hevian throne and deserved death. If that wasn't bad enough, he almost had Drew and I killed."

Cam's face turned paler than usual and was utterly emotionless. "You're kidding me."

"I wish I was."

He punched the wall, somehow creating an indent in the stone. The angry look in his eyes was so fierce that even I took a step back. Shadows swirled around his feet as he began attacking the wall. He muttered strings of elvish curses as he let his rage fly toward the stone. Eventually, he sank to his knees, seemingly exhausted.

"Better?" I asked.

"No," he spat. He looked up at me with a determined face. "I swear I will hunt him down and make him pay for getting you into this mess. He said he would try to help! Did he? No! If anyone deserves punishment, it's him! He was actually starting to get better, and then this happened. That fool! I never should have trusted him after all he has done. Even after what I heard and what I did to his face, he didn't learn. Blast him!"

"Wait, was that silver falcon you?"

"Yes, of course it was me. Falcons don't have grey eyes, and you know that. You just didn't want to let your heart hope that I was back. I wasn't ready to show myself, even if I had already run into you that night," Cam snorted in response.

I was surprised I had apparently seen him twice that night, but it didn't need to be discussed right then.

He continued. "I needed affirmation for the rumors circling around Estal and Heviah. Lo and behold, the rumors of my brother openly aligning himself with our father were true. I *never* should have trusted him."

"Cam, you trusted him because he is still your brother," I said gently as I sat down on the floor in front of him. "It was his choice to betray us and there's nothing you can do to change that now. I doubt he's going to realize his mistakes and he definitely won't repent of them when he sees that you're alive."

"I'm still allowed to punch him the next time I see him, right?"

"Sure."

“Lovely. Now,” he said, changing the subject and standing up again, “we need a plan to get the five of us out of here. You have a fight tonight so maybe I can try to find Drew, Valerie, and Rennan and get them there. Then I could probably cause a distraction to allow you guys to escape and I'll catch up with you later.”

I frowned. “Cam, your plans rely way too heavily on your abilities.”

He scowled at me.

“I do not doubt your abilities—you know that—but I'm still concerned. We're a team, remember? Let us do some of the heavy lifting, too,” I pleaded.

Cam seemed to rethink his plan as he stared at the dented wall for half of eternity.

“Fine, you're right. I try to do too much by myself,” Cam relented. “You just get yourself there, I'll get the others, and then Drew or Valerie can cause a distraction. Rennan…we'll see what he can do when I find him.”

“Why do you say it like that?” I questioned.

Cam shrugged. “I'm sensing something about the wolf that's different. I just hope he's still the same guy I remember.”

“Yeah, same here,” I agreed quietly.

Cam made a soft noise and then took my hands. I looked up into his eyes.

“Don't worry, Scarlet. We'll all get out of here,” he promised. “I'll be back for you with your cousins later.”

“You know of my cousins?”

“Yeah, I was the one who got the Hooded Order to tip them off about you being here," he answered with a mischievous smile.

I grinned and hugged him, thankful that he had sent my cousins my way.

"I really should go now. I've lingered too long already," he said quietly.

"Okay. I'll see you later," I whispered as the elf's form began to shimmer again. "And Cam?"

He raised an eyebrow.

"I'm glad you're alive," I smiled.

He grinned brightly as shadows and mist swirled and passed through the gate. A great grey owl sat on the other side. It nodded to me before it flew off down the hall.

I sighed and sat back on my bed. Now all I could to do was wait for him and my cousins to come for me before the fight would take place.

I heard more footsteps a while later. It was drawing close to sunset now, so I could only assume that my next gladiator fight would be right when light was the trickiest to interpret. That was probably the most unfortunate time of day for a battle because of the harsh rays constantly shining in your eyes. No matter. I had fought at this time of day many times before. What's one more?

"…Exactly, Mr. Elf! It will be a glorious bloodbath! Right after we have a delightful pickle festival!" a male voice I recognized exclaimed from down the hallway.

I wondered what elf he was speaking with. If it was Carter, I would punch his face out. If it was Cam disguised as Carter…I would probably still punch him.

"A pickle festival, you say?" Carter's voice replied. "How would you advertise for a pickle festival?"

I heard Cam's voice in my head. *I'll explain how I did this later. Just know that I am currently acting as Carter so I can be close to everything. The actual fool is in Trehi hiding like the coward he is, so I get to play. Just letting you know so you don't try to kill me.*

I had no way to respond, so I just took noted it as "Carter," Samantha, Serena, and Bartholomew (the one Estalite who always appeared in random places) stepped into view. My cousins stood behind the other two, offering me apologetic glances, obviously being what they meant by not always being able to show kindness. I took it as a cue to be able to act if need be. It was strange seeing this man again after the international argument I had once witnessed. There was still a part of me that wondered if he was totally committed to Estalite rules.

"Time for your battle, maidy," the Estalite said. "Name is Bartholomew Pickle. I'll be supervising your preparations tonight. King says you've got yourself your biggest challenge yet."

He laughed giddily as he pulled the keys to my cell out of his pocket. Cam-as-Carter kept his face neutral as my cell door was unlocked. Bartholomew Pickle gestured for me to come out of the enclosure, and I did so slowly, giving my friends time in case they were planning on doing something.

"Hey, Master Pickle, I think there is something suspicious in her cell,"

Cam stated with an uncanny impression of Carter's voice.

I couldn't believe how much hate swirled up inside me. How could one twin be so amazing and the other so terrible?

Bartholomew glanced at the elf skeptically, but handed him the keys and entered my cell. Naturally, there was nothing there and Cam was being clever. I got out of the way and Cam immediately stepped forward, closed, and locked the cell door behind the Estalite. Bartholomew whipped around and shouted something in his language, but I didn't understand it.

Cam-as-Carter smirked evilly, almost making me believe it was the real Carter right down to the scars. "Sorry, buddy. King's orders."

"Which king?" Bartholomew demanded. "Mine would never lock me in a cell."

Cam shifted back into his own form.

Bartholomew's eyes went wide as he realized Cam was the one Carter and Ladefindel had been trying to retrieve from the river.

"*My* orders. I'm the rightful king and heir to Heviah's throne. Remember that when your friends come find you," Cam answered, confidence filling his voice.

The elf shapeshifted back into Carter's form before leading me and my cousins out of sight from the cell.

When we made it to Sam and Serena's private armory, Cam slumped against the wall and returned to his own form. He didn't seem exhausted physically, but I could tell there were some crazy thoughts running through his mind.

"That ability of yours never ceases to amaze me," Serena commented to break the silence.

I couldn't help but nod in agreement.

Meanwhile, Samantha handed Cam a canteen of water and he took it gratefully. It must have been fresh, because he didn't make a face. My water always tasted like dirty dishwater, but I've mentioned that before.

"It's no big deal," Cam said quietly.

"Not a big deal?" I repeated.

He looked at me and raised an eyebrow, begging me to continue.

I grinned. "Cam, you just freed me and locked up an enemy *and* you still have the keys! I think this might just work."

"And we're going to help, too," Samantha offered with a determined expression.

Serena nodded her head in agreement. "We'll do anything to keep the guards out of the arena while you're making your escape."

"Thank you," Cam said with a nod of his head. He turned to me. "You should get your armor on. Your fight starts very soon."

"Okay. Where are you going?" I asked as he started walking out of the room.

He looked back at me and smiled for no reason. "I'm going to keep watch."

"I cannot think of anyone who would come down here," Sam assured him as she started polishing a couple of switchblades.

Cam didn't look convinced, so he went outside anyway.

"How you managed to get an elf on your side—not to mention care deeply for you—is a complete mystery to me," Serena commented as she watched Cam close the door silently—he did everything silently.

I shrugged, grabbing my armor. "Cameron is different. He doesn't play by the rules of society. He acts as he sees fair."

"He is a king I would follow," Sam decided.

I nodded my head. Cam was someone I would follow, king or not. He was someone I would stand by until one of us died…or until he died a second time.

Serena gestured to my equipment. "Now put on your armor. You need to get to the arena."

"Okay. In case we never see you again after tonight, I wanted to say thank you for everything you've done to help us," I said, smiling at my cousins. "I'm so glad you guys were here. I don't know what we would have done without you."

"You're family, Scarlet," Sam said, putting her hand on my shoulder. "That's what family does. Your friends are close enough to you to be considered our family, too. Especially the elf. He cares deeply for you, and I don't think that love will ever end. You should have seen how excited he was when we met up to get you."

"He didn't have that one creepy smile, did he?" I chuckled.

"No, but he was amazingly determined that you would get out of this," Serena explained. "Now go! He's waiting to take you down there."

I laughed. "Alright! I'm going!"

I finished gearing up and walked outside to where Cam was standing. He was holding his scythe, and I wondered how he had gotten it back. The point was incredibly sharp and it looked exceptionally deadly.

"What are you doing?" I asked him.

His head jerked to face me.

"Inspecting the blade. I named it," he replied as he slung it over his back again. He looked like Carter again as we started walking toward the arena.

"What did you name this one? You already have Egladel."

"Vorngurth. It means 'black death.' Be very careful that you don't get cut by the blade."

"Why?"

He smiled humorlessly. "I'm sure you'll find out sooner or later. I'm bad at avoiding battles, so you'll see it in action sooner than you think."

"'Bad at avoiding battles,'" I repeated with a smile. "You mean you're just eager to solve problems."

"That's one way to put it," he stated with a smile. He dramatically made a sweeping motion to the gates we had just reached. "Oh, look! The arena! This is your stop, miss. I'd take your luggage, but I'm afraid you're about to go into battle and weapons are helpful. Good luck out there. I have a feeling you might need more than just skill tonight. Your opponent is apparently pretty good."

"You're a strange person, Cameron," I decided with a small smile.

He grinned and kissed my head again. Then I put my helmet on and stepped into the arena. I was determined to win this fight.

The crowd was roaring with excitement as I walked out. At this point, I knew enough to raise a weapon to them. The crowd always seemed to love it and would cheer louder. I was the only competitor out here so far, but not for long.

At the other side of the arena, a man emerged from the shadows. He wore a helmet covering his face, had tan skin, and stood tall and proud. He carried a long sword and a small satchel that I guessed was full of throwing stars. There was something familiar about this man, but I couldn't place it.

"Welcome, Estalites, to the fight you've all been waiting for!" King Hezakah shouted over the roars of the spectators.

My opponent and I looked toward his box. I could see Cam disguised as Carter already on one side of the king and Valerie on the other. Cam nodded to me while Valerie watched my adversary.

Hezakah silence the crowd and continued. "Tonight, we have our two champions! We will see who holds more skill and who will rise out of the pits and join my army! Fight!"

I faced my opponent. He charged straight at me, so I braced for the attack. I pulled out my steel battle-axe and raised it right as he swung. He was fast so I had to be ready for another blow. After a few minutes of strong parries, I was able to determine the man's fighting style. I decided to wield my axe in one hand and a knife in the other so I could block and strike at the simultaneously.

I managed to shove the man back. He fell to the ground and grunted, thus encouraging my supporters in the crowd cheered while his booed. The man was quick to roll over and get up again. He launched himself at me, but I spun just in time and knocked him to the ground again.

The crowd started roaring again. It wasn't until I looked at my arm did I realize what they were so excited about. The majority of my left sleeve was torn off, exposing the scars the wild wolf had given me a year or so ago.

"You're gonna pay for that," I muttered as I slung my axe over my back. I took up an offensive stance as I whipped out two daggers.

"Bring it," came the man's muffled voice.

I swung at him, and he did the same. His blow was fast and powerful, but I expertly dodged the attack and landed a passing blow on his leg. He cried out in agony. Before I knew what was happening, the man had forced me onto my knees. That knocked the air out of me somehow, so I knelt there trying to catch my breath.

The crowd was going wild. I looked up at the stands, specifically the king's box. Cam and Valerie were pointing at something, but I couldn't understand what they were trying to communicate. I rolled onto my back so it wasn't turned toward my adversary. I was sure that he had no problem killing me while I was down.

"Any last words?" the man asked, readying his blade.

I shook my head, but I ripped my helmet off so I could get one decent breath. I had pinned my hair up so it wouldn't interfere with the fight, but it now cascaded over my shoulders.

The man went dead still and his weapons clattered on the ground. Then he took off his helmet so I could see who was underneath. He had pale blue eyes and crew cut hair where a silver identification streak cut through the jet black. Two wolfish ears stuck up in surprise, then flattened to his skull.

"*Rennan!?*" I cried. "It was you?!"

I did not think this fighter to be the wolf. His style was so fast and savage that it had been hard to defend against. Not only did I not recognize his style, I didn't recognize *him*. His skin had tanned, and overall, he was stronger than ever before. He *had* changed, just not in the way I had expected. He was absolutely merciless on the battlefield.

"Scarlet! You have no idea how happy I am to see you!" Rennan grinned.

Though he looked like a different person in many ways, his smile hadn't changed, and I was so glad to see that. Perhaps this was the same wolf that I remembered after all. He offered me his hand and I accepted it eagerly.

He looked absolutely relieved to see me. "I was beginning to worry when I hadn't faced you in any fights. I hope you have a plan because I'm sure people have realized that we're friends."

"That's all up to Cam," I answered, looking toward the box.

Cam had disappeared, so I hoped that he was going to get Drew…or to cause a distraction…or both.

Rennan's eyes widened. "Cam is alive?!"

"Yeah, and he's here now. Somewhere. He's supposed to be getting an escape plan in place. I don't know…."

"THAT'S UNFAIR!!" Hezakah bellowed. His face was so red it looked like he was going to explode. "YOU CAN'T HELP EACH OTHER!!"

Valerie stood by, holding a small dagger, ready to defend herself. Rennan spotted her and smiled lovingly. Leave it to Rennan to get mushy when we were literally in a life or death situation.

"They might not be able to, but *I* can!" Valerie shouted as she stabbed Hezakah in the back with her small knife.

The king's eyes widened with shock before rolling back into his head.

Valerie poked him, just to make sure he was dead, and wiped the blood off the blade. She might be brave enough to stab the king, but she was clueless about how to continue a battle.

"Now, Cam!" her voice echoed.

A feral beast roared somewhere outside the arena. All of the audience members started screaming and shuffling nervously as a giant shadow slowly covered the arena. Rennan and I looked to the sky to see a massive grey dragon overhead. Rennan's eyes widened when he realized that the dragon was Cam. I didn't blame him. I had only seen the elf morph into things as large as other people at his maximum. Now he was easily larger than Drew's house in Caso.

Cam the Dragon shot fire at the stands. Some of the flames spilled over the edge of the coliseum's structure, causing yet another town to be set ablaze.

Valerie jumped down into the arena and ran beside us. Rennan quickly hugged her while I nodded in her direction. We only had a few minutes to get out of there before the Estalites started shooting at Cam.

"Where's Drew?" I asked the mermaid, whose eyes were glued to where the fire was spreading. I wasn't excited to see Drew after our last escapade, but he was still a part of the team.

"He said he was coming."

"I'm here!" Drew cried breathlessly. He pulled his satchel open and grabbed four round objects. He avoided my gaze. "Had to find these. I assume the dragon is Cam?"

"Yep," Rennan answered.

The dragon flew down into the arena and lowered a wing for us. We scrambled up onto his back and waited for him to lift off as Drew handed each of us one of the small purple spheres. Rennan inspected his very carefully. His ear twitched.

"What is this?" Rennan asked cautiously.

"Fire grenade. Be careful not to hit Cam when you throw it on the city," Drew explained quickly.

The dragon made a grunting noise as if agreeing with the sorcerer.

Drew snickered. "Cam agrees. On my mark, throw them down."

"Wait!" Valerie cried as we took off.

We quickly grabbed hold of the rough silver scales so we wouldn't fall off. We all looked to the mermaid.

Her concern was evident. "Is there no other way to do this? What about all the innocent people down there? What about the hybrids in captivity?"

"My cousins are doing what they can down there. We just can't hit the palace and the coliseum. They should be able to get as many out as possible. Even still, we shouldn't burn the whole place to the ground," I stated.

I hoped I was right. I would never forgive myself if I really did become the last of my clan.

I patted the dragon's back to get his attention. "Cam! Far side of the city!"

Cam veered north until we were directly on the other side of town. He probably did so just to give the massive amount of people in the coliseum a chance to flee.

We dropped the grenades and they went off thousands of feet below us. Valerie and Rennan appeared to be the most affected by it, which convinced me that the wolf I knew was still in there.

"I can't believe we just blew up almost half the city," Rennan said half to himself as he watched the fire spread from building to building.

Seeing the fires in Bulshkan reminded me of the fires Cam and Drew had started in Hila. Not to mention my horrible nightmare. There seemed to be a recurring sequence….

"Yes. And I have no regrets. I hated it there almost as much as Caso," Drew answered, watching with a stone-cold face as the city burned to cinders.

I shared the sentiment, but I couldn't help feeling bad for the people who were dying down there. I prayed that my cousins were safe as well. Cam picked up on the tension in the air and directed his course south.

We didn't stop flying until we reached the border of Estal and Heviah.

A feeling of dread built in my throat as we touched down. I wasn't looking forward to what we would discover in the most corrupt kingdom in Galerah.

Close Call

"Well, I'd say that was successful," Cam commented when he was back to his normal form. He was flushed from the strain of shifting into something so huge and carrying the four of us such a long distance, but otherwise, he didn't look too bad.

Rennan stared at Cam with icy eyes. "You know, you made all of us think you were dead for a year. How can we be sure you're not a ghost?"

Cam winced, but forced a smile. "Do you really want a joke about ghosts?"

"No."

"That's the spirit," Cam smirked.

Rennan glared at him, and Cam just stared back. Eventually, Cam's expression broke into a creepy, humorless smile. Rennan made a face.

"Okay, so you're real. Where were you?" the wolf demanded.

"It's complicated...."

"Cameron. *Where were you*?"

"In a different dimension."

"Okaaaaay, yeah. Complicated."

"That still doesn't explain why you didn't come back as soon as you realized you weren't dead from that fall," Valerie pouted. Her expression conveyed slight betrayal, but her tone seemed relieved Cam was back.

Cam turned to her and caught her in his steel eyes. His expression was unreadable as he sighed and sunk to the ground.

He muttered something under his breath, likely in elvish, before he started explaining. "Oh, I *was* dead. My body was broken and paralyzed when I hit the water. In that other dimension, I was kept there until they thought it was the right time to send me back. I had no choice in the matter.

Plus, I'm pretty sure time works differently in different dimensions. I've only been here for a couple of months, really. I couldn't find the right opportunity to let you know I returned, so I was working undercover to find anything useful."

"How did you stay hidden for so long?" Valerie asked, seemingly oblivious to the look Cam gave her.

"Valerie, I'm a shape-shifter. It's what we do," he answered. He stood up again and walked over to Rennan. An extremely apologetic expression spread across Cam's face. "Look, I'm sorry for the grief I caused with my death. I would have tried to escape it, but it wouldn't have done any good. That's what I saw in my vision from Shakovi and those *always* come true."

He glanced at me and I felt my cheeks flare up. I don't think anyone else noticed me, though, since Drew looked horrified, Valerie paled, and Rennan's face was hopeful.

In that moment, I realized what I had seen in my vision had come true. I had seen the coliseum and the prison cell. The only thing that hadn't happened was the battle with a man on an alicorn leading the charge. Fear welled inside me when I realized it would soon come to pass.

"Okay, well, now that you're back and apparently not dead like you should be…," Drew tried to say. He let his voice trail off when he saw the narrowed gaze Cam focused at him.

"Are you saying I shouldn't be here?" Cam hissed. Shadows started seeping out of the ground and gathering at his feet.

Rennan, Valerie, and I all took a few steps backward so the demons couldn't touch us. I also panicked because I had no intention of having another one of those things in my head.

"No," Drew said calmly, "I'm just saying that usually when people die, they stay dead. And you're obviously not dead. As I was saying before you interrupted me, I want to come up with a plan of action for the morning."

Valerie groaned. "It's nearly time for bed! Can't we deal with the boring and depressing stuff in the morning and have a little bit of fun tonight? After all, we just escaped the capital. Surely that calls for at least a little celebration."

Cam looked to me. I personally didn't see the harm in it, but I could tell he didn't like it. Drew and Rennan, however, grudgingly agreed with the mermaid. Well, grudgingly in Drew's case. Rennan was fully on board in a matter of seconds. Cam was outvoted, so we did our best to set up a small camp in a grove of trees near the Estal-Heviah border.

The entire time we were on the border, Cam sat where he could see into Heviah. It was as if he wasn't worried about the enemies we had made in Estal, but rather more concerned about returning to his home kingdom. I decided to let him gather his thoughts before trying to talk to him. Instead, I joined the others around the campfire. Drew and I sat on one log while Valerie and Rennan sat on another (technically so was Cam, but he was in a tree).

Drew and I sat in awkward silence.

That is, until he turned to me. "Look, Scarlet, I'm sorry about everything I said about Cam. I should have trusted everything to work out."

"I'm not the one you should apologize to, but I appreciate your concern," I sighed, done being stubborn. "I was still hurting when you said all those things about him being dead and not coming back. I, of all people, know how death works, but I just couldn't bring myself to give up on him."

"I know how that is. Just do one thing for me," Drew requested.

I urged him on.

"Don't take your time with him for granted," Drew pleaded. "Treasure it, and you'll find it to be worth more than all the world's gold."

"I will—you can count on that," I said quietly. "It's a curious thing how you know so much about this topic."

Drew smiled wryly and gazed into the fire. "I've lived a while. I know the pain of heartbreak too well, and I wouldn't wish it on anyone else."

"Like them?" I asked with a smile, gesturing towards Valerie and Rennan.

Drew grinned. "Yeah, them, too."

"I don't know whether to laugh or be happy for them," I chuckled.

They were sitting silently, holding hands while Valerie's head rested on Rennan's shoulder. Drew raised his eyes from the fire to look at the two of them. He smirked slightly.

"Both. Get Cam and he can help get payback," Drew instructed me.

"You know you're asking me to get an extremely moody and dangerous elf out of the tree when he's literally looking into the land that cast him out years ago, right?" I clarified with a raised eyebrow.

Drew didn't seem to see a problem with what he had suggested. "Yep."

"Okay. Just checking," I relented as I stood up from the log. "I'll go talk to him."

I walked to the base of the tree without any question from the two lovers. They weren't paying attention to rest of us and were enjoying each other's company, which I guess was good since I was supposed to get Cam for some payback. I had no idea what it was for this time. Peering up into the tree, I didn't see the elf immediately. However, when I looked higher up, I made out the glint of his armor in the moonlight...at the top of the tree.

I sighed and began to climb.

On my way up, something sailed past my ear. I gazed up to see nothing. That is, until an acorn flew down and hit my arm. For a second, I thought there were crazy squirrels up there, but that wasn't the case.

I squinted to see the pale face of Cam watching me in the upper branches. In his hand he held more acorns. Somehow, I wasn't surprised.

"Hello, Scarlet," he said quietly. He let me climb up to the highest branches without throwing another acorn at me, which I appreciated.

"Strange seeing you up here," I commented, sitting on the branch next to him. I was glad when he didn't try to move away.

Cam looked confused. "What are you talking abou—oh, that was sarcasm, wasn't it?"

"It was," I chuckled. Then I grew serious again. "Cam, are you okay? You haven't exactly seemed like yourself since you've been back. You rarely snap like you did to Drew earlier. Is something wrong?"

He reached for his right temple. "I guess. I've had too much time to think, really. Memories keep resurfacing. It's this place, I'm telling you. I suppressed memories of my betrayal and the beginning of my exile years ago, but now they're coming back."

My eyebrows flew up. "What triggered it, do you know?"

"Carter," he responded sourly. That answer seemed likely enough.

"And being so close to Heviah. That land is filled with my father's poison; can't you feel it? It's like an urge to just fall in step with everyone else, not caring a shred about what beliefs you hold dear."

"And what are your beliefs that are being messed with?"

He looked me directly in the eye, his steel eyes captivating my focus. "That there is a greater being holding our lives and the world in place."

I nodded, and whispered with a smile, "In one thing you have not changed, my friend."

"Hmm?"

"You still speak in riddles."

He grinned, and we fell silent again.

At one point, Cam started tracing his fingers on top of my hand. I let him do it for a few minutes, then I grabbed his hand and wouldn't let go of it until he looked at me. When he did, we both smiled. Cam pulled me closer to him.

Months ago, this might have been awkward. But now? It was reassuring.

"Are you going to be okay?" I asked him in a near whisper.

"Yeah, I'll be fine. Don't worry about me," he replied, leaning his head on mine. "Oh, I said I would explain how you heard my voice in your head."

"That would be nice."

"Yeah, I would imagine so," he said with a small smile. He sighed. "I used a little bit of Ancient Magic to send you a mental message. Before you ask, I didn't see any of your thoughts. I simply projected my message into your head. You don't have to worry about me entering your mind uninvited since I've never figured that part out."

"Well, that's certainly something," I said quietly, not exactly knowing what to think. I decided it would be fine to take his word for it and not worry about anything. So, I changed the subject. "Drew wanted you to come down."

"Why?"

"He said something about revenge on Rennan."

"For teasing me?"

"I don't know."

"It probably is then. Come on. Let's go give Rennan a hard time about actually getting the mermaid romantically interested in him. Any idea how it happened?" Cam asked with a smirk.

"I think it was actually your cliff-side sacrifice that changed him. He's become mellow and strong. And I think Valerie noticed, especially after Carter's betrayal," I guessed.

Cam thought about it for a minute before nodding in agreement.

"Seems likely enough," he decided. Then he sighed and looked at me, gently holding my hand in his. "I'm still so sorry. I didn't want to cause you so much pain in knowing I love you, but I needed you to know."

I smiled weakly and wrapped an arm around him. "It's okay, Cam. I'm glad you told me, despite the pain and loneliness. It made it so much easier when you came back because you made me feel complete again. And it gave me a chance to realize just how important you are to me."

Cam hugged me tightly. I barely caught the "thank you" that slipped out of his lips. I looked over at him and saw a tear running down his cheek. I gently wiped it off and he looked at me. His eyes were pink and teary. I smiled, and then he leaned his head on my shoulder. I pulled him close again.

"Now come on before I start calling you a big softie," I teased. "We have Rennan to mess with, remember?"

Cam sniffled and smiled.

I couldn't believe he was showing this much tender emotion, but I didn't brush it off. I acknowledged that he was fully capable of human emotions, even if he didn't like showing more than one or two most of the time. He was just wary of trusting others so they couldn't stab him in the back. I was honored that he trusted and loved me to be open with his emotions.

"Yeah, you're right. I've spent more than enough time in this tree looking at Heviah," he agreed. He gestured towards the ground. "You go first."

"Why me?"

"Because it's easier for you to go down first."

"There are more branches, you know."

"Well, maybe I just feel like being a gentleman."

"Okay then," I relented as I started climbing down from the highest part of the tree, being careful that I didn't step on a weak branch.

Did he really have to go all the way up to the top?!

Something sharp hit my shoulder. I looked up to see Cam grinning and holding an acorn acorn—obviously proof that he had thrown another one at me.

"Really?! That's not being a gentleman!" I called up to him.

"So? I didn't say what I would be a gentleman about!" Cam laughed gleefully as he swung from the treetop.

He was like a skilled gymnast as he descended, almost looking like he had the ability to fly. He was so adept at moving among the gnarled branches.

Cam effortlessly passed me and made it to the ground gracefully.

He called up to me, “Are you coming?”

“Yes, yes. Be patient!” I called down. “Not everyone has the agility of a bird!”

I reached the bottom a couple minutes later.

Cam offered me his hand with a smug grin.

Trying hard to restrain laughter, I asked, “What are you smiling about?”

“I’m being a gentleman now. Come this way, my lady,” he directed.

I rolled my eyes, but took his hand nonetheless. We rejoined the others back at the campfire.

Drew smirked when he saw us and scooted over on the log to make room.

“Kind of you to finally join us,” the sorcerer stated. “They haven’t moved since I sent Scarlet to get you.”

Cam smirked right back and looked at the wolf and mermaid. They were both still absently staring at the fire, not paying attention to anything that we were doing.

“Oh…they make my job way too easy,” Cam grinned, rubbing his hands together eagerly.

Then he stood up and walked over to the base of the tree and grabbed a couple of leaves. He slowly made his way behind Valerie and stuck them into the base of her ponytail. She didn't notice anything at all, even when Cam started making faces right beside her head.

Drew and I were forced to suppress our laughter as we watched Cam work. He was an absolute genius.

When he had finished messing with Valerie, the elf came back and sat beside me again. At the moment, Rennan was still untouched.

"Are you not doing anything to Rennan?" I whispered, looking at Cam questioningly. My mind did not regard his dealing of torture as fair.

"Oh, I am. But he would notice if I were to put something on his head, unlike Valerie. Once, she didn't notice I tied a bell to her hair for a whole afternoon, so she was constantly wondering why a jingling noise was following her. Heh, it was a good afternoon of watching her go nuts," he explained with a smug grin. "Anyway, I just need to get his attention."

"Not a problem," Drew stated as he summoned some sort of purple magic.

He sent it flying into the campfire and the flames glowed purple long enough for Valerie and Rennan to come back to reality. They looked at each other in surprise before turning to us.

"What are you doing?" Rennan demanded quickly.

He was almost a little intimidating, but as usual, his ear twitched. That always gave him away.

Cam smiled. "I was just talking to Scarlet and Drew and I was wondering if you two actually became a couple."

Rennan and Valerie looked at each other again. Valerie then turned towards Cam, who was trying really hard to keep a straight face.

Valerie hesitated, saying, "Well...it's sort of a convoluted story...."

"All I want to know is if you're a couple."

They both nodded their heads, which made the rest of us cheer and laugh. Cam was the first to regain his composure.

He smiled at Rennan and Valerie. "Good. I'm happy for you guys. You deserve each other and I'm glad the mermaid finally realized that."

He winked at Valerie and she blushed.

Rennan smiled slightly, and then it grew into one of his wide-toothed grins. "What about you and Scarlet, Cam? I'm sure we'd all like to know your answer."

"Ha!! He's turned it against you!" Drew guffawed as Cam's face became somewhat ashen.

I smiled and laid my hand on his shoulder to remind him I could answer, but the elf still didn't move.

I was about to answer for Cam, but the sound of horns echoing through the valley cut me off. Cam immediately seized my hand, some supplies, and bolted for the tree. Drew took the hint and gathered up our small camp (thankfully we hadn't unpacked) and grabbed the other two. We five climbed up into the tree and remained deadly silent.

"What are we…?" Rennan tried to whisper.

Cam clamped his hand over the wolf's mouth and motioned for us all to remain silent. He kept his eyes glued on the ground beneath us. I was careful to make sure I didn't move unless I absolutely had to. I didn't know what we were hiding or fleeing from, but it was enough to freak Cameron out, so it was enough to make me worry.

Seconds later, there was a long sequence of clomping horse hooves and jingling armor. Even through the thick branches of the oak tree, I could see that this was a large battalion of soldiers heading north into Estal.

My only question was: *what kingdom are they from and why are they going into Estal?*

They passed after what felt like eternity.

Cam slowly released his hold on Rennan and dropped from his branch. Though, he didn't actually touch the ground. He went as close to the ground as he dared and swung himself upside down. The elf remained there for a couple minutes before he gave us the all clear to come down.

"What the heck was that?" Valerie immediately asked as she got back to the ground.

"That was prime evil and his soldiers." Cam stated, completely serious.

None of us knew how to respond.

"You mean a creepy doll?" Rennan questioned with a priceless look on his face.

"What the heck—no. It's not that," Cam managed after a few seconds of staring at Rennan, completely dumfounded. "That was my father and one of his legions. Do you know what that means?"

"That you've shown restraint by not facing him down now and getting it over with?" Drew asked, rather unhelpfully. He made it sound like he wanted them to fight.

Cam ran his hands over his face in frustration and glared at Drew.

"No! Come on! If my father is going to Estal, then Trehi is virtually unguarded," Cam cried, pointing south. When we all caught his meaning, and Cam rolled his eyes at our faces. "Seriously. It's not that hard. I'm continuing south tonight, sleep or no. I can't pass up this opportunity."

"Cam, most of us are running on nothing," I interrupted. I got him to look me directly in the eye. "That alone is enough to make this particular mission a bit risky. If what you say about Trehi is true, we're going to need something to get down there. It's a couple weeks' journey at least. Are you sure you're up for it?"

"I know, and I am," Cam answered me. He turned to the rest of our friends, who looked at him expectantly. "I'm sorry. I have to go. The least I can do is give you the choice of coming with me or staying and following later on."

"I'm going to stay back. If this is a trap, we can't all get captured," Drew stated. At least one of us was thinking about that sort of possibility.

"I'm also staying," Valerie agreed with the Drew.

"I go where she goes," Rennan nodded, pointing to Valerie.

Cam nodded his head and turned to me.

"I'm going with you. You need at least one person for backup," I said.

Because he couldn't argue with my defiant answer, Cam cracked a small smile.

"Okay. That's settled. Now I have to figure out how we're going to get to Trehi in the shortest amount of time," Cam sighed, reaching into his satchel and pulling out a folded map. "Air is fastest, but we don't have that option. And I'm not shape-shifting again. That was exhausting."

"You know, Cam, there is another way you can go by air," Rennan said with a knowing smile.

He pulled something out of his pocket and tossed it to Cam, who caught it effortlessly. When the elf looked at it, whatever it was, his eyes widened and he stared at Rennan in shock.

"They gave me that to give you. It only works once, they said," the wolf explained.

Cam grinned widely, not of amusement, but pure gratitude. "Wow. Thank you, Rennan. This means a lot to me."

"Sure thing, old buddy. I wouldn't leave you hanging," Rennan smiled—a real smile this time.

Sure, he had definitely changed. Dealing with death—and apparently resurrection—could change anyone. It calmed me to know that beneath this now-tough exterior, there was still the same wolf I had always known. Some things never change.

"Thank you, guys," Cam said again. "I'll use this in the morning. Until then, we should all try to sleep."

Valerie and Drew nodded. Rennan came over and patted the elf on the back while I just hugged him. We all knew how important this was to Cam. Reclaiming the throne that was rightfully his and trying to defeat his own father was a big deal. I loved Cam more than anything, and I intended to stay with him to the end of this journey.

"Wise idea, Camrade," Rennan agreed, pulling a blanket out of the supplies Drew brought from Bulshkan.

He curled up on the ground near where the fire had been and pulled it over his head. "Good night."

"Good night," Valerie repeated, copying Rennan and laying right beside him.

Drew muttered to himself as he too grabbed a blanket and settled in for the night.

Then Cam turned to me. I thought he was going to say something, but instead, he whisked me off my feet into a massive hug. He completely caught me by surprise, so the only thing I could think to do was pat him on the back.

His soft laugh was muffled by my hair, which had come loose hours ago. I think he put me down another thirty seconds later. When I saw his face, it was both joyful and apprehensive, if that was even possible. Then again, this was Cam. I'd learned anything is possible with this guy.

"I'm sorry. I needed to do that," Cam said with a sheepish expression. "I'm glad you're going with me, Scarlet, but I also couldn't be more worried."

"Why are you worried?" I asked gently. I wanted to reach out to him, but fear had chilled my heart. For some reason, whenever Cam felt something strongly, I couldn't help but be on edge.

"Scarlet, you need to understand this: I have been preparing myself for this mission for half a decade and to confront my father for even longer. I can't just let it pass me by and not do anything about it. It's going to be very dangerous and risky. If my mother is there…I could easily be captured and put to death. If my brother is there…it will likely come to a fight to the death. And my father? Instant death," Cam said, not meeting my eyes. "Anyway, this mission relies on an amazing amount of stealth and secrecy. If just one thing goes wrong…I don't want to lose you again."

He reached for my hand. Since I was completely frozen, I didn't really have the strength to resist. I hugged him again when I came to my senses.

"Cam," I whispered in his ear, "danger or not, I'm coming with you. I'd rather die by your side than be here wondering what I could have done instead."

"Thank you, Scarlet," he whispered back. He held me back where he could see me and smiled. "Get some rest. We have a very long trip ahead of us."

"Okay, good night, Cam," I agreed.

I curled up on the ground under a blanket and tried to fall asleep. The ground, though it was pretty cold, was still softer than the bed in my cell I had somehow survived on for the last year. How my back hadn't died yet, I didn't know. That in and of itself was enough to make me smile, but Cam being back was even better.

"I thought I told you to go to sleep," Cam's voice whispered a few minutes later.

I didn't think he needed to talk so quietly, what with Drew's exceptionally loud snoring.

"I *was* going to sleep," I mumbled, rolling over to face him.

In the darkness, I could see one of his eyebrows arched in suspicion.

"Yeah, right. You've been talking to yourself," he told me, laughing.

"I have?"

He smirked. "Yeah, and it's hilarious."

"Oh, sorry," I blushed.

He smiled. "Don't worry. Now try to get some rest now. Please?"

"Okay. I'll try."

"Thank you. Good night, Scarlet."

"Night."

"Love you."

"Love you, too, Cam."

Filled with warm and joy from that last thought, I slowly drifted off into a peaceful sleep.

I was the first one up the next morning. I was restless, so I decided I would try to find the materials to start a small fire. It wasn't that cold, but we still needed something to rouse us so we could get ready to break camp. I found some usable sticks a couple of particularly sharp rocks to make a spark.

A small fire was blazing when Rennan started to stir. I still couldn't believe how tan he had gotten in Estal, not to mention how serious he had become. I waited patiently for him to open his eyes and come over to the fire.

Eventually, my patience paid off since he walked over and sat next to me on the log, still wrapped up in his blanket.

"Hello," he said.

"Hi," I replied.

"Sooo…."

"This is awkward."

"A little bit, yes. This is the first time it's just been you and I talking to each other in a year, really. It was strange not seeing you."

"It was. Estal was rough on all of us."

"Except for the twins," Rennan spat bitterly.

He didn't bother turning to face me when I sent a curious look in his direction.

"You don't hate Cam now, do you?" I asked quietly.

I feared I would have a breakdown if one of my closest friends decided they didn't like another close friend. Part of me believed that everything was fine, but the other part kept nagging at me and telling me nothing was okay anymore.

Rennan sighed. "I don't hate him—hate is a very strong word. I'm just torn on what I should really be feeling about everyone right now: anger at Carter, love and devotion for Valerie, shock for Cam, or loyalty for you. I feel very conflicted."

"I'm pretty sure we're all pretty conflicted right now," I said.

I had similar feelings and felt just as divided. Though, there was one thing I knew for sure: I was absolutely determined to go to Trehi with Cameron, even if it might result in one or both of us meeting our death.

"We are. We were divided at the cliff, and divided when Carter betrayed us. Now we're dividing again because you and Cam are going to Trehi alone," Rennan commented with a resentful laugh.

I must have made a face, because his ears flattened against his head when he looked at me.

"I'm sorry. I'm being terrible," he groaned softly. "I don't mean it badly toward you and Cam. You guys are still my best friends—previously dead elf or not."

"It's okay. I get it. We're a team, but we're going in different directions. I seriously blame Hezakah and Estal for all of that. If we had never been captured—"

Rennan snapped his fingers. "Hey, did you ever find out what happened to Mongwau and Razil? We saw them at that fateful cliff and then they seem to drop out of the story entirely."

I hung my head. "I know what happened to Razil. The first fight I had in the coliseum was against her, and I won. She's probably dead now since that fight was a year ago. I felt the same way I did when we left Palee—I had gotten my revenge, but I had also lost one of the first people who ever trusted me for who I am."

Rennan wrapped his arm around my shoulders. With Rennan, it was like brotherly affection, which I found as comforting as Cam's embrace in times like these. I never thought my first trip outside of Palee would involve so many trials. Then again, I was the one who had chosen this path so long ago....

"I'm sorry, Scarlet. I guess that's the end of Razil now," Rennan said quietly. "As for Mongwau...he sort of met the same fate."

"What happened?"

"What you might expect. He fell out of the king's favor and found himself in the arena fighting for his life like the rest of us. He almost beat me, but I...uh...sort of stabbed him in the gut."

"On purpose?"

"No! Well, sort of. I was trying to defend myself!" he cried in self-defense. *That* was the Rennan I knew. "He had it coming, especially since he got my cousin dragged into all of this. Wayne was an evil dude, but it's kind of a disgrace to the Penbrooke clan to be taken out by poisonous gas. Did you know that our great, great, great grandfather fought in a war and it took five men, seven arrows, and an axe to take him down?"

"Your great, great, great grandfather sounds an awful lot like a berserker."

"He was! That's what makes Wayne look so puny!"

"You're bizarre sometimes, Rennan, you know that?" I chuckled with a broad smile.

Rennan grinned and gave me the thumbs up sign.

I sighed in relief. "I'm so glad we didn't have to fight each other in that blasted arena until the very end."

"Same here, especially since Cam was blasting fire everywhere. Did he say he was going to shape-shift or did he just do it?" the wolf asked curiously. "But yeah. I'm just glad you took your helmet off. Otherwise, something really bad would have happened."

"Yeah, I'm glad I did, too. And no, he did not tell me he was going to do that," I answered.

"It's kinda nice having him back, isn't it? Even if he stole my thunder yesterday with that ghost joke," Rennan mused, staring at the fire.

I smirked slightly. That joke had been pretty amusing, especially when it was paired with Rennan's facial reaction.

"You have no idea," I said with a small laugh.

Having Cam back was such a relief—I was lost without the unpredictable elf. Not only that, but Cam meant so much to me. Heck, I didn't even realize how important he was to me until he had fallen off that cliff in order to save my life.

We remained silent for a few minutes, enjoying each other's company.

"Scarlet," Rennan said. There was a thoughtful tone to his voice.

I sent him a curious look, arching my eyebrow.

Rennan shifted in his seat, but then continued. "I know you're on your own and with Cam, but I wanted to tell you that I'm adopting you into the Penbrooke clan."

My jaw dropped. "You would adopt me into your family?"

Rennan smiled and nodded. "You've become like a sister to me. Plus, everyone needs a family. Call me crazy, but I've always seen a side to you that's lonely and needs family, even though you wouldn't always see them. I want to be that for you."

"Thank you, Rennan. That means a lot to me," I said with a choking voice. I hugged Rennan and he hugged me back.

Then we heard a snicker from behind us. We both turned around to see Cam standing a few feet away. Figures.

"How long have you been watching us?" Rennan demanded.

He didn't seem mad, more like amused. Honestly, given everything that's happened in the last day, I would not have expected that particular reaction coming from the wolf. I was expecting something a little bit more explosive.

"Long enough to hear that Scarlet has been adopted into a wolf clan," Cam replied as he sat down on my other side. "You know, Rennan, if you were anyone else, I might question why you're sitting so close to Scarlet."

Rennan flushed pink, but grinned. "You do it all the time, Cam. Besides, I have Valerie when she eventually wakes up."

Cam sighed. "You have no rush. You just have to play it safe. Meanwhile, I'm on a time crunch—"

"We are on a time crunch," I corrected, thus triggering a snort from Cam.

"Fine. *We* are on a time crunch," Cam repeated, sending me a glare out of the corner of his eye. He mindlessly spun his signet ring as he continued. "I've already contacted them, and they should be here very soon. At least, they should be if they left right when I sent that message."

"Okay, before you go any further," I interrupted (Cam rolled his eyes at yet another interruption), "who is it exactly that you contacted? You make it sound like they're some amazing thing that's going to save the day."

Rennan and Cam both laughed, much to my chagrin.

Was what I said really that funny or were they just being cruel? Or were they just being guys? Their weirdness really could never be explained by any logical terms. All I knew was that these two had lost themselves in some an inside joke or enjoyment of me looking ridiculous.

"Okay, I contacted Thornebrook and Angelica. One will be able to stay with Rennan, Drew, and Valerie while the other flies us down to Trehi," Cam explained when he regained equanimity.

He seemed to be back to his normal self, despite the weight still resting on his shoulders. Well, normal except for the glint of unexplained mischief that glittered in those steel depths.

"That is actually a really good idea. Rennan, I assume it was yours?" I asked while I tried to keep a smirk off my face.

I turned to Rennan and saw that he had totally picked on what I was laying down.

Cam, however, started making noises in disbelief. One of his weird quirks was that when somebody said something he didn't agree with, he would make random noises instead of using actual words. That also tended to happen while he did different tasks around camp.

"It was, Scarlet," Rennan replied, obviously trying to keep amusement out of his voice as well as his face. He epically failed.

"What?! Scarlet!! I am appalled!" Cam cried. "Are you saying my ideas are terrible?"

His face was so serious that I had a really hard time trying to figure out if he meant it or not. That was something else about this elf—he was a really good actor when he wanted to be—a trait I learned of in Sala when we were trying to lighten the mood of things.

"I—"

"You are! Why have you betrayed me?! I thought you loved me!" he exclaimed as he dramatically fell backward from the log, pretending to faint.

Rennan and I looked down at him and Cam stared up at us. Then all three of us burst into laughter to the point of Rennan and I falling backwards as well.

"Cam, you are a very strange person if you can manage to be perfectly serious one minute and a master thespian the next," Rennan laughed.

"Heh, thanks, Rennan," Cam chuckled.

His laugh was as clear as bells and easy to listen to. It wasn't manic like a hyena hybrid, but it also wasn't forced like those of some merfolk I had heard. It was more like the true laugh of a fox hybrid, which vaguely reminded me of what my father's laugh had been.

"Do I even want to know what happened here?" Drew asked us with a slight scowl as he stood over us.

Cam, Rennan, and I sat up and looked at each other.

Drew threw his arms in the air in defeat. "You know what? Never mind. I have no intention of hearing what the heck happened this time."

"That is a wise idea, sorcerer," Cam agreed quickly.

Okay, so he would do something totally strange in the moment, but he wouldn't relay what happened to someone else only a few minutes later? I didn't understand him.

"Elves," Drew rolled his eyes.

Then he craned his neck up toward the sky and narrowed his eyes. We did the same and saw two winged horses circling above us. Rennan immediately got excited and started calling Thorne. The horses must have heard him because their wide circles started getting closer and closer to the ground until they landed in the clearing with us.

"My lord!" Thornebrook called as he and Angelica both knelt down in their horsey fashion. "We came as soon as we heard your call. All is well, I pray."

Cam inclined his head and bid them rise. I still found it somewhat surprising that these two magnificent creatures recognized an elf as their king. It was amazing that the two creatures respected him enough to regard him as superior when they themselves were legendary animals.

Cam and Rennan both made faces, but Cam was the one who spoke. "That's the thing. My father rode north into Estal last night. It's likely that Trehi is unguarded at the moment, so Scarlet and I need to get down there so we can seize this opportunity before it slips away. We needed your help in getting down there by air."

"Of course, my king," Angelica said gently. She tossed her silver mane and spread her wings. "I would be honored to fly the two of you down to Trehi."

"Thank you," Cam smiled gratefully.

"Thorne, the rest of us will need you to stay in case something really bad happens and we have no way to get out of it ourselves," Rennan explained to the pegasus.

Thorne nodded his head in acknowledgement.

"Since this mission is time sensitive, Angelica should take to the skies rather quickly," the pegasus suggested.

Angelica also nodded and lowered herself so that we could mount. Cam said she didn't need to since he could mount, but the alicorn took the few seconds to remind the elf that I didn't know how to ride a horse.

"When I am king, you are getting riding lessons," he promised me, shooting me a sidelong glance.

I couldn't help but flush red at his comment.

Cam smirked slightly and turned to the others. "Since Valerie isn't up, tell her we say good-bye. With luck, you'll get a smooth welcome into the capital. If you're unlucky, be prepared to fight or break us out of prison or both."

"You are not good at leaving people inspired," Drew remarked. He clapped Cam on the back nevertheless and nodded to me. "We'll be there in a week or so, hopefully. I just hope we don't run into wild beasts. Or death."

"Living is nice," Rennan agreed. He hugged me and patted Cam's shoulder. "Good luck, guys. You're going to need it if you're sneaking into one of the most important cities in the world."

"You're not good at being inspiring either! At least I am when I try!" Cam laughed. "But thanks. We'll see you guys soon. Good luck out there to you, too."

With that, we grabbed what few supplies we could afford to take with us and mounted Angelica. I ended up having to carry Cam's scythe because

I was afraid of the blade hitting me in the arm or something while we were flying. I was still upset that my original daggers had been taken from me in Bulshkan, but I did have replacements that would work until I could reclaim my own.

We slowly rose into the sky, and soon our friends looked like small dots far below us. I tried not to become airsick as I thought about the distance we would cover by air. Cam reached back and pulled my hand forward in an effort to comfort me. It worked, since I somehow managed to stay calm even though we were likely flying into war.

Something to Fight For

"Welcome to the kingdom of Heviah, where everything is green, sparkly, and full of enough evil to last four lifetimes of giants!" Cam shouted over the wind as we crossed the border into elvish territory.

Heviah was beautiful, but at the same time somber. This was the first real glimpse I had gotten of the kingdom that was wrongfully taken from Cam and had shut my people up in exile for over a hundred years. If anyone was fit to rule, it was Cam. He was the man who could change the world for the better.

"Is it always like this?" I questioned, looking at the placid landscape far below us.

"Like what?"

"This quiet?"

"Oh, that. Very few people live in the countryside. The cities are where all the parties are—and that's more in southern Heviah," Cam explained. "I don't know where the central city for stuff like that is these days since I've been gone for so long, but when I lived here, it was in Mystica. We would travel for weeks to get there and then stay for a month."

"How did you survive that? You don't exactly seem like a party person."

"I'm not. I'd always sneak out to read or practice magic or something. To this day, my family doesn't know I'm a master of the Ancient Magic. Well, Carter does, but only because I tested it on him. Oh, when they find out that the very person they were afraid of and cast out knew the arts—"

"Stop, you're brooding."

"But I'm so good at it!"

"You are, but stop it."

"Ah, fine. It's not like I have the greatest chance of surviving this anyway."

"Quit being pessimistic, too."

"But—"

"Stop it! You need something to look forward to…a reason to fight," I decided.

Now he turned around to stare at me. His expression was very questioning. "Alright…if we survive, will you be my queen?"

I was stunned for a second. "Are you serious?"

"Yes."

"And I'm not losing my mind?"

"No, Scarlet, you're not."

"You want a *hybrid* as a queen on the elvish throne?"

"Yes! We both know how we feel. There's no one else who I would rather have as my queen. You are more than capable of co-ruling a kingdom with me. Above all that, I love you more than anything."

"Then yes. Cameron, yes! I would love that," I responded without hesitation.

Grinning, I hugged him from behind so tightly that I could feel his heart beating. That was enough to give both of us a reason to fight. It also meant I stay by Cam's side forever like I felt I was being led toward. My devotion and love for him would never end. The thought of officially pledging myself to him made me smile.

"You two are so sweet together," Angelica told us.

I could have sworn she snickered.

I wondered how long she had been listening to us talk. Still, she didn't seem opposed to a hybrid as queen of an elvish kingdom. Personally, I didn't know what I thought about being royalty if we survived, but the joy of having Cam as my husband overshadowed any doubt I might have had.

"Thanks, Angelica," Cam said as quietly as he could dare and still be heard.

The wind wasn't too bad, though, not like it had been when Cam was a dragon. The gusts that his wings created had been seriously massive. Angelica was like a bird in comparison, gently gliding over the air.

"How long do you think it will take us to get to Trehi at this pace?" Cam asked a while later.

"If the wind is not against us, we may be able to get there in the next couple days. If the wind is against us…perhaps three days," the alicorn responded. "I'm hoping for the early morning since the wind is nice now. Reaching the city under the cover of darkness would be most effective for your mission, really."

"Yeah, I agree. We need the darkness," Cam agreed solemnly. He slow head nods indicated that he was formulating a plan.

My eyebrows knitted together in suspicion. "You aren't planning on using the shadows, are you?"

"Not unless I'm forced to…and I really hope I'm not," Cam responded without looking back at me. "Though, I will admit there's a part of me that knows things are going to come to the point of needing the shadows."

"So do I. Just be careful when you do it. I really don't need you becoming an actual ghost," I said, trying to muster a laugh.

The somber elf snickered at that. He reached back and pulled my hand forward again. I rested my chin on his shoulder, enjoying our closeness.

"Don't worry, I won't let them have overwhelming control over me. I'm the one in charge of them, and they can't hurt me. And they will most certainly never hurt you again," Cam promised me. He meant every word. "See if you can relax a little bit. Your grip feels tense and it's driving me insane."

"Oh, sorry. I'm not used to heights. I can't shape-shift into winged creatures, you know," I apologized, attempting to release some of the tension on my shoulders.

I hadn't realized how tight they were, and once I did, they ached. I wondered how much of it was from sleeping on the ground and how much was just from being in the air without something solid beneath my feet.

"I know you can't," Cam snickered, "but that doesn't mean you have to be so tense!"

"Okay, okay, I get it. I'll try to relax," I chuckled nervously.

Then I tried to change the subject. "So…what was it like growing up here? You said you were exiled when you were nineteen, so you had plenty of time leading up to that."

Cam sighed. "It's painful, but I guess you deserve to know since you'll be living here as well. When Carter and I were little, our parents were renovating the palace so there were a ton of new additions and I wouldn't be surprised if more were made in the years I've been gone. My brother and I always liked to explore the new additions until our mother found us and made us go study or something. The townspeople, most of them anyway, were pretty nice and some I considered friends. They were loyal to me and my cause as I got older, but I don't know if they've held out against my father's dictatorship.

"But yeah. I always liked the country growing up because it was so peaceful. As I got older, I used to go out there for a few days at a time when I could afford to miss my studies. I learned I could shape-shift when I was fifteen, so going out in the wilderness helped me hone that ability. Once I received my sentence, I had even more time on my hands. That is, after I actually figured out what had happened to my life."

I leaned back. I couldn't help but ask, "Was there anyone there who you cared about?"

Cam snickered. "I cared for my family, and I still do, despite the fact that we're on opposite sides of this war. My father caused it, and I will end it by bringing peace to my kingdom and people. But I know that's not what you meant. In the romantic sense, no. I did not care for any woman like I care for you. You're the only one who my heart has fallen for, Scarlet. You always will."

"Okay," I said.

I was relieved there hadn't been anyone else who Cam had once loved. Selfish, perhaps, but I needed to know that. By the time he was banished, he must have already grown to be a good man who would have been well liked by all. Not to mention the fact that he was crown prince to the most influential kingdom in the world.

Cam started laughing out of nowhere.

I waited for him to stop laughing so he could calmly explain what he thought was so entertaining.

He stopped, looked back at me, and then started laughing all over again. "I'm sorry. Your face and the tone in which you asked the question was hilarious."

"I'm glad I could entertain you."

"Hey, I'm choosing to be positive for once instead of focusing on our dreary next few days. Isn't that an improvement from a few minutes ago? If so, I want the credit rightfully mine."

"Fine, you can have your credit," I smiled as I leaned forward to rest my chin on his shoulder again. "I just hope you know you're a unique person, Cameron Woods."

"Good," he stated in a self-satisfied tone. "Now then! On to Trehi and our doom!"

I rolled my eyes. "And you've lost your credit again."

"Scarlet, wake up," Cam's deep, accented voice commanded me.

My eyelids fluttered open. It was dark out, so I couldn't see much of anything around me until my eyes adjusted. When they did, I was able to make out faint outlines of buildings around us thanks to the tiny beams of moonlight illuminating the city. The walls of the buildings glowed in various colors, so I got the feeling they weren't made of stone or wood like I was used to.

"Where are we?" I mumbled as I tried to sit up. "Did I fall asleep?"

My eyes were still groggy as I watched Cameron sit on the ground next to me. He looked at me with concern in his eyes, but I had a feeling that it came from his affection, not the situation. It didn't feel like we were in danger, and he wouldn't have sat down if we were.

"You did. You were out since about noon yesterday. I'd guess it's about three in the morning now. In that time, we reached Trehi because Angelica used some sort of teleporting magic to get us here faster," he answered. Then he considered something else. "Also, I guess you didn't exactly 'fall asleep.' I used a minor enchantment so you could get some rest. And so you know, we're currently in one of the back alleys on the outskirts of the city. Though, you can't really tell because everything here is so nice and regal. Bad for target practice when you're thirteen."

He seemed to be thinking of old memories from when he was a child. I wondered if they were happier than mine.

"Oh. Where's Angelica?"

"She's out in the valley where she's safe, keeping herself hidden using her alicorn magic. She wanted us to get into the city and scout things out. Angelica refuses to leave the area in case we need a really quick escape plan," Cam shrugged. "I would have woken you up sooner, but I thought better of it because we're going to need all the energy we can get."

My eyebrows knitted together and I pursed my lips. "What about you? You probably didn't get any sleep. Honestly, do you even sleep anymore?"

He stared at me, completely serious. Even his eyes seemed blank and distant. "I scheduled a nap for a week from next Tuesday."

I just stared at him, horrified. Then his face broke into a smile.

"I'm kidding!" he chuckled before his smile faded. Then he ran his hands through his hair. "My nerves are firing too much to sleep. I just feel like if I close my eyes, the next time I open them…everything will be gone and everything I've worked years for will be for naught. In times like this, I can't afford that risk because it could either mean starting at square one or death."

"Cam," I began, moving closer to him. "We'll see this through and none of us will lose our lives. I'm sure of it. You have to trust us as we've trusted you. You're a strong man, but even strong men have somebody they can lean on in trying times. No one could do this alone."

He wrapped his arm around me and leaned his head on mine. He didn't say anything for what seemed like forever.

Then he whispered, "Thank you, Scarlet. I needed to hear that. I'm so glad I have you in my life. So…change of topic. I need to do something while we're still under the cover of darkness. Will you join me?"

He stood up and offered me his hand. I took it and he pulled me up.

"It would be silly if I didn't. Anything is better than sitting in an alleyway doing nothing when there's so much we could be doing," I decided.

Cam nodded and had started to lead me out of the small street when he stopped in his tracks at its entrance.

"Your cloak was stolen from you," he realized with wide eyes.

"Yes, my cloak, my daggers, the amber stone, and the picture of me and my family," I confirmed.

He muttered something under his breath as he threw a rock out into the street. I honestly would have liked to see it hit a window or something, but we were trying to keep our cover.

"Why?" I asked.

"I *will* get those back for you," he said firmly. He shrugged, trying to clear his mind. "But if anyone who doesn't support me saw you and realized you were a hybrid in their capital, a riot is going to start. Will you take my cloak? I really don't want you to get caught when I can shape-shift into a townsperson or something."

"I'm not going to be stubborn about it like I was in the Blackshell Inn," I decided, taking his heavy black cloak. How he could survive that thing and his armor and weapons was beyond me. How did he not overheat? "So yes, I accept your cloak."

Cam smirked at the memory. Our stay in the inn had not been a pleasant night. That cat hybrid was still so suspicious in my mind that she popped up into my nightmares from time to time. I wouldn't be surprised if she was another one of those people who had joined Mongwau's cause just to escape Palee. Though, I think the main thing we learned from that inn was to never ask Rennan to cook fly soup.

I put the cloak on and pulled the hood over my head so there the possibility of anyone realizing I am a hybrid was almost nonexistent. Cam, I noticed, shapeshifted into his brother again (most likely to get Carter in trouble or to talk our way out of something if we got caught) when I wasn't looking. I'm not going to deny that I punched him when I saw Carter's face right next to me. Cam protected his ribs for the rest of the night.

"Sooo…where exactly are we going?" I whispered to him after rounding about six corners and walking down three or four empty streets.

Even if I had known Trehi as well as Cam did, I doubt I could have guessed where he was taking me. The elf used so many back roads and alleys that my brain easily got confused at this unearthly hour.

"Uh, the cemetery," Cam replied casually.

"*Why?*"

"Because I want to see if my headstone is still there or if my father has tried to erase me out of the history books as well as existence," he answered. "I know, it sounds weird for an immortal race to have a cemetery...and that I want to go there now. But they're actually pretty small and across the kingdom. Trehi's is devoted to members of the royal family or high-ranking officers."

"But you didn't die...well, you did, but they wouldn't have known about that soon enough to make a headstone."

"Yeah, I know. I'm a living ghost," Cam snorted with bitter amusement. He ducked into another back alley. "Elves are strange, really. We don't just make headstones for those who have died, but also for people who have betrayed the crown. And that would mean I have a headstone somewhere in the blasted cemetery because I opposed my father. Unless, of course, he truly became a heartless beast after he banished his own son and heir and didn't care enough to follow the traditions of our people."

"My mind is boggled so I have no idea what to say to all of that," I decided.

Cam put his hand on my shoulder and laughed softly.

"Yeah, I'm from here and I still don't understand all the traditions and that nonsense. I intend to change some things in addition to making foreign affairs better for everyone involved. Especially the Paleeans. You guys deserve so much better than how you've been treated for the last few centuries," Cam said quietly.

Before I could say anything else, we were greeted by high iron gates attached to the only stone wall I had seen in the entire city. We had reached the cemetery of Trehi.

We walked along the small footpaths of the wooded area in complete silence. There couldn't have been more than around one hundred-fifty graves. After growing up in a kingdom like Palee where deaths were frequent and numerous, it seemed like a really low number. However, Cam (who had returned to his normal form) was so pale in the moonlight that I could tell the number of graves had grown since he had last been here.

"So…where would your headstone be?" I asked Cam as I scanned the ground on either side of me.

All of them so far had names of people that I didn't recognize from any history book. They were all, literally, foreign names of officers and representatives I had never heard of.

Except for one. It was a small, white marble stone that glowed in the moonlight shining through the trees of an oak. Compared to some of the others, it wasn't as clean or well-taken care of. There was moss growing over the top and in some of the engraved words and single letters. I couldn't read it, so I called Cam over to where I was standing.

"Scarlet? Did you find something?" Cam asked from behind me.

I heard him approach and then stop dead in his tracks.

He exhaled softly. "Oh, I see what it is. They actually kept my headstone."

"What does it say?" I asked, noting the conflicting emotions flashing across his face. Whatever it was, it was really bothering him.

Cam sucked in a shallow breath and answered, "*'High Prince Cameron Lester Woods, son of King Tristan Woods. Exiled for conspiring against the crown.'*"

I hadn't heard Tristan's name many times before now, but it seemed regal. However, I had a sneaking suspicion that his heart was colder than the harshest winter.

“I think you did have a family member with power who loved you, Cam, even if it was in their own, cruel way,” I whispered as I grabbed hold of his hand. Then I saw another small rock beside Cam’s. “Whose is that?”

His eyes were distant and empty. He pulled his hand away from me as he leaned down and passed by his headstone. I hadn’t noticed before, but there was another small, white stone beside it. Cam went to work clearing it. He dropped to his knees and went limp when he read the name. He couldn’t stop staring at it.

Somehow, he managed to choke out, “My mother. She’s dead.”

Sure enough, he told me the inscription of the stone read, *“Queen Laralind Woods, wife of King Tristan Woods. Beheaded for betraying the king for supporting her oldest son’s folly.”*

“I’m so sorry, Cam,” I whispered. My heart hurt for him.

I put my hands on his shoulders, but he didn’t move or say anything. He just stared at his mother’s headstone after explaining that date read about three years ago, so she had died sometime since he had been exiled. From what I could tell, this was also right before Carter was given orders by his father to kill Cam. It was heartbreaking how divided his family was. I decided not to mention the fact that I had known that something had happened to his mother but had chosen not to tell him.

“Why?” he croaked. Cam held his face in his hands, shielding it from my sight. “Why did he have to take her, too? Has he not caused enough harm to the world? Did it have to devastate our family as well?!”

He shot to his feet and backed up while still staring at the headstones.

“Cam, what are you doing?”

"Move, Scarlet."

"Cam—"

"MOVE!"

I didn't know what he was going to do, but the force in his voice was terrifying. I quickly ran behind him and braced myself for the worst.

The elf held his hands apart and something dark purple started glowing between them. It grew to the size of an apple and then a small melon. Finally, when it was about the size of a person's head, Cam let out a guttural cry and blasted the orb at the headstones.

Smoke rose around us and I pulled his cloak over us to shield us from the fumes. When it cleared, I lowered the cloak and looked at the rubble. Queen Laralind's headstone was left untouched, but Cam's was completely reduced to smithereens.

Cam wordlessly crept forward and picked up a small part of it, no bigger than the palm of his hand. He came back to my side and opened his fist. In his hand, he held a shard of his headstone that I guessed said "king." The elf scowled and threw it into the rest of the pile.

"What...just...happened...?" I asked quietly. My mind was darting in a thousand different directions with none of them making any sense.

Cam looked at me with a hard expression on his face. Then, mere seconds later, he flung himself onto his back and reduced himself to nothing. "I'm so sorry. I never should have done that with you here. I should have done it while you were still asleep. That blast could have killed you. I'm a fool."

Don't be foolish and assume that you are safe with him. Nay, know that he is the most dangerous person you will ever meet.

"I've told you before that if you're a fool, you're a brave fool," I whispered.

But Mongwau's voice still echoed through my mind. That statement was one thing my late mentor had told me that I would never forget. I was just thankful that the elf and I were fighting for the same cause. There was no telling what would happen if we were enemies. The results would certainly be disastrous.

Cam said nothing, but reached for my hand. I gave it to him and he just lay there, keeping my fingers within his grasp.

"But even a brave fool wouldn't put the one he loves the most at risk," Cam sniffled as he sat up. His nose and ears were pink, so I knew that he was having a really hard time processing his grief. He stared at nothing in particular. "How am I going to destroy the monster without becoming it…?"

"Your heart is too kind to ever belong to a monster. You shouldn't worry about that," I said softly. While still managing to get my point across, I said gently, "Now, are you upset because I was here, or are you upset about your mother?"

Cam looked at me with dead eyes and a tearstained face almost as pale as the moonlight shining down on the headstones.

"Both, I guess," he admitted. "She was my aunt's sister—the one I told you stood with me but was killed. We tried to get my mother to see what my father and brother were becoming, but she simply couldn't understand it. Now that I know her eyes were in fact opened before she died…I just wonder what could have gone differently."

"Many things could have been done differently. For example, we might not have gone to Hila or Caso and met Drew. You could have died of dragon blood. Or the shadows. Or—"

"Okay, I get it. I've almost died too many times."

"My point is. Things are happening like this for a reason. We can't do anything to change them, but we can make sure we're on the right side of this war. You said you believed that there is a greater power holding the world together. If that's so, everything will be taken care of," I stated firmly. I squeezed his hand when he didn't say anything. "Things will work out, Cam. You watch. Now, what's our plan? We can't stay here all night, and I have a sneaking suspicion your mind is anything but silent and peaceful. If it is, then there is something wrong with you."

"You're not wrong," Cam snickered as we both stood up. He looked to the west. "We are going to retake the castle. I have a score to settle and it is not going to be kindly. I've shown them mercy for long enough. No longer. Tonight, they're going to see who Cameron Lester Woods really is."

"Okay, I know that was supposed to be a dramatic, inspiring moment, but I have to say…your middle name is Lester?" I interrupted with a smile.

Cam groaned and face palmed. I couldn't help but laugh.

"Yes, my middle name is Lester. I got the better end of it, though. Carter's middle name is Lenard," Cam grinned wickedly. "My full name is better suited for a king. Carter's implies that he is brave, but he is quite the opposite. I'll go tell him how his story ends. Now come on! I've waited for this night for six years. I'm not going to wait any longer."

"Then let's go. I'm following you!"

Cam flashed another one of his wicked grins then ran through the cemetery. We scaled the wall on the west side ("It's a shortcut to the palace.

It's perfectly safe," he said....) and landed in a garden of thorny rose bushes on the other side.

Cam got out unscathed because he was completely covered and protected, but my arms got torn up. I was thankful for his cloak, though, because it got caught instead of me. While Cam was muttering about how stupid it was to put roses on the other side of a wall, I pulled my hair up into a bun so it wouldn't get in my way.

I was surprised when we mostly took more of the main roads to get to the palace. Cam was also a little less careful in where he walked. If it was a large street, he bared more toward the right. If it was thinner, he strode straight down the center. That man was confusing, so I didn't even try to figure out his reasoning. It was likely based on his own logic, too, which meant it was more complex than it needed to be.

Many of the streets we walked were lined with shops, banquet halls, and various small businesses like bakeries and such. They were also well lit, which was probably what surprised me the most about our route. Normally Cam liked to travel by shadow. Now, he was walking bathed in light from the intricate lanterns. I also noticed that buildings and many other small structures were made of a solid crystal-like substance that sparkled in the light.

Finally, we reached the palace.

The smaller buildings I had seen before had been stunning, but I didn't have words to express the awe I felt when I looked at the palace. It was absolutely breathtaking in the moonlight with all of its towers glinting like pure gemstones in a golden scepter.

Though I compared it to a beautiful scepter, it was more like the crown on top of all the amazing things I had seen since leaving Palee. I was having a very hard time believing how any of Trehi could actually be real. My family's cozy den was a hideous hole in comparison to the palace.

"Open the gates!" boomed Cam's order.

He was not in any shapeshifted form, but rather back to himself, not caring if we were caught anymore. I personally thought it was a risky move and did not hesitate in telling him so. He didn't pay attention to me if he heard me. The gates didn't open, so Cam was forced to blast them open in the same manner that he had obliterated his headstone.

When the smoke cleared, we saw a bridge with two lanterns standing between us and the castle. Cam's face became very determined as he strode forward. Before he could get too far, I caught his shoulder and forced him to look at me. He might have been unwavering in everything else, but there was still softness in his eyes when he looked at me.

"Are you sure you know what you're doing?" I asked him quickly.

Cam nodded his head a single time. "Yes. Are you with me?"

"I'm with you till the end."

"Then let's go."

And so, we went. Jogging across the bridge and only slowing down when torches started bobbing above the walls. Minutes later, a squadron of soldiers burst out of the gates and assumed defensive positions. Their armor was intricate and inlaid with several precious stones—especially on their helmets. Some of the soldiers held bows while others had swords.

"Who are you?" one of the leaders demanded. About a dozen arrows were trained on Cam.

Cam grinned coldly. It was completely terrifying to see this side of him.

"I am Cameron Woods, rightful heir to the throne of Heviah," he answered boldly. "I demand that you let me into my own palace!"

"Nay! We answer to the one and only Hevian King Tristan! His orders stated that we aren't to let anyone into the palace!" the guard shouted angrily. "Lay down your arms and we won't have any trouble."

Now the tips of swords were pointed in our direction as well. Unless we complied, the points would go straight through our hearts

Cam slowly started to lay down his daggers, but then did something I didn't expect.

He kicked the butt of his dagger and it went flying straight into the throat of one of the archers. All arrows were loosed, but a magical shield deflected them.

With a sharp movement of his fingers, three soldiers fell dead. The rest were absolutely petrified. A pale light started glowing around Cam's ankles and was spreading up his body. I realized that he was getting ready to shape-shift.

"You are going to regret that," Cam promised as his eyes began to glow.

Shadows enveloped him and soon a dragon was in his place. It was the same dragon he had transformed into last time, only much smaller. Cam the Dragon blew fire at the guards before turning back into an elf. He nodded to me and then rushed into battle.

Many arrows flew at me, but I either dodged or deflected them with my battle axe. It wasn't my preferred weapon, but I was actually getting pretty good with it. I think with enough practice, I would be able to cause as much damage with it as Cameron did with his scythe.

An arrow almost flew into Cam's back as he wrestled one of the guards to the ground, but I was able to deflect it at the last second. Cam finished with the soldier he was dealing with before he grabbed hold of the one whose arrow I had deflected. He then threw the guard into the river we had crossed to get to the gates. We slashed at the guards until the only one left was the one who had told us to surrender in the first place.

"Tell whoever is currently in charge that the king would like to speak with them," Cam commanded forcefully.

The guard nodded his head in terror and started to turn back to the castle, but then saw something just inside the gates and immediately fled.

"There's no need. I'm right here, *brother*," a familiar voice snarled.

We looked just inside the gates to see Carter, ready for war. He held his helmet in hand and his sword hung at his side, ready for action. He did not look happy to see that Cam was alive. The jagged scars on his left cheek from where Cam as a falcon had sliced him only added to his anger demeanor.

Carter growled, "Father promised me the throne, and I don't intend on letting you take it from me."

Cam was so flustered that he couldn't even speak coherently for a good minute. "*You*? *King*? That man is crazy. The kingdom would fall faster under your rule than Tristan's. You're just as corrupt as he is!"

"You will *never* be king, seron. Just give it up already. You are just something that no one ever wants to deal with and just throws away like garbage. You don't have what it takes to be a true king."

Cam's right eye twitched with agitation. He remained still for about five seconds. In another two, his scythe was out and pointed in Carter's direction.

He scowled. "Yeah? *Prove it!*"

Friends and Enemies

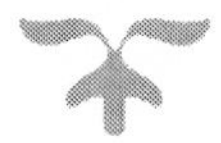

Cam threw himself at his brother faster than I could even blink and faster than Carter could react. Cam swung Vorngurth so swiftly that Carter barely had time to pull up his shield to block the deadly blade. Somehow, Carter managed to hit Cam's ankles and knock him to the ground. Cam cursed and got up quickly. His feet were glowing, so I braced myself for whatever he was going to shape-shift into.

Cam became something I couldn't see with my naked eyes. Maybe he was an insect? I never found out because he swiftly returned to his normal form and kicked Carter forward when he wasn't paying attention. Carter groaned and rolled. He swung wildly at Cam, but the heir was able to dodge every stroke.

I couldn't believe that though both of them were elves, only one of them had sufficient combat skills. In everything I read, all elves were skilled fighters.

That was not the case with Carter. He was about as skilled as a seven-year-old child. He had definitely been right when he admitted that Cam had more of the skill when it came to battle.

"I don't have what it takes? *I don't have what it takes*?!" Cam shouted in fury.

He had managed to flip a struggling Carter onto his back and was now holding Egladel to his throat. Both were very careful not to touch the blade. Smart, because only Cam knew if this one was also cursed.

Cam snapped. "I've been preparing for this moment for years, Carter Woods. How do you figure that I don't have what it takes?"

Carter grinned wickedly. "You've become soft, Cameron, since you met that woman. Yes, you know who I'm talking about. I let myself fall prey to the same thing, but I've discovered that it has gotten me nowhere. She's gone now, and I'm the only one that's left. I've learned the hard way that kingdoms are to be ruled with an iron fist, not kindness. People are meant to be dominated."

Cam stared at his brother in horror. "Where did you get that idea?! People respond to kindness. Ruling with an iron fist doesn't build an empire—it destroys it. Maybe I have become soft since I met her. I don't regret it, and neither does she. It shows that we all have weak spots capable of being exposed. If this is where I'm vulnerable, so be it. I embrace it. It will help me to be a better king than you or our father could ever be."

Carter managed to shove his brother off and reverse the position. Cam, who now had Carter's sword at his throat, did not look happy. This was by far the most unstable I had ever seen him. I wondered how long he had been like this, keeping it all inside for fear of losing it in one untimely moment. Cam struggled like a fish out of water, but couldn't get Carter's foot off his chest.

"A weak spot," Carter scoffed. "Kings don't have weak spots! You're the elder twin, Cameron, but you've always been the imprudent one. No one mourned for you when you were exiled, you know. We were glad to be rid of you like when a tailor throws out their unwanted scraps. You were never accepted here, nor will you ever be. No one could *ever* love you."

I was outraged that Carter could ever call me a weak spot (and because Cam put up a barrier that prevented me from helping him) when he himself had fallen for me for a time. There was no other way to explain the shock and affection I saw from him the one night in Estal that sickened me every time I thought of him. Now I just wanted to see him meet his end. He didn't deserve to live free.

Hot tears streamed down Cam's face as his rage took over again. He violently threw Carter over and kicked his back. Cam was on his feet seconds later holding Vorngurth and Egladel in an attacking position. He was overcome by rage and I knew it was pretty much impossible to control him now.

"You are poison!" Cam yelled as he swung Vorngurth at Carter.

He barely had time to move out of the way. If he were even a second too late, I doubt he would have been able to escape the edge of that accursed blade.

"I *was* loved! You were jealous of me! You always have been!" Cam cried. "I tried to show you kindness, Carter. I really did. For years I tried to be a good brother to you, but you never accepted anything from me. You always have cared for yourself, and it's no different now. Your pride has blinded you to what you have become."

Carter glowered at Cam. "So what? I'll soon be king, just as soon as you and your friends are dead. After that, there is no one who could stop me from conquering all of Galerah. I'll be completely inexorable when I rule the world as an emperor!"

Cam lowered his weapons and sighed. Carter watched him suspiciously. He didn't trust anything that Cam did or said. Honestly, I was surprised that Cam wasn't attacking again. I know I would have.

"Carter, as your rightful king—as your *brother*—I'm asking you one last time to stand down. Come quietly and we won't be forced to do things the messy way. I'll give you a second chance," Cam said softly, offering a hand to his brother.

"You will?" I repeated in surprise.

If I were the one in control of this situation, I would not be giving Carter a second chance. He had done too much harm to ever be given another shot at the good life. It would only be a matter of time before he betrayed us again just to get what he wanted.

I pulled Cam to my side and whispered in his ear, "Cam, are you really sure you want to give *Carter* a second chance? This is the same guy who tried to kill you, watched you die, and then betrayed us."

Cam sighed. "Yes, this is what I have to do. Don't worry, I know exactly what I'm doing."

He gently squeezed my hand before turning back to his brother. Carter was staring at us with a sour look on his face. I didn't even want to know what was going on in that evil head of his. Nothing good, I'd bet. He didn't seem very happy that Cam was showing such affection to me. Then again, Carter was never happy when something wasn't going his way.

"Have you made your choice?" Cam stated in a strong voice.

He sounded way more confident in this approach than I felt, so I was bracing for the worst. Valerie had commented about that feeling once and called it "the effect of Murphy's law." Naturally, none of us knew who this Murphy character was.

Carter scowled. "I do not take orders from you, scum, nor will I ever. I am loyal to King Tristan Woods, Heviah's only sovereign king. I will never bow to another lord."

Cam sighed, long and sad. He looked up at Carter again with a gloomy look in his grey eyes like thunderstorms on a November afternoon. Carter's eyes, meanwhile, were about as cold and unforgiving as an icy tundra.

With a pained frown, Cam said, "So be it. I, King Cameron Woods, banish you forthwith from the Kingdom of Heviah. Should your face ever be seen in my streets again, you will not escape so kindly."

Carter sputtered angrily as Cam turned away.

Cam calmly reached for my hand and our fingers intertwined. The two of us walked past Carter and were a good twenty feet away before trouble began again.

Carter bellowed in rage and the sound of a sword being unsheathed filled the air. Cam immediately released my hand and drew Vorngurth. He swung the blade and it collided with Carter's shield with the sound of splitting wood. Carter grunted, but he didn't fall to the ground from the reverberating force from the blow.

The battle was beginning once more.

"You have no power to banish me! I am a king's son! I am…I am…," Carter seethed, throwing several rushed strikes to Cam, who blocked them patiently and quickly.

"You are banished, Carter. I am king now, and my word is final," Cam said coldly. Any mercy he might have had toward his brother was gone. "Since you have disobeyed my orders, I have the right of the law to deal with you myself."

Carter growled. "Then try to do it! You wouldn't be able to hit the broad side of a barn!"

Cam roared and rushed at Carter again.

I wanted to help, but this was a battle for them to settle; I couldn't interfere.

Both brothers threw vicious attacks at the other. Cam's face and neck got nicked by the tip of Carter's sword, but Carter in turn received several wounds from Egladel. So far, however, no one had been hit by Vorngurth. Eventually, they were moving so fast that they were a blur of silver, teal, and black.

I couldn't tell what was happening until Carter fell to the ground with a cry of agony. Cam stood back with a shocked expression and dropped his weapons. There was a thin trace of blood on the tip of Vorngurth.

Carter had been struck.

"That blade *really* stings," Carter managed. He was clutching his side in a feeble attempt to stem the bleeding. "What curse did you put on that thing?"

Cam's face paled as he stood by his brother's side. Carter went limp and fell over on his back. Blood was beginning to pool around them and the smell of iron filled the air, making made my stomach churn.

"Dead Man's Malediction. Strongest one I could think of," Cam admitted, holding the younger elf up. "I'm sorry, Carter. I wish things could have been different."

"I'm not," Carter spat. With the last of his strength, he protested against being touched by his own brother. "I don't regret what I did, Cameron. I refuse to acknowledge you as king. I would have made a better one than you. Expect my ghost to haunt you for the rest of your life, which won't be much longer. Then you will go where you should be now. You should be coming with me to where you belong."

Cam gaped at him, obviously taken aback. "Carter, I—"

"Save it. It doesn't matter anymore. Good luck surviving Father,

Cameron. You're going to need it," Carter choked out.

Cam just stared as Carter's body began rapidly decaying. Soon, you could see all of his tissues and bones. Then they faded into dust and blew away in the wind. Cam tried to catch the pieces as they floated away, but found no success. Cam bowed his head with a sorrowful expression as he looked at the ground. With the exception of armor, weapons, and the puddle of blood, you never would have known that Carter had even been there.

"Cam," I whispered after a couple minutes of silence.

He didn't move.

"Cam," I said again. "Are you okay?"

"He's gone," Cam murmured, still staring at the ground where Carter had literally faded away. "I killed my own brother."

"Cam, there was nothing else you could have done. Didn't you hear him? Carter chose to take that path knowing he was going to lose in the end," I tried to tell him. "You gave him a chance to turn himself around, but he didn't take it. Carter brought his own death upon himself."

Cam looked up at me with eyes that were full of grief. "But—"

"No buts. It's over and done. There's nothing you can do to bring him back."

"Scarlet…what he said about my weak spot…you're not a weak spot. My love for you is the strongest part me," he said quietly, not able to meet my eyes. "I just wanted you to know that."

I wrapped my arm around his broad shoulders and he leaned into it. "I know, Cam. I know. It's the same for me. Now come on, we have more to do before this night ends."

"You're right," Cam reluctantly agreed as I helped him up.

I let him lean into me as we walked. Neither one of us said anything for a little while.

"Cam?"

"Yes?"

"When this war is over, I want that scythe of yours locked up where it can't turn anyone into ghosts."

Cam chuckled quietly. "Fair enough. That thing is powerful, and I don't want it falling into the wrong hands…which could have grave consequences."

"That's wise, but your sense of humor is terrible. 'Grave consequences.' Really?" I laughed, despite the somber mood that had settled all around us.

Cam smiled somewhat sheepishly and hung his head. "It was necessary."

"Sure, it was."

"It was! Now come on, I have a couple things I need to check out before we can get this palace completely under my control."

"So…what exactly are we supposed to be doing right now?" I whispered as we snuck through the lower levels of the castle.

We had managed to slip in through one of the servant's doors and as far as I knew, we were now wandering around aimlessly. But after a good twenty minutes of searching, Cam still hadn't told me what we were doing.

Cam poked his head around another dark corner. He had been super fidgety the entire time, whereas I was just walking behind him normally. I think he was hyper-aware of everything going on because one wrong move and both of us could end up dead.

"Uh, I kinda need to figure out what officials are here right now because if I meet one of my father's generals in these halls…heh, I'll be a goner," Cam replied with a nervous laugh accompanied by an anxious smile. "If any member of the Woods clan is going to survive the night, it's going to be me."

I pursed my lips. He was jumpy to the point that if I put my hand on his shoulder, he would freak out.

"I like your determination, but your anxiety needs to go," I told him as we ran into another hall.

Cam guided me up a flight of stairs to the second level. I think we were supposed to be looking for the guest bedrooms. Unfortunately, every level was more maze-like and intricate than the last, so it was really hard to keep them all straight. Cam basically grew up in a labyrinth.

For some reason, Cam led me into a supply closet and we hid in there to catch our breath and rest for a couple minutes. He summoned a small purple fire (at least I think it was fire) and sank to the floor. I joined him just so I could get off my feet. Cam didn't answer me for a couple of minutes.

"I'm not trying to be anxious. I'm just trying to be careful…I don't want to blow this for us. This is the only chance we're ever going to get, and I don't really feel like…hey, I just had an idea," the elf said with a suddenly excited expression on his weary face.

I raised an eyebrow, not entirely sure if I should be concerned about whatever this new idea was. “Should I be afraid?”

He grinned deliriously. “No, but this is a crazy plan that may not even work.”

“Cameron, what did you think of?”

“You don’t have to lengthen my name! I just thought maybe we could make a huge ruckus throughout the castle and get the officials out here?” he explained with a hopeful tone while I stared at him skeptically. He randomly waved his hands in the air. “Okay, okay, I know. It’s probably not the best plan I’ve ever come up with—”

“It is not. Not by a long shot.”

“Like I was saying, it’s probably not my best plan, but it would get the officials out here so I can terrify them out of their wits. As far as everyone else is concerned, I’m dead. Unless Carter somehow rose the alarm…’cause then they would know and possibly be expecting me…bah! I don’t care! I’m doing it.”

He got up again and rushed out of the closet, running through the halls and yelling insults and warnings to anyone who could hear him. Not really knowing what to do, I stayed put in the closet and waited for the elf to come back. A few minutes later, when the whole palace seemed to be in an uproar, Cam returned with a very self-satisfied look on his face. He quickly closed the door so nobody would run into it in all the chaos.

“That was fun,” Cam announced, still grinning. He relit his fire so we would be able to see each other again. He eventually became serious after I stared at him long enough. “Okay, so I have good news and bad news.”

I groaned quietly. “I don’t like the sound of that. What’s the bad news?”

"That I don't have any good news, unless you think fighting Heviah's top general is a good thing," Cam answered, hanging his head.

I face palmed and rubbed the bridge of my nose.

He poked my foot with his. "Hey, I know this is probably not how you would have done this, but I have another plan while everything is in chaos."

"This had better be a good one, Cameron," I said firmly.

His faint smile faltered. "Look, I'm sorry. I didn't think that one through. Don't hate me, please."

I sighed. "I don't hate you, Cam. I love you…and that will never change. Now what's your plan?"

He exhaled with relief. Then he grew solemn. "Okay, so I was thinking while I distract—"

"You mean kill."

"Yes, that will be taking place. While I do that, I want you to go down to the dungeons…wait, you don't know your way around here well enough yet. I will take you down to the dungeons and I want you to release any hybrids you may find," Cam said, handing me a key.

I immediately slipped it into my boot's pocket—I wasn't about to lose it.

"Make sense?" he asked.

"Sure, but do you think you could help me down there for a few minutes? We should try to find one of your supporters so they can help me after you leave."

"That is a very good idea. I'll help, and then I've got some generals who need to meet Vorngurth," Cam muttered as he cracked open the door of the closet. He let in the tiniest bit of light, then he snuffed out his flame. Cam turned back to me. "The coast is clear. Ready?"

"Ready as I'll ever be," I answered as my hand found its way to the hilt of one of my daggers.

Cam smiled at me in the dim light. It wasn't one of his wicked ones—it was proud. Proud of what, I did not know.

"That's my Scarlet. You'll do great," he said. He kissed the top of my head and then crept out of the storage closet.

I stood there for a moment, stunned. It was *me* he was proud of. I still couldn't believe that he loved me—a person who was so far from perfect.

Cam stuck his head back in and I could see that he was grinning with amusement. "Well, don't just stand there in shock that I showed affection! We have work to do!"

"You are *so* not helpful!" I chuckled as I followed him through the now-lit halls.

Everything was more alive now that Cam had caused some chaos, but I didn't hear anyone running through the halls. Cam told me at one point that troops were gathering outside, preparing for an attack on the city or the arrival of their king. Heh, little did they know that their king had already arrived, had raised the alarm, and had fun doing it.

Soon we were in the dungeons of Trehi's palace. It was the lowest level of the building and definitely the darkest yet. If Cam hadn't lit another one of his small fires, I'm pretty sure I would have walked into a wall or something.

"How can you even see in here?" I questioned the elf.

"This is weird, but I shapeshifted my eyes to an owl's so I can see in the dark," he replied after making one of his weird noises. "It comes in handy when making a fire is too risky, don't you think?"

"That is not fair. It would be so awesome to do that."

"Eh, sort of. Sometimes it causes—"

"*Cameron*? Cameron Woods? Is that you?" a female voice cried out in the darkness.

Cam's magical flame grew brighter and he held it out away from him so it could spread farther.

It shone on a girl about our age, twenty or so. She had long blonde hair that was intricately braided. Her dress was dirty and her face and arms were covered in grime. Sitting next to her was a guy about the same age. His red hair and clothes were in the same run-down condition his companion's were. Even though both were elves who seemed to know Cam (though I'm sure most elves knew full well who Cam was), they seemed kind enough.

"Kalila? Mayson?" Cam said in amazement. He ran to the door of their cell and grinned widely. "You guys survived! How?!"

"We fled the country a short while after you were exiled," Mayson answered as he stood up. "We came back a couple months ago when that brother of yours was sent out on a mission. Figured it would be safer here. But I can't believe you're here right now! The king declared you dead when Carter returned a year ago!"

Cam smirked. "I was dead, but I'm back. And for the record, *I* am king now. Carter is gone, Hezakah is gone, and now all that's left to do is to get rid of my father."

"That's amazing!" Kalila cried happily.

She vaguely reminded me of what Valerie was like when I first met her. I mentally gagged at the thought and made a mental note to never let this girl come near me with flowers.

"I can't believe that we all survived. No hybrids captured and tortured you, did they?" Kalila asked.

I scowled and Cam snorted. He turned to me and dragged me into the light against my will. Kalila and Mayson's eyes widened.

Cam laughed at their faces. "Guys, this is Scarlet. She's a fox hybrid who has journeyed with me all the way from Palee. We have another hybrid friend in our company, but the rest of the group isn't in the city yet."

Kalila immediately disliked me, but Mayson's reaction was completely different. He seemed to be an elf like Cam who didn't mind the presence of a hybrid in an elvish capital. He asked me several rapid-fire questions, so I did my best to answer while Kalila sulked behind him. Cam thought it was very amusing.

Eventually, I managed to pull my elf aside.

"Cam, who are they?" I asked him quickly, careful not to draw any additional attention to us.

"They're friends of mine from when I attended Trehi's Academy for Nobility before I was exiled. They were always a part of my biggest public speeches, so I'm surprised that my father hasn't put them to death yet. Unless he was going to use them as bait, because then I'd watch your back...especially around Kalila," Cam explained with a slight smile.

I looked at him with a questioning gaze.

He calmly continued. "She had a major crush on me when we were younger. Don't worry about it, though—you're still my future queen."

I sighed in relief and Cam laughed at me. I slapped his arm, and he somehow managed to control himself.

"Okay, your work here is done, sir," I decided. "You have a general to deal with, remember?"

"I know, but it's more fun here. I changed my mind; I'm going to stay here and help. Then we all go up there together," Cam decided. "Also, I don't trust you and Kalila near each other…mostly because I want to protect you from her jealousy."

I rolled my eyes. He had a plan that I had approved! Why did he have to change it?!

I smiled slightly. "That's very sweet of you, Cam. Come on then. We have some work to do."

I reached into my boot and pulled out the key again. I tossed it to Cam. Using magic, he duplicated the key so we could unlock doors at the same time. We needed to find all of the hybrids we could get because they were like me for the longest time—harboring pure hatred for elves. These guys wanted revenge after rotting in the dungeon of the king himself.

"Are we doing this like old times?" Mayson asked as he and Kalila grabbed weapons from the guard room that was conveniently across the hall. Many of the hybrids already had stolen weapons, taken from the guards when they weren't looking, and were now running outside to distract the elvish troops.

"Sort of. I want Kalila to take care of the gates. Make sure nobody gets out of the courtyard," Cam instructed with a glance at the she-elf.

Kalila pouted as she strapped her sword around her waist. I almost laughed as I watched her struggle against her vest as she tried to tie it.

"Why do I have to do the gates?" she whined.

"Because you never learned how to fight with a sword! Plus, you're our resident mechanic so you can handle the gates and all the machinery," Mayson grinned as he threw a pack of arrows to Cam, who caught them effortlessly and put them into his quiver.

Kalila shrugged. "I guess you're right. I'll get the gates lowered."

She walked out of the room without so much as a glance at me. Cam sighed and Mayson rolled his eyes. I wasn't very impressed by the girl—I'd seen squirrel hybrids with more potential than her.

Mayson caught my eye. "Pay no attention to her. She had a major soft spot for Cam back in the day. She doesn't like the fact that he likes another woman better than her."

Cam slapped him, but laughed. "Shut up! That makes me sound old when I'm really not. But yeah. Scarlet, don't worry. Everything is good between us. Why don't you go scout things out? We'll be there in a couple of minutes."

"Okay, fine," I agreed.

Cam smiled at me gratefully and I walked out of the room with a dagger in hand. I considered actually scouting things out, but that wouldn't get me the information I wanted. I instead stayed at the door, trying to listen to Cam's conversation. I realize that it was terrible of me to eavesdrop. That doesn't mean I didn't do it, though.

I heard Mayson snicker. He asked, "A fox hybrid, huh? I hear they're stubborn ones. Did she hate you at first?"

Cam laughed softly. I enjoyed listening to his crisp, clear laugh. It was a calming sound to my ears.

"She did, but she's amazing. Think she'll make a good queen?" Cam asked in return.

My ears were fully alert now. I heard what I assumed to be Mayson clapping Cam's back.

Mayson's voice replied, "I've known her for all of thirty minutes, but she seems like the kind of person I would follow as a queen. You've found a good one, Cameron. And she couldn't have found a more honorable elf."

"Thank you, friend. Now, are you ready to get revenge on the people who cast us out of our homes?"

"Oh yeah. Let's do this," Mayson answered with a very determined tone.

He ran out of the room and barely noticed me as he went past. He patted my shoulder quickly and took off down the hall.

Cam, however, slowly walked out of the room and smirked when he saw me.

"I know you heard that," he informed me. He just laughed when he saw my ear twitch. "I'm not mad, I knew you were going to do it. I wanted you to have assurance that none of this is a mistake. Everything is going to be fine, Scarlet."

"Okay. Thank you, Cam," I said, putting my hand on his shoulder.

He looked down at me, one of his eyebrows was slightly arched. "What have I done to deserve your gratitude?"

"You came into my life when I needed you the most. I wouldn't be the same person I am today if you hadn't shown up in Palee. You've made me change, Cameron Lester Woods, and it's for the better."

"You've changed me, too, Scarlet, and I couldn't be gladder of it," Cam smiled, wrapping his arm around me. He laughed softly. "I find it so amusing that the girls who always chase after me never have a chance and yet the one I love fought me for so long. Don't you?"

"Now that you mention it, it is," I agreed. "Now, are you going to reclaim your kingdom or are you going to stay here and keep laughing about the things that amuse you?"

"Can't I do both?"

"No! We're supposed to be productive, and you are not productive in any way when you're laughing."

"Bah! Fine! I have a general to kill…er, I mean deal with!"

We ran up to the main levels again where Kalila and Mayson were waiting for us. When we asked why they were still there, all they did was point out one of the colossal windows. Cam leaned forward and gripped the ledge. His face paled tremendously. Outside, there were several trebuchets aimed directly at the palace.

"The hybrids have done their part and taken out a good portion of the troops supporting your father," Mayson explained. "They're regrouping in the main hall awaiting your orders."

Cam whipped around to stare at Mayson. "You've got to be kidding me. A bunch of hybrids waiting for orders from *me*?!"

Mayson shrugged. "You're pretty influential, Cam. They're willing to fight for you because of Scarlet. They've seen the way you've treated her just in this short time. They're willing to help you because they want to believe in an age where Paleeans and Hevians can get along as friends and allies."

"I can't believe this day has come," Cam murmured as he watched the sun peek up from behind the mountains to the west and cast its rays all over the courtyard. Cam's face grew hard as he trained his eyes on somebody outside. "Scarlet, come with me. Mayson, Kalila, wait with the hybrids for my signal. Under no other circumstances come out."

"Understood. Come on, Kalila," Mayson said as he started running to the main hall.

Cam and I took off in the opposite direction from them.

"Where are we going? What did you see?" I questioned.

To my dismay, Cam started leading me through back hallways of the palace, which got me lost all over again. I was pretty sure that I would never be able to find my way around this place.

"Not 'what.' 'Who,'" Cam corrected as we reached another door to the outside. He peeked through the crack between the door and the wall, trying to get a view from this new angle. "I saw my grandfather, Ladefindel. He was my mother's father and my own father's second-in-command. We need to take him down. Since my father is out of the kingdom and Carter is dead, command passes to him. Once he's out of the picture, I can fully reclaim the palace."

"He's another family member of yours, though," I objected. All I could think of was that night in Estal when Ladefindel nearly had I and I killed.

"I have no choice, Scarlet," he said, turning to me, his voice tighter than usual. Cam closed his eyes and I saw a single tear run down his cheek. "My family has been divided for so long that it was only a matter of time until this happened. I hate the fact that I'm the one who has had to take lives to get here. Especially...."

"Cam, there's nothing you could have done. I told you that. Carter chose his path, even after you gave him several chances to change his ways."

"You're right. I need to focus on the task at hand. Let's go."

We rushed out into the courtyard. elvish soldiers saw us immediately and drew their swords. Arrows flew at us the second we were in sight. I fully expected one of them to hit us, but somehow, they changed direction before any could find their target.

I looked over at Cam, who had created a force field around us.

"Stop!" Cam commanded in a firm voice.

The soldiers froze so abruptly, which gave me the feeling that Cam had used magic on them. He and I could still move, though, and when he saw that it had worked, he walked straight down the center of the courtyard.

"Who are you?" Ladefindel demanded.

The question was directed at Cam. He knew full well who I was. I could tell from the look on his face that he recognized me as the hybrid who had busted into his meeting with Hezakah in Estal even if he only saw me briefly after our recapture. I was glad he couldn't move his legs, but somehow his mouth still worked. Cam was being too nice to let him speak. I would have killed him just to be done with it. Blast Cam and his manners on the battlefield.

"Your grandson and the rightful king. Don't pretend you don't know who I am," Cam answered, loud enough for everyone to hear. "As you can see, I'm not dead. I've come to give you one last chance to surrender."

Apparently, they could move their lips, too, because the air around us filled with whisperings of "king" and "hybrid." I stuck close to Cam's side. Ladefindel did not look pleased to see either one of us here.

"You have no right to be here," Ladefindel threatened.

Even if he was Cam's grandfather, he looked as young as we did. Light brown hair cascaded over his shoulders and he had piercing grey eyes just like the twins.

Ladefindel snarled, "You don't belong here, Cameron Lester. You are undeserving of the Woods name!"

Cam laughed darkly. "How would you even know? You're not a Woods! You have no power here anymore. I am rightfully your king by law. You and your companions have no choice but to obey *me*."

"Obey an elfling? Ha! We have lived many more years than you, grandson. We have far more experience than you."

The corners of Cam's mouth twitched. "Experience, maybe so, but I've seen enough to know what to do in life. You obeyed my father when he was my age—why should it be any different for me? You are from the dark ages of Heviah when everyone was cruel and wicked. I am breaking that chain and choosing to be kind to my people instead of taking them for granted like my predecessors who exploited their power."

There was more whispering among the soldiers.

"Stop now while you still have the chance!" Ladefindel shouted desperately.

Cam kept advancing until he was standing right in front of his grandfather. I was rather amused when I saw that Cam was a good several inches taller than the other elf. He was also much more intimidating, especially with his scythe in hand.

"*Never*. I didn't stop five years ago; I won't stop now," Cam stated stubbornly. "Since you've not taken the mercy I have tendered, you and your fellow generals are banished from my kingdom. Heviah has a new king, and he does not take kindly to traitors or rebels."

"'Traitors or rebels,'" Ladefindel laughed bitterly. "So says the exile who brought a hybrid into the very kingdom that banished them for their revolts against the crown—for murdering the royal family. Do you know what your father would say about all this? He would tell you that you're a disappointment to him. You don't belong here. You—"

"ENOUGH!" Cam boomed, covering his ears. His eyes were wild and his voice was like a sonic blast throughout the courtyard.

Most people were free to move again, but those loyal to Tristan and Ladefindel remained lifelike statues. The soldiers loyal to Cam bowed deeply when Cam turned to them. Cam inclined his head, but was too troubled to say anything save for giving orders to dispose of all the statues as they saw appropriate with the exception of his grandfather's. He was adamant that his grandfather's statue be put somewhere in the castle for safekeeping for the time being.

Cam caught my hand and we started walking towards the palace again. Many soldiers were shocked to see an elf and a hybrid in such a close relationship, but others were pleased to see our two species getting along. It marked something in history that I doubted had happened before.

All of the elves, however, acknowledged their new king. As we passed, Cam sent several out into the city and palace to alert the people that Tristan had been dethroned during the night and the rightful heir now possessed the crown.

Mayson and Kalila celebrated when we came back inside because they were pleased to see Cam in command even if he hadn't been officially crowned yet. Kalila ignored me the whole time and focused on Cam, as expected. I was used to it after how Valerie had acted around me. Mayson, on the other hand, was kind enough to acknowledge me even if I hadn't done anything to deserve it. He was another elf who didn't seem to be all bad. I could see why he and Cam were friends—they shared the same values and interests.

Cam and I were able to slip away a while later.

It was about noon when he led me outside into the expansive gardens. We were surrounded by blooming flowers and birds singing happily. Meanwhile, Cam and I were completely silent.

"This is quite an accomplishment," I said to break the silence.

"Yeah, but now we're on the verge of war," Cam replied solemnly.

"We always knew war was unavoidable. At least many of the people here seem to know Tristan was corrupt," I pointed out. "That makes it a lot easier for you to take power."

Cam laughed humorlessly. "If only it were that simple. A lot of the residents in Trehi might know that, sure. But people in the farther reaches of the land practically worship my father because they never hear about his faults. They only know of a savior king who protects our borders. We still need to provide evidence of his corruption for everyone to listen."

"I think we have enough evidence now," I commented. The only response I received was an arched eyebrow prompting me on. "Your father exiled you because he wanted to keep the throne for himself when law clearly says it is rightfully yours. And he publicly killed your mother because she sided with you. For crying out loud, he kept innocent hybrids in his dungeons for no apparent reason! I'd say that's proof enough."

"Yeah, I guess you're right," Cam agreed, drawing himself up a straighter. A little more spring appeared in his step.

We continued walking through the gardens in silence. I guess neither one of us had anything to say, so we enjoyed each other's company and the scenery.

Finally, Cam asked, "So, what do you think of Trehi so far?"

"It's a maze that I don't think I'll ever be able to solve," I admitted with a small laugh. "How did you ever find your way around growing up?"

Cam smiled to himself. "I don't know. I kinda just learned as I went along, I guess."

He led me toward a tree swing. I sat on the swing thinking he was going to join me but no…he insisted climbing into the tree and hung upside down from the branch. He was so formal and serious until he randomly chose to hang from a tree.

Though, I enjoyed seeing the casual, joking side of Cam that he so rarely displayed.

He laughed at me. "What? Did you think I was going to be predictable?"

"I don't know what I thought! I guess I thought you were going to sit next to me," I laughed as I spread out on the swing. I was on my back so I could look up at him. He was grinning, so I took that as good sign—I hated it when he was depressed.

"Why? You know I like trees."

“True enough. I just did not expect that.”

“Ha.”

A shadow swept over the gardens. I was on my feet in seconds and Cam jumped down from his branch. Our hands were on our daggers and ready to fight. Thankfully, no danger came. We sighed in relief when Angelica alighted on the ground in front of us. She bowed her head when she saw Cam.

“My lord! I see that your mission succeeded!” she said cheerfully.

“It’s succeeding for now,” Cam stated flatly. He corrected himself after I elbowed him in the ribs. “Yes, it’s succeeding.”

Optimism was not his strong suit.

“Good. I’m glad to hear that, especially since I’m currently playing the messenger,” Angelica said with a nervous twitch of her tail.

Cam sent me a nervous look before he urged the alicorn on. One of these days, I was going to slap all of his anxiety out of him.

“Well, then, what news?” the elf asked with a look of concern on his face. He was preparing himself for the worst.

“Your friends are on the outskirts of the city as of this morning.”

“You’re holding something back.”

“Sadly, I am.”

“What is it, Angelica?”

Her ear twitched, which reminded me of Rennan’s nervous habit. “They come bearing a scroll with the seal of Tristan.”

Tristan's Challenge

Did Cam wait for any more information? No. Did he wait for me or Angelica? No.

What did he do? He shapeshifted into a falcon and flew off to find the others. I rolled my eyes at his haste. Though I understood the feeling, he still could have waited about five seconds instead of leaving as soon as Angelica said his father's name.

"Well, he's gone now," I muttered as I started walking off.

Angelica trotted beside me.

"I could always fly you out there. It would be faster," she offered with an amused tone.

I mentally face palmed.

Yes, help from the alicorn would be a lot easier than trying to navigate through Trehi on my own when I had only been there for nine hours.

"You know, that would be very helpful," I stated, gratefully accepting her offer.

She helped me climb up on her back; it was my first time riding a horse by myself. Angelica said she would fly smoothly so all I had to do was hold on and try not to fall off. I greatly appreciated her offer because I didn't even know the fundamentals of riding. Cam was right—I needed lessons.

We flew to the outskirts of Trehi and found my friends waiting in the shade a short distance from the main gates. I had no idea the emerald gates even existed. That's what I get for being asleep when we reached the city.

I saw Drew, Rennan, Thorne, and Valerie in the river, but there was no sign of Cam anywhere.

Angelica landed near them. I slid off her back and walked over to the guys. Drew and Rennan were pleased to see that I was alive and unharmed, but there was an strong element of irritation in their expressions and postures.

"What's wrong? Where's Cam?" I questioned when I noticed something was amiss. "I thought he was here."

Drew rolled his eyes and Rennan sighed deeply.

Rennan ran his hand through his hair. "Do you really want to know where he is?"

My hope diminished. "It would be stupid of me not to ask."

Drew muttered something under his breath as he uncrossed his arms. "He's flying north to go back into Estal."

I scowled. "You seriously let him go?"

"He didn't stay long enough for us to talk some sense into him!" Rennan cried, throwing his hands into the air. "That elf is way too stubborn for his own good."

"Agreed. If he had waited long enough for us to explain what happened, we could have formed an actual plan!" Drew commented bitterly.

Before we could shout at each other more, we heard Valerie squeal. We ran over to the river to see what was the matter. She was holding something, but I couldn't tell what it was until we got closer.

"Holy cracker barrel. You actually caught him," Rennan breathed.

That was when I realized Valerie was holding a striking silver falcon. The grey-eyed bird fought violently against her grasp. Valerie was holding it very close to the water, so that could have been why it was struggling.

"Yeah, barely," the mermaid muttered as the bird squirmed again. "I nearly missed, but he wasn't expecting me. I keep threatening to take him for a swim, but he squirms even more."

"Cameron, transform. Now," Drew commanded the bird.

It seemed to give him the evil eye before flying out of Valerie's grip, landing a few feet away as pale mist and shadows surrounded it. Seconds later, a very agitated Cam stood in the falcon's place.

Drew continued sternly. "Don't you dare think about leaving."

"I was going to scout out how many there were!" Cam yelled in protest. His ears were red with anger, but his face was pale from exhaustion. "If Valerie hadn't intercepted me, I would've been back in an hour or so."

"We don't *have* an hour or so," Drew argued irritably.

Cam glared at the sorcerer in a way that only he could. Shadows started creeping into his face, so I put my hand on his shoulder. Cam tensed up and shot me a look out of the corner of his eye. "I love you, but don't touch me."

I pulled him down to where I could whisper directly into his ear. Amazingly, he didn't protest.

"Cam, you're exhausted. We're *all* exhausted. Why don't we go back to the palace and try to get some rest?" I suggested. "Then we can discuss whatever has happened since we last saw each other."

The elf nodded, but only because he knew I wouldn't be convinced otherwise. He said nothing to the others, but he grunted and nudged me. I made a mental note to slap him later.

"We're going to the palace to unwind as much as possible before discussing any of this," I informed the rest of our friends.

Valerie nodded, pulled herself out of the water, and waited for her tail to turn back into legs. Soon she skipped over to Rennan and grabbed hold of his hand. The wolf relaxed immediately.

Drew watched them and a slightly heartbroken expression appeared on his face. I wondered what he was thinking of....

"That sounds good to me. Can we get lunch, too?" Rennan questioned hopefully.

I was glad to see that he still had a mind for food, even after everything we had gone through. Cam cleared his throat and Rennan's wary gaze shifted to the elf. Cam hung his head, but he still spoke.

"Now that I have control of the palace and the city, I'll be able to get us anything we need," Cam stated.

He was barely audible to everyone, so I figured that I needed to get him out of the sun before his energy was completely sapped. It was weird how Cam's already quiet voice got even quieter when he was in the sunlight. He really didn't like the sun.

"I'd hope so, since you're the only one with the power to do it," Drew stated bitterly.

Cam sighed miserably and Drew grunted. Rennan kicked Drew in the shin, causing the sorcerer to yelp.

"Quiet, Drew, that isn't helping anything," the wolf admonished.

Drew glared at Rennan and Cam, but he complied and said nothing.

We took it as a sign that we definitely needed to get to Trehi for food and rest. Otherwise, I'm pretty sure Valerie and I would have been the only ones who would think relatively straight because the men were succumbing to emotions rather than sense. And knowing how volatile Cam and Drew could be and how bent Rennan is on food, we wanted to avoid any trouble.

Still, I wasn't looking forward to seeing whatever this message from

Tristan was. All I knew for certain was that it was anything but good.

Cam led us to a room on the second level of the palace. From what I could tell, the first level was for parties and major events. It was also where the great hall was located. The second level consisted of a library and offices for royalty and nobles who lived in the palace or in the city. I'm pretty sure the third level was more miscellaneous rooms and the fourth was bedroom suites.

Anyway, the elf took us to a room that was just a short way away from the master library. I wondered how long it would be before Cam built a book fortress in there. I'd have to keep an eye out for one when I went exploring.

The room we were brought to was cozy. There were a few couches along the walls and a round table in the corner of the room. One large floor-to-ceiling window overlooked the city below.

Rennan immediately face planted on one of the couches. To my amusement, Valerie started poking his head, but Rennan did not move in the slightest. Meanwhile, Drew warily sat down on another couch. I joined him at the opposite end. Cam, however, sat down at the table, looking down on the sparkling metropolis.

When I saw the uneasy look on his face, I moved to sit next to him.

"What is it?" I whispered to him.

"This room. Memories," he shuddered, pinching the bridge of his nose. He sighed and turned to address the others. "I've already asked one of the maids to bring lunch up for us. It should be here in about twenty minutes or so."

Rennan groaned from the couch. Though, it came out muffled because his face was still buried in the couch. "Aww…I'll never make it that long. I'm starving!"

Valerie sat on the arm of the couch and patted his back. The wolf made a pathetic noise and face planted deeper into the cushions. Drew muttered something under his breath and Cam watched them with a concerned expression. Drew got up and came to sit at the table with us.

"So, what exactly is this room used for?" Drew asked skeptically.

It was like he was carefully inspecting and memorizing every detail of the room in order to use the information in future occasions. Eventually, his eyes rested on Cam, who was completely miserable.

"This was a room where my mother, brother, and I used to wait for my father when he came home from foreign trips. It was used during a time where he was overjoyed to see all of us—before our family became so divided and corrupt. I was seven when we last used it," Cam said quietly.

The tips of his ears and nose turned pink, so I gently held his hand while Valerie came over and hugged him.

"I'm sorry, Cam," Drew said with a contrite expression. His irritation diminished. "I should have realized how hard it would be for you to come back here. I, too, know what it's like to be banished from your home by those you love. I can't imagine I'd ever be as strong as you if I went home."

The corner of Cam's mouth twitched. "Thanks, guys."

Rennan's face popped up from the couch. "Hey, I hate to ruin the moment, but where is that jerk of a brother of yours anyway? I'd love to see him and give him a piece of my mind. Being a prisoner in Estal was *not* my idea of fun."

Cam crashed his head onto the table and moaned.

The three of our friends gasped in shock, each guessing what might have happened, but I just sat there. They had no idea how raw the topic of Carter was and, evidently, Cam was in no shape to explain. I beckoned to the others to come and sit, so they did. They watched Cam with concern, and he still didn't move. Well, he did, but only to put his hands over his head.

"There's no need, Rennan. Carter will no longer be a nuisance to us," I began.

Cam kicked my foot from under the table. I assumed it was for my choice of the word *nuisance*. Okay, I know that Carter was a touchy subject, but it was true. He *was* a nuisance in far more ways than one.

"What happened?" Valerie asked in shock.

"Let me start at the beginning. We left and flew all day, most of which I apparently slept through, and this one"—I jabbed a thumb at Cam—"didn't see the point in waking me until we reached Trehi early this morning. From there, Cam led me through the city to their cemetery where we found his and his mother's headstones," I explained.

Cam lifted his head up long enough to add, "Yeah, we found them and then I blasted mine to smithereens."

"Yes, he destroyed his headstone," I repeated. "After that, we headed straight for the castle so we could try to sneak in. However, Cam wasn't too keen on the sneaking part, so we just strolled directly in, took down the patrols, and were met by none other than Carter Woods."

I paused when I got to the part about the twins' fight. "Ugh, Cam, I can't really explain what happened from there."

Cam slowly peeled himself off the table and leaned back in his chair. He was miserable—all of us could see that plainly.

"He wasn't the person I remembered." Cam's voice cracked. "He was cruel, heartless, and vicious. We…we fought. It was fierce. I offered him mercy as his brother, but Carter refused to accept it. After that, he stirred up my wrath to start the battle all over again. Eventually, I struck him down."

"You slapped him?" Valerie questioned innocently.

"I wish, but no. He was sliced by Vorngurth—my scythe that just so happens to be cursed," Cam said forlornly. "The curse took his life. He rapidly decayed and died without repenting; Carter was true to his wicked ways until his last breath. I am so devastated it happened. I really, *really* am."

"So, he's dead then," Drew clarified.

Cam nodded his head. Both of them fell silent. I don't know if it was some mutual understanding between them, but it was definitely something that neither one of them wanted to share.

The doors were pushed open to reveal Kalila standing in the doorway. She carried trays of food that she laid on the table in front of us. She didn't say anything, but as she was leaving, she laid a hand on Cam's armored shoulder. He patted it and then she walked out of the room.

All the while, Rennan was watching Kalila suspiciously. He looked from her to Cam to me and then back to her.

"Cameron…who was that?" Rennan asked when the elvish girl was gone.

Cam shrugged nonchalantly as he picked up an apple from the basket. "Just a friend from when I was younger."

"Uh huh," Renan said, not quite knowing what to think having met one of Cam's old friends.

He looked at me questioningly, and I just shrugged to let him know that Kalila wasn't getting between Cam and I. It was both touching and amusing about how protective he was of me. His concern made me glad that I now had him as an adoptive brother. Rennan relaxed and started eating the fly-less soup that had been brought up to us.

A few minutes later, Rennan asked, "So what happened after your battle with Carter?"

"Eh, we released the hybrids my father was holding captive," Cam said. "Then we found two of my childhood friends, Kalila included, and retook the castle. The Paleeans rallied and fought under my command. I turned all of my father's supporters into stone statues, and otherwise everything went fine."

Valerie, Rennan, and I all had sour expressions on our faces. After all, the three of us were hybrids, even though Valerie wasn't technically classified as one. I envied the merfolk for that. Regardless, the knowledge of hybrids being locked up for who knows how long made us all bitter and eager for revenge.

"He fails to mention that one of his father's supporters was his grandfather," I added when Cam didn't.

Cam once again kicked my foot from underneath the table.

Too bad, Cameron, I thought.

Everyone needed to know the details so they would know why Cam was so sensitive. It certainly didn't help his heart to know that he had been the one to cause two deaths in his own family in the same day, even if both of them were pretty evil men.

Out of the corner of my eye, I noticed Drew make eye contact with me and subtly nod his head. I suppose it was his way of saying that he had guessed Ladefindel's death was coming all along.

"Gosh, that sounds even more emotionally trying than our day yesterday," Rennan commented. "I feel for you, buddy. I hate being the one in charge and having to deal with something like that involving family members."

Cam was quick to change the subject. "So, what happened with you guys yesterday?"

Rennan opened his mouth to try to explain, but Drew clamped his hand over it. The wolf sent him a nasty look, which Drew ignored. Well, that or he really wasn't in touch with social cues.

"I will be the one to explain because Rennan can't explain anything without exaggeration or sound effects," Drew stated.

"That sounds like Rennan, all right," Cam snickered.

I rolled my eyes. "Or you! Minus the exaggeration. But you do make weird noises all the time!"

"I second that statement!" Valerie cried.

I held out my hand and she slapped it triumphantly.

Cam's lips twitched, but he didn't say anything. He just motioned for Drew to continue.

"So, we were just walking along, trying to head south like we were supposed to. The day hadn't been eventful as we were minding our own business. Eventually, we began hearing the sounds of horse hooves so we asked Thorne if it was him, but it wasn't. He was flying just above the ground," Drew explained quickly. "We picked up the pace, but were soon overtaken by a squadron of Hevian soldiers from the north, and among them was Tristan. He demanded to know if you were hiding nearby, Cam."

Cam looked downright scary. "What did you tell him?"

"Since I had a feeling that you were going to be successful in retaking the city, I told him that you had reclaimed your kingdom," Drew answered.

Cam relaxed slightly, but he was still far from placid. The placidity only veiled the murder lurking in Cam's eyes. I nudged his foot and received a strange look from the corner of his eyes before he turned back to Drew.

A smile tugged at the Drew's lips. "Let me tell you, it could have gotten ugly right there. He was—"

"Wait, I just realized: Carter told everyone here that Cam was dead. Why was Tristan asking for Cam if he thought his son was dead?" Rennan asked.

"My father is not stupid, Rennan. He's cruel and heartless, yes, but he's intelligent. Carter has never exactly been the most trustworthy person concerning important details either—the entire palace knew that," Cam explained pointedly. "My father also knows I'm a lot smarter than I let on. I always have a backup plan. He must have known that I could pull something like this—he just didn't know how or to what extent. He probably guessed that I would have to be around in some way if you guys were pressing on towards the capital. Though, for all he knows, I could be a ghost leading you from beyond the grave right now."

"Chasing ghosts is a bad idea," I decided absent-mindedly. "You find them and then they can kill you."

Cam snickered. "Precisely, Scarlet. So, my point is not to worry. My father will get what's coming to him. But what did he do when you said I was retaking the city?"

"Eh...he gave us a scroll," Rennan shrugged. "Basically, he's giving you three days to surrender the city and your status as heir or he's going to declare war. He is bent on ruling of Heviah and the world for the rest of eternity. Right now, he's conquered the Estalites and is ruling instead of their prince. Did you know that the Estalite prince is some dude named Bartholomew Pickle?"

Cam and I looked at each other and laughed, remembering Bartholomew's priceless expression when we tricked and locked him in the cell. Nobody else understood what we were laughing about, so we moved on.

"Annyywaaayy," Drew continued, "he gave us the scroll and then we immediately headed here. It defines the terms of surrender, but it also says that we could meet sooner and Tristan and Cam could compete in a fight to the death. I almost think war is a better option, but I know a hand-to-hand duel could accomplish more. The choice is up to you, Cam."

"Can I just say that I really hate being me right now?" Cam moaned as put his head on the table again. "So much for the idea of hoping people slip up and tell us what Tristan is planning. Instead, we just have to reclaim everything and face him in life or death battle in front of the whole city! How fun."

I patted his back and he made a noise, therefore proving Valerie's and my point. The mermaid sent me a smug expression.

“You don’t have to make the decision now. I know it’s a tough choice,” Rennan said again. “Like Scarlet said earlier—yes, I heard you say this—every single one of us is exhausted. Now that we’ve all eaten at least a little bit, I say we should try to sleep before anything important gets decided.”

“I love it when you act all smart,” Valerie dreamily remarked as she stared at Rennan.

The wolf smiled, but tried not to show it. He was really bad at covering up his pleasure.

“I’m in favor,” I agreed.

Somehow, we managed to pry Cam off the table and headed up to the fourth level of the palace. I was right after all. There *were* bedroom suites up there! Valerie, Rennan, and Drew each got their own rooms near to the room Cam had chosen for us. He opened the door to reveal a large, open area with two couches facing each other. The grey carpet softened the shining stone. Around the room, I saw four sets of doors.

“The doors on the left lead to a private tower that will take you to all levels of the palace. The one dead ahead leads to a balcony. The other two doors go to individual bedrooms. One is mine and the other is yours,” Cam explained. He rubbed his face to stay awake; he was trying hard to fight off exhaustion.

“Cam, surely you didn’t get this all set up this morning, right?” I asked.

I can’t imagine a room as spectacular as this could be set up in six hours or less with or without elvish skill.

Cam smiled slightly. “That’s the thing…I’ve always liked this room.

There wasn't any particular reason why. But when I met you, I knew I wanted it for us if we ended up together. And then when you came here with me, I thought it would be possible for that dream to become reality. But yeah, I just had the maids clean it up for us."

"That's...actually very sweet...."

"Yeah, that was one of the few good things about my exile. It gave me a chance to figure out what really matters to me. And I'm so glad that I did. I would have found you eventually, but I'm glad we shared this quest. It makes our relationship much deeper and more special to me," Cam said sleepily.

I dragged him over to the couches and we sat down. We were facing each other now. Cam just sat there as we processed everything, and within five minutes, he was fast asleep.

I smiled. He really needed the rest. I doubted that he had ever fully recovered after his most strenuous shape-shift coming out of Bulshkan. His lack of sleep didn't help anything, either. Cam needed to be at the top of his game if he chose to face his father in a fight to the death. If things started to look bad...Drew and Rennan would have to hold me back because I would fight Tristan myself to protect Cam.

"Can I see the scroll...?" Cam asked groggily. His eyes were barely open.

"You're supposed to be asleep," I gently chided him.

"But I'm awake," he argued.

He wasn't. He was still more than half asleep.

"No, Cam, go to sleep. You need the rest."

"Scarlet?"

"Yes?"

"Will you stay here until I wake up? Like in this room?"

"Yes, but why?"

"Because I'll feel safer knowing you're here and not out doing something I would do, like rushing into something dangerous."

I smiled. "I'll stay here, Cam. I'll wait for you to wake up."

I waited for him to respond, but he was already out cold—for sure, that time. I considered trying to get him to move to his bed, but decided against it as he was seemed comfortable here. After all, when was the last time either one of us had slept in a real, comfortable bed? Sala? It was so long ago that it might take some getting used to.

I moved to Cam's couch and leaned my head on his shoulder. He subconsciously reached for my hand and dragged it into his lap. After that, he didn't move at all and I didn't mind it one bit. After everything that had happened, we both needed this time together. I intended to make it last even if I was the only one awake to enjoy it.

Flight of the Silver Bird

Cam woke up a few hours later, still holding my hand in his.

Naturally, I wasn't able to stay awake the whole time I was sitting there with him, so I ended up falling asleep from exhaustion as well.

When I was aware of my surroundings, I discovered that I was completely pushing Cam into the arm of the couch. And I had been using his shoulder as a pillow, armor and all. How could he manage to sleep while wearing the armor? How had *I* managed to sleep on his armor?

"Hey, are you awake?" Cam whispered softly.

I slowly nodded my head as I let my eyes adjust to the dim light we had awoken to. It was now about dusk, which meant that Rennan would soon be making his rant about dinner if he hadn't already found it.

He wrapped an arm around me. "Good. Thank you for staying with me."

"Of course. Why exactly did you want me to, though?" I asked curiously. "You're so strong and independent. Why would you need someone to stay with you?"

Cam stood up to walk the length of the room. He seemed to be more at ease even though he kept rearranging books on the various shelves.

Cam smiled weakly. His face didn't look nearly as tired as it had earlier, but his eyes told me he was still running on fumes. "Even the strongest people have their days of feeling weak. This has been one of those days for me. Don't think that I took the deaths of my brother and grandfather lightly—I didn't. I feel like it's tearing me apart from the inside out. I hate that my father drove our family apart and I'm the one destroying any chance of rebuilding it."

He flopped onto the opposite couch. I remained where I was and stayed quiet. Cam reached his leg out and poked me with his toes. I looked up at him to see him staring at me expectantly.

"What? Do you want me to say something?" I asked.

"Well, lately you've been the wiser between the two of us. After all, didn't you tell me not to cause chaos, even if I did it anyway?"

"Well…uh…."

Cam sighed, stood up, and held his hand out to me. I took it with a questioning glance and asked him what he was doing, but he didn't say anything for a minute.

He nodded to a set of doors. "Here, come with me. It might help clear our minds after the chaos we've been through today. Being outside at night has always been a sort of therapy to me."

"We're going onto the balcony?" I asked with uncertainty as he opened the doors leading outside.

From the balcony, we had a magnificent view of the entire city. It stretched on for miles with all of its tall buildings. Yet, none of them rose nearly as high as us.

Cam nodded and strode forward to lean on the railing. Wind whipped his long hair back and forth over his face. His eyebrows were furrowed in thought and his eyes focused on something far away to the north. I assumed that he was trying to guess what his father might be doing.

Personally, I was trying to think about anything but the fact that Cam might face his father in a fight. Tristan was the only blood family Cam had left (as far as I knew) and if anything unexpected happened…? It could be detrimental to Cam's mental stability.

"What do you think I should do?" Cam asked quietly.

I looked at him. "Do about what, specifically? There are a lot of things that you need to do."

"Thanks for reminding me," Cam sighed. "But I was referring to the challenge my father sent. I'm sorry for flying off like that earlier, by the way. It was rash of me and I should have waited for you."

"You're forgiven, Cam. I understand you were angry at your father and wanted to get control of the situation," I replied. "As for the challenge from Tristan…I personally think you should face him in solo combat. Drew was right. We should try to avoid war as long as we can."

"I'm of the same mind, but I'm afraid my father will expect me to make that choice and plan some sort of trick. He's always thought I'm soft-hearted—that's why he took such great delight in exiling me," Cam scowled. He straightened and then leaned back against the railing. "Like I told Rennan earlier, my father is heartless, but not stupid. We just need a—what was that?"

Cam whipped around to look out at the city again. I couldn't see anything, but the elf obviously heard something.

"What is it?" I whispered.

"Intruder on the palace grounds," Cam answered, searching the ground for movement. "Can you shoot?"

I looked at him, thinking I heard him incorrectly. "What?"

"Can you shoot a bow?" he asked again.

"I've only tried a few times."

"Will you try again?"

"I guess…."

"Good. Go into the main room to the table where all my weapons are. Grab my bow and a few arrows and bring them out here," Cam instructed quickly. "And hurry."

I wanted to question why all his weapons were here, but I thought better of it since Cam always had his weapons with him. I found his bow and quiver of arrows on the table just like he said. I grabbed a few of them and rushed back outside.

"What did you want me to do with them?" I questioned.

"I need you to shoot down into the gardens," he answered, pointing down to flower beds in one of the terrace gardens.

I followed where his finger was pointing and saw some rustling in part of the bushes.

"But why do you want me to shoot? You're much more accurate than me."

Cam smiled mysteriously. "I'm having you shoot because you're going to send me down there. I'm going to shapeshift into something small and ride the arrow. Then I'll turn into my actual form or something and fight the guy…or something."

"That's a lot of 'or somethings' for you, Cameron. Are you sure this is going to work?" I asked with a raised eyebrow.

He scratched the back of his neck, but nodded. "Ninety-nine percent sure it will work."

I sighed, but nocked the arrow to the string while Cam shapeshifted into a spider. For the sake of my sanity, Spider Cam crawled up the side of the marble railing and onto the tip of the arrow. When he had stopped moving, I sucked in a nervous breath and slowly pulled the bowstring back. I released the arrow and it flew towards the target area. I missed the bushes by a few feet, but the arrow didn't land far away.

From where I stood on the balcony, I could see pale light and shadows surround the arrow as Cam appeared in its place seconds later. I heard a cry from the intruder as Cam dragged him out of the bushes.

I couldn't really see what happened, but soon a giant silver falcon was flying towards me with a person in its talons. The bird dropped the person and then landed. Cam soon stood in place of the falcon, looking pleased.

"That was a pretty good shot," Cam grinned as he pushed the now-unconscious intruder up to the wall. "Are you sure you're not good at this?"

"Heh, thanks," I said with a small laugh. "I think I'll leave the archery to you, though. I like my knives and even my axe better than a bow."

Cam laughed. "Fair enough! Now, can you stay here and make sure this guy doesn't wake up?"

"I can, but why?"

"I want to go get Drew and Rennan."

"No mermaid?"

"She's probably sleeping like a rock right now and it's pretty much impossible to wake her up before the sun rises."

"Okay then. Go get them while I wait here."

Cam saluted me and then ran inside the palace again.

I heard the heavy main doors open and close before everything became silent. I stood near the new prisoner, waiting for something to happen. If he moved, I was determined to knock him out again until my friends got back. I would not fail this simple task.

Cam, Drew, and Rennan came to the balcony about five minutes later. Cam now looked stressed, Rennan looked like he was half asleep, and

I couldn't decipher the expression on Drew's face. But as soon as the wolf and sorcerer saw the intruder, Drew became a statue and Rennan jolted awake. He pulled out a dagger from his boot and pressing it to the prisoner's throat.

"Who is that?" Drew demanded, giving the prisoner a death glare.

Cam shrugged his shoulders. Then he crouched down to pull the helmet off the intruder so we could see his face better.

He had tan skin and slicked back black hair that fell down to his shoulders. I had been wrong about this being an elf. I think he was either human or a wizard.

"I don't know who it is, but he isn't someone I've ever seen, even with all my travels during exile," Cam stated as he stood back up. He stared down at the strange man. "I don't like that he's wearing Estalite armor in my city on the day I reclaimed power. Suspicious, isn't it?"

"Very," Rennan and I replied in unison.

"I know who it is, and he should definitely not be here," Drew stated with an edge to his voice. He and this man evidently had some history, which I doubted ended well.

Cam threw his hands up in the air and grunted. "Then why were you asking me if I know who it is? You could have just told us and we could have avoided this entire outburst!"

"Well, I'm sorry for just making sure my eyes are not playing tricks on me," Drew shot back irritably.

Cam made a noise and then fell silent. Rennan urged the sorcerer to explain how he knew the prisoner. I crossed my arms and waited for the answer as well.

Drew sighed. "This is Ahmias. He's a wizard from Bor—Caso. Yep. Caso. He tried to steal a lot of my research to use for his own selfish projects. I know he's also plotted to get himself onto the council through dishonest means."

"He sounds like a delightful person," I said sarcastically.

Drew nodded his head bitterly.

"I would love to kill him now, but law states that a wizard cannot kill another wizard unless they're found guilty of stealing research," Drew glowered over Ahmias.

"But if he *did* steal your research, couldn't you kill him anyway?" Rennan inquired in confusion.

Drew cocked his head at the wolf. "There lies my problem. Such theft would have to be brought to the eyes of the council and they would have to deem it worthy of an execution."

Cam rolled his eyes. "Let me guess, they have no inkling of this whatsoever, so you're bound by the laws?"

Drew nodded his head. "The council is blind to dealings outside of their own. They care nothing for the people—only for themselves and the stupid laws they create to govern those they deem are beneath them."

Rennan laughed nervously. "Heh, after we get things settled with Heviah and Estal, maybe we can overthrow the members of the Mahean Council and put Drew in as front man."

"Yeah, that's not gonna happen," Drew stated coldly. "You'd be getting yourselves in way over your head. Let's try not to start another national uprising."

Cam nodded his head in agreement. Both of them missed the fact that

Rennan was trying to lighten the mood.

"We need to get through this war before we start another one. There's going to be a lot of rebuilding afterward, and none of it is going to happen overnight," the elf stated.

Rennan shrugged in defeat.

"Okay, you three got kind of off topic," I said, trying to bring the men back to what we were talking about in the first place. "We seem to have a spy from Tristan here. There's no evidence that he's not from there, right?"

"I don't know. The symbol on the piece of leather he's carrying isn't the same as Tristan's," Cam pointed out, gesturing towards the leather slip around Ahmias' wrist.

It had the mark of a sword and laurel wreath branded on it—the symbol of an Estalite noble. Cam had shown me the Hevian symbol of a great oak tree on the flags earlier, so I was becoming more familiar with the symbols of nobility. It also explained why he was always fond of oak trees.

Cam's expression was thoughtful. "Perhaps we should—"

Cam was cut off by several blasts of horns from the gates. The elf glanced in that direction before sending a look to Drew, who nodded his head. Cam gave the briefest of nods in return before shape-shifting into a falcon and flying off towards the sounds. Rennan and I turned to Drew, who was busy tying up Ahmias.

"What was that? What is Cam doing?" Rennan frantically questioned as he began helping the sorcerer move the now-secured prisoner.

Drew muttered something under his breath. "The city is being ambushed. Cam is going to find out what it is and he's supposed to come back when he gets his answer."

"This is Cam we're talking about. If he finds out and gets stirred up by it, he's going to engage," I pointed out as we ran through the halls and down to the main level. We needed to make it to the gates fast.

"I hate the fact that you're right, Scarlet," Rennan commented. He suddenly stopped in front of a supply closet on the third level and looked at it for a few seconds. "You know what? Let's leave this guy here and keep going. He's knocked out—what harm can he cause?"

"Both of your points are acknowledged," Drew stated as he spitefully shoved Ahmias into the closet. Then he barricaded it and used some kind of magic spell to secure it from the outside. There would be no escaping the closet, that's for sure. "We need to find Cam so we can prevent him from engaging enemy troops. Let's get out there and—"

"No need," a breathless Cam interrupted from behind us. He was leaning against the wall and clutching his left shoulder. "I'm here."

"What happened to you?" Rennan demanded when he realized that Cam was quite obviously in pain.

I stalked closer to Cam and pried his hand off his shoulder. It was stained bright red. I gasped and released my grip on his hand when I saw the blood-soaked cloth underneath. The faint smell of iron made me nauseous.

"You're injured!" I shouted. "What did you get yourself into?"

"Add to the tally. I almost died again. And I wasn't trying to do it intentionally!" the elf cried in defense. He kept pressure on his wound. "It was my father's fault. He and a small squad of soldiers are out there right now demanding combat with me. He knew I had shapeshifted and was waiting for me, so he shot my wing. I barely managed to make it back here."

"Okay, that's just great. The timeline is moving prematurely and now you have to fight him injured. Could this night get any worse?" Drew ranted, throwing his hands up into the air.

"It can. He has an army *and* mercenaries from almost every kingdom. But get this, they're all waiting for his orders to advance and attack the palace," Cam stated with a bitter smile bordering on a sneer.

Rennan sighed. "We need to do something now. There is no way we can possibly wait since we might be killed at any moment. So, that begs the question: what the heck are we going to do?"

"Uh, first things first, I need my arm bound so I can fight my father and buy us some time," Cam stated through gritted teeth. The pain was starting to get to his head. "Drew, since you know medical…things—for lack of a better term—you can help me with this stupid arrow wound."

"And us? What do you want me and Rennan to do?" I asked.

Cam just looked at me for a second.

"Get Valerie awake and start mustering the troops. I need you two to be ready as well. I want you to go with me when I face my father," Cam said as he bit his lower lip.

Rennan and I nodded and we parted ways. The elf and sorcerer went down to the first levels while Rennan and I headed up to the fourth again.

"Any idea how we're going to wake up the mermaid?" I asked as we approached the door to Valerie's suite.

"Sort of. I just need to drag her out of bed then put her in water," Rennan answered nonchalantly.

I rolled my eyes. "And where are you going to get enough water to accomplish that?"

"Heh, Cam is a master of magic, remember? Like in Sala, our suites turn into whatever we think of as home," Rennan smiled. "I've always thought of my parent's den as home, and Valerie always goes to the area in Sala's castle that is both land and water, but I doubt the magic has the same effect in your suite because it's Cameron. Am I right?"

I smiled slightly. "More or less. Let's just get Valerie so we can prepare the soldiers who are loyal to Cam."

We pushed open the door to enter a room that most definitely reminded me of Sala. There were blues and purples and coral everywhere, so it was quite easy to tell that this room belonged to a mermaid. A pool of water in one corner was opposite a large bed against the wall. As one would expect, Valerie was fast asleep.

After gingerly picking Valerie up, Rennan carried her towards the pool of water. All the while, that mermaid did not wake up or move in the slightest way. She remained completely and utterly still.

"How does she not wake up when you carry her? And why do you have to put her in water?" I asked curiously.

"It takes a lot to wake her up, as I discovered when we stayed in Sala. Valerie also mentioned to me once that she feels everything when she has her tail, which is why she prefers to be in her land form," Rennan explained with a casual shrug. "She should wake up any minute now."

Sure enough, Valerie started stirring as soon as her legs began transforming into her magnificent, sparkling tail. She yawned and panicked when she saw that she was in the water. She jumped out before her tail could completely form. Finally, she turned around to see me and Rennan.

I was just standing there normally, but Rennan just had to smile and wave. Valerie scowled slightly (for the first time in her entire life most likely) and crossed her arms.

"Rennan Clay Penbrooke. You better have a good reason for waking me up. You know what I told you about putting me in the water when I'm asleep," Valerie stated with a very pointed look at the wolf.

I'll admit I found it highly amusing, considering how smitten they were with each other.

"I'm sorry, but this is important. Tristan is literally right outside the gates of Trehi and demands that Cam faces him," Rennan replied as he wrapped an arm around Valerie's shoulders. He was lucky enough to receive an affectionate peck on the cheek. "Not to mention the fact that Cam is now injured going into this thing."

Valerie's gaze shot to me and I held up my hands. The mermaid started pacing. "How did he get himself injured this time? He didn't have a run in with a wild gryphon again, did he?"

"I'll ask about what that means later," I decided before clearing my throat so I could actually answer her question. "He was trying to figure out who had sent the spy that we captured while you were sleeping—you can ask Drew about it later—so he morphed into a falcon to scout out the city, but Tristan shot his wing. Drew is trying to bind it now. They sent us to come get you so we could gather the troops."

She pursed her lips. "Okay, but how can—"

"GUYS! CATCH HIM PLEASE!" Drew yelled from the hallway.

Seconds later, a small silver finch unsteadily flew into the room and crashed into me. It fell to the ground and was immediately surrounded by mist and shadows. Cam stood beside me seconds later, clutching his shoulder with a pained expression on his face. The elf angrily muttered to himself while clutching his arm.

Drew frowned at him disapprovingly. "I *told* you not to fly so far."

"Shut up. I had to get up here and I needed to test flying," Cam muttered crossly.

He sank into one of the chairs that were against the wall in the corner. I hated how the room's shadows accentuated how pale he was becoming.

Drew turned to us to explain. "I bound his arm. Then we were trying to see what he could shape-shift into without further injuring himself. As soon as he turned into a bird, he flew up here before I could stop him. Oh yeah, and he has something important to tell you."

Cam groaned loudly from what I guessed was both pain and irritation. "My father sent another message. He decided he wants to battle me using the traditional standards, which means women cannot be present. And that also means he can play dirty which is just great for the rest of us!"

"So...what does that mean?" I asked, eyes narrowing.

"It means that only Drew and Rennan can come with me," Cam replied bitterly.

Valerie and I immediately started protesting. We fell silent when Cam held up his hand.

"Look, I know this is not the preferred course of action, but it's the only one we're allowed to take," he said in a calm tone that betrayed his frustration. "I'll come up with something that you two can do to help while I ready the troops."

"Is there any sort of mission you can give us that might be useful to avoid or win the war if it comes?" Valerie asked. She was being logical, so Estal might have had a good effect on her. If she continued down that path, she would be a good queen one day. "I'm sure Scarlet would agree that we can't just sit around while you're out there risking your life."

"She speaks the truth," I affirmed.

I would lose my mind if we did nothing. Now that I couldn't even be at Cam's side as he faced his father, I had to do something helpful. I was not going to let my king and future husband be killed by his wicked father.

"I love how this keeps getting more and more hopeless," Cam sighed and ran his good hand through his hair. Then he clapped his hands together. "Okay, girls, there is one thing you can do. There's a group of mercenaries from each kingdom, although I don't think Sala is present in the ranks due to the merfolk being a fairly peaceful people. My point is: you should try to infiltrate the hybrids and see if you can get them to fight for our side."

"That's very risky, Cameron," I began. "But, I think Valerie and I could make it work. What do you think, mermaid?"

"We can do it," Valerie bravely agreed. "Where do you want us to go?"

She looked nervous, but I didn't blame her. It was highly likely for our mission to end in death.

"You're going on the ridge above the main valley. You two should go to the armory before you leave, though," Cam stated quickly. He stood up again and winced when he accidentally moved his arm too much. "I'll come with you so you know where you're going."

Cam said something I didn't catch to Drew and Rennan, and they nodded and rushed out of the room. We waited patiently for the elf, and he joined us a few seconds later. He offered me a weak smile as he stood by my side.

We walked in silence for a few minutes.

"Are you sure you want to do this?" I eventually whispered to him.

Valerie had already scampered ahead to explore the rooms. She would peek in, look around, rejoin us in the hallway, then repeat the process.

"There's no other way, Scarlet. Drew is trying to remember a spell that will help with my shoulder in the battle, but I'll have to act like I'm not injured. Beyond that, there's not much I can do," Cam answered sadly. "I have every assurance, however, that you and Valerie will be successful in your mission."

"Well, that would be great, but our success will mean nothing if you're not alive to celebrate with us," I commented with a meaningful glance in his direction.

"Valerie! Not that way! Left!" Cam shouted as the mermaid started going down the right hand passage way.

She giggled and went left as directed.

Cam turned back to me. "I know, and I'm really going to try to survive this. Listen, I'm having you take the ridge because it's still close to where I'll be battling my father, but it's not violating the stupid traditions."

"Why do I have a feeling you want me to watch for something else?"

"Because I am. If things start going south, Drew and Rennan are able to step in and help me. However, since this is my father we're talking about, things are going to get dirty and we might need more help. That's why I'm sending you with an enchanted crossbow."

"That's still risky. Are you sure this is the best way?"

“As sure as I can be,” he answered. “Down the stairs here, ladies.”

We followed him down the spiral staircase and found ourselves in a massive armory. There were all sorts of weapons surrounding us. Swords, spears, shields, bows, axes, and dozens of other things I didn’t know the names of glinted in the firelight of the large chamber. There were also rows upon rows of battle-ready armor in all different sizes just waiting to be used.

Out of the corner of my eye, I was able to see my friends’ reactions to all the weaponry. Valerie appeared to be somewhat uncomfortable whereas Cam couldn’t be more at home. I wondered how often he had been in here as a child. I was very impressed by the extravagant array of weaponry, but I guess it was fitting since Heviah was a huge kingdom with a pretty decent sized military.

“Okay, you guys should find everything you’ll need in here. There’s armor, weapons, a bunch of other things you might need…I’m forgetting their names right now because the throbbing is starting to get to my head and I think I’ll stop talking now,” Cam rambled on as he strode down random aisles of the armory.

He disappeared for a few seconds and then his head popped up a short while later. His eyes were glowing with excitement. “Hey! I found a morning star!”

“I thought the morning star was in the sky?” Valerie remarked as she followed me closely. She must not have wanted to get lost with sharp objects all around her. “Correct me if I’m wrong, but isn’t it more accurately called the ‘sun’ by you land dwellers? I’ve never paid enough attention to all your terminology of simple things.”

Cam snickered as he started swinging random daggers through the air. He extended his left shoulder too far and yelped in pain as the dagger clattered to the floor a few feet away. He sighed and wearily returned it to its shelf.

"No, you're right, Valerie. It is called the sun and it is not usually my friend. Gah, how am I going to survive a fight with my father if I can't even swing a sword...?" Cam continued muttering to himself as he walked around the armory.

Valerie and I shrugged and went to explore on our own for anything we'd need.

"Was he ever like this in Sala when he stayed with you?" I asked a couple minutes later. Curiosity had gotten the better of me. "Like super excited about weapons and stuff, I mean."

Valerie looked up from the dagger she was inspecting.

"Ha! He was worse. Cameron was always looking for a new weapon to test for us. I don't know if we ever saw those weapons again. Let's just say that merfolk are not the best blacksmiths and Cam had a lot to say about Kevay's craftsmanship," Valerie chuckled as she unbuckled the belt holding her small dagger. "I'm switching these out. Anyway, what you just saw him do is the reason we moved our armory underwater and forge using magic."

"Ha. That's probably wise. That also explains why he carries so many weapons with him on a daily basis," I commented as I switched out my blades. They were nowhere near the high quality as the ones stolen from me, but they were still better (and sharper) than the Estalite daggers I had been using.

"Scarlet!" Cam's voice shouted as he rounded the corner to find us.

He grinned with a pleased expression on his face. In his hands, he held an intricately decorated crossbow. I didn't see any bolts for it, but I assumed we would find some before we left on our mission.

"I found the crossbow that you're going to need," he said excitedly. "Bolts will appear magically when you're ready to use it. Are you ready to go?"

The entire time he was speaking, his right eye twitched. Valerie stifled laughter and I fought to keep a smile off my face.

I answered, "I'm pretty sure we are. And…is your eye okay? It keeps twitching."

Cam grinned like a madman. "*My arm is in major agony and is literally driving me crazy!* You would be astounded at what your mind comes up with to distract you from the pain. Now, let us go before my mind becomes any more chaotic."

"Whatever you say, Camrade," Valerie agreed as she made the universal gesture for crazy behind his back.

I wanted to point out that Cam wasn't nearly as crazy as she and Rennan were, but I decided it wasn't the best time to bring it up. She did have a point that Cam was being stranger than normal, though. It might have just been his way of distracting himself from the inevitable doom he was probably expecting.

We followed Cam back out to the main courtyard, Valerie was making little jokes the whole time. Drew and Rennan were waiting there for us. From what I could tell, they were trying to put the soldiers into formation, but to no avail due to a language barrier.

Cam muttered under his breath before running down the steps to take charge like he should have been doing in the first place. Soon, the elvish soldiers were in battle formation.

"Okay, people, are we all ready to go?" Rennan asked once we were all huddled together.

Valerie and I nodded our heads. I had the crossbow and my axe strapped to my back while Valerie had her small dagger. She insisted upon carrying one after the ordeal in Estal.

"Valerie and I are ready. What about you guys?" I asked.

Drew and Rennan both nodded their heads. Cam was more apprehensive.

"I forgot my armor, so I guess I need that," Cam shrugged.

"Where is it, Cameron?" Drew asked with a slightly arched eyebrow.

For some reason, Rennan started making faces behind the sorcerer's back. Drew apparently noticed and pushed Rennan backwards. They had their moments of being perfectly behaved, but more often than not I saw the guys being complete fools when circumstances allowed it.

"Uh...the room all five of us were in earlier...? Maybe?"

"I'll go find it for you," Drew offered. He started walking away, but then turned around towards us again. "And I will take these two with me."

He grabbed Valerie and Rennan's wrists and proceeded to pull them into the bushes. Drew was promptly kicked out of the bush, so he had no choice but to run into the palace to retrieve the armor like he was supposed to. Valerie and Rennan, however, noticeably remained in the bushes. Cam and I sighed.

"They are bizarre," I muttered.

"You have no idea," Cam agreed.

He reached up to rub his left shoulder.

"Are you sure you're going to be okay for this fight? You're not looking too good," I asked him gently, my voice full of concern.

Cam shifted his gaze to look at me.

"I'm going to be fine—I promise. As long as I have the power to fight and the will to live, nothing is going to kill my determination to win this war and be with you forever," Cam stated with utter confidence.

"Okay. Don't forget that you can rematerialize. Good luck out there, Camrade," I said with a wink.

Cam smirked slightly, and then kissed the top of my head. Valerie squealed from the bushes and then we heard Rennan silence her. Needless to say, there was a little bit of bickering coming from those two. Cam and I just shared an amused smile.

"Valerie and I should head out," I said quietly. My reluctance to leave was growing rapidly.

"Yeah, that would probably be a good thing to do. And don't worry, I'll remember that skill," Cam stated with a nod.

Valerie and I said good-bye to the boys and headed off. I was thankful Cam had given us a map because I doubt I would have known where to go.

Valerie burst into song. "Oo! You and Cam sitting in a tree, K-I-S-S-I-N—"

"I have a crossbow and an axe strapped to my back. Consider your next words very carefully," I warned.

Valerie just laughed. "I'm just saying you guys are adorable together!"

"Quiet and let's go. We've got a war to avoid."

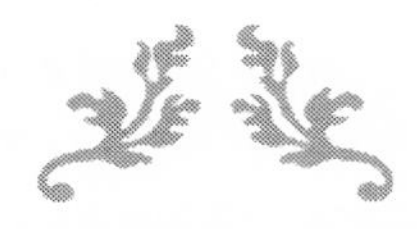

The Calm Before the Storm

"You know, the last time you and I were sent off to do something we ended up getting into a major fight," Valerie mused as we crept through tunnels under the city we had just discovered.

According to the map Cam had given us, there were tunnels all over Heviah. If we followed the map exactly how it directed, we would come out on the ridge right above the valley in a few hours.

"Yeah, it would be best if we didn't repeat that," I chuckled nervously. "There is no room for error at this point in time."

I could recollect our time in Caso far better than I cared to remember what with the incident between Valerie and I and Cam's near-death experience.

"You're right, and I don't think it will happen again. Not if I can help it," Valerie stated with a determined tone. "I've learned a lot since we first left Sala."

With our small amount of light from our tiny torch, I raised an eyebrow in the mermaid's direction. "Oh?"

"Yeah, like the fact that Carter is a jerk and I never should have trusted him, how to fight, that the world isn't as perfect as people want to believe, and that things can't always go my way," Valerie explained. "I've had a lot of time to think about my life so far, too. Goodness, I don't know how people survived around me."

"What? Because half the time you're singing?" I snickered.

"Hey! That was so not what I was going to say!" Valerie laughed as she, to my amusement, lightly slapped my arm. "I was going to say I don't know how you guys could stand me because I was so clueless. On a completely unrelated topic, have you ever met someone who is completely clueless about everything?"

I thought back to anything I could remember from my childhood in Palee. There were always rabbit hybrid cousins that I could never believe survived the massacres. I think their names were Fernando Fluff and Ferdinand Fuzz. Ferdinand was usually pretty nice, but Fernando was pure evil. He liked to hide in people's closets and then slowly cut their hair off as they slept. He was a really weird guy. As strange as they had been, they weren't the strangest people I knew in Palee.

"Uh, all I can think of was a squirrel hybrid family. Their name was Malzeit, which in and of itself was kind of a weird name. But their son—I forget his real name but we always called him 'Dinner' because he always talked about it—was absolutely crazy. He always said he wanted to go to Scottsdale, Tralia because he had a strange attachment to the name 'Scott,'" I recollected.

"You had an interesting childhood, didn't you?" Valerie asked with a slight snort.

Her tone was light, and I assumed she didn't mean anything by it, but I couldn't help but feel a little more deflated than before.

Valerie must have noticed because she seemed to shrink a little bit. "Oh, I'm sorry. I didn't mean to offend you or anything."

"No, it's not your fault," I sighed. "I just have a really hard time letting go of my grief."

"Can I try to help?" Valerie inquired quietly.

I looked at her and the light in her eyes was genuine. I nodded my head to give her my consent.

Valerie's lips hinted at a smile. "Try thinking about anything positive that has happened on this quest since you left Palee. I assume that's where it began for you."

I took a minute to think. "Uh, coming back in contact with Rennan, meeting Cam, and journeying outside of Palee, I guess."

"You make it difficult to see things in the full spectrum!" the mermaid cried in dismay.

"Okay, then what were you thinking?" I asked as we turned down a left-hand passageway. It was starting to feel like the tunnels were warming up, so I assumed we were getting closer to the surface.

"You've made friends and have kept those friendships alive even when times were hard. Rennan told me that he adopted you into his pack so you would have family even if it was by adoption," Valerie stated cheerfully. Then she grinned slyly. "And we are not going to forget that the elf is deeply in love with you!"

"Is that why you two were hiding in the bushes when you were supposed to go with Drew? You were watching us?"

"Eh, more or less, but that's not the point! The point is that lots of good things have happened to you since the beginning of last year. You've got to use the power of positive thinking! Cameron has every ability to defeat his father—and he is going to do it."

"I really hope you're right, Valerie," I stated somewhat hesitantly.

After that, we fell silent. There were some moments when we would strike up a short conversation, but for the most part, we stayed pretty quiet during our hike.

Eventually, I checked the map to make sure we were still going the right way, and I could see the final fork in the road that we needed to take up ahead. That would get us to the ridge. I was glad we hadn't gotten lost yet.

"Come on, we're supposed to take the right-hand tunnel." I told the mermaid.

"Okay!" Valerie chirped as we started trudging in an upwards direction.

We kept going until we felt the warmth of the sun's rays on our faces. It took our eyes a minute to adjust to the bright light. I hadn't realized how dark the tunnels had been. Then again, we had entered the tunnels just after sunrise, so there would have been plenty of time for the sun to heat up.

"So…what's the plan again?" she asked as soon as she was done with her happy sunshine dance.

"Best case, we find the hybrid mercenaries, convince them to be loyal to Cam because he's going to liberate Palee, and then quickly make it back to the gates where we're supposed to watch the fight," I answered, making sure Valerie was still with me. "Worst case, we do all that we can and get as close to Tristan and Cam as possible so we can hear everything."

"Good enough for me," the mermaid shrugged. "Let's go."

Soon we saw a massive gathering of soldiers outside of the city. Despite the huge size, Cam and his troops hadn't arrived yet.

They're trying to buy us some time, I realized.

When I thought about what could be delaying them, I wondered if Drew was working on spells for Cam's shoulder. I still couldn't believe that man had tried flying up four levels of the palace with an injured arm. Wing? I didn't know what to call it.

I'll say one thing: Tristan really knew how to organize an army.

Each group of mercenaries was divided into systematic battalions. From what I could tell, the hybrids were in the very back of the army while Tristan and his officials were at the very front.

That placement would make our task fairly easy because the chances of Tristan seeing us would be significantly lower. We would just have to evade the wizards, who were right in front of the hybrids.

"If I have any luck left on this quest, my cousins are going to be the ones leading the Paleean mercenaries," I whispered.

Valerie and I stealthily moved around behind a rock wall to try to get to where we needed to be.

"You have cousins?!" Valerie cried in amazement.

It was also much louder than I would have dared to speak. I glared at her with exasperation after making sure that nobody had heard us.

Valerie spoke again, this time much quieter. "Why didn't you tell us you have cousins?!"

"I'm pretty sure I mentioned them escaping Bulshkan when Cam shapeshifted into the massive dragon," I muttered, "you people just didn't ask me about it. Plus, there hasn't really been a moment to bring them up because reclaiming Trehi and the challenge from Tristan has taken up most of our time and focus."

"True," Valerie relented with a sigh. "So…are your cousins nice?"

"Yes, and hopefully we all survive so you can meet them sometime," I answered shortly. "Now be quiet. I don't want to give away our position."

Valerie nodded and we continued moving along the lines.

As we crept along, I was able to catch the occasional glimpse of the different groups of mercenaries. Giants from Tralia were in the front, likely protecting the soldiers behind them from projectiles. They were followed by what seemed like the entire Estalite army. Following the Estalites was a fairly large number of Salians, and another large army of elves still loyal to Tristan. The wizards fell in behind the elves and the hybrids in the back.

However, the dwarves and Kevayans were nowhere to be seen. Valerie guessed that her mother had decided not to get involved with this war so they stayed in their own territory. That was good in the sense that it meant that Tristan didn't have water reinforcements. However, since they weren't fighting, Cam also wouldn't have as many allies. With the dwarves and even the trolls unaccounted for, they could be fighting on either side and just didn't reveal their plans to anyone. As far as I knew, Cam hadn't mentioned anything about the Neshans fighting with us.

"It appears that we are vastly outnumbered," I commented quietly.

Valerie nodded her head in somber agreement.

"Let's hope Cam can defeat his father. I don't know how long his army could hold out against forces this vast," Valerie stated as she looked out across the plain.

The hundreds upon hundreds of battle-ready soldiers were overwhelming. Oh, and let's not forget that their leader seemed to wish for nothing more than his own son's death.

Tristan was a monster.

"I'm pretty sure he could hold out in the city for a few weeks, but I wouldn't be too hopeful for anything beyond that," I decided as I kept moving.

Valerie had no choice but to follow me as we drew nearer and nearer to the Paleean mercenaries. Then a thought struck me.

I turned to the mermaid. "I just thought of something."

She raised a curious eyebrow. "What is it?"

"If you try going with me into the Paleean ranks, they're going to realize you're not a Paleean. They're going to see the difference, not to mention smell it," I reminded her.

She made a face. "Are you saying I smell?"

I chuckled. "That is the same thing Cam said to Rennan when we first met each other. But no, most hybrids have sensitive noses, so they're going to be able to tell you're one of the merfolk."

"I suppose that's true," Valerie sighed. "But wouldn't that mean they could smell elf on you've been in the city and near Cam so much?"

"Ugh…there is that. I'll be lucky if I can get out without being discovered first. If I run into my cousins and they're in charge, it won't be a problem since they know me and Cam."

"They've met the Great Wall Jumper?!"

"Okay, you are going to have to tell me stories about Cam because he rarely tells me anything positive about his past. But yes, that's how I got out of my cell in Estal. Now can we please focus?!"

"Yes, yes, yes, we can focus now," the mermaid muttered with a slight scowl. The light in her eyes was still playful and inquisitive (as usual), but she hid it well. "I'll stay here and signal to you if I think anything dangerous is going to happen. Meanwhile, you go see if the hybrids will respond to you and answer to Cam as their king."

"That plan is solid enough for me," I agreed with a shrug.

I was five steps away when I remembered something else that needed to be established. "What will you do if you spot danger?"

"If I need you, I'll give you the signal."

"What signal?"

"I'll imitate the scream of a frightened little girl. In other words, Rennan if you sneak up on him."

I smirked slightly, imagining the wolf jumping sky high from being scared silly. "Okay then. Hopefully this works."

"Just remember the power of positive thinking!"

"Okay, I get it, Valerie," I said with a small smile.

With that, I looked for a chance to break my cover and join the ranks of the hybrid mercenaries. It took a few minutes to find the perfect moment, but eventually I saw an opportunity and took it. I fell into step behind the last line of Paleeans (a bunch of prowling cougar and panther hybrids) and slowly made my way to the front of the line. They didn't seem to care that a stray fighter broke their already-messy ranks.

I was overjoyed when I spotted Samantha and Serena a few yards away. However, my joy became dismay when I realized they were not in the chain of command. They seemed to be among the soldiers who were forced to march south to Trehi and help the tyrant king take over.

As a matter of fact, most of the hybrids (many of whom I recognized from Estal's coliseum fights) looked like they didn't want to be there whatsoever. Of course, there were probably a few who could think of nothing better than tasting elvish blood.

"Serena! Samantha!" I whispered as loudly as I dared.

Somehow, I managed to reach Sam's side. They both looked at me in shock.

"Scarlet! You're alive!" Serena cried with wide eyes.

I was amazed she didn't draw the attention of everyone around us. Her sister quickly quieted her and we resumed speaking in hushed tones, reaching an unspoken agreement to keep our conversation quiet. There was no need to alert the commanding officers to a hybrid who was not supposed to be here.

"For the time being. Did you hear what Tristan is doing?" I asked them quickly.

They shook their heads.

Sam answered, "We only know that Tristan is planning to attack the city his son rightfully reclaimed. Otherwise, we've been kept in the dark. With the death of King Hezakah and Tristan usurping the throne, Serena and I lost our commanding titles and are forced to fight as foot soldiers that are offered as sacrifices in battle with no second thought."

"Well, that's just great," I muttered. "From what I know since I left the capital, Tristan challenged Cameron to a fight to the death. The winner decides the fate of Trehi and the rest of the world. Not only that, but Cam has to go into the fight already injured because Tristan shot an arrow at him while he was in bird form."

"Ah, yes, that's right. Lord Cameron is a shape-shifter," Serena whispered as she remembered the skill Cam displayed in Estal. "Thank you for letting us know, Scarlet, but I'm afraid it was a big mistake for you to come out here."

"Indeed, it was," a sickeningly familiar voice agreed.

Sam and Serena inhaled and backed away from someone I couldn't yet see. Unfortunately, I didn't get to see him because a strong hand hit my face. The shock of it all knocked me backward and I gingerly reached up to my nose which was starting to gush blood. I fought to restrain my fighting instincts.

"You're…dead…," I choked out.

I was hit again and the crowd opened into a huge circle around me.

So much for not being caught.

"You all left me for dead, and that fool Mongwau didn't even try to help me!" the evil man shouted.

The rage cleared enough for me to see a well-built man with blond hair with a grey streak, indicating that he was a grey wolf. It could have been anyone, really, if I hadn't recognized the blinded eye with a scar over it. It was undoubtedly Wayne Penbrooke.

"Well, how were we supposed to care if you were dead when you were trying to kill us?!" I snapped back as I knocked Wayne backwards. "You never should have trusted Mongwau to care about anyone other than himself. Just like you should never trust Tristan to follow through with whatever he promised you!"

"You know nothing of King Tristan! He promised me power and wealth, swearing he would live up to his word. Good kings keep their word no matter what the cost!" Wayne argued.

He grunted, pulled out a dagger and began to swing at me. I growled and kicked the back of his knee. My own blood flew through the air as I spun and struck. Wayne yelled in agony as my sword collided with his thigh.

"Well, he's not a good king! Tristan hates hybrids, Wayne. He will kill you in the end regardless of what he said. He cannot be trusted to do anything except kill you. Right now, he seeks to kill his own son just to keep his power," I said as calmly as I could. "Do you really think he'll keep a hybrid like you or me alive when he is so determined to kill his own son?"

We were in a standstill now, both of us having weapons drawn and ready to fight more.

"Yes, because I will make sure that I keep breathing!" the wolf bellowed as he tackled and held me by my neck. "This is sort of what poisoned gas feels like. The victim feels like they're choking and everything around them starts fading away. I wouldn't have lived if my hatred for you, that stupid elfling, and my cousin hadn't been fueling me. I've been waiting for this moment for a long time, Scarlet Sutton."

Serena gasped and Sam shouted when Wayne's hand pushed down on my throat. I struggled against his grasp with no chance of getting myself out. Black started rimming the edges of my vision.

My heart sank as I heard Valerie's distant shriek.

Several groups of the mercenaries started an uproar that would only lead to trouble and Tristan ultimately finding out about everything we had been trying to do. I hoped it would at least buy Cam some time.

Valerie's shriek had thankfully surprised Wayne enough for him to release his grip on my throat. I sucked in a clear breath as Sam dragged me back from the mad wolf. She and Serena quickly made sure I was still had enough air in me to be able to survive what was still to come.

Two of the fairies soon dragged Valerie over to where we were standing. I had never seen anyone from Salia before, but I had always assumed they would be small, dainty creatures. I was so wrong. They were every bit as athletic and well-built as the elves except two feet shorter, leaner, and had much more defined and chiseled features.

The expression on Valerie's face was extremely apologetic as she met my eyes. It was like she was telling me she was sorry for getting captured, but I couldn't hold that against her because I was guilty of the same thing. We were stuck together in the storm beginning to set in around us. With any luck, we wouldn't be this war's first casualties.

"What is the meaning of this uproar?" a heavily accented voice shouted from somewhere in the crowd.

I registered with unfathomable horror who the accent sounded like.

I lowered my head when a tall man wearing a golden circlet stepped out from the crowd of hybrids surrounding us. His blue eyes glared ice into my very soul. Everything about this man was just cold and harsh from the definition in his face to the angular style in which his hair was cut. He was fearsome.

He declared with a menacing look on his face. "We are mere minutes from battle and you choose *now* to interrupt my preparations? You hybrids need to have a good excuse because I do not feel very forgiving today."

Wayne bowed deeply. His ears flattened against his skull. "Apologies, my lord Tristan. We were experiencing difficulties from these friends of your son the traitor. They tried to breach our troops."

Tristan jerked my chin up and grimly inspected me. "It's the one that fool cares for. Ah, and Coral's girl as well, I see. Cameron has weak allies who shy away from a fight. I will show him what true power and leadership looks like. Tie them up and bring them to the front of the procession. I want the hybrid to see the death of the only thing that has ever dreamed of stopping me."

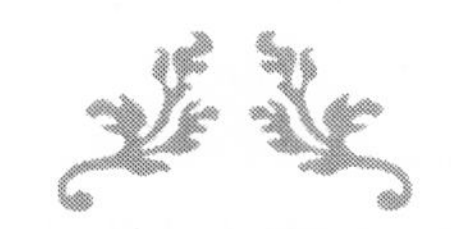

The Exile Returns

Tristan dragged Valerie and me to the front of his army.

Since we were forced to walk directly behind the evil elf, there was no chance to pull anything in an attempt to escape. Wayne followed behind us to personally see to it that we were completely disarmed. I wished our fight would continue just so I could punch that smug smirk off Wayne's face.

I was startled out of my thoughts when I heard Tristan speaking in front of us. My shift back into reality wouldn't have been so bad if I didn't still smell Wayne's blood on my hands, which fueled my anger and instincts. Tristan seemed to understand that and kept Wayne close just to get into my head.

"So. You're the one my son found in Palee. I seem to recall a mission almost twenty years ago where I killed two people, among others, who looked exactly like you," Tristan commented as he caught me in his emotionless gaze.

I merely exhaled in response. My brain refused to process what I had heard and the blood went cold in my veins. On the outside, I might have seemed cool and emotionless, but inside a fire blazed so brightly I thought it would manifest in reality.

He smirked slightly and it sickened me to see how much Cam's smirk resembled his father's. "What did he promise you? A liberated Palee? All you wild animals would run loose. That son of mine is a fool. I knew I should have killed him when I had the chance. I never should have listened to Laralind by letting him live."

"You killed my parents! How can *you* be such a fool? Do you not see how much chaos you have caused in your reign of terror? Because of you, so many families are broken! Your corruption ruined your sons' lives and took Carter's completely. Do they mean nothing to you?" I shot back. There was too much fury boiling under my skin for me to hold my tongue.

Part of me was glad I had learned the answer to who had killed my parents after all those years, but it made me hate Tristan even more. He didn't show even a shred of regret for what he had done to my people—to my *parents*. Because of him, so many children had to grow up as orphans. Palee suffered for centuries all because of one man's greed.

As for my comment about the twins, his face momentarily expressed a look of shock, but the tyrant's eyes narrowed threateningly seconds later.

I scowled. "Palee is in shambles because of the neglect we've been facing for centuries. Our species is dwindling and on the edge of extinction. We're still people who deserve to live."

"You resistance-fighters are all the same," the oppressor muttered under his breath. "You all speak of freedom, but do you know what that would mean? The downfall of Heviah and its allies, that's what. You would tear apart the systems holding this world together. Mark my words, my kingdom will not fall to my bird-brained son who has the help of a stupid girl."

I opened my mouth to speak again, but Valerie sent me a warning look.

Ignoring her, I continued. "But it's not your kingdom anymore. Cameron has control of the capital and the people are rallying to him, not you. Soon, your army will crumble, allowing the rightful king to come home."

Tristan laughed coldly. "Bold words coming from someone who's bound and forced to their knees, but I'll humor you. Suppose Cameron wins this war and I'm defeated. What will he do then? Kill me? He's never had the guts to do anything more dangerous than shoot a bow in the woods. His fear rules him. I'm surprised he survived exile given how timid he was growing up."

Fear is not his master, I thought to myself.

Cam had conquered the shadows and his fear along with them, so there was nothing standing in his way. He was far stronger than anyone could grasp. If he were to unleash his power—even the smallest fraction of it—we would all be facing unimaginable power.

Out loud, I said, "Cameron has become stronger than you will ever comprehend. Just wait and see."

The former dictator clicked his tongue. "Pray that I do not call your bluff, girl. But as for Cameron, I think it's high time for a little family reunion, don't you think? You'll get to watch as I destroy the only obstacle preventing me from obtaining eternal power."

In that moment, I saw how corrupt Tristan truly was. I doubted he even heard half of what he said anymore. Greed and thirst for power had blinded him to what life really was.

I could see what immortality—especially for an elf with royal blood and immense power—could do to their minds. They became so riddled with disease that it would be impossible for them to be healed. I just hoped Cam realized his father was beyond help before he let his love for his family (despite how evil they all were) distract him from the fight.

"Scarlet," Valerie whispered urgently, "Tristan is making us watch the fight while we're bound. The guys are going to see us and freak out. What are we going to do?"

"We need to stay calm and let Cam do his job. He has to win this fight so we can avoid the rest of a war," I whispered back. "We just have to hope he isn't derailed from his task by seeing me bound and that Rennan doesn't break by seeing you in captivity."

"Yeah, they need to stay focused," Valerie began, "and we need to get our weapons back."

"That is not going to happen," Wayne coldly informed us.

I rolled my eyes. I really hated that guy. I wished I were unbound so I could throttle him. It would have been better if he had died from the poison gas like Drew said he had. Then we would have been saved a lot of trouble. If Rennan found out…there's no telling what he would do. All these devastating changes were starting to make my head spin.

"If you two children are done chatting, I have a battle to win," Tristan interrupted as we were forced to march forward again.

I kept trying to snap the ropes tied around my wrists, but I found no success. Valerie wasn't having any better luck. We were bound and our only hope was for Drew to be able to free us or keep Cam level-headed.

Finally, we reached the front of the army where two more of Tristan's generals stood. I guess that made sense since Cam and I had only found Ladefindel in Trehi. It also made sense for Ladefindel, the father of Tristan's late wife, to be the one most trusted to remain in the city. Better to have people you don't trust closer so you can keep an eye on them. As a mercenary, I had learned that early on.

I'm pretty sure we had to wait about an hour until Cam's army poured out of the city gates. The elves loyal to Cam spread out across the valley, and I soon discovered that there was a larger army in Trehi than I had expected. Our chances of victory increased, but it would definitely be difficult to achieve.

Three horses rode out from the gates behind everyone else and the army parted to allow them through. As they approached, we could clearly see Rennan riding Thornebrook and Drew on a unicorn. They wore armor, but no helmets so we could see their faces.

Cam, meanwhile, rode a proud Angelica and was wearing kingly armor that shone silver to match his eyes. He wore a plumed helmet, but we could see his face. I'm not going to lie, my heart fluttered when I saw Cam approaching. Sadly, my dread of what was to come soon overshadowed that feeling.

Cam's eyes widened dramatically when he saw me and Valerie. Amazingly, he kept his composure as he faced his father. The rightful king dismounted and stalked closer to us.

I was both pleased and horrified to see that Cam had brought Vorngurth. Naturally, Egladel hung at his side, but the scythe concerned me greatly. I was afraid Cam would emotionally break for good if he struck his father. He had already lost Carter to the same thing and was still suffering from the emotional consequences.

"It was my understanding that we were doing this by ancient traditions," Cam commented coldly. His tone and expression were equally unwavering.

His face remained utterly emotionless as Tristan grinned smugly. I internally gagged. How Cam was even related to Tristan would be questioned by someone who didn't know them well.

"Ah, we were, but when I found them amongst my army, I had no choice but to bring them forward," Tristan stated with overdramatic gestures. "I expected you to devise a play like that, Cameron. You've always been soft enough to let women do your dirty work. Your aunt and mother were disgraceful enough, but bringing a hybrid into this was uncalled for."

Cam sucked in a breath and scowled. "Aunt Lealia *chose* to fight for the light that continues to fade from the world because of *your* poison. Mother realized her mistake later on, but she was still able to see through the darkness and do something before *you* killed her. Scarlet agreed to help because she believes that good is worth fighting for. They all know what should be in Heviah, a kingdom of elves and light, and it is not here so long as you are on the throne. That's why I've reclaimed it."

He paused before declaring, "I officially banish you."

Tristan laughed callously. "You? Banish me? You must be joking."

Cam frowned. "Am I? We both know your reign is officially over and have illegally been withholding the throne from me and even Carter when you all were under the assumption that I was dead. Did you even realize your other son was killed? Did you ever truly care for either of us?"

"Perhaps I did once, but no more. Your brother is dead, and you should have stayed dead," Tristan commented as he shook his head disdainfully. "It will cause you far less pain when I end your friends' lives. After that, I'll take yours anyway. I intend to make an example of you, Cameron Lester Woods."

"Then why don't you show your backbone and try?" Cam taunted. He cocked his head in a questioning manner and narrowed his eyes. His hand went to his wrist, where he always hid daggers.

Tristan bellowed and rushed at Cam while drawing his shining sword. And just like that, the fight began.

I tried to catch Rennan or Drew's gaze. Rennan was able to meet mine first. The wolf nudged the sorcerer and pointed to us. Drew's eyebrows furrowed when he saw the us bound and captive. The two men started whispering with each other about something (I hoped it was how to free us) while Cam fought like a demon out of the abyss.

As for Cam, he was throwing everything he had at his father. He moved so fast that Tristan didn't know what to expect. Cam's shoulder didn't even seem to bother him—they either used really strong spells or Cam was a good actor.

The only thing saving the tyrant king from several fatal blows was the large shield he carried bearing the Woods' oak tree crest. He did not deserve to bear that crest. Cam was more than worthy, but he instead chose to leave any identifying devices off his armor. He was a rogue warrior.

Tristan tried to throw Cam back using his shield and partially succeeded. Cam stumbled backwards, but was able to strike his father's ankles before hitting the ground. He rolled and was on his feet seconds later. Cam took up a defensive stance and waited for the next attack.

Honestly, I was slightly surprised Cam hadn't tried to use any of his shape-shifting or rematerializing gifts yet, but I was most surprised the shadows hadn't manifested themselves either. I could only guess that Cam was waiting to use any trick until the last possible second because they drained his energy.

Rennan appeared next to us.

"Are you guys okay?" he whispered as he began untying Valerie's bonds.

She grinned happily and kissed his cheek in affection and gratitude. Rennan slightly smiled as the bonds slipped off. He moved on to me.

"Yeah, we're fine, but we need our weapons," I answered. My cords snapped a few seconds later. I rubbed my wrists, glad to be able to move them freely again. "How are you over here right now and why are we not being attacked?"

"Yeah, what she said," Valerie echoed.

She clung closely to Rennan, and I'm sure he was content with that. Comfort was a rare thing on a battle field, especially one that would be as bloody as this one. There was no way things were going to go the way we wanted them to.

Rennan half-smiled. "You can thank Drew. He's currently putting a spell over everyone here and making an illusion of what they want to see. I don't know how that last part works, but I'm pretty sure everyone else thinks I'm still sitting on Thorne and not helping you guys escape."

"Drew never ceases to amaze me," I muttered under my breath.

That man always had something up his sleeve and always waited until the last second to explain what the heck he was planning. That is why I don't always trust sorcerers. They don't like telling you anything.

I turned to Rennan. "Come on, we need to get our weapons."

"That's probably a good idea," Rennan agreed.

We carefully made our way through the mercenaries that had gathered around to watch the battle between a father and his son.

"Um, Rennan? There's something you should probably know," Valerie said, stopping in her tracks.

Rennan stopped walking and turned to look at her. One of his eyebrows arched in curiosity and he motioned for her to continue.

She bit her lip. "There's somebody here that we thought was dead."

"Other than Cam?" Rennan clarified. "This better not be a poorly timed joke."

"Yes, other than Cam. And it's not a joke."

"Who is it then? Spit it out."

"Wayne."

"No, you're messing with me," Rennan denied what the mermaid had said. He put his hands over his ears and refused to open his eyes. "Drew told me he died. This can't be real. I'm dreaming, right? That guy cannot be alive after everything he helped create. If he hadn't fought me in Vareh, I wouldn't be here. Yeah, that's it. I'm dreaming."

Valerie gently pried Rennan's hands off his ears, and he slowly opened his eyes and looked down at Valerie. His nose was turning pink. Valerie gave him a stern gaze and he nodded. The wolf took a deep breath and planted his hand on his sword.

"Okay, I'm done freaking out. Wayne is here, so I just have to avoid him. We were going to get the weapons now, weren't we?"

I nodded. "Yes, Rennan, we were supposed to be getting the—"

A guttural cry echoed through the valley and I knew who it was immediately.

I turned to Rennan in panic. "Weapons. Bring them to me. I have to make sure he's not dead."

Rennan and Valerie nodded and then we ran off in separate directions. I pushed through the crowd, not caring if they caught me. I ran straight to Drew to find out what had happened.

When I was able to see the fight again, Cam was kneeling on the ground with his helmet knocked off. His temple and nose were gushing blood and his shoulder was quite obviously in pain now.

Tristan stood over his son grinning evilly. The former king didn't show any sign of significant injury. He just stood there, waiting to strike the final blow. Drew stood by, looking like he wished he could do something.

"What happened?!" I demanded with a hiss.

"Tristan pulled a dirty trick. That's what happened," Drew replied bitterly. He dismounted so he could speak to me without being overheard.

I watched as Tristan swung his sword towards Cam again. All Cam could do was lift Egladel to block the blow and quickly roll out of the way. Tristan scowled and tried swinging again. Cam rolled onto his back and blocked the swing, but then his grip on Egladel slipped. Tristan saw his chance and pushed his sword straight down.

From my angle, it looked like Tristan stabbed Cam in the chest clear through the armor. My fear was confirmed when I saw his mouth open wide in shock and anguish.

I screamed Cam's name, but he couldn't respond. I moved to run forward, but Drew held me back. I just kept yelling, but neither Cam nor Tristan paid any attention to me. Cam couldn't really do anything, so he basically was a limp form lying on the ground. Tristan, however, was gloating as he pulled his clean sword out of his son's chest.

Tristan bent over to stare Cam in the eye. He grinned wickedly. "Is this too scary for you, saucy boy?"

Cam closed his eyes and smiled.

Drew let me move closer so I could hear what they were saying.

When Cam opened his eyes again, flecks of purple shadow danced in them. "It's hilarious that you think you're scary. I've seen Scary, and you don't have his smile."

Tristan made a face, not understanding the meaning behind Cam's words.

Then Cam jumped up unexpectedly and knocked his father backwards. Tristan was caught off guard, so he flew a few yards. I'm pretty sure Cam had finally used the shadows to enhance his natural strength. He grabbed Vorngurth from the ground and sprinted over to us and briefly smiled when he saw me.

"That stab should have killed you!" I cried in disbelief as I followed Cam over to where Angelica was waiting for him. "And why didn't you kill Tristan when you had the chance?"

At that same moment, Rennan and Valerie ran over and mounted Thorne. The mermaid threw me my weapons and I quickly slung them all over my shoulders as Cam helped me mount the alicorn.

"You told me to remember I can rematerialize, so that's what I did when my father thought he had beaten me. I was going easy on him and making him think I was weak," Cam explained, wiping blood from his face. "I didn't kill him because he came way too close to killing *me*. I need to regroup before I attack him again. Now that I've officially started a war, you are not leaving my sight."

I stared at him with wide eyes the entire time. He exhaled softly as we galloped back to his troops. Warriors from Tristan's army blew their battle horns behind us.

"And how are you going to manage that?" I questioned. "There are thousands of soldiers here combined. Keeping track of *you* is going to be the difficult task. And I hope you have a plan, because your army is vastly outnumbered."

Cam laughed gleefully. "Scarlet Sutton! You should know by now that I always have a twofold plan. Never underestimate an elf who knows battle strategy. We just have to hold out long enough for them to get here. In the meantime, I'm going to take out as many elves and fey as I can so the rest have an easier time."

Angelica, Thorne, and Drew's unicorn (who I later discovered was called "Bothersome Beast" by the sorcerer himself) turned around so we could face our opponents. Cam took a deep breath and guided Angelica out in front of the troops. Cam and I rode back and forth in front of the troops to rally them.

"Men of Heviah! We face our greatest foes: the former King Tristan Woods and the elves who chose to follow him to their deaths. I know what you're all thinking," Cam shouted, eyeing the ranks. "We may be outnumbered for the present, but we are strong and brave. I know some of you have family and friends that joined the tyrant. We all do. After all, I'm fighting my own father. Offer them a chance at redemption, and if they do not wish to take it…then they have chosen their paths. If they are not willing, it is their choice.

"If any of you want to turn back now, this is your chance. There is no shame in turning back. I will understand your decision if that's what you choose to do. But to all of those who are willing to risk their lives in battle for the sake of freedom, prepare yourselves for the battle of the century. If any of us survive today, we will have made history. We will usher in a new age of light and hope. We will not let Tristan take that away from us! We will not let him punish us for fighting for what we believe! So, loyal hybrids and soldiers of Heviah, my friends who have chosen to stand by my side in the deciding hour, rally and fight!"

No one stepped back from the frontlines. Cam grimly nodded in gratitude to his army. In response, every single warrior bowed to their king. I had no doubt that these soldiers would prove themselves loyal to Cam. They would fight with him to the death.

Cam was a born leader—no throne or crown was needed.

We stood on the edges of battle, waiting for the cry of war. Cam sat on Angelica in the center of it all, waiting for the charge. I was seated directly behind him. Drew and his unicorn were to our left while Rennan, Valerie, and Thorne were on our right. We all had weapons drawn and ready for war.

"Guys, whatever happens out there, I want you all to know that it's been an honor to have known and loved you all as my closest friends," Cam said as he watched his father's army advance.

I leaned forward and caught the elf in a hug. He squeezed my hand to express his gratitude.

"So are we. It's been a long journey, but I think everything will work out in the end. Things will change for the better," Rennan said with a smile. "There's nobody else I would rather ride into war with. We're an unstoppable team."

"We are, and we're going to defeat this impossible enemy," Drew agreed with a determined edge to his voice. Far ahead, we saw Tristan's army gather and stop their advance. "This is it, guys. Are you ready?"

"Ready," Cam answered.

Giants sounded their horns and the front battalions of Tristan's army raced forward. They were sure nothing was going to stop them from slaughtering our entire army.

Cam motioned to start advancing. "Hevians! *CHARGE!*"

The Battle for Trehi

I'd love to say that both armies clashed with each other, killed few people, Tristan died, the war ended, and then we lived happily ever after.

Instead, the battle was the bloodiest I had ever seen. Warriors fought both on the ground and in the air. I initially thought the elves were no match for the fairies, but I was mistaken. If you so much as blew on a fairy's wing the wrong way, they wouldn't be able to fly properly for a few minutes.

Naturally, when Cam's troops discovered that, they used their flawless aim with their bows to shoot at the fairies and several fell and died from the impact. On the rare occasion that an arrow flew past a fairy, it would fall and strike one of the enemy soldiers below.

Having never been in an all-out battle with armies of elves fighting in it, I thought their ability to use common weaponry and magic was unprecedented. I was amazed to learn that their arrows would fly to wherever the archer willed them to go. I thought it was a good way to prevent killing one's own troops.

Cam and I rose into the air on Angelica. She fearlessly flew over all the other groups of mercenaries until she was directly over the giants.

Without warning, Cam handed me the reins and jumped off Angelica's back. The alicorn flipped upside down before I could yell at Cam. I screamed as I fell, and landed in a giant pile of something fuzzy. I opened my eyes to discover I was riding a massive, silver bird with a wobbly flight due to an injured wing.

"Why do you do this to me?!" I shouted as Cam flipped to make me freefall again.

Before I hit the ground, he caught me and slowly let me slide off. He immediately returned into his normal form.

I raised an eyebrow when I saw a mischievous smirk on his face. "Was that really necessary?"

"No, but it was fun," Cam replied with a shrug.

A group of enemy elves raced up behind us and Cam quickly drew his scythe. Just like cutting through wheat, Vorngurth sliced through the elves easily. In mere seconds all that was left was a pile of armor.

I stared at Cam with wide eyes.

He scowled. "Yeah, yeah. 'Be careful with where you swing that thing.' I got it."

I pursed my lips. "That's not what I was going to say."

I paused to kill the Estalites who had tried to sneak attack me. All four of them fell to my daggers slitting their throats.

Cam gave me an impressed smile as I spun my daggers and returned them to their sheaths. He gestured for me to continue.

"I was going to say don't do anything stupid. We are so close to coming through this alive, and I intend to hold you to your proposal," I stated with a pointed look at the elf.

He smiled broadly as he battered a couple boar hybrids.

"Don't worry. I'm going to live through this. I'm pretty confident about it now," Cam informed me with a very matter-of-fact expression as he raised a dagger, which just so happened to stab the wizard who was running up behind him. "Now, if you'll excuse me, I have a few giants to kill."

"You are not excused because I'm coming with you," I argued as I followed him through the battle.

He was planning something—the mischievous glint in his eye was unmistakable.

Cam laughed wildly. "Good luck! I'll be shape-shifting to confuse them. Whatever you do, don't kill any giants because it may or may not be me. Keep anything else away from them and please don't get stepped on."

"Okay then," I agreed.

Not having anything else to say for the time being, we battled on. Several times, we were forced to rely on each other's fighting techniques. Cam would often switch places with me to surprise the enemy and have an easier opponent. Soon we were fighting back to back and we were amazingly efficient that way. We made a good team.

Before I knew what was happening, a giant lumbered up to us and started swinging his club at Cam and yelling something completely unintelligible to my ears.

Cam scowled and swung Vorngurth at the giant's knees. I didn't think the curse would be as effective on a fifteen-foot-tall giant, but apparently it was just as deadly as on a normal sized person. The giant panicked as he watched his hands start decaying and fading away into dust.

Other giants noticed what happened to their friend and growled at Cam. The elf had been pretty confident in his quick kill, but now he began to realize his mistake when the other giants began to surround him. Almost immediately, shadows and pale light surrounded him. When it cleared, I noticed that Cam was once again in his dragon form.

Cam the Dragon flew around the heads of the giants and started breathing fire on everything. He landed only long enough for me to climb up on his back. Cam remained fairly steady while I stood up. I swiftly pulled out the magical crossbow and imagined where I wanted to shoot it. A bolt magically appeared on the flight groove. The first one fired and missed two feet to the right.

Cam's voice filled my head. *You have to be absolutely confident you can shoot and aim that thing. Now do it again until you kill the giants. I'm not changing back until you do.*

I sighed at his stubbornness and aimed the crossbow again. I was determined to make the shot. I released the trigger and a giant fell in the valley below, dead. I cheered, but I nearly lost my balance in doing so. I calmed myself down and kept shooting until all of the giants were dead.

When Cam was satisfied with what I had accomplished, he veered left to a "safer" place on the battlefield so he could change back to his elvish form. Once he was back, Cam trapped me in a hug. He let me go a minute later and grinned widely.

"That was amazing! You hit all the giants! I'll make an archer out of you yet," he beamed proudly.

I smiled. I was glad to know I was making a difference in the battle as well encouraging Cam.

Cam grabbed my hand and started pulling me back into battle. "Come on, we're not done yet. We still have to—"

Yet again, and almost unsurprisingly, Valerie's shrill scream cut through the clanging of swords and armor. The scream of a terrified little girl really *was* her signal. I couldn't tell exactly where the sound had come from with all the other noise, but I could tell that they needed our help.

Cam and I sent exchanged worried glances before fighting our way through the hordes of enemy elves. I mostly used my axe since it caused more damage. Since I doubted I would need it again, I broke down the crossbow so I'd have more mobility. Meanwhile, Cam fought with Vorngurth. He also used taunts and insults to draw the enemy closer to us.

I thought it was sort of counterproductive since we were trying to reach Valerie as quickly as we could, but I guess it was helpful in the greater scheme of things. Whenever Cam finished killing whatever it was that he had started fighting, we would continue wading our way through the battlefield until he picked another fight.

We soon got close enough to figure out why Valerie screamed this time. She was being held captive by two wizards: Dione and Krolor. Just like in Mahe, Krolor looked apologetic. However, the hate and fury in Dione's eyes were like a fire that would never be quenched.

Nearby, Rennan was in the middle of a very strenuous duel with Wayne. Both wolves fought ferociously, neither one being able to gain an advantage over the other. Rennan's skills had grown so much in our time in Estal that Wayne was having problems keeping up. Both of them had already been dealt strong blows that had drawn blood. Wayne had a deep gash in his arm and Rennan had blood trickling down his neck.

We didn't think the situation could be any worse, but then we saw Drew in direct combat with Tristan. Tristan was unable to land a hit on the sorcerer, largely due to the fact that Drew kept teleporting directly behind the tyrant (now that I think about it, teleporting had to be how Drew and the others had reached Trehi so fast).

Cam muttered under his breath and a fireball erupted around his father. He raced over to help Drew.

The first thing I did was sprint over to where Valerie was being held by Dione and Krolor. Valerie hadn't stopped struggling against their grips, but she was unable to shake herself free.

"Let her go!" I yelled at the wizards.

Dione sent me a venomous glare.

"Or what? You have *no* power to stop us!" she shouted back at me.

She met Krolor's eyes before letting go of Valerie's wrist. The sorceress drew her sword and charged at me. We exchanged a few swings, before I was finally able to crush her right wrist with my axe. I jumped back when she screamed in agony. She fell to her knees and tried to stop the bleeding.

She sent a withering glare to me. "You!"

"Face it, Dione," I stated firmly, "You're fighting for the wrong side. Tristan will give you nothing."

"You lie! He promised to make me head of foreign affairs so I could take my revenge on you hybrids after all this time! I will have it or I will die!" Dione shrieked.

She brought herself to her feet in an attempt to strike me, but then her whole body started convulsing. Slowly, her limbs became grey and chalky. Dione turned to stone before her sword could hit its mark.

Stunned, I walked around the statue to see Drew standing a few yards away. His arm was extended like he had just cast a spell.

"She had it coming," he announced with a nonchalant shrug before rejoining Cam in battle.

I rolled my eyes with a smile. Then I turned to face Krolor and Valerie. To my astonishment, Valerie was free. Krolor was apologizing to her as well, which confused me further.

"What just happened?" I questioned slowly.

My brain wouldn't comprehend what I was witnessing.

"You've broken the spell the witch cast on me," Krolor answered with a broad grin.

I just blankly stared at the blond man.

He laughed heartily. "Dione cast a spell that bound me to her and basically allowed me to learn nothing. I was like a toddler for centuries, so I'm indebted to you and Andrew for releasing me."

"That sounds miserable," Valerie remarked with a horrified look on her face.

Krolor nodded in agreement.

"Does that mean you're going to fight for Cam instead of Tristan?" I inquired. I kept a cautious hand on the haft my axe in case I received an undesirable answer. Surely Krolor could see that the better king was Cam.

"Indeed, I will. I didn't want to fight for Tristan in the first place. I will consider this service as part of my debt since you are pledged to the young king," Krolor responded with a wink.

I blushed and Valerie's mouth hung open.

"If you'll excuse me, I'm going to go fight for my king *and* queen. Your majesties." With a deep bow, Krolor ran off to join the battle.

Valerie and I remained standing there for a second in silence.

"When did that happen?!" she demanded with a giddy squeal.

"What?"

"You and Cam!! He said king *and* queen!! Why didn't you tell us?!"

"We were about to go into battle! When would we have had an unrushed chance to tell you? Cam and I have been way too distracted with making sure he could fight and everything that we didn't even think of it.

I'm sure you could have figured it out anyway."

"Yeah, but now you're official!"

"Do we have to talk about this right now? Rennan is halfway to the grave and he'll be there soon if we don't do anything," I pointed out, realizing that we should have been helping with the battle instead of talking.

Valerie inspected the battlefield. "I'll go help Rennan bring down Wayne while you help Cam and Drew. Judging by the fact that Drew is somehow in a pit, they could use it."

"Okay, divide and conquer. Works for me," I agreed as we ran off in separate directions.

I intended to sneak attack Tristan and land a blow from behind. Hopefully that would do something helpful, even if that would only be giving Cam and Drew a break.

I tried to keep my eye on the tyrant as I moved through the fighting warriors, but flashes of lights and magic kept getting in my way. Hopefully it was only Drew and Cam who were using the magic. It would be a thousand times harder to win if Tristan had any black magic of his own.

Right as I was about to jump and strike, a kneeling Cam caught my eyes and shook his head. I sent him a quizzical look, but he just shook his head again. Deciding to listen for once, I stayed put and watched Cam stand all the way up. Well, almost all the way. He was slightly hunched from what I guessed was an injury to his side.

"Father, you don't have to do this," Cam tried. "Just surrender and I'll find a way to spare your life."

Tristan cocked his head, but I couldn't see his face.

"What?! No!! Cam, you can't do that after everything he's done!" I shouted before I could control myself.

Drew, Cam, and Tristan all jerked their heads to stare at me.

My blood went cold. I covered my mouth when I realized with dread that I had just blown my chance at sneak attacking Tristan and destroyed whatever plan Cam had developed.

"Indeed not. He has neither the power nor the guts to actually kill me," Tristan taunted his son.

Cam's face became stone still and he didn't move a single muscle.

I, however, was the one who was filled with rage. I threw myself at Tristan and tried to punch his neck. Unfortunately, as my fist hit what should have been flesh, it smashed against ice-hardened rock. I screamed and fell backward, clutching my injured hand. It felt like nearly every bone was broken.

The only rational thought my mind came up with was that this was Tristan's power: he could turn himself into any substance he could think of

Tristan laughed wickedly.

"Scarlet!" Cam shouted as he rushed towards me.

The elf crouched down next to me and ran his hand over mine. He glared at his father before motioning to Drew, who joined us and started wrapping it using shreds of his blue cloak.

Cam stood up again and faced his father. He snarled, "You shouldn't have done that."

"And why not? I can do what I want. I'm the one who has the authority in this kingdom, not you," Tristan growled. "You're just a child—a very ignorant child who has no right to be here. You were exiled for treason."

"On a false charge! I spoke and still speak the truth! I will not be silenced by someone who is corrupted by Evil! He has ruined your mind beyond redemption. *I* have the authority as the rightful king of Heviah, and *you* are the one who needs to leave my kingdom!" Cam shouted.

Shadows started seeping into his features and slowly emerged from the ground like smoke from a chimney.

Cam ignored the shadows as he shouted, "Can you not see how many elves in Trehi alone are fighting against your stolen Estalite army? Are you so blind that you cannot see everyone wanting your tyranny to end? And it's not just Heviah! Every kingdom I've been to longs for the day when your reign ends."

"Then it's a shame that day will never come. I will always reign supreme," Tristan remarked coldly.

"But you don't understand that it will. That is why I'm here and you know that. You've known this day would come for years, yet you didn't allow yourself to think about it," Cam shot back. "Instead, you've let yourself become blind to the corruption in this kingdom and the rest of the world. Can you not even see what your greed and thirst for power has done to our family?"

"All I see happening is my power growing strong enough to defeat you now," Tristan seethed.

He lunged forward to strike again at Cam, but the younger elf deflected the blow with the shadows alone. Tristan watched in fear.

Cam looked furious. "You've become so blind! For years you have ruled with an iron fist. For years I even respected you and what you tried to teach me. But now I see how foolish I was to look up to a man who is cruel, heartless, and utterly unrepenting. I'm done with the games; I'm done with the pretenses. I honestly tried to give you the benefit of the doubt and tried to convince myself that you are the same man I once thought of as 'father.' Now, there is only one way."

"And what is that?" Tristan sneered, obviously trying to cover his cowardice with malice.

"*Amin delotha lle!*"

With that, Cameron let out a guttural cry and shadows exploded around him. They funneled up to the clouds before striking Tristan to the ground along with many, many other enemy soldiers. About a third of Tristan's army now survived. Tristan was down, but he wasn't dead.

The shadows around Cam disappeared, although their presence was still noticeable. They swirled around Cam's hands and turned his eyes a very purple grey.

All I could think of was the evil voice from my dream telling me that we would never succeed and that the world would burn in the flames of war. The flames were never explained, but Cam's shadows looked pretty flame-like to me. I couldn't let them destroy us. We weren't going to die.

"Cam, please don't do this! They don't control you!" I shouted helplessly.

Cam ignored me.

Drew was the one who spoke to me in a far gentler tone than I had ever heard him use.

"Scarlet, let him do it. This is part of his plan," he whispered in my ear.

I tried to listen, but physical and emotional pain made it difficult to pay attention. All I really heard was that Cam had a plan. It was enough for me to sit tight and wait to see the outcome. I used the last of the strength from my weary limbs to keep breathing steadily.

"Cameron! I demand that you stop this right now!" Tristan demanded, fear shaking his voice.

He tried to make himself seem tough, but now that everyone around us had seen his true colors, he couldn't fool us.

Cam just cocked his head.

"I gave you two chances to surrender and you refused. Now you have the nerve to tell *me* to back down?!" Cam seethed. He jerked his arms and shadows shot up out of the ground. They wrapped around Tristan's ankles and pulled him down. "Let me tell you something, Father: I will *not* stand down before you. *I* am rightfully king by law, and *you* have been forced out of power."

"You're a fool," Tristan spat as he struggled against the shadows that kept wrapping themselves tighter around his ankles and hands. The former king roared in agony.

Cam sighed and his eyes returned to their normal grey. The shadows holding Tristan melted back into the ground where they belonged. I would be thrilled if I never saw those demons again in my life.

"I knew you would say that, but somehow I still hoped you wouldn't," Cam stated sadly.

He turned his back on his father and walked back over to me. Cam helped me up to my feet and then we both faced Tristan, whose face was bright red with anger and shame.

"What are you doing?! You're supposed to be fighting me, not helping her!" he fumed. "Are you really going to just let me go? If you do, you will find yourself facing much worse than whatever just happened to you."

Cameron closed his eyes, took a deep breath and stalked up to his father. They stared each other dead in the eye.

"There is nothing that could ever prepare anyone for what's about to happen," Cam said vaguely.

Tristan rolled his eyes. "Blasted fool! Will you stop speaking in riddles?!"

"Sorry, Father, but that's the last thing you'll remember happening," Cam apologized with a greatly saddened expression. "Say hello to Carter and Mother for me."

Before anyone knew what was happening, a knife plunged through Tristan's chest, armor and all. He gasped as his eyes rolled back in his head. He crumpled onto the ground seconds later. Blood poured out of the wound and slid down his armor.

Cam just watched despondently. A single tear rolled down his cheek as he saw the life of his father and last family member fade into oblivion.

Valerie and Rennan approached us a minute later. Rennan saw Tristan's dead body and sighed in understanding. The wolf pulled the bloody dagger out of the dead elf's chest. He wiped it on the grass and returned it to Cam, who quickly sheathed it.

"Well, I think that confirms another name of our elf—Cameron Kingslayer," Rennan announced grimly.

"I can't believe I just did that," Cam whispered, staring at the ground.

Valerie and I both hugged him.

Though he didn't say anything, he gave us both the slightest squeeze.

He just stood there for a minute, then shook his head to break out of his trance. "Come on, our work here is still not done."

Rennan whistled for the horses.

Thorne and Angelica swooped down without a word. Drew's unicorn had been killed a while back in the first charge, so now he mounted Angelica with me behind him. Rennan and Valerie rode Thorne again and Cam shapeshifted into a winged form.

I gasped when I saw him because of how strange it was seeing my Cam in his normal form, but with massive grey wings. All of us took to the skies.

Cam flew down over the fighting armies. "Hevians! To me!"

"What's he doing?" Valerie shouted over the wind.

"He's rallying the troops for one last charge!" I shouted back.

All of Cam's soldiers amassed. We landed right in front of them again and waited for the enemy to gather themselves enough to even try to fight orderly. I would have just attacked them, but I think Cam wanted to give them one last shot at a fair fight. Now that Tristan and his generals were dead, there was nobody capable to lead them; they didn't have a clue what to do.

I turned around so I could see our army. In addition to the elves we had started with, there were hundreds of wizards, hybrids, and Estalites who were being led by Bartholomew Pickle, Krolor, and my cousins. Wayne was nowhere to be seen, so I assumed Valerie and Rennan had managed to finally kill him.

A horn sounded in the distance, but it wasn't from our foes. It was familiar, but wasn't Estalite or Hevian.

The unique horns from Kevay I had found incredibly annoying when I was there sounded amazing at that moment. Valerie cheered when she saw her mother's army on the horizon. All of her cheering got all of the soldiers behind us cheering and celebrating as well.

When they made it within a mile of the battle, the ground started shaking.

Cam grinned as the merfolk closed in. He raised his dagger to the sky and shouted commands in elvish.

The army divided into three parts which were led by Drew, Rennan, and Cam himself. Cam made the call and we rushed out again to surround Tristan's army. Between the loyal Hevians and the Kevayan forces, they were entirely surrounded.

That's when things started to look even brighter.

The ground began splintering beneath the feet of the other army, and panicked soldiers couldn't stop themselves from falling into the pits. Soon, there were only a manageable number of foes remaining. Many of them surrendered, but others jumped into the chasms to meet an untimely death.

Across the field, a short creature crawled out of the ground and bowed to Cam.

That's when I realized Cam's plan included having the merfolk and dwarves launch an attack as soon as Tristan had been killed, thus causing his army to surrender out of fear. It was a risky idea, but in the end it had worked.

Cam nodded to the dwarf in gratitude and it then disappeared back into the ground with its brethren.

Cam's army began to celebrate our victory. Valerie and Rennan ran to

Queen Coral to welcome her, my cousins celebrated with the elves who kept complementing them on their fighting skills, and Drew and Krolor were in deep conversation. Cam, nearly oblivious to everyone else, picked his way through the carnage, undoubtedly trying to find his father's corpse.

Everywhere he went, people reverently whispered the name "Kingslayer."

Knowing that Cam would have difficult time hearing that name, I jogged through the crowd and fell into stride next to him. It was pretty easy to find him since he was one of the tallest people in the crowd. Not to mention the crowd parted so he could pass by. He didn't say anything for the first few minutes I was beside him, but he did grab hold of my good hand, being my left.

"We won, Cam," I stated to break the silence. "You have your kingdom back. Aren't you glad? Now you just have a small rebuilding effort—"

"We," he interrupted. His face didn't give anything away.

I cocked my head at him and hoped his expression would tell me what he meant. "What do you mean?"

"*We* have a rebuilding effort. We both survived, remember so now you're mine forever," Cam grinned happily.

I couldn't help but smile back.

Then a thought occurred to me that made my smile falter.

"Elves live forever, but hybrids aren't immortal. Doesn't that mean I will still die eventually and you won't?" I questioned.

Cam thought about it for a second and then smirked. "Remember what I said about elves having a strange culture? Well, that applies to the immortality thing, too. Because I'm king, I'm able to take a mortal partner and make them immortal with me. Or I could become mortal with you, if that is your desire. It's up to you, because I don't really care either way. I'll still live long enough for my reign to end."

"Is it bad that I'd choose immortality? I mean, it would be hard to see our friends pass on when their times come, but I also want to be around to see the reigns of future generations and help them if possible," I suggested. "I don't want the world to face such sheer darkness because the cycle repeated."

I looked to Cam for a second opinion and he nodded.

"So. What are we doing?" I asked a couple minutes later.

"Finding my father's body. Just because he's an evil parent doesn't mean I can't give him a proper burial. I would have done the same for Carter, but you know what happened with him," Cam replied sadly. His hand became cold and heavy in mine as we searched. "Father's the only one I had left."

"You still have me," I half-smiled.

Cam opened his mouth to say something else, but it never came. He just stared at something that lay on the ground ahead of us. I followed his eyes and saw Tristan's dead body.

I squeezed his hand gently. "Cam...."

"It's all right, Scarlet," he said. "It really is. I'm going to fly back to the city and bury him. I'll be back soon."

"No, I'm coming with you," I stated firmly.

He didn't even try to argue with me. Instead, he nodded before shape-shifting into a dragon. If his injuries bothered him, he didn't do anything to show it during his shape-shift or otherwise. Besides, everyone was still so busy celebrating our victory to notice a giant silver dragon in the middle of the valley. Once the blue light and shadows had cleared, I climbed onto Cam the Dragon's back. He rose off the ground and picked up his father's armored corpse in his claws.

We flew to the city to the graveyard. With both of us working to dig a hole large enough, Tristan was soon buried next to Laralind. I didn't know if she would have wanted that, but Cam needed to see them in the same place one last time. Cam stood back and stared at his parents' graves.

Finally, he sighed and waved his hand, making three new headstones appear in seconds. Cam told me there was one for Laralind, Tristan, and Carter. There were no inscriptions other than their names and when they died.

"Well, that's that then," Cam said to himself.

He turned away with his hands in his pockets. I quickly caught up to him, hooked my arm through his, and leaned my head on his shoulder.

"Don't be sad, Cam. I know you would have loved to see your father and brother enter the light, but you always need to remember that this was their choice. You've made yours, and everything is working out according to plan," I reminded him.

He didn't say anything, but he nodded and pulled his hand out of his pocket so he could hold mine tightly.

"Thanks, Scarlet," he whispered. "I'm so glad I found you."

"So am I, Cam. So am I," I replied, standing up on my toes so I could kiss his cheek.

He turned to face me, grinning. "You missed."

"I did?"

I didn't get a verbal response, but he did respond by kissing me like he had never dared to do before. When he pulled away, I was breathless.

Cam obviously guessed what I was thinking, because he laughed and held me close. He shapeshifted to have the large grey wings again. Then he picked me up and flew to the very top of the palace.

"Look at all this, Scarlet," he breathed as his gaze swept across Trehi and the valleys, mountains, and forest surrounding it. "We're ushering in a new age with the beginning of our reign, and I'd say the future looks pretty bright. We've overcome all odds to reach this moment, and there is no one else I'd rather share it with. Oh, speaking of that, I wanted to give you something."

Cam pulled something out of his pocket and took my left hand. He slipped his signet ring onto my finger.

I stared at him. "What is this for? It's your ring!"

Cam just smiled. "I've secured my place on the throne. This ring secures yours. Of course, no one would dare argue with me because now I have influence over every single kingdom—not that I could care too much. I have you and what is rightfully mine. There's no need for conquest."

"Good, because we have other things that need to be done first," I chuckled. "We need to reestablish peace treaties and liberate Palee. I'm going to start a document for it tomorrow."

"We can worry about that later," Cam interrupted.

He used his wing to move me closer to him and wrapped an arm around my shoulder.

"For now, I want to enjoy this glorious moment with you," he said sweetly. He hugged me close.

"That's completely fine by me," I chuckled, hooking my arm in his.

There was no place I'd rather be than with Cam in that magnificent, triumphant, magical moment.

"I love you, Scarlet."

"I love you, too, Cam."

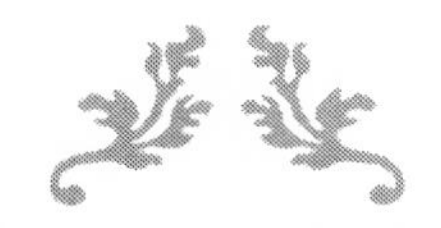

The Coming of the King

I was sitting in my chamber a few days after the battle doing nothing except procrastinating. Why was I procrastinating? Well, it's because I still needed to get ready for my wedding but was still shocked it was actually happening.

Cam and I had decided to put together a wedding a few days after the battle for several reasons. The first was to dispel any social unrest between the eight kingdom's and their rulers; another reason was because representatives of all kingdoms were already present because of the battle. However, Cam's favorite reason was because he wanted to begin the golden age of Heviah with me as his wife.

Cam is exceptionally endearing. He had been willing to pull a few more late nights even though he was more than deserving of sleep in order to get all of our wedding plans completed. For the most part, he let me plan the details and then he took care of them. Of course, he had a few things of his own that he absolutely wanted to add (like the ceremony being at sunset) but I didn't mind being willing to do that. Cam deserved his say as much as I did.

I looked around my large room in our suite.

It was easily larger than my entire den back in Leshee, which would definitely take some time to get used to. I mean, it even had its own small pond and bench! The whole room had a magical aesthetic of a garden on a spring morning. The small flowers that grew in the center of the pond were a beautiful red—my favorite color.

I had mentioned that in passing to Cam once, like way back in Sala, and he seemed to have remembered it—after all, a lot of my bedding and decorations were a calming crimson. I actually liked the room a lot more than I thought I was going to when I first saw it.

A knock on my door echoed through the room.

"Come in!" I called. I tried to put a smile on my face, but that proved difficult because I become more nervous as time passed.

Kalila peeked her head through the doorway.

"Hello," she said, walking in with a basket overflowing with shiny fabric. "Some of the ladies-in-waiting wanted to send this to you."

I looked at the basket, puzzled. "What is it?"

"Wedding dresses that have been used for royal weddings in the past," Kalila shrugged. "They thought it would be another layer of symbolism that your wedding provides to the kingdom. Well, besides everything you and Cam have accomplished."

I heard a slight hitch in her voice. I stared at her, but she didn't look at me.

"Kalila, you aren't jealous, are you?"

She looked slightly taken aback. "Jealous? No! I know I haven't exactly been the warmest to you since we met, but I can assure you it's not jealousy."

"Do you mind me asking what it is, then? I don't want there to be any animosity between us."

"No, I suppose you deserve to know," she sighed. "As I'm sure you're aware, many elves are still reeling from the fact that their exiled prince came back, defeated his tyrant father, and is taking a hybrid as his wife. To be honest, I fall into that category since I never thought Cam would come back—nor did I think he would have fallen in love with a fox hybrid. If you hear anything in my voice, it's because of that shock. All the stories we were ever told were about the foxes being absolute monsters."

I couldn't help but crack a small smile. "I can understand that. Hybrids have similar tales about the elves. However, despite my past line of work, I wouldn't want harm come to you or the rest of the kingdom."

"He was right," Kalila smiled to herself. "You really are a remarkable woman."

"Who said that?"

"Mayson. You have certainly left an impression on him. If you weren't in a relationship with Cam, he might have tried his luck," Kalila laughed. "However, he is fully aware of your standing with Cam and completely respects it. It's not every day that two mortal enemies fall in love and save the world."

"That's kind of an amusing way to say it," I chuckled. Then I let myself grow serious again. "Kalila, regardless of whatever prejudices our people might have given us, I extend my friendship to you."

I held out my hand (which was as good as new after Cam forced me to go to healers) to her. Instead of taking it, she hugged me. I awkwardly patted her back, which she laughed at. I'm still not good at hugs.

"I'd be happy to," she said with a grin. "It will be nice to have a friend who doesn't get easily distracted by weapons. Well, I'm sure you do, but not as much as Cam or Mayson might."

"True," I grinned. "Now, I should probably get ready. It's about an hour until sunset, and I need to have time to find the hall of kings again."

"I'll tell you what. After you get ready, I'll do your hair, and then take you down there. How does that sound?"

"Not going to lie, that sounds great," I smiled gratefully.

With that, Kalila nodded and left the room so I could choose a dress.

None of them caught my eye until I got to the very last one. It was a shining white form-fitting dress with finely glittered sleeves. It was lightweight and not too frilly, but it was a thousand times more elegant than the rest in the basket. I'm not usually a person who would die for dresses, but it was so pretty that I couldn't resist the desire to see it sparkle in the evening sun.

When I called Kalila back in, she was utterly speechless.

Eventually, she said, "You look absolutely stunning."

I smiled slightly. "Thank you. I really liked this one."

"I can understand why. Cam is going to cry when he sees you."

"Why?" I asked with mild concern. "I haven't done anything wrong, have I?"

I knew he was going to cry, but I didn't want it to be because I was wearing a sparkly dress.

"Don't worry—you haven't. But I'll let him be the one to tell you," she responded. "I'll do your hair now, if you'd like."

So she did, but my mind didn't wander far from her comment about Cam. I worried what Kalila's exact intent was, but I had to remind myself that everything was going to be fine. I wasn't going to let any nerves get in the way for my excitement. In the long run, the end results were going to be worth more than my worry.

When Kalila finished putting my hair in an elegant braid that fell to my waist and adorning it with gemstones, she let me add finishing touches of my jewelry before taking me to the throne room.

Along the way, she explained that the palace had been adapted and added to with every king Heviah had had. However, one of the few places that stayed the same throughout the reigns of multiple kings was their throne room. There had been additions made to it, sure, but the basic integrity still remained.

Kalila led me to one of the side rooms where I'd wait until it was time for the ceremony to begin. Then she left to go take her spot with Mayson in the audience, leaving me alone.

That is, until the door burst open and a finely dressed Rennan came in. He stopped dead in his tracks when he saw me. Then he grinned so wide I thought he was going to pull a muscle in his face.

"Who are you and what have you done with Scarlet?!" he cried through his laughter.

Though I knew Rennan was capable of all types of randomness at any point in time, I somehow didn't expect him to say that.

"Rennan, I hope you know you are ridiculous," I laughed. I stood up from my chair and walked over to give him a hug.

He eagerly returned it. "Oh, I know. Coral made that comment to me earlier when I gave Valerie a flower from under the table."

"Why were you under a table?"

"That's none of your concern," Rennan said with a devious look in his eyes. "The only thing you should be worrying about right now is that you don't faint when you see our Camrade."

"And why would that be?"

"Because the guy seriously knows how to dress to impress."

"He *is* an elf of high lineage."

"Yes, but he is a special elf of high lineage," Rennan declared matter-of-factly. Then his exterior of goofiness faded into a softer excitement. "I'm happy for you two. Even though you hated him at first and he rarely trusts anyone, you guys found joy after all your struggles. You are meant for each other. "

I blushed. "Thank you, Rennan."

"Of course," he smiled broadly.

Then the door opened again, revealing Drew and Valerie. Both were dressed in shining clothes that would only be fitting in an occasion such as today's. Valerie's pink layered skirt flowed around her as she danced around the room. Her excitement was practically through the roof.

Even Drew seemed excited. He'd been distant in the last few days for reasons he didn't disclose, but it was touching to see him care enough to dress in a sparkly tunic for my wedding. Still, he insisted on wearing the cloak he always sported. I did notice that he got a new shining amethyst pin for it, though.

"I'm so excited!!!" Valerie shouted as she bear-hugged me.

"Er, I can see that, Valerie," I chuckled as I patted her shoulder.

She released me and latched on to Rennan's hand. "I'm heading into the hall, Rennan. I'll save you a spot."

The wolf smiled and said, "That sounds good to me. I'll see you in a few."

Valerie skipped out of the room, but Drew remained.

"Don't be nervous, Scarlet," Drew said quietly. "Everything is going to go smoothly tonight."

"I know you're right. I just can't help but worry otherwise," I admitted sheepishly.

Drew nodded. "I understand that. But Cameron is in this with you. Nothing matters more than how you treasure each other. Other people's opinions don't matter so much as long as you are content with that."

"Sometimes I really wonder how you're so good with advice," I laughed. "Regardless, thank you, Drew. Your support means a lot to us."

The sorcerer inclined his head and left the room.

When he was gone, Rennan looked to me. "Well, are you ready?"

"Ready as I'll ever be," I answered.

As we walked out of the room, I picked up the bouquet of magnolias that had been left for me. My heart rose in my chest when we stepped in front of the massive doors to the Hall of Kings.

I exhaled. "I can't believe I'm doing this."

"You won't regret it," Rennan reminded me in a gentle tone.

"I know I won't. Thank you for being here, Rennan."

"Of course. You're a sister to me. Any good brother would do this."

I smiled again.

Paleeans, like many other races, have wedding traditions where the father walks the bride to the dais or wherever the ceremony was being held.

Since I lost my father years ago, Rennan had offered to fill the position for me. I was so touched that he would make an offer like that that I cried. Even Cam had told me later on that he thought it was an absolutely kind and thoughtful action from Rennan.

So there we were.

The guards opened up the massive doors to see hundreds of people packed into the Hall. People from every kingdom were present—no one wanted to miss history in the making apparently. They all watched with eager eyes, most of which widened when they saw me.

I ignored all the gawking eyes and tried to focus on the dais ahead.

Before I could focus on the dais, however, my attention was captured by the soaring architecture of the room. Massive columns held up a high, vaulted ceiling. Nearly all the outer walls of the room were made of glass that allowed for a city-wide view. The windows behind the dais were a stained-glass image meant to display the power of the Woods clan.

However, what was even more stunning than the class were the intricately carved, gigantic statues of what I assumed to be previous kings. My heart nearly stopped when I saw the one of Tristan because it was so regal. However, it was also nothing like the man I had met. The statue was cold and condescending—most definitely in Tristan's character—but it also had an air of wisdom that I had failed to see in the tyrant king.

But the best sight in the whole room was below the tree-shaped thrones.

My Cam stood there with a proud smile on his face as he watched me come nearer. He was dressed in shining pale fabrics that glittered just as much as his eyes on a sunny day. They fell around him in gloriously rich folds, portraying him as the king he truly was.

But what I was thrilled to see was his smile. He was genuinely happy. I felt that the light from his smile alone could light the whole city on the darkest night. My heart turned backflips because his joy was so evident.

Rennan squeezed my hand and kissed the top of my head when we reached the steps to the thrones. I smiled at him gratefully before he went to stand with Valerie and Queen Coral in the front row.

Then I turned my attention to Cam, who had tears welling in his eyes.

"You're crying," I whispered with a small smile. I laughed to myself about how right Kalila had been. "Why?"

"Can't a man cry when he sees his beautiful wife-to-be?" He laughed quietly. "That's also the dress my mother wore on her wedding day and in her tapestry. I'm astounded you chose it even though you had no idea who it belonged to. You're absolutely exquisite, Scarlet."

"It was shiny."

He smiled. "I know. I always liked that element of it. Now, it's time."

Cam held out his hand to me, and I took it. Together we walked closer to where one of Heviah's ministers, Xavier Ralk, stood waiting for us. When Cam nodded his head, the minister began the ceremony.

I was kind of surprised to discover that the wedding ceremony was short, but Cam explained that it was abbreviated because he'd made changes because not everything was applicable to our circumstances. He wanted to make sure the important aspects were hit.

"My lord and lady, the rings?" the minister asked.

I reached into the belt pocket that I was wearing (it was an already sewn-in part of the dress) and pulled out a silver ring with an orange stone set in it. The orange was actually a chip off the stone I had brought with me all the way from Palee (Bartholomew had returned it). Mayson had helped me make the ring a surprise for Cam.

Meanwhile, Cam rummaged around in his pocket for an uncomfortably long amount of time.

"Did you lose it?" I whispered with dread.

"No. Here it is," he replied. He held out the ring he was giving me—a smaller, daintier version of his signet ring.

There was a collective sigh around the room.

At Xavier's command, we exchanged rings. Then, when the cheering and clapping quieted down, the minister continued.

"Congratulations, Lord Cameron and Lady Scarlet," Xavier stated. "Are you ready for your coronation?"

"I've been waiting my whole life," Cam answered solemnly.

Xavier nodded and addressed the audience. "Citizens of Heviah and the rest of Galerah, you have gathered here today on the heels of a change of power. With the fall of King Tristan Woods, we have his eldest son, Cameron, to take his place. Today, he ascends to the throne of the king with his wife at his side. Together, they have faced trials to see light return to the world."

After the crowd's explosive cheering, he nodded to Cam, who faced the people.

"My friends, it is an honor to stand before you today with my banishment lifted and the light spreading. To see joy and goodness spread through all lands has been a lifelong dream of mine, and it is empowering to see it come true. Scarlet and I have journeyed through fire and suffering to serve you, which we will do wholeheartedly until it's time for the crown to pass to another. Our reign is not to glorify ourselves, but to serve others and see a change in the world. I, Cameron Woods, make this vow to you."

The entire crowd clapped ecstatically, which brought a smile to Cam's face.

Following their cheers, the crowns were brought to the dais. They were platinum masterpieces, inlaid with silver accents and gemstones with some as dark as night and others as bright as blood. In the fading light of day, the rays cast glittering reflections all around the room.

Cam and I knelt down to be crowned. Xavier gingerly crowned me, whispering a blessing as he did so. Then he turned to Cam, whose robes covered the floor around him. Cam's face was somber as Xavier gently placed the crown on his head. With it, Cam inherited the weight of his ancestor's mistakes, but also the power to fix them.

I was very glad to have met him so many months ago. Though I had hated him at first, knowing Cam had taught me that love really can overcome hate. And not just romantic love, either (though I do love Cam dearly), but Rennan's brotherly love was just as strong. Because of them, the fox clans' conflicts with the elves and wolves were dissolved.

"Rise, my king and queen," Xavier announced.

We stood up and turned, glittering like stars. Cam and I looked at each other and smiled lovingly. He took my hand, kissed it, and we began ascending the steps. We faced the people once more, bowed, and took our seats on our thrones.

I glanced over at Cam, who was majestically seated. He truly was born to be a king.

All heads bowed, acknowledging my loyalty and perseverance to Cam's power and wisdom.

In the next few months, nearly everything was straightened out.

It was absolutely amazing. I never would have thought that such a corrupt world would see the light so soon after its plunge into darkness.

Mahe, Palee, Kevay, Estal, and Nesha had all accepted the new terms for peace readily. The giants of Tralia and the fey folk of Salia were a little bit more difficult to convince (the Salian monarchs didn't like Cam in the least and the giants were thickskulled), but we eventually reached a mutually beneficial resolution.

Since the treaty was signed, there had been more hybrids in Trehi and the rest of Heviah than I had ever seen anywhere in my life. They were so much happier now that they were free because we had all been cornered animals for centuries. It filled me with joy to see my kind liberated after our suffering and it felt so good to have been a part in bringing about a new livelihood for them.

Rennan and I often journeyed north to check on how the rebuilding process was going around Palee. From what we knew, the chiefs of the tribes had gotten together and decided to create a form of government that gave some power to the rest of the people. Valerie called it a "democracy." Naturally, Cam told her it was something that should belong in another world, but here we are. Palee had a "democracy."

Not only that, but the Penbrookes had officially adopted me into their family. Rennan was beyond happy and I was overjoyed to feel so welcomed by them. His parents, Roland and Rainie, were really nice people who liked me from the moment they met me and continued to like me even after we told them a lot about my past. As it turned out, Rennan had an older sister, Lilliana, and two younger brothers named James and Jackson. They were all exceptionally nice in comparison to Wayne and gladly welcomed me (and Cam) into their family.

Concerning Wayne, Rennan told me that he had managed to deal with his cousin in the battle. Rennan didn't say exactly how, but I got the impression that Wayne either died or fled into a self-imposed exile. All I knew for sure was that the rest of the Penbrooke clan was both pleased and grieved about Wayne. They were glad to be rid of his trouble, but were still saddened to lose a family member.

Speaking of Rennan and Valerie, though, they had returned to Sala. Rennan decided to move there to be close to Valerie. Cam and I weren't surprised when we learned we could call him "Prince Rennan" because of his upcoming marriage to Valerie. I was happy for them, of course, but I won't deny a part of me was mildly concerned to see what would happen when they were the ones ruling Kevay. Either way, I was excited for them.

Now that I've explained that much, I might as well explain all that's happened to everyone involved with our journey.

Bartholomew Pickle also had a story about reclaiming his throne. After the Estalites returned to their kingdom, they had reevaluated everything created by Hezakah. Master Pickle found the changes much better suited to his liking when all evil had been purged. When he wasn't locking me in a cell, he really wasn't a bad guy or neighbor.

Kalila and Mayson both were able to return to their lives in Heviah. It turned out they actually lived in a small town to the north of Trehi called Masha. They visited often because of their chosen fields of work. Kalila was an expert on weapons and machinery, so she to inspect the royal armory periodically. Mayson came far more frequently since was a blacksmith who always let Cam test the weapons. He claimed that if Cam thought it was a good weapon, it would work. Consequently, Cam helped in the forges when Mayson visited.

We had decided to appoint Krolor to the head position in Heviah's library as a thank-you for what he had done. In addition to that, he was also one of our personal advisors in international matters. He was exceptionally adept at his job considering he hadn't been able to truly use his skills in years. Krolor was eager to help us. The look in his eyes when we asked him was pure joy; he was so glad to be of service.

Serena and Samantha ended up becoming the chiefs of the fox clans since there were so few of us. They jokingly said they didn't think it was fair if I got to be a queen and a chief, but I honestly didn't care if they co-led our clan. They had also decided to set up their base in the newly rebuilt Leshee in my family's old den. I didn't mind once I had taken everything to Heviah (Shockingly, a lot of Sutton possessions survived the fallen star's fire since the majority of the den was located underground).

After they were situated there, we lost touch. I got the occasional letter saying they were alive and trying to find any other imprisoned hybrids around the world. I sent them aid whenever I could, but the help always came back to Trehi. Eventually, I stopped trying and decided they'd visit when they were ready.

As for Cam and I, we couldn't be happier. For my part, I was so honored to have a home and a loving husband after everything I had been through in my life. Cam was too happy to even bother describing how he felt. Rather, he hugged me every time he saw me and refused to let go.

I'm also very pleased to say that the shadows haven't been seen since the battle. Cam had locked them away just as tightly as I had locked up Vorngurth. I had seen to that scythe myself because I wanted to be the only one who knew where it was. Cam, of course, demanded to know where I had put it (the darkest place in the palace I could find and remember), but I refused to tell him unless it was an emergency. Still, I had a feeling he would find it regardless of whether or not I told him.

The only person I didn't know the whereabouts of was Drew. He had been present at all special events like the weddings, coronations, and peace treaties, but now he seemed to have completely vanished off the face of the earth.

Cam and I worried for him because he had a tendency to be unstable, but Cam assured me that Drew was strong enough to handle whatever happened to him.

The wizard prisoner we had captured just before the battle was also unaccounted for. Rennan and Drew had done a very thorough job of locking Ahmias in a closet, yes, but that evidently hadn't stopped the wizard. He had disappeared without a trace.

Cam, who knew nothing of the escape until several days after everything had calmed down, was irritated the prisoner had gotten away. He had sulked the entire day after he found out. Despite the frustration, we decided to let it go because it would do no good to dwell on something that could very well never be solved.

That was the last four or five months in a nutshell. Hundreds more little events happened every day like small rebel raids, demands of justice for wrongdoings in the towns, or random things Cameron did to amuse us. We had even been successful in stamping out the Serpent's Sons rebellion that had apparently spread all over Heviah in addition to many parts of Salia, Estal, Mahe, Palee, and even in Nesha.

In thinking back on everything, I was so glad it had all happened. It had been rough in some places like when we all thought Cam was dead and when we were stuck in Estal, but it had ended up being for the best.

My mind constantly replayed Mongwau's words about how Cam was the most dangerous man I'd ever meet. I could laugh when I looked back on it now. It was because he was right. Cam *was* the most dangerous man I'd ever met, but not just because of his insane amount of raw power. No, it was also because Cam had forced me to change, learn to love, and to rely on people besides myself.

Believe me, not everyone could have made me do that. Before all of this, I was the most cold-hearted, unforgiving person. Now? I don't think most people from Leshee would be able to recognize me. I guess that one note we had received about the "fox finding more than bones" was right. There was more in life than grieving death, and the quest and Cam helped me realize that.

I'd discovered that love was stronger than any wrath I could ever hold onto, especially the hate I felt from my parents' death. I could let it go now that Tristan was dealt with—I had no hate left. I was beyond glad the first ones I had truly loved other than my blood family was Rennan as an adopted brother and Cameron as my husband and king. They meant more to me than I would ever be able to express.

We had all changed and become stronger as individuals. One thing knowing Cam has taught me is that I can't hold on to the past or let it define me. I had come to accept the fact that I couldn't have prevented the deaths of my parents and grandmother. Though it was painful to lose them, I have come to realize how much more I gained when I let go of my regret. My friendships have become stronger and I know they will never be broken.

By coming with Cam on this quest, I helped the whole world—not just myself. Sure, I gained an incredible husband and loving friends, but I had also accomplished what I had striven for my entire childhood: I had helped liberate my home kingdom and see it restored to its former glory.

I had walked the path of the forgotten.

Epilogue

Drew Cardell?

Is that really what I had called myself?

"Cardell" sounded so stupid in comparison to my actual name. I would have told my new friends, but I couldn't let them know about how I had gotten here and why I couldn't stay. I had received enough trouble when Ahmias—that stupid sorcerer—had found out I could realm jump.

I could never tell my friends I am Andrew Sebastian Casta, sorcerer of Borah. They would ask too many questions and demand to know every single detail of what Borah was like and who lived there and everything about daily life on that blasted island. Questions would lead me far too close to the painful memory of the last time I had seen her.

I gazed at the open locket I held in my hand. Inside was a small picture of the only woman who ever truly understood and loved me unconditionally. What hurts the most is that I love her, too.

I would never forget the way her blonde hair glowed in the sunlight or the way her blue eyes sparkled in the moonlight; I would always remember the way she laughed when I accidentally fell into the river or the way she smiled when she found a new book on her desk.

Annabeth…my beautiful Annabeth. Where are you?

Wind whipped through my hair as I looked up from my palm. I snapped the locket shut and pulled the chain over my head again.

Standing up, I could see all the way into Estal and Mahe, where I had been forced to masquerade for years of my life, trying to figure out how I had been able to cross into a different realm.

I stood on the edge of the barrier. This mountain range separated the Galerah from the Uncharted North. As its name suggested, it was

completely unexplored. It was rumored that everything past the mountains was dead and nothing survived in the frozen wastelands. Cam had mentioned that as well, but never expanded on his experiences.

Cam was going to be upset to learn that I had fallen off the face of the earth. He had been so kind to listen to my trials in searching for my wife and offer his advice. He was a friend that I had never had before, and I was sorry I was going to lose him. But even with the bond we shared and the support he had given me, it was time for me to leave. I had to keep looking for Annabeth.

I needed to leave swiftly. Supposedly, a three-headed dog was rumored to guard the entrance into the north, but I didn't believe that for a second.

A growl echoed through the air.

Okay, maybe there was something to the three-headed dog thing after all.

I climbed down from the rock I was standing on and tried sneaking my way past the entrance into the frozen tundra beyond the mountains. Before I had gotten very far, flames erupted all around me. The snow on the ground hissed as it turned into steam in the intense heat.

"DO YOU GIVE UP YET?" the suffocating voice asked me.

I clenched my jaw. "I thought I told you I'm not giving up no matter what you do to me."

A flame licked my face and I could feel a burn on my right eyebrow. Well, that hair would never grow back.

Flames continued to crackle, as if trying to speak to me. They beckoned me to submit to them, but I resisted with everything I had.

"YOU'RE MAKING A MISTAKE. I COULD TELL YOU WHERE SHE IS. ALL YOU HAVE TO DO IS PLEDGE YOUR LOYALTY TO ME AND NEVER LOOK BACK."

I ran through the wall of flames (which was really stupid because my cloak caught on fire) and into the snow beyond. I unclasped my cloak and let it float away in the wind. I sucked in a breath of the clean air before I broke into a coughing fit.

"Look, I'm flattered that you want me in your service, but no thanks. I kind of have something else going on right now, and it doesn't involve becoming a manservant to an ancient evil who is too cowardly to show me his face," I yelled into the wind.

"INSOLENT BOY. YOU WILL LEARN TO TAUNT THE HAND CONTROLING YOU ALL. THAT GIRL DIDN'T LISTEN TO ME WHEN I SAID YOU WILL BURN IN THE FIRESTORM. NEVER FORGET THAT," the evil voice commanded me. "HEED ME AND YOU MIGHT LIVE. IF NOT…THAT WOMAN OF YOURS WILL DIE."

"No!!" I screamed.

The fire disappeared just as quickly as it had appeared. I shouted again as I threw rocks down into the valleys below.

"No! I will not be controlled by you!" I yelled in defiance. "I will find her myself!"

Mustering all the courage I had, I formed the portal. With any luck, it would take me back to the Lost Isles. I looked back on the land I had come to know. In a way, it was more beautiful than Borah. But Borah was still my home even if the council had deemed me unworthy of my family name.

Eerie howls echoed over the rocks.

I took a deep breath and jumped.

When I came out on the other side, I could see that it was definitely not Borah I had found myself in. It was far greener than the savannah-like climate I was accustomed to. In the distance, there was a castle nestled between two hills and a town spread out in front of it.

"Well, that's just great," I muttered to myself, "but I'm going to find her if it's the last thing it do."

END OF BOOK ONE

Acknowledgements

There are so, so many things that I've been grateful for while writing this book and I have barely a clue of where to start. I don't think I would have been able to do this without the support of my friends, family, and teachers who kept encouraging me through the whole process and teaching me what I needed to know to be able to write and edit a complete novel. There's no way I would have been able to do this without all of their support.

Jada, I'm pretty sure this whole story would be much rougher if you hadn't offered your time and help in editing this thing. I am so grateful for the time you spent with this crazy project of mine. The fact that you were willing to work on this over the summer meant a lot to me and I will eternally be honored that you spent your energy wading through all of the many, many papers in the manuscript.

Mrs. Pope and Mrs. Otheim, I will grin every time Valerie shouts, "Good morning, wonderful people!" The years that I had you as teachers flew by fast. Every time I read any sort of poetry I still remember ranting about Paris—whether it be from Shakespeare or from the Iliad. There were so many great things that have happened in your classes that I won't forget. But in them, my love of English and literature grew into an unquenchable flame. Thank you both so much for the time that you spent preparing lessons, grading papers, and making sure to provide one-on-one help where needed. Without the skills you taught me, I doubt I'd have all the knowledge of character arcs and themes I'd need to write my own novel. My fond memories of you shall live on through the glittery mermaid herself.

Anna, there are certain jokes that will live on in my mind like the Mock Turtle singing "fly soup" in my head. That's not going to come out for years. Thank you so much, my friend, for offering greatly appreciated suggestions to make my plot so much stronger. I don't think it will be quite so easy for me to forget about currency in the Blackshell Inn again, even if it's a minor detail that past (and distracted) Emma overlooked. Your willingness to help edit is greatly appreciated. I will always treasure our friendship; I can't thank you enough for the laughter and encouragement that we have shared. To many more years of book obsessions!

Corin, dearest flying squirrel, though he made only a short appearance in this story, I shall bring back Firequacker! Though, in all seriousness, I can't imagine a more enthusiastic, creative, and hilarious friend to have. I can't imagine life without your smile and evil laughter when you're talking (or as is more often the case, ranting) about books. Or your laughter when saying "sparkles" during movies. Regardless, you're one of the best, most awesome people I've ever met. I'm so grateful to have you as a friend.

Audrey, I can't contain my excitement whenever I see the stunning cover you have drawn for this story. It perfectly captures the determination and courage of Scarlet and the drive she has in reaching her goals. When paired with your skill with color and design, it is one of the most beautiful covers I've ever seen. (And I don't say that out of a bias that it's my book.) I couldn't be more grateful to have such a creative and talented artist as my friend. You've always been a great person to bounce ideas off of you, which as you know, is huge when you're at a crossroads in a story. To all the great randomness and crossovers we have yet to write! *raises sword in excitement*

Marissa, friend of many names (but mostly Hobbit Child), you were the first to know about this story, and you were amazing to test ideas on throughout the writing process. After all, what mind other than yours could think to name a character "Bartholomew Pickle?" He's certainly an unforgettable character for that alone. But in all seriousness, I don't know what I would do without your help in making sense of some of my crazy ideas and how best to execute them in ways that won't lead to incoherent chaos. I will eternally grateful for the time I've spent with you. My friendship with you is worth more than all the glittery things in the world.

Brendan, dearest brother of mine, your constant interruptions in the middle of sentences often brought some of the most interesting shifts in perspective. And they found their way into this story with Rennan constantly interrupting conversations to ask questions. All of your food related questions will never be forgotten. I don't know what I would do without you and your amusing jokes (and historical facts) coming at random points in time. You will forever be the best person to go to for weapon designs. I love you, little brother. And that fact will never change. ;)

My wonderful parents, I cannot thank you enough for all the effort you've put forth to homeschool me and find the resources that helped me as a creative writer. Words cannot describe the love and gratefulness that I have for you guys. Mama and Father, I love you guys so much and I cannot thank you enough for what you've done for me.

And of course, none of this would be possible without my ultimate Creator and Savior, Jesus Christ. *Nothing* would be possible without him.

REALM OF HEROES

Creation of Legends

The Path of the Forgotten

Made in the USA
Coppell, TX
18 September 2020